THE PORTABLE SIXTIES READER

ANN CHARTERS has had a long involvement in reading, collecting, teaching, and writing about the literature of the counterculture. She began collecting books written by Beat writers while still a graduate student at Columbia University, and after completing her doctorate in 1965 she worked together with Jack Kerouac to compile a bibliography of his work. After his death, she wrote the first Kerouac biography and edited the posthumous collection of his *Scattered Poems*. She was the general editor for the two-volume encyclopedia *The Beats: Literary Bohemians in Postwar America*, as well as *The Portable Beat Reader*, and she published a collection of her photographic portraits in a book called *Beats & Company*. More recently she edited two volumes of Kerouac's *Selected Letters*, *The Portable Jack Kerouac*, and *Beat Down to Your Soul: What Was the Beat Generation?*

The Portable

SIXTIES
READER

Edited by

ANN CHARTERS

PENGUIN BOOKS

PENGUIN BOOKS

Published by the Penguin Group

Penguin Putnam Inc., 375 Hudson Street, New York, New York 10014, U.S.A.
Penguin Books Ltd, 80 Strand, London WC2R 0RL, England
Penguin Books Australia Ltd, 250 Camberwell Road, Camberwell,
Victoria 3124, Australia
Penguin Books Canada Ltd, 10 Alcorn Avenue,
Toronto, Ontario, Canada M4V 3B2
Penguin Books India (P) Ltd, 11 Community Centre, Panchsheel Park,
New Delhi–110 017, India
Penguin Books (N.Z.) Ltd, Cnr Rosedale and Airborne Roads, Albany,
Auckland, New Zealand
Penguin Books (South Africa) (Pty) Ltd, 24 Sturdee Avenue,
Rosebank, Johannesburg 2196, South Africa

Penguin Books Ltd, Registered Offices: Harmondsworth,
Middlesex, England

First published in Penguin Books 2003

3   5   7   9   10   8   6   4   2

LIBRARY OF CONGRESS CATALOGING-IN-PUBLICATION DATA
The portable sixties reader / edited by Ann Charters.
p.   cm.—(Penguin classics)
Includes bibliographical references.
ISBN 0 14 20.0194 5
1. American literature—20th century. 2. United States—History—
1961–1969—Literary collections. 3. United States—History—
1961–1969—Sources. 4. Nineteen sixties—Literary collections.
I. Charters, Ann. II. Series.

PS536.2 .P665 2003
810.8'0054—dc21   2002032266

PRINTED IN THE UNITED STATES OF AMERICA
Set in Bembo

Art is an expression of man's desire for life. In and with the work of art, the artist creates an atmosphere for himself, a world, in which he can live according to his secret needs, in which he can experience such sensations as his senses desire, and such emotions as his soul craves.
—Richard Bergh, *Om Konst och Annat*
Stockholm, 1908

CONTENTS

PART ONE
STRUGGLING TO BE FREE:
THE CIVIL RIGHTS MOVEMENT

PART TWO
END IT! AND END IT NOW!
THE ANTI-VIETNAM WAR MOVEMENT

PART THREE
WHY CAN WE NOT BEGIN NEW?
THE FREE SPEECH MOVEMENT AND BEYOND

PART FOUR
"I FEEL LIKE I'M FIXIN' TO DIE": THE COUNTERCULTURE MOVEMENT

PART FIVE
ADRIFT IN THE AGE OF AQUARIUS: DRUGS AND THE MOVEMENT INTO INNER SPACE

PART SIX
LIVING IN THE REVOLUTION:
THE BEATS AND SOME OTHER
LITERARY MOVEMENTS AT THE EDGE

PART SEVEN
OUT OF THE FIRE:
THE BLACK ARTS MOVEMENT AND THE
RESHAPING OF BLACK CONSCIOUSNESS

PART EIGHT
WITH OUR ARMS UPRAISED:
THE WOMEN'S MOVEMENT AND
THE SEXUAL REVOLUTION

PART NINE
IN DEFENSE OF THE EARTH:
THE ENVIRONMENTAL MOVEMENT

PART TEN
TEN ELEGIES FOR THE SIXTIES

PREFACE

The Portable Sixties Reader is a personal anthology. I came of age in that decade, and the historical and cultural events that I participated in during the 1960s have shaped me emotionally and intellectually ever since. In an attempt to convey the spirit of the Sixties in the United States as I experienced it, I have compiled essays, poetry, and fiction by some of America's most gifted writers who also lived through or thought deeply about those turbulent times.

Everyone understands that many of the social and political movements of the Sixties—for example, the battle for civil rights in the United States and the war against the spread of Communism in Southeast Asia—began before the Sixties and continued after that time. But in putting together this anthology, I have defined the Sixties strictly as the ten years of the decade, preferring this digital human construct as my time frame rather than another arbitrary period. I agree with the proposition of historian Arthur Marwick in *The Sixties: Cultural Revolution in Britain, France, Italy, and the United States, c. 1958–c.1974* that "there was a self-contained period (though no period is hermetically sealed), commonly known as 'the sixties,' of outstanding historical significance in that what happened during this period transformed social and cultural developments for the rest of the century."

The contents of this anthology reflect the Sixties because most of the literature included here was created in the Sixties. If I have added later work, I believe that it captures and illuminates important events of the decade—for example, the excerpt from Charles Johnson's novel *Dreamer* (1998), dramatizing Martin Luther King, Jr.'s assassination in 1968, or Yusef Komunyakaa's poems about combat action in Vietnam in his Pulitzer Prize volume *Dien Cai Dau* (1994), or Gloria Steinem's comments on the early years of the women's movement (1971). On rare occasions, I have selected important earlier work published just before the Sixties, if it anticipated the innovative spirit of a later social movement, as in the excerpt from Peter Matthiessen's *Wildlife in America* (1959) in part 9, about the Environmental Movement.

The *Portable Sixties Reader* has been organized into parts beginning with the Civil Rights Movement and continuing to the Anti–Vietnam War Movement, the Free Speech Movement, the Counterculture Movement, drugs and the movement into inner space, the Beats and some other literary movements at the edge, the Black Arts Movement and the reshaping of black consciousness, the Women's Movement and the Sexual Revolution, and the Environmental Movement. It concludes with ten elegies for people who either died or were important in the Sixties. The choice of these topics, and the selection of literature in each of the ten parts, are a result of my decisions. They are not meant to represent the only possible selection of material written by American authors in the Sixties or the only topics relevant to the decade.

For some readers, it will seem that many of my topics need separate anthologies of their own to do them justice. Stewart O'Nan's excellent *The Vietnam Reader* (1998), for example, is a far more inclusive coverage of literature about the war than I could accomplish in this anthology. What I attempted to do in *The Portable Sixties Reader* was to sketch a portrait of the decade by juxtaposing chapters suggesting the evolution of several important social movements during this tempestuous historical period.

Events in the Sixties caused so many Americans to question their basic beliefs about race, patriotism, social roles, and the environment that it became a time when individual expression was encouraged to an unprecedented degree. In selecting the material for this anthology, I have tried to suggest the possibility that American culture as a vital and living force in the Sixties helped to bring about constructive social change through the moral courage and imagination of its writers and artists.

In compiling the literature for *The Portable Sixties Reader,* I also hoped that it would be read in conjunction with my three earlier Penguin anthologies: *The Portable Beat Reader, The Portable Jack Kerouac,* and *Beat Down to Your Soul: What Was the Beat Generation?* Taken together, these four books offer a comprehensive selection of the essays, poetry, and fiction that informed and entertained American readers at midcentury, and challenged many of them to reconsider their attitudes toward themselves and their country. As my friend the folksinger Dave Van Ronk once said, "It's very difficult to write a good political song, but it's remarkably easy to write a bad one." In *The Portable Sixties Reader* I've tried to assemble a volume of what I consider good writing that has contributed to the important tradition of literature of dissent in the United States. I know that books don't change society; people do. But I believe that some books can give people new ideas and help them to revise old ones.

At Penguin Putnam, my editor, Michael Millman, gave me the idea of compiling a Sixties reader. I thank him for suggesting that I organize it by topics and for supporting me through all the stages of this book. My friend Paul Slovak at Penguin Putnam also offered much-appreciated encouragement. Claire Hunsaker was a ready and able editorial assistant. I was fortunate again to work with Bruce Giffords, an expert and sympathetic guide through the copyediting and proofreading of the manuscript at Penguin Putnam. At Bedford Books in Boston, Charles Christensen, Joan Feinberg, Steve Scipione, and Maura Shea, who have helped me to publish my college textbooks of short fiction for the past twenty years, listened to my early ideas about a Sixties anthology and offered useful books and good advice.

With their characteristic grace and generosity, the permissions experts Virginia Creeden and Fred Courtright gave me invaluable assistance for more than a year, the time it took for me to clear the material in the reader. Without the help and resourcefulness of these two generous souls, this anthology would not exist. I am very grateful to them.

Friends who suggested the names of authors and books for me to consider, or helped with my preparation of the manuscript in other ways, include Bruce Barthol, Ed Blair, Susan Blake, Janice and Bill Belmont, Mallay and Nora Charters, Mel and Robert Chatain, Marshall Clements, Betty Colyer, Martin Colyer, Henry Denander, Faith Evans, Jack Foley, Jenny Hartig, Dorothy and Robert Hawley, Donna Hollenberg, Lee Jacobus, Joyce Johnson, Hettie Jones, Betty Levitin, Country Joe McDonald, Marilyn Nelson, Glenn Occhiogrosso, Sally Pleet, Hatto and Sabina Praun, Jim and Janet Robertson, Ed Sanders, Jenny Schuessler, Amanda Sebestyen, Suzie Staubach, John Stokes, Anthony Stoll, and Frederick Usher.

In the fall 2001 semester, students in my graduate seminar on

American Literature in the Sixties at the University of Connecticut in Storrs helped me with the bibliography and background research on my topics. I greatly appreciate the assistance and stimulating company of Amanda Cagle, Rebecca Devers, James J. Donahue, Kimberly Hilton, Tiffanie May, Eveann Mazur, Shelley Mika, and Aaron Sanders. Also at the English Office at UConn, I am grateful to my friends Helen Azevedo-Smith, Doreen Bell, and Rose Kovarovics for frequently getting me out of trouble at the Xerox machine.

Most of all, I want to thank my husband, Samuel Charters, for his help with this book, as with all my other books. It will soon be more than half a century that we have shared our lives—before, during, and after the Sixties—and I have been inspired by his generous spirit throughout all these years. I couldn't work without his unflagging encouragement and applause, tempered with his good critical judgment and helpful suggestions, always.

ANN CHARTERS
STORRS, CONNECTICUT

THE SIXTIES:
A CHRONOLOGY

1960

President Dwight D. Eisenhower calls for modest Civil Rights action in his State of the Union address, urging Congress to appoint federal registrars to enforce Negroes' right to vote in Southern states. In the U.S. Senate, a coalition of liberals and Southern Democrats guts the president's Civil Rights bill, deleting the provision that would make it a federal crime to use violence or threats to obstruct school desegregation. Thurgood Marshall, the attorney for the NAACP (National Association for the Advancement of Colored People) who won the Supreme Court decision outlawing racial segregation in public schools, predicts that resistance to school integration will lead to a period of token integration. The legal fight for integration will stall for years until the 1963 March on Washington gives the impetus for the Civil Rights Act of 1964.

In February, Joseph McNeil, Ezell Blair, Jr., David Richmond, and Franklin McCain—classmates at the all-Negro North Carolina Agricultural and Technical College in Greensboro—stage a sit-in at the lunch counter at the local F. W. Woolworth store. Other restaurant sit-ins follow in 50 other Southern cities. In the fall, four black girls are escorted by federal marshals to first-grade classrooms in two elementary schools in New Orleans, resulting in angry demonstrations by thousands of whites.

Blacks continue to leave the South in large numbers. During this decade, the black population of Washington, D.C., rises from 54 percent to 71 percent; Newark, from 34 percent to 54 percent; Baltimore, from 35 percent to 46 percent; Detroit, from 29 percent to 44 percent; Saint Louis, from 29 percent to 41 percent; and New York City, from 14 percent to 21 percent.

President Eisenhower breaks off diplomatic relations with Cuba after Premier Fidel Castro parades Soviet tanks and artillery in Havana. Castro nationalizes all U.S. property in Cuba. He and Premier Nikita Khrushchev of the Soviet Union meet in New York City to attend the United Nations General Assembly.

The Soviets shoot down the U-2 spy plane piloted over the USSR by Francis Gary Powers, a CIA agent filming the Soviet's long-range ballistic missile operations. Powers draws a ten-year prison sentence but is traded two years later for a Soviet spy in U.S. custody. The Soviets launch *Sputnik V* with a pair of dogs named Streika and Belka; in the U.S., NASA accelerates its plans for putting a man in space.

Congress passes the Clean Water Act. Eisenhower approves an expanded program in the U.S. of underground nuclear explosions. A navy nuclear submarine near Cape Canaveral, Florida, fires a Polaris rocket, which hits a target 1,150 miles away between Bermuda and Puerto Rico. The U.S. Army issues the new M14 automatic rifle with a 20-round magazine, faster than the 8-round weapon used in World War II and Korea.

Currently 2,489,000 people serve in the U.S. military; 3,900,000 in the Soviet military. The Congo wins its independence from Belgium under Patrice Lumumba, the first prime minister of the Democratic Republic of the Congo. He appeals to the Soviets for help in maintaining order.

Syngman Rhee resigns as president of South Korea in his fourth term of office after widespread protest over the fraudulent elections.

War criminal Adolf Eichmann is seized by Israelis in Buenos Aires, Argentina, and tried the following year in Israel for participating in the Nazis' "Final Solution" to exterminate 6 million Jews in Europe. His defense is that he was merely following orders. Found guilty of crimes against humanity, he is hanged in Ramleh Prison near Tel Aviv on June 1, 1962.

OPEC (Organization of Petroleum Exporting Countries) is established by Saudi Arabia, Iran, Iraq, Kuwait, and Venezuela.

Democrats John F. Kennedy and Lyndon B. Johnson win the election over Republicans Richard M. Nixon and Henry Cabot Lodge, Jr. Republicans gain 22 seats in Congress, strengthening the conservative bloc.

Hundreds of UC Berkeley students rally against HUAC (House Un-American Activities Committee) at San Francisco City Hall; police arrest 31 protesters.

Elvis Presley completes his army duty in Germany. Norman Mailer is arrested in Manhattan after stabbing his wife Adele, who later refuses to sign a complaint; Mailer is given a suspended sentence. The Court of Appeals in New York rules that copies of D. H. Lawrence's unexpurgated novel *Lady Chatterley's Lover* can be sent through the mails.

DEATHS: Richard Wright, Albert Camus, Boris Pasternak.

NEW TECHNOLOGY: The Food and Drug Administration approves Enovid and Norlutin as oral contraceptives. By 1966, one of every five American women of childbearing age has a prescription. Also, invention of the first satellite weather station and the Polaroid camera.

THE ARTS: Books: Donald M. Allen (ed.), *The New American Poetry;* Gwendolyn Brooks, *The Bean Eaters;* Gary Snyder, *Myths & Texts;* John Updike, *Rabbit, Run.* Julia Child's *Mastering the Art of French Cooking* introduces provincial American cooks to fine cuisine. Theater: Rodgers and Hammerstein, *The Sound of Music;* Lerner and Loewe, *Camelot;* Lillian Hellman, *Toys in the Attic.* Film: Alfred Hitchcock, *Psycho.* TV: Maynard Krebs, a comic beatnik, featured on *The Many Loves of Dobie Gillis.* Popular Music: Elvis Presley, Frank Sinatra, the Everly Brothers, the Kingston Trio; Pete Seeger and Joan Baez pay tribute to Woody Guthrie at the Newport Folk Festival.

1961

In January, John F. Kennedy takes the oath of presidential office, telling Americans, "Ask not what your country can do for you; ask what you can do for your country." Robert Frost recites a poem at the inauguration, seen and heard by 80 million Americans on television. Kennedy creates the President's Commission on the Status of Women, chaired by Eleanor Roosevelt. Congress approves $30 million for the Peace Corps program, which sends 532 Americans to work in underdeveloped countries by the end of the year. Minimum wage is raised from $1 to $1.25. The average family income before taxes is $7,000. The American Indian Conference meets in Chicago and issues a "Declaration of Indian Purpose" to gain self-determination and preserve Native American heritage.

Protected by detectives, plainclothesmen, FBI agents, and state police, Charlayne Hunter and Hamilton Holmes enroll as sophomores at the University of Georgia. The Civil Rights organizations CORE (Congress of Racial Equality) and SNCC (Student Nonviolent Coordinating Committee) organize "Freedom Buses" with black and white riders traveling through Alabama, Mississippi, and Louisiana. In Birmingham, T. Eugene "Bull" Connor, chief of police, fails to stop the beating of the Freedom Riders or the firebombing of their bus. A federal judge rejects a nonviolence injunction against the Birmingham police and the Ku Klux Klan (KKK). With an escort of highway patrol cars, another group of Freedom Riders heads to Montgomery, but they are beaten by a mob.

Martin Luther King, Jr., preaches to a mass rally at Ralph D. Abernathy's First Baptist Church in Montgomery, but a white mob attacks the church and keeps the parishioners inside until dawn, when 800 National Guardsmen restore peace. Twenty-seven Freedom Riders in two buses travel through Mississippi and arrive in New Orleans. In Albany, Georgia, King is jailed along with 265 other blacks and whites who marched to city hall for a nonviolent prayer demonstration. In New York City, James Lawson, founder of the United African Nationalist Movement, says that "mere crumbs from the tables of an abundant society have made millions of black men angry." Consolidated Edison Company and its union representing 20,000 employees are charged with discrimination against Negroes.

On January 3, 1961, the U.S. severs all diplomatic relations with Cuba. In April, American B-26s bomb Cuban air bases the day before 1,500 anti-Castro soldiers invade the southern coast of Cuba at the Bay of Pigs. They are met by 20,000 Cuban soldiers with Soviet tanks and MIG jets. Within three days, Castro has killed or captured all of the invaders and their American weapons. In December 1962, 1,113 of these "exile fighters" are traded back to the United States in exchange for $53 million in food and medical supplies for Cuba.

Kennedy increases support to the pro-Western government during the escalating civil war in Laos, on the borders of North Vietnam and China. South Vietnamese president Ngo Dinh Diem declares that the struggle against the Communists is "no longer a guerrilla war but a real war." Kennedy sends Green Berets and military advisers to train South Vietnamese troops.

Kennedy meets with Nikita Khrushchev in Vienna to discuss Laos, Berlin, disarmament, and the nuclear test ban. The two leaders agree that nuclear war is to be avoided.

The Soviets detonate a 50-megaton atomic bomb in their Arctic testing ground, 250 times as powerful as the atomic bombs that the U.S. dropped on Hiroshima and Nagasaki.

The Soviets erect an 11-foot concrete wall around their sector in East Berlin to divide the capital city after 20 percent of the East German people have left the Communist-ruled country for West Berlin during the previous decade. More than 250,000 American reservists are called up and 12 months are added to military enlistments. The U.S., Britain, and France agree on a tough allied presence to safeguard West Germany.

Russian cosmonaut Yuri Gagarin becomes the first man in space, making a single orbit around the world in 108 minutes. Test pilot Alan Shepard becomes the first American astronaut in a suborbital flight of 15 minutes in his *Freedom* 7 capsule (Mercury project). Kennedy asks Congress to increase funding to put a man on the Moon.

In New York City, the Port Authority issues a report recommending the establishment of a World Trade Center in lower Manhattan.

DEATHS: James Thurber, Grandma Moses, Carl Jung. UN secretary-general Dag Hammarskjöld dies under mysterious circumstances in a plane crash over battle-torn Northern Rhodesia. Ernest Hemingway commits suicide with a double-barrel shotgun at 61 years old.

THE ARTS: Books: James Baldwin, *Nobody Knows My Name;* William S. Burroughs, *The Soft Machine;* Diane di Prima, *Dinners & Nightmares;* Allen Ginsberg, *Kaddish and Other Poems;* Joseph Heller, *Catch-22;* Jane Jacobs, *The Life and Death of American Cities;* LeRoi Jones, *Preface to a Twenty Volume Suicide Note;* J. D. Salinger, *Franny and Zooey;* Richard Wright, *Eight Men.* Films: Audrey Hepburn in *Breakfast at Tiffany's;* Paul Newman in *The Hustler;* Federico Fellini, *La Dolce Vita.* Dance: 23-year-old Rudolf Nureyev, lead dancer with the Kirov Ballet, seeks asylum in Paris. Art: Pablo Picasso celebrates his eightieth birthday. Theater: Leonard Bernstein, *West Side Story.* Pop music: Bob Dylan debuts in Greenwich Village; Carole King's "Will You Still Love Me Tomorrow," sung by the Shirelles, hits the charts.

1962

President Kennedy appeals to Mississippians to cease their resistance to integration, calling it the most serious challenge to federal authority since the Civil War. Five thousand U.S. troops and 400 U.S. marshals confront a mob of 50,000 whites protesting the enrollment of James Meredith, a Korean War air force veteran, in the University of Mississippi, Oxford. More than a thousand Freedom Riders are jailed in Albany, Georgia, including Martin Luther King, Jr., and Ralph Abernathy. The voter registration drive results in further beatings, arrests, bombings, shootings, and arson.

Congress vetoes Kennedy's Medicare program but allots more than $48 billion for the country's defense budget, including $275 million to South Vietnam's president Diem to fight the Vietcong, Communist guerrillas active in South Vietnam. A force of 11,000 U.S. military personnel, with Marine Corps helicopters, fighter planes, and bombers, unofficially take part in the action.

The Cuban Missile Crisis occurs after President Kennedy learns that the Soviets have placed ballistic missiles in Cuba to counteract the American missles that surround the USSR. The Russians stockpile atomic weapons in Cuba capable of killing 80 million Americans on first attack. Fearing that the Soviets will retaliate by bombing the U.S. or Berlin, Kennedy refuses the plan suggested by his Joint Chiefs of Staff to use a first strike to take out the Cuban missile bases. Instead, the president demands that the Soviets remove their offensive weapons and sets up a naval blockade of Cuba. Tens of thousands of American troops are called up from the reserves and sent to Florida; 40 navy ships man the 500-mile no-pass line at sea. In the first day of the blockade, the Soviets back down and Khrushchev agrees to move the missiles out of Cuba.

Hundreds of college students march for peace to the White House, calling for disarmament, a ban on nuclear weapons tests, and the cancellation of the civil defense program. Kennedy sends out an urn of coffee to warm up the protesters in the bitter winter cold.

SDS (Students for a Democratic Society) publish the Port Huron Statement, written in Port Huron, Michigan, in 1960. Their manifesto advocates participatory democracy and egalitarianism, and is based on the ideas of the radical sociologist C. Wright Mills. It becomes the most important document of the early campus radical movements among white, middle-class college students, who realize their institutions reflect the support of business and military interests intent on enforcing conformism instead of promoting social change.

U.S. ambassador Adlai Stevenson urges the United Nations General Assembly to continue to block China from membership in the UN, condemning China's attack on India along the borders of Communist-held Tibet. French president Charles de Gaulle proclaims Algeria's independence from France.

Colonel John H. Glenn, Jr., orbits the earth three times in the first U.S. manned orbital flight. The Gemini space program costs more than a billion dollars in cost overruns.

DEATHS: e. e. cummings, Isak Dinesen, William Faulkner, Herman Hesse, C. Wright Mills, Marilyn Monroe, Eleanor Roosevelt.

NEW TECHNOLOGY: After the pharmaceutical thalidomide causes severe birth defects to embryos in Europe and the United States, Congress strengthens the FDA's power to enforce the requirement that new drugs sold to the public must be safe as well as effective. Telestar satellites enable television networks to beam live programs worldwide.

THE ARTS: Books: Rachel Carson's *Silent Spring* starts the Environmental Movement in the U.S. James Baldwin, *Another Country;* Helen Gurley Brown, *Sex and the Single Girl;* William S. Burroughs, *The Ticket That Exploded;* William S. Burroughs and Allen Ginsberg, *The Yage Letters;* Euell Gibbons, *Stalking the Wild Asparagus;* Jack Kerouac, *Big Sur;* Ken Kesey, *One Flew Over the Cuckoo's Nest;* Doris Lessing, *The Golden Notebook;* Katherine Anne Porter, *Ship of Fools;* Charles M. Schulz, *Happiness Is a Warm Puppy;* Anne Sexton, *All My Pretty Ones;* John Steinbeck, *Travels with Charlie;* Diane Wakoski, *Coins and Coffins.* Theater: Edward Albee, *Who's Afraid of Virginia Woolf?;* Tennessee Williams, *The Night of the Iguana.* Music: Ray Charles, Bob Dylan; Philharmonic Hall opens at Lincoln Center. John Steinbeck wins the Nobel Prize in literature.

1963

President Kennedy supports Civil Rights legislation after race riots occur in New York, Philadelphia, and Los Angeles. The president sends troops into Alabama after racial violence erupts in Birmingham. There were bombings, demonstrations, mobs, and mass arrests of participants, including comedian Dick Gregory and the children he led in a march to a public park. Attorney General Robert Kennedy travels to Alabama and South Carolina to support voter registration. The University of Alabama integrates its first black students with the help of the National Guard.

In June, after a ten-week period in which there are 758 racial demonstrations and 14,733 arrests in 186 American cities, President Kennedy gives a nationally televised speech, urging his listeners "to treat our fellow Americans as we want to be treated." Four hours later, Medgar Evers, an NAACP official in Jackson, Mississippi, is shot and killed by Byron De La Beckwith. Evers is buried at Arlington National Cemetery. President Kennedy brings his toughest Civil Rights bill to Congress. (It becomes law in 1964 with President Johnson's support.) In response to the actions of the Alabama and Mississippi Freedom Riders, the Interstate Commerce Commission bans overt segregation in public vehicles, requiring that signs be posted stating, "SEATING ON THIS VEHICLE MUST BE REGARDLESS OF RACE, CREED, COLOR, RELIGION, OR NATIONAL ORIGIN."

On August 28, 200,000 people participate in the Civil Rights March on Washington, D.C., and hear Martin Luther King, Jr.'s "I Have a Dream" speech. On September 15, a bomb explodes inside a Birmingham church basement, killing four black girls. Elijah Muhammad, speaking for the Nation of Islam, rejects racial integration in favor of an independent Negro state in America or a return to Africa. On October 10, Robert Kennedy authorizes the FBI to begin wiretapping the telephones of Martin Luther King, Jr., believing erroneously that one of King's closest advisers was an active member of the American Communist Party.

In Saigon, a Buddhist monk self-immolates to protest religious persecution by the repressive Catholic government of President Diem. The CIA backs a coup supporting the murder of President Diem by Major General Duong Van Minh in South Vietnam, while the war against the Vietcong guerrillas escalates. More than 16,000 U.S. servicemen are now involved in the fighting in Indochina.

Kennedy travels to West Berlin to inspect the wall and charms his German audience by saying, *"Ich bin ein Berliner"* ("I am a citizen of Berlin"). A diplomatic Teletype "hot line" is installed between Moscow and Washington after delays hindered messages during the 1962 Cuban Missile Crisis. The Communist government in Iraq is overthrown with the help of the CIA.

In Washington, Congress passes the Clean Air Act. The Supreme Court prohibits recitation of the Lord's Prayer and Bible reading as public school requirements. The president asks Congress to appropriate $4 billion for the space budget in support of the new Apollo program. The Soviets put the first woman in space, as Valentina Tereshkova circles the Earth for more than 70 hours. *Mariner 2* sends back data from Venus to U.S. scientists, showing that life could not be sustained there.

The U.S., the USSR, and Great Britain, along with other nations, sign a test ban treaty stopping all but underground atomic testing, with a provision for on-site inspections. By this time, the Americans have set off 259 nuclear test explosions, the Soviets 126, the British 21, and the French 6.

David Ben-Gurion, prime minister of Israel since its formation in 1948, resigns.

November 22, 1963: President John F. Kennedy is assassinated by Lee Harvey Oswald in Dallas, Texas. Lyndon B. Johnson is sworn in as president. Four days later, Jack Ruby kills Oswald at Dallas Police Headquarters, the first shooting to occur on television.

American pacifist Linus Pauling is awarded the Nobel Peace Prize.

DEATHS: Robert Frost, William Carlos Williams, Clifford Odets, W. E. B. Du Bois, Jean Cocteau, Pope John XXIII, Aldous Huxley, C. S. Lewis, Sylvia Plath.

THE ARTS: Books: Betty Friedan's *The Feminine Mystique* restarts the Women's Rights Movement in the U.S. James Baldwin, *The Fire Next Time;* Allen Ginsberg, *Reality Sandwiches;* Mary McCarthy, *The Group;* Ed Sanders, *Poem from Jail;* Aleksandr Solzhenitsyn, *One Day in the Life of Ivan Denisovich;* William Carlos Williams, *Paterson* [complete]. Film: Elizabeth Taylor and Richard Burton in *Cleopatra;* Alfred Hitchcock's *The Birds;* Jerry Lewis in *The Nutty Professor.* Art: Andy Warhol, Claes Oldenburg, Roy Lichtenstein, Jasper Johns, and other "pop" artists exhibit in New York's Guggenheim Museum. Music: Newport Folk Festival draws a crowd of 47,000 people. The first Beatles album is released in the U.S. Leslie Gore's "It's My Party and I'll Cry If I Want To" is number one on the charts.

1964

President Lyndon Johnson wins the presidential election with the largest popular vote in U.S. history. The Senate passes the Civil Rights bill. The NAACP calls for a boycott of the New York City school system for failing to produce a plan for integration. Fearing riots, a New York judge prohibits "illegal demonstrations" in Harlem by the Progressive Labor Movement, the Harlem Defense Council, and the Community Council on Housing.

The voter registration drive continues in the South, where only 36 percent of the people eligible to vote are listed on the rolls. The NAACP, CORE, and the Southern Christian Leadership Conference (SCLC) form the Council of Federated Organizers (COFO) and recruit white college students to volunteer along with blacks to help people in Mississippi pass the test necessary for registration.

Two white men, Michael H. Schwerner and Andrew Goodman, and a black man, James Chaney—all CORE workers in the project—are beaten and shot by seven members of the KKK in a triple homicide in Philadelphia, Mississippi. Their bodies are recovered 45 days later.

Between June and September, COFO announces 80 beatings, 35 black churches burned, and 30 homes and stores firebombed. By the end of the summer, 1,200 blacks are registered to vote out of 450,000 eligible in Mississippi.

Race riots erupt in New York City; Jersey City, Paterson, and Elizabeth in New Jersey; Chicago, Illinois; Philadelphia, Pennsylvania; and other American cities. Marion D. Green, formerly a captain in the air force, becomes the first black commercial airline pilot after successfully suing Continental Airlines when the courts ban discriminatory hiring by interstate carriers.

In Vietnam, the U.S. destroyer *Maddox*—30 miles offshore in the Gulf of Tonkin—allegedly comes under attack by North Vietnamese ships. The U.S. retaliates with five days of bombing raids in North Vietnam. Congress supports the Gulf of Tonkin Resolution, allowing President Johnson to widen the war in Southeast Asia. He warns the Soviets that the U.S. commitment to Laos and South Vietnam is unlimited. Moscow assures Hanoi of its support. By the end of 1964, there are 23,700 American servicemen in that country, with 164 combat deaths and about 1,000 wounded. Johnson orders a program to reduce the numbers of 19-year-olds registering for the draft who are rejected for health and mental defects.

In Berkeley, Mario Savio, a philosophy major at the University of California, becomes the leader of a student revolt against administrative interference in civil rights advocacy. The Free Speech Movement (FSM) begins the campus revolution of the Sixties with demonstrations for civil rights and against the arms race. Students burn their draft cards to protest the escalating war in Vietnam.

Premier Khrushchev is labeled a "harebrained schemer" by *Pravda* and replaced by Leonid Brezhnev as the leader of the Communist Party. Ernesto "Che" Guevara is dropped as leader of the Cuban United Socialist Revolutionary Party. Communist China explodes its first A-bomb, issuing a bulletin saying that it was "a major contribution . . . in the defense of world peace."

In South Africa, Nelson Mandela is sentenced to life imprisonment at hard labor on Robben Island, the country's maximum security prison, for offenses against the security of the state. He will remain a prisoner in South Africa for the next 27 years.

Congress passes the Water Conservation Act and the Wilderness Act, creating the National Wilderness Preservation System. Title VII of the Civil Rights Act bars employment discrimination on the basis of race and gender.

Surgeon General Luther Terry announces the report *Smoking and Health*, linking cigarettes to the 41,000 annual deaths in the U.S. from lung cancer. Cigarette packages are labeled with the surgeon general's warning that tobacco is hazardous to health.

Twenty-two-year-old Cassius Clay, boasting that he will "float like a butterfly, sting like a bee," wins $465,595 defeating boxing's World Heavyweight Champion Sonny Liston, who refuses to leave his corner after the seventh round. As a member of the Nation of Islam, Clay changes his name to Muhammad Ali.

The *Ranger* 7 spacecraft takes close-up photos of the Moon and collects data for a landing site. Fifty million people view the exhibits at the 1964 World's Fair in New York City, where the theme is "Peace Through Understanding." The fair loses $21 million, most of it paid for by New York City taxpayers.

Neal Cassady drives Ken Kesey and the Merry Pranksters from California to New York in the Further bus. Hippies begin to flock to Haight-Ashbury in San Francisco. Lenny Bruce is found guilty of using obscenity in his act at the Cafe Au Go-Go in Greenwich Village and sentenced to four months in jail. Two years later the conviction is reversed when the judge finds that while Bruce used "coarse, vulgar and profane language which went beyond the bounds of usual candor . . . it was error to hold that the performances were without social importance."

Martin Luther King, Jr., wins the Nobel Peace Prize.

DEATHS: India's prime minister Jawaharlal Nehru; composer Cole Porter; Rachel Carson; Douglas MacArthur.

THE ARTS: Books: *The Warren Report.* The commission chaired by Chief Justice Earl Warren concludes that Lee Harvey Oswald, acting alone, killed John F. Kennedy. Saul Bellow, *Herzog;* Ralph Ellison, *Shadow and Act;* John Le Carré, *The Spy Who Came In from the Cold;* Robert Lowell, *For the Union Dead.* Theater: LeRoi Jones, *Dutchman;* Arthur Miller, *After the Fall.* Films: The Beatles in *A Hard Day's Night;* Sean Connery in *Goldfinger;* Peter Sellers in *Dr. Strangelove or: How I Learned to Stop Worrying and Love the Bomb;* Julie Andrews in *Mary Poppins.* Music: Leslie Gore's "You Don't Own Me," Motown's the Supremes, Stevie Wonder, John Coltrane's *A Love Supreme,* Bob Dylan's "The Times They Are A-Changin'." The Beatles perform on the *Ed Sullivan Show* and draw huge crowds in their public appearances; their record albums sell more than 2 million copies a month. The *East Village Other,* the first counterculture newspaper, is founded in New York City.

1965

The U.S. sustains unprecedented economic prosperity for the fifth consecutive year with 2 percent unemployment among married men and 48 percent of consumer income available for luxury spending. The GNP is high, the cost of living low.

Congress passes 90 bills of President Johnson's "Great Society" plan, including Medicare. He gets funding for programs to fight poverty, to build low-rent housing, and to aid the schools. He also signs Executive Order 11246, banning discrimination against blacks and other minorities. Congress passes the Voting Rights Act and challenges the poll tax.

Martin Luther King, Jr., leads the voter registration drive in Selma, Alabama, where only 65 out of 15,100 eligible blacks are registered. More than 2,000 demonstrators are arrested and 3 men are killed. President Johnson calls for a congressional investigation of the KKK. A Civil Rights march to Montgomery engages 25,000 people, with an escort of nearly 3,000 Alabama National Guardsmen, U.S. troops, and FBI agents. King states, "No wave of racism can stop us now." He also addresses 100,000 people at a UN peace rally to stop the war in Vietnam.

In Watts, a poor black neighborhood in Los Angeles, riots leave 34 people dead after 15,000 National Guardsmen restrain the mobs. More than 4,000 people are arrested, with damages estimated at $175 million. Marvin Jackson coins the phrase "Burn, baby, burn."

Johnson doubles the draft from 17,000 to 35,000 men a month as full-scale war begins in Vietnam, with air strikes north of the truce line dividing the country and American planes dropping napalm bombs. The first battalion of U.S. ground troops arrives in Da Nang. The Soviets send guns, planes, and missiles to Hanoi, where North Vietnamese president Ho Chi Minh also has the support of Communist China. Johnson claims that polls show 56 percent of the American people support his policy of "escalation" in Vietnam, despite peace marches in Washington with signs reading "HEY, HEY, LBJ, HOW MANY KIDS DID YOU KILL TODAY?" By the end of the year, 175,000 American ground troops and 40,000 navy personnel are in Vietnam. There are 1,365 Americans killed in 1965, with more than 5,300 wounded.

Secretary of Defense Robert McNamara announces that 5,000 atomic warheads are stockpiled in the U.S., with the same number stored in Europe to defend NATO. McNamara asks for a 20 percent increase. Students and faculty at university "teach-ins" protest the proliferation of nuclear weapons and the escalating U.S. military involvement in Vietnam.

In China, disputes over ideological purity are spearheaded by Mao Tse-tung and the Gang of Four. During the next decade, Red Guards execute, imprison, or exile to forced labor camps 5 percent of China's population.

Rhodesia declares its independence from Britain, which condemns the act as treason. In South Africa, the Bantu Laws Amendment Act is passed, rescinding the civil rights of 7 million blacks who live in white areas outside designated black reservations.

The United Farm Workers under Cesar Chavez vote to strike the California grape growers in the Central Valley. U.S. auto manufacturers insist that growing air pollution does not warrant smog controls.

In March, Augustus Owsley Stanley III produces his first commercial batch of LSD in Northern California; one year later, manufacture and possession of the drug are declared illegal. Ken Kesey and the Merry Pranksters hold several acid tests in and around San Francisco. A *San Francisco Examiner* article about the Hippie influx into the Haight-Ashbury is headlined "A New Paradise for Beatniks."

Thirty-nine-year-old Malcolm X, leader of the Organization of Afro-American Unity, is shot and killed by Black Muslim gunmen at the Audubon Ballroom in Washington Heights, New York City.

DEATHS: Sir Winston Churchill, Adlai Stevenson, T. S. Eliot, Lorraine Hansberry.

THE ARTS: Books: Naturalist Edwin Way Teale's *Wandering Through Winter* wins the Pulitzer Prize. Claude Brown, *Manchild in the Promised Land;* Lawrence Ferlinghetti, *Where Is Vietnam?;* Alex Haley, *The Autobiography of Malcolm X;* Bob Kaufman, *Solitudes Crowded with Loneliness;* Jack Kerouac, *Desolation Angels;* Timothy Leary et al., *The Psychedelic Reader;* Flannery O'Connor, *Everything That Rises Must Converge;* Lew Welch, *Hermit Poems.* Theater: Michael McClure, *The Beard;* Peter Weiss's *The Persecution and Assassination of Jean-Paul Marat as Performed by the Inmates of the Asylum of Charenton under the Direction of the Marquis de Sade.* Films: Julie Andrews in *The Sound of Music;* the Beatles in *Help.* Dance: Rudolph Nureyev and Dame Margot Fonteyn. Pop music: The Rolling Stones, Diana Ross, Barbra Streisand, Sonny and Cher. Performing with Joan Baez at the Newport Folk Festival, Bob Dylan switches to an electric guitar. The Fugs record their first LP for Broadside/Folkways. In the Bay Area, the counterculture newspaper the *Berkeley Barb* begins publication.

1966

The nonviolent Civil Rights Movement splits over the concept of "Black Power" promoted by a more militant, younger group who want revolutionary action. In June, attempting to encourage the

450,000 unregistered Negroes in the South to go to the polls, James Meredith, now a graduate of the University of Mississippi, is shot by a white man as Meredith begins the "Walk Against Fear," 220 miles, from Memphis to Jackson. Dr. King, the Urban League's Whitney Young, the NAACP's Roy Wilkins, CORE's Floyd McKissick, SNCC's Stokely Carmichael, and thousands of others continue the march and are joined later by Meredith. At night, Mississippi state troopers teargas the marchers in their tents. Carmichael is jailed in Greenwood, Mississippi, and comes out advocating the Black Power doctrine of the new Black Panther Party formed by Bobby Seale, Huey Newton, and Eldridge Cleaver. Wilkins disagrees: "The term 'Black Power' means antiwhite power. We of the NAACP will have none of this." Arriving in Jackson, the marchers attend a rally of 15,000 people at which, unlike the Selma march in 1965, few white supporters are present.

At a demonstration in Chicago to end racial discrimination in housing, schools, and jobs, King is powerless to stop the riots and looting in the slums. National Guard troops begin to carry bayonets. The Black Power cry is met with resistance by angry supporters of white supremacy. Riots erupt in Atlanta, Cleveland, Philadelphia, Providence, and other cities. In Mississippi, more than 80 percent of the 235,000 registered black voters show up at the polls.

Heavy fighting continues in Vietnam, when the U.S. air assaults Operation Rolling Thunder and Operation Strangler encounter effective antiaircraft fire in North Vietnam from advanced Soviet weapons. At the start of the year, 181,000 U.S. servicemen are in South Vietnam; at the end, 400,000. The U.S. suffers 4,800 killed in 1966, the first time our combat deaths exceed those of South Vietnamese soldiers. In China, Chairman Mao Tse-tung launches the Great Proletarian Cultural Revolution.

In the U.S., opposition to the Vietnam War continues to grow. The largest antiwar demonstration to date occurs in a march of more than 20,000 people down Fifth Avenue in New York City. In December, 5,000 students at UC Berkeley boycott classes to protest the suspension of participants in anti–Vietnam War rallies. Students seize the administration buildings at the University of Chicago and City College of New York. Forty percent of the U.S. population is under 25.

Indira Gandhi is elected prime minister of India. Ronald Reagan becomes governor of California. Betty Friedan is elected president of the National Organization for Women (NOW). Medicare coverage starts. The Supreme Court rules that no suspect in any criminal matter can be questioned without first being advised that he or she is entitled to have an attorney present (the Miranda law).

NASA launches four more manned flights into space in the U.S. Gemini program, at the cost of $7.7 billion in the 1966 budget for space research and development. After the Soviets place a 200-pound sphere on the Moon in the first soft landing, the UN approves a treaty forbidding any nation from claiming sovereignty over the Moon or any celestial body. In Pahute Mesa, Nevada, the U.S. sets off a nuclear test blast 50 times more powerful than that of the bomb used on Hiroshima.

Architect Minoru Yamasaki and consulting engineer Leslie Robertson design the World Trade Center buildings in lower Manhattan to be taller than any structure in the world. Offering 10 million square feet of floor space, these are the first skyscrapers specifically designed to survive the impact of a Boeing 707, the largest jet plane at the time. The two World Trade Center towers are completed in 1973.

DEATHS: Lenny Bruce, Buster Keaton, Walt Disney, poet Frank O'Hara, pioneering birth control advocate Margaret Sanger.

THE ARTS: Books: Truman Capote, *In Cold Blood;* Lenore Kandel, *The Love Book;* Tuli Kupferberg and Robert Bashlow, *1001 Ways to Beat the Draft;* Sylvia Plath, *Ariel;* Adrienne Rich, *Necessities of Life;* Anne Sexton, *Live or Die;* Susan Sontag, *Against Interpretation*; Jacqueline Susann, *Valley of the Dolls;* the *Atlantic Monthly* publishes Allen Ginsberg's "The Great Marijuana Hoax." Theater: Harold Pinter, *The Homecoming.* Film: Lynn Redgrave in *Georgy Girl;* Elizabeth Taylor and Richard Burton in *Who's Afraid of Virginia Woolf?* Music: The Metropolitan Opera opens at Lincoln Center with Samuel Barber's *Antony and Cleopatra.* Pop music: The Mamas and the Papas, the Byrds, Simon and Garfunkel. TV: CBS withdraws *The Amos and Andy Show* after blacks protest its racial stereotyping. For the first time, a World Negro Arts Festival is held, in Senegal. The *San Francisco Oracle* is founded.

1967

Black Power demonstrations result in the most violent racial protests in American history. In Newark, Boston, New York City, and other cities, bloody clashes erupt between police and rioters. In Detroit, the toll is 43 dead, 34 injured, 7,000 arrested, 1,300 buildings burned, and 2,700 stores and businesses destroyed. H. Rap Brown, SNCC leader, tells the blacks in Cambridge, Maryland, to burn down the town. In East Saint Louis, he says, "Stop singing and start swinging. Get a gun." Martin Luther King, Jr., Whitney Young, labor leader A. Philip Randolph, and Roy Wilkins continue to urge moderation. The split in the movement is complete.

President Johnson appoints Thurgood Marshall the first black justice to serve on the Supreme Court. Carl Stokes of Cleveland becomes the first black mayor of a major U.S. city.

In Vietnam, Operations Cedar Falls and Junction City escalate the bombing in North Vietnam. Weekly fatalities among American troops rise 33 percent over 1966 figures. Numbers of civilian dead also increase sharply. Congress votes $70 billion for defense, including $20 billion for Vietnam. Johnson asks for a 10 percent tax increase to head off rising deficits in the federal budget due to "an unequal and unjust distribution of the cost of supporting men in Vietnam."

Heavyweight boxing champion Muhammad Ali refuses to be inducted into the U.S. Army, claiming exemption as a Black Muslim minister. He says, "Why should they ask me and other so-called Negroes to put on a uniform and go ten thousand miles from home and drop bombs and bullets on brown people in Vietnam, when so-called Negro people in Louisville are treated like dogs and denied simple human rights?" The U.S. Boxing Commission strips him of his title. Later, Ali recalled, "Back then, black people were brainwashed to think white was supreme. But I loved being a black man. . . . I don't miss fighting. You miss me."

The Women Strike for Peace group organizes anti–Vietnam War protests during the October 16–22 "Stop the Draft" week. Norman Mailer marches with thousands of others to the Pentagon in a peace demonstration organized by David Dellinger's National Mobilization Committee to End the War in Vietnam. In Berkeley, antiwar protesters bomb the draft board office. In New York City, protesters attempting to shut down the armed forces induction center are taken into custody, including Allen Ginsberg and Dr. Benjamin Spock. In Baltimore, Catholic priest Philip Berrigan and two helpers pour blood over Selective Service files.

The Six Day War between Israel, Egypt, and Jordan is won by the Israeli Air Force. Israelis capture Bethlehem and East of Jerusalem from the Jordanians.

Apollo astronauts Virgil Grissom, Edward White, and Roger Chaffee die in a fire during a test at Cape Kennedy, Florida. The USS *Will Rogers* fires a 32,000-pound Polaris missile off Cape Kennedy and hits a target 1,500 miles away, near Antigua, in ten minutes. More than 50 nations sign a treaty to limit military activity in outer space.

The "Summer of Love" takes place in San Francisco, where "flower children" attempt to create a "dropped-out, tuned-in" community in the Haight-Ashbury. In New York City, 10,000 hippies celebrate a "be-in" on Easter Sunday in Central Park's Sheep Meadow, modeled on the "be-in" in San Francisco the previous January.

DEATHS: John Coltrane, Woody Guthrie, Langston Hughes, Dorothy Parker, Carson McCullers, Ernesto "Che" Guevara (in Bolivia).

NEW TECHNOLOGY: On December 2, Dr. Christiaan N. Barnard heads a team of 30 doctors who perform the first successful heart transplant in Cape Town, South Africa; the patient lives until December 31, 1967.

THE ARTS: Books: Mao Tse-tung's *Quotations* is the world's best-selling book. Richard Brautigan, *Trout Fishing in America;* Ann Charters, *A Bibliography of Works by Jack Kerouac;* John Cohen (ed.), *The Essential Lenny Bruce;* John Clellon Holmes, *Nothing More to Declare;* Sue Kaufman, *Diary of a Mad Housewife;* Denise Levertov, *The Sorrow Dance;* Norman Mailer, *Why Are We in Vietnam?;* William Manchester, *The Death of a President;* Marshall McLuhan and Quentin Fiore, *The Medium Is the Massage;* Valerie Solanas, *SCUM Manifesto;* Aleksandr Solzhenitsyn, *Cancer Ward;* William Styron, *The Confessions of Nat Turner;* Hunter Thompson, *Hell's Angels: A Strange and Terrible Saga;* Jean

Toomer's novel *Cane* reprinted for the first time in 42 years. Films: *The Graduate; Bonnie and Clyde; I Am Curious (Yellow)*. Theater: Tom Stoppard's *Rosencrantz and Guildenstern Are Dead*. Hit musical: *Hair*. Pop music: Carole King's "Natural Woman" sung by Aretha Franklin, Jim Morrison and the Doors, Country Joe and the Fish, the Grateful Dead, Jimi Hendrix, the Velvet Underground, Pink Floyd. Top album: The Beatles' *Sgt. Pepper's Lonely Hearts Club Band*. The Monterey Pop Festival draws 50,000 fans. Robert Crumb's comic magazine *Zap #0* is the first underground "comix." *Rolling Stone* magazine begins publication.

1968

In Memphis, after addressing a strike rally in support of the city's sanitation workers in April, Martin Luther King, Jr., is assassinated by James Earl Ray. Mobs in Washington, D.C., Baltimore, Chicago, Kansas City, and other cities take to the streets and are contained by the National Guard and the army. Black members of CORE also try to stop the looting and the fires. In May, the Poor People's Walk draws 50,000 to Washington, D.C. Resurrection City is built on the Mall near the Lincoln Memorial, and demonstrators demand Civil Rights legislation.

In Oakland, Black Panther members Eldridge Cleaver and David Hilliard are charged with attempted murder in a police shootout; Huey Newton is found guilty of killing a policeman, but he later wins an appeal.

In Vietnam, the Vietcong wage a large-scale, unexpected attack, the Tet Offensive, assaulting the U.S. embassy in Saigon, bombing every military base in South Vietnam, and killing 1,113 American personnel in two weeks. Johnson announces that he is halting the bombing of North Vietnam and calls upon President Ho Chi Minh to respond favorably to "this new step of peace." Johnson also announces that he will refuse another term as president. GOP leaders assert that his policies have led to riots and crimes at home and a loss of prestige abroad.

At Columbia University, SDS demonstrators oppose military contracts and the new $11.6 million gym in Morningside Park. Led by Mark Rudd, students occupy campus buildings before the police use what Mayor John Lindsay later termed "excessive force" to oust the demonstrators. Protests also occur at Ohio State, UCLA, Stanford, and other campuses. After students paralyze France with a series of strikes, President De Gaulle raises the minimum wage in France by 35 percent.

In June, Robert Kennedy, a Democratic candidate for the presidency, is assassinated in Los Angeles by Sirhan B. Sirhan, a Jordanian immigrant, in retaliation for the Arab losses in the Six Day War with Israel the previous year.

In August, the Democratic Party convenes in Chicago to elect Hubert Humphrey as their candidate. Mass demonstrations by the Yippies, the hippies, the flower children, and others against the Vietnam War lead to violent confrontations with the Chicago police and the National Guard. In November, Richard Nixon is elected president by a thin margin and pledges to end the war in Vietnam and to restore law and order. New York Democrat Shirley Chisholm becomes the first black woman to serve in the House of Representatives.

George Mitchell and Dennis Banks, two members of the Chippewa tribe, establish the American Indian Movement (AIM). Militant participants in the Women's Movement protest the Miss America beauty pageant in Atlantic City, insisting that women are "no longer enslaved by ludicrous beauty standards." Robin Morgan and members of the Women's International Terrorist Conspiracy from Hell (WITCH) display a banner endorsing the new phrase "Women's Liberation" to television viewers throughout the world.

In Czechoslovakia, Soviet troops invade the country, fire on crowds in Prague, and remove the liberal leader Alexander Dubcek, the Czech Communist Party chief. In Iraq, Saddam Hussein becomes vice president. In Brazil, the ministry of the interior begins a government campaign of genocide against the nation's Indian peoples in order to clear native lands for development. Entire tribes of Amazonian natives are gunned down, poisoned, or deliberately infected with smallpox. Other South American nations will carry out similar programs.

DEATHS: John Steinbeck; Helen Keller; Norman Thomas, six-time presidential candidate on the Socialist ticket; Clyde Warrior, American Indian activist; Neal Cassady, hero of Kerouac's *On the Road*.

THE ARTS: Books: Edward Abbey, *Desert Solitaire;* Donald Barthelme, *Unspeakable Practices, Unnatural Acts;* Carlos Castaneda, *The Teachings of Don Juan: A Yaqui Way of Knowledge;* Eldridge Cleaver, *Soul on Ice;* Allen Ginsberg, *Planet News;* Nikki Giovanni, *Black Judgment;* Etheridge Knight, *Poems from Prison;* Norman Mailer, *The Armies of the Night;* N. Scott Momaday, *House Made of Dawn;* Anne Moody, *Coming of Age in Mississippi;* Tom Wolfe, *The Electric Kool-Aid Acid Test.* Films: Stanley Kubrick's *2001: A Space Odyssey; Midnight Cowboy; Planet of the Apes; Night of the Living Dead; Rosemary's Baby.* Dance: Merce Cunningham, Alvin Ailey. Pop Music: Janis Joplin with Big Brother and the Holding Company; Frank Zappa and the Mothers of Invention; Tiny Tim.

1969

Richard M. Nixon is inaugurated as the thirty-seventh president of the United States of America. Antiwar protests take place in Washington, D.C., during the inauguration, and he watches the parade from behind bulletproof glass. Ralph Abernathy says that the new president's inaugural speech reflects "no sense of urgency, and no sensitivity to the basic problems of hunger, poverty, and race in this nation." Henry Kissinger becomes assistant for national security affairs, going on to be secretary of state in Nixon's cabinet. Runaway inflation and rising unemployment indicate a recession to come.

The Supreme Court rules unanimously that school districts must end segregation "at once," toughening its 1954 decision that desegregation should proceed with "all deliberate speed." Voters in Fayette, Mississippi, elect Charles Evers, the brother of slain Civil Rights leader Medgar Evers, as the first black mayor of a town in that state. Fayette is three-quarters black, but until the Voting Rights Act of 1968, a sufficient number of blacks could not register to vote.

In Vietnam, U.S. soldiers massacre 350 men, women, and children in My Lai. Lieutenant William Calley, Jr., is found guilty of the atrocities. Nixon reduces the number of servicemen in Vietnam from 537,000 to under 500,000. By 1969 the number of American dead totals 30,991 killed in action; by 1973, when the war ends, another 15,499 will be killed. In all, 8,744,000 Americans served in the Vietnam War, as compared with 4,743,826 who served in World War II.

Peace rallies against the war in Vietnam are held in Washington, D.C., and San Francisco. On October 16, 1969, millions of Americans are involved in a one-day Vietnam Moratorium, a national protest organized by college students and joined by groups such as the United Auto Workers.

In Chicago, the trial of the Chicago Eight for disturbances during the 1968 Democratic National Convention results in 175 contempt citations by Judge Julius J. Hoffman. The defendants include Yippies Abbie Hoffman and Jerry Rubin; Black Panther Bobby Seale; Tom Hayden and Rennie Davis of the SDS; David Dellinger; John Froines, a Civil Rights activist; and Lee Weiner, a sociology teacher. All are sentenced to five years in prison for conspiring to set off the police riot at the convention. Four years later the sentences are appealed, and no jail terms are imposed.

In Berkeley, demonstrations against the University of California's plan to repossess a vacant lot turned into a communal garden result in the Battle of People's Park. Police arrest 900 people after firing shotguns to disperse the crowd. National Guardsmen use bayonets and tear gas against student demonstrators at the University of Wisconsin at Madison and the University of North Carolina. Administrators blame "white radicals" from the SDS for the disruptions.

In Greenwich Village, New York City, gays riot against a raid by the vice squad at the Stonewall Inn, initiating the Gay Liberation Movement. The Equal Rights Amendment for Women is still 3 states short of the 38 needed for ratification. A poll shows that the most admired American women are Mamie Eisenhower, Pat Nixon, Ethel and Rose Kennedy, and Jackie Kennedy Onassis.

A group of 78 Native Americans, led by Richard Oakes and Grace Thorpe, angry at the lack of opportunity to study their own cultures, "reclaim" and occupy Alcatraz Island in San Francisco Bay for eighteen months. California becomes the first state to enact a "no fault" divorce law.

A UN advisory group on environmental pollution announces that two-thirds of the world's original forest has been lost to clearance and agriculture.

Palestinian groups organize under the leadership of Yasser Arafat, head of the Palestine Liberation Organization (PLO). They claim responsibility for a terrorist bomb at a large market in Tel Aviv. Golda Meir becomes prime minister of Israel.

DEATHS: Dwight Eisenhower, Ho Chi Minh, Judy Garland, Mary Jo Kopechne, Jack Kerouac.

THE ARTS: Books: Lawrence Ferlinghetti, *Tyrannus Nix?;* Germaine Greer, *The Female Eunuch;* Haki R. Madhubuti, *Don't Cry, Scream;* Michael McClure, *Ghost Tantras;* Kate Millett, *Sexual Politics;* Joyce Carol Oates, *Them;* Ishmael Reed, *Yellow Back Radio Broke-Down;* Carolyn M. Rodgers, *Songs of a Black Bird;* Philip Roth, *Portnoy's Complaint;* Kurt Vonnegut, Jr., *Slaughterhouse-Five;* Al Young, *Dancing.* Theater: Kenneth Tynan, *O! Calcutta!* Films: *Easy Rider;* Haskell Wexler's *Medium Cool* (about the 1968 Chicago Democratic Convention); *Midnight Cowboy; Butch Cassidy and the Sundance Kid.* Pop music: Johnny Cash, Bob Dylan, Leonard Cohen, Creedence Clearwater Revival; the Beatles' *Abbey Road;* the music festivals at Woodstock and Altamont, where the Hell's Angels guards beat, kick, and stab to death a spectator who brandished a gun.

1970 AND BEYOND

By 1970, the population of human beings in the world is 3.6 billion, an increase of 18 percent from 1960.

April 30, 1970—The first celebration of Earth Day. The Environmental Protection Agency is established.

May 4, 1970—At Kent State University, four students protesting the United States' widening the Vietnam War with attacks on Cambodia are shot dead by National Guardsmen during a campus demonstration.

Fall 1970—Jimi Hendrix and Janis Joplin die of drug overdoses.

1971—Ted Hoff invents the microprocessor, the Intel 4004 "computer on a chip." The Twenty-sixth Amendment to the U.S. Constitution gives 18-year-olds the right to vote. Jim Morrison dies of a drug overdose.

1972—The last American ground troops leave Vietnam. The U.S. Senate confirms the House of Representatives' vote for a constitutional amendment banning legal discrimination against women because of their gender (Equal Rights Amendment), which is never ratified. Drs. James Lovelock and Lynn Margulis propose the Gaia Hypothesis, which states that the earth is alive. DDT is banned for agricultural use. Former president Harry S. Truman dies at age 88.

1973—Former president Lyndon B. Johnson dies of a heart attack at age 64. The Supreme Court rules in *Roe v. Wade* to legalize abortion in the United States; the vote is 7 to 2. The military draft is discontinued and the armed forces become all-volunteer.

1982—Dedication of the Vietnam Veterans Memorial in Washington, D.C.

THE PORTABLE SIXTIES READER

PART ONE

STRUGGLING TO BE FREE: THE CIVIL RIGHTS MOVEMENT

*And when we allow freedom to ring, when we let it ring from every
village and hamlet, from every state and city, we will be able to
speed up that day when all of God's children—black men and
white men, Jews and Gentiles, Catholics and Protestants—will be
able to join hands and to sing in the words of the old Negro spiri-
tual, "Free at last, free at last; thank God Almighty, we are free
at last!"*

MARTIN LUTHER KING, JR.
"I HAVE A DREAM"
WASHINGTON, D.C.
AUGUST 28, 1963

THE MODERN CIVIL RIGHTS MOVEMENT in the United States has
its roots in the decades preceding the 1960s. The effects of slavery had
long been woven into the fabric of the nation. Since the Reconstruc-
tion era, racial lynchings—the murder of black men by white mobs—
had become a Southern tradition. They had been so frequent that
Walter Chivers, Martin Luther King, Jr.'s sociology professor at More-
house College, believed that between 1880 and 1922, a lynching
probably occurred every two and a half days in the South. Perhaps
most notable in the movement's taking hold was the 1954 Supreme
Court decision banning segregation in public schools—*Brown v. Board
of Education* (though this had no immediate effect on the unfair "sepa-
rate but equal" practice in the South). The groundswell of the move-
ment continued the next year with the widespread humanitarian
response to the lynching of Emmett Till, a fourteen-year-old school-
boy from Chicago who was visiting relatives in Money, Mississippi.

In 1955, after allegedly whistling at a white woman, Till was sav-
agely beaten, shot, and thrown into the Tallahatchie River with a
metal fan barbwired around his neck. His body was recovered,
brought back to Chicago from Mississippi, and put on display for four
days in an open casket, which was viewed by nearly a hundred thou-
sand people. A photograph of Till's battered, bloated face, juxtaposed
with earlier pictures of him neatly dressed in a shirt and tie, appeared

3

in several black periodicals with large circulations, including *Jet* and the *Chicago Defender*. The story was also covered in many white mainstream magazines and newspapers.

Till's murder affected many people who would become active in the Civil Rights Movement in the following decade, including King, Rosa Parks, and Anne Moody. Three months after a white jury acquitted the white men who had lynched Till, Parks refused to give up her seat to white passengers on a bus in Montgomery and was promptly arrested for disobeying Alabama segregation laws. As a response to her arrest, blacks in Montgomery carried out a successful yearlong boycott of the city buses; their protest resulted in the first integrated bus service in a Southern city, starting December 21, 1956.

At the beginning of the boycott, Martin Luther King, Jr., the twenty-six-year-old minister of the Dexter Avenue Baptist Church in Montgomery, was one of the black leaders who had agreed to support the community action. Early in December 1955, in his first address as president of the Montgomery Improvement Association (MIA; the name was invented by King's close friend the Reverend Ralph Abernathy), King praised Rosa Parks's bravery and exhorted his black audience to stay off the city buses. "Right here in Montgomery when the history books are written in the future, somebody will have to say, 'There lived a race of people, black people, fleecy locks and black complexions, of people who had the moral courage to stand up for their rights, and thereby they injected a new meaning into the veins of history and civilization.' " What began as a black-led bus boycott in Montgomery soon escalated into the most momentous social struggle in postwar America.

For the most part, despite the prevalence of racism throughout the country, mainstream American literature in the 1950s reflected the national mood of complacent satisfaction with the status quo. If the *Brown v. Board of Education* decision had shown that the courts by themselves could not greatly change American society, neither could the work of American writers. Brilliant works of poetry and fiction by black authors, most notably Ralph Ellison's novel *Invisible Man* (1952), helped to raise the consciousness of racial injustice in many readers, but the books didn't change social conditions for black Americans.

The legacy of African-American protest literature created by authors such as Richard Wright (1908–1960), Langston Hughes (1902–1967), Zora Neale Hurston (1891–1960), and W. E. B. Du Bois (1868–1963) was a vital tradition that extended back to Frederick Douglass (1818–1895), Sojourner Truth (1797–1883), and the Negro spirituals. In 1940, in the essay "How 'Bigger' Was Born," Wright explained his creation of the tormented black protagonist of his novel *Native Son* and argued that racism was the central issue for American writers:

> Early American writers, Henry James and Nathaniel Hawthorne, complained bitterly about the bleakness and flatness of the American scene. But I think that if they were alive, they'd feel at home in modern America. True . . . we have only a money-grubbing industrial civilization. But we do have in the Negro the embodiment of a past tragic enough to appease the spiritual hunger of even a James; and we have in the oppression of the Negro a shadow athwart our national life dense and heavy enough to satisfy even the gloomy broodings of a Hawthorne. And if Poe were alive, he would not have to invent horror; horror would invent him.

In the early years of the 1960s, the Civil Rights confrontations begun so courageously by African-Americans in the preceding decade continued to gather momentum. In February 1960, four classmates at the all-Negro Agricultural and Technical College in Greensboro, North Carolina, staged a sit-in at the lunch counter at the local F. W. Woolworth store. More than fifty restaurant sit-ins followed in other Southern cities. In the fall of 1960, federal marshals escorted four black girls to first-grade classrooms in New Orleans through mobs of hostile whites. In 1961 Freedom Riders challenged segregation when they attempted to ride buses through the South. They were savagely attacked and beaten in Alabama, Mississippi, and Louisiana. In the aftermath of the violence, many American authors—both black and white—wrote about the resulting social upheaval that challenged the nation's complacency about racial injustice.

James Baldwin

In 1961 the novelist James Baldwin published an essay about riding the integrated city buses in baffled and demoralized Montgomery after meeting Martin Luther King, Jr., in 1958. Five years older than King, Baldwin thought of the Civil Rights leader as "young Martin." While Baldwin felt King's power, he also had an uneasy presentiment of King's vulnerability, as though King "were a younger, much-loved, and menaced brother." Baldwin's essay, "The Dangerous Road Before Martin Luther King," was included in the February 1961 issue of Harper's. *Baldwin wrote it after he had expressed his alienation from racist American society in two novels,* Go Tell It on the Mountain *(1953) and* Giovanni's Room *(1956), and the nonfiction collection* Notes of a Native Son *(1955). Not long after his article on King, Baldwin published a second collection of essays,* Nobody Knows My Name *(1961), and* The Fire Next Time *(1963), a national bestseller that urged the importance of recognizing all African-Americans as fully empowered American citizens.*

THE DANGEROUS ROAD BEFORE MARTIN LUTHER KING

I FIRST MET Martin Luther King, Jr. nearly three years ago now, in Atlanta, Georgia. He was there on a visit from his home in Montgomery. He was "holed up," he was seeing no one, he was busy writing a book—so I was informed by the friend who, mercilessly, at my urgent request, was taking me to King's hotel. I felt terribly guilty about interrupting him but not guilty enough to let the opportunity pass. Still, having been raised among preachers, I would not have been surprised if King had cursed out the friend, refused to speak to me, and slammed the door in our faces. Nor would I have blamed him if he had, since I knew that by this time he must have been forced to suffer many an admiring fool.

But the Reverend King is not like any preacher I have ever met before. For one thing, to state it baldly, I liked him. It is rare that one *likes* a world-famous man—by the time they become world-famous they rarely like themselves, which may account for this antipathy. Yet King is immediately and tremendously winning, there is really no other word for it; and there he stood, with an inquiring and genuine smile on his face, in the open door of his hotel room. Behind him, on a desk, was a wilderness of paper. He looked at his friend, he looked at me, I was introduced; he smiled and shook my hand and we entered the room.

I do not remember much about that first meeting because I was too overwhelmed by the fact that I was meeting him at all. There were millions of questions that I wanted to ask him, but I feared to begin. Besides, his friend had warned me not to "bug" him, I was not there in a professional capacity, and the questions I wanted to ask him had less to do with his public role than with his private life. When I say "private life" I am not referring to those maliciously juicy tidbits, those meaningless details, which clutter up the gossip columns and muddy everybody's mind and obliterate the humanity of the subject as well as that of the reader. I wanted to ask him how it felt to be standing where he stood, how he bore it, what complex of miracles had prepared him for it. But such questions can scarcely be asked, they can scarcely be answered.

And King does not like to talk about himself. I have described him as winning, but he does not give the impression of being particularly outgoing or warm. His restraint is not, on the other hand, of that icily uneasy, nerve-racking kind to be encountered in so many famous Negroes who have allowed their aspirations and notoriety to destroy their identities and who always seem to be giving an uncertain imitation of some extremely improbable white man. No, King impressed me then and he impresses me now as a man solidly anchored in those spiritual realities concerning which he can be so eloquent. This divests him of the hideous piety which is so prevalent in his profession, and it also saves him from the ghastly self-importance which, until recently, was all that allowed one to be certain one was addressing a Negro leader. King cannot be considered a chauvinist at all, not even incidentally, or part of the time, or under stress, or subconsciously. What he says to Negroes he will say to whites; and what he says to whites he will say to Negroes. He is the first Negro leader in my experience, or the first in many generations, of whom this can be said; most of his predecessors were in the extraordinary position of saying to white men, *Hurry,* while saying to black men, *Wait.* This fact is of the utmost importance. It says a great deal about the situation which produced King and in which he operates; and, of course, it tells us a great deal about the man.

"He came through it all," said a friend of his to me, with wonder and not a little envy, "really unscarred. He never went around fighting with himself, like we all did." The "we" to whom this friend refers are all considerably older than King, which may have something to do with this lightly sketched species of schizophrenia; in any case, the fact that King really loves the people he represents and has—*there-fore*—no hidden, interior need to hate the white people who oppose him has had and will, I think, continue to have the most far-reaching and unpredictable repercussions on our racial situation. It need scarcely be said that our racial situation is far more complex and dangerous than we are prepared to think of it as being—since our major desire is not to think of it at all—and King's role in it is of an unprecedented difficulty.

He is not, for example, to be confused with Booker T. Washington, whom we gratefully allowed to solve the racial problem single-handedly. It was Washington who assured us, in 1895, one year before it became the law of the land, that the education of Negroes would not give them any desire to become equals; they would be content to remain—or, rather, after living for generations in the greatest intimacy with whites, to become—separate. It is a measure of the irreality to which the presence of the Negro had already reduced the nation that this utterly fantastic idea, which thoroughly controverts the purpose of education, which has no historical or psychological validity, and which denies all the principles on which the country imagines itself to have been founded, was not only accepted with cheers but became the cornerstone of an entire way of life. And this did not come about, by the way, merely because of the venom or villainy of the South. It could never have come about at all without the tacit consent of the North; and this consent robs the North, historically and actually, of any claim to moral superiority. The failure of the government to make any realistic provision for the education of tens of thousands of illiterate former slaves had the effect of dumping this problem squarely into the lap of one man—who knew, whatever else he may not have known, that the education of Negroes had somehow to be accomplished. Whether or not Washington believed what he said is certainly an interesting question. But he *did* know that he could accomplish his objective by telling white men what they wanted to hear. And it has never been very difficult for a Negro in this country to figure out what white men want to hear: he takes his condition as an echo of their desires.

There will be no more Booker T. Washingtons. And whether we like it or not, and no matter how hard or how long we oppose it, there will be no more segregated schools, there will be no more segregated anything. King is entirely right when he says that segregation is dead. The real question which faces the Republic is just how long, how violent, and how expensive the funeral is going to be; and this question it is up to the Republic to resolve, it is not really in King's hands. The sooner the corpse is buried, the sooner we can get around to the far more taxing and rewarding problems of integration, or what King calls community, and what I think of as the achievement of nationhood, or, more simply and cruelly, the growing up of this dangerously adolescent country.

I saw King again, later that same evening, at a party given by this same friend. He came late, did not stay long. I remember him standing in the shadows of the room, near a bookcase, drinking something nonalcoholic, and being patient with the interlocutor who had trapped him in this spot. He obviously wanted to get away and go to bed. King is somewhat below what is called average height, he is sturdily built, but is not quite as heavy or as stocky as he had seemed to me at first. I remember feeling, rather as though he were a younger, much-loved, and menaced brother, that he seemed very slight and vulnerable to be taking on such tremendous odds.

I was leaving for Montgomery the next day, and I called on King in the morning to ask him to have someone from the Montgomery Improvement Association meet me at the airport. It was he who had volunteered to do this for me, since he knew that I knew no one there, and he also probably realized that I was frightened. He was coming to Montgomery on Sunday to preach in his own church.

Montgomery is the cradle of the Confederacy, an unlucky distinction which no one in Montgomery is allowed to forget. The White House which symbolized and housed that short-lived government is still standing, and "people," one of the Montgomery ministers told me, "walk around in those halls and cry." I do not doubt it, the people of Montgomery having inherited nothing less than an ocean of spilt milk. The boycott had been over for a year by the time I got there, and had been ended by a federal decree outlawing segregation in the buses. Therefore, the atmosphere in Montgomery was extraordinary. I think that I have never been in a town so aimlessly hostile, so baffled and demoralized. Whoever has a stone to fling, and flings it, is then left without any weapons; and this was (and remains) the situation of the white people in Montgomery.

I took a bus ride, for example, solely in order to observe the situation on the busses. As I stepped into the bus, I suddenly remembered that I had neglected to ask anyone the price of a bus ride in Montgomery, and so I asked the driver. He gave me the strangest, most hostile of looks, and turned his face away. I dropped fifteen cents into the box and sat down, placing myself, delicately, just a little forward of the center of the bus. The driver had seemed to feel that my question was but another Negro trick, that I had something up my sleeve, and that to answer my question in any way would be to expose himself to disaster. He could not guess what I was thinking, and he was not going to risk further personal demoralization by trying to. And this spirit was the spirit of the town. The bus pursued its course, picking up white and Negro passengers. Negroes sat where they pleased, none very far back; one large woman, carrying packages, seated herself directly behind the driver. And the whites sat there, ignoring them, in a huffy, offended silence.

This silence made me think of nothing so much as the silence which follows a really serious lovers' quarrel: the whites, beneath their cold hostility, were mystified and deeply hurt. They had been betrayed by the Negroes, not merely because the Negroes had declined to remain in their "place," but because the Negroes had refused to be controlled by the town's image of them. And, without this image, it seemed to me, the whites were abruptly and totally lost. The very foundations of their private and public worlds were being destroyed.

I had never heard King preach, and I went on Sunday to hear him at his church. This church is a red brick structure, with a steeple, and it directly faces, on the other side of the street, a white, domed building. My notes fail to indicate whether this is the actual capitol of the state or merely a courthouse; but the conjunction of the two buildings, the steepled one low and dark and tense, the domed one higher and dead white and forbidding, sums up, with an explicitness a set designer might hesitate to copy, the struggle now going on in Montgomery.

At that time in Montgomery, King was almost surely the most beloved man there. I do not think that one could have entered any of the packed churches at that time, if King was present, and not have felt this. Of course, I think that King would be loved by his congregations in any case, and there is always a large percentage of church women who adore the young male pastor, and not always, or not necessarily, out of those grim, psychic motives concerning which everyone today is so knowledgeable. No, there was a feeling in this church which quite transcended anything I have ever felt in a church before. Here it was, totally familiar and yet completely new, the packed church, glorious with the Sunday finery of the women, solemn with the touching, gleaming sobriety of the men, beautiful with children. Here were the ushers, standing in the aisles in white dresses or in dark suits, with arm bands on. People were standing along each wall, beside the windows, and standing in the back. King and his lieutenants were in the pulpit, young Martin—as I was beginning to think of him—in the center chair.

When King rose to speak—to preach—I began to understand how the atmosphere of this church differed from that of all the other churches I have known. At first I thought that the great emotional power and authority of the Negro church was being put to a new use, but this is not exactly the case. The Negro church was playing the same role which it has always played in Negro life, but it had acquired a new power.

Until Montgomery, the Negro church, which has always been the place where protest and condemnation could be most vividly articulated, also operated as a kind of sanctuary. The minister who spoke could not hope to effect any objective change in the lives of his hearers, and the people did not expect him to. All they came to find, and all that he could give them, was the sustenance for another day's journey. Now, King could certainly give his congregation that, but he could also give them something more than that, and he had. It is true that it was *they* who had begun the struggle of which he was now the symbol and the leader; it is true that it had taken all of *their* insistence to overcome in him a grave reluctance to stand where he now stood. But it is also true, and it does not happen often, that once he had accepted the place they had prepared for him, their struggle became absolutely indistinguishable from his own, and took over and controlled his life. He suffered with them and, thus, he helped them to suffer. The joy which filled this church, therefore, was the joy achieved by people who have ceased to delude themselves about an intolerable situation, who have found their prayers for a leader miraculously answered, and who now know that they can change their situation, if they will.

And, surely, very few people had ever spoken to them as King spoke. King is a great speaker. The secret of his greatness does not lie in his voice or his presence or his manner, though it has something to do with all these; nor does it lie in his verbal range or felicity, which are not striking; nor does he have any capacity for those stunning, demagogic flights of the imagination which bring an audience cheering to its feet. The secret lies, I think, in his intimate knowledge of the people he is addressing, be they black or white, and in the forthrightness with which he speaks of those things which hurt and baffle them. He does not offer any easy comfort and this keeps his hearers absolutely tense. He allows them their self-respect—indeed, he insists on it.

"We know," he told them, "that there are many things wrong in the white world. But there are many things wrong in the black world, too. We can't keep on blaming the white man. There are many things we must do for ourselves."

He suggested what some of these were:

"I know none of you make enough money—but save some of it. And there are some things we've got to face. I know the situation is responsible for a lot of it, but do you know that Negroes are 10 per cent of the population of St. Louis and are responsible for 58 per cent of its crimes? We've got to face that. And we have to do something about our moral standards. And we've got to stop lying to the white man. Every time you let the white man think *you* think segregation is right, you are co-operating with him in doing *evil*.

"The next time," he said, "the white man asks you what you think of segregation, you tell him, Mr. Charlie, I think it's wrong and I wish you'd do something about it by nine o'clock tomorrow morning!"

This brought a wave of laughter and King smiled, too. But he had meant every word he said, and he expected his hearers to act on them. They also expected this of themselves, which is not the usual effect of a sermon; and that they are living up to their expectations no white man in Montgomery will deny.

There was a dinner in the church basement afterwards, where, for the first time, I met Mrs. King—light brown, delicate, really quite beautiful, with a wonderful laugh—and watched young Martin circulating among church members and visitors. I overheard him explaining to someone that bigotry was a disease and that the greatest victim of this disease was not the bigot's object, but the bigot himself. And these people could only be saved by love. In liberating oneself, one was also liberating them. I was shown, by someone else, the damage done to the church by bombs. King did not mention the bombing of his own home, and I did not bring it up. Late the next night, after a mass meeting in another church, I flew to Birmingham.

I did not see King again for nearly three years. I saw him in Atlanta, just after his acquittal by a Montgomery court of charges of perjury, tax evasion, and misuse of public funds. He had moved to Atlanta and was co-pastor, with his father, of his father's church. He had made this move, he told me, because the pressures on him took him away from Montgomery for such excessively long periods that he did not feel that he was properly fulfilling his ministerial duties there. An attempt had been made on his life—in the North, by a mysterious and deranged Negro woman; and he was about to receive, in the state of Georgia, for driving without a resident driver's license, a suspended twelve-month sentence.

And, since I had last seen him, the Negro student movement had begun and was irresistibly bringing about great shifts and divisions in the Negro world, and in the nation. In short, by the time we met again, he was more beleaguered than he had ever been before, and not only by his enemies in the white South. Three years earlier, I had not encountered very many people—I am speaking now of Negroes—who were really critical of him. But many more people seemed critical of him now, were bitter, disappointed, skeptical. None of this had anything to do—I want to make this absolutely clear— with his personal character or his integrity. It had to do with his effectiveness as a leader. King has had an extraordinary effect in the Negro world, and therefore in the nation, and is now in the center of an extremely complex cross fire.

He was born in Atlanta in 1929. He has Irish and Indian blood in his veins—Irish from his father's, Indian from his mother's side. His maternal grandfather built Ebenezer Baptist Church, which, as I have said, young Martin now co-pastors with his father. This grandfather seems to have been an extremely active and capable man, having been one of the NAACP leaders in Atlanta thirty or forty years ago, and having been instrumental in bringing about the construction of Atlanta's first Negro high school. The paternal grandfather is something else again, a poor, violent, and illiterate farmer who tried to find refuge from reality in drinking. He clearly had a great influence on the formation of the character of Martin, Sr., who determined, very early, to be as unlike his father as possible.

Martin, Sr. came to Atlanta in 1916, a raw, strapping country boy, determined, in the classic American tradition, to rise above his station. It could not have been easy for him in the Deep South of 1916, but he was, luckily, too young for the Army, and prices and wages rose during the war, and his improvident father had taught him the value of thrift. So he got his start. He studied in evening school, entered Atlanta's Morehouse College in 1925, and graduated in June of 1930, more than a year after Martin was born. (There are two other children, an older girl who now teaches at Spelman College, and a younger boy, pastor of a church in Noonan, Georgia.) By this time, Martin, Sr. had become a preacher, and was pastor of two small churches; and at about this time, his father-in-law asked him to become the assistant pastor of Ebenezer Baptist Church, which he did.

His children have never known poverty, and Martin, Sr. is understandably very proud of this. "My prayer," he told me, "was always: Lord, grant that my children will not have to come the way I did." They didn't, they haven't, the prayers certainly did no harm. But one cannot help feeling that a person as single-minded and determined as the elder Reverend King clearly is would have accomplished anything he set his hand to, anyway.

"I equipped myself to give them the comforts of life," he says. "Not to waste, not to keep up with the Joneses, but just to be comfortable. We've never lived in a rented house—and never ridden *too* long in a car on which payment was due."

He is naturally very proud of Martin, Jr. but he claims to be not at all surprised. "He sacrificed to make himself ready"—ready, that is, for a trial, or a series of trials, which might have been the undoing of a lesser man. Yet, though he is not surprised at the extraordinary nature of his son's eminence, he *was* surprised when, at college, Martin decided that he was called to preach. He had expected him to become a doctor or a lawyer because he always spoke of these professions as though he aspired to them.

As he had; and since, as I have said, King is far from garrulous on the subject of his interior life, it is somewhat difficult to know what led him to make this switch. He had already taken pre-medical and law courses. But he had been raised by a minister, an extremely strong-minded one at that, and in an extraordinarily peaceful and protected way. "Never," says his father, "has Martin known a fuss or a fight or a strike-back in the home." On the other hand, there are some things from which no Negro can really be protected, for which he can only be prepared; and Martin, Sr. was more successful than most fathers in accomplishing this strenuous and delicate task. "I have never believed," he says, "that anybody was better than I." That this is true would seem to be proved by the career of his son, who *"never went around fighting with himself, like we all did."*

Here, speculation is really on very marshy ground, for the father must certainly have fought in himself some of the battles from which young Martin was protected. We have only to consider the era, especially in the South, to realize that this must be true. And it must have demanded great steadiness of mind, as well as great love, to hide so successfully from his children the evidence of these battles. And, since salvation, humanly speaking, is a two-way street, I suggest that, if the father saved the children, it was, almost equally, the children who saved him. It would seem that he was able, with rare success, to project onto his children, or at least onto one of them, a sense of life as he himself would have liked to live it, and somehow made real in their personalities principles on which he himself must often have found it extremely dangerous and difficult to act. Martin, Sr. is regarded with great ambivalence by both the admirers and detractors of his son, and I shall, alas, shortly have more to say concerning his generation; but I do not think that the enormous achievement sketched above can possibly be taken away from him.

Again, young Martin's decision to become a minister has everything to do with his temperament, for he seems always to have been characterized by his striking mixture of steadiness and peace. He apparently did the normal amount of crying in his childhood, for I am told that his grandmother "couldn't stand to see it." But he seems to have done very little complaining; when he was spanked, "he just stood there and took it"; he seems to have been incapable of carrying grudges; and when he was attacked, he did not strike back.

From King's own account, I can only guess that this decision was aided by the fact that, at Morehouse College, he was asked to lead the devotions. The relationship thus established between himself and his contemporaries, or between himself and himself, or between himself and God, seemed to work for him as no other had. Also, I think it is of the utmost importance to realize that King loves the South; many Negroes do. The ministry seems to afford him the best possible vehicle for the expression of that love. At that time in his life, he was discovering "the beauty of the South"; he sensed in the people "a new determination"; and he felt that there was a need for "a new, courageous witness."

But it could not have occurred to him, of course, that *he* would be, and in such an unprecedented fashion, that witness. When Coretta King—then Coretta Scott—met him in Boston, where he was attending Boston University and she was studying at the New England Conservatory of Music, she found him an earnest, somewhat too carefully dressed young man. He had gone from Morehouse to Crozer Theological Seminary in Pennsylvania; the latter institution was interracial, which may have had something to do with his self-consciousness. He was fighting at that time to free himself from all the stereotypes of the Negro, an endeavor which does not leave much room for spontaneity. Both he and Coretta were rather lonely in Boston, and for similar reasons. They were both very distinguished and promising young people, which means that they were also tense, self-conscious, and insecure. They were inevitably cut off from the bulk of the Negro community and their role among whites had to be somewhat ambiguous, for they were not being judged merely as themselves—or, anyway, they could scarcely afford to think so. They were responsible for the good name of all the Negro people.

Coretta had perhaps had more experience than Martin in this role. The more I spoke to her, the more I realized how her story illuminates that of her husband. She had come from Lincoln High in Marion, Alabama, to Antioch College in Ohio, part of one of the earliest groups of Negro students accepted there. She was thus, in effect, part of an experiment, and though she took it very well and can laugh about it now, she certainly must have had her share of exasperated and lonely moments. The social mobility of a Negro girl, especially in such a setting, is even more severely circumscribed than that of a Negro male, and any lapse or error on her part is far more dangerous. From Antioch, Coretta eventually came to Boston on a scholarship and by this time a certain hoydenish, tomboy quality in her had begun, apparently, to be confirmed. The atmosphere at Antioch had been entirely informal, which pleased Coretta; I gather that at this time in her life she was usually to be seen in sweaters, slacks, and scarves. It was a ferociously formal young man and a ferociously informal young girl who finally got together in Boston.

Martin immediately saw through Coretta's disguise, and informed her on their first or second meeting that she had all the qualities he wanted in a wife. Coretta's understandable tendency was to laugh at this; but this tendency was checked by the rather frightening suspicion that he meant it; if he had not meant it, he would not have said it. But a great deal had been invested in Coretta's career as a singer, and she did not feel that she had the right to fail all the people who had done so much to help her. "And I'd certainly never intended to marry a *minister*. It was true that he didn't seem like any of the ministers I'd met, but—still—I thought of how circumscribed my life might become." By circumscribed, she meant dull; she could not possibly have been more mistaken.

What had really happened, in Coretta's case, as in so many others, was that life had simply refused to recognize her private timetable. She had always intended to marry, but tidily, possibly meeting her husband at the end of a triumphant concert tour. However, here he was now, exasperatingly early, and she had to rearrange herself around this fact. She and Martin were married on June 18, 1953. By now, naturally, it is she whom Martin sometimes accuses of thinking too much about clothes. "People who are doing something don't have time to be worried about all that," he has informed her. Well, he certainly ought to know.

Coretta King told me that from the time she reached Boston and all during Martin's courtship, and her own indecision, she yet could not rid herself of a feeling that all that was happening had been, somehow, preordained. And one does get an impression, until this point in the King story at least, that inexorable forces which none of us really know anything about were shaping and preparing him for that fateful day in Montgomery. Everything that he will need has been delivered, so to speak, and is waiting to be used. Everything, including the principle of nonviolence. It was in 1950 that Dr. Mordecai W. Johnson of Howard University visited India. King heard one of the speeches Johnson made on his return, and it was from this moment that King became interested in Gandhi as a figure, and in non-violence as a way of life. Later, in 1957, he would visit India himself.

But, so far, of course, we are speaking after the fact. Plans and patterns are always more easily discernible then. This is not so when we try to deal with the present, or attempt speculations about the future.

Immediately after the failure, last June, of Montgomery's case against him, King returned to Atlanta. I entered, late, on a Sunday morning, the packed Ebenezer Baptist Church, and King was already speaking.

He did not look any older, and yet there was a new note of anguish in his voice. He was speaking of his trial. He described the torment, the spiritual state of people who are committed to a wrong, knowing that it is wrong. He made the trials of these white people far more vivid than anything he himself might have endured. They were not ruled by hatred, but by terror; and, therefore, if community was ever to be achieved, these people, the potential destroyers of the person, must not be hated. It was a terrible plea—to the people; and it was a prayer. In *Varieties of Religious Experience,* William James speaks of vastation—of *being,* as opposed to merely regarding, the monstrous creature which came to him in a vision. It seemed to me, though indeed I may be wrong, that something like this had happened to young Martin Luther—that he had looked on evil a long, hard, lonely time. For evil is in the world: it may be in the world to stay. No creed and no dogma are proof against it, and indeed no person is; it is always the naked person, alone, who, over and over and over again, must wrest his salvation from these black jaws. Perhaps young Martin was finding a new and more somber meaning in the command: "Overcome evil with good." The command does not suggest that to overcome evil is to eradicate it.

King spoke more candidly than I had ever heard him speak before, of his bitterly assaulted pride, of his shame, when he found himself accused, before all the world, of having used and betrayed the people of Montgomery by stealing the money they had entrusted to him. "I knew it wasn't true—but who would believe me?"

He had canceled a speaking trip to Chicago, for he felt that he could not face anyone. And he prayed; he walked up and down in his study, alone. It was borne in on him, finally, that he had no right *not* to go, no right to hide. "I called the airport and made another reservation and went on to Chicago." He appeared there, then, as an accused man, and gave us no details of his visit, which did not, in any case, matter. For if he had not been able to face Chicago, if he had not won that battle with himself, he would have been defeated long before his entrance into that courtroom in Montgomery.

When I saw him the next day in his office, he was very different, kind and attentive, but far away. A meeting of the Southern Christian Leadership Conference was to begin that day, and I think his mind must have been on that. The beleaguered ministers of the Deep South were coming to Atlanta that day in order to discuss the specific situations which confronted them in their particular towns or cities, and King was their leader. All of them had come under immensely greater local pressure because of the student sit-in movement. Inevitably, they were held responsible for it, even though they might very well not have known until reading it in the papers that the students had carried out another demonstration. I do not mean to suggest that there is any question of their support of the students—they may or may not be responsible *for* them but they certainly consider themselves responsible *to* them. But all this, I think, weighed on King rather heavily.

He talked about his visit to India and its effect on him. He was hideously struck by the poverty, which he talked about in great detail. He was also much impressed by Nehru, who had, he said, extraordinary qualities of "perception and dedication and courage—far more than the average American politician." We talked about the South. "Perhaps 4 or 5 per cent of the people are to be found on either end of the racial scale"—either actively for or actively against desegregation; "the rest are passive adherents. The sin of the South is the sin of conformity." And he feels, as I do, that much of the responsibility for the situation in which we have found ourselves since 1954 is due to the failure of President Eisenhower to make any coherent, any guiding statement concerning the nation's greatest moral and social problem.

But we did not discuss the impending conference, which, in any case, he could scarcely have discussed with me. And we did not discuss any of the problems which face him now and make his future so problematical. For he could not have discussed these with me, either.

That white men find King dangerous is well known. They can say so. But many Negroes also find King dangerous, but cannot say so, at least not publicly. The reason that the Negroes of whom I speak are trapped in such a stunning silence is that to say what they really feel would be to deny the entire public purpose of their lives.

Now, the problem of Negro leadership in this country has always been extremely delicate, dangerous, and complex. The term itself becomes remarkably difficult to define, the moment one realizes that the real role of the Negro leader, in the eyes of the American Republic, was not to make the Negro a first-class citizen but to keep him content as a second-class one. This sounds extremely harsh, but the record bears me out. And this problem, which it was the responsibility of the entire country to face, was dumped into the laps of a few men. Some of them were real leaders and some of them were false. Many of the greatest have scarcely ever been heard of.

The role of the genuine leadership, in its own eyes, was to destroy the barriers which prevented Negroes from fully participating in American life, to prepare Negroes for first-class citizenship, while at the same time bringing to bear on the Republic every conceivable pressure to make this status a reality. For this reason, the real leadership was to be found everywhere, in law courts, colleges, churches, hobo camps; on picket lines, freight trains, and chain gangs; and in jails. Not everyone who was publicized as a leader really was one. And many leaders who would never have dreamed of applying the term to themselves were considered by the Republic—when it knew of their existence at all—to be criminals. This is, of course, but the old and universal story of poverty in battle with privilege, but we tend not to think of old and universal stories as occurring in our brand-new and still relentlessly parochial land.

The real goal of the Negro leader was nothing less than the total integration of Negroes in all levels of the national life. But this could rarely be stated so baldly; it often could not be stated at all; in order to begin Negro education, for example, Booker Washington had found it necessary to state the exact opposite. The reason for this duplicity is that the goal contains the assumption that Negroes are to be treated, in all respects, exactly like all other citizens of the Republic. This is an idea which has always had extremely rough going in America. For one thing, it attacked, and attacks, a vast complex of special interests which would lose money and power if the situation of the Negro were to change. For another, the idea of freedom necessarily carries with it the idea of sexual freedom: the freedom to meet, sleep with, and marry whom one chooses. It would be fascinating, but I am afraid we must postpone it for the moment, to consider just why so many people appear to be convinced that Negroes would then immediately meet, sleep with, and marry white women; who, remarkably enough, are only protected from such undesirable alliances by the majesty and vigilance of the law.

The duplicity of the Negro leader was more than matched by the duplicity of the people with whom he had to deal. They, and most of the country, felt at the very bottom of their hearts that the Negro was inferior to them and, therefore, merited the treatment that he got. But it was not always politic to say this, either. It certainly could never be said over the bargaining table, where white and black men met.

The Negro leader was there to force from his adversary whatever he could get: new schools, new schoolrooms, new houses, new jobs. He was invested with very little power because the Negro vote had so very little power. (Other Negro leaders were trying to correct *that*.) It was not easy to wring concessions from the people at the bargaining table, who had, after all, no intention of giving their power away. People seldom do give their power away, forces beyond their control take their power from them; and I am afraid that much of the liberal cant about progress is but a sentimental reflection of this implacable fact. (Liberal cant about love and heroism also obscures, not to say blasphemes, the great love and heroism of many white people. Our racial story would be inconceivably more grim if these people, in the teeth of the most fantastic odds, did not continue to appear; but they were almost never, of course, to be found at the bargaining table.) Whatever concession the Negro leader carried away from the bargaining table was won with the tacit understanding that he, in return, would influence the people he represented in the direction that the people in power wished them to be influenced. Very often, in fact, he did not do this at all, but contrived to delude the white men (who are, in this realm, rather easily deluded) into believing that he had. But very often, too, he deluded himself into believing that the aims of white men in power and the desires of Negroes out of power were the same.

It was altogether inevitable, in short, that, by means of the extraordinary tableau I have tried to describe, a class of Negroes should have been created whose loyalty to their class was infinitely greater than their loyalty to the people from whom they had been so cunningly estranged. We must add, for I think it is important, that the Negro leader knew that he, too, was called "nigger" when his back was turned. The great mass of the black people around him were illiterate, demoralized, in want, and incorrigible. It is not hard to see that the Negro leader's personal and public frustrations would almost inevitably be turned against these people, for their misery, which formed the cornerstone of his peculiar power, was also responsible for his humiliation. And in Harlem, now, for example, many prominent Negroes ride to and from work through scenes of the greatest misery. They do not see this misery, though, because they do not want to see it. They defend themselves against an intolerable reality, which menaces them, by despising the people who are trapped in it.

The criticism, therefore, of the publicized Negro leadership—which is not, as I have tried to indicate, always the real leadership—is a criticism leveled, above all, against this class. They are, perhaps, the most unlucky bourgeoisie in the world's entire history, trapped, as they are, in a no man's land between black humiliation and white power. They cannot move backwards, and they cannot move forward, either.

One of the greatest vices of the white bourgeoisie on which they have modeled themselves is its reluctance to think, its distrust of the independent mind. Since the Negro bourgeoisie has so many things not to think about, it is positively afflicted with this vice. I should like at some other time to embark on a full-length discussion of the honorable and heroic role played by the NAACP in the national life, and point out to what extent its work has helped create the present ferment. But, for the moment, I shall have to confine my remarks to its organ, *The Crisis,* because I think it is incontestable that this magazine reveals the state of mind of the Negro bourgeoisie. *The Crisis* has the most exciting subject matter in the world at its fingertips, and yet manages to be one of the world's dullest magazines. When the Reverend James Lawson—who was expelled from Vanderbilt University for his sit-in activities—said this, or something like it, he caused a great storm of ill feeling. But he was quite right to feel as he does about *The Crisis,* and quite right to say so. And the charge is not answered by referring to the history of the NAACP.

Now, to charge *The Crisis* with dullness may seem to be a very trivial matter. It is not trivial, though, because this dullness is the result of its failure to examine what is really happening in the Negro world—its failure indeed, for that matter, to seize upon what is happening in the world at large. And I have singled it out because this inability is revelatory of the gap which now ominously widens between what we shall now have to call the official leadership and the young people who have begun what is nothing less than a moral revolution.

It is because of this gap that King finds himself in such a difficult position. The pressures on him are tremendous, and they come from above and below. He lost much moral credit, for example, especially in the eyes of the young, when he allowed Adam Clayton Powell to force the resignation of his (King's) extremely able organizer and lieutenant, Bayard Rustin. Rustin, also, has a long and honorable record as a fighter for Negro rights, and is one of the most penetrating and able men around. The techniques used by Powell—we will not speculate as to his motives—were far from sweet; but King was faced with the choice of defending his organizer, who was also his friend, or agreeing with Powell; and he chose the *latter* course. Nor do I know of anyone satisfied with the reasons given for the exclusion of James Lawson from the Southern Christian Leadership Conference. It would seem, certainly, that so able, outspoken, and energetic a man might prove of great value to this organization: why, then, is he not a part of it?

And there are many other questions, all of them ominous, and too many to go into here. But they all come, finally, it seems to me, to this tremendous reality: it is the sons and daughters of the beleaguered bourgeoisie—supported, in the most extraordinary fashion, by those old, work-worn men and women who were known, only yesterday, as "the country niggers"—who have begun a revolution in the consciousness of this country which will inexorably destroy nearly all that we now think of as concrete and indisputable. These young people have never believed in the American image of the Negro and have never bargained with the Republic, and now they never will. There is no longer any basis on which to bargain: for the myth of white supremacy is exploding all over the world, from the Congo to New Orleans. Those who have been watched and judged and described for so long are now watching and judging and describing for themselves. And one of the things that this means, to put it far too simply and bluntly, is that the white man on whom the American Negro has modeled himself for so long is vanishing. Because this white man was, himself, very largely a mythical creation: white men have never been, here, what they imagined themselves to be. The liberation of Americans from the racial anguish which has crippled us for so long can only mean, truly, the creation of a new people in this still-new world.

But the battle to achieve this has not ended, it has scarcely begun. Martin Luther King, Jr., by the power of his personality and the force of his beliefs, has injected a new dimension into our ferocious struggle. He has succeeded, in a way no Negro before him has managed to do, to carry the battle into the individual heart and make its resolution the province of the individual will. He has made it a matter, on both sides of the racial fence, of self-examination; and has incurred, therefore, the grave responsibility of continuing to lead in the path he has encouraged so many people to follow. How he will do this I do not know, but I do not see how he can possibly avoid a break, at last, with the habits and attitudes, stratagems and fears of the past.

No one can read the future, but we do know, as James has put it, that "all futures are rough." King's responsibility, and ours, is to that future which is already sending before it so many striking signs and portents. The possibility of liberation which is always real is also always painful, since it involves such an overhauling of all that gave us our identity. The Negro who will emerge out of this present struggle—whoever, indeed, this dark stranger may prove to be—will not be dependent, in any way at all, on any of the many props and crutches which help form our identity now. And neither will the white man. We will need every ounce of moral stamina we can find.

For everything is changing, from our notion of politics to our notion of ourselves, and we are certain, as we begin history's strangest metamorphosis, to undergo the torment of being forced to surrender far more than we ever realized we had accepted.

Martin Luther King, Jr.

Martin Luther King, Jr., smuggled his "Letter from a Birmingham Jail" out of his prison cell during his eight days of solitary confinement in April 1963. His letter is one of the most important, as well as most eloquent, statements clarifying the goals of the Civil Rights Movement. As president of the Southern Christian Leadership Conference (SCLC), King, with more than one hundred associates, organized a complex series of nonviolent demonstrations comprising sit-ins, pickets, marches, and retail boycotts in Birmingham, beginning on April 3, 1963.

After "Bull" Connor, the white police commissioner in the city, obtained a state injunction against the demonstrators, King and Ralph Abernathy led fifty marchers to the assembled police vans and were driven to jail. In his cell, King began writing his letter as a response to an earlier letter from eight "liberal" Alabama clergymen, using the margins of newspapers and scraps of paper supplied by the jail's black trustees. He finished writing it on a pad his attorneys were permitted to leave in his cell. The white ministers had urged King to limit his Civil Rights activities, fearing that his nonviolent resistance would provoke civic disturbance and lead to increasingly violent riots in the streets.

King answered by explaining why segregation contradicted America's democratic foundations and religious heritage. King's book Stride Toward Freedom: The Montgomery Story *(1958), published when he was only twenty-nine years old, had persuaded many people to support the Civil Rights Movement. Five years later, his "Letter from a Birmingham Jail," widely circu-*

lated in the media, attracted such a positive response that financial contributions poured into the SCLC, helping to support the organization's plans for the national March on Washington later in 1963.

LETTER FROM A BIRMINGHAM JAIL

My Dear Fellow Clergymen:

While confined here in the Birmingham city jail, I came across your recent statement calling my present activities "unwise and untimely." Seldom do I pause to answer criticism of my work and ideas. If I sought to answer all the criticisms that cross my desk, my secretaries would have little time for anything other than such correspondence in the course of the day, and I would have no time for constructive work. But since I feel that you are men of genuine good will and that your criticisms are sincerely set forth, I want to try to answer your statement in what I hope will be patient and reasonable terms.

I think I should indicate why I am here in Birmingham, since you have been influenced by the view which argues against "outsiders coming in." I have the honor of serving as president of the Southern Christian Leadership Conference, an organization operating in every southern state, with headquarters in Atlanta, Georgia. We have some eighty-five affiliated organizations across the South, and one of them is the Alabama Christian Movement for Human Rights. Frequently we share staff, educational, and financial resources with our affiliates. Several months ago the affiliate here in Birmingham asked us to be on call to engage in a nonviolent direct-action program if such were deemed necessary. We readily consented, and when the hour came we lived up to our promise. So I, along with several members of my staff, am here because I was invited here. I am here because I have organizational ties here.

But more basically, I am in Birmingham because injustice is here. Just as the prophets of the eighth century B.C. left their villages and carried their "thus saith the Lord" far beyond the boundaries of their home towns, and just as the Apostle Paul left his village of Tarsus and carried the gospel of Jesus Christ to the far corners of the Greco-Roman world, so am I compelled to carry the gospel of freedom beyond my own home town. Like Paul, I must constantly respond to the Macedonian call for aid.

Moreover, I am cognizant of the interrelatedness of all communities and states. I cannot sit idly by in Atlanta and not be concerned about what happens in Birmingham. Injustice anywhere is a threat to justice everywhere. We are caught in an inescapable network of mutuality, tied in a single garment of destiny. Whatever affects one directly, affects all indirectly. Never again can we afford to live with the narrow, provincial "outside agitator" idea. Anyone who lives inside the United States can never be considered an outsider anywhere within its bounds.

You deplore the demonstrations taking place in Birmingham. But your statement, I am sorry to say, fails to express a similar concern for the conditions that brought about the demonstrations. I am sure that none of you would want to rest content with the superficial kind of social analysis that deals merely with effects and does not grapple with underlying causes. It is unfortunate that demonstrations are taking place in Birmingham, but it is even more unfortunate that the city's white power structure left the Negro community with no alternative.

In any nonviolent campaign there are four basic steps: collection of the facts to determine whether injustices exist; negotiation; self-purification; and direct action. We have gone through all these steps in Birmingham. There can be no gainsaying the fact that racial injustice engulfs this community. Birmingham is probably the most thoroughly segregated city in the United States. Its ugly record of brutality is widely known. Negroes have experienced grossly unjust treatment in the courts. There have been more unsolved bombings of Negro homes and churches in Birmingham than in any other city in the nation. These are the hard, brutal facts of the case. On the basis of these conditions, Negro leaders sought to negotiate with the city fathers. But the latter consistently refused to engage in good-faith negotiation.

Then, last September, came the opportunity to talk with leaders of Birmingham's economic community. In the course of the negotiations, certain promises were made by the merchants—for example, to remove the stores' humiliating racial signs. On the basis of these promises, the Reverend Fred Shuttlesworth and the leaders of the Alabama Christian Movement for Human Rights agreed to a moratorium on all demonstrations. As the weeks and months went by, we realized that we were the victims of a broken promise. A few signs, briefly removed, returned; the others remained.

As in so many past experiences, our hopes had been blasted, and the shadow of deep disappointment settled upon us. We had no alternative except to prepare for direct action, whereby we would present our very bodies as a means of laying our case before the conscience of the local and the national community. Mindful of the difficulties involved, we decided to undertake a process of self-purification. We began a series of workshops on nonviolence, and we repeatedly asked ourselves: "Are you able to accept blows without retaliating?" "Are you able to endure the ordeal of jail?" We decided to schedule our direct-action program for the Easter season, realizing that except for Christmas, this is the main shopping period of the year. Knowing that a strong economic-withdrawal program would be the by-product of direct action, we felt that this would be the best time to bring pressure to bear on the merchants for the needed change.

Then it occurred to us that Birmingham's mayoral election was coming up in March, and we speedily decided to postpone action until after election day. When we discovered that the Commissioner of Public Safety, Eugene "Bull" Connor, had piled up enough votes to be in the run-off, we decided again to postpone action until the day after the run-off so that the demonstrations could not be used to cloud the issues. Like many others, we wanted to see Mr. Connor defeated, and to this end we endured postponement after postponement. Having aided in this community need, we felt that our direct-action program could be delayed no longer.

You may well ask, "Why direct action? Why sit-ins, marches, and so forth? Isn't negotiation a better path?" You are quite right in calling for negotiation. Indeed, this is the very purpose of direct action. Nonviolent direct action seeks to create such a crisis and foster such a tension that a community which has constantly refused to negotiate is forced to confront the issue. It seeks so to dramatize the issue that it can no longer be ignored. My citing the creation of tension as part of the work of the nonviolent-resister may sound rather shocking. But I must confess that I am not afraid of the word "tension." I have earnestly opposed violent tension, but there is a type of constructive, nonviolent tension which is necessary for growth. Just as Socrates felt that it was necessary to create a tension in the mind so that individuals could rise from the bondage of myths and half-truths to the unfettered realm of creative analysis and objective appraisal, so must we see the need for nonviolent gadflies to create the kind of tension in society that will help men rise from the dark depths of prejudice and racism to the majestic heights of understanding and brotherhood.

The purpose of our direct-action program is to create a situation so crisis-packed that it will inevitably open the door to negotiation. I therefore concur with you in your call for negotiation. Too long has our beloved Southland been bogged down in a tragic effort to live in monologue rather than dialogue.

One of the basic points in your statement is that the action that I and my associates have taken in Birmingham is untimely. Some have asked: "Why didn't you give the new city administration time to act?" The only answer that I can give to this query is that the new Birmingham administration must be prodded about as much as the outgoing one, before it will act. We are sadly mistaken if we feel that the election of Albert Boutwell as mayor will bring the millennium to Birmingham. While Mr. Boutwell is a much more gentle person than Mr. Connor, they are both segregationists, dedicated to maintenance of the status quo. I have hoped that Mr. Boutwell will be reasonable enough to see the futility of massive resistance to desegregation. But he will not see this without pressure from devotees of civil rights. My friends, I must say to you that we have not made a single gain in civil rights without determined legal and nonviolent pressure. Lamentably, it is an historical fact that privileged groups seldom give up their privileges voluntarily. Individuals may see the moral light and voluntarily give up their unjust posture; but, as Reinhold Niebuhr[1] has reminded us, groups tend to be more immoral than individuals.

We know through painful experience that freedom is never voluntarily given by the oppressor; it must be demanded by the oppressed. Frankly, I have yet to engage in a direct-action campaign that was "well timed" in the view of those who have not suffered unduly from the disease of segregation. For years now I have heard the word "Wait!" It rings in the ear of every Negro with piercing familiarity. This "Wait" has almost always meant "Never." We must come to see, with one of our distinguished jurists, that "justice too long delayed is justice denied."

We have waited for more than 340 years for our constitutional and God-given rights. The nations of Asia and Africa are moving with jetlike speed toward gaining political independence, but we still creep at horse-and-buggy pace toward gaining a cup of coffee at a lunch counter. Perhaps it is easy for those who have never felt the stinging darts of segregation to say, "Wait." But when you have seen vicious mobs lynch your mothers and fathers at will and drown your sisters and brothers at whim; when you have seen hate-filled police-

---

1. American Protestant theologian (1892–1971).

men curse, kick, and even kill your black brothers and sisters; when you see the vast majority of your twenty million Negro brothers smothering in an airtight cage of poverty in the midst of an affluent society; when you suddenly find your tongue twisted and your speech stammering as you seek to explain to your six-year-old daughter why she can't go to the public amusement park that has just been advertised on television, and see tears welling up in her eyes when she is told that Funtown is closed to colored children, and see ominous clouds of inferiority beginning to form in her little mental sky, and see her beginning to distort her personality by developing an unconscious bitterness toward white people; when you have to concoct an answer for a five-year-old son who is asking, "Daddy, why do white people treat colored people so mean?"; when you take a cross-country drive and find it necessary to sleep night after night in the uncomfortable corners of your automobile because no motel will accept you; when you are humiliated day in and day out by nagging signs reading "white" and "colored"; when your first name becomes "nigger," your middle name becomes "boy" (however old you are) and your last name becomes "John," and your wife and mother are never given the respected title "Mrs."; when you are harried by day and haunted by night by the fact that you are a Negro, living constantly at tiptoe stance, never quite knowing what to expect next, and are plagued with inner fears and outer resentments; when you are forever fighting a degenerating sense of "nobodiness"—then you will understand why we find it difficult to wait. There comes a time when the cup of endurance runs over, and men are no longer willing to be plunged into the abyss of despair. I hope, sirs, you can understand our legitimate and unavoidable impatience.

You express a great deal of anxiety over our willingness to break laws. This is certainly a legitimate concern. Since we so diligently urge people to obey the Supreme Court's decision of 1954 outlawing segregation in the public schools, at first glance it may seem rather paradoxical for us consciously to break laws. One may well ask: "How can you advocate breaking some laws and obeying others?" The answer lies in the fact that there are two types of laws: just and unjust. I would be the first to advocate obeying just laws. One has not only a legal but a moral responsibility to obey just laws. Conversely, one has a moral responsibility to disobey unjust laws. I would agree with St. Augustine[2] that "an unjust law is no law at all."

---

2. Early Christian church father (354–430).

Now, what is the difference between the two? How does one determine whether a law is just or unjust? A just law is a man-made code that squares with the moral law or the law of God. An unjust law is a code that is out of harmony with the moral law. To put it in the terms of St. Thomas Aquinas:[3] An unjust law is a human law that is not rooted in eternal law and natural law. Any law that uplifts human personality is just. Any law that degrades human personality is unjust. All segregation statutes are unjust because segregation distorts the soul and damages the personality. It gives the segregator a false sense of superiority and the segregated a false sense of inferiority. Segregation, to use the terminology of the Jewish philosopher Martin Buber,[4] substitutes an "I-it" relationship for an "I-thou" relationship and ends up relegating persons to the status of things. Hence segregation is not only politically, economically, and sociologically unsound, it is morally wrong and sinful. Paul Tillich[5] has said that sin is separation. Is not segregation an existential expression of man's tragic separation, his awful estrangement, his terrible sinfulness? Thus it is that I can urge men to obey the 1954 decision of the Supreme Court, for it is morally right; and I can urge them to disobey segregation ordinances, for they are morally wrong.

Let us consider a more concrete example of just and unjust laws. An unjust law is a code that a numerical or power majority group compels a minority group to obey but does not make binding on itself. This is *difference* made legal. By the same token, a just law is a code that a majority compels a minority to follow and that it is willing to follow itself. This is *sameness* made legal.

Let me give another explanation. A law is unjust if it is inflicted on a minority that, as a result of being denied the right to vote, had no part in enacting or devising the law. Who can say that the legislature of Alabama which set up that state's segregation laws was democratically elected? Throughout Alabama all sorts of devious methods are used to prevent Negroes from becoming registered voters, and there are some counties in which, even though Negroes constitute a majority of the population, not a single Negro is registered. Can any law enacted under such circumstances be considered democratically structured?

Sometimes a law is just on its face and unjust in its application.

---

3. Christian philosopher and theologian (1225–1274).
4. German-born Israeli (1878–1965).
5. German-born American Protestant theologian (1886–1965).

For instance, I have been arrested on a charge of parading without a permit. Now, there is nothing wrong in having an ordinance which requires a permit for a parade. But such an ordinance becomes unjust when it is used to maintain segregation and to deny citizens the First-Amendment privilege of peaceful assembly and protest.

I hope you are able to see the distinction I am trying to point out. In no sense do I advocate evading or defying the law, as would the rabid segregationist. That would lead to anarchy. One who breaks an unjust law must do so openly, lovingly, and with a willingness to accept the penalty. I submit that an individual who breaks a law that conscience tells him is unjust, and who willingly accepts the penalty of imprisonment in order to arouse the conscience of the community over its injustice, is in reality expressing the highest respect for law.

Of course, there is nothing new about this kind of civil disobedience. It was evidenced sublimely in the refusal of Shadrach, Meshach, and Abednego to obey the laws of Nebuchadnezzar,[6] on the ground that a higher moral law was at stake. It was practiced superbly by the early Christians, who were willing to face hungry lions and the excruciating pain of chopping blocks rather than submit to certain unjust laws of the Roman Empire. To a degree, academic freedom is a reality today because Socrates practiced civil disobedience.[7] In our own nation, the Boston Tea Party represented a massive act of civil disobedience.

We should never forget that everything Adolf Hitler did in Germany was "legal" and everything the Hungarian freedom fighters[8] did in Hungary was "illegal." It was "illegal" to aid and comfort a Jew in Hitler's Germany. Even so, I am sure that, had I lived in Germany at the time, I would have aided and comforted my Jewish brothers. If today I lived in a Communist country where certain principles dear to the Christian faith are suppressed, I would openly advocate disobeying that country's anti-religious laws.

I must make two honest confessions to you, my Christian and Jewish brothers. First, I must confess that over the past few years I have been gravely disappointed with the white moderate. I have al-

---

6. Daniel 3.
7. The ancient Greek philosopher Socrates was tried by the Athenians for corrupting their youth through his questioning manner of teaching. He refused to change his ways and was condemned to death.
8. In the anti-Communist revolution of 1956, which was quickly put down by Soviet forces.

most reached the regrettable conclusion that the Negro's great stumbling block in his stride toward freedom is not the White Citizen's Counciler[9] or the Ku Klux Klanner, but the white moderate, who is more devoted to "order" than to justice; who prefers a negative peace which is the absence of tension to a positive peace which is the presence of justice; who constantly says, "I agree with you in the goal you seek, but I cannot agree with your methods of direct action"; who paternalistically believes he can set the timetable for another man's freedom; who lives by a mythical concept of time and who constantly advises the Negro to wait for a "more convenient season." Shallow understanding from people of good will is more frustrating than absolute misunderstanding from people of ill will. Lukewarm acceptance is much more bewildering than outright rejection.

I had hoped that the white moderate would understand that law and order exist for the purpose of establishing justice and that when they fail in this purpose they become the dangerously structured dams that block the flow of social progress. I had hoped that the white moderate would understand that the present tension in the South is a necessary phase of the transition from an obnoxious negative peace, in which the Negro passively accepted his unjust plight, to a substantive and positive peace, in which all men will respect the dignity and worth of human personality. Actually, we who engage in nonviolent direct action are not the creators of tension. We merely bring to the surface the hidden tension that is already alive. We bring it out in the open, where it can be seen and dealt with. Like a boil that can never be cured so long as it is covered up but must be opened with all its ugliness to the natural medicines of air and light, injustice must be exposed, with all the tension its exposure creates, to the light of human conscience and the air of national opinion, before it can be cured.

In your statement you assert that our actions, even though peaceful, must be condemned because they precipitate violence. But is this a logical assertion? Isn't this like condemning a robbed man because his possession of money precipitated the evil act of robbery? Isn't this like condemning Socrates because his unswerving commitment to truth and his philosophical inquiries precipitated the act by the misguided populace in which they made him drink hemlock? Isn't this like condemning Jesus because his unique God-consciousness and

---

9. A member of a southern organization formed to combat the implementation of the *Brown v. Board of Education* decision on the integration of schools.

never-ceasing devotion to God's will precipitated the evil act of crucifixion? We must come to see that, as the federal courts have consistently affirmed, it is wrong to urge an individual to cease his efforts to gain his basic constitutional rights because the quest may precipitate violence. Society must protect the robbed and punish the robber.

I had also hoped that the white moderate would reject the myth concerning time in relation to the struggle for freedom. I have just received a letter from a white brother in Texas. He writes: "All Christians know that the colored people will receive equal rights eventually, but it is possible that you are in too great a religious hurry. It has taken Christianity almost two thousand years to accomplish what it has. The teachings of Christ take time to come to earth." Such an attitude stems from a tragic misconception of time, from the strangely irrational notion that there is something in the very flow of time that will inevitably cure all ills. Actually, time itself is neutral; it can be used either destructively or constructively. More and more I feel that the people of ill will have used time much more effectively than have the people of good will. We will have to repent in this generation not merely for the hateful words and actions of the bad people, but for the appalling silence of the good people. Human progress never rolls in on wheels of inevitability; it comes through the tireless efforts of men willing to be co-workers with God, and without this hard work, time itself becomes an ally of the forces of social stagnation. We must use time creatively, in the knowledge that the time is always ripe to do right. Now is the time to make real the promise of democracy and transform our pending national elegy into a creative psalm of brotherhood. Now is the time to lift our national policy from the quicksand of racial injustice to the solid rock of human dignity.

You speak of our activity in Birmingham as extreme. At first I was rather disappointed that fellow clergymen would see my nonviolent efforts as those of an extremist. I began thinking about the fact that I stand in the middle of two opposing forces in the Negro community. One is a force of complacency, made up in part of Negroes who, as a result of long years of oppression, are so drained of self-respect and a sense of "somebodiness" that they have adjusted to segregation; and in part of a few middle-class Negroes who, because of a degree of academic and economic security and because in some ways they profit by segregation, have become insensitive to the problems of the masses. The other force is one of bitterness and hatred, and it comes perilously close to advocating violence. It is expressed in the various black nationalist groups that are springing up across the nation, the largest and best-known being Elijah Muhammad's Muslim movement.[10] Nourished by the Negro's frustration over the continued existence of racial discrimination, this movement is made up of people who have lost faith in America, who have absolutely repudiated Christianity, and who have concluded that the white man is an incorrigible "devil."

I have tried to stand between these two forces, saying that we need emulate neither the "do-nothingism" of the complacent nor the hatred and despair of the black nationalist. For there is the more excellent way of love and nonviolent protest. I am grateful to God that, through the influence of the Negro church, the way of nonviolence became an integral part of our struggle.

If this philosophy had not emerged, by now many streets of the South would, I am convinced, be flowing with blood. And I am further convinced that if our white brothers dismiss as "rabblerousers" and "outside agitators" those of us who employ nonviolent direct action, and if they refuse to support our nonviolent efforts, millions of Negroes will, out of frustration and despair, seek solace and security in black-nationalist ideologies—a development that would inevitably lead to a frightening racial nightmare.

Oppressed people cannot remain oppressed forever. The yearning for freedom eventually manifests itself, and that is what has happened to the American Negro. Something within has reminded him of his birthright of freedom, and something without has reminded him that it can be gained. Consciously or unconsciously, he has been caught up by the *Zeitgeist*,[11] and with his black brothers of Africa and his brown and yellow brothers of Asia, South America, and the Caribbean, the United States Negro is moving with a sense of great urgency toward the promised land of racial justice. If one recognizes this vital urge that has engulfed the Negro community, one should readily understand why public demonstrations are taking place. The Negro has many pent-up resentments and latent frustrations, and he must release them. So let him march; let him make prayer pilgrimages to the city hall; let him go on freedom rides—and try to understand why he must do so. If his repressed emotions are not released in nonviolent ways, they will seek expression through violence; this is not a threat but a fact of history. So I have not said to my people, "Get rid of your discontent." Rather, I have tried to say that this normal

---

10. That is, the Nation of Islam.
11. The spirit of the times.

and healthy discontent can be channeled into the creative outlet of nonviolent direct action. And now this approach is being termed extremist.

But though I was initially disappointed at being categorized as an extremist, as I continued to think about the matter I gradually gained a measure of satisfaction from the label. Was not Jesus an extremist for love: "Love your enemies, bless them that curse you, do good to them that hate you, and pray for them which despitefully use you, and persecute you." Was not Amos an extremist for justice: "Let justice roll down like waters and righteousness like an ever-flowing stream." Was not Paul an extremist for the Christian gospel: "I bear in my body the marks of the Lord Jesus." Was not Martin Luther an extremist: "Here I stand; I cannot do otherwise, so help me God." And John Bunyan:[12] "I will stay in jail to the end of my days before I make a butchery of my conscience." And Abraham Lincoln: "This nation cannot survive half slave and half free." And Thomas Jefferson: "We hold these truths to be self-evident, that all men are created equal. . . ." So the question is not whether we will be extremists, but what kind of extremists we will be. Will we be extremists for hate or for love? Will we be extremists for the preservation of injustice or for the extension of justice? In that dramatic scene on Calvary's hill three men were crucified. We must never forget that all three were crucified for the same crime—the crime of extremism. Two were extremists for immorality, and thus fell below their environment. The other, Jesus Christ, was an extremist for love, truth, and goodness, and thereby rose above his environment. Perhaps the South, the nation, and the world are in dire need of creative extremists.

I had hoped that the white moderate would see this need. Perhaps I was too optimistic; perhaps I expected too much. I suppose I should have realized that few members of the oppressor race can understand the deep groans and passionate yearnings of the oppressed race; and still fewer have the vision to see that injustice must be rooted out by strong, persistent, and determined action. I am thankful, however, that some of our white brothers in the South have grasped the meaning of this social revolution and committed themselves to it. They are still all too few in quantity, but they are big in quality. Some—such as Ralph McGill, Lillian Smith, Harry Golden,

---

12. English preacher and author (1628–1688); Amos was an Old Testament prophet; Paul, a New Testament apostle; Luther (1483–1546), a German Protestant reformer.

James McBridge Dabbs, Ann Braden, and Sarah Patton Boyle—have written about our struggle in eloquent and prophetic terms. Others have marched with us down nameless streets of the South. They have languished in filthy, roach-infested jails, suffering the abuse and brutality of policemen who view them as "dirty nigger-lovers." Unlike so many of their moderate brothers and sisters, they have recognized the urgency of the moment and sensed the need for powerful "action" antidotes to combat the disease of segregation.

Let me take note of my other major disappointment. I have been so greatly disappointed with the white church and its leadership. Of course, there are some notable exceptions. I am not unmindful of the fact that each of you has taken some significant stands on this issue. I commend you, Reverend Stallings, for your Christian stand on this past Sunday, in welcoming Negroes to your worship service on a nonsegregated basis. I commend the Catholic leaders of this state for integrating Spring Hill College several years ago.

But despite these notable exceptions, I must honestly reiterate that I have been disappointed with the church. I do not say this as one of those negative critics who can always find something wrong with the church. I say this as a minister of the gospel, who loves the church; who was nurtured in its bosom; who has been sustained by its spiritual blessings and who will remain true to it as long as the cord of life shall lengthen.

When I was suddenly catapulted into the leadership of the bus protest in Montgomery, Alabama, a few years ago,[13] I felt we would be supported by the white church. I felt that the white ministers, priests, and rabbis of the South would be among our strongest allies. Instead, some have been outright opponents, refusing to understand the freedom movement and misrepresenting its leaders; all too many others have been more cautious than courageous and have remained silent behind the anesthetizing security of stained-glass windows.

In spite of my shattered dreams, I came to Birmingham with the hope that the white religious leadership of this community would see the justice of our cause and, with deep moral concern, would serve as the channel through which our just grievances could reach the power structure. I had hoped that each of you would understand. But again I have been disappointed.

---

13. The boycott began in December 1955, when Rosa Parks refused to move to the Negro section of a bus.

I have heard numerous southern religious leaders admonish their worshipers to comply with a desegregation decision because it is the law, but I have longed to hear white ministers declare: "Follow this decree because integration is morally right and because the Negro is your brother." In the midst of blatant injustices inflicted upon the Negro, I have watched white churchmen stand on the sideline and mouth pious irrelevancies and sanctimonious trivialities. In the midst of a mighty struggle to rid our nation of racial and economic injustice, I have heard many ministers say: "Those are social issues, with which the gospel has no real concern." And I have watched many churches commit themselves to a completely otherworldly religion which makes a strange, un-Biblical distinction between body and soul, between the sacred and the secular.

I have traveled the length and breadth of Alabama, Mississippi, and all the other southern states. On sweltering summer days and crisp autumn mornings I have looked at the South's beautiful churches with their lofty spires pointing heavenward. I have beheld the impressive outlines of her massive religious-education buildings. Over and over I have found myself asking: "What kind of people worship here? Who is their God? Where were their voices when the lips of Governor Barnett dripped with words of interposition and nullification? Where were they when Governor Wallace gave a clarion call for defiance and hatred?[14] Where were their voices of support when bruised and weary Negro men and women decided to rise from the dark dungeons of complacency to the bright hills of creative protest?"

Yes, these questions are still in my mind. In deep disappointment I have wept over the laxity of the church. But be assured that my tears have been tears of love. There can be no deep disappointment where there is not deep love. Yes, I love the church. How could I do otherwise? I am in the rather unique position of being the son, the grandson, and the great-grandson of preachers. Yes, I see the church as the body of Christ. But, oh! How we have blemished and scarred that body through social neglect and through fear of being nonconformists.

There was a time when the church was very powerful—in the

---

14. George Wallace (1919–1998), then governor of Alabama, opposed admission of black students to the University of Alabama in 1963. Ross Barnett (1898–1988), governor of Mississippi, opposed James Meredith's admission to the University of Mississippi in 1962.

time when the early Christians rejoiced at being deemed worthy to suffer for what they believed. In those days the church was not merely a thermometer that recorded the ideas and principles of popular opinion; it was a thermostat that transformed the mores of society. Whenever the early Christians entered a town, the people in power became disturbed and immediately sought to convict the Christians for being "disturbers of the peace" and "outside agitators." But the Christians pressed on, in the conviction that they were "a colony of heaven," called to obey God rather than man. Small in number, they were big in commitment. They were too God-intoxicated to be "astronomically intimidated." By their effort and example they brought an end to such ancient evils as infanticide and gladiatorial contests.

Things are different now. So often the contemporary church is a weak, ineffectual voice with an uncertain sound. So often it is an arch-defender of the status quo. Far from being disturbed by the presence of the church, the power structure of the average community is consoled by the church's silent—and often even vocal—sanction of things as they are.

But the judgment of God is upon the church as never before. If today's church does not recapture the sacrificial spirit of the early church, it will lose its authenticity, forfeit the loyalty of millions, and be dismissed as an irrelevant social club with no meaning for the twentieth century. Every day I meet young people whose disappointment with the church has turned into outright disgust.

Perhaps I have once again been too optimistic. Is organized religion too inextricably bound to the status quo to save our nation and the world? Perhaps I must turn my faith to the inner spiritual church, the church within the church, as the true *ekklesia*[15] and the hope of the world. But again I am thankful to God that some noble souls from the ranks of organized religion have broken loose from the paralyzing chains of conformity and joined us as active partners in the struggle for freedom. They have left their secure congregations and walked the streets of Albany, Georgia, with us. They have gone down the highways of the South on tortuous rides for freedom. Yes, they have gone to jail with us. Some have been dismissed from their churches, have lost the support of their bishops and fellow ministers. But they have acted in the faith that right defeated is stronger than evil triumphant. Their witness has been the spiritual salt that has preserved the true meaning of the gospel in these troubled times. They

---

15. The Greek New Testament word for the early Christian church.

have carved a tunnel of hope through the dark mountain of disappointment.

I hope the church as a whole will meet the challenge of this decisive hour. But even if the church does not come to the aid of justice, I have no despair about the future. I have no fear about the outcome of our struggle in Birmingham, even if our motives are at present misunderstood. We will reach the goal of freedom in Birmingham and all over the nation, because the goal of America is freedom. Abused and scorned though we may be, our destiny is tied up with America's destiny. Before the pilgrims landed at Plymouth, we were here. Before the pen of Jefferson etched the majestic words of the Declaration of Independence across the pages of history, we were here. For more than two centuries our forebears labored in this country without wages; they made cotton king; they built the homes of their masters while suffering gross injustice and shameful humiliation—and yet out of a bottomless vitality they continued to thrive and develop. If the inexpressible cruelties of slavery could not stop us, the opposition we now face will surely fail. We will win our freedom because the sacred heritage of our nation and the eternal will of God are embodied in our echoing demands.

Before closing I feel impelled to mention one other point in your statement that has troubled me profoundly. You warmly commended the Birmingham police force for keeping "order" and "preventing violence." I doubt that you would have so warmly commended the police force if you had seen its dogs sinking their teeth into unarmed, nonviolent Negroes. I doubt that you would so quickly commend the policemen if you were to observe their ugly and inhumane treatment of Negroes here in the city jail; if you were to watch them push and curse old Negro women and young Negro girls; if you were to see them slap and kick old Negro men and young boys; if you were to observe them, as they did on two occasions, refuse to give us food because we wanted to sing our grace together. I cannot join you in your praise of the Birmingham police department.

It is true that the police have exercised a degree of discipline in handling the demonstrators. In this sense they have conducted themselves rather "nonviolently" in public. But for what purpose? To preserve the evil system of segregation. Over the past few years I have consistently preached that nonviolence demands that the means we use must be as pure as the ends we seek. I have tried to make clear that it is wrong to use immoral means to attain moral ends. But now I must affirm that it is just as wrong, or perhaps even more so, to use moral means to preserve immoral ends. Perhaps Mr. Connor and his policemen have been rather nonviolent in public, as was Chief Pritchett in Albany, Georgia, but they have used the moral means of nonviolence to maintain the immoral end of racial injustice. As T. S. Eliot has said, "The last temptation is the greatest treason: To do the right deed for the wrong reason."[16]

I wish you had commended the Negro sit-inners and demonstrators of Birmingham for their sublime courage, their willingness to suffer, and their amazing discipline in the midst of great provocation. One day the South will recognize its real heroes. They will be the James Merediths,[17] with the noble sense of purpose that enables them to face jeering and hostile mobs, and with the agonizing loneliness that characterizes the life of the pioneer. They will be old, oppressed, battered Negro women, symbolized in a seventy-two-year-old woman in Montgomery, Alabama, who rose up with a sense of dignity and with her people decided not to ride segregated buses, and who responded with ungrammatical profundity to one who inquired about her weariness: "My feets is tired, but my soul is at rest." They will be the young high school and college students, the young ministers of the gospel and a host of their elders, courageously and nonviolently sitting in at lunch counters and willingly going to jail for conscience' sake. One day the South will know that when these disinherited children of God sat down at lunch counters, they were in reality standing up for what is best in the American dream and for the most sacred values in our Judaeo-Christian heritage, thereby bringing our nation back to those great wells of democracy which were dug deep by the founding fathers in their formulation of the Constitution and the Declaration of Independence.

Never before have I written so long a letter. I'm afraid it is much too long to take your precious time. I can assure you that it would have been much shorter if I had been writing from a comfortable desk, but what else can one do when he is alone in a narrow jail cell, other than write long letters, think long thoughts, and pray long prayers?

If I have said anything in this letter that overstates the truth and indicates an unreasonable impatience, I beg you to forgive me. If I have said anything that understates the truth and indicates my having a patience that allows me to settle for anything less than brotherhood, I beg God to forgive me.

---

16. From Eliot's verse play *Murder in the Cathedral*.
17. First black to enroll at the University of Mississippi.

I hope this letter finds you strong in the faith. I also hope that circumstances will soon make it possible for me to meet each of you, not as an integrationist or a civil-rights leader but as a fellow clergyman and a Christian brother. Let us all hope that the dark clouds of racial prejudice will soon pass away and the deep fog of misunderstanding will be lifted from our fear-drenched communities, and in some not too distant tomorrow the radiant stars of love and brotherhood will shine over our great nation with all their scintillating beauty.

> Yours for the cause of Peace and Brotherhood,
> MARTIN LUTHER KING, JR.

Rosa Parks

In Rosa Parks: My Story *(with Jim Haskins, 1992), Rosa Parks described Martin Luther King, Jr.'s nonviolent response to a physical attack by a white man in the audience during a Southern Christian Leadership Conference meeting in the early 1960s. As one of the "unsung heroines of the Civil Rights Movement" (the term is author Lynne Olson's), Rosa Parks was a modest chronicler of her times. However, several militant women active at the Highlander Folk School and at Alabama State College supported Parks's courageous act of civil disobedience when she refused to give up her seat to white passengers on a city bus on December 1, 1955. As the feminist historian Susan Brownmiller understood in her review of Olson's* Freedom's Daughters: The Unsung Heroines of the Civil Rights Movement *(2001),*

> *The often-told story of the Montgomery bus boycott, which Olson repeats in lavish detail, is an excellent illustration of how a complicated scenario gets reduced to a simple narrative that shortchanges, excludes or oversimplifies the contribution of women. In all fairness,*

*King never claimed that he started the boycott, but his
demurrals increasingly sounded like modesty as time
wore on. New to the city in 1955, the personable young
pastor was thrust into the role of the movement's
inspirational leader by the black community's divided
factions. Few would deny that King's anointment was
brilliant and prescient, that the early success and
attention from the news media set him on his public
path. However, the courageous souls who first challenged
the segregated buses, issued the first call for a boycott and
stunned the city by refusing to ride for one thrilling year
were women.*

*Rosa Parks, an NAACP stalwart recently returned
from a workshop for activists run by Septima Clark at
the Highlander Folk School in Tennessee, was neither
a little old lady with tired feet nor the first rider in
Montgomery to be arrested for refusing to give up her
seat to a white and move to the rear. In earlier incidents,
two teenage girls had been jailed for similar acts of
defiance. When word of their arrests spread through the
black community, Jo Ann Robinson, a professor at
Alabama State College, prepared a leaflet. Robinson
had been talking boycott for more than a year. She was
persuaded to hold off after rumors of the teenagers'
imperfect reputations prompted concern in some quarters
that they could not withstand the scrutiny of a public
campaign and litigation.*

*On the night when the 42-year-old Parks—
respectable, married, employed—calmly went to jail as
Montgomery's impeccable symbol of racial injustice,
Robinson and her women's committee sprang into action.
By the following afternoon 35,000 mimeographed flyers
announcing the boycott were all over town. These
significant events preceded the involvement of King and
his ministers' circle, yet after Alabama's bus segregation
laws were struck down by the Supreme Court,
photographers rushed to snap photos of King and
Time's cover story was written as a King profile.
Seemingly secondary in the reams of press coverage was
the militant role of the bus-riding population—the
maids, cooks, and cleaning women for Montgomery's*

white families who had walked or car-pooled for the boycott's duration.

FROM *ROSA PARKS: MY STORY*

BACK IN DETROIT I worked in the home of a seamstress friend, and then later I got a job at a small clothing factory on the west side of the city. In 1961 we moved to a lower apartment on Virginia Park.

I was still traveling around quite a bit, speaking about the bus boycott and the civil-rights movement, which had really gotten active by this time. Dr. King and other ministers had formed the Southern Christian Leadership Conference (SCLC) to fight against segregation in other areas of southern life. I went back south to attend SCLC conventions, and when there was a big march or demonstration, I was there.

I remember one SCLC convention in particular. It was held in Birmingham, Alabama, one of the most viciously segregated cities. That's where whites bombed a church and killed four little black girls. I was sitting in the audience, near the stage. Dr. King was closing the convention with some announcements when a white man from the audience jumped up on the stage and hit Dr. King in the face with his fist, spinning him halfway around. It took everybody by surprise, and before anyone could react, the man was hitting Dr. King again. Dr. King was trying to shield himself from the blows. And then suddenly Dr. King turned around to face the man and just dropped his hands by his sides. The white man was so surprised that he just stared for a moment, long enough for the Reverend Wyatt Tee Walker and some others to get between them.

Dr. King yelled, "Don't touch him! We have to pray for him." Then he started talking quietly to the man, and he kept talking as the man was slowly led off the stage. There seemed to be more attention devoted to calming the man down than to looking after Dr. King.

I went backstage and offered him two aspirins and a Coca-Cola, my remedy for a headache. He was holding a handkerchief full of ice against his face. He later told the convention that he and the man had talked and that the man was a member of the American Nazi Party. The American Nazi Party is a very racist organization. But Dr. King refused to press charges against that man. That, for many of us, was proof that Dr. King believed so completely in nonviolence that it was even stronger than his instinct to protect himself from attack.

I was also at the 1963 March on Washington to push for federal civil-rights laws. Women were not allowed to play much of a role. The March planning committee didn't want Coretta Scott King and the other wives of the male leaders to march with their husbands. Instead there was a separate procession for them. There were also no female speakers on the program, the one where Dr. King gave his famous "I Have a Dream" speech in front of the Lincoln Memorial.

But there was a "Tribute to Women" in which A. Philip Randolph, one of the organizers of the March and the founder of the Brotherhood of Sleeping Car Porters, introduced some of the women who had participated in the struggle, and I was one of them. Another was Josephine Baker, the beautiful dancer and singer who had spent most of her life in Europe but who had stood up for equal rights when she was in the United States. She flew over from Paris just for the March. Marian Anderson sang "He's Got the Whole World in His Hands," and Mahalia Jackson sang "I Been 'Buked and I Been Scorned." Those of us who did not sing didn't get to say anything, as I recall—except for Lena Horne, who was introduced and who then stood and loudly proclaimed, "Freedom." Nowadays, women wouldn't stand for being kept so much in the background, but back then women's rights hadn't become a popular cause yet.

I spoke at the SCLC's seventh annual convention in Richmond, Virginia, the following month. Other people gave reports about the civil-rights movement in a variety of cities. By this time black people in cities and towns all over the South were organizing and demonstrating against segregation.

The civil-rights movement was having a big effect. It didn't change the hearts and minds of many white southerners, but it did make a difference to the politicians in Washington, D.C. The president at that time was Lyndon Baines Johnson, born and raised in Texas. It was he who pushed through the 1964 Civil Rights Act, the most far-reaching legislation since the Reconstruction period after the Civil War. It aimed to guarantee blacks the right to vote and to use public accommodations, and provided for the federal government to prosecute those who did not obey this law. When he signed that act into law, President Johnson said, "We shall overcome," using the words of a song that we had sung many times during the Montgomery bus boycott and that black and white civil-rights workers had sung many times throughout the later struggle.

That Civil Rights Act of 1964 did not solve all our problems.

But it gave black people some protection, and some way to get redress for unfair treatment. There were still more rights to win, and the civil-rights movement continued.

———

Anne Moody

Anne Moody, a member of the younger generation of Civil Rights activists after Rosa Parks, wrote a stirring autobiographical account of her political radicalization in Coming of Age in Mississippi *(1968). She divided her book into four parts: "Childhood," "High School," "College," and "The Movement." Born into a poverty-stricken family of farmhands, she graduated from her local high school for blacks in 1959 with a straight-A average and a basketball scholarship to Natchez Junior College. As a junior at Tougaloo College, she joined the NAACP and participated in a demonstration to picket the state fair in Jackson. The summer of 1962, before Moody's senior year, she joined the Student Nonviolent Coordinating Committee (SNCC) to work in a voter registration drive in the Mississippi Delta.*

In early June the next summer, before her last semester at Tougaloo, Moody was part of a sit-in delegation of black high school and college students trying to integrate the lunch counter at Woolworth in Jackson by sitting at the front counter, reserved for whites, instead of at the back counter. Along with the others, she was threatened with hanging, had her face slapped, and was dragged by her hair away from the counter while the crowd of bystanders chanted "Communist, Communist, Communist." Then the mob started to smear her and the others "with ketchup, mustard, sugar, pies, and everything on the counter." The student beside her was hit on the jaw with brass knuckles; another had "nigger" spray-painted in red on his white shirt. Led out of Woolworth by the president of Tougaloo College, Moody and the other students were taken past a

*line of ninety policemen who "blocked the mob from us. However,
they were allowed to throw at us everything they had collected.
Within ten minutes, we were picked up by the Reverend King in
his station wagon and taken to the NAACP headquarters on
Lynch Street."*

*After this sit-in, Moody understood "how sick Mississippi
whites were. They believed so much in the segregated Southern way
of life, they would kill to preserve it." In* Coming of Age in Mis-
sissippi, *she described her participation in the Civil Rights work-
shops and demonstrations that continued in Jackson in early June
1963, including her four days in jail (along with four hundred
other students) after King's attempt to stage a "pray-in" on the
steps of the post office. Jackson, as she wrote, had become "the
hotbed of racial demonstrations in the South. It seemed as though
most of the Negro college and high school students there were mak-
ing preparations to participate." A few days later, a local judge is-
sued an injunction prohibiting demonstrations.*

FROM *COMING OF AGE IN MISSISSIPPI*

[IN JUNE 1963] an injunction prohibiting demonstrations was issued
by a local judge, naming NAACP, CORE, Tougaloo College, and
various leaders. According to this injunction, the intent of the named
organizations and individuals was to paralyze the economic nerve
center of the city of Jackson. It used as proof the leaflets that had been
distributed by the NAACP urging Negroes not to shop on Capitol
Street. The next day the injunction was answered with another mass
march.

The cops started arresting every Negro on the scene of a demon-
stration, whether or not he was participating. People were being
carted off to jail every day of the week. On Saturday, Roy Wilkins,
the National Director of NAACP, and Medgar Evers were arrested as
they picketed in front of Woolworth's. Theldon Henderson, a Negro
lawyer who worked for the Justice Department, and had been sent
down from Washington to investigate a complaint by the NAACP
about the fairgrounds facilities, was also arrested. It was said that when
he showed his Justice Department credentials, the arresting officer
started trembling. They let him go immediately.

Mass rallies had come to be an every night event, and at each one the NAACP had begun to build up Medgar Evers. Somehow I had the feeling that they wanted him to become for Mississippi what Martin Luther King had been in Alabama. They were well on the way to achieving that, too.

After the rally on Tuesday, June 11, I had to stay in Jackson. I had missed the ride back to campus. Dave Dennis, the CORE field secretary for Mississippi, and his wife put me up for the night. We were watching TV around twelve-thirty, when a special news bulletin interrupted the program. It said, "Jackson NAACP leader Medgar Evers has just been shot."

We didn't believe what we were hearing. We just sat there staring at the TV screen. It was unbelievable. Just an hour or so earlier we were all with him. The next bulletin announced that he had died in the hospital soon after the shooting. We didn't know what to say or do. All night we tried to figure out what had happened, who did it, who was next, and it still didn't seem real.

First thing the next morning we turned on the TV. It showed films taken shortly after Medgar was shot in his driveway. We saw the pool of blood where he had fallen. We saw his wife sobbing almost hysterically as she tried to tell what had happened. Without even having breakfast, we headed for the NAACP headquarters. When we got there, they were trying to organize a march to protest Medgar's death. Newsmen, investigators, and reporters flooded the office. College and high school students and a few adults sat in the auditorium waiting to march.

Dorie Ladner, a SNCC worker, and I decided to run up to Jackson State College and get some of the students there to participate in the march. I was sure we could convince some of them to protest Medgar's death. Since the march was to start shortly after lunch, we had a couple of hours to do some recruiting. When we got to Jackson State, class was in session. "That's a damn shame," I thought. "They should have dismissed school today, in honor of Medgar."

Dorie and I started going down each hall, taking opposite classrooms. We begged students to participate. They didn't respond in any way.

"It's a shame, it really is a shame. This morning Medgar Evers was murdered and here you sit in a damn classroom with books in front of your faces, pretending you don't even know he's been killed. Every Negro in Jackson should be in the streets raising hell and protesting his death," I said in one class. I felt sick, I got so mad with them. How could Negroes be so pitiful? How could they just sit by and take all this shit without any emotions at all? I just didn't understand.

"It's hopeless, Moody, let's go," Dorie said.

As we were leaving the building, we began soliciting aloud in the hall. We walked right past the president's office, shouting even louder. President Reddix came rushing out. "You girls leave this campus immediately," he said. "You can't come on this campus and announce anything without my consent."

Dorie had been a student at Jackson State. Mr. Reddix looked at her. "You know better than this, Dorie," he said.

"But President Reddix, Medgar was just murdered. Don't you have any feelings about his death at all?" Dorie said.

"I am doing a job. I can't do this job and have feelings about everything happening in Jackson," he said. He was waving his arms and pointing his finger in our faces. "Now you two get off this campus before I have you arrested."

By this time a group of students had gathered in the hall. Dorie had fallen to her knees in disgust as Reddix was pointing at her, and some of the students thought he had hit her. I didn't say anything to him. If I had I would have been calling him every kind of fucking Tom I could think of. I helped Dorie off the floor. I told her we'd better hurry, or we would miss the demonstration.

On our way back to the auditorium we picked up the Jackson *Daily News.* Headlines read JACKSON INTEGRATION LEADER EVERS SLAIN.

> Negro NAACP leader Medgar Evers was shot to death when he stepped from his automobile here early today as he returned home from an integration strategy meeting.
>
> Police said Evers, 37, was cut down by a high-powered bullet in the back of the driveway of his home.

I stopped reading. Medgar was usually followed home every night by two or three cops. Why didn't they follow him last night? Something was wrong. "They must have known," I thought. "Why didn't they follow him last night?" I kept asking myself. I had to get out of all this confusion. The only way I could do it was to go to jail. Jail was the only place I could think in.

When we got back to the auditorium, we were told that those who would take part in the first march had met at Pearl Street

Church. Dorie and I walked over there. We noticed a couple of girls from Jackson State. They asked Dorie if President Reddix had hit her, and said it had gotten out on campus that he had. They told us a lot of students had planned to demonstrate because of what Reddix had done. "Good enough," Dorie said, "Reddix better watch himself, or we'll turn that school out."

I was called to the front of the church to help lead the marchers in a few freedom songs. We sang "Woke Up This Morning With My Mind on Freedom" and "Ain't Gonna Let Nobody Turn Me 'Round." After singing the last song we headed for the streets in a double line, carrying small American flags in our hands. The cops had heard that there were going to be Negroes in the streets all day protesting Medgar's death. They were ready for us.

On Rose Street we ran into a blockade of about two hundred policemen. We were called to a halt by Captain Ray, and asked to disperse. "Everybody ain't got a permit get out of this here parade," Captain Ray said into his bullhorn. No one moved. He beckoned to the cops to advance on us.

The cops had rifles and wore steel helmets. They walked right up to us very fast and then sort of engulfed us. They started snatching the small American flags, throwing them to the ground, stepping on them, or stamping them. Students who refused to let go of the flags were jabbed with rifle butts. There was only one paddy wagon on the scene. The first twenty of us were thrown into it, although a paddy wagon is only large enough to seat about ten people. We were sitting and lying all over each other inside the wagon when garbage trucks arrived. We saw the cops stuff about fifty demonstrators in one truck as we looked out through the back glass. Then the driver of the paddy wagon sped away as fast as he could, often making sudden stops in the middle of the street so we would be thrown around.

We thought that they were going to take us to the city jail again because we were college students. We discovered we were headed for the fairgrounds. When we got there, the driver rolled up the windows, turned the heater on, got out, closed the door and left us. It was over a hundred degrees outside that day. There was no air coming in. Sweat began dripping off us. An hour went by. Our clothes were now soaked and sticking to us. Some of the girls looked as though they were about to faint. A policeman looked in to see how we were taking it. Some of the boys begged him to let us out. He only smiled and walked away.

Looking out of the back window again, we noticed they were

now booking all the other demonstrators. We realized they had planned to do this to our group. A number of us in the paddy wagon were known to the cops. After the Woolworth sit-in, I had been known to every white in Jackson. I can remember walking down the street and being pointed out by whites as they drove or walked past me.

Suddenly one of the girls screamed. Scrambling to the window, we saw John Salter with blood gushing out of a large hole in the back of his head. He was just standing there dazed and no one was helping him. And we were in no position to help either.

After they let everyone else out of the garbage trucks, they decided to let us out of the paddy wagon. We had now been in there well over two hours. As we were getting out, one of the girls almost fell. A guy started to help her.

"Get ya hands off that gal. Whatta ya think, ya goin' to a prom or somethin'?" one of the cops said.

Water was running down my legs. My skin was soft and spongy. I had hidden a small transistor radio in my bra and some of the other girls had cards and other things in theirs. We had learned to sneak them in after we discovered they didn't search the women but now everything was showing through our wet clothes.

When we got into the compound, there were still some high school students there, since the NAACP bail money had been exhausted. There were altogether well over a hundred and fifty in the girls' section. The boys had been put into a compound directly opposite and parallel to us. Some of the girls who had been arrested after us shared their clothes with us until ours dried. They told us what had happened after we were taken off in the paddy wagon. They said the cops had stuffed so many into the garbage trucks that some were just hanging on. As one of the trucks pulled off, thirteen-year-old John Young fell out. When the driver stopped, the truck rolled back over the boy. He was rushed off to a hospital and they didn't know how badly he had been hurt. They said the cops had gone wild with their billy sticks: They had even arrested Negroes looking on from their porches. John Salter had been forced off some Negro's porch and hit on the head.

The fairgrounds were everything I had heard they were. The compounds they put us in were two large buildings used to auction off cattle during the annual state fair. They were about a block long, with large openings about twenty feet wide on both ends where the cattle were driven in. The openings had been closed up with wire. It reminded me of a concentration camp. It was hot and sticky and girls were walking around half dressed all the time. We were guarded by four policemen. They had rifles and kept an eye on us through the wired sides of the building. As I looked through the wire at them, I imagined myself in Nazi Germany, the policemen Nazi soldiers. They couldn't have been any rougher than these cops. Yet this was America, "the land of the free and the home of the brave."

About five-thirty we were told that dinner was ready. We were lined up single file and marched out of the compound. They had the cook from the city jail there. He was standing over a large garbage can stirring something in it with a stick. The sight of it nauseated me. No one was eating, girls or boys. In the next few days, many were taken from the fairgrounds sick from hunger. . . .

Eudora Welty

On June 11, 1963, in response to the thousands of demonstrations and arrests throughout the United States, President John F. Kennedy gave a nationally televised speech to announce that he was sending a bill to Congress advocating sweeping Civil Rights reforms. He told the nation, "We are confronted primarily with a moral issue. It is as old as the Scriptures and is as clear as the American Constitution. The heart of the question is whether all Americans are to be afforded equal rights and equal opportunities, whether we are going to treat our fellow Americans as we want to be treated."

A few hours after Kennedy's speech, Medgar Evers, an NAACP official in Jackson, Mississippi, was shot and killed in the driveway outside his home by white supremacist Byron De La Beckwith. Anne Moody described how she tried to organize a demonstration with the students at Jackson State College to protest Evers's death. Shortly after hearing of the murder, Eudora Welty, the eminent novelist and short-fiction author living in Mississippi, wrote a story, "Where Is the Voice Coming From?," in which she imagined herself in Beckwith's consciousness; her story was published in The New Yorker *on July 6, 1963. In the narrative, Evers is called "Roland Summers," and the city of Jackson is renamed "Thermopylae." Evers was buried with full military honors at Arlington Cemetery. After several trials, Beckwith, who often boasted of what he had done, was convicted of murder in 1994.*

WHERE IS THE VOICE COMING FROM?

I SAYS TO MY WIFE, "You can reach and turn it off. You don't have to set and look at a black nigger face no longer than you want to, or listen to what you don't want to hear. It's still a free country."

I reckon that's how I give myself the idea.

I says, I could find right exactly where in Thermopylae that nigger's living that's asking for equal time. And without a bit of trouble to me.

And I ain't saying it might not be because that's pretty close to where *I* live. The other hand, there could be reasons you might have yourself for knowing how to get there in the dark. It's where you all go for the thing you want when you want it the most. Ain't that right?

The Branch Bank sign tells you in lights, all night long even, what time it is and how hot. When it was quarter to four, and 92, that was me going by in my brother-in-law's truck. He don't deliver nothing at that hour of the morning.

So you leave Four Corners and head west on Nathan B. Forrest Road, past the Surplus & Salvage, not much beyond the Kum Back Drive-In and Trailer Camp, not as far as where the signs start saying "Live Bait," "Used Parts," "Fireworks," "Peaches," and "Sister Peebles Reader and Adviser." Turn before you hit the city limits and duck back towards the I.C. tracks. And his street's been paved.

And there was his light on, waiting for me. In his garage, if you please. His car's gone. He's out planning still some other ways to do what we tell 'em they can't. I *thought* I'd beat him home. All I had to do was pick my tree and walk in close behind it.

I didn't come expecting not to wait. But it was so hot, all I did was hope and pray one or the other of us wouldn't melt before it was over.

Now, it wasn't no bargain I'd struck.

I've heard what you've heard about Goat Dykeman, in Missis-sippi. Sure, everybody knows about Goat Dykeman. Goat he got word to the Governor's Mansion he'd go up yonder and shoot that nigger Meredith clean out of school, if he's let out of the pen to do it. Old Ross turned *that* over in his mind before saying to him nay, it stands to reason.

I ain't no Goat Dykeman, I ain't in no pen, and I ain't ask no Governor Barnett to give me one thing. Unless he wants to give me a pat on the back for the trouble I took this morning. But he don't have to if he don't want to. I done what I done for my own pure-D satis-faction.

As soon as I heard wheels, I knowed who was coming. That was him and bound to be him. It was the right nigger heading in a new white car up his driveway towards his garage with the light shining, but stopping before he got there, maybe not to wake 'em. That was him. I knowed it when he cut off the car lights and put his foot out and I knowed him standing dark against the light. I knowed him then like I know me now. I knowed him even by his still, listening back.

Never seen him before, never seen him since, never seen any-thing of his black face but his picture, never seen his face alive, any time at all, or anywheres, and didn't want to, need to, never hope to see that face and never will. As long as there was no question in my mind.

He had to be the one. He stood right still and waited against the light, his back was fixed, fixed on me like a preacher's eyeballs when he's yelling "Are you saved?" He's the one.

I'd already brought up my rifle, I'd already taken my sights. And I'd already got him, because it was too late then for him or me to turn by one hair.

Something darker than him, like the wings of a bird, spread on his back and pulled him down. He climbed up once, like a man under bad claws, and like just blood could weigh a ton he walked with it on his back to better light. Didn't get no further than his door. And fell to stay.

He was down. He was down, and a ton load of bricks on his back wouldn't have laid any heavier. There on his paved driveway, yes sir.

And it wasn't till the minute before, that the mockingbird had quit singing. He'd been singing up my sassafras tree. Either he was up early, or he hadn't never gone to bed, he was like me. And the mocker he'd stayed right with me, filling the air till come the crack, till I turned loose of my load. I was like him. I was on top of the world myself. For once.

I stepped to the edge of his light there, where he's laying flat. I says, "Roland? There was one way left, for me to be ahead of you and stay ahead of you, by Dad, and I just taken it. Now I'm alive and you ain't. We ain't never now, never going to be equals and you know why? One of us is dead. What about that, Roland?" I said. "Well, you seen to it, didn't you?"

I stood a minute—just to see would somebody inside come out long enough to pick him up. And there she comes, the woman. I doubt she'd been to sleep. Because it seemed to me she'd been in there keeping awake all along.

It was mighty green where I skint over the yard getting back. That nigger wife of his, she wanted nice grass! I bet my wife would hate to pay her water bill. And for burning her electricity. And there's my brother-in-law's truck, still waiting with the door open. "No Riders"—that didn't mean me.

There wasn't a thing I been able to think of since would have made it to go any nicer. Except a chair to my back while I was putting in my waiting. But going home, I seen what little time it takes after all to get a thing done like you really want it. It was 4:34, and while I was looking it moved to 35. And the temperature stuck where it was. All that night I guarantee you it had stood without dropping, a good 92.

My wife says, "What? Didn't the skeeters bite you?" She said, "Well, they been asking that—why somebody didn't trouble to load a rifle and get some of these agitators out of Thermopylae. Didn't the fella keep drumming it in, what a good idea? The one that writes a column ever' day?"

I says to my wife, "Find *some* way I don't get the credit."

"He says do it for Thermopylae," she says. "Don't you ever skim the paper?"

I says, "Thermopylae never done nothing for me. And I don't owe nothing to Thermopylae. Didn't do it for you. Hell, any more'n I'd do something or other for them Kennedys! I done it for my own pure-D satisfaction."

"It's going to get him right back on TV," says my wife. "You watch for the funeral."

I says, "You didn't even leave a light burning when you went to bed. So how was I supposed to even get me home or pull Buddy's truck up safe in our front yard?"

"Well, hear another good joke on you," my wife says next. "Didn't you hear the news? The N. double A. C. P. is fixing to send somebody to Thermopylae. Why couldn't you waited? You might could have got you somebody better. Listen and hear 'em say so."

I ain't but one. I reckon you have to tell *somebody*.

"Where's the gun, then?" my wife says. "What did you do with our protection?"

I says, "It was scorching! It was scorching!" I told her, "It's laying out on the ground in rank weeds, trying to cool off, that's what it's doing now."

"You dropped it," she says. "Back there."

And I told her, "Because I'm so tired of ever'thing in the world being just that hot to the touch! The keys to the truck, the doorknob, the bedsheet, ever'thing, it's all like a stove lid. There just ain't much going that's worth holding on to it no more," I says, "when it's a hundred and two in the shade by day and by night not too much difference. I wish *you'd* laid *your* finger to that gun."

"Trust you to come off and leave it," my wife says.

"Is that how no-'count I am?" she makes me ask. "*You* want to go back and get it?"

"You're the one they'll catch. I say it's so hot that even if you get to sleep you wake up feeling like you cried all night!" says my wife. "Cheer up, here's one more joke before time to get up. Heard what *Caroline* said? Caroline said, 'Daddy, I just can't wait to grow up big, so I can marry *James Meredith*.' I heard that where I work. One rich-bitch to another one, to make her cackle."

"At least I kept some dern teen-ager from North Thermopylae getting there and doing it first," I says. "Driving his own car."

On TV and in the paper, they don't know but half of it. They know who Roland Summers was without knowing who I am. His face was in front of the public before I got rid of him, and after I got rid of him there it is again—the same picture. And none of me. I ain't ever had one made. Not ever! The best that newspaper could do for me was offer a five-hundred-dollar reward for finding out who I am. For as long as they don't know who that is, whoever shot Roland is worth a good deal more right now than Roland is.

But by the time I was moving around uptown, it was hotter still. That pavement in the middle of Main Street was so hot to my feet I might've been walking the barrel of my gun. If the whole world could've just felt Main Street this morning through the soles of my shoes, maybe it would've helped some.

Then the first thing I heard 'em say was the N. double A. C. P. done it themselves, killed Roland Summers, and proved it by saying the shooting was done by a expert (I hope to tell you it was!) and at just the right hour and minute to get the whites in trouble.

You can't win.

"They'll never find him," the old man trying to sell roasted peanuts tells me to my face.

And it's so hot.

It looks like the town's on fire already, whichever ways you turn, ever' street you strike, because there's those trees hanging them pones of bloom like split watermelon. And a thousand cops crowding ever'where you go, half of 'em too young to start shaving, but all streaming sweat alike. I'm getting tired of 'em.

I was already tired of seeing a hundred cops getting us white people nowheres. Back at the beginning, I stood on the corner and I watched them new babyface cops loading nothing but nigger children into the paddy wagon and they come marching out of a little parade and into the paddy wagon singing. And they got in and sat down without providing a speck of trouble, and their hands held little new American flags, and all the cops could do was knock them flagsticks a-loose from their hands, and not let 'em pick 'em up, that was all, and give 'em a free ride. And children can just get 'em more flags.

Everybody: It don't get you nowhere to take nothing from nobody unless you make sure it's for keeps, for good and all, for ever and amen.

I won't be sorry to see them brickbats hail down on us for a change. Pop bottles too, they can come flying whenever they want to. Hundreds, all to smash, like Birmingham. I'm waiting on 'em to bring out them switchblade knives, like Harlem and Chicago. Watch TV long enough and you'll see it all to happen on Deacon Street in Thermopylae. What's holding it back, that's all?—Because it's *in* 'em.

I'm ready myself for that funeral.

Oh, they may find me. May catch me one day in spite of 'emselves. (But I grew up in the country.) May try to railroad me into the electric chair, and what that amounts to is something hotter than yesterday and today put together.

But I advise 'em to go careful. Ain't it about time us taxpayers starts to calling the moves? Starts to telling the teachers *and* the preachers *and* the judges of our so-called courts how far they can go?

Even the President so far, he can't walk in my house without being invited, like he's my daddy, just to say whoa. Not yet!

Once, I run away from my home. And there was a ad for me, come to be printed in our county weekly. My mother paid for it. It was from her. It says: "SON: You are not being hunted for anything but to find you." That time, I come on back home.

But people are dead now.

And it's so hot. Without it even being August yet.

Anyways, I seen him fall. I was evermore the one.

So I reach me down my old guitar off the nail in the wall. 'Cause I've got my guitar, what I've held on to from way back when, and I never dropped that, never lost or forgot it, never hocked it but to get it again, never give it away, and I set in my chair, with nobody home but me, and I start to play, and sing a-down. And sing a-down, down, down, down. Sing a-down, down, down, down. Down.

Calvin Trillin

On August 28, 1963, the March on Washington drew nearly a half-million supporters of the Civil Rights Movement from all over the United States. The idea for a massive demonstration in the capital city originated as early as 1941, when A. Philip Randolph, president of the Brotherhood of Sleeping Car Porters, wanted President Franklin D. Roosevelt to guarantee jobs for blacks in wartime industries. Plans for this march were canceled after Roosevelt issued the first executive order protecting black rights since the Emancipation Proclamation.

In 1962 Randolph met with organizer Bayard Rustin to plan another march. Martin Luther King also believed that the time was right, as he told his aides, for "a mass protest." In June 1963, King announced the plans for a march on Washington to lobby for President Kennedy's new Civil Rights bill. At first, Kennedy tried to stop the march, but he couldn't. "We want success in Congress, not just a big show at the Capitol. Some of these people are looking for an excuse to be against us; and I don't want to give any of them a chance to say, 'Yes, I'm for the bill, but I am damned if I will vote for it at the point of a gun.' "

Calvin Trillin described the early morning scene in Washington, D.C., on August 28, 1963, for the "Talk of the Town" column in The New Yorker's issue of September 7, 1963. At that time, the march was the largest political demonstration ever held in the United States. Entertainers on the stage set up at the Washington Monument performed as people assembled for the march, beginning with Joan Baez singing "Oh, Freedom" and "We Shall Overcome," and continuing with Odetta, Josh White, the Albany Freedom Singers, and Bob Dylan (whose song "Blowin' in the Wind," as sung by Peter, Paul, and Mary, was number two on the charts).

The march was broadcast live around the world by the new satellite Telstar, and the three major American television networks all covered the event, their budget of over $300,000 more than twice the march committee's budget. After the marchers walked from the Washington Monument to the Lincoln Memorial, they listened to a program by many distinguished musicians and speakers (mostly male; Josephine Baker, the legendary black entertainer, wearing a Free French uniform decorated with the Legion of Honor, was the only woman speaker). Among the speakers, NAACP president Roy Wilkins announced the death of W. E. B. Du Bois, founder of the NAACP, in Ghana that day. The final speaker, preceded by Mahalia Jackson singing the gospel hymn "I've Been 'Buked and I've Been Scorned," was Martin Luther King, Jr., who began by saying, "I am happy to join with you today in what will go down in history as the greatest demonstration for freedom in the history of our nation." King concluded his "I have a dream" speech by using the words of a Negro spiritual, "Free at last, free at last; thank God Almighty, we are free at last!"

The future novelist and poet Alice Walker, who was a college sophomore in 1963, was in the Washington crowd, perched on the limb of a tree. Later she remembered being "far from the Lincoln Memorial, and although I managed to see very little of the speakers, I could hear everything." When Walker heard King speak of "letting freedom ring" across "the green hills of Alabama and the red hills of Georgia," she responded wholeheartedly to what he "was always uniquely able to make me see: that I, in fact, had claim to the

> *land of my birth. These red hills of Georgia were mine, and nobody was going to force me away from them, until I myself was good and ready to go."*

THE MARCH

WE FLEW TO WASHINGTON the day before the march and, early the next morning, walked from Pennsylvania Avenue past the side entrance of the White House and toward the lawn of the Washington Monument, where the marchers were gathering. It was eight o'clock—three and a half hours before the march was scheduled to move from the Washington Monument to the Lincoln Memorial—and around the Ellipse, the huge plot of grass between the White House grounds and the lawn of the Washington Monument, there were only about half a dozen buses. Most of them had red-white-and-blue signs saying "Erie, Pa., Branch, N.A.A.C.P.," or "Inter-Church Delegation, Sponsored by National Council of Churches of Christ in the U.S.A. Commission on Religion and Race," or "District 26, United Steelworkers of America, Greater Youngstown A.F.L.-C.I.O. Council, Youngstown, Ohio." On a baseball field on the Ellipse, three men were setting up a refreshment stand, and on the sidewalk nearby a man wearing an N.A.A.C.P. cap was arranging pennants that said "March on Washington for Jobs and Freedom. Let the World Know We Want Freedom." Most of the buses were nearly full, and many of the occupants were dozing. Sitting on a bench in front of one of the buses, some teen-agers were singing, "Everybody wants freedom—free-ee-dom."

On the lawn of the Washington Monument, a group of military police, most of them Negroes, and a group of Washington police, most of them white, were getting final instructions. Women dressed in white, with purple armbands that said "Usher" and blue sashes that said "Pledge Cards," were handing out cards to everybody who passed. "I've already contributed to this," a man near us told one of the women. But the card asked for no money; it asked instead that the signer commit himself to the civil-rights struggle, pledging his heart, mind, and body, "unequivocally and without regard to personal sacrifice, to the achievement of social peace through social justice."

Outside march headquarters—a huge tent with green sides and a green-and-white striped roof—workers were setting up a rim of tables. One table held a display of pennants, offering a large one for a dollar and a small one for fifty cents. Inside the tent, a man wearing a CORE overseas cap, a blue suit, an armband with the letter "M" on it, and a badge saying "Assistant Chief Marshal," was testing a walkie-talkie, and another man was issuing instructions to a group of pro- gram salesmen. "Now, everybody report back by nine-fifteen, or whenever they give out," he said. Two or three Negroes were sorting signs that said "The Southern Christian Leadership Conference of Lynchburg, Virginia." In a roped-off area near one end of the tent, the official signs for the march were stacked face down in large piles, most of them covered by black tarpaulins. Next to the signs, in an en- clave formed by a green fence, half a dozen women sat behind a long table. Two signs on the fence said "Emergency Housing." Nearby, three or four television crews had set up their cameras on high plat- forms.

By this time, there were several thousand people on the lawn, many of them gathered around the Monument. An ice-cream truck had managed to drive to within a hundred feet of the Monument and was starting to do an early-morning business. Many of those gathered near the Monument were sitting on the grass, and some were sleep- ing. Three boys dressed in khaki pants and shirts with button-down collars were using their knapsacks for pillows and had covered their faces with black derbies. There were, we thought, surprisingly few knapsacks and sandals in the crowd. Most of the people were neatly dressed, and as they waited for the pre-march program to start, they acted like ordinary tourists in Washington, or like city people spend- ing a warm Sunday in the park. A man took a picture of a couple standing in front of a sign that said "New Jersey Region, American Jewish Congress"; a policeman was taking a picture of two smiling Negro couples; a woman who was selling programs balanced her pro- grams and her purse in one hand and, with the other, took pictures of the sleepers with derbies over their faces.

By nine o'clock, a group of marchers had congregated outside a green fence surrounding a stage that had been set up several hundred yards from the Monument; they were standing six or eight deep against the fence. More people were arriving constantly—some in couples and small groups, others marching in large contingents. A group of young Negroes walked behind a blue-and-gold banner that said "Newman Memorial Methodist Church School, Brooklyn, N.Y., Organized 1900." Another group of Negroes—older, and wearing yellow campaign hats that bore the letters "B.S.E.I.U."—followed four boys who were carrying a long banner that said "Local 144" and two flag-bearers, one carrying the American flag and one carrying a flag that said "Building Services Employees International Union."

In front of the headquarters tent, a group of young people in overalls and T shirts that said "CORE" were marching around in a circle, clapping and singing.

"I'm going to walk the streets of Jackson," one girl sang.

"One of these days," the others answered.

"I'm going to be the chief of police," another sang.

"One of these days," the crowd answered.

Near the singing group, a double line of Negro teen-agers came marching across the lawn. All of them were dressed in black jackets. They had no banners or pennants, and they filed by in silence.

"Where y'all from?" a Negro girl in the CORE group asked one of them.

"From Wilmington, North Carolina," one of the boys replied, and the black-jacketed group walked on silently.

We started toward the stage and happened to come across Bayard Rustin, the deputy director of the march, heading that way with Norman Thomas. Following them up to the stage, we found two other members of the march committee—Courtland Cox, of the Student Non-Violent Coördinating Committee, and Norman Hill, of the Congress of Racial Equality—looking out at the people between the stage and the Monument and talking about the crowd.

At exactly nine-thirty, Ossie Davis, serving as master of ceremonies, tried to begin the pre-march program, but it had to be postponed, because Rustin and Thomas were the only two dignitaries on the stage and many more were expected.

"Oh, freedom," said a voice over a loudspeaker a little later. The program had started, and Joan Baez began to sing in a wonderfully clear voice. "Oh, freedom," she sang. "Oh, freedom over me. Before I'll be a slave, I'll be buried in my grave . . ."

Then came folk songs by Miss Baez; Peter, Paul, and Mary; Odetta; and Bob Dylan. Davis made the introductions, occasionally turning the microphone over to a marshal for an announcement, such as "Mr. Roosevelt Johnson. If you hear me, your child, Larry Johnson, is in the headquarters tent." By ten-thirty, the expanse of grass that had been visible between the crowd around the stage and the crowd around the Monument had almost disappeared, and more people were still marching onto the lawn, carrying signs and banners. Most of the signs identified groups—such as the Alpha Phi Alpha Fraternity and the Detroit Catholics for Equality and Freedom—but some had slogans on them, and one, carried by a white woman who marched up and down the sidewalk in back of the stage, said "What We All Need Is Jesus and to Read the Bible." Another folk singer, Josh White, arrived on the stage while Odetta was singing. White didn't wait for an introduction. He merely unpacked his guitar, handed the cigarette he had been smoking to a bystander, and walked up to the microphone to join Odetta in singing "I'm on the Way to Canaan Land." In a few moments, Miss Baez was also singing, and then all the folk singers gathered at the microphone to finish the song.

At about eleven, Davis announced that the crowd was now estimated at ninety thousand. From the stage, there was no longer any grass visible between the stage and the Monument. Next, Davis introduced a representative of the Elks, who presented the organizers of the march with an Elks contribution of ten thousand dollars; a girl who was the first Negro to be hired as an airline stewardess; Lena Horne; Daisy Bates, who shepherded the nine teen-agers who integrated Central High School in Little Rock; Miguel Abreu Castillo, the head of the San Juan Bar Association, who gave a short speech in Spanish; Bobby Darin; and Rosa Parks, the woman who started the Montgomery bus boycott by refusing to move to the back of the bus.

The official march signs had been passed out, and they began to bob up and down in the crowd: "No U.S. Dough to Help Jim Crow Grow," "Civil Rights Plus Full Employment Equals Freedom."

At about eleven-forty-five, Davis told the crowd that the march to the Lincoln Memorial was going to begin, and suggested that people standing near the Monument use Independence Avenue and people standing near the stage go down Constitution Avenue. We were closer to Constitution Avenue, and as we got onto the street there was a crush of people that for a moment brought back stories of the dangers inherent in a crowd of such a size. But almost immediately the crush eased, and we walked comfortably down shady Constitution Avenue. We noticed that practically nobody was watching the march from the sidelines, and that in the march itself there was a remarkable lack of noise. Occasionally, a song would start somewhere in the crowd, but to a large extent the marchers were silent. A few hundred yards from the Monument, the march was stopped by a man who was holding a sign that said "Lexington Civil Rights Committee" and wearing an armband that said "Mass. Freedom Rider." He asked the people in the front row to link arms, and, beginning to sing "We Shall Overcome," they moved on down the street.

"Slow down, slow down!" the man from Massachusetts shouted

as he walked backward in front of the crowd. "Too fast! You're going too fast! Half steps!"

A few hundred feet farther on, a policeman and an M.P. stood in the middle of the street and split the crowd down the middle. We followed the group to the left, and in a few minutes found ourself standing in a crowd, now even quieter, to the left of the reflecting pool in front of the Lincoln Memorial.

Bob Dylan

In the Sixties, Bob Dylan wrote songs filled with social consciousness, but he rarely referred directly to current events. One of the exceptions occurred at the time of the March on Washington, when he wrote "The Lonesome Death of Hattie Carroll." The song commemorated a crime that had occurred in Maryland earlier in 1963, when William Zanzinger, a wealthy twenty-four-year-old property owner, became enraged at a charity ball because he thought that Hattie Carroll, a fifty-one-year-old waitress serving him dinner, was too slow. He hit her on the head so savagely with his cane that she collapsed and was taken to the hospital, where she died of a suspected brain hemorrhage. Hattie Carroll was the mother of ten children. Zanzinger was charged with murder, but the white jury brought back a verdict of manslaughter and he served only six months in jail.

THE LONESOME DEATH OF HATTIE CARROLL

William Zanzinger killed poor Hattie Carroll
With a cane that he twirled around his diamond ring finger
At a Baltimore hotel society gath'rin'.
And the cops were called in and his weapon took from him

As they rode him in custody down to the station
And booked William Zanzinger for first-degree murder.
But you who philosophize disgrace and criticize all fears,
Take the rag away from your face.
Now ain't the time for your tears.

William Zanzinger, who at twenty-four years
Owns a tobacco farm of six hundred acres
With rich wealthy parents who provide and protect him
And high office relations in the politics of Maryland,
Reacted to his deed with a shrug of his shoulders
And swear words and sneering, and his tongue it was
    snarling,
In a matter of minutes on bail was out walking.
But you who philosophize disgrace and criticize all fears,
Take the rag away from your face.
Now ain't the time for your tears.

Hattie Carroll was a maid of the kitchen.
She was fifty-one years old and gave birth to ten children
Who carried the dishes and took out the garbage
And never sat once at the head of the table
And didn't even talk to the people at the table
Who just cleaned up all the food from the table
And emptied the ashtrays on a whole other level,
Got killed by a blow, lay slain by a cane
That sailed through the air and came down through the
    room,
Doomed and determined to destroy all the gentle,
And she never done nothing to William Zanzinger.
But you who philosophize disgrace and criticize all fears,
Take the rag away from your face.
Now ain't the time for your tears.

In the courtroom of honor, the judge pounded his gavel
To show that all's equal and that the courts are on the level
And that the strings in the books ain't pulled and persuaded
And that even the nobles get properly handled
Once that the cops have chased after and caught 'em
And that the ladder of law has no top and no bottom,
Stared at the person who killed for no reason

Who just happened to be feelin' that way without warnin'.
And he spoke through his cloak, most deep and
    distinguished,
And handed out strongly, for penalty and repentance,
William Zanzinger with a six-month sentence.
Oh, but you who philosophize disgrace and criticize all
    fears,
Bury the rag deep in your face
For now's the time for your tears.

Dudley Randall

On September 15, 1963, three Sundays after the March on Washington, a bomb exploded in the basement of the Sixteenth Street Baptist Church in Birmingham. The church was the meeting place for the Birmingham Civil Rights Movement, since it was close to downtown, where demonstrators had been active for several months. Birmingham was probably the most highly segregated city in the United States; the provocative police commissioner, "Bull" Connor, regularly drove through the streets of black neighborhoods in his personal white armored car. In May 1963, a month after Martin Luther King, Jr., had written his "Letter from a Birmingham Jail," many young people from the local junior high schools, high schools, and colleges participating in demonstrations downtown and in Kelly Ingram Park had also been jailed after being mauled by police dogs and dispersed by firemen wielding water cannon.

On the morning of September 15, the congregation of the Sixteenth Street Baptist Church was celebrating Youth Day, so the church was full of children. The bomb blast killed four young girls and injured twenty-one children. One of the victims was eleven-year-old Denise McNair, whose mother was at home when she heard the explosion. She rushed to the church and searched through the wreckage, unsure if her daughter was dead or alive until she found one of her shoes. Four men were responsible for the bombing. Many years later, Robert Chambliss, a member of the Ku Klux Klan nicknamed "Dynamite Bob," was convicted for his part in the crime and sentenced to a life term in prison in 1977. Herman Frank Cash died untried; and Thomas Blanton, Jr., and Bobby Frank Cherry were finally sentenced to life in prison in 2001 and 2002.

In "Ballad of Birmingham" (1966), the Detroit poet Dudley Randall gave his response to the tragedy. Joan Baez also recorded the song "Birmingham Sunday" (with lyrics by Richard Fariña) about the event, and Spike Lee directed and produced the HBO film 4 Little Girls (1998) to commemorate the lives of Denise McNair, Carole Robertson, Cynthia Wesley, and Addie Mae Collins. As the newscaster Walter Cronkite observed, the bombing was a pivotal event in the struggle for civil rights in the 1960s, forcing the nation to acknowledge the extent of the virulent racial hatred among the whites who resisted integration in the South.

BALLAD OF BIRMINGHAM

(On the bombing of a church in Birmingham, Alabama, 1963)

"Mother dear, may I go downtown
Instead of out to play,
And march the streets of Birmingham
In a Freedom March today?"

"No, baby, no, you may not go,
For the dogs are fierce and wild,
And clubs and hoses, guns and jails
Aren't good for a little child."

"But, mother, I won't be alone.
Other children will go with me,
And march the streets of Birmingham
To make our country free."

"No, baby, no, you may not go,
For I fear those guns will fire.
But you may go to church instead
And sing in the children's choir."

She has combed and brushed her night-dark hair,
And bathed rose petal sweet,
And drawn white gloves on her small brown hands,
And white shoes on her feet.

The mother smiled to know her child
Was in the sacred place,
But that smile was the last smile
To come upon her face.

For when she heard the explosion,
Her eyes grew wet and wild.
She raced through the streets of Birmingham
Calling for her child.

She clawed through bits of glass and brick,
Then lifted out a shoe.
"Oh, here's the shoe my baby wore,
But, baby, where are you?"

Robert Lowell

*Robert Lowell read his poem "For the Union Dead" at the Boston
Arts Festival in 1960 and made it the title poem in his collection*
For the Union Dead *in 1964. At the center of the poem is a ref-
erence to the Civil War hero Robert Gould Shaw, whose sister
Josephine had married into Lowell's old New England family.
Shaw commanded a regiment of black soldiers in the Civil War,
and when he was killed in battle at Fort Wagner, near Charleston,
South Carolina, along with most of his regiment, his body was
buried with his men in a mass grave instead of being returned home
for individual burial in Boston. At the time Lowell's relative
Charles Russell Lowell wrote back to Shaw's wife, Josephine, "I*

*am thankful they buried him 'with his niggers.' They were brave
men and they were his men."*

In the poem, Lowell describes the beautiful bronze memorial
opposite the Boston State House, a bas-relief by Augustus Saint-
Gaudens of Colonel Shaw on horseback in the company of his sol-
diers, that had been put up to honor the Civil War hero and the
members of his Massachusetts Fifty-fourth Regiment. Believing
that fragmentary and so-called insignificant details added up to an
authentic history, Lowell developed his poem by apparently free as-
sociation. Nearly a century after the Civil War, he saw contempo-
rary life in downtown Boston debased by civic corruption and
commercialization. Yet in what critic Helen Vendler recognized as
"the most startling image in the poem," he also acknowledged his
own guilty sense of complicity in his time as a liberal white New
Englander when he described crouching in front of his television set
in Boston, watching "the drained faces of Negro school-children rise
like balloons" while federal marshals tried to enforce the Supreme
Court's Brown v. Board of Education decision in the South.

FOR THE UNION DEAD

"Relinquunt Omnia Servare Rem Publicam."

The old South Boston Aquarium stands
in a Sahara of snow now. Its broken windows are boarded.
The bronze weathervane cod has lost half its scales.
The airy tanks are dry.

Once my nose crawled like a snail on the glass;
my hand tingled
to burst the bubbles
drifting from the noses of the cowed, compliant fish.

My hand draws back. I often sigh still
for the dark downward and vegetating kingdom
of the fish and reptile. One morning last March,
I pressed against the new barbed and galvanized

fence on the Boston Common. Behind their cage,
yellow dinosaur steamshovels were grunting

as they cropped up tons of mush and grass
to gouge their underworld garage.

Parking spaces luxuriate like civic
sandpiles in the heart of Boston.
A girdle of orange, Puritan-pumpkin colored girders
braces the tingling Statehouse,

shaking over the excavations, as it faces Colonel Shaw
and his bell-cheeked Negro infantry
on St. Gaudens' shaking Civil War relief,
propped by a plank splint against the garage's earthquake.

Two months after marching through Boston,
half the regiment was dead;
at the dedication,
William James could almost hear the bronze Negroes
    breathe.

Their monument sticks like a fishbone
in the city's throat.
Its Colonel is as lean
as a compass-needle.

He has an angry wrenlike vigilance,
a greyhound's gentle tautness;
he seems to wince at pleasure,
and suffocate for privacy.

He is out of bounds now. He rejoices in man's lovely,
peculiar power to choose life and die—
when he leads his black soldiers to death,
he cannot bend his back.

On a thousand small town New England greens,
the old white churches hold their air
of sparse, sincere rebellion; frayed flags
quilt the graveyards of the Grand Army of the Republic.

The stone statues of the abstract Union Soldier
grow slimmer and younger each year—

wasp-waisted, they doze over muskets
and muse through their sideburns . . .

Shaw's father wanted no monument
except the ditch,
where his son's body was thrown
and lost with his "niggers."

The ditch is nearer.
There are no statues for the last war here;
on Boylston Street, a commercial photograph
shows Hiroshima boiling

over a Mosler Safe, the "Rock of Ages"
that survived the blast. Space is nearer.
When I crouch to my television set,
the drained faces of Negro school-children rise like
    balloons.

Colonel Shaw
is riding on his bubble,
he waits
for the blessèd break.

The Aquarium is gone. Everywhere,
giant finned cars nose forward like fish;
a savage servility
slides by on grease.

———————————

Malcolm X

*In 1964, Malcolm X gave different versions of his speech "The
Ballot or the Bullet" in several American cities. After he separated
from Black Muslim leader Elijah Muhammad, he spoke more*

*openly about the role that politics and economics played in oppress-
ing blacks. This version is from Malcolm X's delivery of the speech
on April 14, 1964, in Detroit at a rally sponsored by the Group
on Advanced Leadership (GOAL). It was included in* The Auto-
biography of Malcolm X *(1965; written with Alex Haley).
Less than a year after Malcolm X spoke in Detroit, he was killed by
Black Muslim gunmen in Harlem.*

In Claude Brown's bestselling memoir, Manchild in the
Promised Land *(1965), he wrote that "from 1955 through
1959, just about everybody who came out of jail came out a Mus-
lim. By 1959, I had come to the conclusion that few Negroes could
go to any of the city prisons in New York and not come out a Mus-
lim." Still actively recruiting converts, the Black Muslims began as
a radical group in the United States who had broken with Chris-
tianity and turned to Islam. Brown praised the Black Muslim ef-
forts to strengthen Harlem's economy by investing in black-owned
businesses and boycotting white businesses. In the early 1960s, the
Muslims took over Harlem's 125th Street, making street-corner
speeches urging residents of the neighborhood to stick together as a
community. Brown wrote,*

> *The Muslims became a very influential force in Harlem.
> They would never have been able to take over, because
> they couldn't acquire any political power. For one thing,
> many of their recruits had been in jail. Once a person
> goes to jail for a felony, he loses his voting rights. But if
> the Muslims were to run a candidate for Congress in
> Harlem, there might be a good chance that they could
> get enough support.*

*In Chicago, before Malcolm X's assassination, James Baldwin
was invited to dinner with Elijah Muhammad and other Muslim
leaders at their "stately mansion" on the South Side, the headquar-
ters of the Nation of Islam organization. After describing the con-
versation around Elijah Muhammad's dinner table in* The Fire
Next Time *(1963), Baldwin imagined how the United States
would change if the Muslims ever achieved their goal of becoming a
separate nation. Baldwin admitted that his vision was a fantasy,
"although, in an age so fantastical, I would hesitate to say precisely
what a fantasy is."*

THE BALLOT OR THE BULLET

BROTHERS AND SISTERS AND FRIENDS, and I see some enemies.

In fact I think we'd be fooling ourselves if we had an audience this large and didn't realize that there were some enemies present.

This afternoon, we want to talk about *The Ballot or the Bullet. The Ballot or the Bullet* explains itself. But before we get into it, since this is the year of the ballot or the bullet, I would like to clarify some things that refer to me, personally, concerning my own personal position. I'm still a Muslim, that is, my religion is still Islam.

My religion is still Islam. I still credit Mr. Muhammad for what I know and what I am. He's the one who opened my eyes. At present I am the minister of the newly founded Muslim Mosque Incorporated, which has its offices in the Theresa Hotel, right in that heart of Harlem—that's the black belt in New York City. And when we realize that Adam Clayton Powell[1] is a Christian minister, he heads the Abyssinian Baptist Church, but at the same time, he's more famous for his political struggling. And Dr. King[2] is a Christian minister from Atlanta, Georgia—or in Atlanta, Georgia—but he's become more famous for being involved in the Civil Rights struggle. The same as they are Christian ministers, I'm a Muslim minister. And I don't believe in fighting today in any one front, but on all fronts.

In fact I'm a black nationalist freedom fighter.

Islam is my religion, but I believe my religion is my personal business. It governs my personal life and my personal morals. And my religious philosophy is personal between me and the God in whom I believe—just as the religious philosophy of these others is between them and the God in whom they believe. And this is best this way. Were we to come out here discussing religion, we'd have too many differences from the out-start, and we could never get together. So today, though Islam is my religious philosophy, my political, economic, and social philosophy is black nationalism. As I say, if we bring up religion, we'll have differences, we'll have arguments, we'll never be able to get together. But if we keep our religion at home, keep our religion in the closet, keep our religion between ourselves and our

---

1. Congressional representative from New York (1945–1970).
2. Martin Luther King, Jr.

God, but when we come out here, we have a fight that is common to all of us against an enemy who is common to all of us.

The political philosophy of black nationalism only means that the black man should control the politics and the politicians in his own community. The time when white people can come in our community, and get us to vote for them so that they can be our political leaders and tell us what to do and what not to do is long gone. Those days are gone. By the same token, the time when that same white man, knowing that your eyes are too far open, can send another Negro into the community and get you and me to support him, so he can use him to lead us astray, those days are long gone, too.

The political philosophy of black nationalism only means that if you and I are going to live in a black community—and that's where we're going to live, 'cause soon as you move out of the black community into their community it's mixed for a period of time, but they're gone and you're right there by yourself again.

We must, we must understand the politics of our community. And we must know what politics is supposed to produce. We must know what part politics plays in our lives. And until we become politically mature, we will always be misled, led astray, or deceived, or maneuvered into supporting someone politically who doesn't have the good of our community at heart.

So the political philosophy of black nationalism only means that we will have to carry on a program, a political program, of re-education, to open our people's eyes, make us become more politically conscious, politically mature. And then whenever we get ready to cast our ballot, that ballot will be cast for a man of the community who has the good of the community at heart.

The economic philosophy of black nationalism only means that we should own and operate and control the economy of our community. You can't open up a black store in a white community; the white man won't even patronize you. And he's not wrong, he's got sense enough to look out for himself. It's you, it's you who don't have sense enough to look out for yourself.

The white man is too intelligent to let someone else come and gain control of the economy of his community. But you will let anybody come in and control the economy of your community—control the housing, control the education, control the jobs, control the business—under the pretext that you want to integrate. Naw, you're out of your mind.

The economic philosophy of black nationalism only means that we have to become involved in a program of re-education, to educate our people into the importance of knowing that when you spend your dollar out of the community in which you live, the community in which you spend your money becomes richer and richer. The community out of which you take your money becomes poorer and poorer. And because these Negroes who have been misled and misguided are breaking their necks to take their money and spend it with the man, the man is becoming richer and richer and you're becoming poorer and poorer. And then what happens? The community in which you live becomes a slum. It becomes a ghetto. The conditions become run down. And then you have the audacity to complain about poor housing in a run-down community. Why, you run it down yourself, when you take your dollar out.

And you and I are in a double trap because, not only do we lose by taking our money someplace else and spending it, when we try and spend it in *our own* community, we're trapped because we haven't had sense enough to set up stores and control the businesses of our community. The man who's controlling the stores in our community is a man who doesn't look like we do. He's a man who doesn't even live in the community. So you and I, even when we try and spend our money in the block where we live, or the area where we live, we're spending it with a man who when the sun goes down takes that basket full of money in another part of the town.

So we're trapped. Trapped. Double trapped. Triple trapped. Any way we go, we find that we're trapped. And any kind of solution that someone comes up with is just another trap. But the economic philosophy of black nationalism shows our people the importance of setting up these little stores, and developing them and expanding them into larger operations. Woolworth didn't start out big like they are today. They started out with a dime store and expanded and expanded and then expanded until today, they're all over the country and all over the world and they're getting some of everybody's money. Now, this is what you and I— General Motors, the same way, didn't start out like it is. It started out like a little rat-race type operation, and it expanded and it expanded until today it is where it is right now. And you and I have to make a start. And the best place to start is right in the community where we live.

So our people not only have to be re-educated to the importance of supporting black business, but the black man himself has to be made aware of the importance of going into business. And once you and I go into business, we own and operate *at least* the businesses in our community, what we will be doing is developing a situation wherein we will actually be able to create employment for the people in the community. And once you can create some employment in the community where you live, it will eliminate the necessity of you and me having to act ignorantly and disgracefully, boycotting and picketing some cracker someplace else, trying to beg him for a job.

Anytime you have to rely upon your enemy for a job, you're in bad shape.

He is your enemy. You wouldn't be in this country if some enemy hadn't kidnapped you and brought you here.

On the other hand, some of you think you came here on the *Mayflower*.

So, as you can see, brothers and sisters, today, this afternoon, it's not our intention to discuss religion. We're going to forget religion. If we bring up religion, we'll be in an argument. And the best way to keep away from arguments and differences, as I said earlier . . . put your religion at home, in the closet. Keep it between you and your God. Because if it hasn't done anything more for you than it has, you need to forget it anyway.

Whether you are a Christian or a Muslim or a Nationalist, we all have the same problem. They don't hang you because you're a Baptist, they hang you 'cause you're black. They don't attack me because I'm a Muslim, they attack me 'cause I'm black. They attack all of us for the same reason. All of us catch hell from the same enemy. We're all in the same bag. In the same boat. We suffer political oppression. Economic exploitation. And social degradation. All of 'em from the same enemy. The government has failed us. You can't deny that. Anytime you're living in the twentieth century, and you're walking around here singing "We Shall Overcome," the government has failed us.

This is part of what's wrong with you. You do too much singing. Today, it's time to stop singing and start swinging.

You can't sing up on freedom. But you can *swing* up on some freedom.

Cassius Clay[3] can sing. But singing didn't help him to become the heavyweight champion of the world. *Swinging* helped him become the heavyweight champion of the world.

So this government has failed us. The government itself has failed us. And the white liberals, who have been posing as our friends, have failed us. And once we see that all these other sources to which we've

---

3. Prizefighter who, in 1964, took the name Muhammad Ali.

turned have failed, we stop turning to them and turn to ourselves. We need a self-help program. A do-it-yourself philosophy. A do-it-right-now philosophy. An it's-already-too-late philosophy. This is what you and I need to get with. And the only way we're going to solve our problem is with a self-help program. Before we can get a self-help program started, we have to have a self-help philosophy. Black nationalism is a self-help philosophy. What's so good about it, you can stay right in the church where you are and still take black nationalism as your philosophy. You can stay in any kind of civic organization that you belong to and still take black nationalism as your philosophy. You can be an atheist and still take black nationalism as your philosophy. This is a philosophy that eliminates the necessity for division and argument. Because if you are black, you should be thinking black. And if you're a black, and you're not thinking black at this late date, why, I'm sorry for you.

Once you change your philosophy, you change your thought pattern. Once you change your thought pattern, you change your attitude. Once you change your attitude, it changes your behavior pattern. And then you go on into some action. As long as you got a sit-down philosophy, you'll have a sit-down thought pattern. And as long as you think that old sit-down thought, you'll be in some kind of sit-down action. They'll have you sitting-in everywhere.

It's not so good to refer to what you're going to do as a sit-in. Then right there it castrates you. Right there it brings you down. What goes with it? Think of the image of someone sitting. An old woman can sit. An old man can sit. A chump can sit. A coward can sit. Anything can sit. For you and I have been *sitting* long enough and it's time today for you and I to be doing some *standing*. And some *fighting* to back that up.

When we look at other parts of this earth in which we live, we find that black, brown, red and yellow people in Africa and Asia are getting their independence. They're not getting it by singing "We Shall Overcome." No, they're getting it through *nationalism*. It is nationalism that brought about the independence of the people in Asia. Every nation in Asia gained its independence through the philosophy of nationalism. Every nation on the African continent that has gotten its independence brought it about through the philosophy of nationalism. And it will take *black* nationalism to bring about the freedom of twenty-two million Afro-Americans here in this country where we have suffered *colonialism* for the past four hundred years.

America is just as much a colonial power as England ever was. America is just as much a colonial power as France ever was. In fact, America is more so a colonial power than they. Because she's a hypocritical colonial power behind it. What do you call second-class citizenship? Why, that's colonization. Second-class citizenship is nothing but twentieth-century slavery. How are you going to tell me you're a second-class citizen? They don't have second-class citizenship in any other government on this earth. They just have slaves and people who are free. Well, this country is a hypocrite. They try and make you think they set you free by calling you a second-class citizen. Naw, you're nothing but a twentieth-century slave.

Just as it took nationalism to remove colonialism from Asia and Africa, it'll take black nationalism today to remove colonialism from the backs and the minds of twenty-two million Afro-Americans here in this country. Looks like it might be the year of the ballot or the bullet.

Why does it look like it might be the year of the ballot or the bullet? Because Negroes have listened to the trickery and the lies and the false promises of the white man now for too long. And they're fed up. They've become disenchanted. They've become disillusioned. They've become dissatisfied. And all of this has built up frustrations in the black community that makes the black community throughout America today more explosive than all of the atomic bombs the Russians can ever invent. Whenever you got a racial powder keg sitting in your lap, you're in more trouble than if you had an atomic power keg sitting in your lap. When a racial powder keg goes off, it doesn't care who it knocks out the way. Understand this: it's dangerous. Because what can the white man use, now, to fool us? After he put down that march on Washington, and you see all through that now. He tricked you, had you marching down to Washington. Yes, had you marching back and forth between the feet of a dead man named Lincoln and another dead man named George Washington, singing "We Shall Overcome."

He made a chump out of you. He made a fool out of you. He made you think you were going somewhere and you end up going nowhere but between Lincoln and Washington.

So today our people are disillusioned. They've become disenchanted. They've become dissatisfied. And in their frustrations they want action. You can see this young black man, this new generation, asking for the ballot or the bullet. That old Uncle Tom action is outdated. The young generation don't want to hear anything about "The odds are against us." What do we care about odds?

When this country here was first being founded, there were thirteen colonies. The whites were colonized. They were fed up with this taxation without representation. So some of them stood up and said "liberty or death." Well, I went to a white school over here in Mason, Michigan. The white man made the mistake of letting me read his history books. He made the mistake of teaching me that Patrick Henry[4] was a patriot. And George Washington—wasn't nothing nonviolent about old Pat. Or George Washington. "Liberty or death" was what brought about the freedom of whites in this country from the English.

They didn't care about the odds. Why, they faced the wrath of the entire British Empire. And in those days, they used to say that the British Empire was so vast and so powerful that the sun would never set on it. This is how big it was. Yet these thirteen little scrawny states, tired of taxation without representation, tired of being exploited and oppressed and degraded, told that big British Empire, "liberty or death." And here you have twenty-two million Afro-Americans, black people today, catching more hell than Patrick Henry ever saw.

And I'm here to tell you, in case you don't know it, that you got a new, you got a new generation of black people in this country who don't care anything whatsoever about odds. They don't want to hear you old Uncle Tom handkerchief-heads talking about the odds. No.

This is a new generation. If they're going to draft these young black men and send them over to Korea or South Vietnam to face eight hundred million Chinese . . . if you're not afraid of those odds, you shouldn't be afraid of these odds.

Why does this loom to be such an explosive *political* year? Because this is the year of politics. This is the year when all of the white politicians are going to come into the Negro community. You've never seen them until election time. You can't find them until election time. They're going to come in with false promises. And as they make these false promises, they're going to feed our frustrations. And this will only serve to make matters worse. I'm no politician. I'm not even a student of politics. I'm not a Republican nor a Democrat, nor an American. And got sense enough to know it.

I'm one of the twenty-two million black *victims* of the Demo-

---

4. American Revolutionary leader and orator (1736–1799), famous for his pronouncement "Give me liberty or give me death."

crats. One of the twenty-two million black *victims* of the Republicans.
And one of the twenty-two million black *victims* of Americanism.

And when I speak, I don't speak as a Democrat, or a Republican,
nor an American. I speak as a *victim* of America's so-called democracy.
You and I have never seen democracy; all we've seen is hypocrisy.
When we open our eyes today and look around America, we see
America not through the eyes of someone who has enjoyed the fruits
of Americanism, we see America through the eyes of someone who
has been the victim of Americanism. We don't see any American
dream. We've experienced only the American nightmare.

We haven't benefited from America's democracy. We've only suf-
fered from America's hypocrisy. And the generation that is coming up
now can see it, and are not afraid to say it. If you go to jail, so what? If
you're black, you were born in jail. In the North as well as the South.
Stop talking about the South. Long as you're south of the Canadian
border, you're South. . . .

It'll be the ballot or it'll be the bullet. It'll be liberty or it'll be
death. And if you're not ready to pay that price, don't use the word
freedom in your vocabulary.

One more thing: I was on the program in Illinois recently with
Senator Paul Douglas[5] the so-called liberal, the so-called Democrat,
the so-called white man. At which time he told me that our African
brothers were not interested in us in Africa. He says the Africans are
not interested in the American Negro. I knew he was lying. But, dur-
ing the next two or three weeks, it's my intention and plan to make a
tour of our African homeland. And I hope that when I come back I'll
be able to come back and let you know how our African brothers and
sisters feel toward us.

And I know before I go there, that they love us. We're one. We're
the same. It's the same man that colonized them all these years that
colonized you and me too, all these years. And all we have to do now
is wake up and work in unity and harmony and the battle will be
over.

I want to thank the Freedom Now Party in the gold; I want to
thank Milton and Richard Henry for inviting me here this afternoon,
and also the Reverend Cley. And I want them to know that anything
that I can ever do at anytime to work with anybody in any kind of
program that is sincerely designed to eliminate the political, the eco-

---

5. U.S. senator from Massachusetts (1948–1966).

nomic, and the social evils that confront all of our people in Detroit and elsewhere, all you've got to do is give me a telephone call, and I'll be on the next jet right on into the city.

Thank you.

———————————

Alice Walker

Alice Walker reflected on the question "The Civil Rights Movement: What Good Was It?" in an essay written during the winter of 1966–1967. It was her first published essay, and she remembered that it won the three-hundred-dollar first prize in the annual American Scholar *essay contest. Walker had been born and raised in the small town of Eatonton, Georgia. She had felt herself "an exile" in her birthplace because of the social restrictions: white kids could sit at the counter and drink Cokes in the air-conditioned drugstore, but blacks had to buy their Cokes and drink them outside. In 1960, as a high school student, she saw Martin Luther King, Jr., as the first black face on television at her parents' home in Georgia when he was in the process of being arrested for leading a protest march in Alabama. Walker was so moved by what she saw that she decided to become involved in Civil Rights action, starting as a volunteer in a voter registration drive in her home state. In 1973 she brought up the idea of freedom of choice for all Americans in her essay "Choosing to Stay at Home." Before the Civil Rights Movement, few African-American writers born in the South chose to stay there:*

> *In the South, [William] Faulkner, [Eudora] Welty, and [Flannery] O'Connor could stay in their paternal homes and write because although their neighbors might think them weird—and in Faulkner's case, trashy—they were spared the added burden of not being able to use a public toilet and did not have to go through intense emotional struggle over where to purchase a hamburger. What if*

> *[Richard] Wright had been able to stay in Mississippi? I*
> *ask this not because I assumed an alternative direction to*
> *his life . . . but because it indicates Wright's lack of*
> *choice. And that a man of his talent should lack a choice*
> *is offensive. Horribly so.*

In 1970 Walker published her first novel, The Third Life
of Grange Copeland, *inspired by her life as a sharecropper's
daughter. Her second novel,* Meridian *(1976), grew out of her in-
volvement in the racial and gender politics of the Civil Rights
Movement.*

THE CIVIL RIGHTS MOVEMENT: WHAT GOOD WAS IT?

SOMEONE SAID RECENTLY to an old black lady from Mississippi,
whose legs had been badly mangled by local police who arrested her
for "disturbing the peace," that the Civil Rights Movement was dead,
and asked, since it was dead, what she thought about it. The old lady
replied, hobbling out of his presence on her cane, that the Civil
Rights Movement was like herself, "if it's dead, it shore ain't ready to
lay down!"

This old lady is a legendary freedom fighter in her small town in
the Delta. She has been severely mistreated for insisting on her rights
as an American citizen. She has been beaten for singing Movement
songs, placed in solitary confinement in prisons for talking about free-
dom, and placed on bread and water for praying aloud to God for her
jailers' deliverance. For such a woman the Civil Rights Movement
will never be over as long as her skin is black. It also will never be over
for twenty million others with the same "affliction," for whom the
Movement can never "lay down," no matter how it is killed by the
press and made dead and buried by the white American public. As
long as one black American survives, the struggle for equality with
other Americans must also survive. This is a debt we owe to those
blameless hostages we leave to the future, our children.

Still, white liberals and deserting Civil Rights sponsors are quick
to justify their disaffection from the Movement by claiming that it is
all over. "And since it is over," they will ask, "would someone kindly
tell me what has been gained by it?" They then list statistics suppos-
edly showing how much more advanced segregation is now than ten

years ago—in schools, housing, jobs. They point to a gain in conservative politicians during the last few years. They speak of ghetto riots and of the survey that shows that most policemen are admittedly too anti-Negro to do their jobs in ghetto areas fairly and effectively. They speak of every area that has been touched by the Civil Rights Movement as somehow or other going to pieces.

They rarely talk, however, about human attitudes among Negroes that have undergone terrific changes just during the past seven to ten years (not to mention all those years when there was a Movement and only the Negroes knew about it). They seldom speak of changes in personal lives because of the influence of people in the Movement. They see general failure and few, if any, individual gains.

They do not understand what it is that keeps the Movement from "laying down" and Negroes from reverting to their former *silent* second-class status. They have apparently never stopped to wonder why it is always the white man—on his radio and in his newspaper and on his television—who says that the Movement is dead. If a Negro were audacious enough to make such a claim, his fellows might hanker to see him shot. The Movement is dead to the white man because it no longer interests him. And it no longer interests him because he can afford to be uninterested: he does not have to live by it, with it, or for it, as Negroes must. He can take a rest from the news of beatings, killings, and arrests that reach him from North and South— if his skin is white. Negroes cannot now and will never be able to take a rest from the injustices that plague them, for they—not the white man—are the target.

Perhaps it is naïve to be thankful that the Movement "saved" a large number of individuals and gave them something to live for, even if it did not provide them with everything they wanted. (Materially, it provided them with precious little that they wanted.) When a movement awakens people to the possibilities of life, it seems unfair to frustrate them by then denying what they had thought was offered. But what was offered? What was promised? What was it all about? What good did it do? Would it have been better, as some have suggested, to leave the Negro people as they were, unawakened, unallied with one another, unhopeful about what to expect for their children in some future world?

I do not think so. If knowledge of my condition is all the freedom I get from a "freedom movement," it is better than unawareness, forgottenness, and hopelessness, the existence that is like the existence of a beast. Man only truly lives by knowing; otherwise he simply performs, copying the daily habits of others, but conceiving nothing of his creative possibilities as a man, and accepting someone else's superiority and his own misery.

When we are children, growing up in our parents' care, we await the spark from the outside world. Sometimes our parents provide it—if we are lucky—sometimes it comes from another source far from home. We sit, paralyzed, surrounded by our anxiety and dread, hoping we will not have to grow up into the narrow world and ways we see about us. We are hungry for a life that turns us on; we yearn for a knowledge of living that will save us from our innocuous lives that resemble death. We look for signs in every strange event; we search for heroes in every unknown face.

It was just six years ago that I began to be alive. I had, of course, been living before—for I am now twenty-three—but I did not really know it. And I did not know it because nobody told me that I—a pensive, yearning, typical high-school senior, but Negro—existed in the minds of others as I existed in my own. Until that time my mind was locked apart from the outer contours and complexion of my body as if it and the body were strangers. The mind possessed both thought and spirit—I wanted to be an author or a scientist—which the color of the body denied. I had never seen myself and existed as a statistic exists, or as a phantom. In the white world I walked, less real to them than a shadow; and being young and well hidden among the slums, among people who also did not exist—either in books or in films or in the government of their own lives—I waited to be called to life. And, by a miracle, I was called.

There was a commotion in our house that night in 1960. We had managed to buy our first television set. It was battered and overpriced, but my mother had gotten used to watching the afternoon soap operas at the house where she worked as maid, and nothing could satisfy her on days when she did not work but a continuation of her "stories." So she pinched pennies and bought a set.

I remained listless throughout her "stories," tales of pregnancy, abortion, hypocrisy, infidelity, and alcoholism. All these men and women were white and lived in houses with servants, long staircases that they floated down, patios where liquor was served four times a day to "relax" them. But my mother, with her swollen feet eased out of her shoes, her heavy body relaxed in our only comfortable chair, watched each movement of the smartly coiffed women, heard each word, pounced upon each innuendo and inflection, and for the duration of these "stories" she saw herself as one of them. She placed herself in every scene she saw, with her braided hair turned blond, her two hundred pounds compressed into a sleek size-seven dress, her rough dark skin smooth and *white*. Her husband became "dark and handsome," talented, witty, urbane, charming. And when she turned to look at my father sitting near her in his sweat shirt with his smelly feet raised on the bed to "air," there was always a tragic look of surprise on her face. Then she would sigh and go out to the kitchen looking lost and unsure of herself. My mother, a truly great woman who raised eight children of her own and half a dozen of the neighbors' without a single complaint, was convinced that she did not exist compared to "them." She subordinated her soul to theirs and became a faithful and timid supporter of the "Beautiful White People." Once she asked me, in a moment of vicarious pride and despair, if I didn't think that "they" were "jest naturally smarter, prettier, better." My mother asked this: a woman who never got rid of any of her children, never cheated on my father, was never a hypocrite if she could help it, and never even tasted liquor. She could not even bring herself to blame "them" for making her believe what they wanted her to believe: that if she did not look like them, think like them, be sophisticated and corrupt-for-comfort's-sake like them, she was a nobody. Black was not a color on my mother; it was a shield that made her invisible.

Of course, the people who wrote the soap-opera scripts always made the Negro maids in them steadfast, trusty, and wise in a home-remedial sort of way; but my mother, a maid for nearly forty years, never once identified herself with the scarcely glimpsed black servant's face beneath the ruffled cap. Like everyone else, in her daydreams at least, she thought she was free.

Six years ago, after half-heartedly watching my mother's soap operas and wondering whether there wasn't something more to be asked of life, the Civil Rights Movement came into my life. Like a good omen for the future, the face of Dr. Martin Luther King, Jr., was the first black face I saw on our new television screen. And, as in a fairy tale, my soul was stirred by the meaning for me of his mission—at the time he was being rather ignominiously dumped into a police van for having led a protest march in Alabama—and I fell in love with the sober and determined face of the Movement. The singing of "We Shall Overcome"—that song betrayed by nonbelievers in it—rang for the first time in my ears. The influence that my mother's soap operas might have had on me became impossible. The life of Dr. King, seeming bigger and more miraculous than the man himself, because of all he had done and suffered, offered a pattern of strength and sincerity I felt I could trust. He had suffered much because of his simple belief in nonviolence, love, and brotherhood. Perhaps the majority of men could not be reached through these beliefs, but because Dr. King kept trying to reach them in spite of danger to himself and his family, I saw in him the hero for whom I had waited so long.

What Dr. King promised was not a ranch-style house and an acre of manicured lawn for every black man, but jail and finally freedom. He did not promise two cars for every family, but the courage one day for all families everywhere to walk without shame and unafraid on their own feet. He did not say that one day it will be us chasing prospective buyers out of our prosperous well-kept neighborhoods, or in other ways exhibiting our snobbery and ignorance as all other ethnic groups before us have done; what he said was that we had a right to live anywhere in this country we chose, and a right to a meaningful well-paying job to provide us with the upkeep of our homes. He did not say we had to become carbon copies of the white American middle class; but he did say we had the right to become whatever we wanted to become.

Because of the Movement, because of an awakened faith in the newness and imagination of the human spirit, because of "black and white together"—for the first time in our history in some human relationship on and off TV—because of the beatings, the arrests, the hell of battle during the past years, I have fought harder for my life and for a chance to be myself, to be something more than a shadow or a number, than I had ever done before in my life. Before, there had seemed to be no real reason for struggling beyond the effort for daily bread. Now there was a chance at that other that Jesus meant when He said we could not live by bread alone.

I have fought and kicked and fasted and prayed and cursed and cried myself to the point of existing. It has been like being born again, literally. Just "knowing" has meant everything to me. Knowing has pushed me out into the world, into college, into places, into people.

Part of what existence means to me is knowing the difference between what I am now and what I was then. It is being capable of looking after myself intellectually as well as financially. It is being able to tell when I am being wronged and by whom. It means being awake to protect myself and the ones I love. It means being a part of the world community, and being *alert* to which part it is that I have joined, and knowing how to change to another part if that part does not suit me. To know is to exist: to exist is to be involved, to move about, to see the world with my own eyes. This, at least, the Movement has given me. . . .

What good was the Civil Rights Movement? If it had just given this country Dr. King, a leader of conscience, for once in our lifetime, it would have been enough. If it had just taken black eyes off white television stories, it would have been enough. If it had fed one starving child, it would have been enough.

If the Civil Rights Movement is "dead," and if it gave us nothing else, it gave us each other forever. It gave some of us bread, some of us shelter, some of us knowledge and pride, all of us comfort. It gave us our children, our husbands, our brothers, our fathers, as men reborn and with a purpose for living. It broke the pattern of black servitude in this country. It shattered the phony "promise" of white soap operas that sucked away so many pitiful lives. It gave us history and men far greater than Presidents. It gave us heroes, selfless men of courage and strength, for our little boys and girls to follow. It gave us hope for tomorrow. It called us to life.

Because we live, it can never die.

Charles Johnson

Charles Johnson, born and educated in Illinois, was radicalized as a college student by the visit of the black activist-poet Amiri Baraka (LeRoi Jones) to the campus of Southern Illinois University in the late 1960s. "Baraka said a black artist should bring his talent back home to black people." Johnson published his first novel, Faith and the Good Thing, *in 1974, attempting what he considered "a genuinely philosophical black American fiction, which I don't think existed before the work of Jean Toomer, Richard Wright, and Ralph Ellison." In 1988 he published a book of essays,* Being and Race: Black Writing Since 1970, *and two years later he won the National Book Award for his novel* Middle Passage, about the journey of captive slaves from Africa to America. In 1998 Johnson published Dreamer, a fictional portrayal of Martin Luther King in the last months of his life.

In the plot of the novel, the narrator, Matthew, a young man who along with his girlfriend, Amy, is working on King's staff, has found an ex-con named Chaym Smith who physically resembles King so closely that King has reluctantly agreed to use him as a stand-in whenever public appearances seem especially dangerous. But as the protest demonstrations swirl out of control in Chicago and Memphis, King moves irrevocably toward the moment of his own tragic death from an assassin's bullet on April 4, 1968. Here are chapters 12 and 13, the conclusion of Dreamer, beginning with King's reflections after the disastrous protest march in Memphis.

FROM *DREAMER*

12

It was the greatest mistake of his life, and he had no one but himself to blame. Sitting with his arms folded across his knees beside an equally baffled and speechless Abernathy in the Rivermont Hotel, he stared, his face squeezed shut, at televised scenes of bloodshed and civil breakdown on the downtown streets of Memphis. He'd been out there just minutes before, leading a crowd of six thousand down Main Street from the Clayborn Temple to protest the city's blatantly racist treatment of black sanitation workers. They'd marched all of three blocks before he heard glass breaking in clothing stores behind him. Turning, he saw black teenagers, some wearing stocking caps to hold their processed hair in place, pillaging shoes and suitcoats priced at $89.95 through plate-glass windows, then the police moving toward them, and he'd cried out, "Stop this, I won't lead a violent march," but it was too late. Evil was free. To save his life aides pulled him into a passing car, sped through the police barricades, and delivered him, not back to the black-owned and -operated Lorraine Motel, but to a deluxe hotel in a white neighborhood overlooking the Mississippi.

"God Almighty, we waltzed right into this one." Abernathy's eyes watered as he watched cops with butchwax crew-cuts driving elderly black demonstrators in raincoats from the empty streets onto sidewalks, where they pinned them to the pavement, jamming their knees into the backs of anyone who resisted. "Why the devil didn't somebody do their homework before we got here?"

"Ralph, you've got to get me out of Memphis."

"Soon," Abernathy said. "As soon as we can settle things here."

"I don't think I can take any more—"

"Tomorrow. We've got a flight in the morning."

"Ralph . . ."

"Yes?"

"Am I doing any good?"

"I think you know the answer to that."

"No," he said. "No, I don't."

In the next room the phone was ringing. There was pounding on the hotel's door. From what he could tell, the hallway was filled with people. James Lawson's folks, no doubt. And reporters—they were always at his heels, asking him to comment on everything colored men did on this earth, or analyze every new political development, forever asking him for answers, predictions, opinions. In his youth, right out of B.U., he had four answers for any question the media posed to him. Fifteen years later what he wanted most for himself— for Martin—was a brief withdrawal, a retreat for meditation and reflection. But now they had a bona fide catastrophe, one with his name attached to it. One they could say destroyed his beliefs forever.

Abernathy let his head fall back on the sofa; he stared at the white ceiling. Then, abruptly, he said, "ML, you've got to talk to them."

His insides were shaking. Brackish fluids from his belly kept climbing up his throat, and he kept swallowing to force down the backwash. The room was swimming. It felt wrong, all of it. Outside the window of his two-bedroom suite, in a garden that made him think of Gethsemane, trees were leaved lusciously, the quiet was broken only by songbirds while downtown the police were painting the streets with blood. He clamped shut his eyes. Now he understood the meaning of Paul's words, "I die daily."

"Not now . . ."

"You want me to run interference?"

"Please, I can't see anybody right now." His voice shook. "Buy me some time."

Abernathy gave him a pat on his shoulder, then pulled his suitcoat off the back of the chair, slipped his arms through the sleeves, adjusted his tie, and went to answer the door. Once Abernathy was gone, he threw up on the sofa. Then he put his head in his trembling hands and cried until he felt clean. He'd wept often and easily in 1967, trailing tears across a continent, from Atlanta to Washington, from New York to Marks, Mississippi, where in preparation for the ambitious Poor People's Campaign he'd interviewed black tenant workers with teeth colored like Indian corn. In their tin-roofed shacks he saw barefoot children, their stomachs bloated, wearing clothes woven from dirt: babies living in conditions as miserable as those of the Untouchables in India, but

Gandhi had given them a different title, Harijans ("children of God"), and the government officials he and Coretta met were sincere in their commitment to programs aimed at alleviating the suffering of a class it had despised and oppressed for centuries. If there, he wondered, then why not in the wealthiest nation in the world? If America had done so many special things to suppress Negroes, why couldn't it do something special for them? Other ministers, black and white—particularly white ones from rich churches—reminded him that when Jesus was in Bethany at the house of Simon the leper, a woman brought him costly fragrant oil, which set his disciples to complaining, "To what purpose is this waste when the ointment might have been sold for much and given to the poor," and to this Jesus replied, "Ye shall have the poor always with you." Indeed, white preachers cited this often; they were the ones he chastised in his "Letter from Birmingham City Jail," and to them he replied with a passage of his own: "If a man say, I love God, and hateth his brother, he is a liar: for he that loveth not his brother whom he hath seen, how can he love God whom he hath not seen?" But the words of Christ were the horn of his salvation. Poverty would always exist, he knew that. Prejudice, so hydra-headed, could never entirely be eliminated. He knew that too; but no piety from the pages of Scripture could ever justify the fact that the world's suffering poor in the modern era were predominantly black and brown, women and children.

Later that night, as he drank to dull the pain in his mouth (he'd ground down on his teeth and crushed a filling), he watched baton-wielding motorcycle policemen, jackbooted and jacketed, wade into black rioters on Main Street. Three thousand National Guardsmen and a phalanx of olive-green tanks and trucks rumbled like thunder into town, imposing a dusk-to-dawn curfew. Reports coming through the television told of two hundred eighty arrested, sixty-two clubbed and wounded, and one sixteen-year-old boy killed. No matter what anyone said, that death was on his soul. His critics were right—sometimes he was a damned poor organizer. But how could he oversee everything? Be everywhere at once? He felt he was caught in a current sweeping him relentlessly forward, one in which he was drowning, unable to catch his breath or keep his head above water as the waves propelled him helplessly on like a man hurtling over Niagara Falls. Abernathy ordered from room service but could not get him to touch a thing on the tray. Or speak, for he felt dim in understanding, weak in flesh, and cold in his heart.

He paced the turquoise carpeted floors of their hotel room in his stocking feet, thinking of that dead teenage boy, blowing cigarette smoke, his collar open and sweat-stained, retracing every step that had directed him away from the prodigious work of preparing for the Poor People's Campaign, with its impossible logistics, to leading this tragic march for the sanitation workers. At first, their problems with Mayor Henry Loeb seemed peripheral to the Movement and did not draw his attention until the day, February 12, when thirteen hundred black workers went on strike after the city refused to recognize their union and rejected its demands for a ten percent wage increase and benefits. They marched, wearing and carrying signs proclaiming "I AM a Man." Negroes in the Memphis community rallied behind the strikers, who now and then skirmished with the police. They listened to civil rights leaders at Mason Temple Church urge them not to return to their jobs before their demands were met. Mayor Loeb's response was to dig in, refusing to talk to their representatives, and he promised to fire all the strikers. The city brought forth an injunction to halt demonstrations on the workers' behalf. Local ministers decided there was only one man who could shore up their battle against Loeb, whom blacks had hugely voted against during his campaign for office.

As Abernathy dozed, he went back to the television, turning the volume down low, on his face the flickering television's glow as the full-scale riot raged on. Transfixed, unable to turn away from the violence, he remembered how he'd turned James Lawson's request to address a Memphis rally over and over in his mind. The timing seemed wrong. He was in the midst of raising money for the proposed three-month spring offensive for the poor, an assault that would force Congress to directly confront economic injustice in America and realize a dream long nurtured by predecessors such as A. Philip Randolph. But how could he turn away from this other just cause? These black sanitation workers needed a nationally visible champion. Earlier in the year two black crewmen were crushed in a grisly accident caused by a garbage truck's compressor. In early February sewer workers were sent home for a day because of bad weather, but while whites received a full day's wage, the blacks were only paid for two hours. The injustices in Memphis were clear, for, as Marx might put it, the sanitation workers provided "socially necessary labor" without which the city would smother in its own sludge. Yet despite the value of their work, these men, who tramped every day down hot alleyways with the filth of the affluent packed in plastic tubs on their backs, and swept away rats and maggots and the stench of so-called civilized life so the wealthy could move about in clean homes and bright workplaces—these invisible men in Memphis, whose clothes were perpetually scented with the waste of others, were denied the most basic forms of decency. Their situation perfectly mirrored the point he wanted to drive home with the Poor People's Campaign. One of his aides jokingly remarked that he was always operating two steps ahead of where he actually was. Perhaps, the aide suggested, he needed to get over his inability to say no to anyone in need, a comment he brushed aside, pointing out that his tour of Mississippi would bring him near Memphis, and once there he would carefully test the waters to see how deep he should dive in.

It so happened that the waters in Memphis were pleasantly warm and felt just fine. On March 18, he spoke to an enthusiastic crowd of nearly seventeen thousand that hung on his every word as he told them to put aside their class differences and join ranks behind the striking garbagemen, whom he called "as significant as the physician, for if he doesn't work, disease is rampant." For every sentence he sang, the crowd sang back, That's right! and Hallelujah! They stamped their feet, they cheered, and he got into the swing of it, strengthened by their energy, at one with their hopes and dreams of dignity. The injunction wouldn't stop them, he said. Nothing would turn them around because they were tired, so tired, from working day and night and never seeing a living wage. Their men were sick of having their manhood denied, their wives and daughters of being domestic servants. The crowd rocked to his preaching that Monday night, roared its approval. And why not? This was Tennessee and he was a son of the South. There were no nationalists here. The Black Power plague hadn't infected Memphis, not like in Chicago. He was home again. He understood these good, Galilean people. He was of them, and they were happily in the palm of his hand, just as in Birmingham and Montgomery. Lord have mercy! This was what he'd needed for so long, and in that giddy, feel-good moment he made them a promise. If they marched to-gether on Friday, if every working man and woman joined in, and the children too, then they would win. And he promised himself he would lead them.

It should have been a triumphant march, an exuberant overture, or trial run for the Poor People's Campaign. The problems began when his flight from New York to Memphis was late by two hours. The parade started without him. A little before noon Abernathy met him at the airport and hurried him to the Clayborn Temple; then he was rushed by car toward the front of six thou-sand restless, edgy Tennesseans already on the move. In the backseat, peering out, he realized something was very wrong. This wasn't a line of protesters. It felt more like an undisciplined mob. Toward its end he saw young people hold-ing up placards that read "Black Power Is Here." They were the Invaders, his driver said. None of them cared for his message of nonviolence—they were dis-ciples of Stokely and Rap Brown—and they had threatened to disrupt the march if they were not included. Fact was, they'd been a problem since the Memphis strike began. "And you didn't tell me?" he asked, grabbing the front seat and pulling himself forward, which jostled his driver. Great Peter only knew why they'd held back this information. He struck the seat and his driver jumped, hunching his shoulders, bringing the car to a stop. Up ahead, the police were closing off Main Street. It was too late to turn back. Whither-soever he went he knew he would find them, the violent in spirit, the herren-moralists, the Nietzscheans. Turning the door handle, lifting himself out of the car, he silently said a prayer, knowing that men of conviction had to act, *though always on the basis of partial information, blindly forging ahead and hoping for the best. The word for this from time immemorial, he knew, was faith.*

Which lasted all of three blocks, then died in downtown Memphis. Most of the marchers returned home or to their churches. But the Invaders, who had used the march as a cover, fought on, firing at the police, turning over cars, setting fires and smashing store windows.

He was still watching the news reports when Abernathy padded sleepily from the bedroom. His friend of sixteen years plopped down beside him on the sofa, yawning and knuckling his red-rimmed eyes. Always his nearness was bracing. As friends they had the habit of each other, like siblings, and he could talk candidly with him. They complemented and in many ways completed each other, though he knew that from their first meeting in Montgomery Abernathy had, in his own words, burned with envy at his big-city learning and confidence.

"Do you good to get some sleep, ML," Abernathy said. "Things out there have to settle down sooner or later."

"Maybe they shouldn't."

"What?"

"If we believe in peace, maybe we should get out of the way and let the separatists and segregationists, the Invaders and racists, black anti-Semites and Klansmen, go at each other in a full-scale war." He coughed, his voice slipping a scale. "They're two of a kind. Just different in color. I can't believe they'll ever change. Hate is too easy. Nonviolence as a way of life may be asking too much of people. Maybe it goes against the grain of something tribal in our genes. Or against the ego. Or the carnal mind, which can only perceive in terms of polarities. If I have to choose between seeing men as fallen angels or risen apes, I prefer the former. You know that. But the apes, black and white, are out there. And their goal is to make the world a jungle. I say, let them kill each other and tear it all down, then God-hungry men and women can make a fresh start."

"You don't mean that . . ."

"I do."

"I think you're just tired."

"Yes, I am. And I think it's over, Ralph."

"No, that's just—"

"Let me finish. I'm not saying we haven't accomplished a great deal. We have. But where can I go from here? After this? Can I keep developing? What can I do? God, I haven't read a book in years! These reporters ask me about the Tet offensive, the Middle East, the Kerner Commission report, and I haven't had one blessed hour to study any of it in depth, but I'm expected to

keep on giving speeches, so I do, making it up as I go along. That's shallow. It's skating along the surface when I need to go deeper into things. Into myself, if I'm going to give back anything of value. I feel trapped, like I'm stuck in a hole. I remember from Crozer, in a paper I wrote, that's what the word suffering *means in Sanskrit:* Dukkha. 'Duk,' bad, 'kah,' hole." *He let his breath roll out.* "What I'm trying to say is that if every day doesn't add knowledge, wisdom, and the ability to live life and increase our capacity to love, we are already dead. Does that make any sense?"

"Yes, and what I think is you should get some rest."

"I'll sleep here on the sofa. And, Ralph?"

"Yes?"

"Thanks."

It was quarter to four.

Abernathy stood, clicked off the television and then the lights, and, after tossing a blanket over his friend, returned to his own bedroom.

In the darkness, on the stiff cushions of the sofa, he tossed and turned, trying to find a comfortable position that might beckon sleep, grappling with the perennial dilemma of his public ministry, how to end evil without creating evil; then mercifully his eyelids grew heavy. In the region between waking and slumber he relived his trip to Kerala, feeling the heat, and watching the locals hang pots on coconut trees to collect their milk; but the heat fermented the sweet milk, which became so intoxicating that crows sipping from the pots fell drunkenly to the ground and stumbled about cawing at the wrong time of day. For a few moments he dreamed of journeying there again for the rest he needed so badly, and to probe deeper into their concept of Maya—the world as itself a cradle-to-crypt dream, in which all men were caught and only the blessed allowed to awaken. He looked at his watch. Four-fifteen. He sat up slowly, knowing this was all the sleep he would have this night. Knowing he would have to return to Tennessee. To make things right. To undo the damage. The Washington campaign would have to be postponed. In Memphis, nonviolence was being tested—he was on trial. Already he was clear on the new itinerary. Check out of this room. Call his wife. Hold a press conference. Fly back to Atlanta for a furious week of meticulous preparations, then return to this wartorn city for a second demonstration and, for himself, a fuller, deeper, and more perfectly realized broken heart.

13

On the evening of April 4 (Thursday) one hundred and twenty-five American cities began erupting in flame: a prophet had fallen. Pronounced dead at 7:05 P.M. The electrifying, awful report that a metal-jacketed .30-06 bullet brought down the man who was the nation's moral conscience, ripping away the right side of his jaw and neck, severing his spine on the second-floor balcony of the Lorraine Motel, spread through this splintered world like a declaration of war. There came a confusion of tongues in a house divided against itself. "Nonviolence is a dead philosophy," proclaimed Floyd McKissick, "and it was not the black people that killed it. It was the white people that killed nonviolence, and the white racists at that." So many agreed with McKissick. "Get your gun," shouted Stokely Carmichael. "When white America killed Dr. King, she declared war on us!" The rioting and looting that Citizen King had loathed lasted for ten days in a blood-drenched decade that left everyone perpetually short of breath. In Texas, white students cheered when they heard he was dead. (I am not ashamed to say I hated them.) In Washington, D.C., seven hundred blazes blackened the sky. Tendrils of smoke drifted through windows in the White House, where Lyndon Johnson designated Sunday, April 7, a day of national mourning. Flags were lowered to half-staff. Schools closed. The baseball season was postponed. Three networks broadcast his funeral for six hours. Docks were shut down. Pope Paul VI cried out that this "cowardly and atrocious" killing of our better brother "weighed on the conscience of mankind." It was four and a half years since JFK's murder. Four years since Malcolm X's. Robert Kennedy (only two months away from the bullet that would end his life in Los Angeles) had three extra telephones installed in Coretta's home and chartered an Electra jet to bring the body of Atlanta's finest son—now dwelling in a house not made with hands, eternal in the heavens—home to lie in state in the Sisters' Chapel of Spelman College. We had never, I knew, been equal to him, or to the transcendent tasks he called us to perform. He was destined for vaticide. Before this ritualistic blood ceremony, this foundation sacrifice, ended, forty-six people were dead. Whites, pulled from their cars, were beaten mercilessly and stabbed. Two thousand six hundred people were injured. Another twenty-one thousand were arrested, myself and Amy among them at an April 5 demonstration in Chicago, where I'd returned to school.

By Tuesday of that longest week in modern history, I stood in sweltering heat outside Ebenezer Baptist Church in Atlanta, travel-worn and with a bad case of trench mouth. The corners of my eyes were crusted after the long drive from Illinois. My hair was uncombed and dry, the scent in my clothes was the aroma of sweat commingled with fried chicken eaten on the road. My mind felt like a freshly opened grave. I was one of sixty thousand people encircling the building where King was baptized and raised, listening, on a sun-heavy street beneath a cerulean sky, to Dr. L. Harold DeWolf and Rev. Ralph Abernathy on a loudspeaker because we—Amy, Mama Pearl, and myself—were unable to get inside, where nearly eight hundred mourners filled the pews. These, of course, were the dignitaries: Carmichael, who came with his bodyguards, entertainers like Harry Belafonte, Sammy Davis Jr., and Dick Gregory, all of whom had marched arm-in-arm with King. (Marlon Brando pledged ten percent of his earnings to the Cause.) The politicians were there too, particularly the ones running for president that fall (Eugene McCarthy and Richard Nixon, but Hubert Humphrey came instead of LBJ), and we saw the nation's other grand woman of sorrows, Jacqueline Kennedy, enter the crowded church as well. On and on they came to pay their last respects in public, the hypocrites and true bearers of homage to the colored man who died for our collective racial sins and spiritual failures. I felt no need to be inside with them, but as I listened to Abernathy's eloquent speech, my head felt light. My knees buckled a little. Amy, perspiring on her upper lip, put her arm around my waist to steady me. "Are you going to be okay?" I didn't know the answer to that, or to a thousand other questions that had troubled my sleep since King fell in the crosshairs of that high-powered rifle.

But this much I did know:

The day before he died, the sky above Memphis was turgid, the spring air moistened and charged by electricity from a thunderstorm the night before. As I said, I was back in school, studying Brightman, as he'd asked me to do, but I called his hotel on the evening of the third. The whole city knew where he was staying because his room number had been broadcast on several radio stations. He'd picked the Lorraine Motel to stay at after an article appeared in a Memphis paper criticizing him for running away to the Rivermont after the earlier aborted march down Beale Street (it was Bureau copy, of that I was convinced). When he returned to Memphis, detectives assigned to protect him met King at the airport but left after someone in his entourage shouted, "We don't want you here." Local organizers hurried him off to the Lorraine, lodgings that one of his aides, Hosea Williams, found confusing, since they had never stayed there before. He was originally given a room (306) on the ground floor, then reassigned to the second floor (305), and Abernathy was put in the first room. I reached him at about 4 P.M. Tired, he said all he wanted to do that evening was rest before spending most of the next day with organizers for the march. He'd toyed with the idea of finding someone to substitute for him at a rally he was slated to attend at the Mason Temple, and in the end decided to let Abernathy do it for him.

But when Abernathy reached the Mason Temple he found the crowd clamoring for King. That night they would accept no stand-ins. Wearily, the minister changed out of his pajamas and was driven to the temple in pounding rain with Andrew Young and Jesse Jackson (wearing bluejeans and a brown jacket). Without a text, he thundered oratory that made the audience forget the storm lashing the temple's windows. "I want you to know tonight that we as a people will get to the Promised Land," he said. "I'm so happy tonight. I'm not worried about anything. I'm not fearing any man. Mine eyes have seen the glory of the coming of the Lord. I have a dream this afternoon that the brotherhood of man will become a reality . . . With this faith we will be able to achieve this new day, when all God's children—black men and white men, Jews and Gentiles, Protestants and Catholics—will be able to join hands and sing with the Negroes in the spiritual of old. 'Free at last! Free at last! Thank God Almighty we are free at last!' " And when he was done, and turned away from the bank of gleaming microphones, it seemed he fell, exhausted, toward Abernathy, who rushed with outthrown arms to embrace and steady him on his feet.

He and his staff decided to postpone the march for the sanitation workers until Monday. His plan that Wednesday was to visit Rev. Samuel Kyles's home for dinner on Thursday evening. Somewhere I'd heard that on the third he'd dined on catfish, buttered black-eyed peas, and a tossed salad at the Four Way Grill. He asked me, "How is Chaym? The last time we talked, you said you hadn't seen him, that two men came by the farmhouse . . ."

"Yes," I said. "That's right. It's been weeks."

"Do you think those government men killed him?"

"Honestly, I don't know, sir." And I did not. All that was left of Chaym Smith were a few of his deeds and products: paintings, sketchbooks, and his saxophone, which I was learning to play by paying for private lessons with a graduate student in Columbia College's Music Department. Sometimes I sat doing meditation "with seed," as it was called, journeying through passages I'd committed to memory from the spiritual traditions of the world. Occasionally I volunteered at the poorer churches, temples, synagogues, and mosques, though I belonged to none. Now and then when I thought of it, I practiced the Tai Chi Chuan form he'd taught me. And I no longer worried about defining myself or being wrong. "I just pray he's all right."

"So do I. We've had too many casualties already. If it's not Division Five after us, then it's COINTEL-PRO or COMINFIL. Since sixty-three we've had more break-ins than I can remember, and they've planted informants everywhere and . . . Wait, I think someone's calling me—I'd better go."

"Good night," I said, "and God bless you."

"Good-bye, Matthew."

It was the last time we'd spoken. (Why, when he said that, did he sound so like Socrates bidding farewell to Crito?) Later, when I pored over the flood of news reports, trying to make sense of his slaying, my hands shaking, I found only conundrums, as if I was prying open a Chinese puzzle box. The deeper I descended, the funnier-looking these fish appeared. The man in charge of the police and fire departments, I discovered, was Frank Holloman, who'd been with the Bureau for twenty-five years. He and Hoover were friends. In fact, Holloman once ran the Atlanta office of the FBI, which kept the Kings under surveillance. In other words, the Bureau had Memphis locked up tight. Yet King had no security—his own people had run them off because they didn't trust the police. The city had assigned two detectives, one of them a black man named Ed Reddick, to be in Fire Station 2, just south of the Lorraine Motel. It was a good location for keeping an eye on the motel, but on that Wednesday two black firemen—Norvell Wallace and Floyd Newsom—were pulled off the job. People said different things about that, and none of them made sense to me. Someone told the firemen there was a threat made against them (some said this was Reddick), so they were transferred, allegedly for their own safety. (Reddick said he did not have them transferred.) But then, Reddick was pulled away too; a Secret Service man from D.C. met him at the station and said there was a contract out on his life, so they sent him home. Yet—and yet—some Negroes called Detective Reddick a spy who felt that one of the black firemen was a militant sympathetic to the strikers. This welter of conflicting "facts," of so many testimonies that contradicted one another, was dizzying, and I swear I didn't have a cross-eyed guess as to who was telling the truth.

And the facts grew stranger with each new string I pulled. James Earl Ray, a drifter and escaped convict sentenced in 1960 to twenty years in the Missouri State Penitentiary for armed robbery (aliases: Eric Galt, Harvey Lomeyer, John Willard) with a white Mustang bearing Alabama license plate 1-38993, but no motivation for murdering King, was being hunted as the prime suspect for the shooting.

But, I wondered, as any sane man would, if a real assassin might leave behind so many fingerprinted items (shaving cream, clippers, a radio with Ray's prison I.D.) to clearly identify him on the street outside Bessie Brewer's boardinghouse at 422½ South Main Street? No, that was more than I could accept. In his FBI wanted poster, in his history, Ray perfectly fit the image of a patsy. Or a fool.

The gun, a 760 Remington Gamemaster, was never swabbed to determine if it had been fired. And the copper-jacketed bullet sent to the FBI didn't match—or so I read—the one extracted from King. That bullet entered his lower jaw and cheek one and a half inches below his mouth, hit the jawbone, reentered above the collarbone, then went down (left) through his neck. It was visible as a node in his left shoulder under the skin. Had he lived, he would have been a vegetable. (And who among us could have beared seeing him that way?) According to the physician who removed the bullet in St. Joseph's Hospital, it was intact, its end flattened out. A whole bullet weighed 150 grams. The one dug out of King was 4.7 grams and 3.0 inches round. But that was not the same bullet that found its way with other evidence to Washington, D.C.

Complicating things further, and giving me more sleepless nights than I cared to count, were the claims of two black witnesses at the Lorraine when King went down, one foot stuck in the railing of the balcony, his shoe off, a cigarette crushed in his hand; they claimed they saw a plume of white smoke rise up from the large, hedgelike bushes at the back of the boardinghouse. One was Solomon Jones, King's driver in the limousine, borrowed from a funeral parlor, which was to take King, musician Ben Branch, and Jackson to Rev. Kyles's home. Jones said he saw a man in those bushes. So did Earl Caldwell, a journalist sent to Memphis (his editor at the *New York Times,* he said, wanted him to "nail" King) who heard the shot, followed by someone yelling, "Get low!" People were ducking everywhere in the courtyard, but Caldwell saw a crouching white figure in the bushes, wearing overalls and looking up at the balcony. All those bushes were cut down on April 5 by the police, who said—and I winced at their words—they needed to clear the area to look for evidence.

Inside Ebenezer Church, a choir began singing the minister's favorite hymns, "When I Survey the Wondrous Cross" and "In Christ There Is No East Nor West." Time stood still. The crowd was quiet, intense. A knot gathered in my throat. (I was thinking how, according to Andrew Young, when King fell on that balcony, Jesse Jackson covered his palms with the minister's blood, wiped them on his sweater;

then the next day he flew to Chicago to appear bloodstained before the press, declaring he'd held a dying King in his arms. That was untrue, said Young, and I was haunted by the feeling that this act of theater and falsity, this photo-op, would define the spirit of the black struggle for decades after the minister's demise. Had he not said to Carmichael, "I've been used before"?) Then my heart gave a slight jump when Abernathy played a recording of King's sermon, "The Drum Major Instinct," which the minister had delivered at Ebenezer earlier in the year, on February 4, taking his text from Mark 10:35, where James and John, the sons of Zebedee, approach Jesus with their desire to sit beside him in Glory. King's bronze voice, that startling basso profundo, washed over the crowd in skin-prickling waves and reverberated in the ether.

"There is, deep down within all of us, an instinct. It's a kind of drum major instinct—a desire to be out front, a desire to lead the parade, a desire to be first. And it is something that runs a whole gamut of life . . . We all want to be important, to surpass others, to achieve distinction, to lead the parade. Alfred Adler, the great psychoanalyst, contends that this is the dominant impulse . . . this desire for attention . . . Now in adult life, we still have it, and we really never get by it. We like to do something good. And you know, we liked to be praised for it . . . But there comes a time when the drum major instinct can become destructive. And that's where I want to move now . . . Do you know that a lot of the race problem grows out of the drum major instinct? A need that some people have to feel superior. Nations are caught up with the drum major instinct. I must be first. I must be supreme. Our nation must rule the world . . . but let me rush on to my conclusion, because I want you to see what Jesus was really saying . . . Don't give it up. Keep feeling the need for being important. Keep feeling the need for being first. But I want you to be first in love. I want you to be first in moral excellence. I want you to be first in generosity. That's what I want you to do . . ."

Pallbearers brought out King's bier, loading it onto a flatbed farm wagon pulled by two mules—a striking, martyrial phaeton symbolic of the Poor People's Campaign that consumed King's last days. The funeral bells tanged and the wagon began its long trek halfway across Atlanta to Morehouse College, where Rev. Benjamin Mays would give the eulogy. A slow march. A sorrowful march with the mules chacking beneath a sun that burned mercilessly overhead. We fell in behind fifty thousand mourners following the procession. I heard the clop-clop of the mules' heels on hot concrete. Along the way, spectators crowded the sidewalks, a herd of multicolored humanity guilty of sloth, pride, anger, gluttony, covetousness, envy, lust, and acedia. Some dropped to their knees to pray. In spite of myself, my face broke. Amy took my hand, intertwining her fingers with mine, and I took her grandmama's. Dressed in black, Mama Pearl had to be hot, there on a spring day in Atlanta, with the crush of bodies that closed us in. Her skin was sweat-streaked. She was weeping as we walked, her mouth quivering. I gave her my handkerchief.

"He was a beautiful man. I know he's got his jeweled ring and purple robe. And he liked my rugala." She dabbed at her eyes and handed back my handkerchief, rumpled and moist, and thanked me for it.

"*Sama-sama.*"

"How's that again, Matthew?"

"Nothing. I was just thinking—"

"About who killed Dr. King?" asked Amy.

"No," I said. "I know that."

"Who?"

"We all did."

Amy shot me a look, all irritation, as the throng labored with a cautious tread, one that said she couldn't see herself as responsible. But I saw. I understood. We'd killed him—all of us, black and white—because we didn't listen when he was alive, though this was, of course, the way of things: no prophet was accepted in his own country. Even before his death, we were looking for other, more "radical" black spokesmen. The Way of agapic love, with its bottom-less demands, had proven too hard for this nation. Hatred and compe-tition were easier. Exalting the ethnic ego proved far less challenging than King's belief in the beloved community. We loved violence—verbal and physical—too dearly. Our collective spirit, the *Geist* of our era, had slain him as surely as the assassin's bullet that cut him down. We were all Cainites. And deservedly cursed. Did we not kill the best in ourselves when we killed King? Wasn't every murder a suicide as well?

All around us, the crowd of the apostates kept pace behind the wagon, concrescing. Walking on, the air now a bright shimmer, I be-lieved in each of us there was a wound, an emptiness that would not be filled in our lifetime. But we could not stop if we wanted to, or go backward.

Amy pressed a little nearer to me, squeezing my hand. "What do you think he'd want us to do now?"

"Excuse me, keep moving forward. If we stop, we'll fall and be trampled."

"Matthew?"

"Eh?"

Her eyes swung up, searching my face. "What about Chaym? Where do you think he is?"

I dropped my gaze, watching my feet and those of the sinners in front of me. I thought hard. "Everywhere . . ."

That seemed to satisfy her, and she smiled as the crowd of the contrite rolled on like a piece of the sea, both of us but waves blending perfectly with its flow, our fingers interlaced, and perhaps she felt, as I did, that if the prophet King had shown us the depths of living possible for those who loved unconditionally in a less than just universe engraved with inequality, and that only the servants should lead, then Chaym had in his covert passage through our lives let us know that, if one missed the Galilean mark, even the pariahs, the fatherless exiles, might sometimes—and occasionally—doeth well.

Amen.

PART TWO

END IT! AND END IT NOW! THE ANTI-VIETNAM WAR MOVEMENT

Om a ka ca ta ta pa ya sa svaha
As you shoot down the Vietnamese girls and men
in their fields
Burning and chopping,
Poisoning and blighting,
So surely I hunt the white man down
in my heart.

GARY SNYDER, "A CURSE ON THE MEN
IN WASHINGTON, PENTAGON" (1967)

LIKE THE ESSAYS, STORIES, AND POEMS written as a response to the Civil Rights Movement, most of the literature of the Anti–Vietnam War Movement came out of personal responses to either specific events of the war or to the rushing tide of events making history. From 1961 to 1965, the first years that American armed forces were involved in Vietnam, the majority of the books published about the conflict were political and historical works, and they were not against the war. However, as novelist Stewart O'Nan wrote in *The Vietnam Reader* (1998), "With the notable exception of *The Green Berets* [Robin Moore's 1965 report as an investigative journalist], nearly all the Vietnam fiction and poetry of note that came out between 1965 and 1973 was antiwar, and most appeared after 1968, when even such establishment figures as trusted evening newscaster Walter Cronkite conceded on air that the war was unwinnable."

In 1961, after years of internal conflict during the Cold War, South Vietnamese president Ngo Dinh Diem declared that the struggle of South Vietnamese soldiers against Communist forces from North Vietnam was "no longer a guerrilla war but a real war." Since 1949, when the Nationalist forces in China fell to the Communists led by Mao Tse-tung, the Americans had feared that other Asian nations would join the Communist Bloc, which was also expanding into Eastern Europe. In the 1950s, the United States fought the spread of Communism in Korea, a military engagement that lasted three years at the cost of the lives of fifty-four thousand American soldiers. By 1954, when the French withdrew from Vietnam, the country was divided in two—the north, controlled by Ho Chi Minh's Communist forces, and the south, controlled by President Diem's allegedly prodemocracy government, supported by the United States.

The recently elected U.S. president John F. Kennedy sent Green Beret troops and military advisers to train South Vietnamese troops, but in the early Sixties, the attention of most Americans was focused primarily on Communist premier Fidel Castro in nearby Cuba. As Lawrence Ferlinghetti wrote in "One Thousand Fearful Words for Fidel Castro" (published as a thirty-five-cent folded broadside by City Lights Press in San Francisco after the poet returned from a visit to Cuba in December 1960),

> I am sitting in Mike's Place trying to figure out
> >what's going to happen
> >without Fidel Castro
> Among the salami sandwiches and spittoons
> >I see no solution
> >It's going to be a tragedy

On the back of the broadside, Ferlinghetti stated, "There are not one thousand words here. The author has left room for a happier ending, in case the relentless hostility of government and press in the U.S. should somehow not triumph in the end." To date, the poet has not added the "happier ending."

After the Bay of Pigs fiasco in 1961, the United States began to develop biological weapons to use against Cuba and continued to stockpile its growing arsenal of nuclear weapons. As one of Eisenhower's last presidential acts in 1960, he had approved an expanded program of underground nuclear explosions in the United States. Soon afterward, the Soviets detonated a 50-megaton bomb in their Arctic testing ground, 250 times more powerful than the atomic bombs that the United States had dropped on Hiroshima and Nagasaki.

By September 1961, the self-assurance felt by Americans after the country's victory over Fascism in World War II was beginning to be replaced by fear and anxiety. That month, *Life* magazine described the nuclear capability of the superpowers as threatening an unprecedented scale of mass destruction, since theoretically the United States and the USSR could destroy 96 percent of each other with their stockpiled bombs and missiles. The writer Flannery O'Connor understood in her essay "Some Aspects of the Grotesque in Southern

Fiction" (1961) that "since the eighteenth century, the popular spirit of each succeeding age has tended more and more to the view that the ills and mysteries of life will eventually fall before the scientific advances of men, a belief that is still going strong even though this is the first generation to face total extinction because of these advances." The work of many American writers and intellectuals began to reflect their increasing despair at the prospect of nuclear destruction.

Thomas Merton

The threat of a global thermonuclear war was foremost in many people's minds in 1962, during the Cuban Missile Crisis, when President John F. Kennedy set up a naval blockade and forced the Soviets to move their missiles out of Cuba. College students marched on Washington, calling for a ban on nuclear weapons. One of the most eloquent poems by an American author against the use of atomic weapons was "Original Child Bomb," published in 1962 by Thomas Merton (1915–1968), a Catholic monk at the Abbey of Our Lady of Gethsemani near Bardstown, Kentucky. Merton became a well-known writer with the success of his autobiography, The Seven Storey Mountain, *in 1948. In the early 1960s, he focused on social criticism in his work, and he created his own verse form, abandoning meter, poetic diction, and imagery, and using flat, undramatic language in order to report what the critic George Woodcock recognized as "facts that are at the same time so banal and inhuman that they became the images of their own inherent horror." The "original child bomb" is the literal translation of one of the "poetic" names the Japanese found for the bomb that destroyed Hiroshima on August 6, 1945. Merton originally subtitled his poem "points for meditation to be scratched on the walls of a cave"—presumably the one in which any survivors of an atomic war would be living.*

ORIGINAL CHILD BOMB

1: In the year 1945 an Original Child was born.
The name Original Child was given to it by
the Japanese people, who recognized that it was
the first of its kind.

2: On April 12th, 1945, Mr. Harry Truman
became the President of the United States,
which was then fighting the second world war.

Mr. Truman was a vice president who became
president by accident when his predecessor died
of a cerebral hemorrhage. He did not know
as much about the war as the president before
him did. He knew a lot less about the war
than many people did.

About one hour after Mr. Truman became
president, his aides told him about a new bomb
which was being developed by atomic
scientists. They called it the "atomic bomb."
They said scientists had been working on it for
six years and that it had so far cost two
billion dollars. They added that its power was
equal to that of twenty thousand tons of
TNT. A single bomb could destroy a city. One of
those present added, in a reverent tone, that
the new explosive might eventually destroy the
whole world.

But Admiral Leahy told the President the
bomb would never work.

3: President Truman formed a committee of
men to tell him if this bomb would work, and if
so, what he should do with it. Some
members of this committee felt that the bomb
would jeopardize the future of civilization.
They were against its use. Others wanted it to
be used in demonstration on a forest of
cryptomeria trees, but not against a civil or
military target. Many atomic scientists warned
that the use of atomic power in war would
be difficult and even impossible to control. The
danger would be very great. Finally, there
were others who believed that if the bomb were
used just once or twice, on one or two Japanese
cities, there would be no more war. They
believed the new bomb would produce eternal
peace.

4: In June 1945 the Japanese government
was taking steps to negotiate for peace. On one
hand the Japanese ambassador tried to
interest the Russian government in acting as a
go-between with the United States. On the
other hand, an unofficial approach was made
secretly through Mr. Allen Dulles in Switzerland.
The Russians said they were not interested
and that they would not negotiate. Nothing was
done about the other proposal which was
not official. The Japanese High Command was
not in favor of asking for peace, but wanted
to continue the war, even if the Japanese
mainland were invaded. The generals believed
that the war should continue until everybody
was dead. The Japanese generals were
professional soldiers.

5: In the same month of June, the President's
committee decided that the new bomb
should be dropped on a Japanese city. This
would be a demonstration of the bomb on a
civil and military target. As "demonstration" it
would be a kind of a "show." "Civilians"
all over the world love a good "show." The
"destructive" aspect of the bomb would
be "military."

6: The same committee also asked if America's
friendly ally, the Soviet Union, should be
informed of the atomic bomb. Someone
suggested that this information would make the
Soviet Union even more friendly than it was
already. But all finally agreed that the
Soviet Union was now friendly enough.

7: There was discussion about which city
should be selected as the first target. Some
wanted it to be Kyoto, an ancient capital
of Japan and a center of the Buddhist religion.
Others said no, this would cause bitterness.

As a result of a chance conversation, Mr.
Stimson, the Secretary of War, had recently
read up on the history and beauties of Kyoto. He
insisted that this city should be left untouched.
Some wanted Tokyo to be the first target,
but others argued that Tokyo had already been
practically destroyed by fire raids and
could no longer be considered a "target." So
it was decided Hiroshima was the most
opportune target, as it had not yet been bombed
at all. Lucky Hiroshima! What others had
experienced over a period of four years
would happen to Hiroshima in a single day!
Much time would be saved, and "time is
money!"

8: When they bombed Hiroshima they would
put the following out of business: The
Ube Nitrogen Fertilizer Company; the Ube Soda
Company; the Nippon Motor Oil Company;
the Sumitomo Chemical Company; the
Sumitomo Aluminum Company; and most of
the inhabitants.

9: At this time some atomic scientists
protested again, warning that the use of the
bomb in war would tend to make the
United States unpopular. But the President's
committee was by now fully convinced that the
bomb had to be used. Its use would arouse
the attention of the Japanese military class
and give them food for thought.

10: Admiral Leahy renewed his declaration that
the bomb would not explode.

11: On the 4th of July, when the United States
in displays of fireworks celebrates its
independence from British rule, the British and
Americans agreed together that the bomb
ought to be used against Japan.

12: On July 7th the Emperor of Japan
pleaded with the Soviet Government to act as
mediator for peace between Japan and the
Allies. Molotov said the question would
be "studied." In order to facilitate this "study"
Soviet troops in Siberia prepared to attack
the Japanese. The Allies had, in any case, been
urging Russia to join the war against Japan.
However, now that the atomic bomb was
nearly ready, some thought it would be better
if the Russians took a rest.

13: The time was coming for the new bomb to
be tested, in the New Mexico desert. A name
was chosen to designate this secret operation. It
was called "Trinity."

14: At 5:30 A.M. on July 16th, 1945, a
plutonium bomb was successfully exploded in
the desert at Almagordo, New Mexico. It
was suspended from a hundred foot steel tower
which evaporated. There was a fireball a
mile wide. The great flash could be seen for a
radius of 250 miles. A blind woman miles
away said she perceived light. There was a cloud
of smoke 40,000 feet high. It was shaped
like a toadstool.

15: Many who saw the experiment expressed
their satisfaction in religious terms. A
semi-official report even quoted a religious book
—The New Testament, "Lord, I believe, help
thou my unbelief." There was an atmosphere
of devotion. It was a great act of faith.
They believed the explosion was exceptionally
powerful.

16: Admiral Leahy, still a "doubting Thomas,"
said that the bomb would not explode when
dropped from a plane over a city. Others may

have had "faith," but he had his own variety of
"hope."

17: On July 21st a full written report of
the explosion reached President Truman at
Potsdam. The report was documented by
pictures. President Truman read the report and
looked at the pictures before starting out
for the conference. When he left his mood was
jaunty and his step was light.

18: That afternoon Mr. Stimson called on
Mr. Churchill, and laid before him a
sheet of paper bearing a code message about
the successful test. The message read
"Babies satisfactorily born." Mr. Churchill was
quick to realize that there was more in this
than met the eye. Mr. Stimson satisfied
his legitimate curiosity.

19: On this same day sixty atomic scientists who
knew of the test signed a petition that the
bomb should not be used against Japan
without a convincing warning and an
opportunity to surrender.

At this time the U.S.S. Indianapolis, which
had left San Francisco on the 18th, was
sailing toward the Island of Tinian, with some
U 235 in a lead bucket. The fissionable material
was about the size of a softball, but there
was enough for one atomic bomb. Instructions
were that if the ship sank, the Uranium was
to be saved first, before any life. The
mechanism of the bomb was on board the U.S.S.
Indianapolis, but it was not yet assembled.

20: On July 26th the Potsdam declaration was
issued. An ultimatum was given to Japan:
"Surrender unconditionally or be destroyed."

Nothing was said about the new bomb. But
pamphlets dropped all over Japan
threatened "an enormous air bombardment"
if the army would not surrender. On July 26th
the U.S.S. Indianapolis arrived at Tinian and the
bomb was delivered.

21: On July 28th, since the Japanese High
Command wished to continue the war,
the ultimatum was rejected. A censored version
of the ultimatum appeared in the Japanese
press with the comment that it was "an
attempt to drive a wedge between the military
and the Japanese people." But the Emperor
continued to hope that the Russians, after
"studying" his proposal, would help to
negotiate a peace. On July 30th Mr. Stimson
revised a draft of the announcement that was to
be made after the bomb was dropped on the
Japanese target. The statement was much
better than the original draft.

22: On August 1st the bomb was assembled in an
air-conditioned hut on Tinian. Those who
handled the bomb referred to it as "Little Boy."
Their care for the Original Child was devoted
and tender.

23: On August 2nd President Truman was
the guest of His Majesty King George VI
on board the H.M.S. Renown in Plymouth
Harbor. The atomic bomb was praised. Admiral
Leahy, who was present, declared that the
bomb would not work. His Majesty George VI
offered a small wager to the contrary.

24: On August 2nd a special message from the
Japanese Foreign Minister was sent to the
Japanese Ambassador in Moscow. "It is
requested that further efforts be exerted . . .
Since the loss of one day may result in a

thousand years of regret, it is requested that you
immediately have a talk with Molotov."
But Molotov did not return from Potsdam until
the day the bomb fell.

25: On August 4th the bombing crew on Tinian
watched a movie of "Trinity" (the
Almagordo Test). August 5th was a Sunday but
there was little time for formal worship.
They said a quick prayer that the war might end
"very soon." On that day, Col. Tibbetts,
who was in command of the B-29 that was to
drop the bomb, felt that his bomber ought
to have a name. He baptized it Enola Gay, after
his mother in Iowa. Col. Tibbetts was a well
balanced man, and not sentimental. He did not
have a nervous breakdown after the bombing,
like some of the other members of the crew.

26: On Sunday afternoon "Little Boy"
was brought out in procession and devoutly
tucked away in the womb of Enola Gay.
That evening few were able to sleep. They were
as excited as little boys on Christmas Eve.

27: At 1:37 A.M. August 6th the weather scout
plane took off. It was named the Straight
Flush, in reference to the mechanical action of a
water closet. There was a picture of one,
to make this evident.

28: At the last minute before taking off Col.
Tibbetts changed the secret radio call
sign from "Visitor" to "Dimples." The Bombing
Mission would be a kind of flying smile.

29: At 2:45 A.M. Enola Gay got off the ground
with difficulty. Over Iwo Jima she met her
escort, two more B-29s, one of which was called
the Great Artiste. Together they proceeded
to Japan.

30: At 6:40 they climbed to 31,000 feet, the
bombing altitude. The sky was clear. It was a
perfect morning.

31: At 3:09 they reached Hiroshima and
started the bomb run. The city was full of sun.
The fliers could see the green grass in
the gardens. No fighters rose up to meet them.
There was no flak. No one in the city
bothered to take cover.

32: The bomb exploded within 100 feet of the
aiming point. The fireball was 18,000 feet
across. The temperature at the center of
the fireball was 100,000,000 degrees. The
people who were near the center became
nothing. The whole city was blown to bits and
the ruins all caught fire instantly
everywhere, burning briskly. 70,000 people
were killed right away or died within a
few hours. Those who did not die at once
suffered great pain. Few of them were soldiers.

33: The men in the plane perceived that the
raid had been successful, but they thought of
the people in the city and they were not
perfectly happy. Some felt they had
done wrong. But in any case they had obeyed
orders. "It was war."

34: Over the radio went the code message that
the bomb had been successful: "Visible
effects greater than Trinity . . . Proceeding to
Papacy." Papacy was the code name for Tinian.

35: It took a little while for the rest of Japan
to find out what had happened to Hiroshima.
Papers were forbidden to publish any
news of the new bomb. A four line item said
that Hiroshima had been hit by incendiary

bombs and added: "It seems that some damage
was caused to the city and its vicinity."

36: Then the military governor of the
Prefecture of Hiroshima issued a proclamation
full of martial spirit. To all the people
without hands, without feet, with their faces
falling off, with their intestines hanging
out, with their whole bodies full of radiation,
he declared: "We must not rest a single day in
our war effort . . . We must bear in mind
that the annihilation of the stubborn enemy is
our road to revenge." He was a
professional soldier.

37: On August 8th Molotov finally summoned the
Japanese Ambassador. At last neutral
Russia would give an answer to the Emperor's
inquiry. Molotov said coldly that the Soviet
Union was declaring war on Japan.

38: On August 9th another bomb was dropped
on Nagasaki, though Hiroshima was still
burning. On August 11th the Emperor
overruled his high command and accepted the
peace terms dictated at Potsdam. Yet for three
days discussion continued, until on August
14th the surrender was made public and final.

39: Even then the Soviet troops thought
they ought to fight in Manchuria "just a little
longer." They felt that even though they could
not, at this time, be of help in Japan, it
would be worth while if they displayed their
good will in Manchuria, or even in Korea.

40: As to the Original Child that was now born,
President Truman summed up the philosophy
of the situation in a few words. "We found
the bomb" he said "and we used it."

> 41: Since that summer many other bombs have
> been "found." What is going to happen?
> At the time of writing, after a season of brisk
> speculation, men seem to be fatigued by the
> whole question.

———————————

IN THE MID-1960s, instead of nuclear war, the United States in-volved itself in another conventional war in Southeast Asia, apparently undeterred by the heavy losses of American troops in the previous decade's engagement in Korea. First the CIA backed a coup in South Vietnam supporting the assassination of unpopular Catholic President Diem by Major General Duong Van Minh. Then in 1964, the U.S. destroyers *Maddox* and *C. Turner Joy* reported an alleged attack by North Vietnamese torpedo boats in the Gulf of Tonkin, thirty miles offshore of Vietnam. The "attack" was later demonstrated to have originated in a mistaken radar signal, but nevertheless Congress sup-ported the Gulf of Tonkin Resolution, officially authorizing Presi-dent Johnson to wage war in Southeast Asia.

Full-scale war was under way in 1965, when President Johnson ordered air strikes on Communist targets over North Vietnam and sent the first battalion of U.S. ground troops to Da Nang. In August 1965, Robert Lowell—active in peace groups—went to Washington to ad-dress a student antiwar protest demonstration. In November the poet Robert Bly participated in another Washington demonstration. His poem "At a March Against the Vietnam War, Washington, Novem-ber 27, 1965" described the mood of the demonstrators, alert to the pal-pable presence of evil behind the serene autumn afternoon in the city:

> Newspapers rise high in the air over Maryland.
>
> We walk about, bundled in coats and sweaters in the
>   late November sun.
> Looking down, I see feet moving
> Calmly, gaily,
> Almost as if separated from their bodies.

> But there is something moving in the dark somewhere
> Just beyond
> The edge of our eyes: a boat
> Covered with machine guns
> Moving along under trees.

By the end of 1965, 175,000 American troops and 40,000 navy personnel were in South Vietnam; twelve months later, 400,000 U.S. service men were fighting there. In 1966, the United States suffered 4,800 fatalities, the first year American combat deaths exceeded those of the South Vietnamese soldiers. That year antiwar demonstrations were organized on college campuses throughout the United States, as well as in Washington, and antiwar activists grouped together to offer support to student draft resisters.

———————

Susan Sontag

In the summer of 1966, the editors of Partisan Review *sent out a questionnaire. It began, "There is a good deal of anxiety about the direction of American life. In fact, there is reason to fear that America may be entering a moral and political crisis." Readers of the magazine were invited to respond to seven specific questions: "(1) Does it matter who is in the White House? Or is there something in our system which would force any President to act as Johnson is acting? (2) How serious is the problem of inflation? the problem of poverty? (3) What is the meaning of the split between the Administration and the American intellectuals? (4) Is white America committed to granting equality to the American Negro? (5) Where do you think our foreign policies are likely to lead us? (6) What, in general, do you think is likely to happen in America? (7) Do you think any promise is to be found in the activities of young people today?"*

Susan Sontag, noted essayist and author of Against Interpretation *(1966), a provocative statement about the intellectual roots of social and cultural movements, was one of the readers of* Partisan Review *who received the questionnaire. Her response, along with contributions by many others, including Martin Duberman, Michael Harrington, Tom Hayden, Robert Lowell, and Diana Trilling, appeared in the magazine's winter 1967 issue.*

WHAT'S HAPPENING IN AMERICA
(1966)

EVERYTHING THAT ONE FEELS about this country is, or ought to be, conditioned by the awareness of American *power:* of America as the arch-imperium of the planet, holding man's biological as well as his historical future in its King Kong paws. Today's America, with Ronald Reagan the new daddy of California and John Wayne chawing spareribs in the White House, is pretty much the same Yahooland that Mencken was describing. The main difference is that what's happening in America matters so much more in the late 1960's than it did in the 1920's. Then, if one had tough innards, one might jeer, sometimes affectionately, at American barbarism and find American innocence somewhat endearing. Both the barbarism and the innocence are lethal, outsized today.

First of all, then, American power is indecent in its scale. But also the quality of American life is an insult to the possibilities of human growth; and the pollution of American space, with gadgetry and cars and TV and box architecture, brutalizes the senses, making gray neurotics of most of us, and perverse spiritual athletes and strident self-transcenders of the best of us.

Gertrude Stein said that America is the oldest country in the world. Certainly, it's the most conservative. It has the most to lose by change (sixty percent of the world's wealth owned by a country containing six percent of the world's population). Americans know their backs are against the wall: "they" want to take all that away from "us." And, I think, America deserves to have it taken away.

Three facts about this country.
America was founded on a genocide, on the unquestioned assumption of the right of white Europeans to exterminate a resident, technologically backward, colored population in order to take over the continent.

America had not only the most brutal system of slavery in modern times but a unique juridical system (compared with other slaveries, say in Latin America and the British colonies) which did not, in a single respect, recognize slaves as persons.

As a country—as distinct from a colony—America was created mainly by the surplus poor of Europe, reinforced by a small group who were just *Europamüde,* tired of Europe (a literary catchword of the 1840's). Yet even the poorest knew both a "culture," largely invented by his social betters and administered from above, and a "nature" that had been pacified for centuries. These people arrived in a country where the indigenous culture was simply the enemy and was in process of being ruthlessly annihilated, and where nature, too, was the enemy, a pristine force, unmodified by civilization, that is, by human wants, which had to be defeated. After America was "won," it was filled up by new generations of the poor and built up according to the tawdry fantasy of the good life that culturally deprived, uprooted people might have at the beginning of the industrial era. And the country looks it.

Foreigners extol the American "energy," attributing to it both our unparalleled economic prosperity and the splendid vivacity of our arts and entertainments. But surely this is energy bad at its source and for which we pay too high a price, a hypernatural and humanly disproportionate dynamism that flays everyone's nerves raw. Basically it is the energy of violence, of free-floating resentment and anxiety unleashed by chronic cultural dislocations which must be, for the most part, ferociously sublimated. This energy has mainly been sublimated into crude materialism and acquisitiveness. Into hectic philanthropy. Into benighted moral crusades, the most spectacular of which was Prohibition. Into an awesome talent for uglifying countryside and cities. Into the loquacity and torment of a minority of gadflies: artists, prophets, muckrakers, cranks, and nuts. And into self-punishing neuroses. But the naked violence keeps breaking through, throwing everything into question.

Needless to say, America is not the only violent, ugly, and unhappy country on this earth. Again, it is a matter of scale. Only three million Indians lived here when the white man arrived, rifle in hand, for his fresh start. Today American hegemony menaces the lives not of three million but of countless millions who, like the Indians, have never even *heard* of the "United States of America," much less of its mythical empire, the "free world." American policy is still powered by the fantasy of Manifest Destiny, though the limits were once set by the borders of the continent, whereas today America's destiny embraces the entire world. There are still more hordes of redskins to be mowed down before virtue triumphs; as the classic Western movies explain, the only good Red is a dead Red. This may sound like an exaggeration to those who live in the special and more finely modulated atmosphere of New York and its environs. Cross the Hudson. You find out that not just *some* Americans but virtually all Americans feel that way.

Of course, these people don't know what they're saying, literally. But that's no excuse. That, in fact, is what makes it all possible. The unquenchable American moralism and the American faith in violence are not just twin symptoms of some character neurosis taking the form of a protracted adolescence, which presages an eventual maturity. They constitute a full-grown, firmly installed national psychosis, founded, as are all psychoses, on the efficacious denial of reality. So far it's worked. Except for portions of the South a hundred years ago, America has never known war. A taxi driver said to me on the day that could have been Armageddon, when America and Russia were on collision course off the shores of Cuba: "Me, I'm not worried. I served in the last one, and now I'm over draft age. They can't get me again. But I'm all for letting 'em have it right now. What are we waiting for? Let's get it over with." Since wars always happen Over There, and we always win, why not drop the bomb? If all it takes is pushing a button, even better. For America is that curious hybrid—an apocalyptic country and a valetudinarian country. The average citizen may harbor the fantasies of John Wayne, but he as often has the temperament of Jane Austen's Mr. Woodhouse.

To answer, briefly, some of the questions:

1. I do *not* think that Johnson is forced by "our system" to act as he is acting: for instance, in Vietnam, where each evening he personally chooses the bombing targets for the next day's missions. But I think there is something awfully wrong with a *de facto* system which allows the President virtually unlimited discretion in pursuing an immoral and imprudent foreign policy, so that the strenuous opposition of, say, the Chairman of the Senate Foreign Relations Committee counts for exactly nothing. The *de jure* system vests the power to make war in the Congress—with the exception, apparently, of imperialist ventures and genocidal expeditions. These are best left undeclared.

However, I don't mean to suggest that Johnson's foreign policy is the whim of a clique which has seized control, escalated the power of the Chief Executive, castrated the Congress, and manipulated public opinion. Johnson is, alas, all too representative. As Kennedy was not. If there is a conspiracy, it is (or was) that of the more enlightened national leaders hitherto largely selected by the Eastern-seaboard plutocracy. They engineered the precarious acquiescence to liberal goals that has prevailed in this country for over a generation—a superficial consensus made possible by the strongly apolitical character of a decentralized electorate mainly preoccupied with local issues. If the Bill of Rights were put to a national referendum as a new piece of legislation, it would meet the same fate as New York City's Civilian Review Board. Most of the people in this country believe what Goldwater believes, and always have. But most of them don't know it. Let's hope they don't find out.

4. I do not think white America is committed to granting equality to the American Negro. So committed are only a minority of white Americans, mostly educated and affluent, few of whom have had any prolonged social contact with Negroes. This is a passionately racist country; it will continue to be so in the foreseeable future.

5. I think that this administration's foreign policies are likely to lead to more wars and to wider wars. Our main hope, and the chief restraint on American bellicosity and paranoia, lies in the fatigue and depoliticization of Western Europe, the lively fear of America and of another world war in Russia and the Eastern European countries, and the corruption and unreliability of our client states in the Third World. It's hard to lead a holy war without allies. But America is just crazy enough to try to do it.

6. The meaning of the split between the Administration and the intellectuals? Simply that our leaders are genuine yahoos, with all the exhibitionist traits of their kind, and that liberal intellectuals (whose deepest loyalties are to an international fraternity of the reasonable) are not *that* blind. At this point, moreover, they have nothing to lose by proclaiming their discontent and frustration. But it's well to remember that liberal intellectuals, like Jews, tend to have a classical theory of politics, in which the state has a monopoly of power; hoping that those in positions of authority may prove to be enlightened men, wielding power justly, they are natural, if cautious, allies of the "establishment." As the Russian Jews knew they had at least a chance with the Czar's officials but none at all with marauding Cossacks and drunken peasants (Milton Himmelfarb has pointed this out), liberal

intellectuals more naturally expect to influence the "decisions" of administrators than they do the volatile "feelings" of masses. Only when it becomes clear that, in fact, the government itself is being staffed by Cossacks and peasants, can a rupture like the present one take place. When (and if) the man in the White House who paws people and scratches his balls in public is replaced by the man who dislikes being touched and finds Yevtushenko "an interesting fellow," American intellectuals won't be so disheartened. The vast majority of them are not revolutionaries, wouldn't know how to be if they tried. Mostly a salaried professoriat, they're as much at home in the system when it functions a little better than it does right now as anyone else.

7. Yes, I do find much promise in the activities of young people. About the only promise one can find anywhere in this country today is in the way some young people are carrying on, making a fuss. I include both their renewed interest in politics (as protest and as community action, rather than as theory) and the way they dance, dress, wear their hair, riot, make love. I also include the homage they pay to Oriental thought and rituals. And I include, not least of all, their interest in taking drugs—despite the unspeakable vulgarization of this project by Leary and others. . . .

Denise Levertov

The writer Denise Levertov wrote many poems protesting the escalating war, such as "Life at War," included in The Sorrow Dance *(1967), and "Overheard over S.E. Asia," published in* Footprints *(1972), the year she traveled to Hanoi, North Vietnam, at the invitation of the Women's Union and Writers' Union. In 1968 she told the interviewer E. G. Burrows that her participation in antiwar groups grew naturally out of her work as a poet:*

> *I have found myself as a poet, long before this particular involvement, saying things in poems which I think have moral implications. I think that if one is an articulate*

> *person, who makes certain statements, one has an*
> *obligation as a human being to back them up with one's*
> *actions. So I feel that it is poetry that has led me into*
> *political action and not political action which has caused*
> *me to write poems more overtly engaged than those I*
> *used to write, which is something that has happened to*
> *me, but that is just a natural happening. I've always*
> *written rather directly about my life and my concerns at*
> *any particular time.*

Levertov made clear that her writing against the Vietnam War was meant as a personal statement, not as propaganda for the antiwar movement. "I think there is no abrupt separation between so-called political poetry and so-called private poetry in an artist, who is in both cases writing out of his own inner life." She felt that her activism cut across political ideologies and was not following a party line:

> I don't think that this happens in the peace movement
> in this country, where so many poets in the last two or
> three years have been increasingly writing poems overtly
> concerned with war, because the peace movement in this
> country is not an ideology, is not a monolithic
> organization with a party line, which a person enters
> and gives up his own conscience and thought and
> becomes subservient to that ideology. The peace
> movement in this country is just an agglomeration of
> individuals. Some people say this is a weakness, that it
> would have more power or more efficiency if it were
> better organized. I think its great underlying strength is
> that it is composed of individuals who do whatever they
> do—do their thing—because their own conscience leads
> them to it, and the proliferation of organizations within
> the peace movement is a reflection of that fact. I think
> it's basically a strength.

LIFE AT WAR

The disasters numb within us
caught in the chest, rolling
in the brain like pebbles. The feeling
resembles lumps of raw dough

weighing down a child's stomach on baking day.
Or Rilke said it, "My heart . . .
Could I say of it, it overflows
with bitterness . . . but no, as though

its contents were simply balled into
formless lumps, thus
do I carry it about."
The same war

continues.
We have breathed the grits of it in, all our lives,
our lungs are pocked with it,
the mucous membrane of our dreams
coated with it, the imagination
filmed over with the gray filth of it:

the knowledge that humankind,

delicate Man, whose flesh
responds to a caress, whose eyes
are flowers that perceive the stars,

whose music excels the music of birds,
whose laughter matches the laughter of dogs,
whose understanding manifests designs
fairer than the spider's most intricate web,

still turns without surprise, with mere regret
to the scheduled breaking open of breasts whose milk
runs out over the entrails of still-alive babies,
transformation of witnessing eyes to pulp-fragments,
implosion of skinned penises into carcass-gulleys.

We are the humans, men who can make;
whose language imagines *mercy,*
lovingkindness; we have believed one another
mirrored forms of a God we felt as good—

who do these acts, who convince ourselves
it is necessary; these acts are done

to our own flesh; burned human flesh
is smelling in Viet Nam as I write.

Yes, this is the knowledge that jostles for space
in our bodies along with all we
go on knowing of joy, of love;

our nerve filaments twitch with its presence
day and night,
nothing we say has not the husky phlegm of it in the
    saying,
nothing we do has the quickness, the sureness,
the deep intelligence living at peace would have.

OVERHEARD OVER S.E. ASIA

"White phosphorus, white phosphorus,
mechanical snow,
where are you falling?"

"I am falling impartially on roads and roofs,
on bamboo thickets, on people.
My name recalls rich seas on rainy nights,
each drop that hits the surface eliciting
luminous response from a million algae.
My name is a whisper of sequins. Ha!
Each of them is a disk of fire,
I am the snow that burns.
                    I fall
wherever men send me to fall—
but I prefer flesh, so smooth, so dense:
I decorate it in black, and seek
the bone."

Robert Bly

As the Vietnam War continued, both mainstream and radical presses in the United States kept up the antiwar protest in magazines and books. Three of the most notable were 1001 Ways to Beat the Draft *(1966) by Tuli Kupferberg and Robert Bashlow, a wacky illustrated pamphlet offering half-serious [#1: "Grope J. Edgar Hoover in the silent halls of Congress"] and not-so-serious [#2: "Get thee to a nunnery"] suggestions. In 1967* Writers Take Sides on Vietnam *included Denise Levertov's passionate statement:*

> *I am absolutely opposed to the U.S. war of aggression in Vietnam. Not only is it an unjustifiable interference hypocritically carried on in the name of "freedom" while in fact its purpose is to further the strategic ends of a government whose enormous power has destroyed the morality of its members; but it is being waged by means of atrocities. . . . Violence always breeds more violence and is never a solution even when it temporarily seems to be. Violence of this magnitude, even if the ultimate holocaust it is swiftly leading to is averted—i.e., if we at least stop in time to avoid a still larger war—promises a dreadful future for America, full of people tortured and distorted with the knowledge (conscious or unconscious) of what we have done.*

In 1968 the writer Diane di Prima edited War Poems *for the Poets Press in New York City, including work by poets associated with the Beat and Black Mountain groups, such as Allen Ginsberg, LeRoi Jones, Gary Snyder, Philip Whalen, Robert Duncan, Charles Olson, and Robert Creeley. Di Prima contributed her poem "To the Unnamed Buddhist Nun Who Burned Herself to Death on the Night of June 3, 1966." Gregory Corso opened the collection with a poem beginning "The winds of Babylon / whirl over this God-sick nation."*

Many poets expressed their feelings about the war in Vietnam in works meant for public performance. Robert Bly recalled in his volume Selected Poems *(1986) that*

> the Vietnam War and the revulsion against it came
> down like a rainstorm and carried us away. . . . The
> Vietnam War changed the way I lived: the psychic
> urgency dissolved calmness for most of us, and actively
> opposing the war meant an end to long periods of
> solitude.
>   Reciting political poems at Vietnam gatherings, I
> experienced for the first time in my life the power of
> spoken or oral poetry. A briefly lasting community
> springs to life in front of the voice, like a flower
> opening—it can be a community either of excitement or
> of feeling. The community flowers when the poem is
> spoken in the ancient way—that is, with full sound,
> with conviction, and with the knowledge that the
> emotions are not private to the person speaking them.

Composing "The Teeth Mother Naked at Last," Bly chose to write in a long line that he felt embodied "power in a direct way. I wrote in a line adapted from earlier poets that throws or catapults itself into the outer world, and composed a number of passages while reciting." City Lights Books published "The Teeth Mother Naked at Last" in 1970. Bly also included it in Sleepers Joining Hands *(1973).*

THE TEETH MOTHER NAKED AT LAST

I

Massive engines lift beautifully from the deck.
Wings appear over the trees, wings with eight hundred
   rivets.

Engines burning a thousand gallons of gasoline a minute
   sweep over the huts with dirt floors.

The chickens feel the new fear deep in the pits of their
   beaks.
Buddha with Padma Sambhava.

Meanwhile, out on the China Sea,
immense gray bodies are floating,
born in Roanoke,
the ocean on both sides expanding, "buoyed on the dense
    marine."

Helicopters flutter overhead. The death-
bee is coming. Super Sabres
like knots of neurotic energy sweep
around and return.
This is Hamilton's triumph.
This is the advantage of a centralized bank.
B-52s come from Guam. All the teachers
die in flames. The hopes of Tolstoy fall asleep in the ant
    heap.
Do not ask for mercy.

Now the time comes to look into the past-tunnels,
the hours given and taken in school,
the scuffles in coatrooms,
foam leaps from his nostrils,
now we come to the scum you take from the mouths of the
    dead,
now we sit beside the dying, and hold their hands, there is
    hardly time for good-bye,
the staff sergeant from North Carolina is dying—you hold
    his hand,
he knows the mansions of the dead are empty, he has an
    empty place
inside him, created one night when his parents came home
    drunk,
he uses half his skin to cover it,
as you try to protect a balloon from sharp objects. . . .
Artillery shells explode. Napalm canisters roll end over
    end.
800 steel pellets fly through the vegetable walls.
The six-hour infant puts his fists instinctively to his eyes to
    keep out the light.
But the room explodes,
the children explode.
Blood leaps on the vegetable walls.

Yes, I know, blood leaps on the walls—
Don't cry at that—
Do you cry at the wind pouring out of Canada?
Do you cry at the reeds shaken at the edge of the sloughs?
The Marine battalion enters.
This happens when the seasons change,
This happens when the leaves begin to drop from the trees
    too early
"Kill them: I don't want to see anything moving."
This happens when the ice begins to show its teeth in the
    ponds
This happens when the heavy layers of lake water press
    down on the fish's head, and send him deeper, where his
    tail swirls slowly, and his brain passes him pictures of
    heavy reeds, of vegetation fallen on vegetation. . . .
Hamilton saw all this in detail:

*"Every banana tree slashed, every cooking utensil smashed, every
    mattress cut."*

Now the Marine knives sweep around like sharp-edged jets;
    how beautifully they slash open the rice bags,
the mattresses . . .
ducks are killed with $150 shotguns.

Old women watch the soldiers as they move.

II

Excellent Roman knives slip along the ribs.

A stronger man starts to jerk up the strips of flesh.

*"Let's hear it again, you believe in the Father, the Son, and the
    Holy Ghost?"*

A long scream unrolls.

More.

*"From the political point of view, democratic institutions are being
    built in Vietnam, wouldn't you agree?"*

A green parrot shudders under the fingernails.
Blood jumps in the pocket.
The scream lashes like a tail.

"Let us not be deterred from our task by the voices of dissent. . . ."

The whines of the jets
pierce like a long needle.

As soon as the President finishes his press conference, black
    wings carry off the words,
bits of flesh still clinging to them.

★   ★   ★

The ministers lie, the professors lie, the television lies, the
    priests lie. . . .
These lies mean that the country wants to die.
Lie after lie starts out into the prairie grass,
like enormous caravans of Conestoga wagons. . . .

And a long desire for death flows out, guiding the
    enormous caravans from beneath,
stringing together the vague and foolish words.
It is a desire to eat death,
to gobble it down,
to rush on it like a cobra with mouth open

It's a desire to take death inside,
to feel it burning inside, pushing out velvety hairs,
like a clothes brush in the intestines—

This is the thrill that leads the President on to lie

★   ★   ★

Now the Chief Executive enters; the press conference
    begins:
First the President lies about the date the Appalachian
    Mountains rose.
Then he lies about the population of Chicago, then he lies
    about the weight of the adult eagle, then about the
    acreage of the Everglades

He lies about the number of fish taken every year in the Arctic,
   he has private information about which city *is* the capital of
   Wyoming, he lies about the birthplace of Attila the Hun.

He lies about the composition of the amniotic fluid, and he
   insists that Luther was never a German, and that only the
   Protestants sold indulgences,

That Pope Leo X *wanted* to reform the church, but the
   "liberal elements" prevented him,
that the Peasants' War was fomented by Italians from the
   North.

And the Attorney General lies about the time the sun sets.

★   ★   ★

These lies are only the longing we all feel to die.
It is the longing for someone to come and take you by the
   hand to where they all are sleeping:
where the Egyptian pharaohs are asleep, and your own
   mother,
and all those disappeared children, who used to go around
   with you in the rings at grade school. . . .

Do not be angry at the President—he is longing to take in
   his hand
the locks of death hair—
to meet his own children dead, or unborn. . . .
He is drifting sideways toward the dusty places

III

This is what it's like for a rich country to make war
this is what it's like to bomb huts (afterwards described as
   "structures")
this is what it's like to kill marginal farmers (afterwards
   described as "Communists")

this is what it's like to watch the altimeter needle going mad

*Baron 25, this is 81. Are there any friendlies in the area? 81 from
   25, negative on the friendlies. I'd like you to take out as many*

*structures as possible located in those trees within 200 meters
east and west of my smoke mark.*

diving, the green earth swinging, cheeks hanging back, red
pins blossoming ahead of us, 20-millimeter cannon fire,
leveling off, rice fields shooting by like telephone poles,
smoke rising, hut roofs loom up huge as landing fields,
slugs going in, half the huts on fire, small figures running,
palm trees burning, shooting past, up again; . . . blue sky
. . . cloud mountains

This is what it's like to have a gross national product.

It's because the aluminum window shade business is doing
so well in the United States that we roll fire over entire
villages
It's because a hospital room in the average American city
now costs $90 a day that we bomb hospitals in the North

It's because the milk trains coming into New Jersey hit the
right switches every day that the best Vietnamese men
are cut in two by American bullets that follow each other
like freight cars

This is what it's like to send firebombs down from air-
conditioned cockpits.

This is what it's like to be told to fire into a reed hut with
an automatic weapon.

It's because we have new packaging for smoked oysters that
bomb holes appear in the rice paddies

It is because we have so few women sobbing in back rooms,
because we have so few children's heads torn apart by high-
velocity bullets,
because we have so few tears falling on our own hands
that the Super Sabre turns and screams down toward the earth.

It's because taxpayers move to the suburbs that we transfer
populations.

The Marines use cigarette lighters to light the thatched
   roofs of huts
because so many Americans own their own homes.

IV

I see a car rolling toward a rock wall.
The treads in the face begin to crack.
We all feel like tires being run down roads under heavy
   cars.

The teen-ager imagines herself floating through the Seven
   Spheres.
Oven doors are found
open.
Soot collects over the doorframe, has children, takes courses,
goes mad, and dies.

There is a black silo inside our bodies, revolving fast.
Bits of black paint are flaking off,
where the motorcycles roar, around and around,
rising higher on the silo walls,
the bodies bent toward the horizon,
driven by angry women dressed in black.

       ★   ★   ★

I know that books are tired of us.
I *know* they are chaining the Bible to chairs.
Books don't want to remain in the same room with us
   anymore.

New Testaments are escaping . . . dressed as women . . .
   they go off after dark.
And Plato! Plato . . . Plato wants to go backwards. . . .
He wants to hurry back up the river of time, so he can end
   as some blob of sea flesh rotting on an Australian beach.

V

Why are they dying? I have written this so many times.
They are dying because the President has opened a Bible
   again.
They are dying because gold deposits have been found
   among the Shoshoni Indians.

They are dying because money follows intellect!
And intellect is like a fan opening in the wind—

The Marines think that unless they die the rivers will not
    move.
They are dying so that the mountain shadows will continue
    to fall east in the afternoon,
so that the beetle can move along the ground near the fallen
    twigs.

VI

But if one of those children came near that we have set on
    fire,
came toward you like a gray barn, walking,
you would howl like a wind tunnel in a hurricane,
you would tear at your shirt with blue hands,
you would drive over your own child's wagon trying to
    back up,
the pupils of your eyes would go wild—

If a child came by burning, you would dance on a lawn,
trying to leap into the air, digging into your cheeks,
you would ram your head against the wall of your bedroom
like a bull penned too long in his moody pen—

If one of those children came toward me with both hands
in the air, fire rising along both elbows,
I would suddenly go back to my animal brain,
I would drop on all fours, screaming,
my vocal cords would turn blue, so would yours,
it would be two days before I could play with my own
    children again.

VII

I want to sleep awhile in the rays of the sun slanting over
    the snow.
Don't wake me.
Don't tell me how much grief there is in the leaf with its
    natural oils.
Don't tell me how many children have been born with

stumpy hands all those years we lived in St. Augustine's
 shadow.
Tell me about the dust that falls from the yellow daffodil
 shaken in the restless winds.
Tell me about the particles of Babylonian thought that still
 pass through the earthworm every day.
Don't tell me about "the frightening laborers who do not
 read books."

Now the whole nation starts to whirl,
the end of the Republic breaks off,
Europe comes to take revenge,
the mad beast covered with European hair rushes through
 the mesa bushes in Mendocino County,
pigs rush toward the cliff,
the waters underneath part: in one ocean luminous globes
 float up (in them hairy and ecstatic men—)
in the other, the teeth mother, naked at last.

Let us drive cars
up
the light beams
to the stars . . .

And return to earth crouched inside the drop of sweat
that falls
from the chin of the Protestant tied in the fire.

———————————

David Lance Goines

*Individual college students of draft age in the United States created
their own tactics of resistance to avoid the Selective Service order to
report for duty. David Lance Goines, a student active in the Free*

Speech Movement at the University of California at Berkeley, was reclassified 1-A when President Johnson increased the draft quotas in 1966 and 1967. At that time, twenty thousand soldiers were being shipped out of the Oakland Induction Center every month. In "Let Sleeping Dogs Lie," a chapter in Goines's book The Free Speech Movement *(1993), he described the strategy he devised to delay his induction into the armed forces until the end of the war.*

LET SLEEPING DOGS LIE

I PARTICIPATED in a few marches and demonstrations, and did the obligatory public incineration of the draft card. Most of my time, though, was spent behind a printing press. The revolution ran on paper and ink and the Berkeley Free Press was where it all came from. The antiwar and civil rights movements kept us running at full capacity.

In response to the difficulties of addressing the nonstudent, nonactivist population (preaching to the saved was fun, but what we wanted was to win some souls from Satan), we came up with a clever technique. What piece of paper will no one throw away, will people actually pass along to someone else, regardless of political inclination? You got it. Money, banknotes, the old mazoola, scratch, gelt, yenom. We ordered up dozens of rubber stamps saying "Get out of Vietnam," and simply stamped both sides of every bill that went through our hands. The idea caught on, and it was the unusual Dead President that wasn't the grudging bearer of this message. As a further protest, it was common to see ordinary American-flag postage stamps affixed upside down, as a symbol of distress.

In the middle of summer 1966, I drew the unwelcome attentions of the government when, quite gratuitously, I sent a letter to my draft board that began:

Gentlemen: Please remove my name from your mailing list, as I am no longer interested in your organization.

And continued in much the same vein for several pages. I really don't know why I did this. It seems unreasonable in retrospect, but this was about the time that I was doing my best to win the "all-time most civil rights arrests" award, and getting busted for possession of a smart mouth and failure to kiss ass was more or less my style.

I had registered for the draft when I turned eighteen, and had gone to the Oakland draft board for a preliminary physical. The result was that I was classified 4-F, because of my poor eyesight. As a student, I hadn't bothered to get reclassified 2-S, figuring that a 4-F was good enough. Of course, the Army can draft anybody, anytime, for any reason, but the need for half-blind rabble-rousers is so limited that I felt myself safe.

I guess that the letter was the last straw, or perhaps it merely drew me to their attention, but a month or so later I received the official communication that turns the blood to icewater:

Greetings from the President of the United States. You have been selected . . .

Drafted. Reclassified 1-A and drafted, sure as God made little green apples. Shit, oh dear.

My draft physical (which I passed with flying colors, even though I couldn't count my fingers at arm's length without my glasses on) ended with an intelligence test. The Army Alpha is cleverly designed, consisting of four sets of basic questions, increasing in difficulty and contrived to show just about everything that the Army wants to know about how well educated you are and where your intellectual strengths might lie. The four types of questions concern mathematics, diagrams of exploded boxes that indicate spatial conceptualization, word skills, and comparison of objects or ideas—the "A shoe is to a foot as a glove is to a: 1) hand 2) arm 3) head 4) leg" kind. There are twenty-five of each kind of question, making a hundred questions all told. I believe that there is a time limit of an hour. I got them all correct but one, further arousing the mistrust of the sergeant in charge.

After the test, the group of conscripts was asked to sit at school desks and write a short essay. I am not at all sure what we were asked to write about, perhaps it was the Army, or patriotism, or America. I took the opportunity to vomit out a Niagara of vitriol, revealing in excessive detail my feelings about the war, the Army, the draft, the president and the government in general. I was still writing long after everyone else had gone. The same suspicious sergeant took the thick sheaf of papers from me, and said that they would be contacting me in the near future.

Sure enough, Army Intelligence called me up in about a week, wanting to chat. On the advice of my attorney, Art Wells, we met in his office. They would ask questions, and as soon as I would climb up on the soapbox, Art would shut me up.

I had recently finished reading C. Northcote Parkinson's humorous but deadly accurate book analyzing the nature of bureaucracies, *Parkinson's Law,* wherein he gives useful advice about how to get things from them when they wish to obstruct and, more important, how to avoid giving them something when you don't want to. In this case, the thing they wanted that I didn't want to give them was me. Basically, his advice was: Write the bureaucracy a letter, and time the response. This reveals the period in which the letter will sit on somebody's desk, along with your file. When the letter has been answered, the file will be returned to its proper place. Next, write them another letter, and if the time for a response is just about the same, you have discovered the period of time that your file is moving around within the office. Now, start writing letters within the period of response. Subject matter is unimportant, as they must respond to everything, without regard to content. Since your file now is kept in constant motion and never gets back into the filing cabinet where it belongs, but is always in transition from one department to another, *sooner or later, they will lose it!* When you stop getting replies, stop writing immediately, and you will essentially have ceased to exist, as far as they are concerned. I did just that. I wrote letters like,

Dear Sirs:
    As I am not the sole surviving son of a veteran killed, wounded or missing in action, I request a deferment for this reason.
    Thank you for your attention to this matter.

Dear Sirs:
    As I am not currently the sole support of my family, I request a deferment for this reason.
    Thank you for your attention to this matter.

Dear Sirs,
    As I am not currently enrolled in an accredited four-year college or university, I request a deferment for this reason.
    Thank you for your attention to this matter.

Dear Sirs,

As I am not an ordained minister of the Gospel, Catholic priest, or rabbi, I request a deferment for this reason.

Thank you for your attention to this matter.

And so on and so forth, *ad nauseam*.

My correspondent was a seriously dumb young woman named Debby Dirt or something like that, with big, loopy, subliterate handwriting—the kind that has little circles over the lowercase *i*'s, and happy faces in them if she is cheerful or wants to seem so. This poor child was the officer in charge of my case, and had a hell of a time figuring what I was up to.

Dr. Jerry Rosenfield wrote a letter to the draft board that stated, in essence, that I would make one damned piss-poor soldier, that inducting me into the armed services would be to court a resounding failure, that they had better try it on somebody else. I do not remember that there was a response.

Sure enough, after some time of this they lost my file, and I heard nothing whatever from them until late 1972. By then the war was over, and my ass was saved. The file had, apparently, fallen (or been pushed) down behind a filing cabinet. I guess now with everything on computers, this trick won't work anymore. But it might!

Ann Charters

As David Lance Goines suggested, the antiwar demonstrations involved many different kinds of people, alike only in their determination to make it clear that they did not support America's involvement in the war in Vietnam. There were so many marches and sit-ins and teach-ins in the second half of the 1960s that I felt I came of age with many thousands of other people in demonstrations against the Vietnam War. I participated in four of them, all

*very different as the war escalated toward the end of the decade,
when the demonstrations got more serious, more belligerent, and
more bloody. As they changed, I also changed, and nothing after-
ward was ever quite the same.*

HOW TO MAINTAIN A PEACEFUL
DEMONSTRATION

I.

I WENT ON MY FIRST DEMONSTRATION in the late spring of 1966,
a few months after I had completed the requirements for my doctor-
ate in American literature at Columbia University. I had a one-year
appointment to teach freshmen in the general studies program there,
but my husband, Sam, and I had just moved along with our Irish set-
ter puppy downtown into a one-bedroom East Village apartment on
Saint Mark's Place in New York City. Sam had supported me by
working as a record producer for the two and a half years it took for
me to earn the degree, but once settled in the apartment, he took off
for a trip around the world. I missed him, but I was also enormously
happy that I was no longer a student. The exams and papers were fin-
ished. I was nearly thirty years old, and for as long as I could remem-
ber, I had been either going to school, or waiting to go back to
school. Now I was free.

My dissertation had been about nineteenth-century American
writers in the Massachusetts Berkshires, but I had no desire to revise it
for publication. I wanted to do something else, but I didn't have a
clue about what that could be. The United States' involvement in the
war in Vietnam had been growing while I had been a doctoral stu-
dent at Columbia, but I hadn't joined any of the organizations on
campus in 1963 or 1964—if there were any—that were organizing
students to protest the draft. It was still early days for the Peace Move-
ment then. Until the end of 1965 I was too immersed in taking
classes, passing my exams, and defending my dissertation to have time
to go to activists' meetings, such as the New York Workshop in Non-
violence that prepared students to go south for Civil Rights demon-
strations.

Now that I had more time, I pursued my hobby of collecting
books by Beat writers. I began to browse in the back corners of mid-
town Manhattan bookstores, looking for cheap remaindered copies of
Kerouac novels; in the used magazine stores off Times Square, I

hunted for back issues of mainstream magazines like *Esquire* and *Escapade* that had Kerouac articles or Ginsberg poems in them. In my East Village neighborhood, I investigated the sparsely stocked Peace Eye Bookstore, set up in what had once been a kosher meat store by the poet Ed Sanders. It featured odd items, such as the piles of mimeographed issues of *Fuck You: A Magazine of the Arts,* which Sanders published with his underground press. At the time, I was completely in the dark about how something as apparently ephemeral as "Beat Generation literature" could become an absorbing research subject for a literary scholar whose dissertation topic had been Bryant, Hawthorne, Melville, and Thoreau.

The light dawned on the day of a massive Anti–Vietnam War Parade on Fifth Avenue. Early in the afternoon I took the subway uptown at Astor Place with a sense of doing something on my own that felt absolutely right, like going to bookstores. There wasn't anything special about the mood of the people riding the subway, but when I got out at Seventy-seventh Street and walked over from Lexington Avenue to where the demonstrators were waiting to assemble on Fifth Avenue, the side streets were full of people who seemed to be walking with a special sense of purpose. I hadn't arranged to meet anyone, and suddenly I was aware that I didn't know a soul.

I wandered around, looking into the faces of strangers, feeling uneasy. People were gathering in little clumps, most of them young adults like me or middle-aged, with a scattering of teenagers and old folks. Some were casually holding banners or signs stapled to sticks. Groups of people with armbands lettered MARSHAL were talking among themselves. Everyone was dressed informally. A lot of people were wearing sneakers. I had watched Saint Patrick's Day parades march on Fifth Avenue, but I'd never given any thought as to how they were organized. I began to feel confused, not knowing what I was supposed to do, yet I didn't want to go home. I loitered by the curb, behind a row of yellow police barricades set up along Fifth Avenue, waiting to be shown the way.

The demonstration had been announced for two P.M., and just about the time it was supposed to start, the peace marshals shouted that we should take our places, and that everyone had to march in a group. Their commands took me by surprise. I had assumed that we would all come individually to Fifth Avenue and then somehow we would fall into line and start marching. Now suddenly I was being asked to choose a group, not form a group. Which group did I belong to?

Apparently everyone had come prepared but me. People assembled, straightened out their cloth banners, and lifted their signs into the air. I could see that they were all labels for different groups. In the next few minutes I saw bunches of teachers organizing under banners, along with other clusters of people who were doctors, lawyers, librarians, members of neighborhood action committees, Jews, Catholic workers, Irishmen, activists from New Jersey insurance offices, peaceniks from Connecticut. Some groups included mothers and fathers pushing baby carriages and strollers with small children—the march was offering me an apparently unending stream of possibilities. Where did I belong?

Totally confused, I reminded myself that the easiest way to formulate a self-definition was to say that what you do is who you are. What did I do? Up to then, the strongest identity I felt was being a graduate student. But I had just graduated, so that wasn't true anymore. Should I join the marching group of middle-aged people carrying a teacher banner who had just walked past where I was standing? Not yet—I had only a part-time job. Something in me shied away from the teacher label. Okay then, was I a Jew? That was a more difficult question than it seemed. Of course I was a Jew by birth, but I didn't practice my religion and I had married a lapsed Episcopalian. Would I be a hypocrite to march with a group of people who labeled themselves Jews Against the War? Was I splitting hairs? What else could I be? Who was I? Where was the marching group of Irish setter owners? Or the assemblage of amateur pianists like myself dedicated to Scott Joplin ragtime or to collecting Jack Kerouac books?

Suddenly cutting through my jumbled thoughts and the press of the crowd surging around me, I heard the instantly recognizable, penetrating cacophony of the Fugs, the raunchy group of folk musicians who played informal concerts in my neighborhood on the Lower East Side. Over my right shoulder I saw the entire band scuffling down Fifth Avenue, Ed Sanders in the front linked with Tuli Kupferberg and Allen Ginsberg, followed by a ragged line of other musicians and a pack of howling acolytes. The music triumphed over my sense of an identity crisis. Now I knew where I belonged—my joyful response to the music was unmistakable.

Wasn't it Hemingway or some other existentialist who said if you felt good about something, then it was morally right? The idea of joining the gang demonstrating against the war in Vietnam by bellowing out the racy lyrics of "Kill for Peace" and "Slum Goddess from the Lower East Side" unquestionably made me feel good. I was one in spirit with the gaggle of provocative poets and their raucous loved ones strumming strings and banging on percussion instruments and carrying crudely lettered peace signs, proudly marching with the Fugs. I knew their songs, because I'd heard the band play in the East Village. I'd bought their first record the previous fall, and I sang along with them when I washed the dishes or cleaned my apartment. Without hesitation my feet left the curb and I squeezed between the police barricades onto Fifth Avenue to join Ed Sanders's entourage. There was no mistaking the feeling—I was finally among my own people. I was home.

II

Nearly eighteen months later, I marched again to protest the war in Vietnam. The front pages of the *New York Times* were full of war headlines, and with the escalation of combat, the country was split in two. You were labeled either a hawk—for the war—or a dove—against the war. I was definitely a dove.

By October 21, 1967, when I participated in my second antiwar demonstration, I had made friends in New York City who were also—like Sam and myself—adamantly against the war in Vietnam. One of my new friends was Rusty Kalish. I had met her when Sam recorded her husband, Gil, and the young violinist Paul Zukofsky playing the Charles Ives piano-violin sonatas in 1964. Rusty—her curly hair was a striking shade of red—and her husband lived with their three kids and a well-dusted black Steinway grand piano in a sprawling apartment on the Upper West Side. Besides taking care of her young children, Rusty was also going to graduate school part-time, completing a degree in mathematics so she would be able to become a college teacher.

My well-organized friend also somehow found the time to join a group of West Side mothers engaged in the Peace Movement. She showed me the full-page announcements in magazines in which Martin Luther King endorsed a program called "Vietnam Summer," a call for ten thousand volunteers to spend the summer of 1967 in five hundred communities educating people to lead demonstrations against the war. The program was modeled on the 1964 Mississippi Freedom Summer Project, which mobilized thousands of students and young people in the struggle against racial injustice. This time the Vietnam

Summer program targeted the inner-city ghettos, to encourage the young men who were questioning their obligation in a racist society to fight the war overseas.

One day in early October 1967, Rusty phoned to invite me to join her friends on a day trip to Washington, D.C. I still wasn't enthusiastic about joining groups, but she told me it would be a "mammoth demonstration." I was innocent enough to think that I would make a difference by helping to swell the numbers of people attending the march. Rusty told me that her friends had arranged everything. All I had to do was pack myself a lunch and show up on time in the early morning to catch the bus chartered to transport us to and from Washington.

Joining Rusty in a line of women like myself, eager to demonstrate against a war we hated, I began the journey in high spirits. It felt good to be traveling together. I studied the piece of paper handed to me on the bus by a motherly woman wearing an armband lettered MARSHAL. The single-spaced text filling both sides of the paper had been neatly typewritten and mimeographed. It was headed in block letters and here is what it said:

A WORD TO THE WISE:
MAINTAINING A PEACEFUL DEMONSTRATION

Permits for the rallies, the march, the picketing and vigiling on the mall of the Pentagon have been assured us. Problems may arise, but serious trouble is unlikely, especially for those not committing civil disobedience. This is a peaceful demonstration. Our purpose is to protest the violence of the administration, not to contribute to it.

All of us should think through our actions in different situations. People will always have different responses, but in general the following policies are good:

1. Listen to Marshals—they have been trained to intercept and isolate provocative situations.
2. Don't answer back to counter-demonstrators or hecklers.
3. Attempt to remain calm—be firm, but not provocative.
4. Violent or potentially violent situations are

made worse by violent responses or frightened
retreat. Make it your responsibility, also, to
calm others.

5. In most situations, it is better not to run. If you
   run *from* the police, you may encourage them
   to be bullies. If you run *at* them, you may
   cause them to panic and act irrationally.
   Remember: the police are often scared when
   dealing with a crowd. If you can act toward
   them in a way that makes them less tense, they
   are much less apt to behave brutally.

6. Don't accept or spread rumors. Check with
   marshals for accurate information.

7. Always remain with a group—but stay with the
   official line of march. Do not follow "wildcat"
   groups or individuals.

8. Do not respond to provocative acts initiated by
   "demonstrators." Disengage from and isolate
   persons whose behavior seems likely to
   produce trouble. GET THE NEAREST
   MARSHAL to deal with the situation.

For those planning to participate in Civil Disobedience:

If the demonstration proceeds according to plan, direct
action will begin at the Pentagon at around 4:00 P.M. follow-
ing an announcement by Dave Dellinger. A small commit-
tee will have surveyed the situation, and depending on the
nature of the police preparations, will instruct Dave to give
the appropriate directions.

Trained marshals will guide people to the spots where they
will be most effective. We do not intend to rush police lines,
or attempt to enter the Pentagon by force. Nevertheless, we
will persist in a determined effort to impede its operations
and to stand our ground for as long as this is feasible—at
least until Monday, noon, October 23.

In case of attack, we should attempt to remain as calm and
unaggressive as possible. Use the various self-protective
techniques that have been developed to blunt the force of

physical attack. In any event, listen to the instructions of marshals, attempt to control your natural anger or fear, and remain calm.

If police start making arrests, one technique is to impede their progress by going limp, i.e., making the police carry you to the paddy wagon, rather than walking. Going limp is considered a form of resisting arrest in Virginia, but not in D.C. Its advantage is that, when done *en masse,* it prolongs the action for hours, sometimes days.

> *"There is no way to peace—peace is the way."*
> A. J. MUSTE

Arriving in downtown Washington, a few blocks from the Lincoln Memorial, we joined the thousands of people congregated there to listen to speeches before marching to the Pentagon. Rusty told me that Dr. Benjamin Spock and others from the organization Women Strike for Peace had arranged for the rally to begin at the Lincoln Memorial so that women and children could disperse in comparative safety before the actual march started if the mood of the crowd seemed dangerous.

Everything seemed mellow when we gathered in ragged lines, four abreast, to walk over Arlington Memorial Bridge to the Pentagon. At the beginning of the march, there were thousands of law enforcers on hand to maintain order. Norman Mailer later estimated 1,500 Metropolitan Police, 2,500 Washington, D.C., National Guardsmen, about 200 U.S. marshals, and hundreds of government security guards, and White House and Capitol police. An additional 6,000 troops from the Eighty-second Airborne, MP units from California and Texas, and 20,000 troops were stationed outside the city on alert. This was no frolicking promenade down Fifth Avenue like the first march I had attended.

I had personal contact with none of the law-enforcement officers in Washington. After crossing the bridge without incident, my friends and I stood around and listened to speeches for an hour or so while we ate our bag lunches and sipped our cartons of apple juice. Then in the late afternoon we drifted over to the parking lot with hundreds of other women to find the buses that would transport us back to New York City and our families. On another side of the Pentagon, Mailer was listening to the music of the Fugs and preparing himself to storm the barricades. But like the majority of people at the march, Rusty and I were intent on maintaining a peaceful demonstration. I was satisfied with my protest in Washington; it was clear that our group of mothers for peace had added to the crowd. I was still so naive that I felt that the presence of a large number of people would persuade the government to take our antiwar stance seriously.

III

By the end of 1969, there were protest demonstrations every month against the war. I kept a scrapbook for my two-year-old daughter, Mallay, and in it there is a clipping from the *New York Times* of November 15, 1969, a few days after my thirty-third birthday. The article is headlined "LIE-IN HELD IN CENTRAL PARK TO SYMBOLIZE THE DEAD IN VIETNAM." The accompanying photograph shows more than two thousand people lying in the grass in Central Park, each holding a black balloon or a white balloon. The line under the photo reads "Antiwar demonstrators show black balloons for those who have died and white for future victims."

Earlier that afternoon—it was a chilly, damp, bleak November Friday—I finished teaching, went home to change into a windbreaker and blue jeans, and then rode the subway from Brooklyn Heights up to Central Park. I don't recall how I heard about the demonstration, but when I came up the stairs out of the subway exit, I saw organizers standing nearby distributing thousands of black and white balloons. I took two of them and trudged across Sheep Meadow to find myself an empty space between the bodies sprawled out on the lawn. There I lay down with strangers. Later, in Mallay's scrapbook, I wrote under the newspaper photo, "Look closely & you'll find Annie lying in the heap of bodies protesting the Vietnam War. It was mucky on the ground, but everybody was there TOGETHER—holding hands with balloons in long ragged lines, listening to the drumrolls and the bugle playing taps, going down together."

I didn't regard the afternoon lying with my balloons in Central Park as a march, or even as much of a demonstration. The organizers had estimated that ten thousand people would show up, but there were many fewer of us there. The event was so dispirited that when I got back home, I told Sam that I felt nothing much had happened: I was just being used as a body. I was beginning to lose my faith that peace demonstrations could stop the war. Then the next morning I read in the *New York Times* that FBI agents had persuaded suburban bus companies to cancel their contracts at the last minute, so fewer groups of demonstrators from out of town had transportation into Manhattan. That explained the subdued mood of the people handing out the balloons. As the war escalated, I was learning that the game could get rough.

IV

Less than six months later, on April 30, 1970, President Richard Nixon ordered U.S. troops into Cambodia. There were immediate demonstrations on American college campuses. On May 1, Nixon, chatting with a group of people from the Pentagon, criticized "these bums" on college campuses who burn books and "blow up buildings." On May 2 and 3, more students joined in the protests against both the invasion of Cambodia and the Black Panther trial in New Haven, Connecticut. Then, on May 4, during a campus antiwar demonstration, National Guard troops fired on and killed four Kent State University students. Nixon's response had been to tell reporters, "This should remind us all again that when dissent turns to violence it invites tragedy." Enough.

The week took on its own momentum. May 5, the New Mobilization Committee to End the War in Vietnam called for a massive demonstration on Saturday, May 9, at Lafayette Square, across from the White House. They anticipated a crowd of 35,000 (50,000 to 100,000 people actually came). Protests erupted on 225 campuses on May 6. May 7, 5,000 U.S. troops were placed on special alert in Washington for Saturday's demonstration. May 8, Nixon approved plans for a crowd to gather on the Ellipse, south of the White House. At least 200 colleges closed down with student strikes organized by the National Student Association.

This time Sam and I wanted to attend the Saturday demonstration in Washington together. We had New York friends who had recently moved to Georgetown along with their daughter, Juliana, who was Mallay's closest playmate. We couldn't reach our friends by phone, so we sent a telegram, asking if we could stay with them and leave Mallay there while we went to the Ellipse. They telegraphed back: "Dearest Charters, Will take Mallay with us Saturday. Please come. Susan, Bart and Juliana." This was complicated, because although we had been close friends for nearly three years while we lived in the same apartment building in Brooklyn Heights, they hadn't been involved in protests against the war in Vietnam. In fact, they had friends in Nixon's government who had arranged a job for Bart in Washington in finance and banking.

Late Friday, while we were packing to drive to Georgetown, I received a second telegram, this one from my brother in Los Angeles. My father had died suddenly of a heart attack. I phoned our travel agent and booked myself a flight from Washington to Los Angeles on Sunday afternoon, the day after the demonstration. My father had been ill for many years, but I was still upset. I wanted to help my mother and brother in Los Angeles, yet it was unthinkable not to go to Washington first. So Sam and I put our suitcases in the car and drove down with Mallay, who stayed awake the entire trip, not understanding that Juliana wasn't waiting for her around the next bend in the highway. When we got to Georgetown at ten P.M., Mallay woke up her friend, and the two little girls stayed awake until the early hours of the morning. We sat talking to Susan and Bart, all of us apprehensive about the next day's demonstration. After the shootings at Kent State, none of us were sure of what would happen next.

Late the next morning, after Susan helped me pack a lunch of peanut butter sandwiches and juice, Bart dropped us off near the Ellipse to join the many thousands of people gathered there. He told us to think of him and Susan, while they watched Mallay, but we noticed that he carefully didn't say that we should march for them. It was warm in the sun, and crowds milled around the speakers' platform. We were given black paper armbands to wear, in memory of the four slain students. I put mine on, but I felt troubled doing it, thinking of my father lying in a funeral home in Los Angeles. We also took a copy of the mimeographed paper distributed by the marshals. Headlined "Preparation for the Demonstration," it spelled out our situation in simple terms:

1. Women: wear pants; don't wear earrings or jewelry.
2. Everyone: wear heavy shoes. Don't wear glasses unless necessary. Wear a sweater or a heavy coat.
3. Bring plastic goggles if gas is expected.
4. Bring a handkerchief for protection of nose and mouth in case of gas. Bring Vaseline to cover exposed skin.
5. Carry phone numbers of a lawyer or legal defense office and medical facilities.
6. Never carry drugs at a demonstration.
7. Bring cigarettes (if you smoke); candy bars in case you get busted.
8. Never take an address book with you.

9. Never carry a penknife or anything else that could be construed as a concealed weapon.
10. Carry a small first-aid kit if you have one.
11. Think through your reasons for being at the demonstration.
12. Think about the possible situations that may arise and how you should respond to them.
13. Come psychologically as well as physically prepared.
14. Know the area you are in and how to get out of it in case of trouble.
15. Have some idea of what you are doing, why you are doing it, and the possible consequences.   PEACE

It was clear from just reading the list that everyone was expecting trouble from the police and the military troops massed all around us. The atmosphere was tense. We stood on the grass and listened to Jane Fonda and the other speakers gathered on a platform. We'd heard the speeches before, but this moment seemed different. After Kent State, there was an angry sense of purpose, and more people assembled than we had ever seen before. Sam told me that in November 1965, when he came to Washington for his first antiwar demonstration, he joined a crowd of less than fifty people. Then the organizers spaced everyone out on the sidewalk, kneeling ten or twelve feet apart, and the FBI photographers came, bent down in front of each person, and took a quick mug shot.

This time, Sam had decided to do something on his own. Standing in the crowd, he told me that if he could get past the parade marshals assembled in front of us, he was going to attack the White House. I was startled, but I knew immediately what I wanted to do. I said that I wouldn't follow him, but I'd wait and get him out of jail. When the parade began, we could hear Allen Ginsberg chanting "Om Om" somewhere ahead, even if we couldn't see him, in an effort to calm the crowd and stave off violence. The sun gleamed down on us, rising higher in the sky, getting hotter. It was well past noon.

Following directions, we assembled by chance with a group of students from Juilliard, musicians who reminded me of my students at the community college where I was teaching in New York City, except that these young men and women joked nervously that they had to be very careful of their hands. Most people wore jeans and T-shirts, but it was so hot that Sam took off his shirt. We walked slowly, moving in fits and starts, packed closely together, toward the White House, talking about New York concerts and classical music recordings.

Our group was carrying four simulated coffins, wooden frames with black paper stapled to them, which I thought were intended to be symbolically delivered to Nixon in the White House. Sam and I each took hold of the side of a coffin, staying together in the crowd. I was glad to be participating in the march, yet I tore off my armband, because my father had died and I felt that I wanted my armband to be for him, even more than I mourned the four Kent State students. Then something unexpected happened. As the procession of thousands of people began to turn a corner, we encountered parade marshals—mostly college students trying to keep peace—who told us to march away from the White House, to turn right at the corner. Behind the marshals, we could see the police barricades.

Sam looked at me and said that he was not going to turn right at the corner. It had been a long, hot march, and he wasn't going to turn away and follow the Juilliard students. I stayed at his side as he pushed past the marshals. We broke through the barricades and found ourselves caught up in a new group of marchers, who were headed toward the White House. By the time we had gone two blocks we were surrounded by a different crowd. The Juilliard students had evaporated. Around us were men who struck me as being older and tougher than the students. I thought they looked like bikers or professional demonstrators; probably some were undercover agents. Every one of them looked strong and muscular, wearing gloves and helmets and bandannas and plastic goggles, ready for the tear gas.

We kept walking, pressed tightly together. Gradually we got close enough to the White House at Seventeenth and H Streets NW to see that the fence around the lawn was ringed with buses parked nose to tail. It was impossible for a person to squeeze between them. In front of the buses was a line of police. The marshals hurried to stay ahead of us, shouting, "Don't throw stones! Don't attack!" But around us, angry people were shouting back, ready to throw stones.

Sam broke away from me and moved ahead, supporting the front end of a coffin, trying to get past the police and take the coffin over the bus. I moved back, away from the massing crowd of men, watching to see what would happen to Sam. Some men were taunting the police. Other marchers helped Sam climb the side of the bus, still holding on to the flimsy coffin. For a brief moment, perched on the top of the bus, he caught a clear view of the White House lawn. It was filled with a line of soldiers standing shoulder to shoulder in gas masks, attaching bayonets to their weapons.

Seized by policemen, Sam was hurled off the bus. Luckily the men gathered behind him cushioned his fall. He pushed through the demonstrators to join me at the curb, and we stayed in the middle of the street for the rest of the afternoon. Frightened that the police would throw their tear gas canisters to disperse us, I asked Sam how I'd know tear gas; what did it smell like? He answered, "You'll know." When tear gas began to drift over the crowd a block away, the marshals offered us their canteens of water so we could moisten our cotton bandannas and hold them over our faces. Most of the tear gas didn't reach our section of the street. But someone close by told us that he had once been hit by a tear gas canister, and rumors circulated like crazy.

It was very noisy in the crowd, with shouts and sirens and the chaotic sound of fifty thousand people talking at once. For the most part, we stayed calm, aware that the police couldn't arrest all of us. We decided to wait until six P.M. We knew that we couldn't do anything, but we insisted that we would not leave. If Nixon looked out of his White House window, he couldn't help but see us. That gave me enormous satisfaction somehow. The police understood that we weren't going to try to do anything more, so there was a tense, wary feeling of truce. We were hot and sweaty, but we stayed. I kept moving between the street and the shade of the sidewalk, alternating between my deep concern for Sam, in the company of the potentially rowdy demonstrators, and my desire not to get arrested so I could get back to little Mallay in Georgetown with our friends.

At six P.M. it was time to leave. Slowly we walked back to our friends' house. Mallay had been playing all afternoon with Juliana, and both children greeted us with smiles. Susan and Bart took us inside, offered us cool drinks and dinner while we slumped on the floor of their living room. A couple of their friends were there, the man a businessman like Bart. They looked at us, sunburned and tired, and asked us what we had been through. When Bart's friend left, he said to Sam with a smile, "I'm going to the White House tomorrow to meet Nixon. Is there anything you want me to tell him?"

In Washington we had come face-to-face with two irreconcilable sides of America—the angry protest on the streets and the generous hospitality of our friends, people we had known for years whose jobs were dependent on a president whose actions we detested and feared.

I was confused. There was no way to resolve the situation. Later that evening, Bart put on the television news, which he and Susan had already seen at six o'clock. I remember Sam continued to lie on the floor, too tired to shower, reluctant to dirty the white slipcovers on the sofas and chairs. All of us watched the film of him climbing the bus, attempting to hurl his simulated coffin onto the White House lawn. None of us had much to say by the end of the evening.

The next morning, I took a plane to Los Angeles for my father's funeral while Sam and Mallay spent a few more hours with our friends before driving back home to Brooklyn Heights. I never marched in another anti–Vietnam War demonstration.

Norman Mailer

The March on Washington in October 1967 to protest the escalating war in Vietnam was one of the major peace demonstrations of the 1960s. Denise Levertov and her husband, Mitchell Goodman, along with Robert Lowell, Norman Mailer, Grace Paley, and many other writers, helped to plan the demonstration, which involved turning in thousands of draft cards collected from male students on college campuses throughout the country to the Justice Department on October 16, and marching on the Pentagon five days later.

The novelist Norman Mailer, author of the 1948 bestseller The Naked and the Dead, *about the Second World War, and other books, including* Why Are We in Vietnam? *(1967), wrote about his involvement in the October 1967 March on Washington in* The Armies of the Night *(1968). He subtitled his book "History as a Novel / The Novel as History."*

Writing in the third person about himself with a deliberately egocentric prose style in Part One ("History as a Novel: The Steps of the Pentagon"), Mailer described his series of adventures over the four days leading up to the confrontation at the Pentagon, with his friends Robert Lowell and Dwight Macdonald, against the military police. In Part Two ("The Novel as History: The Battle of the Pentagon"), his mood darkened when he chronicled the end of the march. He reported on the experiences of the more radical demonstrators, mostly members of the Students for a Democratic Society and a smaller group of "unattached elements who had once called themselves the Revolutionary Contingent, but had been unable to function together because of many arguments on the proper style of their militancy." Before being dragged off to jail, this group forced a brutal confrontation with the military troops surrounding the Pentagon as midnight approached and the permit allowing the time for the march expired.

In choosing a title for his book, Mailer alluded to the crisis of faith expressed in the well-known poem "Dover Beach," composed by the English writer Matthew Arnold in 1867. A century later, it was also Mailer's theme in The Armies of the Night. *"Dover Beach" concludes,*

> *Ah, love, let us be true*
> *To one another! for the world, which seems*
> *To lie before us like a land of dreams,*
> *So various, so beautiful, so new,*
> *Hath really neither joy, nor love, nor light,*
> *Nor certitude, nor peace, nor help for pain;*
> *And we are here as on a darkling plain*
> *Swept with confused alarms of struggle and flight,*
> *Where ignorant armies clash by night.*

Mailer understood, as he wrote in his book, that the stakes were particularly high at the Washington demonstration. While the entire world looked on, the basic principles of American democracy were being tested during the antiwar protests, the Civil Rights demonstrations, and the student riots occurring simultaneously at the end of the 1960s throughout the United States:

> *An open white riot in the streets of the Capital after the summer riots in the Negro ghettos would telegraph a portrait of America to Global Village as an explosively unstable nation, therefore a dangerous nation on whom to count for long-term alliances since the explosiveness gave every sign of increase. Moreover, the possibility of a number of white Americans seriously wounded or*

*killed by police, troops, or U.S. Marshals after the
government's refusal to permit civil disobedience was even
worse to contemplate.*

The Armies of the Night *was Mailer's most dramatic and
powerful statement of his belief that President Lyndon Johnson and
his advisers had brought the United States to a point of crisis. In his
final paragraph, Mailer voiced his fear that their government would
"probably give birth, and to what?—the most fearsome totalitarian-
ism the world has ever known?" In the section titled "A Con-
frontation by the River," he described his arrest by the military
police guarding the Pentagon.*

A CONFRONTATION BY THE RIVER

IT WAS NOT MUCH of a situation to study. The MPs stood in two
widely spaced ranks. The first rank was ten yards behind the rope, and
each MP in that row was close to twenty feet from the next man. The
second rank, similarly spaced, was ten yards behind the first rank and
perhaps thirty yards behind them a cluster appeared, every fifty yards
or so, of two or three U.S. Marshals in white helmets and dark blue
suits. They were out there waiting. Two moods confronted one an-
other, two separate senses of a private silence.

It was not unlike being a boy about to jump from one garage
roof to an adjoining garage roof. The one thing not to do was wait.
Mailer looked at Macdonald and Lowell. "Let's go," he said. Not
looking again at them, not pausing to gather or dissipate resolve, he
made a point of stepping neatly and decisively over the low rope.
Then he headed across the grass to the nearest MP he saw.

It was as if the air had changed, or light had altered; he felt im-
mediately much more alive—yes, bathed in air—and yet disembodied
from himself, as if indeed he were watching himself in a film where
this action was taking place. He could feel the eyes of the people be-
hind the rope watching him, could feel the intensity of their existence
as spectators. And as he walked forward, he and the MP looked at one
another with the naked stricken lucidity which comes when absolute
strangers are for the moment absolutely locked together.

The MP lifted his club to his chest as if to bar all passage. To
Mailer's great surprise—he had secretly expected the enemy to be
calm and strong, why should they not? they had every power, all the

guns—to his great surprise, the MP was trembling. He was a young Negro, part white, who looked to have come from some small town where perhaps there were not many other Negroes; he had at any rate no Harlem smoke, no devil swish, no black, no black power for him, just a simple boy in an Army suit with a look of horror in his eye, "Why, why did it have to happen to me?" was the message of the petrified marbles in his face.

"Go back," he said hoarsely to Mailer.

"If you don't arrest me, I'm going to the Pentagon."

"No. Go back."

The thought of a return—"since they won't arrest me, what can I do?"—over these same ten yards was not at all suitable.

As the MP spoke, the raised club quivered. He did not know if it quivered from the desire of the MP to strike him, or—secret military wonder—was he now possessed of a moral force which implanted terror in the arms of young soldiers? Some unfamiliar current, now gyroscopic, now a sluggish whirlpool, was evolving from that quiver of the club, and the MP seemed to turn slowly away from his position confronting the rope, and the novelist turned with him, each still facing the other until the axis of their shoulders was now perpendicular to the rope, and still they kept turning in this psychic field, not touching, the club quivering, and then Mailer was behind the MP, he was free of him, and he wheeled around and kept going in a half run to the next line of MPs and then on the push of a sudden instinct, sprinted suddenly around the nearest MP in the second line, much as if he were a back cutting around the nearest man in the secondary to break free—that was actually his precise thought—and had a passing perception of how simple it was to get past these MPs. They looked petrified. Stricken faces as he went by. They did not know what to do. It was his dark pinstripe suit, his vest, the maroon and blue regimental tie, the part in his hair, the barrel chest, the early paunch—he must have looked like a banker himself, a banker gone ape! And then he saw the Pentagon to his right across the field, not a hundred yards away, and a little to his left, the marshals, and he ran on a jog toward them, and came up, and they glared at him and shouted, "Go back."

He had a quick impression of hard-faced men with gray eyes burning some transparent fuel for flame, and said, "I won't go back. If you don't arrest me, I'm going on to the Pentagon," and knew he meant it, some absolute certainty had come to him, and then two of them leaped on him at once in the cold clammy murderous fury of all cops at the existential moment of making their bust—all cops who secretly expect to be struck at that instant for their sins—and a surprising force came to his voice, and he roared, to his own distant pleasure in new achievement and new authority—"Take your hands off me, can't you see? I'm not resisting arrest," and one then let go of him, and the other stopped trying to pry his arm into a lock, and contented himself with a hard hand under his armpit, and they set off walking across the field at a rapid intent quick rate, walking parallel to the wall of the Pentagon, fully visible on his right at last, and he was arrested, he had succeeded in that, and without a club on his head, the mountain air in his lungs as thin and fierce as smoke, yes, the livid air of tension on this livid side promised a few events of more interest than the routine wait to be free, yes he was more than a visitor, he was in the land of the enemy now, he would get to see their face.

Robert Chatain

Much of the writing against the war in Vietnam was created by people who saw active duty there. Robert Chatain was drafted into the army after his graduation from Columbia College in 1965. His original conception for his story "On the Perimeter" was to write twenty-four fragments describing a typical twenty-four-hour day of his assignment in Vietnam. The sections in this excerpt appeared in New American Review *13 in 1971.*

FROM ON THE PERIMETER

Zone

THE TATTERED JUNGLE beyond the barbed wire had been declared a free-fire zone in late June. Looking forward to spending at least five of my remaining ten weeks of war in permanent duty on the bunker line (the unofficial transfer was complete; even my "Visit Gay, Historic Vietnam" poster had been torn from the AG barracks wall and sent along with me to the ordnance company's security platoon, so determined was Colonel Hamilton to purge from his new command any taint of the pacifist subversion he had uncovered), I decided to free-fire.

I had access, over the weeks, to M-14's, M-16's, machine guns, grenade launchers, and an occasional pistol. The M-14 had been my weapon in basic training; I was a good shot. With it I could cut down plant stalks at ten meters, hit beer cans and bottles at thirty; I drew beads on man-sized stumps and bushes as far away as I could see them and was sure some of my shots found their targets. I could also kill birds.

The M-16 I found disappointing. Its horizontal drift gave me trouble. Its ugly black stock was not long enough for my reach. The pistol grip fell awkwardly into my palm. Its sight was blunt. Obviously the weapon had not been designed for target practice. Remembering an old account of Marines dead on the slopes of Hill 881 with their M-16's broken down beside them, I wondered what it had been designed for.

The M-60 machine gun was a thrill. Fire at a patch of bare earth produced satisfying explosions of dirt, leaves, garbage, and anything else lying in the radius of my bullets. With a short burst one evening I tore a metal water can to shreds. The next night I opened up on the struts and wires of the old crippled powerline support tower I had begun to think of almost as a friend. Most of the rounds went through into empty air.

The powerlines were also a good place to aim the M-79 grenade launcher. If I connected, the grenades exploded high above the ground and fragmentation pellets clattered on the worn steel.

I discovered that pistols demanded more practice than I could manage without attracting attention. Free-fire was permitted, but some discretion was expected. Exorbitant waste of ammunition was discouraged. At the infrequent moments when a pistol found itself in my hand I shot at the rats foraging openly in the barbed wire for scraps of food. I never hit them.

I did this free-firing at dusk, after the trucks had gone back across no-man's-land through the interior perimeter gate into the ammunition depot; if the sergeant on my section of the perimeter called, I could explain that I was testing my bunker's arsenal. Firing after dark always drew such panic from the neighboring bunkers that I soon gave it up. Firing at dawn—I never fired at dawn. Dawn did not seem like the right time to fire.

Once I would have been ashamed to find myself willingly associating with these weapons. But I was alone. The guns were clean, well-made, efficient, impersonal. And I suppose that the problem of my former negative feelings toward weaponry had been solved. Guns were of some use, I admitted. In the proper circumstances I think I could have shot Colonel Hamilton without batting an eye.

Maze

A rat's sleek head caught in the red beam of the flashlight triggered somber, fretful ruminations. How deep do they burrow? How many live in this hill with me? How do they know to avoid the pale yellow sticks of rat poison scattered in the corners of the bunker and outside under the clean starlight? Intelligent rats, well-fed on candy bars and C-ration tins, uninterested in poison. Their squeaks as they prowled around the base of my high perch on the stacked ammunition boxes. Their scuttling down below my dangling feet with cockroaches and scorpions. Don't reach down there, not for ammunition, not for anything. If you drop something, leave it until morning. Thousands in this mound of earth. Holes in the floorboards, holes in the walls, holes in the heavy timbers overhead. The sandbag slope alive with rats scurrying in the moonlight. Nocturnal. Remaining in tunnels during the day. Long tunnels, winding back upon themselves, coiling for miles. VC moving south in such tunnels, some captured with stories of traveling two hundred miles underground. Black-clad VC no older than fifteen sitting with their backs to dirt tunnel walls, singing. Underground hospitals. Operations underground, emergency lights flickering. Underground at Dien Bien Phu the wounded finding their wounds infested with maggots. The maggots beneficial, eating rotten tissue, leaving healthy. Time passing slowly. The wounded lying in darkness tended by blind worms.

I shifted my position. The rat vanished into its cavity.

Test

Just before midnight the sound of a jeep on the perimeter road pulled me to the back of the bunker. Without hesitation I challenged the man who emerged; I was an old hand at the game. He identified himself as a corporal on official business. I let him climb the catwalk. He dropped into the bunker next to me and told me to relax. I relaxed. The corporal struck a match and studied his watch. I loaned him my flashlight. I saw that he carried a clipboard and a folded piece of paper. At what must have been precisely midnight, he ceremoniously handed me the paper. I asked him what the hell it was. "Black handicap message," he announced.

"What the hell is that?"

He seemed surprised. "A black handicap message," he repeated.

I looked at the piece of paper, unfolding it, and read only a small group of neatly typed numbers.

"It's a test," he said. "Don't you know what to do?"

Obviously I did not know what to do.

The corporal shook his head and sighed. "You guys are all supposed to know what to do with one of these. That's the way it goes, you don't know what you're doing, they don't know what they're doing, and I sure don't know what I'm doing."

"So what's it all about?" I asked.

"All right," he said, "you call your command bunker and tell the sergeant you've got a black handicap message. You read off the numbers. The sergeant copies them down and passes them on."

"Should I do it now?"

"Yeah, you should do it now."

I cranked the field phone, reached the sergeant in Bunker 12, gave him my information, and hung up. The corporal retrieved his piece of paper and turned to go.

"Hold it," I said. "What the hell is going on?"

He explained. A black handicap message tested the efficiency of communications along the chain of command. Originating in my humble bunker, those numbers would be passed from one headquarters to the next until they arrived at the Pentagon itself. Crucial to the test was not only correct transmission of the number series, but also the amount of time required to pass information through command channels. "Are you bullshitting me?" I asked.

"Would anyone come way out here in the middle of the night to bullshit you?" The corporal hoisted himself up out of the bunker and descended the catwalk to his jeep.

"Hey, how long does it usually take?" I asked.

"I don't know. A couple of hours. Who gives a shit?" He

wheeled his jeep around on the narrow road and raced back along the perimeter into the night, anxious for the safety of the depot.

Miami

The passing of the broom from one bunker to the next was a time-honored ritual that had survived the earlier attacks on the ammunition depot, the physical deterioration of the bunkers during the months since their construction, even the coming of the monsoon and subsequent reduction in the amount of dust to be swept from the bunks and floorboards. No one remembered when the last inspection of the bunker line had been made, but still the broom passed every night. It was a good chance to catch up on the news.

"You hear about Fine?"

"No."

"Got orders for the Congo. Diplomatic mission. Far out."

"Hm."

"You haven't heard about the new offensive in September?"

"No."

"Supposed to be a big offensive in September, big as Tet."

"Hm."

"You hear about all the fucking money they dug up near Qui Nhon?"

"No."

"A hundred and fifty grand, all in fifty-dollar bills. The Treasury Department says there isn't supposed to be any fifty-dollar bills over here. We're paying for both fucking sides of this war."

"Hm."

"You hear about the Republicans?"

"No."

"Nominated Richard Nixon."

"Hm."

Perfume

We lit up any time after midnight. No one traveled the perimeter road after midnight.

"Ah-ha!"

Voice and boots on the catwalk startled us.

"What is that delightful odor? Could it be—? Yes, I think it is!"

A stranger climbed unhindered into our bunker. I was too stunned even to try to challenge him. But there was nothing to fear. He was a PFC from that night's reaction force, out alone for a hike and a smoke.

"We've got an IG. The fools are awake cleaning the barracks. I snuck out."

We got acquainted.

"Let me lay some of this on you people."

I inhaled.

The stranger went his way.

One of the two guards spending the night with me slept; in slow motion, the other climbed onto the upper bunk. "Jesus, what a buzz I've got. Wow, I can't stand up, I've got to sit down. Wow, I think I might get sick."

I draped my arm over the machine gun and bored into the luminous jungle with my eyes.

Product

The C-rations had been packed a long time ago, everybody knew, but nobody knew just when, perhaps as far back as World War II. Most of the food tasted pretty good, considering. Inside the unmarked gray cardboard cartons there were tins of "main dish," various small tins (cheese and crackers in one, fruit dessert in another, etc.), and cellophane bags containing fork, napkin, salt, pepper, sugar, dehydrated cream, and ten cigarettes. Of the main dish selections, some were choice (tuna, ham), some not so choice (veal, hamburgers), some inedible (bacon and eggs). All of the tins were olive green; contents were printed in black according to a standard form, noun first, adjectives trailing with their commas. Brand name appeared only as a means of identifying the packer. I visualized dozens of cartoon factories turning out these uniform dark green tins and gray cardboard boxes, selfless owners and managers eschewing profitable competition to serve their country, patriotic stockholders approving, grim-faced workers unaware of any change.

In the bunkers we encountered one major problem with C-rations: the familiar ingenious government-issue P-38 can opener was not included in every C-ration box. In fact, finding a P-38 in your box was a little like finding a prize in a package of breakfast cereal. It was something to cherish, because those C-ration cans were *hard*. They conformed to *government specifications.* They were *tin cans,* not aluminum cans or vinyl-covered cardboard cans. With a good pair of pliers and a lot of time you could worry one open; artful wielding of a bayonet produced primitive but satisfactory results; blunt instruments cracked the cans but wasted most of their contents; shooting them, although entertaining, was not a good idea nourishment-wise; various other schemes occurred to me at various times, but a P-38 was the only guaranteed method of success. Without one, you might go hungry. I knew several men who carried them around their necks where they hung their dog-tags. One man wore a P-38 on the same chain with his crucifix.

Chicago

First I heard that large demonstrations were planned, which was to be expected, and that the Mayor had announced he would keep order, which was also to be expected. Then I heard that twenty thousand troops would be on hand and that sixty black GI's had staged a sit-down strike at Fort Hood when ordered to go. From an amateur political analyst I understood that Gene had no chance, George had no chance, and if Hubert didn't take it on the first ballot, Teddy would get the nod. I was reminded that labor troubles in the city had affected transportation and communications. I discovered that the FBI had unearthed plans to dump LSD into the city's water supply. I read that the Unit Rule had been abolished, a "peace plank" had been proposed by a minority of the Platform Committee, and Georgia's Lester Maddox group had not been seated pending the outcome of a challenge by a rival delegation. A sergeant told me about a lot of violence in Lincoln Park. I found out that the peace plank had been respectably defeated. I was informed that city police had apparently gone crazy, injuring hundreds of people. A crowd had been pushed through the plate-glass window of the Hilton Hotel's Haymarket Lounge, someone reported. I saw a remarkable *Stars and Stripes* headline which read, "Police Storm Hotel, Beat McCarthy Aides." There was speculation that newsmen were being deliberately assaulted. I learned that Hubert Humphrey had received the Democratic nomination. I was told of a silent candle-light parade by delegates from the Amphitheater to the Loop.

Riot

The MP was unsympathetic. "We'll let them live in their own filth as long as they want."

"You mean they're still loose?"

"Loose? Hell, no. They got one part of the compound, is all. They're not going anywhere."

"Did some escape?"

He shrugged. "Hard to tell, with all the records gone. May be a couple of weeks before they get a good head count."

"I wonder if a guy named Forbes was in the stockade."

"No idea."

"Larry Forbes. He was in for pot. I understood that they were going to move all the narcotics guys to Okinawa."

"I don't know. I don't think so." He lit a cigarette and glanced at the rain heading toward us.

"Was a guy named Haines Cook still there?"

"What, do you know everybody in LBJ?"

I chuckled nervously.

"The whole deal was chicken-shit," the MP said.

"But somebody got killed, didn't he?"

"Yeah. Big deal. One out of seven hundred."

"Out of how many?"

"About seven hundred, more or less. Give or take a few."

"In that one spot? I've seen it; it's only two blocks long!"

"It's a lot smaller than that now, and most of what's left is charcoal."

A few drops of rain fell.

"I've got to take off, I'm going to get wet," the MP said.

"Did you guys use tear gas?"

"Shit yeah."

"Many people get hurt?"

"Mostly them."

"How come you went in?"

"Well, what are you going to do? Let a bunch of militants take the place over?"

Rain was falling harder. On the road the other men in the detail struggled to secure a tarpaulin over the trailer-load of old ammunition they had collected from the bunker. At my feet, my new shells gleamed in their fresh boxes.

"What's the status of things now?" I asked.

"Most everyone is sleeping outside; the fucking Afros are fenced off by themselves. When they feel like giving their right names, they can come out."

"I guess technically it was the worst stockade riot in Army history."

The MP sneered. "Technically."

Garbage

As I approached the magic thirty-day mark, that date when I could no longer be reassigned, transferred, lent out on temporary duty, or otherwise fucked with, the orderly room sent me an out-processing slip and told me to begin working on it. The next day an order arrived removing me from the guard roster and dumping me back into Headquarters Company as a nominal duty soldier, although I was expected to spend most of my time staying out of everybody's way. Reshevsky let me know that I was not supposed to report back to the AG Section. This was fine with me.

On the last night out I caught a ride from the bunker line directly back to the company area. Hart was driving; it seems that Colonel Hamilton had overheard one of his monologues on death and had reassigned him to the supply room. I sat in the cab of the truck with him. His headlights didn't work and he wanted to make it back before the light failed; he asked me about a short cut along the perimeter road to the construction work at the new supply battalion warehouses. I had seen jeeps travel off in that direction, so we gave it a try. Hart must have missed the turn. We wound up in pitch darkness somewhere southeast of Long Binh looking for the 1st Aviation helipad. I spotted a glow on our left and we drove overland toward it. Hart bounced the truck through a series of shallow trenches and then we were in the midst of the Long Binh garbage dump. The stench was dizzying. Murky fires flickered and smoldered. Smoke blinded us. I climbed out on the running board and tried to tell Hart which way to turn. The engine stalled. Hart began to cry. I considered it, but collapsed instead into helpless laughter.

Michael Herr

Until Esquire *magazine sent Michael Herr to Vietnam in 1967 to write an article about the Americanization of Saigon, he had been reviewing films for the* New Leader. *Herr was in Khesanh during the Vietcong siege. He later told an interviewer, "You lost your noncombatant status very quickly, because nobody thought they were going to get out alive. At first I didn't feel like I was covering anything. I just felt very lost."*

Herr's Dispatches *(1977) exposed the moral dilemma of the American presence in Vietnam. In Herr's awareness of his own complex but always unheroic role as a war correspondent, the war had found its ideal reporter. As Stewart O'Nan understood, the book "takes the reader seemingly everywhere in-country by chopper, touching down with Herr in the middle of the first rock 'n' roll war. While Herr is writing nonfiction, he never lets the reader assume his objectivity, often focusing on his own strange, even parasitic role in the proceedings." After completing* Dispatches, *Herr went to Hollywood to work on the scripts for two Vietnam war films,* Apocalpyse Now *and* Full Metal Jacket.

FROM *DISPATCHES*

THE DEATH OF MARTIN LUTHER KING intruded on the war in a way that no other outside event had ever done. In the days that followed, there were a number of small, scattered riots, one or two stabbings, all of it denied officially. The Marine recreational facility in China Beach in Danang was put off-limits for a day, and at Stud we stood around the radio and listened to the sound of automatic-weapons fire being broadcast from a number of American cities. A southern colonel on the general's staff told me that it was a shame, a damn shame, but I had to admit (didn't I?) that he'd been a long time asking for it. A black staff sergeant in the Cav who had taken me over to his outfit for dinner the night before cut me dead on the day that we heard the news, but he came over to the press tent later that night and told me that it shouldn't happen that way. I got a bottle of Scotch from my pack and we went outside and sat on the grass, watching the flares dropping over the hillside across the river. There were still some night mists. In the flarelight it looked like heavy snow, and the ravines looked like ski trails.

He was from Alabama and he had all but decided on a career in the Army. Even before King's murder he had seen what this might someday mean, but he'd always hoped to get around it somehow.

"Now what I gonna do?" he said.

"I'm a great one to ask."

"But dig it. Am I gonna take 'n' turn them guns aroun' on my own people? Shit!"

That was it, there was hardly a black NCO anywhere who wasn't having to deal with that. We sat in the dark, and he told me that when he'd walked by me that afternoon it had made him sick. He couldn't help it.

"Shit, I can't do no twenny in this Army. They ain' no way. All's I hope is I can hang back when push comes t' shove. An' then I think, Well, fuck it, why should I? Man, home's jus' gonna be a hassle."

There was some firing on the hill, a dozen M-79 rounds and the dull bap-bap-bap of an AK-47, but that was over there, there was an entire American division between that and us. But the man was crying, trying to look away while I tried not to look.

"It's just a bad night for it," I said. "What can I tell you?"

He stood up, looked at the hill and then started to leave. "Oh, man," he said. "This war gets old."

At Langvei we found the two-month-old corpse of an American stretched out on the back of a wrecked jeep. This was on the top of the small hill that opposed the hill containing the Special Forces bunkers taken by the NVA in February. They were still in there, 700 meters away. The corpse was the worst thing we'd ever seen, utterly blackened now, the skin on the face drawn back tightly like stretched leather, so that all of his teeth showed. We were outraged that he had not been buried or at least covered, and we moved away and set up positions around the hill. Then the ARVN moved out toward the bunkers and were turned back by machine-gun fire. We sat on the hill and watched while napalm was dropped against the bunkers, and then we set up a recoilless rifle and fired at the vents. I went back to Stud. The next day a company of the Cav tried it, moving in two files on high and low ground approaching the bunkers, but the terrain between the hills offered almost no cover, and they were turned back.

That night they were rocketed heavily, but took no serious casualties. I came back on the third day with Rick Merron and John Lengle of the Associated Press. There had been heavy airstrikes against the bunkers that night, and now two tiny helicopters, Loaches, were hovering a few feet above the slits, pouring in fire.

"Man, one Dink with a forty-five could put a hurtin' on those Loaches they'd never come back from," a young captain said. It was incredible, those little ships were the most beautiful things flying in Vietnam (you had to stop once in a while and admire the machinery), they just hung there above those bunkers like wasps outside a nest. "That's sex," the captain said. "That's pure sex."

One of the Loaches rose suddenly and flew over the hill, crossed the river and darted into Laos. Then it circled quickly, dipped, flew directly over us and hung there. The pilot radioed the captain.

"Sir, there's a gook di-di-ing down the trail into Laos. Permission to kill him."

"Permission given."

"Thank you," the pilot said, and the ship broke its suspended motion and sped toward the trail, clearing its guns.

A rocket whistled by, missing the hill, and we ran for the bunkers. Two more came in, both missing, and then we moved out for the opposite hill one more time, watching the machine-gun slits for fluttering blips of light with one eye and checking the ground for booby traps with the other. But they had abandoned it during the night, and we took it without a shot, standing on top of the bunkers, looking down into Laos, past the remains of two bombed-out Russian tanks, feeling relieved, victorious and silly. When Merron and I flew back to Stud that afternoon, the two-month-old corpse rode with us. No one had covered him until ten minutes before the chopper had picked us up, and the body bag swarmed with flies until the motion of the rising chopper shook them off. We got out at Graves Registration with it, where one of the guys opened the bag and said, "Shit, this is a *gook!* What'd they bring him *here* for?"

"Look, Jesus, he's got on our uniform."

"I don't give a fuck, that ain't no American, that's a fucking *gook!*"

"Wait a minute," the other one said. "Maybe it's a spade. . . ."

Tim O'Brien

In the 1970s, after the American troops pulled out of Vietnam, our involvement in the war led to an outpouring of novels, poetry, memoirs, and films about the conflict. Titles included novelists Ron Kovic's Born on the Fourth of July *(1976), Philip Caputo's* A Rumor of War *(1977), James Webb's* Fields of Fire *(1978), and Tim O'Brien's* If I Die in a Combat Zone, Box Me Up and Ship Me Home *(1973),* Northern Lights *(1975),* Going After Cacciato *(1978),* The Nuclear Age *(1981, 1985), and* In the Lake of the Woods *(1994). American women writers also created strong fiction about the war, including Louise Erdrich's* Love Medicine *(1984) and Bobbie Ann Mason's* In Country *(1985).*

Tim O'Brien, generally regarded as the major writer of Vietnam War fiction, was drafted shortly after his college graduation in 1968 and served two years in the U.S. Army, one of them as an infantryman in Vietnam. There he became a sergeant and received a Purple Heart. The Things They Carried *(1990) is a collection of interlinked stories narrated by a character named Tim O'Brien, who is both the real-life author and his fictional double. This narrative strategy allows O'Brien to explore the bottomless reserves of guilt he feels about his participation in the war, especially about his feeling of responsibility for the deaths of members of his own company, as well as the Vietcong he was brought in to kill. As he wrote in his "Notes" to* The Things They Carried,

> *For years I'd felt a certain smugness about how easily I had made the shift from war to peace. A nice smooth glide—no flashbacks or midnight sweats. The war was over, after all. And the thing to do was go on. So I took pride in sliding gracefully from Vietnam to graduate school, from Chu Lai to Harvard, from one world to another. In ordinary conversation I never spoke much about the war, certainly not in detail, and yet ever since my return I had been talking about it virtually nonstop through my writing. Telling stories seemed a natural, inevitable process, like clearing the throat. Partly catharsis, partly communication, it was a way of grabbing*

> *people by the shirt and explaining exactly what had*
> *happened to me, how I'd allowed myself to get dragged*
> *into a wrong war, all the mistakes I'd made, all the*
> *terrible things I had seen and done.*

O'Brien never resolved his complex feelings about his war ex-periences in The Things They Carried, *even if in the act of sto-rytelling, he hoped to show that you can "objectify your own experience. You separate it from yourself. You pin down certain truths. You make up others. You start sometimes with an incident that truly happened . . . and you carry it forward by inventing inci-dents that did not in fact occur but that nonetheless help to clarify and explain." O'Brien's emotional conflict in the stories is ulti-mately always about himself and his own role in the war, even when he is ostensibly describing violent combat action or other soldiers, as in "The Man I Killed."*

THE MAN I KILLED

HIS JAW WAS IN HIS THROAT, his upper lip and teeth were gone, his one eye was shut, his other eye was a star-shaped hole, his eyebrows were thin and arched like a woman's, his nose was undamaged, there was a slight tear at the lobe of one ear, his clean black hair was swept upward into a cowlick at the rear of the skull, his forehead was lightly freckled, his fingernails were clean, the skin at his left cheek was peeled back in three ragged strips, his right cheek was smooth and hairless, there was a butterfly on his chin, his neck was open to the spinal cord and the blood there was thick and shiny and it was this wound that had killed him. He lay face-up in the center of the trail, a slim, dead, almost dainty young man. He had bony legs, a narrow waist, long shapely fingers. His chest was sunken and poorly mus-cled—a scholar, maybe. His wrists were the wrists of a child. He wore a black shirt, black pajama pants, a gray ammunition belt, a gold ring on the third finger of his right hand. His rubber sandals had been blown off. One lay beside him, the other a few meters up the trail. He had been born, maybe, in 1946 in the village of My Khe near the central coastline of Quang Ngai Province, where his parents farmed, and where his family had lived for several centuries, and where, dur-ing the time of the French, his father and two uncles and many neigh-bors had joined in the struggle for independence. He was not a

Communist. He was a citizen and a soldier. In the village of My Khe, as in all of Quang Ngai, patriotic resistance had the force of tradition, which was partly the force of legend, and from his earliest boyhood the man I killed would have listened to stories about the heroic Trung sisters and Tran Hung Dao's famous rout of the Mongols and Le Loi's final victory against the Chinese at Tot Dong. He would have been taught that to defend the land was a man's highest duty and highest privilege. He had accepted this. It was never open to question. Secretly, though, it also frightened him. He was not a fighter. His health was poor, his body small and frail. He liked books. He wanted someday to be a teacher of mathematics. At night, lying on his mat, he could not picture himself doing the brave things his father had done, or his uncles, or the heroes of the stories. He hoped in his heart that he would never be tested. He hoped the Americans would go away. Soon, he hoped. He kept hoping and hoping, always, even when he was asleep.

"Oh, man, you fuckin' trashed the fucker," Azar said. "You scrambled his sorry self, look at that, you *did,* you laid him out like Shredded fuckin' Wheat."

"Go away," Kiowa said.

"I'm just saying the truth. Like oatmeal."

"Go," Kiowa said.

"Okay, then, I take it back," Azar said. He started to move away, then stopped and said, "Rice Krispies, you know? On the dead test, this particular individual gets A-plus."

Smiling at this, he shrugged and walked up the trail toward the village behind the trees.

Kiowa kneeled down.

"Just forget that crud," he said. He opened up his canteen and held it out for a while and then sighed and pulled it away. "No sweat, man. What else could you do?"

Later, Kiowa said, "I'm serious. Nothing *anybody* could do. Come on, stop staring."

The trail junction was shaded by a row of trees and tall brush. The slim young man lay with his legs in the shade. His jaw was in his throat. His one eye was shut and the other was a star-shaped hole.

Kiowa glanced at the body.

"All right, let me ask a question," he said. "You want to trade places with him? Turn it all upside down—you *want* that? I mean, be honest."

The star-shaped hole was red and yellow. The yellow part seemed to be getting wider, spreading out at the center of the star. The upper lip and gum and teeth were gone. The man's head was cocked at a wrong angle, as if loose at the neck, and the neck was wet with blood.

"Think it over," Kiowa said.

Then later he said, "Tim, it's a *war*. The guy wasn't Heidi—he had a weapon, right? It's a tough thing, for sure, but you got to cut out that staring."

Then he said, "Maybe you better lie down a minute."

Then after a long empty time he said, "Take it slow. Just go wherever the spirit takes you."

The butterfly was making its way along the young man's forehead, which was spotted with small dark freckles. The nose was undamaged. The skin on the right cheek was smooth and fine-grained and hairless. Frail-looking, delicately boned, the young man would not have wanted to be a soldier and in his heart would have feared performing badly in battle. Even as a boy growing up in the village of My Khe, he had often worried about this. He imagined covering his head and lying in a deep hole and closing his eyes and not moving until the war was over. He had no stomach for violence. He loved mathematics. His eyebrows were thin and arched like a woman's, and at school the boys sometimes teased him about how pretty he was, the arched eyebrows and long shapely fingers, and on the playground they mimicked a woman's walk and made fun of his smooth skin and his love for mathematics. The young man could not make himself fight them. He often wanted to, but he was afraid, and this increased his shame. If he could not fight little boys, he thought, how could he ever become a soldier and fight the Americans with their airplanes and helicopters and bombs? It did not seem possible. In the presence of his father and uncles, he pretended to look forward to doing his patriotic duty, which was also a privilege, but at night he prayed with his mother that the war might end soon. Beyond anything else, he was afraid of disgracing himself, and therefore his family and village. But all he could do, he thought, was wait and pray and try not to grow up too fast.

"Listen to me," Kiowa said. "You feel terrible, I know that."

Then he said, "Okay, maybe I *don't* know."

Along the trail there were small blue flowers shaped like bells. The young man's head was wrenched sideways, not quite facing the flowers, and even in the shade a single blade of sunlight sparkled against the buckle of his ammunition belt. The left cheek was peeled back in three ragged strips. The wounds at his neck had not yet clotted, which made him seem animate even in death, the blood still spreading out across his shirt.

Kiowa shook his head.

There was some silence before he said, "Stop *staring.*"

The young man's fingernails were clean. There was a slight tear at the lobe of one ear, a sprinkling of blood on the forearm. He wore a gold ring on the third finger of his right hand. His chest was sunken and poorly muscled—a scholar, maybe. His life was now a constellation of possibilities. So, yes, maybe a scholar. And for years, despite his family's poverty, the man I killed would have been determined to continue his education in mathematics. The means for this were arranged, perhaps, through the village liberation cadres, and in 1964 the young man began attending classes at the university in Saigon, where he avoided politics and paid attention to the problems of calculus. He devoted himself to his studies. He spent his nights alone, wrote romantic poems in his journal, took pleasure in the grace and beauty of differential equations. The war, he knew, would finally take him, but for the time being he would not let himself think about it. He had stopped praying; instead, now, he waited. And as he waited, in his final year at the university, he fell in love with a classmate, a girl of seventeen, who one day told him that his wrists were like the wrists of a child, so small and delicate, and who admired his narrow waist and the cowlick that rose up like a bird's tail at the back of his head. She liked his quiet manner; she laughed at his freckles and bony legs. One evening, perhaps, they exchanged gold rings.

Now one eye was a star.

"You okay?" Kiowa said.

The body lay almost entirely in shade. There were gnats at the mouth, little flecks of pollen drifting above the nose. The butterfly was gone. The bleeding had stopped except for the neck wounds.

Kiowa picked up the rubber sandals, clapping off the dirt, then bent down to search the body. He found a pouch of rice, a comb, a fingernail clipper, a few soiled piasters, a snapshot of a young woman standing in front of a parked motorcycle. Kiowa placed these items in his rucksack along with the gray ammunition belt and rubber sandals.

Then he squatted down.

"I'll tell you the straight truth," he said. "The guy was dead the second he stepped on the trail. Understand me? We all had him zeroed. A good kill—weapon, ammunition, everything." Tiny beads of sweat glistened at Kiowa's forehead. His eyes moved from the sky to the dead man's body to the knuckles of his own hands. "So listen, you best pull your shit together. Can't just sit here all day."

Later he said, "Understand?"

Then he said, "Five minutes, Tim. Five more minutes and we're moving out."

The one eye did a funny twinkling trick, red to yellow. His head was wrenched sideways, as if loose at the neck, and the dead young man seemed to be staring at some distant object beyond the bell-shaped flowers along the trail. The blood at the neck had gone to a deep purplish black. Clean fingernails, clean hair—he had been a soldier for only a single day. After his years at the university, the man I killed returned with his new wife to the village of My Khe, where he enlisted as a common rifleman with the 48th Vietcong Battalion. He knew he would die quickly. He knew he would see a flash of light. He knew he would fall dead and wake up in the stories of his village and people.

Kiowa covered the body with a poncho.

"Hey, you're looking better," he said. "No doubt about it. All you needed was time—some mental R&R."

Then he said, "Man, I'm sorry."

Then later he said, "Why not talk about it?"

Then he said, "Come on, man, talk."

He was a slim, dead, almost dainty young man of about twenty. He lay with one leg bent beneath him, his jaw in his throat, his face neither expressive nor inexpressive. One eye was shut. The other was a star-shaped hole.

"Talk," Kiowa said.

———

Ron Kovic

Ron Kovic wrote Born on the Fourth of July *as a nonfiction account of his stint as a Marine in Vietnam and its painful aftermath. The dedication of his book reads "For my country and its people,*

happy birthday." Physically disabled from his wounds in combat,
Kovic was shipped back to the United States, where he waged an
emotionally debilitating war with the Veterans Administration. As
critic Stewart O'Nan understood, Kovic's narrative showed his
"progression from an idealistic teenager to a scared and bitter patient
and finally to a committed political activist." Born on the Fourth
of July was published in 1976; the director Oliver Stone made the
book into a popular movie in 1989. Here are the opening pages of
Kovic's poignant memoir.

FROM *BORN ON THE FOURTH OF JULY*

THE BUS TURNED OFF A SIDE STREET and onto the parkway, then into Queens where the hospital was. For the first time on the whole trip everyone was laughing and joking. He felt himself begin to wake up out of the nightmare. This whole area was home to him—the streets, the parkway, he knew them like the back of his hand. The air was fresh and cold and the bus rocked back and forth. "This bus sucks!" yelled a kid. "Can't you guys do any better than this? I want my mother, I want my mother."

The pain twisted into his back, but he laughed with the rest of them—the warriors, the wounded, entering the gates of St. Albans Naval Hospital. The guard waved them in and the bus stopped. He was the last of the men to be taken off the bus. They had to carry him off. He got the impression that he was quite an oddity in his steel frame, crammed inside it like a flattened pancake.

They put him on the neuro ward. It was sterile and quiet. I'm with the vegetables again, he thought. It took a long while to get hold of a nurse. He told her that if they didn't get the top of the frame off his back he would start screaming. They took it off him and moved him back downstairs to another ward. This was a ward for men with open wounds. They put him there because of his heel, which had been all smashed by the first bullet, the back of it blown completely out.

He was now in Ward 1-C with fifty other men who had all been recently wounded in the war—twenty-year-old blind men and amputees, men without intestines, men who limped, men who were in wheelchairs, men in pain. He noticed they all had strange smiles on their faces and he had one too, he thought. They were men who had played with death and cheated it at a very young age.

He lay back in his bed and watched everything happen all around him. He went to therapy every day and worked very hard lifting weights. He had to build up the top of his body if he was ever going to walk again. In Da Nang the doctors had told him to get used to the idea that he would have to sit in a wheelchair for the rest of his life. He had accepted it, but more and more he was dreaming and thinking about walking. He prayed every night after the visitors left. He closed his eyes and dreamed of being on his feet again.

Sometimes the American Legion group from his town came in to see him, the men and their wives and their pretty daughters. They would all surround him in his bed. It would seem to him that he was always having to cheer them up more than they were cheering him. They told him he was a hero and that all of Massapequa was proud of him. One time the commander stood up and said they were even thinking of naming a street after him. But the guy's wife was embarrassed and made her husband shut up. She told him the commander was kidding—he tended to get carried away after a couple of beers.

After he had been in the hospital a couple of weeks, a man appeared one morning and handed him a large envelope. He waited until the man had gone to open it up. Inside was a citation and a medal for Conspicuous Service to the State of New York. The citation was signed by Governor Rockefeller. He stuck the envelope and all the stuff in it under his pillow.

None of the men on the wards were civilian yet, so they had reveille at six o'clock in the morning. All the wounded who could get on their feet were made to stand in front of their beds while a roll call was taken. After roll call they all had to make their beds and do a general clean-up of the entire ward—everything from scrubbing the floors to cleaning the windows. Even the amputees had to do it. No one ever bothered him, though. He usually slept through the whole thing.

Later it would be time for medication, and afterward one of the corpsmen would put him in a wheelchair and push him to the shower room. The corpsman would leave him alone for about five minutes, then pick his body up, putting him on a wooden bench, his legs dangling, his toes barely touching the floor. He would sit in the shower like that every morning watching his legs become smaller and smaller, until after a month the muscle tone had all but disappeared. With despair and frustration he watched his once strong twenty-one-year-old body become crippled and disfigured. He was just beginning to understand the nature of his wound. He knew now it was the worst he could have received without dying or becoming a vegetable.

More and more he thought about what a priest had said to him in Da Nang: "Your fight is just beginning. Sometimes no one will want to hear what you're going through. You are going to have to learn to carry a great burden and most of your learning will be done alone. Don't feel frightened when they leave you. I'm sure you will come through it all okay."

——————

Janice Mirikitani

During the Vietnam War, the young Japanese-American poet Janice Mirikitani was struck by a newspaper photograph of the face of a Vietnamese woman who bore an unmistakable resemblance to Mirikitani's grandmother. In the poem "Attack the Water," Mirikitani expressed her painful sense of connection with the suffering caused by war at all times and in all countries throughout the world. Mirikitani's poem was included in David Hsin-Fu Wand's anthology Asian–American Heritage *(1974).*

ATTACK THE WATER

My first flash
on the newsprint/face
she could have been
obachan[1]
back then/just after
the camps
when the land/dried/up
no water for months.

———
1. The Japanese word for *grandmother.*

In town,
they would not sell
to japs.
we had to eat what
we could grow
that's only natural
when there is nothing
else
nothing
          else.

we ate rice with roots & rooster legs.

          Vietnamese woman
          her face etched old
          by newsprint/war
          mother/grandmother
          she has borne them all
          (have they all died?)

                    flash!!

          "they are bombing the waterways

          "this new offensive
          which has previously/been/avoided/
          for humanitarian/reasons/
          will/seriously/jeopardize/
          their/food/situation."

Obachan
sitting
breathing heavily
in the sun
watching her pet rabbits
(she loved them like children)
which one/
tonight?
i still remember her eyes
drawing the blood
like water.

And the rice—
there were maggots
in the rice.
no water
to flush/them/out.

> Up river
> bodies floated in My Chanh
> eyes eaten by crabs
> flushed onto the land—
> fly food.
> "They are attacking the water.
> when all else fails
> attack the water."

Obachan
would chew
the food first/spit
out maggots.
Grandchildren
ate the spit-flushed rice.

> when all else fails
> attack the water.

———————————

Yusef Komunyakaa

Memories of the traumatic events of the war in Vietnam are the source of the poetry of Yusef Komunyakaa in Dien Cai Dau, *a collection of poems chronicling his experiences as a journalist in Vietnam, which won the Pulitzer Prize for poetry in 1994. "Tunnels," "Hanoi Hannah," " 'You and I Are Disappearing,' " "2527th Birthday of the Buddha," "Prisoners," and "Facing It," Komun-*

yakaa's response to the Vietnam Veterans Memorial in Washington, D.C., are from this volume. "Nude Interrogation" was included in Thieves of Paradise *(1998).*

TUNNELS

Crawling down headfirst into the hole,
he kicks the air & disappears.
I feel like I'm down there
with him, moving ahead, pushed
by a river of darkness, feeling
blessed for each inch of the unknown.
Our tunnel rat is the smallest man
in the platoon, in an echo chamber
that makes his ears bleed
when he pulls the trigger.
He moves as if trying to outdo
blind fish easing toward imagined blue,
pulled by something greater than life's
ambitions. He can't think about
spiders & scorpions mending the air,
or care about bats upside down
like gods in the mole's blackness.
The damp smell goes deeper
than the stench of honey buckets.
A web of booby traps waits, ready
to spring into broken stars.
Forced onward by some need,
some urge, he knows the pulse
of mysteries & diversions
like thoughts trapped in the ground.
He questions each root.
Every cornered shadow has a life
to bargain with. Like an angel
pushed against what hurts,
his globe–shaped helmet
follows the gold ring his flashlight
casts into the void. Through silver
lice, shit, maggots, & vapor of pestilence,

he goes, the good soldier,
on hands & knees, tunneling past
death sacked into a blind corner,
loving the weight of the shotgun
that will someday dig his grave.

HANOI HANNAH

Ray Charles! His voice
calls from waist-high grass,
& we duck behind gray sandbags.
"Hello, Soul Brothers. Yeah,
Georgia's also on my mind."
Flares bloom over the trees.
"Here's Hannah again.
Let's see if we can't
light her goddamn fuse
this time." Artillery
shells carve a white arc
against dusk. Her voice rises
from a hedgerow on our left.
"It's Saturday night in the States.
Guess what your woman's doing tonight.
I think I'll let Tina Turner
tell you, you homesick GIs."
Howitzers buck like a herd
of horses behind concertina.
"You know you're dead men,
don't you? You're dead
as King today in Memphis.
Boys, you're surrounded by
General Tran Do's division."
Her knife-edge song cuts
deep as a sniper's bullet.
"Soul Brothers, what you dying for?"
We lay down a white-klieg
trail of tracers. Phantom jets
fan out over the trees.
Artillery fire zeros in.

Her voice grows flesh
& we can see her falling
into words, a bleeding flower.

"YOU AND I ARE DISAPPEARING"

—Björn Håkansson

The cry I bring down from the hills
belongs to a girl still burning
inside my head. At daybreak
        she burns like a piece of paper.

She burns like foxfire
in a thigh-shaped valley.
A skirt of flames
dances around her
at dusk.
        We stand with our hands
hanging at our sides,
while she burns
        like a sack of dry ice.
She burns like oil on water.
She burns like a cattail torch
dipped in gasoline.
She glows like the fat tip
of a banker's cigar,
        silent as quicksilver.
A tiger under a rainbow
    at nightfall.
She burns like a shot glass of vodka.
She burns like a field of poppies
at the edge of a rain forest.
She rises like dragonsmoke
    to my nostrils.
She burns like a burning bush
driven by a godawful wind.

2527TH BIRTHDAY OF THE BUDDHA

When the motorcade rolled to a halt, Quang Duc
climbed out & sat down in the street.
He crossed his legs,
& the other monks & nuns grew around him like petals.
He challenged the morning sun,
debating with the air
he leafed through—visions brought down to earth.
Could his eyes burn the devil out of men?

A breath of peppermint oil
soothed someone's cry. Beyond terror made flesh—
he burned like a bundle of black joss sticks.
A high wind that started in California
fanned flames, turned each blue page,
leaving only his heart intact.
Waves of saffron robes bowed to the gasoline can.

PRISONERS

Usually at the helipad
I see them stumble-dance
across the hot asphalt
with croaker sacks over their heads,
moving toward the interrogation huts,
thin-framed as box kites
of sticks & black silk
anticipating a hard wind
that'll tug & snatch them
out into space. I think
some must be laughing
under their dust-colored hoods,
knowing rockets are aimed
at Chu Lai, that the water's
evaporating & soon the nail
will make contact with metal.

How can anyone anywhere love
these half-broken figures
bent under the sky's brightness?
The weight they carry
is the soil we tread night & day.
Who can cry for them?
I've heard the old ones
are the hardest to break.
An arm twist, a combat boot
against the skull, a .45
jabbed into the mouth, nothing
works. When they start talking
with ancestors faint as camphor
smoke in pagodas, you know
you'll have to kill them
to get an answer.
Sunlight throws
scythes against the afternoon.
Everything's a heat mirage; a river
tugs at their slow feet.
I stand alone & amazed,
with a pill-happy door gunner
signaling for me to board the Cobra.
One day, I almost bowed
to such figures walking toward me,
& I can't say why.
From a half-mile away
trees huddle together,
& the prisoners look like
marionettes hooked to strings of light.

NUDE INTERROGATION

DID YOU KILL ANYONE OVER THERE? Angelica shifts her gaze from
the Janis Joplin poster to the Jimi Hendrix, lifting the pale muslin
blouse over her head. The blacklight deepens the blues when the
needle drops into the first groove of "All Along the Watchtower." I
don't want to look at the floor. *Did you kill anyone? Did you dig a hole,
crawl inside, and wait for your target?* Her miniskirt drops into a rainbow
at her feet. Sandalwood incense hangs a slow comet of perfume over

the room. I shake my head. She unhooks her bra and flings it against a bookcase made of plywood and cinderblocks. *Did you use an M-16, a hand-grenade, a bayonet, or your own two strong hands, both thumbs pressed against that little bird in the throat?* She stands with her left thumb hooked into the elastic of her sky-blue panties. When she flicks off the blacklight, snowy hills rush up to the windows. *Did you kill anyone over there? Are you right-handed or left-handed? Did you drop your gun afterwards? Did you kneel beside the corpse and turn it over?* She's nude against the falling snow. *Yes.* The record spins like a bull's eye on the far wall of Xanadu. *Yes,* I say. *I was scared of the silence. The night was too big. And afterwards, I couldn't stop looking up at the sky.*

FACING IT

My black face fades,
hiding inside the black granite.
I said I wouldn't
dammit: No tears.
I'm stone. I'm flesh.
My clouded reflection eyes me
like a bird of prey, the profile of night
slanted against morning. I turn
this way—the stone lets me go.
I turn that way—I'm inside
the Vietnam Veterans Memorial
again, depending on the light
to make a difference.
I go down the 58,022 names,
half-expecting to find
my own in letters like smoke.
I touch the name Andrew Johnson;
I see the booby trap's white flash.
Names shimmer on a woman's blouse
but when she walks away
the names stay on the wall.
Brushstrokes flash, a red bird's
wings cutting across my stare.
The sky. A plane in the sky.
A white vet's image floats
closer to me, then his pale eyes

look through mine. I'm a window.
He's lost his right arm
inside the stone. In the black mirror
a woman's trying to erase names:
No, she's brushing a boy's hair

———————

PART THREE

WHY CAN WE NOT BEGIN NEW?
THE FREE SPEECH
MOVEMENT AND BEYOND

A little while ago, something happened to me,
While I was taking a walk through the old U.C.
In front of Sproul Hall I was told to grab a seat,
When somebody hands me an apple to eat . . . so I ate it.
Figured I'd better stick around though, and see what it was all
  about.

Well, after I got done eating the fruit, I feeled the heel of a combat
  boot.
It was the cops, all right, and they was making their way
To a car with a roof like a big ash tray . . .
People on top of it . . . inside of it . . . all around it . . .
  bedpans out the window.

I'd knew'd then and there it was speeches they was making,
And all around me I could hear the eggs breaking,
And the sulphur stinks, and the Ex-Lax in our drinks,
I was wondering who would do these things.
Found out, though . . . soon enough. . . .

DAVE GENESEN, "FREE SPEECH DEMONSTRATION
TALKING BLUES" (1964)

IN MAY 1969, Governor Ronald Reagan called in the National Guard to maintain order in Berkeley after an angry crowd rioted in a futile effort to stop the University of California's repossession of a vacant lot a few blocks from the campus that had been landscaped by local citizens as a People's Park. The "Battle of Berkeley" was so intense that the police arrested nine hundred people after firing shotguns to disperse the crowd. One of the demonstrators, James Reston, was killed. As National Guardsmen patrolled the Berkeley streets, Governor Reagan summoned the university faculty to a meeting in order to rebuke them for having allowed students to organize their Free Speech Movement (FSM) in 1964.

The meeting was stormy. Refusing to listen to the protests of the professors, who insisted that the governor was out of touch with the

students and that his authoritarian methods of discipline were out-
dated and ineffectual, Reagan finally gathered his papers and prepared
to leave. As the film *Berkeley in the Sixties* documents, before Reagan
left the room, he spoke the last, bitter words: "All of this began the
first time some of you who know better—and are old enough to
know better—let young people think that they have the right to
choose the laws they would obey as long as they were doing it in the
name of social protest."

In the fall of 1964, the FSM began at the UC campus in Berke-
ley after the administration revoked permission for Civil Rights
activists to pass out literature outside Sather Gate at Bancroft and
Telegraph Avenues, the main southern entrance to the university.
Many of the student activists had spent their summer vacation regis-
tering black voters in Mississippi. Six months earlier, inspired by Civil
Rights action in the South, students had protested discriminatory hir-
ing at San Francisco hotels by staging a demonstration at the Sheraton
Palace Hotel. They utilized nonviolence strategies that led to the ar-
rest of a hundred students. After a trial, none of the convictions were
upheld, and the hotels agreed to employ black workers.

Attempting to placate the university trustees, who were alarmed
that students at the largest public university in the country were fo-
menting labor unrest in San Francisco, President Clark Kerr tried to
curb the activists on campus. Many members of the Board of Regents
supported FBI director J. Edgar Hoover's belief in an international
Communist conspiracy plotting to control for its own evil purposes
the naive students at the Berkeley campus, where there were top
secret, federally funded nuclear laboratories. Kerr denied students a
forum to spread information about off-campus events supporting so-
called liberal causes, such as meetings to plan Civil Rights demonstra-
tions and debate the testing of nuclear weapons. On September 30,
1964, eight students were suspended for "illegal activity" at tables
near Sather Gate.

The next day, when former student Jack Weinberg defied the
ban and set up a table to distribute Civil Rights literature, the campus
police were called in. They arrested Weinberg for trespassing and
placed him in a squad car on Sproul Plaza inside the Sather Gate. A
mob (only one out of nine was actually enrolled at the university)
quickly surrounded the car so that it couldn't be moved. Weinberg,
who later originated the slogan "Don't trust anyone over thirty," sat in
the car for two days, while thousands of bystanders gave speeches,

sang songs, and milled about. Mario Savio, a junior at UC Berkeley, took off his shoes to stand on top of the car and address the crowd. He was such an engaging speaker that he became the leader of the activists. On October 2, an agreement was reached stipulating that the fate of the eight suspended students would be turned over to the Academic Senate Committee on Student Conduct.

By mid-October, the Campus Committee on Political Activity (CCPA) was formed. When the Berkeley faculty and administration continued to insist on regulating the content of "free speech" expressed on campus, the students protested that they should be able to advocate as they saw fit, arguing that "if civil authorities don't find the advocacy illegal, or don't act against it, then the students should be immune from university discipline."

In early November, the FSM representatives again set up their tables at Sather Gate, despite the administrative ban, and the suspension of the eight students was lifted. But after a series of articles by Pulitzer Prize–winning reporter Ed Montgomery in the *San Francisco Examiner* depicting the FSM as a "Marxist-dominated" plot to disrupt American colleges, and a meeting of the university's regents on November 20, 1964, President Kerr announced severe punishment for the previously suspended students and proposed a single rule to cover the issue of free speech. He stipulated that "campus facilities . . . may be used . . . for planning, implementing, raising funds, recruiting participants for lawful off-campus action, not for unlawful off-campus action."

The response of the FSM leaders was to threaten a sit-in unless the administration agreed to drop all charges against FSM leaders, guarantee no further disciplinary action, allow political activity on campus, and persuade the regents that only the courts should regulate the content of on-campus political expression determined by a faculty-student committee. The administration ignored the FSM demands. On December 2 and 3, the demonstrators initiated a sit-in, occupying the four floors of Sproul Hall, the main campus administration building. At 3:45 A.M. on December 3, then-Governor Pat Brown ordered the police to arrest the demonstrators. Twelve hours later, after eight hundred students had been taken off to jail, the building was cleared.

By the end of December, the Committee on Academic Freedom of the Berkeley division of the Academic Senate released its recommendations, ending the battle. They authorized the FSM to hold its political rallies on the steps of Sproul Hall. This opened the door for Civil Rights and anti–Vietnam War demonstrations on the Berkeley campus, which were held nearly every day at noon.

To raise money for their organization, the FSM had published a pamphlet of songs in the fall of 1964. *The Free Speech Songbook* ("Songs of, by, and for the F.S.M.") sold for a quarter as the "suggested donation." They were inspired by the songs composed during the years of the Depression by American folksingers such as Woody Guthrie for socialist labor movement organizations. **Lee Felsenstein** wrote the introduction, which began,

> Throughout the free speech controversy it has been evident that the administration has assumed that the students would act as individuals who could be easily frightened away by a token exercise of authority. They expected that we would act with the same regard for precedent and pecking order that they had. The record has shown that we have acted more commendably.
>
> From the beginning we have acted as a group, a community which would suffer no individual to be singled out for punishment for what all had done or should have done. We have never turned our backs and hoped that the problem would go away if we ignored it. That course was consistently taken by the Administration, and their problems did not go away, but increased. Finally, they admitted defeat on December 3rd by calling in hundreds of policemen to drag the problems off to jail.
>
> The press has been almost uniformly unfavorable to us, to say the least. But there are among us many people who know from the examples of the IWW and the CIO that a good song lasts far longer and has a wider circulation than any editorial.
>
> And so the songs were written, for the most part individually by students caught up in the movement. The subjects are many, and more songs are constantly being written. . . . **Dave Mandel** wrote "Battle of Berkeley Talking Blues" which satirizes the events surrounding the October demonstrations. "Put My Name Down" was written by myself for Nov. 9th when the FSM again set up more tables and gave the Deans more names than they could handle. This is also the subject of Dan Paik's "There's a Man Taking Names."

"Hey, Mister Newsman" by **Richard Kampf** addresses itself to those journalists who pay more attention to unconventional dress than to the issues involved. . . . **Richard Schmorleitz,** press secretary of the FSM, found time from his duties to write "I Walked Out in Berkeley" along with **Dan Paik.** . . . There are more, for which I do not have space to mention.

These, then, are our songs, and they constitute a powerful weapon. No amount of sanctimonious speeches can stop them, no number of frantically summoned policemen can capture and imprison them. Sing them loud and sing them often. You will be helping to fight the battle for Constitutional rights.

The songs composed by the Berkeley students were taken up by socially committed performers like Phil Ochs and Joan Baez, who came to campus with their guitars to rouse the crowds at the demonstrations. The little song pamphlet also included a page of Christmas carols written as part of a songwriting project by Joe La Penta, Ken Sanderson, Dusty Miller, and Barry Jablon. It contained new titles such as "We Three Deans" (instead of "We Three Kings") and "O, Come All Ye Mindless," as well as new lyrics to be sung to such familiar old tunes as "Jingle Bells":

> Oski Dolls, Pompon Girls,
> U.C. all the way!
> Oh, what fun it is to have
> your mind reduced to clay!
> Civil rights, politics
> just get in the way.
> Questioning authority
> when you should obey.

A 45-rpm recording of the Christmas carols titled "Joy to U.C." sold so well that the demonstrators who packed Sproul Hall on December 3 sang the new words to the Christmas carols as well as other FSM songs to help keep up their spirits as the police entered the building and began to work over the crowd.

Dave Mandel

BATTLE OF BERKELEY TALKING BLUES

Let me tell you a tale of campus sin,
Of tables and regents and a big sit-in,
The day the students built a mountain
Atop a police car near Ludwigs fountain . . .
Defying law and order . . . thinking, God forbid!

It all started out near Sather Gate,
September 30th was the fateful date,
The rebels sat, tin cans in hand,
A threat to traffic on the Regents' land . . .
Sabotage by the I.S.C.; the Intracampus Slate Conspiracy.

The rebels were ousted, the tables banned,
The deans thought they had won their hand . . .
Then came a sight they never thought they'd see,
A genuine sit-in in the halls of Big C . . .
Civil Disobedience . . . an essay come alive . . . education
   in action.

Then Sproul Hall spoke in tones of woe:
"From our marble steps you'll have to go;
We wouldn't threaten, but we'll tell you true,
We might be forced to suspend you too!"
"Policy, y'know . . . regulations . . . we can back 'em up,
   too. Call out Knowland's police."

The students left the steps that night
But returned to the tables in a show of might.
The cops tried to split them, but to no avail;
Four hundred gladly went to jail . . .
   or built their own . . . a jail surrounded on all sides by
   prisoners!

Then came a show of patriotic might
Rotten eggs bursting by the dawn's early light;
Red-blooded lads from Fraternity Lane
Proudly upholding Cal's great name, shouting
   "We want our car . . . we want our . . . we want . . .
   we . . . . . . "

Friday eve brought a glorious sight
800 cops just itchin' for a fight;
Clark was bluffing, Mario knew,
But they signed a pact and the cops withdrew . . .
They'll write a book about it . . . they'll call it *A Motorcycle
   For Your Thoughts*.

The FSM is now in action;
At the Multi-U there's a multi-faction.
Free speech is coming 'cause some spoke out . . .
To get our rights we'll have to shout,
But don't worry . . . it's o.k. if you wake the people up,
   'cause morning's come.

———————————

Lee Felsenstein

PUT MY NAME DOWN

Chorus:
I'm going to put my name down, brother, where do I sign?
        Sometimes you have to lay your body on the
           line,
        We're going to make this campus free
        And keep it safe for democracy
        I'm going to put my name down!

(Chorus)

We can't solicit funds, I thought you knowed,
That would be a hideous crime, 'way down the road,
I got a brother in a southern jail,
And he needs money for his bail, so
I'm going to put my name down!

(Chorus)

We're going to have Clark Kerr's job, I thought you
    knowed,
We're going to see him unemployed, 'way down the road,
We're going to give him that good old deadline,
Make that headline or make that breadline,
I'm going to put my name down!

(Chorus)

Take the students back, they said, I thought you knowed,
At least until you've proven them guilty, 'way down the road,
Clark Kerr simply uttered "No,"
The Constitution's red, you know,
I'm going to put my name down!

(Chorus)

We're going to break the rules, I thought you knowed,
Yes we're going to talk and think, 'way down the road,
What do we want, why the mess?
The Constitution, nothing less!
I'm going to put my name down!

(Chorus)

Richard Kampf

HEY MR. NEWSMAN

Hey Mister Newsman, how come you're taking pictures
   of me? (2x)
Is it 'cause of my long hair
Or 'cause of my boots up to my knees?

Hey Mr. Newsman, Abe Lincoln, he had long hair too (2x)
Or did you want Abe Lincoln
Would have a crewcut just like you?

You call me a Commie, say that all my friends are red, (2x)
But we've been freezing here for freedom
While you've been sleeping in your nice warm bed.

Don't know if I'm subversive, just want to say what I please.
   (2x)
Strange how us subversives
Keep fighting for democracy.

Yes, my hair is long, and I haven't shaved in days, (2x)
But fighting for my freedom
While clean-cut kids just look the other way.

My boots are old, and my collars don't button down (2x)
But you don't need no tuxedo
When you're fighting for the rights of man.

———

Dan Paik

THERE'S A MAN TAKING NAMES

(Chorus) There's a man goin' round takin' names (2x)
You may take my buddy's name,
But you gotta take me just the same.
There's a man goin' round takin' names.

I read my Constitution long ago (2x)
I read the Bill of Rights, read it nice and slow
I don't know much but this I know
They ain't got no right to take my name.

There's freedom in the air, baby mine (2x)
If it's a crime to speak your mind
I may be guilty, but I'm feeling fine
There's freedom in the air, baby mine.

Tell me which side are you on, baby mine (2x)
You gonna stop, turn, hide your face
Just when it looks like we'll win this race?
Which side are you on, baby mine.

———————————

Richard Schmorleitz and Dan Paik

I WALKED OUT IN BERKELEY

As I was out walking one morning in Berkeley,
As I walked out in Berkeley one day,
I spied an old man all sad and dejected
His hands they were shaking, his hair it was gray.

"I see by your books, boy, that you are a student"
These words he did say as I tried to go by,
"Come sit down beside me and hear my sad story"
He then shook his head and he gave a deep sigh.

"It is here on the campus that I am the Chancellor
I push the buttons and run the whole show,
These are my children but now they're ungrateful
They think they are adults, they think they are grown.

"Can you hear them shouting and screaming and singing?
They think they're so smart and they think they're so strong
They want to make speeches but never say nice things,
But they're only students so they're in the wrong.

"They stopped my cop car and kept making speeches,
Those beatniks and communists sat in my hall.
We can do without them, they always cause trouble,
This school'd look its best with no students at all."

It was then that I left him to go to my classes
But I heard some voices and noticed a crowd.
I left off my studies and listened to their side,
I gathered my books and sat down on the ground.

I wish he had been there to watch and to listen,
To hear what all of those students did say.
It wasn't a final or even a midterm
But we showed we'd learned something at Berkeley
    that day.

(Repeat first verse)

———————————

David Lance Goines

David Lance Goines described his arrest with hundreds of other students in Sproul Hall on December 3, 1964, in his book The Free Speech Movement *(1993). He subtitled it "Coming of Age in the 1960s." There was little doubt, as Eldridge Cleaver later wrote in* Soul on Ice *(1968), that the "spontaneous [Civil Rights] protests on southern campuses over the repressive measures of their college administrations" had shown the way for the Berkeley students. As Cleaver understood, "In countless ways, the rebellion of the black students served as catalyst for the brewing revolt of the whites."*

FROM *THE FREE SPEECH MOVEMENT*

HERE THEY COME! Get ready!"

"Don't link arms; go limp and make them carry you. Do *not* resist in any way. All you have to tell them is your name, and be sure to ask for a lawyer and a phone call. Does everybody have a dime? Don't answer any other questions. When you telephone, call Arrest Central. Give your own name and the names of everybody with you, and say where you are. We want to keep track of everybody. Make sure you've taken anything sharp, like pens and pencils, out of your pockets. Take off your buttons, the sharp pins could stick you. Girls, make sure you've taken off any dangly earrings. No tied scarves, take off your necklaces or bracelets. If you see any instances of brutality, get the officer's badge number."

The cops start with the people nearest the elevator, and methodically work their way through the tightly packed crowd. I'm about two-thirds of the way down the hall, leading singing. It's amazing—I can remember every word to every song I've ever heard. Usually I have trouble, and bog down after a verse or two. Not this morning. Civil rights songs, FSM Christmas carols, Leadbelly songs, chain-gang chants, spirituals, folk songs—anything I can think of that has a call-and-response; it doesn't much matter, what's important is that we keep on clapping and singing. Everybody's excited, but it's a fragile sort of excitement. Some of the girls look like they're going to cry. That would never do.

Ain't gonna let nobody turn me 'round, turn me 'round, turn me 'round . . .

. . . we shall not, we shall not be moved, just like a tree standing by the water, we shall not be moved.

One of the cops points at me, two others nod their heads.

God gave Moses the rainbow sign, no more water but fire next time.

. . . and before I'll be a slave, I'll be buried in my grave, and I'll fight for my right to be free.

Lots of yelling up near the elevator. Girls' screams.

. . . deep in my heart, I do believe, we shall overcome some day.

They get closer and closer, and I guess they've gotten tired of my voice, because they skip over a bunch of kids to get at me. The girl next to me gives me a hard hug; she's shaking like a leaf, and hasn't got any color at all in her face, eyes as big as saucers. I look up at the giant policemen looming over me. My stomach turns over.

"You are the forty-third person to be arrested this morning. Will you walk or do we have to carry you?"

No answer.

Two officers pick me up with a "come-along" hold, and involuntarily I rise to my feet, cursing and trying not to show that it hurts; I don't want to frighten the others. It feels like they're trying to break my wrist. I clamp my mouth shut. I can hear the singing starting up again behind me. At the end of the corridor, they toss me underhand into the elevator.

The basement smells like sweat. An officer pats me down, but without much conviction. Pretty slim pickin's among these college kids. The guy behind me gets the once-over-lightly, too.

Another officer holds a piece of paper with a number on it in front of me. Flash. "Turn to the right." Flash. It's 5:06 AM.

"Empty your pockets." The policeman puts everything into a paper envelope. "You can keep your smokes."

"Name?"

"David Goines."

"Age?"

"Nineteen."

"Address?"

"2252 Bancroft, Berkeley."

"Race?"

"Human."

The policeman checks off "Caucasian," giving me a weary "nobody likes a wise-ass" look.

"Give me your right hand." As he fingerprints me. "Give me your left hand." He repeats the process. None too gentle about it, either. I wipe my fingers on my pants.

There's no room anywhere for us to be held and more students are piling in every minute, so we're escorted out to an Alameda County Sheriff's bus, barred windows painted over with grimy white. I light up. I swear to God, the first drag on that cigarette is better than sex. Sitting in the bus for half an hour while it fills, swapping stories about what we've seen and what's happened, singing more songs just to show them, and all the kids outside around the busses, that we're not slowing down for a minute.

> *If you're ever in Berkeley*
> *Well, you better walk right,*
> *You better not picket,*
> *Or sit-in all night.*
> *Or Alameda sheriffs will arrest you*
> *And the boys will take you down,*
> *And before you get free speech,*
> *You're jailhouse bound.*
> *Let the midnight special*
> *Shine its light on me . . .*

Then the Greyhound bus station smell of diesel exhaust as we take off on a long ride to we-don't-know-where. My wrist has stopped hurting. Dawn is just breaking as we file off the bus into the holding tank at Santa Rita.

Early December, and cold as a brass bra. I don't have a coat. I had one when we went into Sproul Hall at noon, but somewhere along the line I gave it to somebody. They run us through a police-paperwork gauntlet and herd us off in untidy groups to empty, dim barracks. Chilly, but we're issued thin scratchy blankets from a pile. Army-surplus bunk beds set up every which way, bare springs with a stingy striped mattress folded up on top. The whole operation looks like it was thrown together with no notice. Chattering excitedly among ourselves, waiting to see what happens now. No cops around anywhere. Nobody I'm with has ever been arrested before. After a while, most of us are asleep. Around noon we get a bologna sandwich.

Two in the morning and the lights come on without any warning; we stagger off through the unfamiliar compound, bright lights on lampposts and guard towers puncturing the darkness, guards at the head and tail of our straggling column. That sick feeling of not enough sleep and being abruptly awakened heart-pounding where am I what's happening. Wish I had a cup of hot coffee. Somebody's gotten our bail together, and we're being processed out. A faculty member greets me at the gate; parked on the side of the highway are hundreds of cars: faculty and Berkeley citizens waiting to take their students home.

THE RULES OF THE GAME . . . WHEN YOU'RE BUSTED:[1]

IF STOPPED ON THE STREET, DON'T act furtive. Don't try to throw anything away, swallow anything, etc.

COOPERATE when asked innocuous questions, i.e, name, address—BUT if they ask to search you or your car or packages, etc., say NO. YOU HAVE THIS RIGHT. If they search you anyway, evidence so obtained will not stand up in court. If searched over your objections, get names and addresses of witnesses.

ASK the police if you are under arrest, if not, then there is generally no right to search you.

IF YOU ARE UNDER ARREST, the police must, according to the California Penal Code, do the following:

> § 841. [Informing person arrested.] The person making the arrest must inform the person to be arrested of the intention to arrest him, of the cause of the arrest, and the authority to make it, except when the person making the arrest has reasonable cause to believe that the person to be arrested is actually engaged in the commission of or an attempt to commit an offense, or the person to be arrested is pursued immediately after its commission, or after an escape. [Enacted 1872; Am. Stats. 1957, ch. 2147, § 3.]
>
> Method of making arrest: § 835.
>
> *Annotation:* See 3A McK. Dig. Arrest, §§ 13–16; Cal. Jur.2d Arrest §§ 21, 23, Searches and Seizures § 49; 4 Am. Jur. 43.

---

1. This document and "Wanted: Hip Cops," which follows on p. 207, were handed out on the streets of Berkeley during the FSM demonstrations.

If the police don't volunteer this information, ASK them . . .

> § 836. [Arrests by peace officers: Arrest under warrant or without warrant.] A peace officer may make an arrest in obedience to a warrant, or may without a warrant, arrest a person:
>
> 1. Whenever he has reasonable cause to believe that the person to be arrested has committed a public offense in his presence.
>
> 2. When a person arrested has committed a felony, although not in his presence.
>
> 3. Whenever he has reasonable cause to believe that the person to be arrested has committed a felony, whether or not a felony has in fact been committed. [Enacted 1872; Am. Stats. 1957, ch. 2147, § 2.]

DON'T RESIST ARREST . . .

> A peace officer who makes or attempts to make an arrest need not retreat or desist from his efforts by reason of the resistance or threatened resistance of the person being arrested; nor shall such officer be deemed an aggressor or lose his right to self-defense by the use of reasonable force to effect the arrest or to prevent escape or to overcome resistance. [Added by Stats. 1957, ch. 2147, § 11.]
>
> *Annotation:* See Cal. Jur.2d Arrest § 26.

REMEMBER, IF YOU ARE UNDER ARREST, THE SEARCH IS VALID. DON'T RESIST.

WANTED

HIP COPS

We know it's a heavy trip, but there are more than 30 vacancies on the Berkeley Police force. If hip people do not apply and go on to fill those vacancies, we'll get more of the same old stuff and have the same old hassles! Put yourself on the line—and get some change for it, too. **Starting pay for Berkeley officers is $782 per month.**

We want PEACEmen, not POLICEmen
If you are sane;
If you love children and other growing things;
If you do not like the use of force when gentleness will work;
If you will defend justice for all, regardless of race, appearance or politics;
If you believe that all people should be free to live their own lives if they do not harm others;
If you value people for themselves, not for their money or dress—
THEN WE NEED YOU TO REMOLD "THE MAN" AND HIS JOB.

MINIMUM REQUIREMENTS—Applicants must:
1. Be between 20 and 29 years old.
2. Have completed two years of college.
3. Be 5'-8" or taller and of proportionate weight.
4. Have a valid driver's license.
5. Be in good health and physical condition.
6. Have at least 20/70 correctable or 20/30 eyesight.
You must also be willing to undergo a medical examination, take a loyalty oath, and have a background check. You must be a United States citizen but need not live in Berkeley.

TO MAKE APPLICATION—Write to: Berkeley Police Department, Personnel Dept., 2100 Grove Street, Berkeley
Call: 841-0200
Recruiting information is available free from the Berkeley Police Department.

IF YOU APPLY—If you are hip (black, white, red, yellow or brown) and decide to apply, please notify the BBC or the Berkeley branch of the ACLU. We want to be sure that you are hired without prejudice as to your appearance, race, or background. BBC Patrol can be reached at 526-6370. ACLU can be reached at 548-0921, or at 1919 Berkeley Way.

Published as a public service by **The Better Berkeley Council**, 1534 Grove Street, Berkeley

Allen Ginsberg

*In November 1965 another demonstration march was planned in
Berkeley to protest the draft and the war in Vietnam. The Free
Speech Movement invited poet Allen Ginsberg to suggest ways to
deflect the violence if the local Hell's Angels motorcycle gang, who
supported the war as patriotic American citizens, attacked the stu-
dent demonstrators. Ginsberg's suggestions were published in the*
Berkeley Barb *on November 19, 1965, under the title "Demon-
stration or Spectacle As Example, As Communication or How to
Make a March/Spectacle."*

DEMONSTRATION OR SPECTACLE
AS EXAMPLE, AS COMMUNICATION
OR
HOW TO MAKE A MARCH/SPECTACLE

IF IMAGINATIVE, pragmatic, fun, gay, happy, *secure* Propaganda is is-
sued to mass media in advance (and pragmatic leaflets handed out days
in advance giving marchers instructions) the parade can be made into
an exemplary spectacle on how to handle situations of anxiety and
fear/threat (such as specter of Hell's Angels or specter of Commu-
nism) to manifest by concrete example, namely the parade itself, how
to change war psychology and surpass, go over, the habit-image-
reaction of fear/violence.

That is, the parade can embody an example of peaceable health
which is the reverse of fighting back blindly.

Announce in advance it is a safe march, bring your grandmother
and babies, bring your family and friends. Open declarations, "We
aren't coming out to fight and we simply will not fight."

We have to use our *imagination*. A spectacle can be made, an unmis-
takable statement OUTSIDE the war psychology which is lead-
ing nowhere. Such statement would be heard around the world with
relief.

The following suggestions manifest or embody what I believe to
be the conscious psychology of latent understanding of the majority
of the youth and many elders who come out to march.

And once clearly enunciated by the leaders of the march will be clearly understood and acted upon by them. Necessary to TRUST the communal sanity of the marchers who already demonstrated that community when they first SAT DOWN.

Needed: an example of health which will paralyze the Angels and also manifest itself thru mass media reportage.

N.B. A negative psychology, of becoming scared by threats, adrenaline running in neck, uprush of blood to head, blind resentment, self-righteousness, fear, anger and active return of violence is exactly what the [Hell's] Angels' "power structure" press and fuzz THRIVE ON what the young people who come [to] march don't want and are dragged by what will decrease the number who come and discourage the great many on the fence who would come to a good scene.

The following are specific suggestions for organizing march and turning marchers on to their roles in the demonstration.

1. Masses of flowers—a visual spectacle—especially concentrated in the front lines. Can be used to set up barricades, to present to Hell's Angels, police, politicians, and press and spectators whenever needed or at parade's end. Masses of marchers can be asked to bring their own flowers. Front lines should be organized and provided with flowers in advance.
2. Front lines should be the psychologically less vulnerable groups. The Women for Peace or any other respectable organization, perhaps a line of poets and artists, mothers, families, professors. This should also be announced (publicized in advance).
3. Marchers should bring crosses, to be held up in front in case of violence; like in the movies dealing with Dracula. (This for those who use crosses or Jewish stars.)
4. Marchers who use American flags should bring those: at least one front row of American flags and myriad in the spectacle.
5. Marchers should bring harmonicas, flutes, recorders, guitars, banjos and violins. (Those who don't use crosses or flags.) Bongos and tambourines.
6. Marchers should bring certain children's toys (not firecrackers or balloons which cause noise hysteria)

which can be used for distracting attackers: such as sparklers, toy rubber swords, especially the little whirling carbon wheels which make red-white-blue sparkles, toy soldiers.

7. In case of heavy anxiety, confusion or struggle in isolated spots marchers could be led in
>   Sit Down
>   Mass Calisthenics
>   In case of threat of attack marchers could intone en masse the following mantras:
>   The Lord's Prayer
>   Three Blind Mice (sung)
>   OM (AUM) long breath in unison
>   Star Spangled Banner
>   Mary Had a Little Lamb (spoken in unison)

8. More interesting Zen/Spectacle SIGNS
>   As In Oakland So In Vietnam
>   Everybody's Made Of Meat
>   Nobody Wants To Get Hurt—Us Or Them
>   Everybody's Wrong Including U.S.
>   Hell's Angels Vietcong Birch Society
>   DON'T FLIP
>   We Love You Too

9. Candy bars carried by marchers to offer Hell's Angels and police.

10. Marchers encouraged to carry copies of the Constitution if they have them; or can buy them.

11. Little paper halos to offer Angels, police and spectators and patriots.

12. A row of marchers with white flags and many white flags in mass.

13. Those who have movie cameras bring them and take pictures of spectacle or any action. (To combine for documentary film which could be used in court in case of legal hassles later, and also to circulate for propaganda and profits.) Monitors who can should have cameras.

OTHER MORE GRANDIOSE POSSIBILITIES.

14. Corps of student newsmen to interview newsmen, propagandize and soften and charm TV crews etc.

15. Small floats or replicas in front:

> Christ with sacred heart and cross (invite church groups to prepare)
>
> Buddha in meditation (invite Zen people to come march and meditate on floats)
>
> George Washington, Lincoln, Whitman, etc. (float or living masquerade)
>
> Thoreau behind bars (float)
>
> Hell's Angels float—with halos, happy, praying (no ugly provocative caricature)
>
> Birch Society float (old ladies in tennis sneakers)
>
> Dixieland Band float dressed as Hitler Stalin Mussolini
>
> Napoleon and Caesar (See "Universal Soldier" song).

16. At first sign of disturbance, public address systems swing into vast sound to loud *Beatles* "I Wanna Hold Your Hand" and marchers instructed to dance (if not doing calisthenics or Lord's Prayer). (These could be schematized as strategy 1, 2, 3, etc. for diverting crowd and angels from violence.)

17. The Mime Troupe in costume a block down the march, walking doing pantomime.

18. Sound tracks with Bay area rock 'n' roll bands every 2 blocks, Jefferson Airplane, The Charlatans, etc. (These bands have their own sound systems.) Family Dogg people might be able to arrange this. This scheme to pick up on the universal youth rockroll protest of Dylan, "Eve of Destruction," "Universal Soldier," etc. and concretize all that consciousness in the parade.

19. Front (or toward front)—toy army in costume, Civil War or Revolutionary War or WWI uniforms and signs.

> NO MORE
>
> LEAVE ME ALONE

Addenda: Pre-March Propaganda

1. Muslims, unions etc. all invited to join *inside* the masses.

2. Leaflets with above instructions to marchers how to channel their anxiety and respond to attack.

3. Daily delegations to Hell's Angels to talk to them, pestering them in advance.

4. Petitions and letters and news releases to papers setting tone of march: Petitions to [Gov.] Brown, open letter to Hell's Angels—one news release (We're NOT going to fight); open letters to Young Republicans, Democrats, Birchers, Army, Johnson etc. All the propaganda suggested at Tuesday meeting—conferences with Oakland police to force them to keep peace.

5. Emphasize in propaganda TRUST THE MARCHERS to be hip, calm and tranquil with a sense of humor and not get sidetracked into frustration/personal violence.

6. Perhaps as propaganda, an imaginary ladies corps to pull down Hell's Angels pants in case of attack, or a (theoretical) corps of trained fairies to seduce them in mid-battle. This is a sort of press release joke to lighten the atmosphere.

Hunter Thompson

Hunter Thompson, the talented journalist who became a historian of the counterculture, published his first book in 1967, titled Hell's Angels: A Strange and Terrible Saga. *At the time he was a national correspondent for the* Reporter *and the* Nation, *while he moonlighted as a contributor to* Spider *magazine, a publication of the Free Speech Movement at Berkeley. In his book about the Hell's Angels, he described introducing them in 1965 to the young novelist Ken Kesey. Kesey was then living near La Honda, south of San Francisco, after having left his home in Perry Lane, Palo Alto, where he had written* One Flew Over the Cuckoo's Nest *(1963).*

The Angels enjoyed the LSD and the girls at Kesey's parties, but in 1966, despite Ginsberg's attempt to calm everyone down,

*the motorcycle gang clashed with Berkeley students during an
anti–Vietnam War protest march from the Berkeley campus to the
Oakland Army Terminal. In Thompson's account, he attempted to
clarify the complicated relationship between the Angels, the Berkeley
students, and the Oakland police.*

FROM *HELL'S ANGELS*: THE DOPE CABALA AND A WALL OF FIRE

BY LATE SUMMER OF 1965 the Angels had become a factor to be
reckoned with in the social, intellectual and political life of northern
California. They were quoted almost daily in the press, and no half-
bohemian party made the grade unless there were strong rumors—
circulated by the host—that the Hell's Angels would also attend. I was
vaguely afflicted by this syndrome, since my name was becoming as-
sociated with the Angels and there was a feeling in the air that I could
produce them whenever I felt like it. This was never true, though I
did what I could to put the outlaws onto as much free booze and ac-
tion as seemed advisable. At the same time I was loath to be responsi-
ble for their behavior. Their pre-eminence on so many guest lists
made it inevitable that a certain amount of looting, assault and rapine
would occur if they took the social whirl at full gallop. I recall one
party at which I was badgered by children and young mothers because
the Angels didn't show up. Most of the guests were respectable Berke-
ley intellectuals, whose idea of motorcycle outlaws was not consistent
with reality. I told the Angels about the party and gave them the ad-
dress, a quiet residential street in the East Bay, but I hoped they
wouldn't come. The setting was guaranteed trouble: heaping tubs of
beer, wild music and several dozen young girls looking for excitement
while their husbands and varied escorts wanted to talk about "alien-
ation" and "a generation in revolt." Even a half dozen Angels would
have quickly reduced the scene to an intolerable common denomina-
tor: Who will get fucked?

It was Bass Lake all over again, but with a different breed of
voyeur: this time it was the Bay Area's hip establishment, who adopted
the Angels just as eagerly as any crowd of tourists at a scraggy Sierra
beer market.[1] The outlaws were very much the rage. They were big,

---

1. It reminded me of a cartoon in *The Realist* showing the World's Fair Poverty
Pavilion. [Footnotes are by Hunter Thompson.]

dirty and titillating . . . unlike the Beatles, who were small, clean and much too popular to be fashionable. As the Beatles drifted Out, they created a vacuum that sucked the Hell's Angels In. And right behind the outlaws came Roth saying, "They're the last American heroes we have, man." Roth was so interested in the Angels that he began producing icons to commemorate their existence—plastic replicas of Nazi helmets with swinging slogans ("Christ was a Hype") and Iron Crosses, which he sold on the teen-age market from coast to coast.

The only problem with the Angels' new image was that the outlaws themselves didn't understand it. It puzzled them to be treated as symbolic heroes by people with whom they had almost nothing in common. Yet they were gaining access to a whole reservoir of women, booze, drugs and new action—which they were eager to get their hands on, and symbolism be damned. But they could never get the hang of the role they were expected to play, and insisted on ad-libbing the lines. This fouled their channels of communication, which made them nervous . . . and after a brief whirl on the hipster party circuit, all but a few decided it was both cheaper and easier, in the long run, to buy their own booze and hustle a less complicated breed of pussy.

The only really successful connection I made for the Angels was with Ken Kesey, a young novelist[2] living in the woods near La Honda, south of San Francisco. During 1965 and '66 Kesey was arrested twice for possession of marijuana and finally had to flee the country to avoid a long prison term. His association with the Hell's Angels was not calculated to calm his relationship with the forces of law and decency, but he pursued it nonetheless, and with overweening zeal.

I met Kesey one afternoon in August at the studios of KQED, the educational TV station in San Francisco. We had a few beers at a nearby tavern, but I was forced to leave early because I had a Brazilian drum record to take out to Frenchy at the Box Shop. Kesey said he'd come along, and when we got there he made a great hit with the four or five Angels still on the job. After several hours of eating, drinking and the symbolic sharing of herbs, Kesey invited the Frisco chapter down to La Honda for a party on the coming weekend. He and his band of Pranksters had about six acres, with a deep creek between the house and the highway, and a general, overcrowded madness in the private sector.

---

2. *One Flew Over the Cuckoo's Nest* and *Sometimes a Great Notion.*

As it happened, nine marijuana charges against the Kesey menagerie were dropped on Friday; this was duly noted in the Saturday papers, which appeared in La Honda just about the time Kesey was posting a sign on his gate saying: THE MERRY PRANKSTERS WELCOME THE HELL'S ANGELS. The sign, in red, white and blue, was fifteen feet long and three feet high. It had a bad effect on the neighbors. When I got there, in the middle of the afternoon, five San Mateo County sheriffs' cars were parked on the highway in front of Kesey's property. About ten Angels had already arrived and were safely inside the gate; twenty others were said to be en route. The pot was boiling nicely.

I had brought my wife and small son along, and we wanted to go down to the beach for a short meal before joining the festivities. Several miles down the road I stopped at the general store in San Gregorio, a crossroads community with no real population but which serves as a center for the surrounding farms. The store was quiet back around the tool, produce and harness sections, but up front at the bar, things were loud and edgy. The folks were not happy about the goings-on up the road. "That goddamn dope addict," said a middle-aged farmer. "First it's marywanna, now it's Hell's Angels. Christ alive, he's just pushin our faces in the dirt!"

"Beatniks!" said somebody else. "Not worth a pound of piss."

There was talk of divvying up the ax handles in the store and "goin up there to clean the place out." But somebody said the cops were already on the job: "Gonna put em in jail for good this time, every damn one of em . . ." So the ax handles stayed in the rack.

By nightfall Kesey's enclave was full of people, music and multicolored lights. The police added a nice touch by parking along the highway with their own lights flashing . . . red and orange blips lighting up the trees and the sheer dirt cliff across the road. Earlier that spring the Kesey estate had been raided by seventeen cops and a half dozen dogs, led by a notorious federal narcotics agent named Willie Wong. Kesey and twelve of his friends were arrested on marijuana charges, but most of these had to be dropped due to peculiarities in the search warrant. Shortly after the raid Agent Wong was transferred out of the district, and the local police made no further attempts to breach the gates. They contented themselves with lurking on the highway across the creek and checking out all those coming and going. Local sheriff's deputies stopped and questioned a steady stream of college professors, vagrants, lawyers, students, psychologists and high-style hippies. There was not much the police could do except run radio checks for unpaid traffic citations, but they did this with unflagging determination. Now and then they would roust an obvious drunk or somebody completely stoned, but during several months of intense vigil their only actual arrests netted less than a half dozen traffic fugitives.

Meanwhile, the parties grew wilder and louder. There was very little marijuana, but plenty of LSD, which was then legal. The cops stood out on the highway and looked across the creek at a scene that must have tortured the very roots of their understanding. Here were all these people running wild, bellowing and dancing half naked to rock-'n'-roll sounds piped out through the trees from massive amplifiers, reeling and stumbling in a maze of psychedelic lights . . . WILD, by God, and with no law to stop them.

Then, with the arrival of the Hell's Angels, the cops finally got a handle—a raison d'être, as it were—and they quickly tripled the guard. Kesey had finally gone over the line. A bunch of beatniks and college types eating some kind of invisible drug was a hard thing to deal with, but a gang of rotten thugs on motorcycles was as tangible a menace as the law could hope for. . . .

In the language of politics and public relations the Angels "peaked" in the fall of 1965. The Labor Day Run to Kesey's was a letdown of sorts, because towns all over the country were braced for the invasion, waiting to be raped and pillaged. The National Guard was called out at such far-flung points as Parker, Arizona, and Claremont, Indiana. Canadian police set up a special border watch near Vancouver, British Columbia; and in Ketchum, Idaho, the locals mounted a machine gun on the roof of a Main Street drug-store. "We're ready for those punks," said the sheriff. "We'll put half of em in jail and the other half in the graveyard."

The Angels' jaunt to La Honda was a sad anticlimax for the press. The outlaws did a lot of strange, high-speed traveling, but it was not in the realm of the five W's. One of my memories of that weekend is Terry the Tramp's keynote speech delivered to the police on the highway. He got hold of a microphone tied up to some powerful speakers and used the opportunity to unburden his mind . . . addressing the police in a very direct way, speaking of morals and music and madness, and finishing on a high, white note which the San Mateo sheriff's department will not soon forget:

"Remember this," he screamed into the mike. "Just remember that while you're standing out there on that cold road, doin your righteous duty and watchin all us sex fiends and dope addicts in here having a good time . . . just think about that little old *wife of yours* back home with some dirty old Hell's Angel crawlin up *between her thighs!*" Then a burst of wild laughter, clearly audible on the road. "What do you think about that, you worthless fuzz? You gettin hungry? We'll bring you some chili if we have any left over . . . but don't hurry home, let your wife enjoy herself."

It was hard to know, in the triumphant chaos of that Labor Day, that the Angels were on the verge of blowing one of the best connections they'd ever had. Busting up country towns was old stuff, and the cops were getting tense about it. The hippie drug scene was a brand-new dimension—a different gig, as it were—but as the Vietnam war became more and more a public issue the Angels were put in a bind.

For several months they'd been drifting toward political involvement, but the picture was hazy and one of the most confusing elements was their geographical proximity to Berkeley, the citadel of West Coast radicalism. Berkeley is right next door to Oakland, with nothing between them but a line on the map and a few street signs, but in many ways they are as different as Manhattan and the Bronx. Berkeley is a college town and, like Manhattan, a magnet for intellectual transients. Oakland is a magnet for people who want hour-wage jobs and cheap housing, who can't afford to live in Berkeley, San Francisco or any of the middle-class Bay Area suburbs.[3] It is a noisy, ugly, mean-spirited place, with the sort of charm that Chicago had for Sandburg. It is also a natural environment for hoodlums, brawlers, teen-age gangs and racial tensions.

The Hell's Angels' massive publicity—coming hard on the heels of the widely publicized student rebellion in Berkeley—was interpreted in liberal-radical-intellectual circles as the signal for a natural alliance. Beyond that, the Angels' aggressive, antisocial stance—their *alienation,* as it were—had a tremendous appeal for the more aesthetic Berkeley temperament. Students who could barely get up the nerve to sign a petition or to shoplift a candy bar were fascinated by tales of the Hell's Angels ripping up towns and taking whatever they wanted.

---

3. Oakland's official population is nearly four hundred thousand, but it is the center of a vastly urban sprawl called the East Bay, with a population of about two million—more than twice the size of San Francisco.

Most important, the Angels had a reputation for defying police, for successfully bucking authority, and to the frustrated student radical this was a powerful image indeed. The Angels didn't masturbate, they raped. They didn't come on with theories and songs and quotations, but with noise and muscle and sheer balls.

The honeymoon lasted about three months and came to a jangled end on October 16, when the Hell's Angels attacked a Get Out of Vietnam demonstration at the Oakland-Berkeley border. The existential heroes who had passed the joint with Berkeley liberals at Kesey's parties suddenly turned into venomous beasts, rushing on the same liberals with flailing fists and shouts of "Traitors," "Communists," "Beatniks!" When push came to shove, the Hell's Angels lined up solidly with the cops, the Pentagon and the John Birch Society. And there was no joy that day in Berkeley, for Casey had apparently gone mad.

The attack was an awful shock to those who had seen the Hell's Angels as pioneers of the human spirit, but to anyone who knew them it was entirely logical. The Angels' collective viewpoint has always been fascistic. They insist and seem to believe that their swastika fetish is no more than an antisocial joke, a guaranteed gimmick to bug the squares, the taxpayers—all those they spitefully refer to as "citizens." What they really mean is the Middle Class, the Bourgeoisie, the Burghers—but the Angels don't know these terms and they're suspicious of anyone who tries to explain them. If they wanted to be artful about bugging the squares they would drop the swastika and decorate their bikes with the hammer and sickle. That would really raise hell on the freeways . . . hundreds of Communist thugs roaming the countryside on big motorcycles, looking for trouble.

The first clash came on a Saturday afternoon, at the midway point of a protest march from the Berkeley campus to the Oakland Army Terminal, a shipping point for men and matériel bound for the Far East. Some fifteen thousand demonstrators moved down Telegraph Avenue, one of the main streets of Berkeley, and came face to face—at the city limits—with a four-hundred-man wall of Oakland police wearing helmets and holding riot sticks at port arms. They were deployed in a flying wedge formation, with Police Chief Toothman in the central, ball-carrier's position, giving orders over many walkie-talkies. It was obvious that the march was not going to cross the Oakland line without a fight. I approached the confrontation from the Oakland side—but even with a tape recorder, camera and press credentials, it took almost thirty minutes to get through the no man's land of the police wall. Most people—even some legitimate journalists—were turned back.

So it is still beyond my understanding how a dozen Hell's Angels, obviously intent on causing trouble, managed to filter through and attack the leaders of the protest march as they came forward to confer with Chief Toothman. Tiny led the charge, swinging at anyone unlucky enough to be in his way. The Angels were quickly subdued by Berkeley police, but not before they managed to punch a few people, tear up some signs and rip microphone wires off the march leaders' sound truck. This was the infamous struggle that resulted in the cop's broken leg.

It was all a misunderstanding, the hipster commandos said, explaining the attack: the Angels were duped by the cops, their heads had been turned by secret Right Wing money, and they would certainly adjust their allegiance just as soon as they knew the score.

But the score was a lot more complicated than the hipsters realized. Another Vietnam protest was scheduled for mid-November, and in the meantime there were numerous meetings between the antiwar brain trust and the Hell's Angels. Barger would sit in his living room and listen patiently to everything the Vietnam Day Committee had to say, then brush it all aside. The Berkeley people argued long and well, but they never understood that they were talking on a different frequency. It didn't matter how many beards, busts or acid caps they could muster; Sonny considered them all chickenshit—and that was that.

The Angels, like all other motorcycle outlaws, are rigidly anti-Communist. Their political views are limited to the same kind of retrograde patriotism that motivates the John Birch Society, the Ku Klux Klan and the American Nazi Party. They are blind to the irony of their role . . . knight errants of a faith from which they have already been excommunicated. The Angels will be among the first to be locked up or croaked if the politicians they think they agree with ever come to power.

During the weeks preceding the second march on the Oakland Army Terminal, Allen Ginsberg spent much of his time trying to persuade Barger and his people not to attack the marchers. On the Wednesday before the march Ginsberg, Kesey, Neal Cassady, some of Kesey's Pranksters and a group of Angels met at Barger's house in Oakland. A lot of LSD was taken, foolish political discussion was resolved by phonograph voices of Joan Baez and Bob Dylan, all concluding with the whole group chanting the text of the *Prajnaparamita Sutra,* the Buddhist Highest, Perfect Wisdom Sermon.

The outlaws had never met anyone quite like Ginsberg: they considered him otherworldly. "That goddamn Ginsberg is gonna fuck us *all* up," said Terry. "For a guy that ain't straight at all, he's about the straightest sonofabitch I've ever seen. Man, you shoulda been there when he told Sonny he loved him . . . Sonny didn't know *what* the hell to say."

The Angels never really understood what Ginsberg meant, but his unnerving frankness and the fact that Kesey liked him gave them second thoughts about attacking a march that he obviously considered a Right Thing. Shortly before the November march, Ginsberg published this speech in the *Berkeley Barb:*

TO THE ANGELS

by Allen Ginsberg

These are the thoughts—anxieties—of anxious marchers
That the Angels will attack them
for kicks, or to get publicity, to take the heat off
themselves
or to get the goodwill of police & press &/or
right wing Money
That a conscious deal has been made with Oakland
police
or an unconscious rapport, tacit understanding
mutual sympathy
that Oakland will lay off persecuting the Angels
if the Angels attack & break up the March &
make it a riot
Is any of this true, or is it the paranoia of the less
stable-minded marchers? . . .

Despite Ginsberg's pleas, Sonny told me a week before the march that he was going to meet it with "the biggest bunch of outlaw bikes anybody ever saw in California." Allen and his friends meant well, he said, but they just didn't know what was happening. So it came as a real surprise when, on November 19—the day before the march—the Angels called a press conference to announce that they would not man the barricades. The explanation, in the form of a mimeographed press release, said: "Although we have stated our intention to counter-demonstrate at this despicable, un-American activity, we believe that in the interest of public safety and the protection of the good name of

Oakland, we should not justify the V.D.C.[4] by our presence . . . because our patriotic concern for what these people are doing to our great nation may provoke us to violent acts . . . [and that] any physical encounter would only produce sympathy for this mob of traitors."

Kay Boyle

The writer Kay Boyle, teaching at San Francisco State University in the midst of a long and distinguished career as a novelist, poet, essayist, and memoirist, sympathized with her radical students and went to jail for demonstrating with them. "Testament for My Students, 1968–1969" was the title poem of her 1970 Doubleday collection, published when she was sixty-eight years old.

"BSU" in Boyle's poem refers to the Black Student Union at San Francisco State University, which was part of a loose coalition of student programs, including the Tutorial Program (a one-on-one tutoring program that taught kids who were then called "disadvantaged children"), the Experimental College (which administered student-designed classes and brought in outside lecturers, such as Steward Brand and others), and the Community Involvement Program (which was designed to help local communities organize around their needs and issues).

Janice Belmont, who was an undergraduate at San Francisco State University in the 1960s, understood that the Black Student Union pointed up a real difference between the demonstrations at UC Berkeley and at SFSU. She explained:

> *Part of the protest in the earlier FSM movement*
> *involved the realization that students at Berkeley were*
> *being stamped out in cookie-cutter fashion in order to fit*
> *into the corporate structure. This raised the issue of what*
> *an education at a prestigious university is for. The FSM*

---

4. Vietnam Day Committee, the radical Berkeley group organizing the demonstration.

*pointed to an early recognition of the change in the
objectives of university education. We at the more
working class institution across the Bay had no illusions
about any of this and were beginning to concentrate on
developing student organizations that had ties to the
communities from which we came. A sympathetic
student advisor at SFSU and money for jobs from the
Economic Opportunity Program helped make this
possible. By the time of the Berkeley demonstrations a
tightly organized group of student programs was a
presence on the SFSU campus and in the student
government. Although the friction between these
programs increased as the rhetoric of the Black Student
Union heated up, the establishment of a Black Studies
Program was one of the primary demands of the student
demonstrations at SFSU.*

TESTAMENT FOR MY STUDENTS, 1968–1969

Each year you came jogging or loping down that hall
Bearded or not, sweet emissaries from Arizona
Montana, Illinois, Mass., beneath the light silk hair
Or the dark, or the natural crown, skulls crushable, ribs
   breakable
This year and last wearing sandals in order to run fast
At your temples pools of blood always trembled
And I would see them spill.

Lodged in the red partitions of your hearts
(Where your fathers reigned for a brief time)
On the palpitating thrones of auricle left or ventricle right
Legs crossed, fluently at ease, sat such brothers as Baudelaire
Melville, Poe, sometimes Shakespeare, Genet, Rimbaud; or
   sisters
Like Dickinson, Brontë, Austen, needlepoint set aside for
   that afternoon
Or Gertrude Stein telling you over and over how
   Americans were doggedly made
Your fingers, even though broken, crazily beckoned

These brothers and sisters and others to you, in your lungs
Enough breath remained to summon them all by name.
These lines are set down for a reason that's suddenly gone
    out the window
For I can recall now only your faces: Woodie Haut, Shawn
    Wong, Rebhun, Turks, Alvarado
And how many more. Or I catch now and then the sound
    of a voice
From a long way away, saying something like: "Poetry is for
    the people
And it should represent the people." (You can say that
    again, Woodie)
Or saying: "If the academic poets want to keep poetry for
    themselves, then
They're no different from the administration of this college
Which wants to keep education for the select few. I am
    inclined
To agree with Eldridge Cleaver and the BSU that you are
    part of the problem
Or else you are part of the solution." Or maybe Alvarado's
    voice can be heard
Barely whispering under the campus trees: "Don't make
    too much noise
You might wake up the middle class."

Once I read in a book that the ear of the Oriental records
    sound so swiftly
So sharply, that the falling of a rose petal from a vase will
    rouse him
From his sleep. That spring, Shawn Wong awoke to see the
    mounted police charge, yet
It was "the small white flowers trampled in the grass, and
    the blood
Of poets lying near the broken stems" that stirred his gentle
    dreams
Or Rebhun will flip aside the armor of arrogance he wears
    to type on the required paper
"If you wish to see mankind, look into the glass. If you
    look long enough
One man will become ten men, and then a hundred men,
    and then a thousand.

We saw the police striking out in a sadly strange fury. Each
    time
The baton fell on bone, the pain was felt by all of us. For
Behind the physical manifestations of our fervor we are one
    man
Asking for another world, a world in which we are less
    tools
Of an impersonal power, and ten or a hundred or a
    thousand men of flesh and blood."

The Ungarbled Story That Unfolded Before Me

Well, the incident I want to tell you about came to pass in a college
small enough to put in your pocket. In the northern sticks of Califor-
nia it was, where a middle-aged white professor got up on the audito-
rium stage to introduce a black psychiatrist to what was left of a
student body scattered in the seats on a rainy afternoon. The two
principal characters had beards, but no two beards could have been
more different one from the other. The black man's was a handsome
addition to his face. The professor's was thin and ailing, but still he
had managed to train it to do his bidding. Whenever he turned his
shrunken head, the point of his beard jerked accusingly in still another
direction, indicating with severity that education lay, if you were only
able to see it, in that dusty corner right over there.

"Dr. Parnassus is not just a psychiatrist who is black," the profes-
sor began this memorable introduction. "He is a *black* psychiatrist. I
hope you can all grasp that distinction." For some reason nobody in
the audience said: "Right on, brother" as he stood looking out over
the auditorium, his beard pointing this way and then that. The black
psychiatrist himself had instantly become expendable as he sat on the
stage fingering his yellow silky tie. "There are not many around,"
continued the professor, and this was certainly the truest thing that
had been said that afternoon, for the psychiatrist was the only black
face within a mile or two.

And then the professor turned to the exciting subject of himself.
For a number of years, he said, he had been interested in the problems
of minority groups, and in particular in the black man in the black
ghetto. ("I say, that's awfully good of you, old crutch," said somebody
out of the top drawer of my English mementos.) And now the profes-

sor charmed everyone there with the avowal that he was about to lay
the foundation for, or to initiate, or else to inaugurate, a course at this
up and coming institution for the study of a Black Studies Program,
and his beard waved sparsely in the direction of the psychiatrist. "I
hope to have many eminent black scholars come to talk here on the
subject of a study for the development of what may eventually be-
come, we hope," he said.

"Those who have been closely involved in educational proce-
dures," the professor proceeded, excluding the audience from that
happy experience, "have established beyond question that there is no
possibility of successfully inaugurating—or initiating, if you prefer—
or, indeed, laying the foundations for, any course unless that inaugu-
ration or initiation has been preceded by a long term study in depth
of what it may be advisable to undertake at some future time." There
was a perceptible movement of restlessness among the seated, includ-
ing the psychiatrist, and the professor's beard jerked toward the door
marked "Exit," but no one rose to go. It could have been that no one
in the history of the college had ever got up and walked out in distaste
for what was being said.

The students in this place wore marvelously clean tan Levis, and
navy blue windbreakers. The young men's hair was splendidly
trimmed, and the girls' hair was anything but long and untamed.
They all had regular shoes on their feet. It was another era entirely,
and the things the professor was saying kept carrying us even farther
back on the assembly line of his eager self-esteem. "This is somewhat
of a pilot course I am initiating," were his words. "I might say it took
a good deal of personal ingenuity to get it started, for it has a touch of
revolutionary daring about it." (Oh, how dreary, dreary, can the pur-
veyors of education be if you let them get out of hand for even two
minutes, and this is what had taken place. That's what rock and roll is
for; I knew it with sweet exhilaration then. It's the only thing loud
enough to drown out the voices of the cautious of our day.) "A pre-
study of a Black Studies Program could scarcely be considered anar-
chistic in concept," the professor hastened to add, his beard ready to do
battle for him if it came to that. "Wisdom and reason are not the most
popular words in our current vocabulary, but I still find them useful.
This semester will be devoted to studying with patience and wisdom
what reasonable procedure we can develop which will lead . . ."

There are times when there is nothing left to do but take a decision, and now that moment had come. It would have been taken even had the psychiatrist, after glancing at his wristwatch, not risen to the occasion and made one step in the direction of the lectern. The professor turned his head in irritation and the words died in his mouth. His beard pointed directly to the chair that the psychiatrist had vacated, but the black man had no intention of sitting down again. He tapped the crystal of his watch with his long forefinger. "I have a plane to catch in about three-quarters of an hour. I have to get back to Watts," he said, and so he was allowed to laugh out loud.

> Each year their eyes, midwestern gray or cattle-range blue
> Or jet like the ghetto, held visions of what might be
>   achieved
> They wrote of the river bank that colonized men slide
>   down
> In Fanon's prose, to cleanse themselves of the violence of
>   the dance
> Or wrote: "We all sense the pressure of black passion
> We lose balance in the presence of the black man's frenzied
> Momentum toward autonomy. The urgent tempo with
>   which
> He hurls himself at life dazzles us." When I see Victor Turks
> Again I'll ask him if he was listening when Sartre spoke
> For the dead Fanon, saying that all the inexcusable, the
>   uncondonable acts
> Of violence on the part of those at bay are neither sound
>   nor fury
> Nor the resurrection of savage instincts, but are part of
> The anguished process of man as he re-creates his lost
>   identity.
> "We should accept the black man's advances toward self-
>   possession," Victor kept writing
> Looking up for a moment from *Les Fleurs du Mal, Le Diable
>   au Corps*
> "As the means of his salvation. Let *him,* for once, not the
>   white man
> Not the European, not Western civilization, but *him* set the
>   example
> For us all to follow." It might be in this way, the trembling
>   wind

And the young midwestern voices whistled softly, that we
   could regain
Our lost humanity. There were many more. There was
   Father Jim Hietter
Muted laughter, muted grief, melodious student, saying to
   me
That Christian hate had masqueraded for so long as
   Christian love
The time had come to call it by its rightful name. "Stuff
   your holiday stomachs,"
He wrote at Christmas. "Paint your world with colored lights
And sleep   sleep   sleep
There is Police on Earth, and Eichmann carols the
   countdown
To the Christ child's birth."

There were others, among them Chris Miller who bought
   ankle-high sneakers
With air vents, like portholes, near the soles. He loved
   them so
That he walked with his dark head lowered to watch the
   pure white
Canvas keeping pace with his thoughts, his talk. "A self
Which does not transcend itself is dead," he said. I see the
   sideways
Shy, dark smile and the pointed chin. "So let me rise into
   life
And die naked like an animal, which I am," he wrote, "and
   be buried
In my mother's earthy body, to rot, and to fertilize the soil.
   Thus
Death will be my final offering to God."

You were not afraid of death, sweet emissaries from Arizona
Montana, Mass., and Illinois; or of mace, or of handcuffs or
   clubs
And there's one thing more: you bore the terrible
   knowledge
That colonized men and poets wear their sharpest pain on
   the surface
Of their flesh, like an open sore

But this year the writers you honored were, with the crack
   of a baton
Turned suddenly to stone. Their tongues were hacked from
   their throats
By bayonets, and the blows came steadily, savagely, on the
   exquisite
Brittleness of bone. What good were the poets to you then,
   Baudelaire, Whitman
Rimbaud, Poe? "All the good in the world!" you shouted out
Through the blood in your mouths. They were there beside
   you on
The campus grass, Shakespeare, Rilke, Brontë, Radiguet
Yeats, Apollinaire, their fingers on the pulse in your wrists
Their young arms cradling your bones.

Andrew Gordon

In Thomas Pynchon's early novel The Crying of Lot 49 *(1965),
he described the student activists on the UC Berkeley campus dur-
ing the late summer of 1964 (shortly before the administration pro-
voked their demonstrations) through the eyes of his protagonist,
Oedipa, who compares the scene before her with her own tranquil-
ized memories of being an undergraduate there a decade earlier.*

> *It was summer, a weekday, and midafternoon; no time
> for any campus Oedipa knew of to be jumping, yet this
> one was. She came downslope from Wheeler Hall,
> through Sather Gate into a plaza teeming with corduroy,
> denim, bare legs, blonde hair, hornrims, bicycle spokes in
> the sun, bookbags, swaying card tables, long paper
> petitions dangling to earth, posters for undecipherable
> FSM's, YAF's, VDC's, suds in the fountain, students
> in nose-to-nose dialogue. She moved through it carrying*

*her fat book, attracted, unsure, a stranger, wanting to feel
relevant but knowing how much of a search among
alternate universes it would take. For she had undergone
her own educating at a time of nerves, blandness and
retreat among not only her fellow students but also most
of the visible structure around and ahead of them, this
having been a national reflex to certain pathologies in
high places only death had the power to cure, and this
Berkeley was like no somnolent Siwash out of her own
past at all, but more akin to those Far Eastern or Latin
American universities you read about, those autonomous
culture media where the most beloved of folklores may be
brought into doubt, cataclysmic of dissents voiced,
suicidal of commitments chosen—the sort that bring
governments down. But it was English she was hearing
as she crossed Bancroft Way among the blonde children
and the muttering Hondas and Suzukis; American
English. Where were Secretaries James and Foster and
Senator Joseph, those dear daft numina who'd mothered
over Oedipa's so temperate youth? In another world.*

A quarter-century later in his novel Vineland *(1990), Pyn-
chon captured a much grittier sense of the Berkeley revolt as the
FSM drifted into anarchy in the late 1960s, when he dramatized
the reckless mood of the students and the brutal violence on the
streets as the state militia used tear gas and rubber bullets to disperse
the unruly crowds of demonstrators. In* Vineland, *the character DL,
a woman biker looking for action, arrives on the scene just in time to
rescue Frenesi, a Berkeley graduate student who has been filming
the riots close to campus.*

> *What [DL] found was Frenesi, who'd been out with her
> camera and a bagful of bootlegged ECO stock since
> dawn, finally ending up on Telegraph Avenue filming a
> skirmish line of paramilitary coming up the street in riot
> gear, carrying small and she hoped only rubber-bullet-
> firing rifles. Last time she looked she'd been at the front
> edge of a crowd who were slowly retreating from the
> campus, trashing what they could as they went. When
> the film roll ended and she came up out of the safety of
> her viewfinder, Frenesi was alone, halfway between the
> people and the police, with no side street handy to go*

dodging down. Hmm. Shop doors were all secured with chain, windows shuttered with heavy plywood. Her next step would've been to go ahead and change rolls, get some more footage, but to go rooting around in her bag right now could only be taken as a threat by the boys in khaki, who'd come close enough that even above the lingering nose-wrenching ground note of tear gas she could still begin to smell them, the aftershave, the gunmetal in the sun, the new-issue uniforms whose armpits by now were musky with fear.

Careening by on a flashy Czech motorcycle, DL lifts Frenesi onto the backseat and carries her away out of danger. "*Skidding among piles of street debris and paper fires, over crumbled auto glass, trying not to hit anybody lying on the pavement, up onto some side-walk and around the corner at last and down the long hillside to the Bay flashing in the late sun they escaped, in a snarling dreamrush of speed and scent.*" The two young women are in a jagged mood of exhilaration and defiance after surviving the dangerous action on the street. Ravenously hungry, they head for a Berkeley restaurant:

*They sat devouring cheeseburgers, fries, and shakes in a waterfront place full of refugees from the fighting up the hill, all their eyes, including ones that had wept, now lighted from the inside—was it only the overhead fluo-rescents, some trick of sun and water outside? no . . . too many of these fevered lamps not to have origin across the line somewhere, in a world sprung new, not even defined yet, worth the loss of nearly everything in this one. The jukebox played the Doors, Jimi Hendrix, Jefferson Airplane, Country Joe and the Fish. . . . Frenesi gestured with her burger, trailing drops of separating ketchup and fat, each drop warped by the forces of its flight into swirling micropatterns of red and beige, and—
"It's the Revolution, girl—can't you feel it?"*

Andrew Gordon described a quieter evening in "*Smoking Dope with Thomas Pynchon: A Sixties Memoir*" in The Vine-land Papers: Critical Takes on Pynchon's Novel *(1994). Gor-don was a self-styled "Berkeley hipster" graduate student in the late 1960s. His encounter with Pynchon in 1967 ended in "an all-night burger palace on University Avenue," the scene the novel-ist later incorporated into* Vineland.

SMOKING DOPE WITH THOMAS
PYNCHON: A SIXTIES MEMOIR

THIS IS A STORY about the sixties: it's about me and some friends of mine, it's about Berkeley, and it's about Pynchon. It's about a decade in which we were all young together and thought we would stay young forever. Berkeley was our Vineland, a dream of a perfect new world. The time was ripe, America was ours, and we were going to change the world: Paradise Now or Apocalypse Now.

Neither one happened. As the decades pass, is anything left of that refuge, that Vineland, apart from memory and isolated dreams? Where are the sixties now? Where are we? And where is Thomas Pynchon?

Ultimately, I suppose this story is all about me. Everything you write always is, disguise it as you may. I don't know what I can tell you about Thomas Pynchon, but I can tell you something about myself, about the impact that the sixties and Berkeley and Pynchon had on me. *Vineland* looks back on the late sixties, and I'm going to look back on 1964–67, from ages nineteen to twenty-two, when I was first going out into the world on my own and when my life became enmeshed with Pynchon's fictions. I want to trace some of the parallels between life and fiction.

According to his friend Jules Siegel, when Pynchon lived in Mexico in the sixties, "the Mexicans laughed at his mustache and called him Pancho Villa." There's a hoary old joke whose punch line goes, "Did I know Pancho Villa? *Hombre,* we had lunch together!" Mine goes, "Did I know Thomas Pynchon? Man, we smoked dope together!" Except it's no joke; it really happened.

I often feel that way about the 1960s in America: they were no joke, they really happened to us, and they happened to me, although in retrospect they boggle the imagination and seem too incredible to be real. The truth of the sixties is stranger than fiction. As Philip Roth wrote about the period, "is it possible? is it happening?" ("Writing American Fiction" in *Reading Myself and Others*, 121). That's why the sixties have so rarely been captured well in American fiction, except by a few authors such as Pynchon: if somebody told you the history of the decade as a story, you wouldn't believe it. You'd wonder: Is this for real? Is this some kind of joke? Is it supposed to be farce or tragedy? You wouldn't know how to feel, to laugh or to cry.

And although I met Thomas Pynchon one evening in Berkeley in June of 1967, I cannot say I really know him. He remains for me a figure as mysterious and ungraspable as Pancho Villa, a dope-smoking guerrilla warrior of the imagination, disappearing into his Mexican desert.

I consider Pynchon a quintessential American novelist of the 1960s because he came of age as an artist during that entropic decade and shows its stamp in all his work: *V.* (1963) covers the century from 1898 to 1956, but most of it was composed during the Kennedy years, and its zany mood reflects the liberatory burst of energy of the Thousand Days, that peculiar mix of Camelot idealism and Cold War paranoia also found in Heller's *Catch-22* (1961) and Kesey's *One Flew Over the Cuckoo's Nest* (1962). *The Crying of Lot 49* (1966) is set in the relatively innocent sixties of the early Beatles (when they were still the Adorable Moptops and the Fab Four) and of legal LSD. Nevertheless, all the attraction, danger, and destructive tendencies of the New Left and the counterculture are prophesied in the insidious underground web of the Tristero. *Gravity's Rainbow* (1973), ostensibly about World War II, was written during the Vietnam War and indirectly reflects that topsy-turvy time; Pynchon also sneaks in references to Malcolm X, Kennedy, and Nixon. Slothrop in *Gravity's Rainbow* discovers what many young Americans found out in the late sixties: that our Magical Mystery Tour in the zone of Vietnam was a love affair with death, that the war never ends, and that your own country is your enemy. We weren't in Kansas anymore, the Wicked Witch of the West was after us, but there was no Yellow Brick Road and no kindly Wizard to come to the rescue. Finally, *Vineland* (1990) is the sixties revisited from the perspective of the eighties, about all the unresolved issues, about our sympathy for the Devil and our betrayal of the revolution, and about the long arm of the Nixonian counterrevolution continuing under Reagan. And whether or not his four novels are set in the sixties, they are ultimately all *of* the sixties, and always conjure up the contradictory moods of that decade and evoke the peculiarly mixed response.

I was introduced to Pynchon's fiction in the fall of 1964 at Rutgers by Richard Poirier: *V.* was the last novel assigned that semester in his course on the twentieth-century American novel. I immediately glommed on to Pynchon the way I had to Kerouac in the late fifties. He had an epic, wild, wide-ranging imagination. He was hip, he was funny, alternately farcical and profound. He also had modernist traits:

he was learned, complex and allusive, and he liked to write about wastelands (even in the early sixties, in many English departments T. S. Eliot was still God). That Pynchon was camera-shy added to the mystique: he actually lived by the Joycean ethic of "silence, exile, and cunning"!

Unlike Kerouac, Pynchon appealed to two sides of me: the adolescent and the cerebral—the anarchist and the intellectual. Nevertheless, I connected Pynchon to Kerouac because both wrote about restless post–WW II young Americans. Except that Kerouac's heroes were filled with romantic angst and an unfulfilled yearning to burn like Roman candles, whereas Pynchon's were clowns, schlemiels, and human yo-yos, bouncing between farce and paranoia. Kerouac was of the cool fifties; he wrote jazz fiction. But Pynchon was of the apocalyptic sixties; he wrote rock and roll.

Fall 1964 was my last semester at Rutgers. I had enough credits to graduate, and had already been accepted to study English at Berkeley the next fall. I was a New York City boy, but the east couldn't hold me anymore; for years, I had been California dreaming. All I'd ever known of life was school. The summer after high school I had retraced part of Kerouac's route in *On the Road;* now I was ready to live like a Pynchon hero, to start bouncing around the globe like a human yo-yo. Restless and terrifically naive—in other words, a perfect schlemiel—I boarded a boat for Europe in February 1965, just after my twentieth birthday, ostensibly to learn French in Paris but mostly, as it turned out, to bum around. A last fling before graduate school. Fiction imitates life, but life also imitates fiction, in an endless feedback loop: I soon found myself yo-yoing in a Pynchonesque narrative involving historical change, illegal substances, FBI agents, farce, and paranoia.

By June of 1965, I was broke and lonesome and took the Cunard line home from England; I got back just in time to graduate with my class. Despite my insistent letters and packages of French perfume, my girlfriend of the fall had moved on to another guy.

I returned to a different country than the one I had left four months earlier. The first teach-in on the war had been held at Rutgers that spring. The number-one tune was no longer the Beatles' sweet chant, "I Want to Hold Your Hand"; now people were listening instead to the angry, insistent lament of the Rolling Stones, "(I Can't Get No) Satisfaction." A chemistry major told me about his experiences with a new wonder drug called LSD. He said he had found nirvana and met God. I thought, if it could do that for this schnook, then what could it do for me? I ingested 250 micrograms and wound up in the hospital.

I didn't realize at the time that I had fallen into a Pynchon novel and that the author was about to appear on the scene.

In the fall of 1966 I was writing a seminar paper on *V.* for a graduate course taught by Sheldon Sacks. Sacks was a sweet man and an inspiring teacher, a formalist and neo-Aristotelian of the Chicago school of R. S. Crane; out of place at Berkeley, he soon returned to the University of Chicago, where he edited *Critical Inquiry* and died much too young. Sacks and Frederick Crews—then in his Freudian phase—were my most influential teachers at Berkeley in the late sixties.

Briefly, I argued that *V.* was organized less as a novel than as a moral fable or apologue, and that its message read, "Keep cool but care." Anyway, that's what I believed then; I was a lot more certain about many things in the late sixties than I am now. Maybe that's the message I read because that's the way I was trying to live: cool but caring, a Berkeley hipster.

But I found *V.* so dense that it took my entire paper just to begin to explicate the first chapter. I never went further: I was overawed by Pynchon's complex and daring imagination and intimidated by his learning. Nevertheless, I lived with that novel for a time. And, in a curious way, the novel led me to Pynchon when I wasn't even trying to find him.

I used to carry around a dog-eared paperback of *V.* (I have it still, scotch-taped together. How could I give it up? It has all my notes!) I turned friends on to Pynchon; we became cognoscenti, sharing favorite lines of dialogue: "Oh, man, [. . .] an intellectual. I had to pick an intellectual. They all revert" (111) or "You're turning our marriage into a trampoline act" (113). Later we would similarly appropriate *The Crying of Lot 49,* sending each other letters with the stamps pasted upside down and penciling on the envelopes "W.A.S.T.E." Once again, fiction was infiltrating life.

One friend, a woman graduate student, noticed me carrying *V.* and said, "Oh, are you reading that? I know the guy who wrote it." I was naturally skeptical about her claim and asked if this mysterious Pynchon really existed and if he was a man or a committee.

She said she had met him in Berkeley in 1965 and that they stayed in touch. She asked if I minded if she sent Pynchon my paper. I gave her a copy, suspecting that it would vanish into a black hole.

Several months later, she mentioned that "Tom" had read my paper and liked it, thought it a lot more perceptive than the reviewers' comments. I thanked her but still wondered what kind of game she was playing.

From time to time, she dropped convincing-sounding details about Pynchon. She said he picked his friends carefully and that they guarded his privacy. She said he had written a second novel in haste and for money and that he was not too proud of it; that would be the just-published *Crying of Lot 49*. She claimed he had people help him with research and that he was working on an endless novel in which all of his friends would appear, including her. Is *Gravity's Rainbow* a roman à clef? If there is ever a biography of Pynchon, someone should investigate that angle. I once combed through *Gravity,* searching for the character who is supposed to be her; there are just too many, and I couldn't be sure.

In fact, she reminded me most of Rachel Owlglass in *V.:* she was a bright, lovely Jewish woman who liked to mother people. I was half in love with her but I was also friends with the guy she was living with. They later married and divorced; she claims he's in *Gravity's Rainbow* too.

One night in June of 1967, my Pynchon connection phoned me at my apartment on Shattuck Avenue. Pynchon was in town, staying with her and her boyfriend. He'd been living in L.A., flown up to Seattle to visit friends from Boeing, and on his way back to L.A. had stopped off for a day in Berkeley. She said, "Tom wants to meet you."

This was like a command audience with the pope. I kick-started my motorcycle and, I think, made it across town to her place near San Pablo Avenue before she had time to put down the phone.

Many years later, I ran into her at a literature conference and she revealed some unexpected details about herself and Pynchon. They weren't just friends; they had been lovers and lived together in Berkeley for a while in 1965. She described him as being then a "prematurely middle-aged" young man with "a lot of hang-ups." She claimed she was the first to turn him on to dope. They broke up because of the "hang-ups," but they remained friends and corresponded. From time to time, he would reappear suddenly and unexpectedly in her life—the last time at her wedding, with a wedding present of a kilo of Michoacán (a superior brand of Mexican weed).

That night in June of 1967 she made it clear on the phone that I was not to ask Pynchon about his work—past, present, or future. Just what did that leave me to talk about with him, I wondered as I drove across town, burning with anticipation. Yet I still had the nagging feeling that, like Oedipa Maas, I might be the victim of an elaborate hoax, that there would be no Pynchon at her apartment, just an imposter—or perhaps a locked door with a mail slot marked with the sign of a muted posthorn.

She had a tiny, one-bedroom house, living room separated from bedroom by a bead curtain. As I entered, the room was flooded with a pungent aroma and enough smoke to induce an immediate contact high; I coughed. A long, lanky young man was methodically rolling joints on the table; his stash box was a One-a-Day Brand Multivitamin pill bottle. He carefully finished rolling and extended the bomber to me, saying, "Hey, man, would you like a joint?" (This was Berkeley, 1967; people really talked that way back then.) I took a toke gladly; it was obvious by the fog in the room that they were way ahead of me.

This man, who was introduced to me as Thomas Pynchon, appeared to be in his late twenties. I'm six foot one, but he was taller than I, about six two or three. He wore a corduroy shirt and corduroy pants, both green, and a pair of those brown, ankle-high suede shoes known as desert boots. He was lean, almost emaciated, and his eyes were wasted. His hair was thick and brown and he had a ragged, reddish brown soup-strainer mustache; I wondered if he had grown it to hide his teeth, which were crooked and slightly protruding.

Pynchon was evidently a man of few words. I wanted very much to talk with him, to sound him out, at least to get him to laugh, but as we sat on the floor and passed around buzz bombers and grew progressively more zonked, he didn't say much, just listened intently as our hostess and host and I talked. The conversation was disjointed, grass talk consisting of little bits and revelations (Leslie Fiedler had just been busted for possession of marijuana) and silly stoned jokes, like the one about the woman who traded in her menstrual cycle for a Yamaha. I thought of Pynchon as a Van der Graaf machine, one of those generators that keeps building static electricity until a lightning bolt zaps between the terminals.

All of a sudden, he pulled out of his pocket a string of firecrackers and asked, "Where can we set these off?"

"Why don't we blow up the statue of Queen Victoria?" I replied.

"O wow, man, have you read that book?" Pynchon said. He'd caught my allusion to Leonard Cohen's novel *Beautiful Losers,* recently released in paperback. Cohen's hero actually does blow up a statue of Victoria, a typically sixties symbolic gesture. I was pleased to finally get a response from Pynchon, yet I still felt like the overeager grad student trying too hard to impress the prof.

There were no Victorian monuments to explode in Berkeley, so we drove instead to the marina and set off the fireworks by the bay. We walked by the water, past junkpiles, setting off cherry bombs and running like hell. A midnight ritual: four heavily stoned people hearing the snap, crackle, and pop, watching the dazzle against the black mud and the midnight waters. At that moment, halfway around the world in Vietnam, equally stoned soldiers were probably admiring in the same way the rocket's red glare.

Suddenly, for some inexplicable reason, everyone had the munchies and I suggested an all-night burger palace on University Avenue, probably the only restaurant open at that hour. It was a huge fluorescent Burgertown. As we sat at formica-topped tables and ate greasy sleazeburgers, Pynchon slouched in the booth, long thin legs in green Levis sprawled out, pensively biting his nails. Then he ripped a styrofoam coffee cup into tiny, meticulous shreds. He had dissipated, tired eyes like Robert Mitchum's.

The place featured a colorful old baroque Wurlitzer jukebox. We fed the machine streams of quarters: the Beatles' "Strawberry Fields" and Country Joe's "Not So Sweet Martha Lorraine." Pynchon chose Procol Harum's "A Whiter Shade of Pale" and the Stones' "Ruby Tuesday," which remain for me associated with that night.

In *Vineland,* after DL rescues Frenesi from the Berkeley street-fighting,

> They sat devouring cheeseburgers, fries, and shakes in a wa-
> terfront place full of refugees from the fighting up the hill,
> all their eyes, including ones that had wept, now lighted
> from the inside—was it only the overhead fluorescents,
> some trick of sun and water outside? no . . . too many of
> these fevered lamps not to have origin across the line some-
> where, in a world sprung new, not even defined yet, worth
> the loss of nearly everything in this one. The jukebox played
> the Doors, Jimi Hendrix, Jefferson Airplane, Country Joe
> and the Fish. [. . .] Revolution all around them, world-class
> burgers, jukebox solidarity. (117–18)

DL and Frenesi's "jukebox solidarity" doesn't last. And that night in 1967 I made the mistake of introducing Pynchon to an acquaintance of mine who happened to be in the restaurant, the manager of a local rock band; they became engrossed in a technical conversation about music, and I was lost.

The last thing I recall is sitting with Pynchon in the open back of a red pickup truck, freezing, as we rocketed up into the Berkeley hills. The fog slid in like satin, so thick the water dripped on me. Suddenly, out of a cloud, San Francisco materialized below us. It was dawn.

Later that morning Pynchon caught a plane back to L.A. I never saw him again.

Donald Barthelme

The humorist Donald Barthelme wrote "The Police Band" as a tongue-in-cheek short story with a narrator sympathetic to the perspective of an atypical Sixties law enforcement officer. It was included in Barthelme's early collection Unspeakable Practices, Unnatural Acts *(1968). As a postmodernist writer, he was often criticized for creating ironic works of fiction that offered unsettling reflections of his times. Barthelme replied, "Art is not difficult because it wishes to be difficult, rather because it wishes to be art. However much the writer might long to be straightforward, these virtues are no longer available to him. He discovers that in being simple, honest, straightforward, nothing much happens."*

THE POLICE BAND

IT WAS KIND OF THE DEPARTMENT to think up the Police Band. The original impulse, I believe, was creative and humanitarian. A better way of doing things. Unpleasant, bloody things required by the line of duty. Even if it didn't work out.

The Commissioner (the old Commissioner, not the one they have now) brought us up the river from Detroit. Where our members had been, typically, working the Sho Bar two nights a week. Sometimes the Glass Crutch. Friday and Saturday. And the rest of the time wandering the streets disguised as postal employees. Bitten by dogs and burdened with third-class mail.

What are our duties? we asked at the interview. Your duties are to wail, the Commissioner said. That only. We admired our new dark-blue uniforms as we came up the river in canoes like Indians. We plan to use you in certain situations, certain tense situations, to alleviate tensions, the Commissioner said. I can visualize great success with this new method. And would you play "Entropy." He was pale, with a bad liver.

We are subtle, the Commissioner said, never forget that. Subtlety is what has previously been lacking in our line. Some of the old ones, the Commissioner said, all they know is the club. He took a little pill from a little box and swallowed it with his Scotch.

When we got to town we looked at those Steve Canyon recruiting posters and wondered if we resembled them. Henry Wang, the bass man, looks like a Chinese Steve Canyon, right? The other cops were friendly in a suspicious way. They liked to hear us wail, however.

The Police Band is a very sensitive highly trained and ruggedly anti-Communist unit whose efficacy will be demonstrated in due time, the Commissioner said to the Mayor (the old Mayor). The Mayor took a little pill from a little box and said, We'll see. He could tell we were musicians because we were holding our instruments, right? Emptying spit valves, giving the horn that little shake. Or coming in at letter E with some sly emotion stolen from another life.

The old Commissioner's idea was essentially that if there was a disturbance on the city's streets—some ethnic group cutting up some other ethnic group on a warm August evening—the Police Band would be sent in. The handsome dark-green band bus arriving with sirens singing, red lights whirling. Hard-pressed men on the beat in their white hats raising a grateful cheer. We stream out of the vehicle holding our instruments at high port. A skirmish line fronting the angry crowd. And play "Perdido." The crowd washed with new and true emotion. Startled, they listen. Our emotion stronger than their emotion. A triumph of art over good sense.

That was the idea. The old Commissioner's *musical* ideas were not very interesting, because after all he was a cop, right? But his police ideas were interesting.

We had drills. Poured out of that mother-loving bus onto vacant lots holding our instruments at high port like John Wayne. Felt we were heroes already. Playing "Perdido," "Stumblin'," "Gin Song,"

"Feebles." Laving the terrain with emotion stolen from old busted-up loves, broken marriages, the needle, economic deprivation. A few old ladies leaning out of high windows. Our emotion washing rusty Rheingold cans and parts of old doors.

This city is too much! We'd be walking down the street talking about our techniques and we'd see out of our eyes a woman standing in the gutter screaming to herself about what we could not imagine. A drunk trying to strangle a dog somebody'd left leashed to a parking meter. The drunk and the dog screaming at each other. This city is too much!

We had drills and drills. It is true that the best musicians come from Detroit but there is something here that you have to get in your playing and that is simply the scream. We got that. The Commissioner, a sixty-three-year-old hippie with no doubt many graft qualities and unpleasant qualities, nevertheless understood that. When we'd play "ugly," he understood that. He understood the rising expectations of the world's peoples also. That our black members didn't feel like toting junk mail around Detroit forever until the ends of their lives. For some strange reason.

He said one of our functions would be to be sent out to play in places where people were trembling with fear inside their houses, right? To inspirit them in difficult times. This was the plan. We set up in the street. Henry Wang grabs hold of his instrument. He has a four-bar lead-in all by himself. Then the whole group. The iron shutters raised a few inches. Shorty Alanio holding his horn at his characteristic angle (sideways). The reeds dropping lacy little fill-ins behind him. We're cooking. The crowd roars.

The Police Band was an idea of a very romantic kind. The Police Band was an idea that didn't work. When they retired the old Commissioner (our Commissioner), who it turned out had a little drug problem of his own, they didn't let us even drill anymore. We have never been used. His idea was a romantic idea, they said (right?), which was not adequate to the rage currently around in the world. Rage must be met with rage, they said. (Not in so many words.) We sit around the precinct houses, under the filthy lights, talking about our techniques. But I thought it might be good if you knew that the Department still has us. We have a good group. We still have emotion to be used. We're still here.

Abbie Hoffman

*The radical activist Abbie Hoffman wrote "Che's Last Letter," sup-
posedly composed by the Cuban revolutionary hero Che Guevara,
who died in 1967 while fighting in Bolivia. In the 1960s, Che be-
came the great symbol of the "freedom fighter" to college students in
the United States and Europe, and posters of him in a guerrilla sol-
dier's uniform with black beard and beret sold widely. "Che's Last
Letter" was part of what Hoffman called "a little plot Jerry Rubin,
Ed Sanders and I worked up, with plans 'to discover the letters in
the Bolivian jungles' and sell them to* Ramparts. *We blew it
though and they ended up in* The Realist *for free."*

CHE'S LAST LETTER

To the youth of the United States:

I WRITE TO YOU huddled in blankets. Damp, shivering, cold, tem-
porarily dejected over recent military setbacks. We are somewhere in
the jungles of Bolivia surrounded by the enemy, cut off from all sup-
plies. Struggling against immense odds. My thoughts turn to the
young people struggling for a chance at life in the bowels of plastic
America cut off from the lifeline of human existence. For you, like us,
we are also surrounded. I recall the time I worked as a waiter in [a]
Miami Beach hotel and my frequent visits to New York and know
that people in the second half of the twentieth century are not des-
tined to play out their lives in either the jungles of Bolivia or Manhat-
tan. Surely the destiny of man was to lift himself out of the jungle.
Out of an economic system that forced him to behave like a beast of
prey. Out of a corresponding socio-religious system that cherished
money and greed and hatred and inhumanity. I know you will say,
"We know all that but what do you offer? More killing? A subtle
change in things? What is so revolutionary about your revolution?"
But of course you are cynical. Your universities teach you to be eter-
nal cynics, a cynicism that can be only drowned in alcohol and diet
pills and psychoanalysts and golf. Forget your cynicism. There is no

one who has more respect for life than a revolutionist. I am by profession a doctor. I found, however, to heal bodies under an inhuman system such as existed then and now in my native Argentina was corrupt. So I left to join Fidel and the others and help in my small way to build the revolution in Cuba. What we did was to establish a model to show that under great oppressive odds radical social change can take place. You must shed the bandages bound around your eyes by the press in your country. You must go to Cuba and experience what has happened there over the past ten years.

Even as we realized victory in Cuba, we knew that the battle had just begun. For a revolution, in order to be a true revolution, must be a world revolution. To achieve that world revolution, you the children of the Yankees must lend a hand. You must vomit forth your cynicism in the streets of your cities. You must mount an unrelenting attack on everything the bastards that rule your country hold dear. You must refuse to serve in their armies, you must reject the heroin offered in their universities, you must become clogs in their productive machinery. Your struggle will be a long and arduous one. It will not come easy. There are no guide rules to apply to revolution. Each country is unique and your struggle is the most unique of all, for your repression is of a very peculiar nature. Search for brothers and sisters in the struggle. Steel yourself inside for the oppressive blows that will greet each new victory. Learn patience. Learn how to survive. It will not be all hardship and suffering as others have warned. What is suffering, comrades? Even as I write knowing death is coming over that hill not five hundred yards away I would not go back to being a respected professional in a system I detested. That is the true death of the spirit. No, although my health is failing, physical death is approaching and our plans here have met with disaster, I know we have won. Not for ourselves but for those who will follow us into these jungles of reality and into the jungles of their own minds to strike that blow for freedom. Men of revolutionary vision and action are sprouting everywhere. Like wild flowers bursting the overpowering prison of cement roads they grow [in] Vietnam, Angola, Guatemala, Paris and now even in the heart of the Steel Goliath. Little Davids strike hard and deep. Venceremos.

CHE

William S. Burroughs

*By 1968, the year before the Berkeley Free Speech Movement
ended in the conflict over People's Park, the radical student move-
ment had spread worldwide, with protests in Japan, France, Ger-
many, and Italy, as well as on college campuses throughout the
United States. The literary fallout from the radical demonstrations
peaked at the Chicago Democratic Convention, after President
Johnson announced that he would not seek reelection. William Bur-
roughs, Terry Southern, and the French writer Jean Genet were
commissioned by* Esquire *to cover the convention. Burroughs's
report, "The Coming of the Purple Better One," appeared in the
November 1968 issue of the magazine.*

THE COMING OF THE
PURPLE BETTER ONE

SATURDAY AUGUST 24, 1968: Arrive O'Hare Airport, Chicago.
First visit in 26 years. Last in Chicago during the war where I exer-
cised the trade of exterminator.

"Exterminator. Got any bugs lady?"

"The tools of your trade," said the customs officer touching my
cassette recorder.

Driving in from the airport note empty streets newspapers in the
wind a ghost town. Taxi strike bus strike doesn't account for the feel-
ing of nobody here. Arrive Sheraton Hotel where I meet Jean Genet.
He is dressed in an old pair of corduroy pants no jacket no tie. He
conveys a remarkable impact of directness confronting completely
whoever he talks to.

Sunday August 25: Out to the airport for the arrival of McCarthy.
An estimated fifteen thousand supporters there to welcome him
mostly young people. Surprisingly few police. Whole scene touching
and ineffectual particularly in retrospect of subsequent events.

Monday August 26: We spend Monday morning in Lincoln Park
talking to the Yippies. Jean Genet expresses himself succinctly on the
subject of America and Chicago.

"I can't wait for this city to rot. I can't wait to see weeds growing through empty streets."

May not have to wait long. Police in blue helmets many of them wearing one-way dark glasses stand around heavy and sullen. One of them sidles up to me while I am recording and says: "You're wasting film."

Of course the sound track does bring the image track on set so there is not all that much difference between a recorder and a camera.

Another sidles up right in my ear. "They're talking about brutality. They haven't seen anything yet."

The cops know they are the heavies in this show and they are going to play it to the Hilton.

Monday night to the Convention Hall. Cobblestone streets smell of coal gas and stockyards. No place to park. Some citizen rushes out screaming. "You can't park here! I'll call the police! I'll have your car towed away!"

Through line after line of police showing our credentials and finally click ourselves in. Tinny atmosphere of carnivals and penny arcades without the attractions. The barkers are there but no freaks no sideshows no scenic railways.

Up to Lincoln Park where the cops are impartially clubbing Yippies newsmen and bystanders. After all there are no innocent bystanders. What are they doing here in the first place? The worst sin of man is to be born.

Tuesday August 27: The Yippies are stealing the show. I've had about enough of the convention farce without humor barbed wire and cops around a lot of nothing.

Jean Genet says: "It is time for writers to support the rebellion of youth not only with their words but with their presence as well."

It is time for every writer to stand by his words.

Lincoln Park Tuesday night: The Yippies have assembled at the epicenter of Lincoln Park. Bonfires, a cross, the demonstrators singing *The Battle Hymn of the Republic.*

He hath loosed the fateful lightning of his terrible swift sword.

"Wet a handkerchief and put it in front of your face. . . . Don't rub your eyes."

He is trampling out the vintage where the grapes of wrath are stored.

"Keep your cool and stay seated."

He has sounded forth the trumpet that shall never call retreat.

"Sit or split."

At this point I look up to see what looks like a battalion of World

War I tanks converging on the youthful demonstrators and I say, "What's with you Martin you wig already?"

He just looks at me and says: "Fill your hand stranger." And hauls out an old rusty police force from 1910 and I take off across Lincoln Park tear-gas canisters raining all around me. From a safe distance I turn around to observe the scene and see it is a 1917 gas attack from the archives. I make the lobby of the Lincoln Hotel where the medics are treating gas victims. The Life-Time photographer is laid out on a bench medics washing his eyes out. Soon he recovers and begins taking pictures of everything in sight. Outside the cops prowl about like aroused tomcats.

Wednesday August 28: Rally in Grant Park to organize a march to the Amphitheatre. I am impressed by the organization that has been built here. Many of the marshals wear crash helmets and blue uniforms. It is difficult to distinguish them from the police. Clearly the emergent Yippie uniform is crash helmet, shoulder pads, and aluminum jockstrap. I find myself in the second row of the nonviolent march feeling rather out of place since nonviolence is not exactly my program. We shuffle slowly forward the marshals giving orders over the loudspeaker.

"Link arms. . . . Keep five feet between rows. . . . You back there watch what you're smoking. . . . Keep your cool. . . . This is a nonviolent march. . . . You can obtain tear-gas rags from the medics. . . ."

We come to a solid line of cops and there is a confab between the cops and the marshals. For one horrible moment I think they will let us march five bloody miles and me with blisters already from walking around in the taxi strike. No. They won't let us march. And being a nonviolent march and five beefy cops for every marcher and not being equipped with bulldozers it is an impasse. I walk around the park recording and playing back, a beauteous evening calm and clear vapor trails over the lake youths washing tear gas out of their eyes in the fountain. Spot of bother at the bridge where the pigs and national guardians have stationed themselves like Horatio but in far greater numbers.

So out to the Convention Hall where they don't like the look of us despite our electronic credentials being in order and call a Secret Service man for clearance. We get in finally and I play back the Grant Park recordings and boo Humphrey to while away the time as they count votes to the all too stupid and obvious conclusion.

What happened Wednesday night when the guard dogs broke loose again is history.

I have described the Chicago police as left over from 1910 and in a sense this is true. Daley and his nightstick authority date back to turn-of-the-century ward politics. They are anachronisms and they know it. This I think accounts for the shocking ferocity of their behavior. Jean Genet, who has considerable police experience, says he never saw such expressions before on allegedly human faces. And what is the phantom fuzz screaming from Chicago to Berlin, from Mexico City to Paris? "We are REAL REAL REAL!!! REAL as this NIGHTSTICK!" As they feel, in their dim animal way, that reality is slipping away from them. Where are all the old cop sets, Clancy? Eating your apple twirling your club the sky goes out against your back. Where are the men you sent up who came around to thank you when they got out? Where is the gold watch the chief gave you when you cracked the Norton case? And where are your pigeons, Clancy? You used to be quite a pigeon fancier remember the feeling you got sucking arrests from your pigeons soft and evil like the face of your whiskey priest brother? Time to turn in your cop suit to the little Jew who will check it off in his book. Won't be needing you after Friday.

The youth rebellion is a worldwide phenomenon that has not been seen before in history. I don't believe they will calm down and be ad execs at thirty as the establishment would like to believe. Millions of young people all over the world are fed up with shallow unworthy authority running on a platform of bullshit. There are five questions that any platform in America must answer not with hot air but with change on a basic level.

1. Vietnam: As I recollect the French were in there quite some years and finally pulled out to repeat the same mistake in Algeria. History tells us this is a war that cannot be won. Perhaps it is not intended to be won but merely as provocation and pretext to start a war with Red China. Looks like some folks figure the only answer to this mess is blow the set up and start over. May have happened several times before what we call history going back about 10,000 years and the human actor being about 500,000 years on set, give a little take a little, so what was he doing for the 480,000 years unaccounted for? If we have come from stone axes to nuclear weapons in ten thousand years this may well have happened before. Brion Gysin has put forward the theory that a nuclear disaster in what is now the Gobi Desert destroyed the civilization that had made such a disaster possible and incidentally gave rise to what he terms "Albino freaks," namely the white race. Any case if we don't want to see the set go America should get out of Vietnam and reach an immediate agreement with Red China.

2. *Alienated youth:* The only establishment that is supported by its young people is Red China. And that is why the State Department does not want Americans to go there. They do not want Americans to realize that any establishment offering young people anything at all will get their support. Because the western establishments are not offering anything. They have nothing to declare but their bad intentions. Let them come all the way out in the open with their bad intentions, declare a Secret Service overwhelming majority, and elect a purple-assed baboon to the Presidency. At this dark hour in the history of the penny arcade, Wednesday troubling all our hearts, the aggressive Southern ape suh fought for you in the perilous Kon-Tiki Room of the Sheraton.

3. *Black Power:* Find out what they want and give it to them. All the signs that mean anything indicate that the blacks were the original inhabitants of this planet. So who has a better right to it?

4. *Our police and judicial system:* What would happen if all the cotton-picking, stupid-assed, bible-belt laws passed by bourbon-soaked state legislators were actually enforced together with all federal and city laws? If every businessman who chiseled on his income tax by one dollar was caught and jailed? If every drug offender was caught and jailed? If every violator of all the laws penalizing sex acts between consenting adults in private was caught and jailed? How many people would be in jail? I think 30,000,000 is a very conservative estimate. And how many cops would it take to detect and arrest these criminals? And how many guards to keep them confined? And how many judges parole officers and court personnel to process them? And how much money would this cost?

Fix yourself on 30,000,000 violators in vast internee camps all united to scream with the inflexible authority of one big mouth. "We want gymnasiums! Libraries! Swimming pools! We want golf courses! Country clubs! Theatres!"

And with every concession they scream for MORE! MORE! MORE!

"The internee delegation in a meeting with the President today demanded as a prerequisite for any talks the 'immediate and unconditional removal of the so-called guards.' "

Senator Bradly rose in the Senate to question the wisdom of setting up what he termed "a separate state of dubious loyalty at the very core of our nation."

"We want tanks! Planes! Submarines!"

"An ominous atmosphere smogged the capital today as peace talks with the internee delegation bogged down."

"We want a space program! We want an atom bomb!"

"The number of internees is swelling ominously . . . forty million . . . fifty million . . . sixty million . . . 'America is a thin shell around a pulsing core of sullen violators.' "

"Today the internees exploded their first atom bomb described as 'a low yield nuclear device.' "

"It may be low yield but it's right on our back porch," said Senator Bradly plaintively.

"Today the internees signed a mutual assistance pact with Red China."

As regards our judicial system there are three alternatives:

A. Total enforcement. Is either of our distinguished candidates for the Presidency prepared to support the computerized police terror that such enforcement would entail?

B. An admission that the judicial system is a farce and the laws not really intended to be enforced except in a haphazard sporadic fashion. Is either candidate prepared to make such an admission?

C. Get some bulldozers in here and clean out all this garbage and let no state saloon reel to his drunken feet and start braying about state rights. Is either candidate prepared to advocate the only sensible alternative?

5. *The disappearing dollar:* 1959 Minutes To Go: "I'm absolutely weak I can only just totter home the dollar has collapsed." Figuring ten years time lag the dollar should collapse in 1969. There is something wrong with the whole concept of money. It takes always more and more to buy less and less. Money is like junk. A dose that fixes on Monday won't fix on Friday. We are being swept with vertiginous speed into a worldwide inflation comparable to what happened in Germany after World War I. The rich are desperately stockpiling gold, diamonds, antiques, paintings, medicines, food, liquor, tools and weapons. Any platform that does not propose the basic changes necessary to correct these glaring failures is a farce. What is happening in America today is something that has never happened before in recorded history: *Total confrontation.* The lies are obvious. The machinery is laid bare. All Americans are being shoved by the dead-

weight of a broken control machine right in front of each other's faces. Like it or not they cannot choose but see and hear each other. How many Americans will survive a total confront?

In Last Resort the Truth

The scene is Grant Park Chicago 1968. A full-scale model of *The Mayflower* with American flags for sails has been set up. A. J. in his Uncle Sam suit steps to a mike on the deck.

"Ladies and gentlemen it is my coveted privilege and deep honor to introduce to you the distinguished Senator and former Justice of the Supreme Court Homer Mandrill known to his many friends as the Purple Better One. No doubt most of you are familiar with a book called *African Genesis* written by Robert Ardrey a native son of Chicago and I may add a true son of America. I quote from Mr. Ardrey's penetrating work: 'When I was a boy in Chicago I attended the Sunday School of a neighborhood Presbyterian church. I recall our Wednesday-night meetings with the simplest nostalgia. We would meet in the basement. There would be a short prayer and a shorter benediction. And we would turn out all the lights and in total darkness hit each other with chairs.'

"Mr. Ardrey's early training tempered his character to face and make known the truth about the origins and nature of mankind. 'Not in innocence and not in Asia was mankind born. The home of our fathers was the African highland on a sky-swept savannah glowing with menace. The most significant of all our gifts was the legacy bequeathed us by our immediate forebears a race of terrestrial, flesh-eating, killer apes. . . . Raymond A. Dart of the University of Johannesburg was the strident voice from South Africa that would prove the southern ape to be the human ancestor. Dart put forward the simple thesis that Man emerged from the anthropoid background for one reason only: because he was a killer. A rock, a stick, a heavy bone was to our ancestral killer ape the margin of survival. . . . And he said that since we had tried everything else we might in last resort try the truth. . . . Man's original nature imposes itself on any human solution.'

"The aggressive southern ape suh, glowing with menace, fought your battles on the perilous veldts of Africa 500,000 years ago. Had he not done so you would not be living here in this great city in this great land of America raising your happy families in peace and prosperity. Who more fitted to represent our glorious Simian heritage than Homer Mandrill himself a descendant of that illustrious line? Who else can restore to this nation the spirit of true conservatism that imposes itself on any human solution? What candidate is better fitted for the highest office in the land at a time when this great republic is threatened by enemies foreign and domestic? Actually there can be only one candidate: the Purple Better One your future President."

To *The Battle Hymn of the Republic* an American flag is drawn aside revealing a purple-assed mandrill (thunderous applause). Led to the mike by Secret Service men in dark suits that bulge suggestively here and there the Purple Better One blinks in bewilderment.

The Technician mixes a bicarbonate of soda and belches into his hand. He is sitting in front of three instrument panels, one labeled P.A. for Purple Ass, one labeled A. for Audience, a third P. for Police. (Crude experiments with rhesus monkeys have demonstrated that small currents of electricity passed through electrodes into the appropriate brain areas can elicit any emotional or visceral response: rage, fear, sexuality, vomiting, sleep, defecation. No doubt with further experimentation these techniques will be perfected and electromagnetic fields will supersede the use of actual electrodes imbedded in the brain.) He adjusts dials as Homer's mouth moves to a dubbed speech from directional mikes. The features of other candidates are projected onto Homer's face from a laser installation across the park so that he seems to embody and absorb them all.

"At this dark hour in the history of the republic there are grave questions troubling all our hearts. I pledge myself to answer these questions. One question is the war in Vietnam which is not only a war but a holy crusade against the godless forces of international communism. And I say to you if these forces are not contained they will engulf us all." (Thunderous applause.) "And I flatly accuse the administration of criminal diffidence in the use of atomic weapons. Are we going to turn a red white and blue ass to the enemy?" (No! No! No!) "Are we going to fight through to victory at any cost?" (Yes! Yes! Yes!) "I say to you we will win if it takes ten years. We will win if we have to police every blade of grass and every gook in Vietnam." (Thunderous applause.) "And after that we are going to wade in and take care of Chairman Mao and his gang of cutthroat slave drivers." (Thunderous applause.) "And if any country shall open its mouth to carp at the great American task well a single back-handed blow from our mighty Seventh Fleet will silence that impotent puppet of Moscow and Peking.

"Another question is so-called Black Power. I want to go on record as saying I am a true friend to all good Darkies everywhere." (To wild applause a picture of the world-famous statue in Natchitoches Louisiana flashes on screen. As you all know this statue shows a good old Darkie with his hat in his hand and is dedicated to All Good Darkies Everywhere.) Homer's voice chokes with emotion and tears drip off his purple nose. "Why when I was fourteen years old our old yard Nigrah Rover Jones got runned over by a laundry truck and I cried my decent American heart out. And I have a deep conviction that the overwhelming majority of Nigrahs in this country is good Darkies like Rover Jones. However we know that there is in this country today another kind of Nigrah and as long as there is a gas pump handy we all know the answer to that." (Thunderous applause.) "And I would like to say this to followers of the Jewish religion. Always remember we like nice Jews with Jew jokes. As for Niggerloving communistic agitating Sheenies well just watch yourself Jew boy or we'll cut the rest of it off." (That's telling em Homer.) What about the legalization of marijuana? "Marijuana! Marijuana! Why that's deadlier than cocaine. And what are we going to do about the vile America-hating hoodlums who call themselves hippies, Yippies, and chippies? We are going to put this scum behind bars like the animals they are." (Thunderous applause.) "And I'll tell you something else. A bunch of queers, dope freaks, and degenerated dirty writers is living in foreign lands under the protection of American passports from the vantage point of which they do not hesitate to spit their filth on Old Glory. Well we're going to pull the passports off those dope freaks." (The Technician pushes a sex button and the Simian begins to masturbate.) "Bring them back here and teach them to act like decent Americans." (The Simian emisses, hitting the lens of a Life-Time photographer.) "And I denounce as Communist-inspired the rumors that the dollar collapsed in 1959. I pledge myself to turn the clock back to 1899 when a silver dollar bought a steak dinner and a good piece of ass." (Thunderous applause as a plane writes September 17, 1899, across the sky in smoke.) "I have heard it said that this is a lawless nation that if all the laws in this land were truly enforced we would have thirty percent of the population in jail and the remaining seventy percent on the cops. I say to you if there is infection in this great land it must be cut out by the roots. We will not fall into slack-assed permissive anarchism. I pledge myself to uphold the laws of America and to enforce these hollowed statutes on all violators regardless of race, color, creed or position." (Thunderous applause.) "We will overcome all our enemies foreign and domestic and stay armed to the teeth for years, decades, centuries."

A phalanx of blue-helmeted cops shoulder through the crowd. They stop in front of the deck. The lead cop looks up at A. J. and demands: "Let's see your permits for that purple-assed son of a bitch."

"Permits? We don't have any permits. We don't have to show you any stinking permits. You are talking suh to the future President of America."

The lead cop takes a slip of paper from his shirt pocket and reads MUNICIPAL CODE OF CHICAGO . . . Chapter 98, Section 14: "No person shall permit any dangerous animal to run at large, nor lead any such animal with a chain, rope, or other appliance, whether such animal be muzzled or unmuzzled, in any public way or public place." He folds the paper and shoves it back into his shirt pocket. He points at the Purple Better One. "It's dangerous and we got orders to remove it."

A cop steps forward with a net. The Technician shoves the rage dial all the way up. Screaming, farting, snarling, the Simian leaps off the deck onto the startled officer who staggers back and goes down thrashing wildly on the ground while his fellow pigs stand helpless and baffled not daring to risk a shot for fear of killing their comrade. Finally the cop heaves himself to his feet and throws off the Simian. Panting, bleeding, he stands there his eyes wild. With a scream of rage the Purple Better One throws himself at another patrolman who fires two panicky shots which miss the Simian and crash through a window of the Hilton in the campaign headquarters of a conservative Southern candidate. A photographer from The London *Times* is riddled with bullets by Secret Service men under the misconception he has fired from a gun concealed in his camera. The cop throws his left arm in front of his face. The Simian sinks his canines into the cop's arm. The cop presses his gun against the Simian's chest and pumps in four bullets. Homer Mandrill thuds to the bloody grass, ejaculates, excretes and dies. A. J. points a finger at the cop.

"Arrest that pig!" he screams. "Seize the assassin!"

A. J. was held in $100,000 bail which he posted in cash out of his pocket. Further disturbances erupted at the funeral when a band of vigilantes who call themselves the White Hunters attempted to desecrate the flag-draped body as it was carried in solemn procession through Lincoln Park on the way to its final resting place in Grant Park. The hoodlums were beaten off by A. J.'s guard of Korean Karate experts. The Daughters of the American Revolution who had gathered in front of the Sheraton to protest the legalization of marijuana were charged by police screaming, "Chippies! Chippies! Chippies!" And savagely clubbed to the sidewalk in a litter of diamonds, teeth, blood, mink stoles and handbags.

As the Simian was laid to rest under a silver replica of *The Mayflower* a statue of the Purple Better One in solid gold at the helm, A. J. called for five minutes of silent prayer in memory of our beloved candidate, "Cut down in Grant Park by the bullets of an assassin. . . . A Communistic Jew Nigger inflamed to madness by injections of marijuana. . . . The fact that the assassin had, with diabolical cunning, disguised himself as a police officer indicates the workings of a far-flung communistic plot the tentacles of which may reach into the White House itself. This foul crime shrieks to high heaven. We will not rest until the higher-ups are brought to justice whoever and wherever they may be. I pledge myself to name a suitable and worthy successor. We will overcome. We will realize the aspirations and dreams that every American cherishes in his heart. The American dream can be must be and will be realized. I say to you that Grant Park will be a shrine for all future Americans. In the words of the all-American poet James Whitcomb Riley

> "Freedom shall a while repair
> To dwell a weeping hermit there."

Edward Sanders

Nearly thirty years after the Democratic Convention of 1968, the poet Edward Sanders, one of the founding members of the Fugs, included his eyewitness account of what had happened that summer in Chicago in 1968: A History in Verse *(1997). His long poem describes the most disruptive political rally of the Sixties, which ushered in the backlash among the American electorate that resulted in*

repressive Republican governments under Presidents Richard Nixon
and Ronald Reagan. In the section of 1968 titled "Yeats in the
Gas," Sanders described his response to a comment by his friend,
the folksinger Phil Ochs, after they had experienced the brutal treat-
ment of the Chicago police during the Democratic Convention.

YEATS IN THE GAS

Phil Ochs later mentioned how
in the horror of the gas and the clubs
he thought of Yeats

"I was in the worst police brutality," he said, "right when they
charged up by the Hilton. I was between the charging cops and the
crowd and I raced into a doorway in the nick of time. . . . While rac-
ing away from the tear gas, I just had a sensation of Yeats. I thought of
Yeats (laughs) for some reason."

I wondered about that for years
till it dawned that he might
have been thinking of Yeats' poem
"Easter 1916"

and its repeated line
A terrible beauty is born

That is, those crazy youth and not-so-youth
their hasty signs, their hasty props, their
                                        hasty yells
were transformed in the
                Chicago injustice
                so that
A terrible beauty was born

"Chicago has no government,"
                        said Allen Ginsberg a few weeks later.
"It's just anarchy maintained by pistol. Inside the
convention hall it was rigged like an old Mussolini strong-arm
scene—police and party hacks everywhere illegally, delegates
        shoved around and kidnapped, telephone lines cut."

and, in opposing it,
A terrible beauty was born

I was in a "don't say hello/don't say goodbye"
                                    mood
and wanted to get out of the hell of Chicago
to the safety of Avenue A
            where the street-sweeping trucks
                                    still used water

It all seemed so senseless
            I filed away the clips I cut
    of the action in Chicago
    the leaflets and fliers
                    and let them rest in a box for 28 years

———————————

PART FOUR

"I FEEL LIKE I'M FIXIN' TO DIE": THE COUNTERCULTURE MOVEMENT

Haight-Ashbury is a "new" reality. Yet it shuns reality. It hides in capsules, needles, garish costumes, and defensive egos.

Haight-Ashbury is love. Yet it hates the establishment, the wars, the enforcers of society's "justice," and often itself. It is beset by internal feuding, bickering, power politics, and apathy. None of these "qualities" know love. It scorns the "straights," it ignores laws, it jaywalks and continually snarls traffic on Haight Street. It advocates rebellion. It is a dredge on the economy. It is dishonest.

Haight-Ashbury is a rebellion from conformity . . . to conformity.

Haight-Ashbury has fallen. Haight-Ashbury is a failure. May we have many more failures like it.

THE FAILURE OF HAIGHT-ASHBURY/LOVE GENERATION
[1960s MIMEOGRAPH HANDOUT]

LATE IN 1969, in a manifesto titled "Foreplay," Abbie Hoffman spelled out the essential difference that he saw between political and cultural revolution:

Political revolution leads people into support for other revolutions rather than having them get involved in making their own. Cultural revolution requires people to change the way they live and act in the revolution, rather than passing judgments on how the other folks are proceeding. The cultural view creates outlaws; politics breeds organizers.

In the Sixties, the difference between the literature that came out of the Civil Rights Movement, the Anti–Vietnam War Movement, and the Free Speech Movement, and the literature that evolved out of the Counterculture Movement, defined the difference between politics and culture. The two occasionally combined, as when Country Joe McDonald composed the words to "I Feel Like I'm Fixin'-to-Die Rag" as a biting, iconoclastic warning to his listeners during the Vietnam War. But Country Joe was primarily, like Hoffman, a cultural revolutionary, an outlaw.

As Hoffman understood, the rebellious inhabitants of the new communities, such as the Haight-Ashbury hippies in San Francisco, shared the feeling that "I'm not angry over Vietnam and racism and imperialism. Naturally, I'm against all that shit but I'm *really* pissed cause my friends are in prison for dope and cops stop me on the street cause I have long hair. I'm guilty of a conspiracy, all right. Guilty of creating a liberated land in which we can do whatever the fuck we decide."

There were several public celebrations of the brief, media-beleaguered cultural revolution of the Sixties—among them, the sunrise of the movement at the Be-Ins in San Francisco's Golden Gate Park and New York City's Central Park during the winter and summer of 1967; the three-day rock festival at Woodstock, New York, in August 1969; and the daylong concert four months later at the Altamont racetrack in the hills east of Livermore, California, that signaled what the earlier Welsh poet Dylan Thomas might have called "the dying of the light." Since live performance and the appearance of spontaneity were essential to the spirit of self-expression within the movement, the artistic achievement of the counterculture flourished in the decade's music, theater, and poster art as much as in literature.

Country Joe McDonald

In protest songs such as "I Feel Like I'm Fixin'-to-Die Rag," "Talking Non-Violence," and "Superbird," Country Joe McDonald created witty lyrics that continued the earlier protest tradition of American composers like Woody Guthrie and Malvina Reynolds. McDonald's words expressed the pacifist feelings of his generation. After producer Sam Charters recorded Country Joe and the Fish playing "Fixin' to Die Rag" for Vanguard Records in 1966, the song became the anthem of the anti–Vietnam War movement throughout the world. After the war, McDonald continued to sing his song, but his audience changed as he lent his support to raise money to benefit the Vietnam Veterans Movement for soldiers and nurses who had served their country.

Country Joe McDonald wrote the lyrics for "Janis" as a tribute to Janis Joplin, lead singer for Big Brother and the Holding Company, another of the rock groups popular in the Bay Area. In April 1967, writing a letter to her mother, Joplin told her family how well things were going for her in San Francisco, where she was "becoming quite a celebrity among the hippies."

Later in the letter, Janis described her new boyfriend at the time: "He's head of Country Joe and the Fish, a band from Berkeley. Named Joe McDonald, he's a Capricorn like me & is 25 & so far we're getting along fine. Everyone in the rock scene just thinks it's the cutest thing they've ever seen. It is rather cute actually."

I FEEL LIKE
I'M FIXIN'-TO-DIE RAG

Now come on all of you big strong men
Uncle Sam needs your help again
Got himself in a terrible jam
Way down yonder in Vietnam
Put down your books pick up your gun
Gonna have a whole lotta fun.

Chorus:
And it's 1,2,3 what are we fighting for?
Don't ask me I don't give a damn
The next stop is Vietnam.
And it's 4,5,6,7 open up the Pearly Gates
Well, there ain't no time to wonder why
Woopee, we're all gonna die.

Well come on Generals and let's move fast
Your big chance has come at last
Now you go out and get those reds
The only good Commie is one that's dead
You know that peace can only be won
When you've blown them all to kingdom come.

Chorus

Hey come on Wall Street don't be slow
Why man this is war a go-go
There's plenty good money to be made
Supplying the army with the tools of the trade
Just have to pray if they drop the bomb
They drop it on the Viet Cong.

Chorus

Now come on mothers throughout the land
Pack your boys off to Vietnam
Come on fathers don't hesitate
You send your sons off before it's too late
And you can be the first one on your block
To have your boy come home in a box.

Chorus

TALKING NON-VIOLENCE

Gather 'round me, children, be you black or brown
If you're yellow or white just stick around.
Gonna tell ya 'bout some new times a-comin'
'bout all us Americans sittin' 'round lovin'
   one another, playin' games, workin'
   and singin' together.

Now don't be bashful, don't be shy,
We got a new brand a lovin' we're gonna try,
Just move in close and give me your hand
And together we'll march across this land
   Usin' peaceful, ever-lovin', non-violent resistance.

But first let me explain—and listen close to me—
It ain't gonna be easy—nobody said it be.
The road to freedom is muddy and wide,
You'll trip and stumble, you'll slip and slide,
   But you gotta get up, patch your shoes, wipe off the
   Mud, and keep on a'goin'.

But wait a minute 'fore you get in line.
Hold on now 'fore you pick up that sign.
Stand up straight and look in your brain,
Have you got the fare for the Freedom Train?
   Don't cost much, but baby, it costs!
   Don't get nothin' for nothin'!

When the petition comes, are you ready to sign?
When the pickets come, will you get in line?
When the dogs, the hoses, the clubs and jails
Start movin' in close, will you stand and not fail
   the cause, man? I mean your cause!
   Will you stand?

But don't get excited 'cause I ain't through,
There's more than fightin' you've got to do.
You've got to keep smilin' no matter what's said,
You've got to love that man beatin' you on the head.
   Love him till his hate's all dead.
   Hold out your hand, and keep it out!

And now my children, if you've listened well
To everything I've had to tell,
And if you're tired of sniffin' and crawlin' on the ground
Tired of hatin' and bein' alone,
   Then take my hand and grab that sign,
   Freedom's comin' and we don't want to be left behind.

SUPERBIRD

Look up yonder in the sky now,
Oh, what is that I pray?
It's a bird, it's a plane, it's a man insane,
It's my president L.B.J.
He's flyin' high, way up in the sky,
Just like Superman.
But I've got a little piece of kryptonite,
Yes, I'll bring him back to land.

Chorus:
Come out, Lyndon, with your hands held high,
Drop your guns, baby, and reach for the sky.
We've got you surrounded and you ain't got a chance,
Gonna send you back to Texas—make you work on your
   ranch.
Ya ya—oh ya.

He can call Super Woman and his Super Dogs
But it sure won't do him no good.
Ya, I found out why from a Russian spy
He ain't nothin' but a comic book.
We'll pull him off the stands
And clean up the land,
Yes, we'll have a brand new day.
What is more, I got the Fantastic Four
And Doctor Strange to help him on his way.

[Chorus]

JANIS

Into my life on waves of electrical sound
And flashing lights she came
Into my life with the twist of a dial
The wave of her hand
The warmth of her smile
And even though I know that you and I
Could never find the kind of love we wanted together
    Alone
I find myself missing you and I
You and I, you and I, you and I.

It's not very often
That something special happens
And you and I happen to be that
Something special for me
And walking on grass
Where we rolled and laughed
In the moonlight

I find myself thinking
Of you and I, you and I— You.

Into my eye come visions of patterns
Designs the image of her I see,
Into my mind the smell of her hair
The sound of her voice—we once were there

And even though I know that you and I
Could never find the kind of love we wanted together
    Alone
I find myself missing you and I
You and I— You.

━━━━━━━━━━

Douglas Blazek

*Along with rock music, small-press publications and underground
periodicals flourished in the Sixties counterculture. The poet and
editor Douglas Blazek published, as he recalled, "in hundreds of
magazines that contributed to the ferment of the Sixties. Not only
did I help light the fire with these poems, but I also stirred the pot
by editing the magazine* Ole, *which was dedicated to making po-
etry dangerous." The scholar George Butterick listed 147 periodi-
cals active in the 1960s in volume 16 of the* Dictionary of
Literary Biography *on "The Beats: Literary Bohemians in Post-
war America." Some were long-lasting, such as Diane di Prima's*
Floating Bear, *Ed Sanders's* Fuck You/A Magazine of the
Arts, *and the City Lights'* Journal for Protection of All Be-
ings, *among many others.*

In the essay "On Small Press as Class Struggle," included in
Editor's Choice: Literature & Graphics from the U.S. Small
Press, 1965–1977, *Merritt Clifton recognized that small presses
gave a voice to working-class writers in the Sixties and endured
through and beyond the storms of the decade, largely because the
people running them—unlike rock musicians and poster artists and
inhabitants of hippie communes—could make themselves indistin-
guishable from the mainstream.*

> *Small pressmanship can accordingly be linked to such
> other movements as the civil rights struggle, the antiwar
> protests, and feminism. But unlike these, small
> pressmanship is not a mass movement. To begin with, it*

> *does not concern the average citizen. Small pressmanship*
> *is by definition a minority viewpoint concerning what are*
> *minority interests already. It is not an obvious activity;*
> *unless one looks for inkstains beneath fingernails, the*
> *small pressman cannot be told from his more docile*
> *neighbor, who watches television, accepting intelligentsia*
> *verdicts on what to think or not think.*

As a book reviewer, Blazek wrote his blazing prose in "THE little PHENOMENA" for the East Village Other *newspaper early in 1968. His column caught his live-wire enthusiasm about what was happening in the small-press scene.*

THE little PHENOMENA

LITERATURE IS NOW A WHEEL OF FIRE and it's burning a new cycle into the skulls of more people than even before—mostly young people who first heard of gas chambers instead of jolly ice cream cones & ferris wheels. There is more direct communication, more involvement in life, more concern for the acts & paths of man in literature than ever before & 90% of this fire is located in the little magazines & small press publications that slither out of ungodly mimeos & breadsucking offsets & even out of a few ambitious speed-veined hand letterpresses.

Three of the magazines most infested with the fire are ENTRAILS No. 4 ($1, 283 E. Houston, N.Y.C. 10002), HORSESHIT No. 2 ($2, Scum Pub. Co., Box 361, Hermosa Beach, Cal. 90254), & THE WILLIE (50c, c/o 1379 Masonic, S.F. 94117).

ENTRAILS is edited by Mike Berardi in lieu of Gene Bloom (busy proselytizing inmates of Sing Sing while serving out a grass bust) & is simply loaded with insanity, ennui slayers & dementia cacklers. Read about the new identification procedure called "Dickprinting." Read about the hilarious judge who said "1½ to 3 years, Sing Sing." Read about the nun who said "FUCK." Read a review of the 1967 Spring/Summer Sears Catalogue. Also, a reprinting of the hard to get underground creamery, HUNGER, by E. R. Baxter, plus fantastic prose & poesy by Fred Dawson, Sid Rufus, Charles Bukowski, Rich Krech, Harold Norse, Willie, Runcible Wagner & even myself.

HORSESHIT is a magazine not recommended for children or

idiots. It can, in words as well as drawings, stand up to our Animal Farm in D.C. & say FUCK YOU & refuse to creep off in fear of pot-shots, cream pies or Jack Rubyisms. Nearly all the art work spreads our toad glum faces into radiant laughter sparklers & there are two MUSTS as far as prose: "The Last Words of Jefferson Monroe Before He Was Torn To Pieces On The Floor Of Congress" & "A Killer?" "Yes, Sir." "One Of Our Soldiers Is A Killer?" "Yes, Sir." "Good God!" a story that picks up the ax where Dalton Trumbo (JOHNNY GOT HIS GUN) put it down.

The last little jewel is THE WILLIE, a maverick little mimeo that has more guts than Sam Bass robbing a 90 m.p.h. Santa Fe super chief. The whole pleasure of this wild-ass death stomper is the spirit of its editor, Willie the Snort Gobbler, who is a minor legend in S.F.—land a la Kerouac. Wear asbestos gloves & red shades when you pick up this rag—IT IS HOTTER THAN FIRE! IT IS THE UNIVERSE'S WHITE LIGHT! Complete with reviews, statements, ejaculations, etc. by Willie, & poems by Bukowski, Brown Miller, Kent Taylor, Geo Montgomery, Steve (Earth Rose) Richmond, Norse, Jesus Christ, d. a. levitation, Wagner, Cauble, Grapes, Kiennolz, Wantling (& myself, again) this magazine, available at all bookstores, butcher shops & Cosmic Pastry Parlors, is the greatest bargain Woolworths never thought of!

Reading an article on what a doctor terms "the new pornography": "At one time, pornography generally referred to obscenity with regard to sex. But, since every aspect of sex has received so much exposure in recent years, there is little excitement roused in reading about it."

Which is all very interesting. If sex is not the thing to get busted for, then it must be death. I logically deduct that Jim Lowell, d. a. levy, Lenore Kendal (THE LOVE BOOK) and Steve Richmond (FUCK HATE) were busted for either publishing or selling books that pertain to death and "offend good taste." How ironic when one considers that these people have all been such pro-life, vibrant, and alive individuals, espousing a reverence for life rather than an exploitation and promiscuous use of it.

If this new pornography is now the rage of smuthunters, I sure wish they would catch on in Cleveland, Santa Monica and S.F. In case they don't I strongly urge you, demand, even threaten you to buy (no fair reading in the store, then putting it back on the shelf, creeps) A TRIBUTE TO JIM LOWELL ($2 / Asphodel Bookshop / 306 Superior Ave. W / Cleveland, Ohio 44113). The book, a compendium on censorship, serving a weighty value for anyone interested in fascism, as well as being a tribute to the owner of one of the gutsiest bookshops in the world—such people as Bukowski, Cauble, Cunliffe, DeLoach, Dowden, Ferlinghetti, Kryss, Laughlin, Levertov, Lowell, Lowenfels, MacDonald, McClure, Miller, Olson, Selby, Sorrentino, Wagner, Wantling, Weissner, Williams, levy and myself all get to spew into the eyes of the Storm Troopers.

Other items of interest that stem from the diabolical underworld & contain samples of both the old & the new pornography (hmmmm) are FREE LOVE PERIODICALLY #2 (50c / Asphodel Bookshop), which reprints levy's VISUALIZED PRAYER FOR THE AMERICAN GOD—a swastika formed by pointillistic $$-signs. We are also informed in this wild mimeo that d. a. levy's tribute issue, YOU CAN HAV YR FUCKIN CITY BACK, will be coming out soon for $1.50, available from The Asphodel Bookshop, which ought to be another compendium of censorship to mate with the Lowell Tribute. Also coming an RJS / GENE BLOOM STEVE RICHMOND TRIBUTE (price unknown). POEMS FROM THE MIND JAIL by Dominique is a small hand-wrought pamphlet with silk-screen cover that is very intriguing & the poems are surprizingly endearing (25c / Asphodel Bookshop).

From Wisconsin comes QUIXOTE (22 Henry St. Madison); it has no price listed but I'm sure $1 will procure you a copy & you should procure it because there is a trump card in every issue—a joker as well—something to amuse the intellect & to elevate the boob. A Quixote Supplement entitled THE DESTRUCTION OF PHIL-ADELPHIA by Mike Maggid is an amazing concoction of poetry, collages, drawings, prose & ??? (meaning the undefinable).

Two pamphlets from Great Lakes Books (733 E. Clarke Milwaukee 53212) are liable to cause a little harm to stagnant minds (come on, censors, attack!): MAYORS OF MARBLE by Morgan Gibson & PRELUDE TO INTERNATIONAL VELVET DEBUTANTE by Gerard Malanga. Malanga is good when he is not soaking his typer in the sensationalism of Warhol & The Gang, but here he is soaking. Gibson is good & doesn't soak, suck or sack—he knows not sleep, his brain cells are always saluting new levels of perception.

Now for the treat, the strawberries with whipped cream that has nothing to do with wet-dreams, baby—KARMA CIRCUIT by Harold Norse, $2.75, Nothing Doing in London Press, 10 Blacklands Tr., Sloane Sq., London SW3). Norse has only had three books previous to this one, all excellent but antediluvian by the standards he sets here, plus a special issue of OLE magazine which included tributes, letters, & various bits by Baldwin, Burroughs, Nin, Bukowski, W. C. Williams, Paul Carroll, etc. (which is still available in some bookshops for $1).

Several of these poems were first published in that special issue of OLE & are reissued here along with many new ones—all of which are saturated with genius—a word I don't understand but seems to be used as the tantamount in praise.

Norse is his own man, with his own visions & he can synchronize them so beautifully into poems that I often wonder whether he was conditioned to think by other worldly beings instead of mere earthlings. Unfortunately, there are only 500 of these books printed—but that should increase the drama; only a selected few will know these poems—because of that the flavor will be more poignant than ever conceived.

Emmett Grogan

Perhaps the preeminent chronicler of the counterculture's activities in San Francisco in the mid-1960s was Emmett Grogan (Eugene Leo Michael Emmett Grogan), who published his outspoken memoir Ringolevio *in 1972. In the book, Grogan described how he and others in San Francisco founded the Diggers, a loosely organized group who shunned publicity but tried to make the counterculture in the Haight-Ashbury district of the city a functioning community by opening "free stores" and supplying food to the needy.*

Grogan had little tolerance or respect for the people who he thought were using the counterculture to further their own careers or to enrich their own pockets. His account of the San Francisco Human Be-In was scathingly candid, in contrast to the thousands of sentimental words poured out by media hacks on the spectacle.

Along with local rock bands, Allen Ginsberg, Gary Snyder, Jerry Rubin, and Timothy Leary were the stars of the event, advertised as a "Gathering of the Tribes."

Agitprop theater thrived during the height of the counterculture movement. Grogan supported the idea that

Theater is fact/action . . . the Diggers [were perceived] as life-actors, and their activities as theater, because it provided a very good cover and satisfied the curiosity of the authorities and general public, as well as exciting the hipper members of the New Left. Of course, it was just a superficial description of what was really going on—the same thing as classifying the Saint Valentine's Day Massacre as "Theater of Cruelty." It was simply an account of the casual, outward, conscious style of the Diggers and some of the things they did, and not an examination of the heightened awareness of the intrinsic essence of the Digger operation or its motives. The elements of guerrilla theater and street events were merely accessories contingent upon the fundamental reality of Free Food, the free stores, the free goods, and the free services made available to the people. The San Francisco Diggers attempted to organize a solid, collective, comparative apparatus to provide resources sufficient for the people to set up an alternative power base, which wouldn't have to depend on either the state or the system for its sustenance.

FROM *RINGOLEVIO*

THE HUMAN BE-IN was publicized as a "Gathering of the Tribes," but it was actually more a gathering of the suburbs with only a sprinkling of nonwhites in the crowd of three hundred thousand. It was a showcase for beaded hipsterism with only one stage for the assembly to face. On it sat the HIP [Haight Independent Proprietors] merchants, their consultants, and several psychedelic superstars, while the Quicksilver Messenger Service, the Airplane and The Grateful Dead played their sets over a PA system guarded by Hell's Angels who were asked to do so after several incidents had occurred. The turkeys had been made into thousands of sandwiches under John-John's supervi-

sion, and the bread was salted down with crushed acid. Gary orga-
nized the free distribution of the sandwiches to those who looked like
they needed something to eat, physically or spiritually. Afterwards,
Emmett[1] walked to one side of the stage and stood below it, watching
the so-called luminaries of the alternative culture. He felt a sense of
anger and despair over the way the Be-In had been set up and pre-
sented. Their advertising had assembled three hundred thousand peo-
ple, and all they gave them was a single stage with a series of schmucks
schlepping all over it, making speeches and reciting poetry nobody
could hear, with interludes of music. It was even more incredible to
Emmett that the crowd crushed forward for a better spot where they
could stargaze at the feeble spectacle. The HIP merchants had invited
the Berkeley radicals to participate in the Be-In, as a placating gesture
to the left-wing, liberal media. They were more than happy to come,
of course, and were represented on the stage by the baby-fat runt
himself, Jerome Rubin. All made up in the image of a true Russian
theorist complete with a Trotsky-Stalinesque moustache, he called for
a marriage between the Haight-Ashbury and Berkeley tribes, pro-
claiming that "our smiles are our political banners and our nakedness
is our picket sign!" He was awed and shaken by the enormity of the
crowd and several times he seemed about to wet his pants, ecstatic
over his getting to speak to so many at once. But he was afraid to be-
gin sounding like the cornball square he is, so he gave up the micro-
phone after a few minutes and sat down to ask his gooseberry, Stew
Alpert, whether he had come on like a hippie or an old straight. Stew
Alpert is to Jerome Rubin what Clyde Tolson is to John Edgar
Hoover and he was quick to assure him that he flashed everyone with
his ability to make hip-sounding remarks and even shocked some
with his new image. Timothy Leary followed and he seemed to be a
bit juiced, only able to mumble, "Tune-in, turn-on, drop-out," once
or twice to the crowd before he sat back down with that same old
shit-eating grin all over his face.

Allen Ginsberg, like everyone on the stage, was pleased with the
giant, press publicity–engineered turn-out of people. He even ap-
peared to believe that the mere assembling of such a crowd was a su-
perworthy achievement in itself, negating any need for further action.
In a way it did. Since the body count of three hundred thousand as-
sured the HIP and their friends of worldwide media coverage, why

---

1. Emmett Grogan, like Norman Mailer, refers to himself by name in his third-
person narrative.

give the press anything to photograph or write about other than the people who gathered? That way it was one great big fashion show, that's all.

More ham chewers trooped up to the mike and kept saying how wonderful it was with all that energy in one place at the same time. Just being. Being together—touching, looking, loving, embracing each other—that's what it was all about, they said: "The New Consciousness!" Then, the mantra began: *"We are one!" "We are one!"* Three hundred thousand people shouted repeatedly that they were one, and Emmett just sat on the grass and watched them pretend, wondering how long it was going to take before people stopped kidding themselves.

Someone parachuted out of a single-engine plane into the middle of the meadow and several thousand people began swearing that they just saw a vision of God. Poet Gary Snyder ended it all by blowing on a conch shell and everyone turned toward the falling sun and walked toward the Pacific Ocean to watch the dusk from the beach.

Later that evening and throughout the following week, the mass media kept applauding and broadcasting the news about what they called the dawning of a new era for the country and for the world. They pointed out that everything had been peaceful with no fights among the *gigantic crowd* of three hundred thousand. Well, no large, serious slugfests, at least. Just a few dozen minor stompings. The love shuck was given momentum by all the coverage, and the press even began calling the Love Ghetto of Haight-Ashbury things like "Psychedelphia" and "Hashbury." The HIP merchants were astounded by their own triumph in promoting such a large market for their wares. They became the Western world's taste makers overnight and built a power base upon their notoriety and their direct line into the mass media. The city's officialdom began to take the HIP leadership class a little more seriously. They held public conferences with them about token problems, like the rerouting of the municipal buses to avoid clogging up the Haight Street traffic, which was already overburdened with squares, shopping for a far-out purchase to bring back to suburbia.

Emmett was angry. He didn't give a fuck about how much bread the HIP merchants were making, or particularly care that only a chosen few in the community were actually benefiting from these profits. He was simply angered by the outrageous publicity that the Haight Independent Proprietors had created to develop new markets for the merchandising of their crap—angry about how their newsmongery was drawing a disproportionate number of young kids to the district that was already overcrowded—thousands of young, foolish kids who fell for the Love Hoax and expected to live comfortably poor and take their place in the district's kingdom of love. Angry with most of the heads in the community who were earning a dollar doing something, like the rock musicians, and kidding themselves by feeling that all the notoriety was good and would bring more money into the underground and expand the HIP shops, providing more jobs for those who wanted them. The truth was that the disastrous arrival of thousands too many only meant more money for the operators of fly-by-night underground-culture outfits, the dope dealers, and the worst of the lot, the shopkeepers who hired desperate runaways to do piece-work for them at sweatshop wages. It was a catastrophe and there was nothing to be done except leave, or try to deal with it as best one could. Whenever someone sought to reveal the truth of the situation, they were put down, ignored or dismissed as being unhip by the long-haired, false-bottomed hipsters who had money in the bank. Emmett understood that he might be making a mistake by judging his anonymity more important than exposing the hype that was going down, but he felt it would be dumb to open his mouth to the media. He would only end up as down payment for the future of a mob of middle-class kids who were just experimenting with hunger—young-sters who were playing hooky from suburbia to have an adventure of poverty. He felt that most of them would return to the level of society which bred them but he also knew that some of them would never, ever get back home to compare their stories of wantage with their parents' "You'll-never-know-what-it-was-like" tales of the Depression.

"Emmett Grogan" had become an anonym to the public and he understood that. It would have been relatively easy for him to have captured the media spotlight, gain recognition, and finesse his own acclamation as a leader by broadcasting to the youth of the nation, telling them to stay where they were because they had been deceived. But it already seemed too late to stop them. They were thoroughly duped into coming to the Haight-Ashbury and they were eagerly on their way and there was nothing to be done. He decided to continue in his attempt to effect something substantial and relevant to cope with the oncoming invasion, instead of exchanging his anonymity for the notoriety which would have accompanied his denunciation of the HIPs as pigs to the press.

He had been dealing in Free Food for over four months now, and things like Free Food do something to a person when he keeps them going for a long time. They tend to give him a healthy respect for reality and a deep disdain for the fake political ploys of the fraudulent Left. And so, he went on as a Digger, doing things that were, at least, pertinent and to the point of some community need, and he left the performance of trivial, unavailing antics to the fatuous publicity seekers who were most of the self-proclaimed radical spokesmen of his generation.

His seemingly resolute adherence to anonymity confused the political careerists, and he enjoyed watching them try to figure out whether he was just a sucker or someone with an angle up his sleeve. But he never thought about the semantics or tactics of politics long enough for him to become bitter. His work kept him too tired and busy to want to hassle himself about mere words and people who did nothing but use them. There was, however, a large group of men in the city who functioned only with words, but whose use of them was very important to Emmett. They were the poets who first broadcast the news to him—the news that he now needed to know. They had all come to San Francisco for a sort of reunion, using the activity surrounding the Human Be-In as their point of convergence. Emmett wanted to meet and speak with all of them and was knocked out when Richard Brautigan told him that the poets felt the same way about the Diggers and wanted to have a poetry reading for them.

The arrangements were quickly made for a reading to be held in Gino and Carlo's bar in the beat section of North Beach. It was advertised by word of mouth, and by a newspaper columnist as a "benefit for the Diggers." So many poets showed up to read that night, and so many people came to listen, that the gathering had to be divided in half between Gino's and another bar, forcing the poets to walk back and forth to each place if they wanted their poetry to be heard by everyone.

The people who made up the audience that night had been reading news stories and had been hearing about the Diggers and "their philanthropic social work" for months, but never anything about where the Diggers got the money to do all those things. So when the word went out that the reading was to be a benefit for the Diggers, they naturally assumed that meant a donation. But it didn't. There was no admission or cover charge or money collected in either bar—it was all free. Allen Ginsberg and Gary Snyder accidentally passed a hat around Gino's for a collection, however, while the Diggers were arranging things at the other location. When Emmett and [Peter]

Coyote arrived, the money had already been collected and the hat was given to them. But, instead of accepting it, the two immediately asked for everyone's attention and announced that there was a· mistake. "The only type of benefit that could be thrown for the Diggers is one where everything is free!" Then, they gave the hat to the bartender and told him to count the money out on the bar in front of everybody, and to continue buying rounds for the crowd for as long as the bread held out.

"That's a Digger benefit!" laughed Coyote, and everyone applauded.

And Gary Snyder remarked to Allen Ginsberg, "Did you see that? They gave it all away—back to the people!" The money lasted a long time because there was a lot of it in that hat. "An awful lot of it," Emmett had thought when it was handed to him. It was far into the morning before the sound of poetry turned into conversation, and everyone agreed that a good time was had by all. The only other poets the people would like to have seen there that night were Charles Olson and Gregory Corso, but they were well represented, even though they hadn't been able to make it to San Francisco.

———————

R. G. D a v i s

Among the hundreds of experimental theater groups that thrived in the Sixties—perhaps most notably Peter Schumann's Bread and Puppet Theatre in New York City, and the Living Theatre in New York City and Europe—the San Francisco Mime Troupe was one of the most successful. R. G. Davis with the Mime Troupe wrote A Minstrel Show or: Civil Rights in a Cracker Barrel *as an extension of his work with nontraditional theater. He recalled that the minstrel show*

> evolved out of working for five years in the avant garde
> movement and on Commedia dell'arte in the parks,

*outside the establishment's usual theatrical venues and
even outside buildings. Over a period of time we collected
a performance piece that exceeded the anti-white or
pro-black shows of Amiri Baraka, rather focusing on
racism in a racist society and also within the left. Not
content to puncture the misdemeanors of the middle class,
we challenged the assumptions of superficial integration
without socio-economic change.*

Davis credited Saul Landau, an activist and filmmaker who
later produced the film Que Hacer *(1970)* about Chile, for pro-
viding "half the script and much of the political savvy. Juris Svend-
son the critique, John Broderick, Jason Marc Alexander the guts of
the down dirty, popular culture that arose from our nine months of
research and rehearsal." The music for the San Francisco Mime
Troupe's production of Minstrel Show *was written by the composer
Steve Reich, who also provided the score for the fourteen-minute
film* O Dem Watermelons, *photographed and edited by Bob
Nelson with a script by Landau and the cast of the show; it was
shown during the stage performances in 1966. As director and actor
in* Minstrel Show, *Davis was most concerned with what he consid-
ered "the visual aspect, the kinesthetic aspect" of each performance.
This description of the play is from Davis's book* The San Fran-
cisco Mime Troupe: The First Ten Years *(1975).*

A MINSTREL SHOW OR:
CIVIL RIGHTS IN A CRACKER BARREL

IN 1964, when I first thought about doing a show on racism, *The
Blacks* by Genet came to mind. I had seen the New York production
and was fascinated by its possibilities. Although I was dubious about
the relevance of the play, I thought if I could find Black Muslims (not
knowing what they were like at the time) or black activists, I could
achieve a quality not obtained in the New York production. I hoped
to reach a strength and depth rarely achieved by using non-political
actors. Roger Blins's production of *The Blacks* in Paris had used polit-
ically hip actors and reports of the performances indicated a far
greater confrontation with audience consciousness.

My search ended for a number of reasons: the lack of performers;
Black Muslims and Black nationalists were not about to consider

Genet's play; we couldn't mount a production like I envisioned without some organization and we had none; and the rights for the production had been sewn up by the New York producers, who made sure that no one did the production unless they profited, which, of course, meant few productions. The choice of play faded from possibility, but the hope of using politically active people as performers stayed on.

The search for relevant material on civil rights continued until one of us (either Nina, Saul or myself) happened upon the idea: why not write a play—write a minstrel show. The idea was nurtured by finding out that minstrel shows were a part of our cultural heritage from 1830 to 1920 and, at its peak, there were three hundred floating companies, from town to city, amateur and professional, rapping out: "Mr. Bones, who was dat chicken Ah saw you wid de odder night?" We realized that by doing an original minstrel show, or an adaptation of an old one, we would be following the line we had established with commedia: adaptations or returning it to 1600s commedia; and, of course, we would get right into the problem of racism—ours and everyone else's—by unearthing those stereotypes, clichés, cornballs and all that Uncle Tom jive.

Our first cast was memorable. I placed some ads and sent out a few press releases, announcing we were holding auditions for a minstrel show. In 1965, racial activists were for integration. The first call was attended by about fifteen people—some white, some black—who came to our Capp Street theatre. I told them we were going to go through some difficult personal and political confrontations and I wanted to be as out-front as possible. I said, "We are going to unearth the garbage of our culture and sort it out. For example: we would like to open the show with something like 'eeny meany miney moe, catch a nigger by the toe . . .'" This little rhyme had been taught to me as a kid, probably by my Negro maid, and we were going to get it up and out and use it for what it was worth. I blushed on saying that rhyme in front of blacks, but that was the essence of the minstrel show.

Selecting performers for a show that was not yet written was difficult. Although none of us had seen a minstrel show, Amos and Andy, the Marx Brothers' darkie movies, Stepin Fetchit and Rochester were in our consciousness. We knew much of the stereotypical racism was pounded soft by WASPish thinking and we expected to have a rough go.

We auditioned and auditioned. Finally, one day Roy and Willie Ballard walked into the studio with a group of black-bereted street

politicos. They had been famous in demonstrations at the Sheraton Palace and now were working the Cadillac sit-ins. (Cadillac sold more cars to Negroes, and, it followed, why not demand Negro Cadillac salesmen! Some of us saw the Cadillac Row issue like Paul Jacobs, who said: "And the difference between a white goniff and a black goniff?")

I didn't discuss political tactics with Roy or Willie Ballard because they brought along Willie Hart and Jason Marc Alexander. Roy looked particularly macho and interesting as a type, but was no stage performer. His brother couldn't keep a beat. But Jason was flash and Willie was a natural. I think they auditioned by singing. Willie Hart led them in one of those intertwined quartet sets that black kids do on the street: four voices in four-part harmony. Willie Hart underplayed his character, Hokus, who was a country Stepin Fetchit; while Jason played a snappy urban street hood. Both guys were essential to the creation of the show and stayed in the entire two-year run. We never did find a permanent third black to match these two, although, in the early rehearsals, we worked with a great performer who was five feet wide and six feet tall, played piano, could dance and sing, and was a fine actor. He left. The show was merciless and each joke was self-critical. He couldn't stand up to the scrutiny of the form: racism, white or black. He did not dig the politics or the jokes at his size. He would not admit that he was twice the width of any one performer and we found out later that he hadn't noticed he was Negro until the age of twenty-one.

We collected a number of whites from various sources: John Broderick from commedia days, the curly-haired kid who could bullshit back at Jason. Both about twenty-two, they didn't give a shit for racism, so they would just slam insults back and forth. More sophisticated, I found myself embarrassed by John's slinging, but it was great for all of us. Jason got hit sometimes and he did some hurting in turn.

I had presumed that I would play a part, but I could not. It took all of my time to try and figure out the show. We finally got Kai Spiegal, who had played Père Ubu, to take on the endman, Klinker. Six minstrels, three white, three black, all in black face, powder satin-blue tails, black fright wigs and white lips and eyes. They were out of sight. In the dark, they were crazy. We decided that we would use blacks and whites—yes, integrated—but all playing in black face, so that the audience would have to struggle through the performance trying to figure out which were black and which were white. The process would unnerve them and fuck up their prejudices.

The spirit of commedia ran through the Minstrel Show, stereotypical characters, exaggerated gestures, masks, in this case blackface with white parts that were particularized by each performer, and the whole show was done in presentational form. The element that made the show particularly American, and in part an American commedia, was that it was based upon the many years of minstrel show history in the collective theatrical conscience of the United States. We not only knew of Amos and Andy, the Black Crows and a few solo comics, but we discovered that the country had been criss-crossed for eighty years by traveling groups. At its peak three hundred–odd companies performed in blackface doing musical numbers and nigger jokes. Minstrel types were imbedded in white unconsciousness: even though the books didn't talk much about popular forms, we saw the show's stereotypes in oppressed ghetto characters. Whereas our commedia poked holes in American stuffiness, the minstrel show up-chucked the unmelted pieces from the melting pot.

The Interlocutor in rehearsal was played by Saul, but it was important to have an older man, someone with a deep voice and a presence like the traditional ringmaster—a circus ringmaster. The only example of an Interlocutor I had seen was in the Russian circus, an adult figure to the childlike clown.

For the minstrel show we found an older man who was a little slow but who had a deep, rich voice. While the kids squeaked, he would bellow. Somehow or other, money got in the way and he expected to get paid for each rehearsal. About a week before we opened the show for in-house previews, he quit. As always, I found myself on stage in a top hat with some stupid make-up, trying to play a basso profundo. I could make some of the bullshit, but I knew I was on only for a short while. We needed a taller actor, too, somebody who could look down on the six-foot Willie Hart.

Robert Slattery worked on the waterfront as a longshoreman and had been involved in political activity in the Bay Area. He walked in, looked down at me with his great, mature, stone WASPish face like a fine Clark Kent, tough and determined. I can't remember auditioning him. It was a miracle, and how can anyone audition miracles? Slattery was so hard and cornball that he was almost impossible to replace. When he got tired of us, we tried others who gave different interpretations, but when Slattery came out on stage, you knew white America was in the middle of these screaming, ranting darkies and that he was the thing to be attacked. He was no paper tiger, he was strong, imposing and he had the show in his hands. He was the perfect ringmaster.

We placed our stereotypes (Stepin Fetchits, even radical blacks) in conflict with Mr. America. The stage conflict had to reflect the observable social conditions, otherwise it would have been fantasy and dream therapy, rather than politically relevant. The movement had yet to develop a strong radical leadership. Malcolm X was just clearing the ground for many blacks and some whites. The Panthers had not begun to talk tough yet. We had to investigate why the civil rights movement objected to Uncle Tom.

Uncle Tom, it turns out, was not as horrible as I imagined. The minstrel show darkie is a variation of a Tom, either drawl outside and quick-witted inside (Stupidus from Roman mime, Pulcinella from commedia) or the snappy, urbane dude (Sanio, Roman; Brighella, commedia). The lower classes develop great means of survival and Uncle Tom, even in Harriet Beecher Stowe's novel, is a survival character. A Christian slave who, rather than tell on his escaped companions, suffers a beating (the martyr), yet he doesn't flee. In struggling to leap out of the slavish obedience to racist America, civil rights lambasted the Uncle Tom; however, not in this show. We raised him to smart alec, to wise conniver, to brute threat to white man's existence, and learned to respect him.

In addition to our social analysis, we had to deal with the personal liberation of each actor; not only to incorporate some material we might find in each performer but also to make sure that the individuals would present the collective point of view. I asked each actor to talk privately into a tape recorder about the time he first realized his black, white or ethnic identity. We learned a lot. Jason and Willie had torturous early experiences. Willie saw his father run across the path of a milk truck. The driver, furious that he almost hit the man, yelled out: "You fuckin' nigger . . ." His father didn't say anything. Marc Alexander lived with his mother, who was a mammie to some white kids. He went to play with the black kids down the road and they threw him in a box and called him "whitey," while they kicked the box around. Don Pedro Colley, at twenty-one, walked into a dining room in some college in Oregon and didn't sit at the table with all the blacks, but with the whites. They pointed to the black table. White-Spanish-descent kid, Julio Martinez, said, "We were never prejudiced against Negroes. Of course, we were never taken for Negroes."

All of us heard these important "coming-of-age moments." Those who had realized early their skin color or ethnic origins understood our show and created its whip-like intensity. Performers who had not experienced the existential racial twist until very late never stayed on long.

We worked on the show for nine months, constructing it slowly. After the fourth month, I increased rehearsals to twice a week and there was a demand for money. Jason and Willie needed it; the whites looked on with interest. We began to pay five dollars a week to each performer. Increasing the number of days of rehearsal, but keeping the pay the same, we finally got our show moving enough to see run-throughs and rehearsals of the whole thing. Music was put together by various banjo players. The choreography or scene management I put together with the help of Jason and some stuff by John Broderick. We did a tambourine, shoutin', stompin', cake-walk for the opener that was a minstrel show version of a commedia warm-up. It was practiced till everyone was swinging together. It opened to a roar of applause and when the Interlocutor came on and gave out with the glib, "Gentlemen, beee seated . . ." (the traditional opener), we had warmed up the house.

Minstrel shows had a particular format which we simply imitated. The cross-fire was quick, rapid-fire cornball gags between minstrel and interlocutor.

> [Viz: Read very fast in minstrel lilt; Interlocutor—straight white man; Minstrel—exaggerated Tom]

Talk:
Inter: Gentlemen, be seated. *[All sit except Gimme.]*
Gimme: Wish I was rich, wish I was rich, wish I was rich.
Inter: I heard you the first time, Mr. Gimme.
Gimme: Did you? But de fairy gimme three wishes, and dem was it.
Inter: Where did you see a fairy?
Gimme: On a ferry-boat. *[All guffaw. Gimme sits.]*
Inter: Mr. Bones, are you a Republican or a Democrat?
Bones: *[jumping up]* Oh, I'm a Baptist.
Inter: Come, come. Whom did you vote for last time?
Bones: Robinson Crusoe.
Inter: What did he run for?
Bones: Exercise. *[All yuk yuk; Bones stays standing with Interlocutor.]*
Inter: Now, cut out the foolishness. Are you a Republican or a Democrat?

Bones: Democrat.
Inter: And your wife is also a Democrat?
Bones: She was, but she bolted.
Inter: Bolted the party?
Bones: No, just me. When I come home late, she bolts de door. *[All guffaw.]*

Although there was some original material in the show, brilliant stuff improvised by the minstrels or written by Saul Landau, the basic format and material had been "gleaned" from the old minstrel shows. I read hundreds of pages of cross-fire, picking out the most appropriate gags I could find: those with a bit of political relevance and ones we could make funny. There were probably tons of garbage done in the old minstrel shows and only some of it was usable in 1965. Cross-fire, the heart of the minstrel show, was actually no more than a traditional routine between two performers: the straight man and his clown. When minstrel shows faded away, vaudeville took their place with duos like Weber and Fields or Gallagher and Scheen, who did cross-fire dialogues, but without the other six or ten minstrels.

We followed the cross-fire with a traditional Stump Speech on Evolution, done by John Broderick in the style of a Southern senator (couldn't tell if he was black or white), then a great song: "Old Black Joe" first sung in part by the minstrels, who turned their backs to the audience in pseudo-piety, bowed their heads as the Interlocutor recited. One of the minstrels didn't bow his head completely and began to masturbate (simulated) as the dramatic recital continued. There was the complete opposition of elements working toward hysteria. The tone and presentation of "Old Black Joe" by Bob Slattery was superb, something like Laurence Olivier or Paul Robeson, and directly behind him this blue-coated crazy whippin' it off. The cops could barely write it all down fast enough, the heavy ideologues winced or winked at the childishness, but thousands got hysterical.

The Interlocutor finished off his portion of the song with a rendition of "Old Black Joe" in flamboyant Spanish:

> Se fueron los dias buenos
> Cuando mi corazon era joven y feliz
> Se fueron tambien mis amigos buenos
> De las sueldos de algodón.
> Se pasaban, se pasaban para una tierra mejor, eso lo se.

Escucho las voces suaves llamando me
VIEJO NEGRITO JOSE.

He dissolved in tragic tears and was led off center by one of the minstrels who took pity on him. The others began to march around and Klinker jumped up on the chair and shouted in platdeutsch (à la Nazi), to the marching minstrels:

Grammaphone gesellschaft,
Volkswagen uber alles;
Hansel und Gretel in der Schwarzwald.

They stopped marching. He came down stage and ended the number with a bark to the audience, "Alta Swartza Jeuden." The minstrels jived him back to his chair and we resumed the "rational" format of the minstrel show.

Bones asked the Interlocutor for permission to tell the folks something and, of course, the Interlocutor allowed:

Bones: I am here, my friends, to speak before you, one and
        all, to honor a very festive occasion.
Group: Yeh, Ho hum. *[yawns]*
Bones: For it has been proclaimed throughout this land by
        the President hisself, as sure as he is the leader of this
        humble band of people, that one week will be set aside
        every year at the same time so that we can *all* take pride
        in the accomplishments of the past. So, we for you are
        going to retrace back through the years and the ages the
        history of the colored race as glorious as the Bible's
        pages. Yes, at times, things looked very bleak for the
        black man—
Group: And very black for the bleak man!
Bones: But it is changed, for Nego History Week will tell
        you all how it really happened. How we balance out on
        the great ledger book of time, and who was who in literature, so that we looks mighty fine, and deserving of a
        week unto ourselves.
(Note: Negro has no "r" in the Minstrel Show text, we said
        Nego.)

Nego history went on with mimetic and verbal demonstrations to portray Crispus Attucks, the first black man to be killed in the War for Independence; Toussaint L'Ouverture, an articulate spokesman of black revolution; Booker T. Washington and his relations with Teddy Roosevelt; George Washington Carver and the peanut; black soldiers in Vietnam; and a jail scene with Martin Luther King, which ended in a rising tide of black power images. We punctured some of the exaggerated claims for three of the heroes, cut into the Uncle Tomism in Booker T. and the absurdity of a poor black man killing yellow men for an imperialist (racist) power.

Nego History ended with the minstrels banging chairs on stage, yelling at the audience, "We're brave. We're strong. Black is beautiful. Blood in the streets. Revenge." About to get out of control, the Interlocutor rushes in to calm the darkies. We picked up the tempo with cross-fire. Then the Interlocutor suggested that Gimme and Snowball "improvise" a "chick/stud scene." (Terrible ruse, but in fake minstrel style, we could yassa boss it to believability. Nothing was assumed as truth.)

The chick/stud scene was the breaking point of the show. If Nego History didn't bruise emotions and hidden treasures, then the sight of a black stud picking up a white chick in a bar and taking her home to bed usually succeeded. The magic of the show was the unearthing of stereotypical images, placing them on stage, making them move rapidly from cornball black jokes (minstrel racism) to radical black (radical puncturing) jokes thus transforming a stereotypical image into a radical image. The speed of the performance and the shift from level to level, cornball to cornstalk, caught prejudices offguard and exposed them.

THE CHICK-STUD SCENE

[As the dialogue begins, the minstrels turn their backs to the audience to give better focus to the chick and stud, who are standing in spots separated by ten feet of empty space, both facing into light and audience.]

Stud: For Christ's sake, if you got something to say, say it.
Chick: What's wrong?
Stud: Nothing's wrong, baby, you got a problem and I was just solving it for you. Felt pretty good, didn't it. Yeah, the white man invented that problem for the black man to solve.

Chick: You really can't have a relationship with me just as a person.

Stud: Baby, you came up here with me willingly, and lay down on that bed and spread your white legs, and humped up and down and moaned in my goddam ear. You was horny for black, baby, a black body on top of you, and now you think it's disgusting and cheap.

Chick: Well, I didn't need you!

Stud: What? what was all that moaning and groaning and oh–how–I–love–it about? Tell me you didn't like that.

Chick: I wanted you to feel good, but you're not man enough to accept it. You can't even be a good lover: if you can't take you can't give.

Stud: That's a cliché. You don't know who I am.

Chick: And you! You may have the body of a man, but emotionally you're a child. You can't know me as a woman.

Stud: Woman! Ain't no body tole you, baby? You ain't nothin but a white chick. You're status and satisfaction and revenge. You're pussy and pale skin and you know no white man can satisfy you like I can. Now me, I'm different; I'm all NEGRO, with the smell of Negro, and the hair of Negro, and all the goddam passion of Africa and wild animals. I haven't got the same hang-ups, have I?

Chick: I feel sorry that so many bad things have happened to you. I really want to love you, because you need love.

Stud: You're a whore.

Chick: Don't say that!

Stud: You're a whore. You're trying to sell me something. You want me to buy what you've got. You've got guilt and you're selling it to me under a different label. You love Negroes, but I'm a man, and you can't love me if you love Negroes.

Chick: But I can. I want to. I lied. You did satisfy me. You were majestic and you were tender. Did you think I wouldn't notice your tenderness. You do want to love me. You need to love me.

Stud: Sheeeeet, you been reading too much James Baldwin.

[*Mimetic reaction: She takes off mask and skirt, holds them before her, moves tenderly, pleadingly toward stud, offering herself. He be-*]

comes cool, frightened. Mask and skirt continue toward him, swing-ing and coming on. Angry, stud lunges for the imaginary neck of the mask and skirt figure. He strangles the image, as the other min-strel lowers the image to the floor. Stud discovers that the skirt is not filled, is empty, kicks it. First minstrel still has mask on hands, be-gins to laugh; as other minstrels laugh and scream, he pursues black stud off stage with threatening pink mask. Blackout.]

The news of the show spread, unearthing various worried liber-als. One such junior executive ran the cultural affairs program at Western Washington State College in Bellingham. He came down to Seattle to see the show before letting us on his campus. He took me out for a drink: 7-Up and Four Roses! And he talked officiously, fi-nally explaining that he and the cultural committee wanted to print a one-page statement explaining their position on the show—a dis-claimer. "Sure," I said. He then asked if we would do a modified ver-sion. I said, "No, absolutely not." Worried, but not beaten, he agreed to honor our contract. We went up to Bellingham a few days later and there was an eight-by-ten statement posted about how they didn't be-lieve it was their right to censor, but the cultural affairs committee wanted to warn the audience. . . . With that kind of statement, the audience was looking to be "shocked." No show in the world can come up to the excitement level of a nervously expectant audience.

To compensate and void the effect of this disclaimer, Bob Slattery agreed to go out on stage and say in his most stentorian, serious tone:

Ladies and Gentlemen: We are happy to be here through the gracious invitation of your Cultural Affairs Committee. With due respect to their position, as stated in the flyer, we don't wish to create any trouble and will perform the *modi-fied* version of our minstrel show. We hope you enjoy it.

We then went onstage and performed the whole fucking thing as done in all the other performances.

The first half of the show was never drastically changed, because it was a gem; it moved, slapped and disturbed. From the cornball, hoky opening to cross-fire, jolly jokes, to stump speech, the show was a fast-paced parody of traditional minstrel and monkey logic. The song "Old Black Joe" loosened the screws and Nego History was a solid piece of historical satire, the chick/stud scene got under the skin and was topped off by Watermelon.

Bob Nelson, Landau and I, with members of the Troupe, conceived, wrote and played in a movie about the life and death of a watermelon or thirty ways of doing in or getting done in by a symbol. The film, "Oh, Dem Watermelons," won award after award for its rapid-fire hysterical insight. In the production, the live sound was made by the cast, who chanted a Steve Reich repetitive round, as the audience viewed the film. "Watermelon, wa-ter-mel-on—WATERMELON, etc." The repetition of sound increased as the film came to a close, and the watermelon started chasing people up streets and up steps. The Interlocutor came to center stage and announced:

> And now, ladies and gentlemen, there will be a fifteen-minute intermission, during which time we will have dancing on the stage. The minstrels will go among you and take a partner. . . . house lights, music, please."

The minstrels leapt off stage into the audience, whooping it up. The music turned up a rhumba, the Black Muslim song, "White Man's Heaven is a Black Man's Hell." We wouldn't even let them get away during the break.

The minstrels picked up blond women to dance with on stage and, of course, made approaches to the various women. The intermission was designed to illustrate blacks and whites dancing and spill the action from stage to the audience. Most of the actors did it with gusto. They picked up chicks and copped onto the sexual energy aroused by the show. The chick/stud scene was a theatrical depiction of a symbolic scene; however, the realities of the dancing section bothered me.

The second half was composed of two playlets: a cop/kid scene, based upon the Gilligan killing in New York's Harlem that touched off the riot of 1964; and a bathroom scene written by Saul and worked out by the cast in a clear and precise depiction of the social problems of the period. The cop/kid scene was always improvised and was difficult to recapture. The bathroom scene takes to print more easily.

> *[Bones, Inkspot and Gimme come on with signs: "Nigger" apron, "White" and "Negro" vests. Two minstrels set up door and one is flushing a toilet. Negro and white approach the bathroom door:]*
> White: After you.

Negro: No, after you.

White: Oh, go ahead, I can wait.

Negro: No, you were here first, I insist—

White: No—*[more ad libbing by both]*

Nigger: *[enters, listens to debate, anxious to get inside, pushes through]* After *me*. Shit, you goin' to stand there and debate who is going to take de first piss?

Negro: *[enters bathroom]* Where's your manners? You're the kind that gives our race a bad image.

Nigger: In dat case, I moves on over since you have to go so bad. Dere's room enough for two.

Negro: That's not what I meant.

Nigger: Oh, who gives a damn what you meant. *[flushes toilet, pantomimes combing hair]*

White: Maybe I should leave and that way it would be less crowded.

Nigger: Wait a minute, boss, you mean you didn't even have to go? What de hell you come in here for and cause all dis trouble? You one of dem peeverts?

Negro: *[to white]* Pay no attention, sir. He's probably drunk.

Nigger: Fuck you. Why you got to kiss de white man's ass?

Negro: Watch your language. Remember where you are.

Nigger: I know where I am. I'm in de pissin' room and I come in here to take one. I don't know what you come in here for, but it sure wasn't for pissin'.

Negro: If you were any kind of civilized human being, you would move aside and let the customers use the facilities first. I'm going to report you to the manager.

Nigger: If you like de manager so much you can go ahead and piss in his room.

White: I can see what you're up against. It's very difficult to deal with an uneducated person.

Negro: I agree.

Nigger: *[to white]* Shit, man—you need an education to learn to piss more than one in a commode. And you *[to Negro]*—you need an education, you white ass-kisser.

Negro: I resent that, you street nigger! *[Goes to punch him. White man intervenes.]*

White: Now wait a minute, let's be reasonable about this. Use some reason.

Nigger: *[pulls out razor]* Here's my reason. I'm gonna settle
     something with Mr. Ass Kisser. *[Negro hides behind
     white]* You chicken shit, Mr. Ass Kisser, you ain't no
     nigger no more. Don't even carry a blade to defend
     yourself. Mighty educated.
Negro: Cool it, baby—we're brothers! Dere's de white man!
White: Don't kill me, I didn't say anything. Honest.
Nigger: Yeah, no one says nothin' to me except clean dis and
     do dat. Well, now I'm saying something. One of you is
     goin' to get it, and maybe both. All I gotta do is figure
     out which one of you I hates the most. *[freeze]*

People thought we were on their side, thought it was a civil
rights integration show. Not so, we were cutting deeper into preju-
dices than integration allowed. We poked not at intolerance, but tol-
erance. We were not for the suppression of differences; rather, by
exaggerating the differences we punctured the cataracts of "color
blind" liberals, disrupted "progressive" consciousness and made peo-
ple think twice about eating watermelon.

Sally Tomlinson

*Sally Tomlinson summarized the symbiosis between popular music
and art at the height of the counterculture in San Francisco, when
rock bands and psychedelic concerts at the local dance halls were ex-
traordinary mixed-media events. She wrote her essay "Psychedelic
Rock Posters: History, Ideas, and Art" for the catalog of the San
Diego Museum of Art show of poster art,* High Societies: Psy-
chedelic Rock Posters of Haight-Ashbury. *The exhibition in
the California museum was held from May 26 to August 12,
2001. Tomlinson's footnotes follow her essay.*

PSYCHEDELIC ROCK POSTERS:
HISTORY, IDEAS, AND ART

IT BEGAN IN LATE 1965, with music. In the months that followed a group of merrymakers became a community in San Francisco, drawn together around music-oriented gatherings they called dance concerts. This youthful group was not aware that their collective, experimental lifestyle would be known all over the world by 1967. As the music of the Bay Area grew more popular, a poster-making industry came into being to promote it, and over time the posters have become recognized as a sophisticated art form. Yet the context in which these works were made remains as elusive as it is fascinating.

The term used to refer to the group's lifestyle and ideology was taken from the name of the neighborhood they adopted—Haight-Ashbury. This actual intersection of streets in San Francisco near Golden Gate Park was also a point of confluence for the ideas held by thousands of young people. They were idealistic, baroquely dressed, and hungry for rock music and hallucinogenic drugs, mistrustful of the "establishment," and drawn to the tenets of Eastern spirituality.

Between 1965 and 1967 they gathered in the streets and parks, and in the dancehalls, where loud music and sensory-bombarding light shows claimed the night. One dancehall visitor describes the "disorienting" sensation of entering the environment: "You'd have to stop moving just to gain your equilibrium; it would bowl you over."[1]

The light shows are gone, the music has changed, and drugs have gotten harder and less mainstream. The two most ephemeral experiences of the mid-sixties—the dance-concert environment and hallucinogenic drugs—are preserved in the posters' colors, images, and texts. The light, sound, and spirit of the era seem almost present in the dizzying patterns and charged hues.

"Psychedelic" Defined

The term "psychedelic," which means "mind expanding" or "mind manifesting," was coined by psychiatrist Humphrey Osmond in 1957. Dr. Osmond used the term to refer to the psychic and visual effects of LSD, a mind-altering substance that in the late fifties was gaining acceptance in the psychiatric community as a drug of therapeutic value.[2] When the use of LSD and other drugs, such as marijuana, psilocybin mushrooms, peyote, and its synthetic counterpart, mescaline, became popular within the sixties youth culture, the term "psychedelic" was extended to include the art that reproduced some of the drugs' visual effects. Certain writers, however, use the term "psychedelic" indiscriminately to describe all the poster art created through 1971, including examples that are more directly influenced by Surrealism and Art Nouveau.

Walter Medeiros, arguably the most articulate writer on the poster art of the sixties counterculture, describes the visual qualities of the posters that connote the psychedelic experience. These include "dense patterns" of both form and lettering and what Medeiros calls "hot colors adjacent to each other, which causes edges of forms to vibrate or flow in a way similar to the visual experiences of LSD or mescaline."[3] Nearly illegible styles of lettering might also be added to the characteristics of psychedelic poster art.

A Brief History of the Hippies

The hippies did not originate many of the activities and philosophies that would become synonymous with their name; indeed, they did not even originate their name. According to Haight-Ashbury chronicler Charles Perry, it was the beats who first coined the term as a derisive nickname for "junior grade hipsters."[4] The beats had preceded the hippies as a San Francisco subculture, claiming the North Beach district for themselves in the 1950s and early 1960s. Many elements of the hippie ethos derived from beat interests. The beats, like the hippies, had rallied around experimental music; for the beats it was jazz. It was the beats who began playing with the light-show elements that were later codified by hippie artists[5] and who first spoke openly about using hallucinogenic or psychotropic drugs. Beat literature documents the group's permissive attitudes toward sex well before the birth-control pill allowed the sixties youth to separate sex from morality. Years before the hippies arrived, some beats subscribed to the tenets of Eastern spiritual disciplines such as Zen Buddhism. The beat poets Allen Ginsberg and Gary Snyder encouraged the hippies' interest in these philosophies. The hippies were not even the first to dress unusually as a way to set themselves apart from middle-class society. The all-black costume of the beats had come before the hippies' thrift store gear, vivid colors, and busy fabric patterns.

What did distinguish the hippies from their counterculture fore-runners were their greater numbers, which allowed them to organize as a community in a way the beats had never attempted to do. Even more significant were the philosophical differences between the two groups: the optimistic, joyful attitude of the hippies contrasted sharply with the beats' brooding outlook.[6]

The Merry Pranksters and the Charlatans, 1965–1966

The genesis of the dance concerts that so galvanized the hippie community can be traced to a simultaneous two-part explosion in 1965: author Ken Kesey's rollicking "Acid Tests" in the Bay Area and the freewheeling western-theme performances by a band named the Charlatans in Virginia City, Nevada.

Beginning in November, Kesey and his communal group of Merry Pranksters hosted their public gatherings at various locations around San Francisco—at Palo Alto, Muir Beach, Stinson Beach, and other places. The Pranksters' idea of a good time was to spike the punch with LSD and turn up the volume of the music performed by Kesey's house band, who would later be called the Grateful Dead. The room was wired with a speaker system that allowed the Pranksters to broadcast suggestions and sound effects—sometimes humorous, sometimes terrifying—to an audience largely under the influence of hallucinogenic drugs, and then to watch what happened.[7] The Acid Test announcements were hand drawn, with every blank space filled, and they demonstrated a kind of absurd humor that would color later efforts. One early example contained a fingerprint with the caption "Now you can tell which one is us."

The Charlatans, an "alternative" band from San Francisco, had begun holding their events in Nevada during the summer of 1965, before Kesey's parties were open to the public. Virginia City was a "frontier" town, and the band performed at the Red Dog Saloon, a bar remodeled to resemble a turn-of-the-century watering hole. The Charlatans and their audiences decked themselves out in Old West– and Edwardian-style dress to match the character of both the town and the bar, and marijuana and LSD figured heavily in their frolics.

The Charlatans created their own announcements in a graphic style that combined black-and-white line drawings with Old West motifs. These posters made humorous use of the fantastic claims of traveling medicine shows and circuses and would influence later poster creators. On one of their posters the Charlatans were described as "The Limit of the Marvelous."

A few other music and dance venues existed in 1965 as well. In the fall, Jefferson Airplane vocalist Marty Balin opened a club called the Matrix, a folk-rock venue that hosted the Jefferson Airplane as its house band. (The Airplane did not yet have its signature sound: vocalist Grace Slick would not join the group until later in the year.)[8] On a smaller scale a man named Chet Helms, who later managed Big Brother and the Holding Company and brought Janis Joplin from Texas to sing with the band, organized fifty-cent concerts in the basement of a twenty-room house at 1090 Page Street in Haight-Ashbury.[9]

Those who attended the earliest dance concerts had such a good time that they wanted to expand and continue the fun. The first and most significant concert in the city proper was hosted in October 1965 by members of a communal group from Pine Street who called themselves the Family Dog, some of whom had lived in Virginia City the previous summer. Their objective was to provide a fun-filled musical event and a place for people to dance. The first dance concert, called "A Tribute to Dr. Strange," was held at the Longshoremen's Hall in the Fisherman's Wharf area. The poster advertising it was another hand-drawn effort, this one by Alton Kelley. *San Francisco Chronicle* music critic Ralph Gleason reported that the evening was attended en masse by young people dressed in "exotic costumes that would have delighted the wildest party-giver."[10]

The original Family Dog gave only three performances. Its final dance concert, in November 1965, was called "Tribute to Ming the Merciless," in honor of a Marvel Comics magician who could travel between dimensions via mind power. On the same evening as the Ming concert, San Francisco Mime Troupe manager Bill Graham hosted a fundraising party. The Mime Troupe had a constant need for infusions of cash to cover legal fees because its public performances, which always included obscenities, were never granted city permits, and brushes with the law were frequent. Various bands played, including the Airplane and Frank Zappa's Mothers of Invention, both of whom had performed earlier at the Ming dance. The Mime Troupe event was held in a loft used by the Jefferson Airplane as a rehearsal hall, and the crowd so overwhelmed the space that hundreds had to be turned away.[11]

The word about music in the Bay Area was beginning to spread, and Haight-Ashbury was the focal point. The San Francisco bands favored exploratory music with long guitar riffs, lyrics that meandered almost as much as the music did, contrasting rhythms, and a mixed repertoire that included hillbilly, rock and roll, and Indian ragas, occasionally interspersed with the screeching feedback of an amplified guitar. What audiences were hearing at the dance concerts in 1965 and the following year offered a radical alternative to the catchy tunes and simple, often insipid lyrics being played on AM radio stations, and the early concerts whetted a hunger for more. San Francisco State College, which was near the Haight, provided a receptive audience, especially for benefits and free concerts in the park. The demand inspired the earliest rock promoters to create more demand, and so the birth of rock poster art followed on the heels of the musical innovations.

Organizing the Music, 1966–1967

Two figures predominate as poster-art patrons in the formative years of Haight-Ashbury—Bill Graham and Chet Helms. After the enormous success of his Mime Troupe benefits, Graham recognized the concerts' lucrative potential and capitalized on it. He rented an old club called the Fillmore Auditorium at the corner of Geary and Fillmore streets in the predominantly African-American Fillmore district, and his second Mime Troupe benefit was held there on December 10, 1965. The event drew 3,500 people.[12]

Graham also helped produce the Trips Festival in early 1966. He collaborated with the Merry Pranksters and Ken Kesey, who had been charged with possession of marijuana and was freed on bail. The Trips evening was held at the Longshoremen's Hall on three nights, January 21–23, 1966, and 10,000 people attended.[13]

After the original members of the Family Dog held their last dance concert in the fall of 1965, Chet Helms assumed both the name and the business enterprise in early 1966. From February through early April, Helms and Graham shared the Fillmore Auditorium. The Family Dog concerts were held on certain nights and Graham's shows on others. Then Graham took a lease on the building without alerting Helms to his intentions. The displaced Helms responded by taking over a turn-of-the-century dance academy called the Avalon Ballroom at Sutter and Van Ness. The Avalon featured red-flocked wallpaper, crenellated balconies, and gilt trim, Victorian features that appealed to the hippie aesthetic.[14] Every weekend beginning in April

1966 dance concerts took place at both halls. The two promoters had very different styles, as *San Francisco Examiner* columnist Philip Elwood remarked:

> Hiking up the steep stairs into the Fillmore Auditorium, the first thing you saw was the box office on the landing; the second thing you saw, at the head of the stairs, was Bill Graham, checking tickets, distributing free apples, and noisily ejecting stoned-out troublemakers. . . . Bill had one eye on the box office, another on the unruly crowd; one ear on the music's format—he liked to be on stage, to introduce acts and make sure the crowds of hippies knew who he was— and another ear picking up crowd reaction.
>
> Helms is Graham's opposite. Walk in the Avalon's lobby, hike up the stairs and chances are . . . there will be no one to sell a ticket, or collect it. Helms will be jumping around in the middle of the dance floor, enjoying himself. The musicians love Helms and the Avalon but often they don't get their guarantee ($$). . . .[15]

The Love Pageant Rally, October 1966

The seminal period in the development of the Haight-Ashbury community was the year between June 1966 and July 1967. Many celebratory events and free gatherings were held in Golden Gate Park in addition to the performances at the Avalon and Fillmore. One of the most memorable celebrations was the Love Pageant Rally, organized to publicly mourn a new law that would make LSD illegal in California effective October 6, 1966. The men who produced the pageant, Allen Cohen[16] and Michael Bowen, decided that a celebration on that day would help avert a possible protest demonstration against the law. They felt a protest would be a needless continuation of "old forms" (their words) in which "the police always held the physical advantage."[17]

A leaflet circulated to publicize the rally declared that "the first translation of this prophesy into political action" would begin at 2:00 P.M. in the Panhandle, a section of Golden Gate Park, to "affirm our identity, community and innocence from influence of the fear addiction of the general public as symbolized by this law." The leaflet also suggested the means of celebratory expression: "Bring the color gold, bring photos of personal saints and gurus and heroes of the underground. . . . Bring children . . . flowers . . . flutes . . . feathers . . . bands . . . beads . . . banners, flags, incense, chimes, gongs, cymbals, . . . [and] symbols." An estimated seven to eight hundred people thronged to the park in response.[18]

A week after the Love Pageant Rally, a group of self-styled revolutionaries called the Diggers, who had emerged from the ranks of the Mime Troupe, began distributing free food every afternoon in Golden Gate Park. In the months that followed the Diggers would also create a free store, where people could donate clothing or pick up others' used articles, and free "crash pads" to accommodate new arrivals to Haight-Ashbury.[19]

The Be-In, January 1967

The celebratory event that drew the most media attention, "A Gathering of the Tribes for a Human Be-In," took place in January 1967. The Be-In was better advertised and better attended than the Love Pageant had been. Several posters were created for it, including one by Stanley Mouse, who collaborated with the organizer of the event, Michael Bowen, and the photographer Casey Sonnabend.

Rick Griffin also created a poster for the event. The purpose of the Be-In was to bring together disparate factions of the Bay Area youth culture, namely the Berkeley political activists and San Francisco's "spiritual generation," which had begun to feel somewhat estranged. The *San Francisco Oracle*, Haight-Ashbury's own influential alternative newspaper, proclaimed the Be-In "a union of love and activism previously separated by categorical dogma and label mongoring [sic]."[20] The East Bay's underground paper, *The Berkeley Barb*, reported with a more political slant: "The spiritual revolution will be manifest and proven. . . . Fear will be washed away; ignorance will be exposed to sunlight; profits and empire will lie drying on deserted beaches; violence will be submerged and transmuted in rhythm and dancing."[21]

For the Be-In, attended by an estimated 25,000 people, Timothy Leary made his first Bay Area public appearance, and beat poets Allen Ginsberg and Gary Snyder led the crowd in rhythmical Hindu mantras dedicated to "the coming Buddha of Love." A self-described "Indian incarnate" announced to the crowd: "Brothers, the spirit of the New Messiah may not be coming to us, but *from* us!"[22] It seemed like the dawn of a new era that promised peace, greater spiritual awareness, and a sense of clearer purpose for all humanity. The mass optimism affected even the Hell's Angels: during the concerts by the leading Bay Area bands the wires to the amplifiers were mysteriously cut, and, after repairs were made, the sound system was guarded by an uncharacteristically peaceful contingent of the motorcycle club.

The Be-In riveted media attention. Articles were published in national magazines[23] and newspapers, launching a media blitz on Haight-Ashbury that would continue through the following summer. Waves of new youths arrived, along with celebrities—two of the Beatles, Russian ballet dancer Rudolf Nureyev with his dance partner, Dame Margot Fonteyn, and the mayor of Delhi, India—as well as sociologists and curious tourists, all eager to witness the unique social phenomenon firsthand.[24]

The Summer of Love, 1967

It became clear that the city of San Francisco would have to prepare for an influx of visitors during the coming summer. On April 5, 1967, a press conference was held by concerned members of the Haight-Ashbury community, who announced the formation of the Council for a Summer of Love.[25] Residents and business owners, the city council, and the police department all braced themselves to deal with the impact of a huge number of new arrivals. Plans were made for supplying housing, food, and medical care.

Yet, in spite of advance planning, the city was overwhelmed. The media attention, the success of the San Francisco bands, and, to some degree, the posters that publicized the music contributed to drawing an estimated 75,000 to San Francisco during the summer of 1967, setting in motion a process of change that would profoundly affect Haight-Ashbury. The number of people who arrived for the Summer of Love, and the character of many of them, contributed to the rapid decline of the community. The media portrayal of the Haight was selective, sensationalizing "free love," free drugs, and free food. *Newsweek* reported in February: "There are no hippies who believe in chastity . . . or see even marriage itself as a virtue. Physical love is a delight—to be chewed upon as often and freely as a handful of sesame seeds. 'Sex is a psychedelic,' said Gary Goldhill, 38, an Englishman who gave up radio scriptwriting to live as a painter in the Haight-Ashbury area. . . . Virtually every hippie has taken LSD."[26]

In an article published in *The New York Times Magazine* in May 1967, Hunter Thompson noted:

Marijuana is everywhere. People smoke it on the sidewalks, in doughnut shops, sitting in parked cars or lounging on the grass in Golden Gate Park. . . . Some of the rock bands play free concerts in [the] pàrk for the benefit of those brethren who can't afford the dances. An at-home entertainment is nude parties at which celebrants paint designs on each other. . . . Drugs have made formal entertainment obsolete in the Hashbury. . . . [He quotes one resident]:". . . I have no money, no possessions. . . . We take care of each other. There's always something to buy beans and rice for the group, and someone always sees that I get grass or acid. . . ."[27]

Monterey Pop, June 1967

When word got out about the Summer of Love, two men involved with the Los Angeles rock music industry, Lou Adler and Alan Pariser, organized the Monterey Pop Festival, held on June 16–18, 1967. Others who had a hand in organizing the event were John Phillips of the Mamas and the Papas and Beatles publicist Derek Taylor.[28] The charity-fundraising festival was intentionally patterned after the Be-In and was billed as "three days of music, love and flowers." It was even advertised with a San Francisco–style poster. By this time it was apparent, according to music historian Charlie Gillett, that something new was going on in the San Francisco music scene:

During 1966, a new generation of groups was formed in San Francisco who made no attempt to shape their repertoire and approach to the requirements of top forty radio. . . . [The] San Francisco–based groups seemed to embody something closer to the original carefree spirit of rock 'n' roll than [what] had been represented in the records made by the professional careerists in Los Angeles. A new generation of journalists . . . cultivated this impression, acclaiming the new musicians as visionaries with a spiritual purity that could permanently alter art, politics, and society.[29]

Representatives of "the San Francisco sound" performed for the estimated 55,000 to 90,000 who attended Monterey Pop. The bands included the Jefferson Airplane, Big Brother and the Holding Company, the Grateful Dead, Moby Grape, the Electric Flag, the Miller

Blues Band, Quicksilver Messenger Service, and the Butterfield Blues Band. Jimi Hendrix, who was then hardly known, set his guitar on fire at the end of his set. Berkeley-based Country Joe and the Fish also performed, along with the Who, the Mamas and the Papas, Buffalo Springfield, Otis Redding, Ravi Shankar, and other newly formed and well seasoned groups.[30] The Jefferson Airplane had already made its mark on radio station popularity charts, but most of the other San Francisco bands had never cut a record.[31] Rock music executives attended the festival en masse. Their mission, made possible by apparently limitless bank accounts, was to entice the resolutely "noncommercial" Bay Area musicians to sign recording contracts.[32] D. A. Pennebaker filmed the event, and release forms were thrust at the musicians as they mounted the stage. The San Francisco musicians had agreed in advance not to sign the releases, but in the end only the Grateful Dead held out and was not filmed. Big Brother performed a second time after music mogul Albert Grossman convinced vocalist Janis Joplin to appear in the film. Her soul-churning performance in a gold lamé dress was the sensation of the festival and made her an overnight star. The result of the event, even before the release of the film, was the emergence of many of the bands from the Haight-Ashbury "underground" into the bright lights of national attention.

Poster Chronology

Between 1965 and 1967 poster commissions came from both commercial and nonprofit sources. There were the Charlatans' early gigs in San Francisco and concerts at the Matrix. A wave of posters made for benefit concerts soon followed: the Week of the Angry Arts, a protest against the war in Vietnam; the Children's Adventure Day Camp Benefit; and an event for the theater troupe called the Committee, featuring the Charles Lloyd Quartet. The First Annual Love Circus inspired its own protest—from the audience—because of the hefty $3.50 admission charge. (Most concerts cost $2.50 to $3.00.)

During the first half of 1967 the posters created for the Fillmore and the Avalon met with tremendous success. They had been issued in editions of three hundred in early 1966. By the following year they were being printed by the thousands every month, with reprints of the more popular designs appearing at the same time.[33] The media took note. Bill Graham's poster sales—up from 59,000 in December 1966 to 112,000 the following February—were reported in *Time* magazine.[34] Graham said he sometimes printed between 100,000 and 150,000 posters a week and shipped them all over the world.[35] Other national magazines also touted the poster phenomenon in 1967, and the Oakland Museum assembled its own collection.[36] John Cipollina, guitarist for the Quicksilver Messenger Service, reported that when his band traveled across the country young people who had never heard the band's recordings were drawn to the shows by the posters.[37]

Chet Helms responded to the demand for posters by dividing his Family Dog organization into two businesses in early 1967, with one division exclusively for poster sales and distribution.[38] The San Francisco style of poster art had taken off and was influencing artists as far away as New York and London.

The Development of Psychedelic Poster Design

Before mid-1965 music events had usually been advertised by posters modeled on the ones used to promote boxing matches. These were straightforward rectangular designs that included photos of the performers and clear block-style lettering. The earliest psychedelic handbills and posters broke away from the simplicity of the "boxing style" and the guiding principle of all commercial design: utter readability. The most novel early psychedelic works are perhaps best described as "tabletop doodles"[39] and included the posters and handbills created for the Red Dog Saloon, the Acid Tests, and the Family Dog dances. The "busyness" of the earliest San Francisco posters nearly obscured the bands' names. It was not so much the musical quality they advertised as the promise of an all-out good time, suggested by the undulating graphics and "fun" lettering styles. The compromised legibility caught on as a stylistic feature of later posters, and, as the fame of Haight-Ashbury grew, it was perhaps this element above all that came to be associated with the San Francisco style of rock posters.

To understand the posters' illegibility, consider the context of their origins. The hippies rejected middle-class values, including the nine-to-five job, accumulated wealth, and major purchases such as cars. As a result, many people traveled Haight-Ashbury on foot and had ample leisure time for "hanging out" and for poring over posters tacked to telephone poles at eye level. Posters that took time to unravel spoke to hippie values. According to poster historian Walter Medeiros, deciphering the posters required concentration, which dovetailed handily with "the state of mind which occurs when high on [marijuana and/or psychedelic substances]," in which there is often an "intense visual involvement in details."[40]

Chet Helms had great influence on psychedelic poster iconography. He provided the artists for the first Avalon Ballroom posters with visual images and humorous phrases. Helms contributed this to Wes Wilson's poster *The Quick and the Dead*: "Don't look for premiums or coupons as the cost of the tobacco blended in CAMEL cigarettes prohibits the use of them." He also created themes for dance concerts, such as "Hubmobile-8 (A Free-Wheeling Vehicle)" and "Laugh Cure." It was Helms who established the logo for the Family Dog. He borrowed an image of a Native American fur trader from the *American Heritage Book of Indians* and collaged a marijuana joint or pipe onto it. For the first portraits of the Family Dog "father," Helms added a benediction he had seen on a bathroom wall: "May the Baby Jesus shut your mouth and open your mind."[41] . . .

Notes

1. Leslie Nelson, conversation with the author, March 2, 2001.

2. Martin A. Lee and Bruce Shlain, *Acid Dreams: The CIA, LSD and the Sixties Rebellion* (New York, 1985), p. 55. The term "mind manifesting" is a literal translation of "psychedelic"; "mind expanding" is the definition used by the scientist who discovered LSD, Albert Hofmann, who wrote *LSD: My Problem Child*, trans. Jonathan Ott (Los Angeles, 1983), p. 176.

3. Walter Medeiros. "San Francisco Rock Concert Posters: Imagery and Meaning" (M.A. thesis, University of California, Berkeley, 1972), p. 14. Hereafter cited as Medeiros, "Posters."

4. Some beats felt the hippies were interested only in getting stoned and having a good time instead of pursuing more serious (beat) interests such as poetry or jazz. Charles Perry, *The Haight-Ashbury: A History* (New York, 1984), p. 5. Hereafter cited as Perry.

5. Funk artists Wally Hedrick and Charles Yerby had produced light shows with homemade projectors years before Haight-Ashbury. Thomas Albright, *Art in the San Francisco Bay Area, 1945–1960* (Berkeley and Los Angeles, 1985), pp. 84–85. As early as 1952 State College Professor Seymour Locks, who was not a beat, produced a light show for a conference of art educators. Locks used hollow slides and glass dishes filled with pigments. With overhead and regular projectors he broadcast images created by stirring and swirling the pigments. The same method was used by dancehall light-show artists in the late 1960s. Perry, p. 87.

6. The beats are described by historian Leonard Wolf as "dark, silent, moody, lonely, sad," and the hippies as "bright, vivacious, ecstatic, crowd-loving and joyful." The beats were, Wolf points out, the first generation of artists and writers to emerge during the era of the bomb. Leonard Wolf, *Voices from the Love Generation* (Boston and Toronto, 1968), p. xxi. Hereafter cited as Wolf.

7. Described in Tom Wolfe, *Electric Kool-Aid Acid Test* (New York, 1968), pp. 214–17; Perry, pp. 34–35.

8. Ralph Gleason, *The Jefferson Airplane and the San Francisco Sound* (New York, 1969), p. 29. Hereafter cited as Gleason.

9. Jack McDonough, *San Francisco Rock: The Illustrated History of San Francisco Rock Music* (San Francisco, 1985), p. 6. Hereafter cited as McDonough. The house was in the care of Peter Albin, who later became a member of Big Brother and the Holding Company.

10. Gleason, pp. 2–6.

11. McDonough, p. 7.

12. Ibid.

13. Gene Sculatti and Davin Seay, *San Francisco Nights: The Psychedelic Music Trip, 1965–1968* (New York, 1985), p. 60. Hereafter cited as Sculatti and Seay.

14. Ibid., p. 70.

15. Philip Elwood, reprinted in "Rockin' Back in Time for Helms Tribute," *San Francisco Examiner*, April 22, 1994, p. D–15.

16. Cohen was a poet who founded the Haight-Ashbury chronicle, *The San Francisco Oracle*, in September 1966. Perry, p. 88.

17. Ibid., p. 96.

18. Ibid.

19. Ibid., pp. 97–98. Leonard Wolf describes the Diggers as opposed to the "premises of culture based on profit, private property, and power" (Wolf, p. 117). Todd Gitlin covers the Diggers' activities in *The Sixties: Years of Hope, Days of Rage* (New York, 1989), pp. 222–41. Perry discusses the Diggers' civic activities, p. 220.

20. Ibid., pp. 121–22.

21. Ibid.

22. Ibid., p. 122. See also Steven Levine, "The First American Mehla," *The San Francisco Oracle*, January 1967, quoted in Jerry Hopkins, ed., *The Hippie Papers: Notes from the Underground Press* (New York, 1968), pp. 20–22.

23. *Newsweek* was one. "Dropouts With a Mission: The Hippies," February 6, 1967, pp. 92–95. Hereafter cited as *Newsweek*.

24. Perry, pp. 217, 224, 226–27; Gleason, p. 276.

25. Perry, p. 171.

26. *Newsweek*, pp. 92–95.

27. Hunter S. Thompson, "The 'Hashbury' Is the Capital of the Hippies," *The New York Times Magazine*, May 14, 1967, pp. 28–29, 120–24.

28. Charlie Gillett, *The Sound of the City* (New York, 1970), pp. 343–54. Hereafter cited as Gillett. Sculatti and Seay, p. 162.

29. Gillett, pp. 350, 352.

30. Sculatti and Seay, p. 182; Gillett, p. 354.

31. The song "Somebody to Love" from the Airplane's first album, *Takes Off*, had made the top-forty lists, indicating "distinct commercial possibilities" for San Francisco musicians; "White Rabbit" from the same album would catch on later in the year (Gillett, p. 354). Big Brother had been signed by Mainstream, but as a result of Monterey Pop, Columbia paid a "transfer fee" to put them under their own contract (ibid.).

32. McDonough, p. 16. Gillett (p. 354) says the record company producers were "throwing caution and control to the winds."

33. Later printings were 5,000 (Walter Medeiros, *From Frisco With Love: An Introduction to the Dance Concert Poster Art*, exhibition catalogue, San Francisco Museum of Modern Art, October 6–November 21, 1976, p. 3). Ralph Gleason says the early posters were printed 500 at a time and that by 1968 printings were up to 25,000 (Gleason, p. 293).

34. "Nouveau Frisco," *Time*, April 7, 1967, p. 67.

35. McDonough, p. 59.

36. *Life*, September 1, 1967, pp. 36–41; *Newsweek*, March 6, 1967, p. 87; and a Dugald Stermer essay in *Communication Arts* are quoted in McDonough, p. 57, although no source is given. The Oakland Museum had begun collecting posters in early 1966 (Perry, p. 218); Ralph Gleason states that museums in New York, London, and Europe asked the bands for posters (Gleason, p. 63).

37. Sculatti and Seay, p. 108.

38. Perry, p. 134; Paul D. Grushkin, *The Art of Rock: Posters from Presley to Punk* (New York and London, 1987), pp. 80–81.

39. Poster artist Victor Moscoso used this term to describe specific early efforts (lecture, October 15, 2000, San Rafael Masonic Hall, during an exhibition of his work).

40. Medeiros, "Posters," p. 13.

41. Ibid., pp. 6–7.

Editor's note: After further research, it has been determined that at no time did the average print run of BGP posters exceed about 2,000 copies. In a few cases, more posters were printed. The average "edition" run was 300 to 500 copies.

Michael Lydon

Two outdoor rock musical spectacles attracting many thousands of young people ended the decade of the Sixties—the Woodstock music festival in upstate New York in August 1969, followed four months later by the concert at the Altamont Speedway in Northern California. The Altamont concert resulted in a riot near the stage in which the Hell's Angels attacked and stabbed to death one of the spectators, an eighteen-year-old young man named Meredith Hunter. Reporter Michael Lydon was among the crowd at Altamont on December 6, 1969. His article "The Rolling Stones—At Play in the Apocalypse" was published in 1970 in Ramparts Magazine *and expanded in a chapter profiling the* Rolling Stones *in his book* RockFolk: Portraits from the Rock 'n' Roll Pantheon *(1971), the version included here.*

THE ROLLING STONES—AT PLAY IN THE APOCALYPSE

IT ALL CAME DOWN AT ALTAMONT on that strange day. A cold sun alternated with bright clouds, and 300,000 young Americans stepped into the future (or was it?), looked at each other, and were frightened by what they saw. It was the biggest gathering in California (the population of San Francisco is 756,000) since the Human Be-In three years before, not only in numbers but in expectation. In common with all the voluntary mass events of the sixties—was the Sproul Hall sit-in the first?—it would, all believed, advance the trip, i.e., reveal some important lesson intrinsic to and yet beyond its physical fact. The 300,000, all in unspoken social contract, came not only to hear music, but to bear living testimony to their own lives.

The Stones as well as the audience—and whether such a distinction should or could be made was one of the day's questions. They had wanted it to be in San Francisco's Golden Gate Park, their gift to the city and its culture. As their long hair, outrageous manners, and music had helped make San Francisco possible, San Francisco had helped make the past three years possible. Like thousands before them, the Stones were coming to say thank you. They hoped it would be in all senses a free concert, an event spiritually outside the commercial realm of the tour. It both was and was not. Neither the tour's footnote nor quite its denouement, that long Saturday was the drama's second and enigmatic ending which proved all endings as false and hard to mark as beginnings.

When the Stones left for Muscle Shoals, first Sam, then Jo, Ronnie and John, flew to San Francisco. Sam was met at the plane by Rick Scully, a long-time manager of the Grateful Dead, and concert planning began at the Dead's office and communal ranch. The Dead, hosts of more free concerts than any other band, are still the best embodiment of the San Francisco spirit that in 1967 captured the imagination of the world. True if harried believers in the psychedelic revolution, the Dead promised full cooperation (which they never gave the ill-fated Wild West), and the concert seemed to be in good if freaky hands. On Tuesday no site had been secured; by Wednesday morning the director of the Sears Point Raceway promised his grounds free of charge. Chip and his crew, aided by the Dead's extended family, started moving tons of equipment to the drag strip north of San Francisco. Then came the problems.

An essential element of free concerts is simplicity. You want to hear music? Okay, do it! Get a place, a source of power, a few flatbed trucks or a stage, a few bands, spread the word, trust to God, and have the thing. But this free concert was also a Stones concert, free or not, and everybody wanted a piece of the action. Hustlers of every stripe swarmed to the new scene like piranhas to the scent of blood.

The Sears Point man got cold feet or itchy palms or both and asked for six thousand dollars, plus five thousand dollars to be held in escrow against possible damages. Costs mounted on a dozen fronts; fearful of huge losses, Ronnie decided on a film designed for a TV special to be made by the Maysle brothers, who had already been shooting the final stages of the tour. Any profits would go to charity—"as yet unspecified," said John. The actual owners of the raceway, a Hollywood-based company called Filmways Corporation, which had promoted two of the town's concerts, heard about that and demanded film distribution rights as part of their fee. Ronnie refused, and Filmways, overriding their local management, responded by upping the fee to $100,000.

That was late Thursday. The San Francisco papers and radio stations were announcing Sears Point as the site, and a large volunteer vanguard had already encamped. That blatantly colorful attorney,

Melvin Belli, offered his help in the fight with Filmways; Ronnie accepted it. The Dead office was abandoned as the HQ, and was replaced by Belli's office in San Francisco's financial district, and by Ronnie's suites in the posh Huntington Hotel. Managers of local bands started calling to get their groups on the stage for the priceless exposure; the city's rival Top-40 stations, KFRC and KYA, started running hourly bulletins, each trying to be the unofficial "Stones Station." Underground KSAN-FM, which had had the best coverage early in the week, was slowly edged out. Communes of ordinary hippies offering their services were rebuffed. The radical community, suspicious from the start, started talking about the festival as "one more shuck."

By midmorning Friday, Filmways was still adamant, but then got left when another track, this one a stock car oval called Altamont, offered its several hundred acres of rolling hills. Track director Dick Carter thought it would be "great publicity." The half-built stage at Sears Point was dismantled, and radio stations blasted the new directions with frantic assurances that, yes, the Stones concert was still on.

By late Friday afternoon the concert was the sole and obsessive topic of hip conversation, and Altamont a familiar name. KFRC had on-the-spot reporters on every spot worth being on, and KYA's DJ's bemoaned the fact that "some stations are trying to turn something that should be free and groovy into a commercial event." Both stations carried hi-fi store ads for "all new stereo tape recorders so *you* can make the Stones concert more than a memory." The scores of equipment trucks got to Altamont, fifty miles east of Berkeley, by early Friday evening; a huge volunteer crew worked like ants under blue floodlights amid a growing tangle of wires, planking and staging. "No one will be allowed on the grounds until 7:00 A.M. Saturday, so *stay home,*" was the broadcast word, but by midnight there were traffic jams miles from the site. The Stones got to the Huntington by ten, exhausted. In Alabama they had heard only the confusing rumors, but were determined to go ahead. "We'll have it in a bloody parking lot if we have to," said Keith. He and Mick flew out to see Altamont. Mick went back to get some sleep; Keith stayed all night.

As the stage crew labored, a few thousand people who had missed the roadblocks slept before the stage or stood by campfires; other thousands waited behind a fence for official opening time. I wandered from fire to fire; place was immediately made for any stranger, and joints steadily circled the impromptu hearths. I made scores of friends I'll never see again.

One girl told me solemnly that it would be a heavy day "because the sun, Venus, Mercury, and some other planet are all in Sagittarius, and the moon's on the Libra-Scorpio cusp." Another presented me with a grotesque doll made by her dead husband. "He lives in the doll; I know it," she said, nodding her head uncontrollably. "He sees everything." I said I was sorry. "Oh, that's okay, he was shot through the heart and lungs and the liver, but I really don't mind, 'cause he must have been meant to die, and anyway, I have the doll." Still nodding and smiling, she took it back and wrapped it in her shawl.

They came from everywhere. Two boys boasted that they had seen the Stones in LA, Chicago, Philly, and Palm Beach without ever buying a seat; someone countered by saying he had been to fourteen festivals plus Woodstock. A girl said she was from Akron, had run away to New Orleans, got an abortion in Houston, and had been on her way to Seattle ("I heard it's groovy there"), when she met a dealer in Phoenix who took her to San Francisco, then split to avoid a bust. "It's all so far out," she said. Somebody with a phonograph played *Abbey Road* over and over. The spindly light towers grew tall, generators roared, helicopters clattered overhead, and as night became grey dawn, Altamont looked strikingly like the mad consummation of Fellini's *8½*.

At 7:00 A.M. the gates are opened. Over the hill and down into the hollow by the stage comes a whooping, running, raggle-taggle mob. From sleeping bags peer sleepy heads that duck back as the mob leaps over them and dashes between them. In minutes the meadow is a crush of bodies pressed so close that it takes ten minutes to walk fifty yards. Only the bravest blades of grass still peep up through the floor of wadded bedding. On and on comes the crowd; by ten it spreads a quarter mile back from the stage, fanning out like lichen clinging to a rock.

There are the dancing beaded girls, the Christlike young men, and smiling babies familiar from countless stories on the "Love Generation," but the weirdos too, whose perverse and penetrating intensity no camera ever captures. Speed freaks with hollow eyes and missing teeth, dead-faced acid heads burned out by countless flashes, old beatniks clutching gallons of red wine, Hare Krishna chanters with shaved heads and acned cheeks. Two young men in filthy serapes and scraggly beards lean against a crushed and brightly painted derelict veteran of the Demolition Derby. In the brims of their cowboy hats are little white cards: "Acid $2." A shirtless black man stands in the center of a cheering circle. "I have in my hand," he barks, "one little purple tab of 100 percent pure LSD. Who wants this cosmic jewel?" A dozen hands reach out eagerly. "Who really wants it?" "I do, I do, I want it, me, me, me." "Going, going, gone to that freaky chick with the blue bandana." He tosses it to her, and reaches again into his leather bag. "I have in my hand one cap of mescaline, guaranteed organic. . . ."

Two middle-aged men with pinched Okie faces set up a card table and hawk Rolling Stones programs left over from another tour. They've only sold a few when a milling crowd of radicals surrounds them. "It's free, man, nothing is sold today." "Better give the stuff away, man, or we'll rip it off in the name of the people." The men are frightened. A kid dashes up and grabs a handful of the glossy books. The table collapses. One man scoops the programs from the dirt, the other brandishes the table in wild-eyed defense. They retreat, walking backwards, as the brave guerrillas search for other targets.

Face by face, body by body, the crowd is recognizable, comprehensible. As ugly beautiful mass, it is bewilderingly unfamiliar—a timeless lake of humanity climbing together through the first swirling, buzzing, euphoric-demonic hours of acid. Is this Bosch or Cecil B. DeMille; biblical, medieval, or millennial? Are we lost or found? Are we *we*, and if we are, who are we?

Whoever or whatever, we are *here, all* here, and gripped by the ever-amazing intensity of psychedelics, we *know* that this being here is no accident but the inevitable and present realization of our whole lives until this moment. One third of a million post-war boom babies gathered in a Demolition Derby junkyard by a California freeway to get stoned and listen to rock 'n' roll—is that what it has all been about? And someone, thinking maybe to help feed us, brought a split-open crate of dirty, wilted cabbage heads. They got kicked around in the dust until they rolled under cars and were forgotten.

Some call us Woodstock West, but we are not. Woodstock was a three-day encampment at which cooperation was necessary for survival; it was an event only because it became an event. The Altamont crowd is *demanding* that an event come to pass, be delivered, in a single day; should it go bad—well, it'll be over by evening. And it's four months later, and it's California, where inevitably everything is that wee but significant bit less known, less sure, less safe. . . .

And more political; if concert isn't the right word for the day, festival isn't either. The week's maneuverings, still known only by rumor, have raised a hard edge of suspicion; the day's vibes include aggressive paranoid frequencies that demand self-justification. Some come in bitter mourning for two Chicago Black Panthers shot to death just days before; a concert without confrontation would be frivolous escapism for them. But it is more than the radicals; large segments of the crowd share a dangerous desire to tighten up that festival idea a few notches, to move to a new level—just how weird can you stand it, brother, before your love will crack?

It isn't that the morning is not a groove; it is, friendly enough and loose. But . . . but what? There is too much of something; is it the people, the dope, the tension? Maybe it is the *wanting,* the concentration, not just of flesh, but of unfulfilled desire, of hope for (or is it fear of) deliverance. ("There must be some way out of here, said the joker to the thief; there's too much confusion, I can't get no relief.") What is our oppression that in escaping it we so oppress ourselves? Have we jammed ourselves together on these sere hills miles from home hoping to find a way out of such masses? If that is our paradox, is Altamont our self-made trap? And yet . . . might we just, in acting out the paradox so intensely, transcend it?

The Jefferson Airplane are on stage, knocking out "3/5's of a Mile in 9/10's of a Second" with a mad fury—when suddenly all eyes rivet on an upraised pool cue. It is slashing downward, held by a mammoth Hell's Angel, and when it hits its unseen target there is a burst of water as if it had crushed a jellyfish. A wave of horror ripples madly across the crowd. The music stops and the stage is full of Angels in raunchy phalanx. The music starts, falters, stops. Thousands hold their breath and wave pathetic V signs. No one wants the Angels. A few scream, "Pigs, pigs." The odds against the Angels are maybe five-thousand to one, but the crowd is passive and afraid. The Angels stay on stage, sure of their power.

Now something is definitely wrong, but there is no time or space to set it right. The Angels become the villains, but why are they here? They just came, of course, as they always do, but, we hoped, as friends. Since Ken Kesey faced them down and turned them on, San Francisco has had a sentimental romance with the Angels: the consummate outlaws, true rolling stones, street fighting men: they're so bad they're good, went the line. It turns out later that they were actually hired by the Stones on the suggestion of the Dead; their fee, five-hundred-dollars worth of beer. But now their open appetite for violence mocks our unfocused love of peace; their grim solidarity, our fearful hopes of community.

Community? It just doesn't feel like that anymore. Though participants in the whole rite, we are not actively engaged in it; we are spectators who came to "see" the Stones, passive voyeurs hoping, like all voyeurs, that "something" will happen. But since we're just watching, we can say we're not to blame—it's the Stones and the Angels, the Stars, they did it all, so they're to blame, right? The *I Ching* says all communities must have a leader, but every community member must be willing to become that leader at any time.

So we're all voyeurs, but what do you have to do in late 1969 to get 300,000 people to watch it?

The day drags on. Many leave; as many more arrive. Invisibly and inevitably the crowd squeezes toward the stage until the first fifty yards around it are suffocatingly dense. Occasionally it becomes too much for someone, and while twitching in the grip of some apocalyptic vision ("We are all going to die, we are all going to die, right here, right here, we've been tricked!"), he is carried by friends to the medical tent for some Thorazine and, if he's lucky, some thoughtful attention.

Darkness begins to fall. "The Stones are here." "I saw their helicopter." "Somebody said they're not gonna show." The lights come on, and a new wave sweeps thousands more toward the stage. The stage itself is so full that it is sagging in the center. The Angels continue their random attacks. "The Stones are here." "That's why they turned on the lights."

In fact, they are—packed into a tiny trailer filled with stale smoke and spilled food. Charley's happy; he needs only to get through this final set and he can go home to Shirley and Serafina. Mick is upset; as he got off the helicopter a freak had rushed him, screaming, "I hate you, I hate you," then punched him in the face. For all his presence, Mick Jagger is not fearless; on tour, when the engine of one small chartered plane had flamed briefly as it coughed to a start, Mick leapt from his seat, crying that the plane was about to explode. Keith, up all night and in the trailer all day, is exhausted. Crying girls peer and shout through the small screen windows. Jo Bergman is huddled in a corner waiting for it to be over. Ronnie cracks nervous jokes.

It is time. Surrounded by security men, they squeeze the few yards to a tent directly behind the stage. Mick Taylor, Keith, and Bill tune up. A dozen Angels stand guard, punching at faces that peek through holes in the canvas. They are ready. The Angels form a wedge; they file between two equipment trucks, up four steps, and they are there. It is fully dark now but for the stage; in its incandescence, the Rolling Stones are as fine as ever. Mick bows low, sweeping his Uncle Sam hat wide in an ironic circle, and on Keith's signal, the band begins "Jumping Jack Flash." That incredible moment is there again. In those first seconds when Keith's shirt is sparkling, and Charley has just set his big cymbal shimmering with a snap of his right wrist, and Mick bends forward biting out the first defiant words, that enormous pressure of wants, material and spiritual, dissolves— phisst! like that in thin air. For it is just that moment, that achievement of perfect beauty after impossible trial, that is the object of all those longings.

> *'Cause it's all right now,*
> *In fact it's a gas,*
> *I'm Jumping Jack Flash,*
> *It's a gas gas gas!*

And then it is irrevocably gone. Four Angels flash from behind the amps, one vaulting almost over Charley's head. One jumps from the stage, and the crowd scatters into itself in total panic. There appears to be a fight. Then it seems to be over. The music goes on. Again: more Angels, this time wandering around among the Stones. They stop playing.

"Fellows, fellows," says Mick, "move back, won't you, fellows?" His sarcasm gets him through, and they start again. Trouble for the third time, and it is serious. Two Angels (I saw two) wade deep into the crowd. There are screams. Rows of faces fishtail away before these thugs from some very modern nightmare. Boos rise from the mass of the crowd who can't see what's wrong and who just want the show to go on. The band starts again, but something unmistakably weird is still going on down in front. A few kids escape to the stage, streaking to the safety of its far corners. Sam comes out. He has been begging this crowd all day for cooperation; his voice is flat and hoarse.

"This is an important announcement. Someone has been hurt and a doctor is leaving the stage right now; that's him with his arm raised, he's got a green jacket on. Will you please let him through. Someone has been badly hurt."

Security men are begging that all those who do not absolutely need to be on the stage leave it. I leave, not unhappily, and walk through the burnt-out campfires, small piles of trash, and rakishly tilted motorcycles behind the stage, then up a slope where the kids are standing on cars, maybe thirty to a car. A girl comes by asking for her friends; she has cut her leg on barbed wire and wants to go home, but she lost her friends with the car at noon.

The Stones are going again, and the crowd is with them. We can't see them, but the music sounds good—not great, not free festival great, but no one hopes for that anymore. It is enough that it is here. Around me a few people are dancing gently. The morning's dope is wearing off; all the trips are nearly over. We do glimpse the basket flying through the air, trailing petals. We all cheer one last massive cheer. Friends find friends; the crowd becomes fragments that get into cars that back up on the freeway for miles and for hours. Luckily it is only about eight; but it feels like the very end of the night. The only want left is for rest. I realize that the Grateful Dead did not get a chance to play and figure that I won't go to any more of these things.

In the days that follow, the free concert becomes "the disaster at Altamont." There is wide disagreement on what happened and what it meant; everyone, it seems, had their own day, and that was, we all say, one of the problems. The only common emotion is disappointment and impotent sorrow. "If only . . . if only. . . ." The papers report that there were three births (though later the figure cannot be substantiated) and four deaths. Mark Feiger, twenty-two, and Richard Savlov, twenty-two, friends who had recently moved to Berkeley from New Jersey, were killed when a car on its way out to the freeway plowed into their campfire hours after the concert was over. A young man with long hair, moustache, and sideburns, with a metal cross through his pierced right ear, still listed as "John Doe," stumbled stoned into an irrigation canal and drowned. Another, a young black man, Meredith Hunter, was stabbed, kicked, and beaten by Angels right before the stage while the Stones were playing. His body was battered so badly that doctors knew, the moment they reached him, there was no chance to save him.

So far, no murder charges have been brought. It was not until a week later, when someone asked me about it, that I even considered the possibility that the police, whom no one would have wanted at Altamont in the morning, would actually investigate the horrendous act that closed it and bring any person or persons to trial. We all seemed beyond the law at Altamont, out there willingly, all 300,000 of us, Stones and Angels included, and on our own. And anyway the tour is over.

Robert Hunter

Among the many articles about the concert at Altamont was one by rock critic Ralph J. Gleason in the San Francisco Chronicle *on December 8, 1969. Gleason's indictment of the Altamont affair, and the controversy over what had happened at the concert, provoked Robert Hunter, lyricist for the Grateful Dead, to write "New Speedway Boogie." The song was first performed by the band on December 20, 1969, at the Fillmore Auditorium in San Francisco.*

NEW SPEEDWAY BOOGIE

Please don't dominate the rap Jack
if you got nothing new to say
If you please don't back up the track
This train got to run today

Spent a little time on the mountain
Spent a little time on the hill
Heard some say better run away
Others say you better stand still

Now I don't know but I been told
it's hard to run with the weight of gold
Other hand I heard it said
it's just as hard with the weight of lead

Who can deny? Who can deny?
it's not just a change in style
One step done and another begun
in I wonder how many miles?

Spent a little time on the mountain
Spent a little time on the hill
Things went down we don't understand
but I think in time we will

Now I don't know but I been told
in the heat of the sun a man died of cold
Do we keep on coming or stand and wait
with the sun so dark and the hour so late?

You can't overlook the lack Jack
of any other highway to ride
It's got no signs or dividing lines
and very few rules to guide

Spent a little time on the mountain
Spent a little time on the hill
I saw things getting out of hand
I guess they always will

I don't know but I been told
if the horse don't pull you got to carry the load
I don't know whose back's that strong
Maybe find out before too long

One way or another
One way or another
One way or another
this darkness got to give
One way or another
One way or another
One way or another
this darkness got to give

———

Sherman Alexie

Many years after the Woodstock festival, Native American writer Sherman Alexie created a narrator who shared his memories of his father's anecdotes about the Sixties in "Because My Father Always Said He Was the Only Indian Who Saw Jimi Hendrix Play 'The Star-Spangled Banner' at Woodstock." Alexie made it a chapter in The Lone Ranger and Tonto Fistfight in Heaven *(1993), the collection of short stories that first brought him national recognition.*

In the story, the narrator wonders if his father "wasn't the only Indian" at Woodstock. Actually, several Native Americans from the Indian Arts and Crafts School in New Mexico set up an "Indian village" to sell moccasins and jewelry on the festival grounds near Wavy Gravy's Hog Farm site. According to Bill Belmont, the artists' coordinator for Country Joe and the Fish at Woodstock, "a brisk trade in Plains artifacts took place amidst the turmoil."

BECAUSE MY FATHER ALWAYS SAID HE WAS THE ONLY INDIAN WHO SAW JIMI HENDRIX PLAY "THE STAR-SPANGLED BANNER" AT WOODSTOCK

DURING THE SIXTIES, my father was the perfect hippie, since all the hippies were trying to be Indians. Because of that, how could anyone recognize that my father was trying to make a social statement?

But there is evidence, a photograph of my father demonstrating in Spokane, Washington, during the Vietnam war. The photograph made it onto the wire service and was reprinted in newspapers throughout the country. In fact, it was on the cover of *Time*.

In the photograph, my father is dressed in bell-bottoms and flowered shirt, his hair in braids, with red peace symbols splashed across his face like war paint. In his hands my father holds a rifle above his head, captured in that moment just before he proceeded to beat the shit out of the National Guard private lying prone on the ground. A fellow demonstrator holds a sign that is just barely visible over my father's left shoulder. It read MAKE LOVE NOT WAR.

The photographer won a Pulitzer Prize, and editors across the country had a lot of fun creating captions and headlines. I've read many of them collected in my father's scrapbook, and my favorite was run in the *Seattle Times*. The caption under the photograph read DEMONSTRATOR GOES TO WAR FOR PEACE. The editors capitalized on my father's Native American identity with other headlines like ONE WARRIOR AGAINST WAR and PEACEFUL GATHERING TURNS INTO NATIVE UPRISING.

Anyway, my father was arrested, charged with attempted murder, which was reduced to assault with a deadly weapon. It was a high-profile case so my father was used as an example. Convicted and sentenced quickly, he spent two years in Walla Walla State Penitentiary. Although his prison sentence effectively kept him out of the war, my father went through a different kind of war behind bars.

"There was Indian gangs and white gangs and black gangs and Mexican gangs," he told me once. "And there was somebody new killed every day. We'd hear about somebody getting it in the shower or wherever and the word would go down the line. Just one word. Just the color of his skin. Red, white, black, or brown. Then we'd chalk it up on the mental scoreboard and wait for the next broadcast."

My father made it through all that, never got into any serious trouble, somehow avoided rape, and got out of prison just in time to hitchhike to Woodstock to watch Jimi Hendrix play "The Star-Spangled Banner."

"After all the shit I'd been through," my father said, "I figured Jimi must have known I was there in the crowd to play something like that. It was exactly how I felt."

Twenty years later, my father played his Jimi Hendrix tape until it wore down. Over and over, the house filled with the rockets' red glare and the bombs bursting in air. He'd sit by the stereo with a cooler of beer beside him and cry, laugh, call me over and hold me tight in his arms, his bad breath and body odor covering me like a blanket.

Jimi Hendrix and my father became drinking buddies. Jimi Hendrix waited for my father to come home after a long night of drinking. Here's how the ceremony worked:

1. I would lie awake all night and listen for the sounds of my father's pickup.
2. When I heard my father's pickup, I would run upstairs and throw Jimi's tape into the stereo.
3. Jimi would bend his guitar into the first note of "The Star-Spangled Banner" just as my father walked inside.
4. My father would weep, attempt to hum along with Jimi, and then pass out with his head on the kitchen table.
5. I would fall asleep under the table with my head near my father's feet.
6. We'd dream together until the sun came up.

The days after, my father would feel so guilty that he would tell me stories as a means of apology.

"I met your mother at a party in Spokane," my father told me once. "We were the only two Indians at the party. Maybe the only two Indians in the whole town. I thought she was so beautiful. I figured she was the kind of woman who could make buffalo walk on up to her and give up their lives. She wouldn't have needed to hunt. Every time we went walking, birds would follow us around. Hell, tumbleweeds would follow us around."

Somehow my father's memories of my mother grew more beautiful as their relationship became more hostile. By the time the divorce was final, my mother was quite possibly the most beautiful woman who ever lived.

"Your father was always half crazy," my mother told me more than once. "And the other half was on medication."

But she loved him, too, with a ferocity that eventually forced her to leave him. They fought each other with the kind of graceful anger that only love can create. Still, their love was passionate, unpredictable, and selfish. My mother and father would get drunk and leave parties abruptly to go home and make love.

"Don't tell your father I told you this," my mother said. "But there must have been a hundred times he passed out on top of me. We'd be right in the middle of it, he'd say *I love you*, his eyes would roll backwards, and then out went his lights. It sounds strange, I know, but those were good times."

I was conceived during one of those drunken nights, half of me formed by my father's whiskey sperm, the other half formed by my mother's vodka egg. I was born a goofy reservation mixed drink, and my father needed me just as much as he needed every other kind of drink.

One night my father and I were driving home in a near-blizzard after a basketball game, listening to the radio. We didn't talk much. One, because my father didn't talk much when he was sober, and two, because Indians don't need to talk to communicate.

"Hello out there, folks, this is Big Bill Baggins, with the late-night classics show on KROC, 97.2 on your FM dial. We have a request from Betty in Tekoa. She wants to hear Jimi Hendrix's version of 'The Star-Spangled Banner' recorded live at Woodstock."

My father smiled, turned the volume up, and we rode down the highway while Jimi led the way like a snowplow. Until that night, I'd always been neutral about Jimi Hendrix. But, in that near-blizzard with my father at the wheel, with the nervous silence caused by the dangerous roads and Jimi's guitar, there seemed to be more to all that music. The reverberation came to mean something, took form and function.

That song made me want to learn to play guitar, not because I wanted to be Jimi Hendrix and not because I thought I'd ever play for anyone. I just wanted to touch the strings, to hold the guitar tight against my body, invent a chord, and come closer to what Jimi knew, to what my father knew.

"You know," I said to my father after the song was over, "my generation of Indian boys ain't ever had no real war to fight. The first Indians had Custer to fight. My great-grandfather had World War I, my grandfather had World War II, you had Vietnam. All I have is video games."

My father laughed for a long time, nearly drove off the road into the snowy fields.

"Shit," he said. "I don't know why you're feeling sorry for yourself because you ain't had to fight a war. You're lucky. Shit, all you had was that damn Desert Storm. Should have called it Dessert Storm because it just made the fat cats get fatter. It was all sugar and whipped cream with a cherry on top. And besides that, you didn't even have to fight it. All you lost during that war was sleep because you stayed up all night watching CNN."

We kept driving through the snow, talked about war and peace.

"That's all there is," my father said. "War and peace with nothing in between. It's always one or the other."

"You sound like a book," I said.

"Yeah, well, that's how it is. Just because it's in a book doesn't make it not true. And besides, why the hell would you want to fight a war for this country? It's been trying to kill Indians since the very beginning. Indians are pretty much born soldiers anyway. Don't need a uniform to prove it."

Those were the kinds of conversations that Jimi Hendrix forced us to have. I guess every song has a special meaning for someone somewhere. Elvis Presley is still showing up in 7-11 stores across the country, even though he's been dead for years, so I figure music just might be the most important thing there is. Music turned my father into a reservation philosopher. Music had powerful medicine.

"I remember the first time your mother and I danced," my father told me once. "We were in this cowboy bar. We were the only real cowboys there despite the fact that we're Indians. We danced to a Hank Williams song. Danced to that real sad one, you know. 'I'm So Lonesome I Could Cry.' Except your mother and I weren't lonesome or crying. We just shuffled along and fell right goddamn down into love."

"Hank Williams and Jimi Hendrix don't have much in common," I said.

"Hell, yes, they do. They knew all about broken hearts," my father said.

"You sound like a bad movie."

"Yeah, well, that's how it is. You kids today don't know shit about romance. Don't know shit about music either. Especially you Indian kids. You all have been spoiled by those drums. Been hearing them beat so long, you think that's all you need. Hell, son, even an Indian needs a piano or guitar or saxophone now and again."

My father played in a band in high school. He was the drummer. I guess he'd burned out on those. Now, he was like the universal defender of the guitar.

"I remember when your father would haul that old guitar out and play me songs," my mother said. "He couldn't play all that well but he tried. You could see him thinking about what chord he was going to play next. His eyes got all squeezed up and his face turned all red. He kind of looked that way when he kissed me, too. But don't tell him I said that."

Some nights I lay awake and listened to my parents' lovemaking. I know white people keep it quiet, pretend they don't ever make love. My white friends tell me they can't even imagine their own parents getting it on. I know exactly what it sounds like when my parents are touching each other. It makes up for knowing exactly what they sound like when they're fighting. Plus and minus. Add and subtract. It comes out just about even.

Some nights I would fall asleep to the sounds of my parents' lovemaking. I would dream Jimi Hendrix. I could see my father standing in the front row in the dark at Woodstock as Jimi Hendrix played "The Star-Spangled Banner." My mother was at home with me, both of us waiting for my father to find his way back home to the reservation. It's amazing to realize I was alive, breathing and wetting my bed, when Jimi was alive and breaking guitars.

I dreamed my father dancing with all these skinny hippie women, smoking a few joints, dropping acid, laughing when the rain fell. And it did rain there. I've seen actual news footage. I've seen the documentaries. It rained. People had to share food. People got sick. People got married. People cried all kinds of tears.

But as much as I dream about it, I don't have any clue about what it meant for my father to be the only Indian who saw Jimi Hendrix play at Woodstock. And maybe he wasn't the only Indian there. Most likely there were hundreds but my father thought he was the only one. He told me that a million times when he was drunk and a couple hundred times when he was sober.

"I was there," he said. "You got to remember this was near the end and there weren't as many people as before. Not nearly as many. But I waited it out. I waited for Jimi."

A few years back, my father packed up the family and the three of us drove to Seattle to visit Jimi Hendrix's grave. We had our photograph taken lying down next to the grave. There isn't a gravestone there. Just one of those flat markers.

Jimi was twenty-eight when he died. That's younger than Jesus Christ when he died. Younger than my father as we stood over the grave.

"Only the good die young," my father said.

"No," my mother said. "Only the crazy people choke to death on their own vomit."

"Why you talking about my hero that way?" my father asked.

"Shit," my mother said. "Old Jesse WildShoe choked to death on his own vomit and he ain't anybody's hero."

I stood back and watched my parents argue. I was used to these battles. When an Indian marriage starts to fall apart, it's even more destructive and painful than usual. A hundred years ago, an Indian marriage was broken easily. The woman or man just packed up all their possessions and left the tipi. There were no arguments, no discussions.

Now, Indians fight their way to the end, holding onto the last good thing, because our whole lives have to do with survival.

After a while, after too much fighting and too many angry words had been exchanged, my father went out and bought a motorcycle. A big bike. He left the house often to ride that thing for hours, sometimes for days. He even strapped an old cassette player to the gas tank so he could listen to music. With that bike, he learned something new about running away. He stopped talking as much, stopped drinking as much. He didn't do much of anything except ride that bike and listen to music.

Then one night my father wrecked his bike on Devil's Gap Road and ended up in the hospital for two months. He broke both his legs, cracked his ribs, and punctured a lung. He also lacerated his kidney. The doctors said he could have died easily. In fact, they were surprised he made it through surgery, let alone survived those first few hours when he lay on the road, bleeding. But I wasn't surprised. That's how my father was.

And even though my mother didn't want to be married to him anymore and his wreck didn't change her mind about that, she still came to see him every day. She sang Indian tunes under her breath, in time with the hum of the machines hooked into my father. Although my father could barely move, he tapped his finger in rhythm.

When he had the strength to finally sit up and talk, hold conversations, and tell stories, he called for me.

"Victor," he said. "Stick with four wheels."

After he began to recover, my mother stopped visiting as often. She helped him through the worst, though. When he didn't need her anymore, she went back to the life she had created. She traveled to powwows, started to dance again. She was a champion traditional dancer when she was younger.

"I remember your mother when she was the best traditional dancer in the world," my father said. "Everyone wanted to call her sweetheart. But she only danced for me. That's how it was. She told me that every other step was just for me."

"But that's only half of the dance," I said.

"Yeah," my father said. "She was keeping the rest for herself. Nobody can give everything away. It ain't healthy."

"You know," I said, "sometimes you sound like you ain't even real."

"What's real? I ain't interested in what's real. I'm interested in how things should be."

My father's mind always worked that way. If you don't like the things you remember, then all you have to do is change the memories. Instead of remembering the bad things, remember what happened immediately before. That's what I learned from my father. For me, I remember how good the first drink of that Diet Pepsi tasted instead of how my mouth felt when I swallowed a wasp with the second drink.

Because of all that, my father always remembered the second before my mother left him for good and took me with her. No. I remembered the second before my father left my mother and me. No. My mother remembered the second before my father left her to finish raising me all by herself.

But however memory actually worked, it was my father who climbed on his motorcycle, waved to me as I stood in the window, and rode away. He lived in Seattle, San Francisco, Los Angeles, before he finally ended up in Phoenix. For a while, I got postcards nearly every week. Then it was once a month. Then it was on Christmas and my birthday.

On a reservation, Indian men who abandon their children are treated worse than white fathers who do the same thing. It's because white men have been doing that forever and Indian men have just learned how. That's how assimilation can work.

My mother did her best to explain it all to me, although I understood most of what happened.

"Was it because of Jimi Hendrix?" I asked her.

"Part of it, yeah," she said. "This might be the only marriage broken up by a dead guitar player."

"There's a first time for everything, enit?"

"I guess. Your father just likes being alone more than he likes being with other people. Even me and you."

Sometimes I caught my mother digging through old photo albums or staring at the wall or out the window. She'd get that look on her face that I knew meant she missed my father. Not enough to want him back. She missed him just enough for it to hurt.

On those nights I missed him most I listened to music. Not always Jimi Hendrix. Usually I listened to the blues. Robert Johnson mostly. The first time I heard Robert Johnson sing I knew he understood what it meant to be Indian on the edge of the twenty-first century, even if he was black at the beginning of the twentieth. That must have been how my father felt when he heard Jimi Hendrix. When he stood there in the rain at Woodstock.

Then on the night I missed my father most, when I lay in bed and cried, with that photograph of him beating that National Guard private in my hands, I imagined his motorcycle pulling up outside. I knew I was dreaming it all but I let it be real for a moment.

"Victor," my father yelled. "Let's go for a ride."

"I'll be right down. I need to get my coat on."

I rushed around the house, pulled my shoes and socks on, struggled into my coat, and ran outside to find an empty driveway. It was so quiet, a reservation kind of quiet, where you can hear somebody drinking whiskey on the rocks three miles away. I stood on the porch and waited until my mother came outside.

"Come on back inside," she said. "It's cold."

"No," I said. "I know he's coming back tonight."

My mother didn't say anything. She just wrapped me in her favorite quilt and went back to sleep. I stood on the porch all night long and imagined I heard motorcycles and guitars, until the sun rose so bright that I knew it was time to go back inside to my mother. She made breakfast for both of us and we ate until we were full.

PART FIVE

ADRIFT IN THE AGE OF AQUARIUS: DRUGS AND THE MOVEMENT INTO INNER SPACE

I propose, then, that everybody, including the President and his and our vast hordes of generals, executives, judges and legislators of these States go to nature, find a kindly teacher or Indian peyote chief or guru guide, and assay their consciousness with LSD. Then, I prophesy, we will all have seen some ray of glory or vastness beyond our conditioned social selves, beyond our government, beyond America even, that will unite us into a peaceable community.

ALLEN GINSBERG, "PUBLIC SOLITUDE" (1967)

IN THE 1960S, the hallucinogenic drug LSD-25 became widely available for the first time. The High Priest of Psychedelia was **Timothy Leary,** who offered a brief history of this hallucinogenic agent in his article "Turning on the World," published in the July 1968 issue of *Esquire* magazine. The major portion of Leary's essay described how while still a Harvard professor in 1960, he gave hallucinogenic mushrooms to Allen Ginsberg, who had been interested in expanding his consciousness for more than a decade, as the titles of several of his poems suggest: "Marijuana Notation" (1951), "Laughing Gas" (1958), "Mescaline" (1959), "Lysergic Acid" (1959), and "Aether" (1960). Drugs, both men agreed, would be the primary agency for change in the social and cultural revolution that seemed imminent at the time.

An earlier professor at Harvard University had also been an enthusiastic drug experimenter as a way to alter consciousness. More than a half century before Leary, the philosopher William James, the founder of both pragmatism and behavioral psychology, used nitrous oxide as an agent that would assist him in the investigation of hallucinatory experience. As James wrote in *The Varieties of Religious Experience* (1902):

> . . . our normal waking consciousness, rational consciousness as we call it, is but one special type of consciousness, whilst all about it, parted from it by the filmiest of screens, there lie potential forms of consciousness entirely different. . . . No account of the universe in its totality can be final which

leaves these other forms of consciousness quite disregarded
. . . they forbid a premature closing of our accounts with
reality.

James had no intention of making himself the leader of a cult that
would try to create a new world utopia, which is what Leary tried to
do after he was dismissed from Harvard in 1963. Nor did two others
before Leary, Aldous Huxley and Alan Watts, who also wrote about
their psychedelic experiments in two influential books published after
World War II: Huxley's *Doors of Perception* (1954) and Watts's *The Joy-
ous Cosmology: Adventures in the Chemistry of Consciousness* (1962).

In book after book, Leary proselytized for the cause of psychic
revolution, trying to convert young people to his point of view, suc-
cinctly expressed in his slogan "Turn on, tune in, drop out." Two of
his book titles in 1968 suggest his ambition: *The Politics of Ecstasy*
(1968) and *High Priest* (1968). As Leary told a BBC interviewer the
previous year, LSD was a miracle drug, "the sacrament that will put
you in touch with the ancient two-million-year-old wisdom inside
you," besides freeing you "to go on to the next stage, which is the
evolutionary timelessness, the ancient reincarnation thing we always
carry inside."

Timothy Leary

TURNING ON THE WORLD

BY THE FALL OF 1960 there was in existence an informal international network of scientists and scholars who had taken the psychedelic trip and who foresaw the powerful effect that the new alkaloids would have on human culture. The members of this group differed in age and temperament, and had varying ideas about tactics, but the basic vision was common to all—we believed these wondrous plants and drugs could free man's consciousness and bring about a new conception of man, his psychology and philosophy.

There was Albert Hofmann, who had invented LSD, who dreamed the utopian dream, but who was limited by the cautious politics of Sandoz Pharmaceuticals. What a frustrating web his genius had woven for Sandoz. How could a medical-drug house make a profit on a revelation pill?

Sandoz knew they had patented the most powerful mind-changing substance known to man. They expected to make millions when the psychiatric profession learned how to use LSD, and they were continually disappointed to discover that human society didn't want to have its mind changed, didn't want to touch a love-ecstasy potion.

In 1960 a top executive of Sandoz leaned across the conference table and said jokingly to me, LSD isn't a drug at all. It's a food. Let's bottle it in Coca-Cola and let the world have it. And his legal counsel frowned and said that foods still come under the jurisdiction of the Food and Drug Administration.

By 1966, when LSD was crowding Vietnam for the headlines, officials of Sandoz Pharmaceuticals were groaning, We wish we had never heard of LSD.

> *I do really wish to destroy it! cried Frodo. Or well, to have it destroyed. I am not made for perilous quests. I wish I had never seen the Ring! Why did it come to me? Why was I chosen?*
> —The Lord of the Rings

There were the detached philosophers—Aldous Huxley, Father Murray, Gerald Heard, Alan Watts, Harry Murray, Robert Gordon Wasson—who knew that the new drugs were reintroducing the platonic-gnostic vision. These men had read their theological history and understood both the glorious possibility and the angered reaction of the priestly establishment. They were not activists but sage observers.

Then there were the turned-on doctors—psychiatrists who had taken the trip, and came back hoping to fit the new potions into the medical game. Humphrey Osmond, witty, wise, cultured, had invented the name psychedelic and tolerantly wondered how to introduce a harmony-ecstasy drug into an aggressive-puritanical social order. Sidney Cohen, Keith Ditman, Jim Watt, Abram Hoffer and Nick Chewelos hoped to bring about a psychiatric renaissance and a new era of mental health with the new alchemicals.

And there was that strange, intriguing, delightful cosmic magician called Al Meyner, the rum-drinking, swashbuckling, Roman Catholic frontier salesman who promoted uranium ore during the Forties and who took the trip and recognized that LSD was the fissionable material of the mind and who turned on Osmond and Hoffer to the religious mystical meaning of their psychotomimetic drug. Al Meyner set out to turn on the world and flew from country to country with his leather bag full of drugs, claiming to have turned on bishops and obtained *nihil obstat* from Pope John. When the medical society complained that only doctors could give drugs, Meyner bought himself a doctor's degree from a Kentucky diploma mill and swept through northern California turning on scientists and professors and God seekers.

Right from the beginning this dedicated group of ring bearers was rent with a basic disagreement. There were those who said work within the system. Society has assigned the administration of drugs to the medical profession. Any non-doctor who gives or takes drugs is a dope fiend. Play ball with the system. Medicine must be the vanguard of the psychedelic movement. Any nonmedical use of psychedelic drugs would create a new marijuana mess and set back research into the new utopia.

The medical point of view made little sense to religious philosophers. Aldous Huxley called the psychedelic experience a gratuitous grace. His vibrant flame-colored wife, Laura, agreed. So, in gentle tones, did Huston Smith and Alan Watts and Gerald Heard.

And so did Allen Ginsberg, who had discovered the Buddha nature of drugs along with other writers.

I had been visited by most of the psychedelic eminences by this time and was under steady pressure to make the Harvard psychedelic research a kosher-medically-approved project. Everyone was aware of the potency of Harvard's name. Timothy, you are the key figure, said Dr. Al Meyner; I'm just old deputy-dog Al at your service. But the message was clear: Keep it respectable and medical.

And now here was Allen Ginsberg, the secretary-general of the world's poets, beatniks, anarchists, socialists, free-sex/love cultists.

November 26, 1960, the sunny Sunday afternoon that we gave Allen Ginsberg the mushrooms, started slowly. First in the cycle of breakfasts at noon were my son Jack Leary and his friend Bobbie, who had spent the night. Bobbie went off to Mass. When I came down I found Donald, an uninvited raccoon hipster-painter from New York, solemnly squatting at the table gnawing at toast and bacon. Frank Barron, who was visiting, and the poets, Allen Ginsberg and Peter and Lafcadio Orlovsky, remained upstairs and we moved around the kitchen with that Sunday-morning hush, not wanting to wake the sleepers. Lafcadio, Peter's brother, was on leave from a hospital.

About twelve-thirty the quiet exploded into family noise. Bobbie was back from church where he had excitedly told his father about the party we had given the night before for the Harvard football team and how I had given the boys, Bobbie and Jack, a dollar each for being bartenders.

I toted up the political profit and loss from this development. The Harvard football team rang up a sale. But the boys bartending? Bobbie's father is Irish so that's all right. All okay.

Then wham, the door opened and in flooded Susan Leary, my daughter, with three teen-age girls, through the kitchen, upstairs to get clothes, down to make a picnic lunch, up again for records, out, and then back for the ginger ale.

By now the noise had filtered upstairs and we could hear the late sleepers moving around and the bathroom waters running, and down came Frank Barron, half-awake, to fry codfish cakes for his breakfast. And then, Allen Ginsberg and Peter. Allen hopped around the room with nearsighted crow motions cooking eggs, and Peter sat silent, watching.

Afterward the poets fell to reading the *Times* and Frank moved upstairs to Susan's room to watch a pro football game on TV. I told Allen to make himself at home and got beers and went up to join Frank. Donald the painter had been padding softly around the house watching with his big, soft creature eyes and sniffing in corners and at the bookcase and the record cabinets. He had asked to take mushrooms in the evening and was looking for records of Indian peyote drum music.

At dusk, Allen Ginsberg, hunched over a teacup, peering out through his black-rimmed glasses, the left lens bisected by a break, started telling of his experiences with ayahuasco, the fabled visionary vine of the Peruvian jungles. He had followed the quest of Bill Burroughs, sailing south for new realms of consciousness, looking for the elixir of wisdom. Sitting, sweating with heat, lonely in a cheap hotel in Lima, holding a wad of ether-soaked cotton to his nose with his left hand and getting high and making poetry with his right hand, and then traveling by second-class bus with Indians up through the Cordillera de los Andes and then more buses and hitchhiking into the Montaña jungles and shining rivers, wandering through steaming equatorial forests. Then the village Pucallpa, and the negotiations to find the *curandero* [guide], paying him with *aguardiente,* and the ritual itself, swallowing the bitter stuff, and the nausea and the colors and the drums beating and sinking down into thingless void, into the great eye that brings it all together, and the terror of the great snake coming. The old *curandero,* wrinkled face bending over him and Allen telling him, *culebra,* and the *curandero* nodding clinically and blowing a puff of smoke to make the great snake disappear and it did.

> *The fate of fire depends on wood; as long as there is wood below, the fire burns above. It is the same in human life; there is in man likewise a fate that lends power to his life.*   —I Ching

I kept asking Allen questions about the *curandero.* I wanted to learn the rituals, to find out how other cultures (older and wiser than ours) had handled the visionary business. I was fascinated by the ritual thing. Ritual is to the science of consciousness what experiment is to external science. I was convinced that none of our American rituals fit the mushroom experience. Not the cocktail party. Not the psychiatrist. Not the teacher-minister role. I was impressed by what Allen said about his own fear and sickness whenever he took drugs and about the solace and comforting strength of the *curandero,* about how good it was to have someone there who knew, who had been to those far regions of the mind and could tell you by a look, by a touch, by a puff of smoke that it was all right, go ahead, explore the strange world, it's all right, you'll come back, it's all right, I'm here back on familiar old human earth when you need me, to bring you back.

Allen was going to take the mushrooms later that night and he was shaping me up to help him. Allen was weaving a word spell, dark eyes gleaming through the glasses, chain-smoking, moving his hands, intense, chanting trance poetry. Frank Barron was in the study now, and with him Lafcadio Orlovsky.

A car came up the driveway and in a minute the door opened, and Donald, furry and moist, ambled in. He had brought his friend, an anthropology student from Harvard, to be with him when he tripped. Donald asked if his friend could be there during the mushroom session. I liked the idea of having a friend present for the mushrooms, someone to whom you could turn at those moments when you needed support, so I said, Sure, but he couldn't take the pills because he was a university student. Everyone was warning us to keep our research away from Harvard to avoid complications with the university health bureau and to avoid the rumors. He wasn't hungry so I mixed him a drink and then I got the little round bottle and pulled out the cotton topping and gave Donald 30 mg. and Allen Ginsberg 36.

Allen started bustling around getting his cave ready. I brought Susan's record player up to his room and he took some Beethoven and Wagner from the study and he turned out the lights so that there was just a glow in the room. I told him we'd be checking back every fifteen minutes and he should tell me if he wanted anything.

By the time I got downstairs Donald was already high, strolling around the house on dainty raccoon feet with his hands clasped behind his back, thinking and digging deep things. I stayed in the study writing letters, reading the *Times.* I had forgotten about the anthropology student. He was waiting in the kitchen.

After about thirty minutes I found Donald in the hallway. He called me over earnestly and began talking about the artificiality of civilization. He was thinking hard about basic issues and it was obvious what was going on with him—clearing his mind of abstractions, trying to get back behind the words and concepts.

*And if he succeeds in assigning the right place to life and to fate,
thus bringing the two into harmony, he puts his fate on a firm foot-
ing. These words contain hints about the fostering of life as handed
on by oral tradition in the secret teachings of Chinese yoga.*

—I Ching

The anthropology student was standing by, watching curiously,
and Donald asked if he minded leaving so that he could talk to me
privately. Anthro went back to the kitchen and Donald continued
talking about the falseness of houses and machines and deploring the
way man cut himself off from the vital stuff with his engines and
structures. I was trying to be polite and be a good *curandero* and sup-
port him and tell him, great boy, stay with it and work it out.

Susan came back from her friends' about this time and went up-
stairs to her homework, and I followed her up to check on Allen. He
was lying on top of the blanket. His glasses were off and his black
eyes, pupils completely dilated, looked up at me. Looking down into
them they seemed like two deep, black, wet wells and you could look
down them way through the man Ginsberg to something human be-
yond. The eye is such a defenseless, naïve, trusting thing. PROFESSOR
LEARY CAME INTO MY ROOM, LOOKED IN MY EYES, AND SAID I WAS
A GREAT MAN. THAT DETERMINED ME TO MAKE AN EFFORT TO LIVE
HERE AND NOW.   —Allen Ginsberg

Allen was scared and unhappy and sick. And still he was lying
there voluntarily, patiently searching, pushing himself into panics and
fears, into nausea, trying to learn something, trying to find meaning.
Shamelessly weak and shamelessly human and greatly classic. Peter
was lying next to him, eyes closed, sleeping or listening to the record.
I GOT NAUSEOUS SOON AFTER—SAT UP IN BED NAKED AND SWAL-
LOWED DOWN THE VOMIT THAT BESIEGED FROM MY STOMACH AS IF
AN INDEPENDENT BEING DOWN THERE WAS REBELLING AT BEING
DRAGGED INTO EXISTENCE.

On the way downstairs I checked Susan's room. She was curled
up on the carpet, with her books scattered around her and reading in
the shadows. I scolded her about ruining her eyes and flicked on the
two wall bulbs. Downstairs Frank was still at the study desk. Anthro
was wandering in the living room and told me that Donald had gone
outside. The rule we had set up was that no one would leave the
house and the idea of Donald padding down Beacon Street in a mys-
tic state chilled me. Out on the front porch I turned on the two rows
of spotlights that flooded the long winding stone stairs and started

down, shielding my eyes and shouting Donald. Halfway down I heard him answering back and saw him standing under an oak tree on the lower lawn. I asked him how he was, but he didn't talk, just stood there looking wise and deep. He was barefoot and higher than Piccard's balloon. I want to talk to you, but first you must take off your shoes. Okay, why not? I sat down to unlace my shoes and he squatted alongside and told about how the machines complicate our lives and how cold and hot were abstractions and how we didn't really need houses and shoes and clothes because it was just our concepts that made us think we needed these things. I agreed with him and followed what his mind was doing, suspending for a moment the clutch of the abstract but at the same time shivering from the November wind and wanting to get back behind the warm glow of the windows.

The young anthropology student was standing in the hallway. I told him that Donald was doing fine, great mystical stuff, philosophizing without concepts. He looked puzzled. He didn't want a drink or food. I walked upstairs and found the door to Allen's room closed. I waited for a while, not knowing what to do and then knocked softly and said softly, Allen I'm here now and will be back in a few minutes. *Paradise Lost*, A BOOK I'D NEVER UNDERSTOOD BEFORE—WHY MILTON SIDED WITH LUCIFER THE REBEL IN HEAVEN.

I GOT UP OUT OF BED AND WALKED DOWNSTAIRS NAKED, ORLOVSKY FOLLOWING ME, CURIOUS WHAT I WOULD DO AND WILLING TO GO ALONG IN CASE I DID ANYTHING INTERESTINGLY EXTRAVAGANT. URGING ME ON IN FACT, THANK GOD.

Susan was sitting cross-legged on her bed brushing her hair when there came a patter of bare feet on the hallway carpet. I got to the door just in time to see naked buttocks disappearing down the stairway. It was Peter. I was grinning when I went back to see Susan. Peter is running around without any clothes on. Susan picked up her paraphernalia—curlers, brush, pins, and trotted up to the third floor. I headed downstairs.

When I got to the study Frank was leaning back in his chair behind the desk, grinning quizzically. In front of the desk looking like medieval hermits were Allen and Peter, both stark naked. I WENT IN AMONG THE PSYCHOLOGISTS IN STUDY AND SAW THEY TOO WERE WAITING FOR SOMETHING VAST TO HAPPEN ONLY IT REQUIRED SOMEONE AND THE MOMENT TO MAKE IT HAPPEN—ACTION, REVOLUTION. No, Allen had on his glasses and as I came in he peered out at me and raised his finger in the air. Hey, Allen, what goes on? Allen had a holy gleam in his eye and he waved his finger. I'm the Messiah.

I've come down to preach love to the world. We're going to walk through the streets and teach people to stop hating. I DECIDED I MIGHT AS WELL BE THE ONE TO DO SO—PRONOUNCED MY NAKEDNESS AS THE FIRST ACT OF REVOLUTION AGAINST THE DESTROYERS OF THE HUMAN IMAGE.

Well, Allen, that sounds like a pretty good idea. Listen, said Allen, do you believe that I'm the Messiah? THE NAKED BODY BEING THE HIDDEN SIGN. Look, I can prove it. I'm going to cure your hearing. Take off your hearing machine. Your ears are cured. Come on, take it off, you don't need it. AND GRABBED THE TELEPHONE TO COMMUNICATE MY DECISION—WANTED TO HOOK UP KHRUSHCHEV, KEROUAC, BURROUGHS, IKE, KENNEDY, MAO TSE-TUNG, MAILER, ETC.

Frank was still smiling. Peter was standing by, watching seriously. The hearing aid was dumped on the desk. That's right. And now your glasses, I'll heal your vision too. The glasses were laid on the desk too. ALL IN ONE TELEPHONE LINE AND GET THEM ALL TO COME IMMEDIATELY TO HARVARD TO HAVE SPECTRAL CONFERENCE OVER THE FUTURE OF THE UNIVERSE.

Allen was peering around with approval at his healing. But Allen, one thing. What? Your glasses. You're still wearing them. Why don't you cure your own vision. Allen looked surprised. Yes, you're right. I will. He took off his glasses and laid them on the desk.

Now Allen was a blind Messiah squinting around to find his followers. Come on. We're going down to the city streets to tell the people about peace and love. And then we'll get lots of great people onto a big telephone network to settle all this warfare bit.

Fine, said Frank, but why not do the telephone bit first, right here in the house. Frank was heading off the pilgrimage down the avenue naked.

Who we gonna call, said Peter. Well, we'll call Kerouac on Long Island, and Kennedy and Khrushchev and Bill Burroughs in Paris and Norman Mailer in the psycho ward in Bellevue. We'll get them all hooked up in a big cosmic electronic love talk. War is just a hang-up. We'll get the love-thing flowing on the electric Bell Telephone network. Who we gonna call first, said Peter. Let's start with Khrushchev, said Allen.

Look, why don't we start with Kerouac on Long Island. In the meantime, let's pull the curtains, said Frank. There's enough going on in here so I don't care about looking outside. Allen picked up the white telephone and dialed Operator. The two thin figures leaned forward wrapped up in a holy fervor trying to spread peace. The dear noble innocent helplessness of the naked body. They looked as though they had stepped out of a quattrocento canvas, apostles, martyrs, dear fanatic holy men. Allen said, Hello, operator, this is God, I want to talk to Kerouac. To whom do I want to talk? Kerouac. What's my name? This is God. G-O-D. Okay. We'll try Capitol 7-0563. Where? Northport, Long Island. There was a pause. We were all listening hard. Oh. Yes. That's right. That's the number of the house where I was born. Look, operator, I'll have to go upstairs to get the number. Then I'll call back.

Allen hung up the receiver. What was all that about, Allen? Well, the operator asked me my name and I said I was God and I wanted to speak to Kerouac and she said, I'll try to do my best, sir, but you'll have to give me his number and then I gave her the number of my mother's house. I've got Kerouac's number upstairs in my book. Just a minute and I'll get it.

Back at the phone, Allen was shouting to Jack. He wanted Jack to come up to Cambridge and then he wanted Jack's mother to come too. Jack had a lot to say because Allen held the phone, listening for long spaces. Frank was still sitting behind the desk smiling. Donald and the anthro student were standing in the hallway looking in curiously. I walked over to explain. Allen says he is the Messiah and he's calling Kerouac to start a peace and love movement. Donald wasn't interested. He went on telling me about the foolishness of believing in hot and cold. It occurred to me that Allen and Peter were proving his point. The phone call continued and finally I walked back in and said, Hey, Allen, for the cost of this phone call we could pay his way up here by plane. Allen shot an apologetic look and then I heard him telling Jack, Okay, Jack, I have to go now, but you've got to take the mushrooms and let's settle this quarrel between Kennedy and Khrushchev. BUT NEEDED MY GLASSES—THOUGH HAD YELLED AT LEARY THAT HE DIDN'T NEED HIS EARPIECE TO HEAR THE REAL VIBRATIONS OF THE COSMOS. HE WENT ALONG WITH ME AGREEABLY.

Allen and Peter were sitting on the big couch in the living room and Allen was telling us about his visions, cosmic electronic networks, and how much it meant to him that I told him he was a great man and how this mushroom episode had opened the door to women and heterosexuality and how he could see new womanly body visions and family life ahead. BUT THEN I BEGAN BREATHING AND WANTING TO LIE DOWN AND REST. Peter's hand was moving back and forth on Allen's shoulder. It was the first time that Allen had stood up to Jack and he was sorry about the phone bill but wasn't it too bad that Khrushchev and Kennedy couldn't have been on the line and, hey, what about Norman Mailer in that psychiatric ward in Bellevue, shouldn't we call him.

I don't think they'd let a call go through to him, Allen. Well, it all depends on how we come on. I don't think coming on as Allen Ginsberg would help in that league. I don't think coming on as the Messiah would either. Well, you could come on as big psychologists and make big demanding noises about the patient. It was finally decided that it was too much trouble.

Still *curandero,* I asked if they wanted anything to eat or drink. Well, how about some hot milk. IF I ATE OR SHIT AGAIN I WOULD TURN BACK TO MERE NON-MESSIAH HUMAN. Allen and Peter went upstairs to put on robes and I put some cold milk in a pan and turned on the stove. Donald was still moving around softly with his hands behind his back. Thinking. Watching. He was too deep and Buddha for us to swing with and I later realized that I hadn't been a very attentive *curandero* for him and that there was a gulf between Allen and him never closed and that the geographic arrangement was too scattered to make a close loving session. Of course, both of them were old drug hands and ready to go off on their own private journeys and both wanted to make something deep and their own.

Anthro's role in all of this was never clear. He stood in the hallway watching curiously but for the most part we ignored him, treated him as an object just there but not involved and that, of course, was a mistake. Any time you treat someone as an object rest assured he'll do the same and that was the way that score was going to be tallied.

We ended up with a great scene in the kitchen. I bustled around pouring the hot milk into cups, and the poets sat around the table looking like Giotto martyrs in checkered robes. Lafcadio came down and we got him some food and he nodded yes when I asked him about ice cream and Allen started to talk about his visions and about the drug scene in New York and, becoming eloquent, wound up preaching with passion about the junkies, helpless, hooked, lost, thin, confused creatures, sick and the police and the informers. I SAW THE BEST MINDS OF MY GENERATION DESTROYED BY MADNESS, STARVING HYSTERICAL NAKED, DRAGGING THEMSELVES THROUGH THE NEGRO STREETS AT DAWN LOOKING FOR AN ANGRY FIX. And then we started planning the psychedelic revolution. Allen wanted everyone to have the mushrooms. Who has the right to keep them from someone else? And there should be freedom for all sorts of rituals too. The doctors could have them and there should be *curanderos,* and all sorts of good new holy rituals that could be developed and ministers have to be involved. Although the church is naturally and automatically opposed to mushroom visions, still the experience is basically religious and some ministers would see it and start using them. But with all these groups and organizations and new rituals, there still had to be room for the single, lone, unattached, non-groupy individual to take the mushrooms and go off and follow his own rituals—brood big cosmic thoughts by the sea or roam through the streets of New York, high and restless, thinking poetry, and writers and poets and artists to work out whatever they were working out.

Allen Ginsberg hunched over the kitchen table, shabby robe hiding his thin white nakedness, cosmic politician. Give them the mystic vision. They'll see it's good and honest and they'll say so publicly and then no one from the police or the narcotics bureau can put them down. And you're the perfect persons to do it. Big serious scientist professors from Harvard. That's right. I can't do it. I'm too easy to put down. Crazy beatnik poet. Let me get my address book. I've got lots of connections in New York and we'll go right down the list and turn them all on.

Now Allen Ginsberg, stooping over the kitchen table peering at his address book. There's Robert Lowell and Muriel Rukeyser, and LeRoi Jones. And Dizzy Gillespie. And the painters. And the publishers. He was chanting out names of the famous and the talented. He was completely serious, dedicated, wound up in the crusade. I'M NEARSIGHTED AND PSYCHOPATHIC ANYWAY. AMERICA, I'M PUTTING MY QUEER SHOULDER TO THE WHEEL.

And so Allen spun out the cosmic campaign. He was to line up influentials and each weekend I would come down to New York and we'd run mushroom sessions. This fit our Harvard research plans perfectly. Our aim there was to learn how people reacted, to test the limits of the drug, to get creative and thoughtful people to take them and tell us what they saw and what we should do with the mushrooms. Allen's political plan was appealing too. I had seen enough and read enough in Spanish of the anti-vision crowd, the power-holders with guns, and the bigger and better men we got on our team the stronger our position. And then, too, the big-name bit was intriguing. Meeting and sharing visions with the famous.

It was around midnight. Donald still seemed high and would walk in and out of the room, silently, hands behind his back, Talmudic raccoon, studying the kitchen crowd seriously, and then padding out. The anthropology student had joined us around the table. We had given him something to drink and he was listening to the conversation and saying nothing. He made some comment about schedules back to Cambridge and it was time for him to make the last train, so I drove him down to the station. He asked some questions about the scientific meaning of the mushroom research and it was clear that he didn't understand what had happened and what we were doing. There wasn't time to explain and I felt badly that he had been dragged into a strange situation. We had made the rule that people could bring their friends when they took the mushrooms and this seemed like a good idea for the person taking the mushrooms but it was just beginning to dawn on me that the problem never was with the person taking the drug but rather the people who didn't. Like Brother Toriblo, the Spanish monk, who talked about cruelty and drunkenness caused by the Sacred Mushrooms. It's okay to bring a friend, but he should take the mushrooms with you. And poor Anthro, it turned out, wasn't even a friend of Donald's and as it turned out didn't like him and was clearly bewildered by and critical of what he had seen and heard and the nakedness of the poets. His train was about due and I was too preoccupied by what Allen had been saying to feel like explaining to Anthro. The uneasy feeling persisted and I suggested that he not tell people about the mystic visions and the naked crusaders because this might be misunderstood and he said he wouldn't talk about it and we shook hands and he left.

That was Sunday night. By Monday afternoon the rumors were spreading around Harvard Yard.

Beatniks. Orgies. Naked poets. Junkies. Homosexuality. Drug parties. Tried to lure a decent naïve graduate student into sin. Wild parties masquerading as research. Queers. Beards. Criminal types.

The chairman of my department called me. What the hell is going on, Tim? Two graduate students have come to me indignant—demanding that your work be stopped.

I laughed. I'll send you the reports from the session as soon as they are typed. It was a good session. God would approve. We're learning a lot.

> *The disapproving gaze of the establishment was on us. You should fear the wary eyes of the servants of Sauron were the words of Elrond. I do not doubt that news . . . has already reached him, and he will be filled with wrath.*   —The Lord of the Rings

In the months that followed we began to see ourselves as unwitting agents of a social process that was far too powerful for us to control or more than dimly understand. A historical movement that would inevitably change man at the very center of his nature, his consciousness.

We did sense that we were not alone. The quest for internal freedom, for the elixir of life, for the draught of immortal revelation was not new. We were part of an ancient and honorable fellowship which had pursued this journey since the dawn of recorded history. We began to read the accounts of earlier trippers—Dante, Hesse, René Daumal, Tolkien, Homer, Blake, George Fox, Swedenborg, Bosch, and the explorers from the Orient—tantrics, Sufis, Bauls, Gnostics, hermetics, Sivaites, sadhus.

From this moment on my days as a respectable establishment scientist were numbered. I just couldn't see the new society given birth by medical hands, or psychedelic sacraments as psychiatric tools.

From this evening on my energies were offered to the ancient underground society of alchemists, artists, mystics, alienated visionaries, dropouts and the disenchanted young, the sons arising.

Diane di Prima

New York poet Diane di Prima was a guest with her husband, Alan Marlowe, and their children at the estate in Millbrook, New York, where Tim Leary and his family were living in the fall of 1966. In "The Holidays at Millbrook—1966," di Prima described how she cooked Thanksgiving dinner for the assorted dancers, musicians, singers, and poets in residence, including a Canadian reporter who missed dinner because he had unknowingly imbibed large quantities of sherry laced with acid (LSD-25), along with Leary and his wife, Rosemary.

THE HOLIDAYS AT MILLBROOK—1966

THANKSGIVING DAY DAWNED CLEAR. I got up later than usual (8:30 or so) and made it down to the kitchen, grimly resolved to eat a breakfast, DO NO COOKING, and leave again for a leisurely day at home. After cooking all three Millbrook meals for some 50 people for over a month, I had had it with the spacious and picturesque kitchen, and the eternal Beatles on the kitchen phonograph.

When I got to the "main house" I found that Kumar, our Hindu poet friend, had already arrived from New York with hashish and gossip, and many other people were converging from Massachusetts, Washington, and farther afield. The parking lot beside the big house, with its great gouges and holes—from the legendary trip when Timothy & Co. had decided to get rid of all the pavement in the world, starting in their own back yard and heading down the Taconic State Parkway—was full to capacity with everything from old pickup trucks to a solitary silver Porsche, and the house was filling rapidly. It was clearly necessary to do some cooking—none had been started yet—and I had a sinking feeling that I wasn't going to escape, after all.

Sure enough, Alan had volunteered to cook one of the four huge turkeys, and he conned me into "starting" it for him. Naturally, I looked up from the first motions to find him gone, and wound up cooking the turkey, and several gallons of cranberry sauce, and a cauldron of candied yams, while Alan made off for parts unknown. It was a soft, warm day, doors and windows were open, velvet draperies blowing, and wind; goats, dogs and children all wandering in and out.

There was a football game before lunch on the lawn in front of the main house. Timothy loves football, baseball, softball—has a big rah-rah streak which some find very lovable—and is constantly pressing his guests into some strenuous sport-like activity, which leaves them usually with sprained backs and sore leg muscles and sour dispositions—until the next round of drinks, food, meditation, or grass sets them up again. The more ornamental girls gathered round to cheer. The rest of us went on with the cooking.

I noticed that Alan had managed to escape the football game as well as the turkey. Found out later that he had retired to sweep the back porch of the pseudo-Swiss chalet that he and I lived in with the children—a really charming little building of wood and stone, known to Millbrook inmates as "the bowling alley" (it had indeed been built, with its myriad stone balconies and three-inch-thick shingles, as a bowling alley and billiard room for the first owner). Whenever things get to be too much for Alan, he sweeps.

He showed up for lunch, though, which was baked Virginia ham, split pea soup, beer and other goodies set out on the front porch of the main house, and in the main dining room. The kids wheeled their tricycles up and down the porch while we ate, looking out over the sweep of the lawn turning brown from the recent frosts. Alexander, my three-year-old, drank a half a can of beer and fell out on a mattress in the main dining room and slept till dinnertime.

The light came in, and faded, and I was still in the kitchen. A familiar feeling. Around 5:30, Jean McCreedy, Tim's secretary, came in and offered to candy the yams in my stead if I wanted to rest before dinner. I went back up to the bowling alley dead tired, to change clothes.

DeeDee Doyle was up there, reading and reminiscing. DeeDee was a California speed freak and old friend, who had sought refuge with us a few days before, when her old man had gone a little too berserk, even for her. She was wanting "something pretty to wear," and so we pulled gowns and capes and old shawls out of the closet and spread them about, and I put Bob Dylan on the phonograph.

DeeDee picked a costume, complete down to rhinestone pins and necklace, and put up her hair while she told me how years ago she had given Dylan a book of Michael McClure's, and how it had turned him on. Dylan later bought McClure an auto harp which changed his style for a while: he sang his poetry readings, wrote songs, grew his hair. Dylan had wanted her to live with him, "but I chose to go with Bad Bruce," said DeeDee a little sadly, making up her eyes.

I pulled on a coral gown and black velvet cape, braided some pearls into my hair, stuffed all the remaining clothes back into the closet, and returned to the main house to go to the john. (The bowling alley had no toilet facilities—no running water at all, in fact—nor any heat, except for a very small fireplace, more decorative than functional, which, during the winter ahead, usually managed to heat the huge room we lived in to about 40 or 50 degrees.)

At the main house I found Bali Ram. Bali is a Nepalese temple dancer. He had come to the States a few years before with Bill Haines, who was then arranging tours for groups of eastern dancers, musicians, etc. Bill was now head of the Sri Ram Ashram, a motley crew who occupied the second floor of the Millbrook main house at this time. The Ashram had 28 members, mostly young longhairs, to whom Tim had recently given asylum when they were thrown out of their former home, the Ananda Ashram in Monroe by the staid older members of that organization. The older members owned the land, and controlled the board of directors; the younger members had come to work the garden and pass the summer. They decided to stay and squatted, more or less, till the arrival of a large number of police and private detectives made it unfeasible for them to remain. The Sri Ram Ashram boasted several colorful and talented members. There was Jean-Pierre Merle, grandson of Raymond Duncan, and third-generation vegetarian: a skilled painter, sandalmaker, potter, and flute player, a slight young man who looked positively frail till you saw him in action. There was Tambimuttu, the Indian-British poet with a strong English accent, a friend of Auden &c., and founder of the little magazine of the '50s, *Poetry London–New York*. And there was Bali.

Bali was in full costume, about to begin a dance recital in the "music room" when I came in, and I immediately sat down to watch. He is a great dancer, and today he danced the dedication to Shiva—with which he opens all his concerts—particularly well. He changed, did a narrative dance from the Mahabarata, changed again, and danced the Nataraja, which I had never seen before. In it, he actually portrays Shiva doing his dance of the destruction of the cosmos, and ends in the pose on all the statues of the dancing Shiva: one hand raised in the "have no fear" mudra, the other pointing to his lifted foot, which represents liberation/enlightenment. I have never found any of Bali's dancing as moving as I did today. (Bill Haines told me later that Bali had been dedicated to Shiva as an infant, and given to the temple at the age of six, to begin his training.)

After the dance recital, nearly everyone was as out of it as I was, no one seemed to want to move, or talk. Allen Ginsberg took out his finger cymbals, and he and Peter began to sing a *kirtan,* starting with the "Hare Krishna" mantra that nearly everyone there knew. I stole that opportunity to try and make it back up to the bowling alley to gather up Alan and whoever else might want to come and sing. But I was to have a rude shock.

I left the music room by the sliding doors that open onto the main entry hall of the house, and there in the hall narrowly missed being knocked down by a giant of a man who was literally hurling himself about, from banister to wall, barely missing the huge gilded mirror and shouting "I have been Vi-o-la-ted!" over and over again to an astonished and immobilized audience.

Turned out that he was one Ted Cook, Canadian reporter, who, while being wined and entertained by Timothy in his study on the third floor, had inadvertently imbibed a large quantity of acid. It seems Timothy had offered him the choice of some perfectly straight bourbon or scotch, but he had secretly decided on the sherry he had seen in the cabinet, and when everyone else was otherwise occupied he wandered off and helped himself to a good-sized glass of same. The sherry happened to be one of the three bottles of liquor which held our new stash.

And now it seemed he was very shook up. Well, it served him right, I figured. Not simply because it ain't cool to drink liquor which ain't offered, but—dig this—he had done a full-length movie about acid for CBC or something without ever having touched the stuff. That old black karma, catching up with him. I ducked as he made another howling lurch for the stairs and went on back to the bowling alley.

By the time I came back to the main house with Alan and our friend Zen (who lived downstairs from us in the bowling alley, where he devoured large quantities of morning glory seeds almost daily, and played his trumpet) *kirtan* had broken up: the howls and curses of Ted Cook had proved to be too much for everyone. Most of our guests were milling about aimlessly, making small talk and waiting for dinner, while the more competent—and the more paranoid—members of the community crashed around outside, coatless and flashlightless in the winter twilight, trying to find Ted Cook who had burst out of the house, surging through the masses of folk around him.

The general fear was that he would find his way to the highway (a good half mile away) and all hell would break loose with the local folk. We sat constantly on this powder keg at Millbrook, dissuading ecstatic first-time trippers from calling their wives in Virginia, tromping resolutely by the side of energetic ones who had decided to go for a long hike, feeding yoga, breathing exercises, niacin, or Thorazine to persistent bad-trippers—handling any and all drug crises as best we could alone.

Dinner was finally ready. I made a quick run back home with Ed, to wake up Mini, my four-year-old, who had consented to take a nap on my sworn oath that I would get her up in time to eat. The shouts of Ted Cook could be heard in the distance as we went up the path to the bowling alley, and I heard myself muttering, "If this is Thanksgiving, what will Christmas be like?"

At the bowling alley there was also a heap of presents that had to be brought back to the main house, Alan having, the day before, bought a gift for each of the eleven Millbrook children. There was absolutely no money at Millbrook at this time—times of total financial drought alternated there always with times of dizzying plenty— but that didn't stop Timothy, who handed us a blank check and told us to fill it out for whatever amount we needed. And so, Alan had decided that presents were in order, and had bought sweaters, toys, mittens, etc., at the huge shopping center in Poughkeepsie at the same time as the turkeys, yams, and other goodies.

Ed carried Mini, who was still half asleep, and an armload of packages, and I lugged a huge shopping bag full of presents back to the main house.

Dinner was very good and very luxurious, in the way that feasts always feel luxurious when the house is full and there is more than enough of everything. I heaped a big paper plate for myself and stashed it in a cupboard, and then I went to check out the rest of my family.

Found Jeanne, my eight-year-old, asleep in Suzie Blue's room on the top floor, her hair full of pincurls. She had been planning on a dazzling and glamorous entrance at dinner time. I woke her just enough to ask if she wanted to come on downstairs and join the festivities. But just at this point, Ted Cook, who had been captured in the ruined formal garden behind the "meditation house" was standing among the extra turkeys in the butler's pantry, alternately shouting horrifically in some abrupt, violent fright, and murmuring beatific nonsense at those who were trying to calm him. Jeanne listened to the noises from downstairs for a while, and decided judiciously to stay where she was. She asked me to bring her a dinner, which I painfully did, handling cape and gown and tray most clumsily on the stairs. She and Suzie settled themselves in, cozy and snug, getting high and watching television.

I finally got around to eating, settled halfway up the first flight of stairs in the entry hall, as the dining room was way too crowded. Alan passed by, looking totally out of his mind. He was working on his third plate and his sixth glass of wine. I told him what was going on upstairs, which hugely delighted him, and he went on up to join Jeanne and Suzie in front of the TV version of *Jason and the Argonauts*.

Soon after this, we had the *kirtan* that Ted Cook had interrupted before dinner, and Ted Cook brought it about. He had wandered out of the butler's pantry and settled down on a black trunk in the small entry hall, his trip still struggling between good and bad. Allen Ginsberg followed closely behind and sat down on the floor next to him. The hall was small, cold and drafty, and the floor was tiled and very hard. Allen began to sing mantras to Ted, and slowly a crowd gathered in spite of the discomfort. We brought cushions and our dinner plates, and sat on the ground or in each other's laps, squeezed into that tiny space.

We sang for over two hours: "Hare Krishna," "Hare Om Namo Shivaya," "Om Sri Maitreya"—one after another of Allen's favorites. Kumar, our Hindu friend, with Naomi, one of his two women, me and the kids, Howie from the Ashram, Karen Detweiler, a young blonde witchgirl who kept a cauldron in the Millbrook forest, Judy Mayhan, our blues singer, Jackie Leary, Tim's son, and many of the Ashram people—all joined together in singing for this strange, frightened man whom no one of us had known two or three hours before. He slowly relaxed; his Buddha-nature began to shine forth—reluctantly at first, and then stronger as our energy built. He finally became perfectly joyous, joined us in singing a Shiva mantra over and over, and after a long time was able to wander about and join in the throng in which a good third of the guests were probably as stoned as he.

I had learned a lot from watching the kindness and understanding that Allen had so spontaneously held out to a fellow creature. That *kirtan* remains to this day the most moving I've ever been in. But the day was to hold one more heavy learning experience for me.

I heard from Joel Kramer that Tim, who hadn't been downstairs to eat at all, was on a high dosage "session" (usual Millbrook terminology for tripping), and that he "had to be seen to be believed." I was naturally a little curious to know what that meant—to see what Tim was into. So I went on up to the third floor, first stopping in Suzie Blue's room to ask Alan if he had seen Tim since he turned on. Alan nodded and said, in his best rhetorical style, "I'll never be angry with him again." When I asked him why, he said simply, "Go in and see for yourself."

I knocked on the door to Timothy and Rosemary's room, and opened it. The space in the room was warped—a funny kind of visual effect curved it somehow, as if it were in a different space-time continuum. I have since talked to other old-time trippers and hangers-around-trippers about this, and they all admit to seeing something similar at some point when they came "cold" upon people who were on a very high dosage of acid. The visual effect is a bit like the "heat waves" that show around a candle flame, or a hot car in the summer sun, or the waves that rise from the hot asphalt of a highway in the

desert. I have seen it a few times since. I remember waking one night
later that winter when Alan Marlowe and John Wieners were tripping
in the bowling alley and seeing the air around them curved in the
same way—some kind of high-energy charge that becomes visible.
But this was the first time I had ever seen anything like it, and it liter-
ally made me gasp.

Stepping into the room was like stepping into another dimen-
sion. Timothy looked at me from a million light-years away, from a
place of great sadness and loneliness and terrible tiredness, and after a
long time he formed the one word "Beloved." I knelt down to where
they were sitting side-by-side on the rug in front of a cold, dark fire-
place, and kissed him and Rosemary, spent a moment holding their
hands and looking into their eyes, and then went away as quietly as I
could, leaving them to each other.

It turned out later that the sherry which had set Ted Cook off
was what Tim and Rosemary had also had that day. Nobody ever
managed to figure out how strong it was. What had happened was
this: a new shipment of acid had arrived in powder form. Timothy
dumped half the powder in a two-pound coffee can, dumped in a
quart of vodka, sloshed it around, and poured it back in the vodka
bottle. He then repeated the process with the other half of the powder
and a second quart of vodka. After that, to save whatever might be
sticking to the coffee can, he poured in a fifth of sherry to rinse it
out. It was this sherry that dominated the events of that Thanks-
giving.

Carlos Castaneda

*Perhaps the most original book about consciousness expansion pub-
lished at the height of the 1960s interest in drug culture was the
work of Carlos Castaneda, a graduate student doing anthropological
research in Arizona and Sonora, Mexico. Castaneda's doctoral dis-*

sertation, published in 1968 as The Teachings of Don Juan: A Yaqui Way of Knowledge, *was a description of his five-year relationship with an old Sonora shaman, or magic man, a Yaqui Indian named Juan Matus.*

With the encouragement of his professors at UCLA, Castaneda began his research in 1961, convinced "that there was very little time left for the thought processes of the Native American cultures to remain standing before everything was going to be obliterated into the mishmash of modern technology," and that "the phenomenon under observation, whatever it may have been, was a bona fide subject for inquiry, and deserved my utmost care and seriousness."

Under the tutelage of the Yaqui Indian sorcerer, Don Juan Matus, Castaneda set himself the task of understanding the cognitive processes of the shaman's world, which he soon understood to be intrinsically different from his own way of perceiving everyday reality. In the process of Castaneda's initiation into the sorcerer's world, the graduate student used three hallucinogenic plants: peyote, Jimson weed, and mushrooms. Don Juan attempted to teach his disciple a new way of seeing: *"the act of perceiving energy directly as it flows in the universe."*

As Castaneda commented in his new introduction to The Teachings of Don Juan *in 1998, thirty years after its first publication by the University of California Press,*

> The internalization of the processes of a different cognitive system *always began by drawing the shaman initiates' total attention to the realization that we are beings on our way to dying. Don Juan and the other shamans of his lineage believed that the full realization of this* energetic fact, *this irreducible truth, would lead to the acceptance of the new* cognition.

The result of the student's effort to acquire wisdom from his teacher was that his consciousness was transformed. As Castaneda said, "Most of the processes which I have described in my published work had to do with the natural give and take of my persona as a socialized being under the impact of new rationales. . . . After years of struggle to maintain the boundaries of my persona intact, those boundaries gave in." Later critics have challenged the authenticity of the field research documented in The Teachings of Don Juan, *insisting that Castaneda's book is a work of fiction. Regardless of its*

status in the academic discipline of anthropology, it has become a
Sixties classic wherein Castaneda attempted to describe his effort to
absorb the "total cognitive revolution" that Don Juan Matus was
offering him during his long apprenticeship.

FROM *THE TEACHINGS OF DON JUAN*

Introduction

IN THE SUMMER OF 1960, while I was an anthropology student at the University of California, Los Angeles, I made several trips to the Southwest to collect information on the medicinal plants used by the Indians of the area. The events I describe here began during one of my trips. I was waiting in a border town for a Greyhound bus talking with a friend who had been my guide and helper in the survey. Suddenly he leaned toward me and whispered that the man, a white-haired old Indian, who was sitting in front of the window was very learned about plants, especially peyote. I asked my friend to introduce me to this man.

My friend greeted him, then went over and shook his hand. After they had talked for a while, my friend signaled me to join them, but immediately left me alone with the old man, not even bothering to introduce us. He was not in the least embarrassed. I told him my name and he said that he was called Juan and that he was at my service. He used the Spanish polite form of address. We shook hands at my initiative and then remained silent for some time. It was not a strained silence, but a quietness, natural and relaxed on both sides. Though his dark face and neck were wrinkled, showing his age, it struck me that his body was agile and muscular.

I then told him that I was interested in obtaining information about medicinal plants. Although in truth I was almost totally ignorant about peyote, I found myself pretending that I knew a great deal, and even suggesting that it might be to his advantage to talk with me. As I rattled on, he nodded slowly and looked at me, but said nothing. I avoided his eyes and we finished by standing, the two of us, in dead silence. Finally, after what seemed a very long time, don Juan got up and looked out of the window. His bus had come. He said good-bye and left the station.

I was annoyed at having talked nonsense to him, and at being seen through by those remarkable eyes. When my friend returned he tried to console me for my failure to learn anything from don Juan. He explained that the old man was often silent or noncommittal, but the disturbing effect of this first encounter was not so easily dispelled.

I made a point of finding out where don Juan lived, and later visited him several times. On each visit I tried to lead him to discuss peyote, but without success. We became, nonetheless, very good friends, and my scientific investigation was forgotten or was at least redirected into channels that were worlds apart from my original intention.

The friend who had introduced me to don Juan explained later that the old man was not a native of Arizona, where we met, but was a Yaqui Indian from Sonora, Mexico.

At first I saw don Juan simply as a rather peculiar man who knew a great deal about peyote and who spoke Spanish remarkably well. But the people with whom he lived believed that he had some sort of "secret knowledge," that he was a "brujo." The Spanish word *brujo* means, in English, medicine man, curer, witch, sorcerer. It connotes essentially a person who has extraordinary, and usually evil, powers.

I had known don Juan for a whole year before he took me into his confidence. One day he explained that he possessed a certain knowledge that he had learned from a teacher, a "benefactor" as he called him, who had directed him in a kind of apprenticeship. Don Juan had, in turn, chosen me to serve as his apprentice, but he warned me that I would have to make a very deep commitment and that the training was long and arduous.

In describing his teacher, don Juan used the word "diablero." Later I learned that diablero is a term used only by the Sonoran Indians. It refers to an evil person who practices black sorcery and is capable of transforming himself into an animal—a bird, a dog, a coyote, or any other creature. On one of my visits to Sonora I had a peculiar experience that illustrated the Indians' feeling about diableros. I was driving at night in the company of two Indian friends when I saw an animal that seemed to be a dog crossing the highway. One of my companions said it was not a dog, but a huge coyote. I slowed down and pulled to the side of the road to get a good look at the animal. It stayed within range of the headlights a few seconds longer and then ran into the chaparral. It was unmistakably a coyote, but it was twice the ordinary size. Talking excitedly, my friends agreed that it was a very unusual animal, and one of them suggested that it might be a diablero. I decided to use an account of the experience to question the

Indians of that area about their beliefs in the existence of diableros. I talked with many people, telling them the story and asking them questions. The three conversations that follow indicate what they felt.

"Do you think it was a coyote, Choy?" I asked a young man after he had heard the story.

"Who knows? A dog, no doubt. Too large for a coyote."

"Do you think it may have been a diablero?"

"That's a lot of bull. There are no such things."

"Why do you say that, Choy?"

"People imagine things. I bet if you had caught that animal you would have seen that it was a dog. Once I had some business in another town and got up before daybreak and saddled up a horse. As I was leaving I came upon a dark shadow on the road which looked like a huge animal. My horse reared, throwing me off the saddle. I was pretty scared too, but it turned out that the shadow was a woman who was walking to town."

"Do you mean, Choy, that you don't believe there are diableros?"

"Diableros! What's a diablero? Tell me what a diablero is!"

"I don't know, Choy. Manuel, who was riding with me that night, said the coyote could have been a diablero. Maybe you could tell me what a diablero is?"

"A diablero, they say, is a brujo who changes into any form he wants to adopt. But everybody knows that is pure bull. The old people here are full of stories about diableros. You won't find that among us younger people."

"What kind of animal do you think it was, doña Luz?" I asked a middle-aged woman.

"Only God knows that for sure, but I think it was not a coyote. There are things that appear to be coyotes, but are not. Was the coyote running, or was it eating?"

"It was standing most of the time, but when I first saw it, I think it was eating something."

"Are you sure it was not carrying something in its mouth?"

"Perhaps it was. But tell me, would that make any difference?"

"Yes, it would. If it was carrying something in its mouth it was not a coyote."

"What was it then?"

"It was a man or a woman."

"What do you call such people, doña Luz?"

She did not answer. I questioned her for a while longer, but without success. Finally she said she did not know. I asked her if such people were called diableros, and she answered that "diablero" was one of the names given to them.

"Do you know any diableros?" I asked.

"I knew one woman," she replied. "She was killed. It happened when I was a little girl. The woman, they said, used to turn into a female dog. And one night a dog went into the house of a white man to steal cheese. The white man killed the dog with a shotgun, and at the very moment the dog died in the house of the white man the woman died in her own hut. Her kin got together and went to the white man and demanded payment. The white man paid good money for having killed her."

"How could they demand payment if it was only a dog he killed?"

"They said that the white man knew it was not a dog, because other people were with him, and they all saw that the dog stood up on its legs like a man and reached for the cheese, which was on a tray hanging from the roof. The men were waiting for the thief because the white man's cheese was being stolen every night. So the man killed the thief knowing it was not a dog."

"Are there any diableros nowadays, doña Luz?"

"Such things are very secret. They say there are no more diableros, but I doubt it, because one member of a diablero's family has to learn what the diablero knows. Diableros have their own laws, and one of them is that a diablero has to teach his secrets to one of his kin."

"What do you think the animal was, Genaro?" I asked a very old man.

"A dog from one of the ranchos of that area. What else?"

"It could have been a diablero!"

"A diablero? You are crazy! There are no diableros."

"Do you mean that there are none today, or that there never were any?"

"At one time there were, yes. It is common knowledge. Everybody knows that. But the people were very afraid of them and had them all killed."

"Who killed them, Genaro?"

"All the people of the tribe. The last diablero I knew about was S———. He killed dozens, maybe even hundreds, of people with his sorcery. We couldn't put up with that and the people got together and took him by surprise one night and burned him alive."

"How long ago was that, Genaro?"

"In nineteen forty-two."

"Did you see it yourself?"

"No, but people still talk about it. They say that there were no ashes left, even though the stake was made of fresh wood. All that was left at the end was a huge pool of grease."

Although don Juan categorized his benefactor as a diablero, he never mentioned the place where he had acquired his knowledge, nor did he identify his teacher. In fact, don Juan disclosed very little about his personal life. All he said was that he had been born in the Southwest in 1891; that he had spent nearly all his life in Mexico; that in 1900 his family was exiled by the Mexican government to central Mexico along with thousands of other Sonoran Indians; and that he had lived in central and southern Mexico until 1940. Thus, as don Juan had traveled a great deal, his knowledge may have been the product of many influences. And although he regarded himself as an Indian from Sonora, I was not sure whether to place the context of his knowledge totally in the culture of the Sonoran Indians. But it is not my intention here to determine his precise cultural milieu.

I began to serve my apprenticeship to don Juan in June, 1961. Prior to that time I had seen him on various occasions, but always in the capacity of an anthropological observer. During these early conversations I took notes in a covert manner. Later, relying on my memory, I reconstructed the entire conversation. When I began to participate as an apprentice, however, that method of taking notes became very difficult, because our conversations touched on many different topics. Then don Juan allowed me—under strong protest, however—to record openly anything that was said. I would also have liked to take photographs and make tape recordings, but he would not permit me to do so.

I carried out the apprenticeship first in Arizona and then in Sonora, because don Juan moved to Mexico during the course of my training. The procedure I employed was to see him for a few days every so often. My visits became more frequent and lasted longer during the summer months of 1961, 1962, 1963, and 1964. In retrospect, I believe this method of conducting the apprenticeship prevented the training from being successful, because it retarded the advent of the full commitment I needed to become a sorcerer. Yet the method was

beneficial from my personal standpoint in that it allowed me a mo-
dicum of detachment, and that in turn fostered a sense of critical
examination which would have been impossible to attain had I partic-
ipated continuously, without interruption. In September, 1965, I vol-
untarily discontinued the apprenticeship.

Several months after my withdrawal, I considered for the first
time the idea of arranging my field notes in a systematic way. As the
data I had collected were quite voluminous, and included much mis-
cellaneous information, I began by trying to establish a classification
system. I divided the data into areas of related concepts and proce-
dures and arranged the areas hierarchically according to subjective im-
portance—that is, in terms of the impact that each of them had had
on me. In that way I arrived at the following classification: uses of hal-
lucinogenic plants; procedures and formulas used in sorcery; acquisi-
tion and manipulation of power objects; uses of medicinal plants;
songs and legends.

Reflecting upon the phenomena I had experienced, I realized
that my attempt at classification had produced nothing more than an
inventory of categories; any attempt to refine my scheme would
therefore yield only a more complex inventory. That was not what I
wanted. During the months following my withdrawal from the ap-
prenticeship, I needed to understand what I had experienced, and
what I had experienced was the teaching of a coherent system of be-
liefs by means of a pragmatic and experimental method. It had been
evident to me from the very first session in which I had participated
that don Juan's teachings possessed an internal cohesion. Once he had
definitely decided to communicate his knowledge to me, he pro-
ceeded to present his explanations in orderly steps. To discover that
order and to understand it proved to be a most difficult task for me.

My inability to arrive at an understanding seems to have been
traceable to the fact that, after four years of apprenticeship, I was still a
beginner. It was clear that don Juan's knowledge and his method of
conveying it were those of his benefactor; thus my difficulties in un-
derstanding his teachings must have been analogous to those he him-
self had encountered. Don Juan alluded to our similarity as beginners
through incidental comments about his incapacity to understand his
teacher during his own apprenticeship. Such remarks led me to be-
lieve that to any beginner, Indian or non-Indian, the knowledge of
sorcery was rendered incomprehensible by the outlandish characteris-
tics of the phenomena he experienced. Personally, as a Western man,

I found these characteristics so bizarre that it was virtually impossible to explain them in terms of my own everyday life, and I was forced to the conclusion that any attempt to classify my field data in my own terms would be futile.

Thus it became obvious to me that don Juan's knowledge had to be examined in terms of how he himself understood it; only in such terms could it be made evident and convincing. In trying to reconcile my own views with don Juan's, however, I realized that whenever he tried to explain his knowledge to me, he used concepts that would render it "intelligible" to him. As those concepts were alien to me, trying to understand his knowledge in the way he did placed me in another untenable position. Therefore, my first task was to determine his order of conceptualization. While working in that direction, I saw that don Juan himself had placed particular emphasis on a certain area of his teachings—specifically, the uses of hallucinogenic plants. On the basis of this realization, I revised my own scheme of categories.

Don Juan used, separately and on different occasions, three hallucinogenic plants: peyote (*Lophophora williamsii*), Jimson weed (*Datura inoxia* syn. *D. meteloides*), and a mushroom (possibly *Psilocybe mexicana*). Since before their contact with Europeans, American Indians have known the hallucinogenic properties of these three plants. Because of their properties, the plants have been widely employed for pleasure, for curing, for witchcraft, and for attaining a state of ecstasy. In the specific context of his teachings, don Juan related the use of *Datura inoxia* and *Psilocybe mexicana* to the acquisition of power, a power he called an "ally." He related the use of *Lophophora williamsii* to the acquisition of wisdom, or the knowledge of the right way to live.

The importance of the plants was, for don Juan, their capacity to produce stages of peculiar perception in a human being. Thus he guided me into experiencing a sequence of these stages for the purpose of unfolding and validating his knowledge. I have called them "states of nonordinary reality," meaning unusual reality as opposed to the ordinary reality of everyday life. The distinction is based on the inherent meaning of the states of nonordinary reality. In the context of don Juan's knowledge they were considered as real, although their reality was differentiated from ordinary reality.

Don Juan believed the states of nonordinary reality to be the only form of pragmatic learning and the only means of acquiring power. He conveyed the impression that other parts of his teachings were incidental to the acquisition of power. This point of view permeated don Juan's attitude toward everything not directly connected with the states of nonordinary reality. Throughout my field notes there are scattered references to the way don Juan felt. For example, in one conversation he suggested that some objects have a certain amount of power in themselves. Although he himself had no respect for power objects, he said they were frequently used as aids by lesser brujos. I often asked him about such objects, but he seemed totally uninterested in discussing them. When the topic was raised again on another occasion, however, he reluctantly consented to talk about them.

"There are certain objects that are permeated with power," he said. "There are scores of such objects which are fostered by powerful men with the aid of friendly spirits. These objects are tools—not ordinary tools, but tools of death. Yet they are only instruments; they have no power to teach. Properly speaking, they are in the realm of war objects designed for strife; they are made to kill, to be hurled."

"What kind of objects are they, don Juan?"

"They are not really objects; rather, they are types of power."

"How can one get those types of power, don Juan?"

"That depends on the kind of object you want."

"How many kinds are there?"

"As I have already said, there are scores of them. Anything can be a power object."

"Well, which are the most powerful, then?"

"The power of an object depends on its owner, on the kind of man he is. A power object fostered by a lesser brujo is almost a joke; on the other hand, a strong, powerful brujo gives his strength to his tools."

"Which power objects are most common, then? Which ones do most brujos prefer?"

"There are no preferences. They are all power objects, all just the same."

"Do you have any yourself, don Juan?"

He did not answer; he just looked at me and laughed. He remained quiet for a long time, and I thought my questions were annoying him.

"There are limitations on those types of powers," he went on. "But such a point is, I am sure, incomprehensible to you. It has taken me nearly a lifetime to understand that, by itself, an ally can reveal all the secrets of these lesser powers, rendering them rather childish. I had tools like that at one time, when I was very young."

"What power objects did you have?"

"*Maíz-pinto,* crystals, and feathers."

"What is maíz-pinto, don Juan?"

"It is a small kernel of corn which has a streak of red color in its middle."

"Is it a single kernel?"

"No. A brujo owns forty-eight kernels."

"What do the kernels do, don Juan?"

"Each one of them can kill a man by entering into his body."

"How does a kernel enter into a human body?"

"It is a power object and its power consists, among other things, in entering into the body."

"What does it do when it enters into the body?"

"It immerses itself in the body; it settles on the chest, or on the intestines. The man becomes ill, and unless the brujo who is tending him is stronger than the bewitcher, he will die within three months from the moment the kernel entered into his body."

"Is there any way of curing him?"

"The only way is to suck the kernel out, but very few brujos would dare to do that. A brujo may succeed in sucking the kernel out, but unless he is powerful enough to repel it, it will get inside him and will kill him instead."

"But how does a kernel manage to enter into someone's body?"

"To explain that I must tell you about corn witchcraft, which is one of the most powerful witchcrafts I know. The witchcraft is done by two kernels. One of them is put inside a fresh bud of a yellow flower. The flower is then set on a spot where it will come into contact with the victim: the road on which he walks every day, or any place where he is habitually present. As soon as the victim steps on the kernel, or touches it in any way, the witchcraft is done. The kernel immerses itself in the body."

"What happens to the kernel after the man has touched it?"

"All its power goes inside the man, and the kernel is free. It becomes just another kernel. It may be left at the site of the witchcraft, or it may be swept away; it does not matter. It is better to sweep it away into the underbrush, where a bird will eat it."

"Can a bird eat it before the man touches it?"

"No. No bird is that stupid, I assure you. The birds stay away from it."

Don Juan then described a very complex procedure by which such power kernels can be obtained.

"You must bear in mind that maíz-pinto is merely an instrument, not an ally," he said. "Once you make that distinction you will have no problem. But if you consider such tools to be supreme, you will be a fool."

"Are the power objects as powerful as an ally?" I asked.

Don Juan laughed scornfully before answering. It seemed that he was trying hard to be patient with me.

"Maíz-pinto, crystals, and feathers are mere toys in comparison with an ally," he said. "These power objects are necessary only when a man does not have an ally. It is a waste of time to pursue them, especially for you. You should be trying to get an ally; when you succeed, you will understand what I am telling you now. Power objects are like a game for children."

"Don't get me wrong, don Juan," I protested. "I want to have an ally, but I also want to know everything I can. You yourself have said that knowledge is power."

"No!" he said emphatically. "Power rests on the kind of knowledge one holds. What is the sense of knowing things that are useless?"

In don Juan's system of beliefs, the acquisition of an ally meant exclusively the exploitation of the states of nonordinary reality he produced in me through the use of hallucinogenic plants. He believed that by focusing on these states and omitting other aspects of the knowledge he taught I would arrive at a coherent view of the phenomena I had experienced.

I have therefore divided this book into two parts. In the first part I present selections from my field notes dealing with the states of nonordinary reality I underwent during my apprenticeship. As I have arranged my notes to fit the continuity of the narrative, they are not always in proper chronological sequence. I never wrote my description of a state of nonordinary reality until several days after I had experienced it, waiting until I was able to treat it calmly and objectively. My conversations with don Juan, however, were taken down as they occurred, immediately after each state of nonordinary reality. My reports of these conversations, therefore, sometimes antedate the full description of an experience.

My field notes disclose the subjective version of what I perceived while undergoing the experience. That version is presented here just as I narrated it to don Juan, who demanded a complete and faithful recollection of every detail and a full recounting of each experience. At the time of recording these experiences, I added incidental details in an attempt to recapture the total setting of each state of nonordinary reality. I wanted to describe the emotional impact I had experienced as completely as possible.

My field notes also reveal the content of don Juan's system of beliefs. I have condensed long pages of questions and answers between don Juan and myself in order to avoid reproducing the repetitiveness of conversation. But as I also want to reflect accurately the overall mood of our exchanges, I have deleted only dialogue that contributed nothing to my understanding of his way of knowledge. The information don Juan gave me about his way of knowledge was always sporadic, and for every spurt on his part there were hours of probing on mine. Nevertheless, there were innumerable occasions on which he freely expounded his knowledge.

In the second part of this book I present a structural analysis drawn exclusively from the data reported in the first part. Through my analysis I seek to support the following contentions: (1) don Juan presented his teachings as a system of logical thought; (2) the system made sense only if examined in the light of its structural units; and (3) the system was devised to guide an apprentice to a level of conceptualization which explained the order of the phenomena he had experienced.

———

N. Scott Momaday

Native American writer N. Scott Momaday described the traditional peyote ceremony in his novel House Made of Dawn *(1968), winner of the Pulitzer Prize. The following year, Momaday became the most influential Native American writer of his generation after the publication of his next book,* The Way to Rainy Mountain. *In* House Made of Dawn, *Momaday emphasized the importance of oral tradition and ritual in the lives of contemporary Jemez Pueblo Indians. This selection is from the chapter "The Priest of the Sun."*

FROM *HOUSE MADE OF DAWN*

TOSAMAH, ORATOR, PHYSICIAN, Priest of the Sun, son of Hummingbird, spoke:

" 'Peyote is a small, spineless, carrot-shaped cactus growing in the Rio Grande Valley and southward. It contains nine narcotic alkaloids of the isoquinoline series, some of them strychnine-like in physiological action, the rest morphine-like. Physiologically, the salient characteristic of peyote is its production of visual hallucinations or color visions, as well as kinesthetic, olfactory, and auditory derangements.' Or, to put it another way, that little old woolly booger turns you on like a light, man. Daddy peyote is the vegetal representation of the sun."

The Priest of the Sun was going to conduct a prayer meeting, and he had painted himself for it. The part in his hair was a bright yellow line; there were vertical red lines on either side of his face; and there were yellow half moons under his eyes. He was a holy, sinister sight. Everything was ready. He stepped upon the platform with a gourd rattle and staff in one hand and the paraphernalia satchel in the other. One by one the celebrants followed and sat down in a circle. Cristóbal Cruz was the fireman, Napoleon Kills-in-the-Timber the drummer.

The fire blazed in a pan at the center of the circle. The Priest of the Sun sat west of the fire, between the fireman and the drummer. Before him was the low earthen altar in the shape of a crescent, horns to the east. It rose from either end to the center, where there was a small flat space, a kind of cradle for the father peyote. There was a fine groove which ran the length of the altar; the groove symbolized the life of man from birth, ascending from the southern tip to the crest of power and wisdom at the center, and thence in descent through old age to death at the northern tip. When everyone was seated in place, the Priest of the Sun laid a bunch of sage sprigs on the altar, and there he placed the fetish.

The drum was a potbellied, cast-iron, three-legged No. 6 trade kettle with the bail ears filed off, half filled with water in which live coals and herbs were dropped. The buckskin head was made taut, and the sound of the drum was mellow and low like distant thunder. The Priest of the Sun spread a clean white cloth before him on the floor, and on this he placed the things which he removed from the paraphernalia satchel:

1. A fine fan of fancy pheasant feathers.
2. A slender beaded drumstick.
3. A packet of brown cigarette papers.
4. A bundle of sage sprigs.
5. A smokestick bearing the sacred water-bird symbol.
6. A pouch of powdered cedar incense.
7. An eagle-bone whistle.
8. A paper bag containing forty-four peyote buttons.

The first ceremony was begun. The Priest of the Sun made a cigarette out of Bull Durham and brown paper, then passed the makings to his left. When everyone had made a cigarette, Cruz took up a burning stick and handed it to Tosamah. The Priest of the Sun lit his cigarette and passed the stick to his left. When all were smoking, he prayed, saying, "Be with us tonight." Then he held his cigarette out to the fetish, that it also might smoke. Others prayed.

The incense-blessing ceremony followed. The Priest of the Sun sprinkled dry rubbed cedar on the fire, then made four circular motions toward the flames, holding in his hand the bag of peyote buttons. Having done this, he removed four of the buttons and passed the remainder to his left. Kneeling, he bruised a tuft of sage between his palms, inhaling deeply of the scent, and rubbed his hands on his head and chest, shoulders and arms and thighs. The others imitated him, first holding out their hands to receive the blessing of the incense, then rubbing themselves.

Then all the celebrants ate of the peyote buttons, spitting out the woolly centers. From then on until dawn there were songs, prayers, the sound of the rattle and the drum. The fire leaped upward from the pan in a single flame, and the flame wavered and danced. Everyone was looking at it, and after a while there was a terrible restlessness, a sheer wave of exhilaration in the room. There was no center to it; it was everywhere at once. Everyone felt himself young and whole and powerful. No one was sick or weary. Everyone wanted to run and jump and laugh and breathe deeply of the air. Everyone wanted to shout that he was hale and playful and everlastingly alive, but no one said anything; they waited. And directly the fire stood still, and everyone grew sad. There was a great falling down of the spirit, and everyone rocked back and forth in misery and despair. The flames gave off wisps of black smoke, and an awful sense of grief rose up in the room. Everyone thought of death, and the thought was overwhelming in itself. Everyone was caught up in the throes of a deadly depression.

There was general nausea, and the dullest pain of the mind. And slowly, slowly the flame hardened and grew bright. It receded to a point at the depth of vision; there was a pale aura all about it, and in this there began to radiate splinters of light, white and red and yellow. And the process of radiation quickened and grew. At last there was nothing in the world but a single point of light, brilliant, radiant to infinity; and from it there arose in the radiance wave upon wave of purest color, rose and red and scarlet and carmine and wine. And to these was added a sudden burst of yellow: butter and rust and gold and saffron. And final fire—the one essence of all fires from the beginning of time, there in the most beautiful brilliant bead of light. And flares of blue and green emerged from the bead and burst, and it was not the blue and green of turquoise and emeralds, or of water and grass, but far more intensely beautiful than these, crystalline and infused with the glare and glitter of the sun. And there was sound. The gourd danced in Tosamah's hand, and there was a rushing and rolling of rain on the roof, a rockslide rumbling, roaring. And beneath and beyond, transcendent, was the drum. The drumbeats gathered in the room and the flame quivered to the beat of the drum and thunder rolled in the somewhere hills. The sound was building, building. The first and last beats of the drum were together in the room and the gulf between was growing tight with sound and the sound was terrible and deep, shivering like the pale, essential flame. And then the sound did not diminish but backed away to the walls, and everyone waited. And at the center of the circle, rising and holding over the fetish and the flame, there were voices, one after another:

Henry Yellowbull:
"Be with us tonight. Come to us now in bright colors and sweet smoke. Help us to make our way. Give us laughter and good feelings always. Listen, I want to honor you with my prayer. I want to give something, these words. Listen."

Cristóbal Cruz:
"Well, I jes' want to say thanks to all my good frens here tonight for givin' me this here honor, to be fireman an' all. This here shore is a good meetin', huh? I know we all been seein' them good visions an' all, an' there's a whole lot of frenhood an' good will aroun' here, huh? I jes' want to pray out loud for prosper'ty an' worl' peace an' brotherly love. In Jesus' name. Amen."

Napoleon Kills-in-the-Timber:
"Great Spirit be with us. We gone crazy for you to be with
us poor Indi'ns. We been bad long time 'go, just raise it hell
an' kill each others all the time. An' that's why you 'bandon
us, turn you back on us. Now we pray to you for help. Help
us! We been suffer like hell some time now. Long, long time
'go we throw it in the towel. Gee whiz, we want be frens
with white mans. Now I talk to you, Great Spirit. Come
back to us! Hear me what I'm say tonight. I am sad because
we die. The ol' people they gone now . . . oh, oh. They tol'
us to do it this way, sing an' smoke an' pray. . . . [Here Kills-
in-the-Timber began to wail, and his body quaked with
weeping. No one was ashamed, and after a time he regained
possession of himself and went on.] Our childrens are need
your help pretty damn bad, Great Spirit. They don' have no
respec' no more, you know? They are become lazy, no-
good-for-nothing drunkerts. Thank you."

Ben Benally:
"Look! Look! There are blue and purple horses . . . a house
made of dawn. . . ."

At midnight there was a lull in the sound and motion of the
world. The fire was going out, and the circle of men swayed in and
out very slowly to the small, pulsating flame. And from every angle of
vision, there at the point of the flame was the fetish; it seemed to swell
and contract in the silence, and the odor of sage became so heavy in
the room that it burned in the nostrils. The Priest of the Sun arose
and went out. Far off a juke box began to fill one corner of the night
with brassy music, and there were occasional sounds of traffic in the
streets. Then in the agony of stasis they heard it, one shrill, piercing
note and then another, and another, and another: four blasts of the
eagle-bone whistle. In the four directions did the Priest of the Sun,
standing painted in the street, serve notice that something holy was
going on in the universe.

Ken Kesey

Peyote was also the drug of choice for novelist Ken Kesey when he wrote the first pages of One Flew Over the Cuckoo's Nest *(1963). While Kesey's experiences with LSD in scientific experiments at a California hospital gave him the idea for the novel, he wrote in* Kesey's Garage Sale *(1973):*

> *Peyote, I used to claim, inspired my Chief narrator [in Cuckoo's Nest], because it was after choking down eight of the little cactus plants that I wrote the first three pages. These pages remained almost completely unchanged through the numerous rewrites the book went through, and from this first spring I drew all the passion and perception the narrator spoke with during the ten months' writing that followed. That the narrator happened to be an Indian, despite my having never known an Indian before, I attributed to the well-known association between peyote and certain tribes of our Southwest: "The drug's reputation is bound to make one think of our red brothers," was how I used to explain it to admiring fans.*

From a hideout in Mexico in 1966, Kesey wrote his "Letters from Mexico" to Larry McMurtry, his novelist friend from the Stanford University creative writing seminar they both took with editor Malcolm Cowley. Kesey had left the United States to avoid being convicted of possessing marijuana. A few months later, Kesey returned to the West Coast, served a short jail sentence, and settled down to live with his wife and children on a cattle farm in Oregon. In 1968 Tom Wolfe published The Electric Kool-Aid Acid Test, *his bestselling account of Kesey's cross-country bus ride with the Merry Pranksters in June 1964 and his "Acid Test" LSD parties at his home in La Honda, California, and at various locations around San Francisco in 1965.*

LETTERS FROM MEXICO

Larry:

Phone calls to the state min. 8 bucks a piece besides was ever a good board to bounce my favourite ball of bullshit offen, it was you. And with the light steady enough to instruct where the end of the breakwater is out across the bay, ocean calm and warm fifty feet from mine here in outside under tarp beside that cursed bus and kids asleep inside, first time in some moons I feel like bouncing a jubilant ball.

I feel good. Healthy, tanned, standing happily tall again after too many stooped hours ambling stiffly about fink ridden Mexico as the white-haired, bespectacled and of course mild-mannered reporter, Steve Lamb, I am chancing here a stretch or two in full daylight as Sol Almande, Prankster Extraordinaire.

Is relatively now. In between here and whatever furthest time back my pen touches lies many an experience, no small amount of achievements and a tidy sum of insights. I was never one to happen through the market place *any* place on this world without grabbing on to whatever my fancy and my resourcefulness could compromise upon.

Cut to

(longshot right down on rooftop of San Francisco North Beach—levels, ladders, asphalt squares. At first glance almost a set—semi-symbolic University theatre clever Jewish director type of stage set—then a man and a young woman interrupt the parallel arrangement of horizontal surfaces. On a thin and rather ragged mattress, $1\frac{1}{2}$ inch foam in blue cover, shape indicates it was a pad for the back of station wagon. The man has all the usual stigmata of the bohemian in vogue at that period . . . a bohemian crowding that age when "its time the goddam ninny stopped actin like them snotty Vietniks and dope fiends and acted his age." No longer even the argument of ideals and escape, just pure social outrage, voiced by the fleecy image of daddy-mama-and-other-dear-but-square-ones.

(He has partially balded and has been sick long enough it is difficult to know if he is 25 or 35. Hair boils wildly from his head in thick kinky blond locks. His neck and torso are thick and muscular though he is not short as those built thus usually are. His face is excited but tired, lopsided with the strain faces show after too long forced to smile diplomatically. The girl almost as big as her companion, matching his six feet in height but not his weight. Her hair is long and reddish brown; dark appearing cool black except where the light occasionally sets off the reddish lustre. Her eyes almost identical hue, and quite large. Rather like the eyes of an Irish setter pup just turning from awkward carefree frolic to the task of devotion. Her face is young and pretty despite a too broadness and her manner is ornery and fun-loving as she and her companion banter over the plans for the forthcoming Trips Festival. Their talk concerns personalities and wiring problems.)

"With that big new speaker"—the girl is on the optimistic side of the banter—"we'll be able to wire that place so you can hear a *flea* fart!"

"Hasn't happened yet," the man says. Pessimism nowhere near the strength of her mood.

"With this many days to get it set up? Always before we were in the hall that night and maybe set up before we finished in the morning. We got almost a week till Friday."

"I hope Stewart gets that Albright business straight. Fillmore was enough of us getting booted out at two."

"Just when we got this system working good," she agreed, a bit too unanimously.

"Just when we got everything to where we could quit playing with wires and start playing. No more of that shit. Stewart's got to have the cops, managers, *every*body cooled completely before we get so deep into it that it'll be obvious we don't plan to pull out."

"Because without the Pranksters the Festival will be just another rock and roll dance."

"Just another Family Dog."

"Right!" the girl agrees this time her tone shrewd and curt as well as confident.

The pair lie on their stomachs chins on hands looking down 4 storeys to the alley below. As they talk they each occasionally scrape from the asphalt rooftop large gravels to toss down (and see?

Cut back now

See? Just as the pair see a police car pull in, park in the alley, and red light in the hillside drive 50 yards to my left blinks in the dawn—do I learn *any*thing? Or once again lie loaded and disbelieving as two cops climb 5 storeys to drag me to cooler?

Oh well; a man could get piles sit too long one spot.

Stay tuned,
Kesey

Larry: This at Puerto Vallarta not long after news leak set me scrambling.

For a long time now he had been sitting watching a fruitless surf, sitting sadly staring out with a swarm of situations and the fact that he could illiterate up a f—ing storm in the flush, flush, lush lush lush of Mexico.

He had seen a fish, yellow tail tuna's broken leap. Two times now. Both times had been good. And he hoped that he could see it leap again without turning into Hemingway. But his hopes proved vain. For he went back and rewrote rearranged picked and changed for a full half-hour when it leapt the third.

And after that he was compelled to spend another ten until clang! Somebody! not just humble hermit crabs any more but a tourist a noise a *federale?* sound of jeep. Clang Clang Clang sudden reappearance of hatted American followed by mex! roar again of jeep—then—ah—the two turn, leave. WHOP! of surf again into that crack left by the fear change of their leaving. Still around though, close. What if they should connect his sitting alone writing with the KESEY CAVORTS IN PUERTO VALLARTA headline? He opened his other pad, let the coloured part show: always do a quick sketch pass off image as artist.

And beneath these everlasting the call I hear. Grit and take it. Maybe I gotta kind of grit-your-teeth-and-grin-John-Wayney sorta zen. And sometimes the third "It's all shit" followed by, slower, slyer, "but it's all *good* shit."

Until he achieved a levelling with a three-sided palm hut housing empty bottles an empty cot and doodlebug holes thick and heavy about in the dust indicating a bad year for ants. Also some of those scrawny trees with those greeny things—not coconuts but mangoes or papas or one of those tropical gizmos he hadn't got to know because he hadn't really come to believing in them yet.

"Wellsir, this place might just hold me a spell," he drawled and took off his shirt. Ten minutes later he was smoking the 3 roaches rolled together in a cone and examining with his knife one of the green gizmos as it bled meekly white in his lap. The innards were white and meek and full of pale little rabbit pills. A papaya, he surmised, and mighty young papaya to be put to the sword, let alone the tooth. He hid its remains lest some Mex uncle tom hermit come back up to his shack and see his prize papaya caught redhanded dead before its prime, unzipped his fly to let his sweating nuts air out, and leaned back into twilighting crickets to ring his planetarium, see what the next moment was going to bring.

And was suddenly alert to a rare alarm—"Ritual, Ritual," it whispered, faint. The alarm starts and startles beat an even bigger fear. That he wasn't taking care of his job. Mex returns shorts swims suspicious—maybe sketch now? And had they put out a reward for Chrissakes every f—ing peon in the *state* after his ass and 75 pesos? Okay. If this is them straight out the surf over the rocks he'd checked out earlier go under turn sharp left far under as he could swim *voices!* clang clang again this could be the show un-f—ing believable as it seemed but by god it was keep loose or get busted maybe five years five years even staying outside bars playing stacked low game as pawn not even player, five years against possibility of getting snuffed while staying loose. That pat. All the time. And he knew why. He was at last being forced to the brink of his professed beliefs. Of all that he had babbled about for years now being brought up continually for actual down-to-the-wire testing!

"OOO OOOO!" God almighty! Now some fool over the rocks there wailing like a ghost! "OOO OOO!" A signal? Door slams. Man is hot again. Shows up again take out pen and draw the f—er fast. Only possibility against true foe as well as 3rd level foe like american fink. *Draw* him. *Write* him. *Imagine* him into plot always and then believe all that crap you've been claiming about altering by accepting. Believe it! Or you are a goner, m'boy, a walking dead man for evermore fading finally inaudible like the voices mumbling litanies in the cathedral!

So having vowed thus—and having checked to find the Mex working on the road above—he resolutely dug up his stash, lit up the next to last joint in all of Mexico, and just leaning back to embark once again upon the will of God—Ka-BOOOM!—up the hill dynamiting? Now that's a ka-boom of a different colour. I'd go watch them do a little blasting. "And have every Gringo driving past" another voice interrupted "pointing at you gawking there's Ken *Kee-zee,* Mabel!"

In short, this young, handsome, successful, happily-married-three-lovely-children father, was a fear-crazed dope fiend in flight to avoid prosecution on 3 felonies god knows how many misdemeanours and seeking at the same time to sculpt a new satori from an old surf and—in even shorter—mad as a hatter.

Once an athlete so valued he had been given the job of calling signals from the line and risen into contention for nationwide amature wrestling crown, now he didn't know if he could do a dozen push-ups. Once possessor of phenomenal bank account and money waving from every hand now it was all his poor wife could do to scrape together 8.00 dollars to send as getaway money to Mexico. But a few years previous he had been listed in *Who's Who* and asked to speak to such auspacous gatherings as the Wellsley Club in Dahlahs and now they wouldn't even allow him to speak at a VDC gathering. What was it that had brought a man so high of promise to so low a state in so short a time? Well the answer can be found in just one short word, my friends, in just one all-wellused syllable.

Dope!

And while it may be claimed by some of the addled advocates of these chemicals that our hero is known to have indulged in drugs *before* his literary success we must point out that there was evidence of his literary prowess *well before* the advent of the so called psychedelic into his life but *no evidence at all* of any of the lunatic thinking that we find thereafter!

> (Oh yeah, the wind hums
> time ago—time ago—
> the rafter drums and the walls see
> . . . and there's a door to that bird
> in the sa-a-a-apling sky
> time ago by—
>
> Oh yeah the surf giggles
> time ago time ago
> of under things killed when
> bad was banished and all the
> doors to the birds vanished
> time ago then.)

And thought then "Let my winds of whatever thru and out of this man-place paranoia be damned and into the jungle—

"Where its *really* scary."

The road he'd reached was a Mexican fantasy that had petered out for the same reason his heart and lungs were working so hard now—too steep. He sat down in the road looking out at the sea. No cars had been along the road—what reason? it petered out right there? when? time ago?—since the last rainfall.

The sky had clouded. The sun, nearing its setting, vanished through the clouds into the sea thump! a car on the road above. Stops. Starts. Probably the workers but—he stands, effecting a satori smile—

> If you gonna ride the
> wind
> Ride the fat and ride the thin
> Ride the soft and ride the boney
> time ago—time ago
> because there ain't no other
>   poney
> time ago agin.

. . . Someone approaching!

He waits. Long time. It creaks closer and comes out in the very last of the jungles fading light. A little honeybear of a thing. He is delighted and tries to whistle it over but it turns as soon as it senses his presence and sckuffles back. And the mosquitoes get him up and moving again.

Kesey

Larry:

Isn't it a drag? interrupted right in the middle of the past to have to out into the world and actually *deal* with it. The past don't come The End Twentieth Century Fox and you can get up walk home and tell people who it was because it's over.

Because it isn't over. Up on the same hill I saw red lights. To shit, and while I'm at it peek over the edge see what the FB Eyes are looking at this morning. *Plus* "don't forget the San Mateo Sheriff's office, a lot of them are taking vacations in Mexico for the specific purpose of bringing you in."

Is some of the news Faye brings from USA.

By the time I get sit it's full grey dawn. A slate fan of clouds rattle above the Sierra Madre Occidental. Egrets gulls and grackles rise calling from the backwater across the highway, flapping overhead to the beach behind me to early-bird the worm. Bells ring across the bay in town 20 or 30 times—mexican chime code still a complete mystery. Be able to crack it in a few weeks tho, sir; at most one month. "A *month*! By God, Mister, you think I want information of such stature in time for the *Universal Wake?* Strange vehicles sculking around the rocks not five minutes ago *who knows* they're cops American or Mexican? A manta ray cruzing the beach like a frigging doberman out of the K9 Korp, and out in the bay some brand new contrivance like never before floated water before—great rustproof triangle would cover a *city block* with all three points of the vessel running black and yellow steel pools big around as these tugs that went out to nose around and were waved off *sticking straight into the sky 3 times as high as the hotel over in town yonder*—and you tell me *a month?* Well, mister, you figure that bell code pronto. I need to know the time within the frigging hour or you'll be playing with those slide rules and charts up in *Ancorage!*"

The old captain pivots smartly and stalks off, returning the frightened salute of the younger officer who was stammering at the departure.

The horizon was colouring now in the east; it reminded the officer of paintings speed painters at Bakersfield County Fair splashed onto white fibreboard in one minute flat—3 dollars apiece 2 for five bucks—still hanging when he enlisted; a rectangular sunrise, one on each side of FDR.

The bells chimed again. Barely moments since the last ringing. No ryme or reason, pattern or possibility. "In an *hour?*" In fact, for all anybody knew, it might be the Police Chiefs Idiot daughter at the rope again. He shivered. To have to check *that* out again. And find an armless and legless unfortunate—result of food poisoning; the mother 2 months after conception nearly dieing from a can of bad green beans paralysing development of the embryonic limbs and producing a, well, child with an alarmingly lovely face—features that might have posed for Leonardo's *Pietà* despite the fact that closer examination revealed the mouth to be but two beautiful lips sealed forever over a skull that showed no evidence of an oral opening whatsoever. Below the cute nose the bone ran in a solid fortress to the chin. A quick tracheotomy by a clever intern was all that saved the poor creature from asphyxiation moments after birth. X-rays and a 3/16 in carpenter's auger finally afforded the infant the luxury of breathing from her nostrils instead of a hole between her collar-bones, but a mouth the doctors were unable to provide. X-rays showed a complete absence of tongue, glottis, throat, or any cavity whatsoever where the mouth might be jenny-rigged.

"We're feeding the little darling through her nose," the doctors informed the grief-crazed mother (the father, so claimed those of the sisters at the cathedral, unfortunately unhampered by any oral malfunction, who just happened to be the one who had purchased the evil can of beans, expired not many weeks after the birth as a result of botulism—rumour had it he left the hospital immediately after his legless, armless, and mouthless offspring, to buy all the canned green beans the market-place could provide, take out a large life insurance policy (which proved worthless owing to a ridiculously small mistake made in the forms by the distraught father) and lock himself in a secret out-of-town hotel hide-away eating beans, letting them set, opened, adding houseflies and horned toads, recapping them, recapping and days later eating until he either successfully bred and consumed the proper poison, or until his system surrendered under the constant onslaught of beans and flies).

"But if you disregard the child's ah deficiencies," the doctors consoled the grief-freaked mother when they decided she might try to follow her husband's lead, "she is a very *very* lovely child."

"*Already* she has the most expressive eyes I've *ever* in all my *years* witnessed," a kind old nurse added. "She'll be a beautiful girl! The two of you will do fine. God will see to it."

This was adequate to drive mother and infant from the canned goods into the nunnery, where the mother found St Teresa and crocheting, and the child did grow into a very *very* lovely girl. The medical men in their haste to get a potential suicide and/or mercy killing off the hospital grounds had benevolently neglected to inform the mother that the X-rays indicated very little more space for brain than mouth, and the girl had exhausted this area by the time she was 3 or 4. After that the mother or one of the other sisters could frequently be seen pulling a wagon about the cathedral in which was propped a face that grew yearly more and more strikingly beautiful.

"Who gives a snap how *pretty* the girl is," the young officer grumbled, returning to his office in the decoding department, "when you climb ten miles of treacherous ol ladder to find her swinging on the bell-rope *like that*." He shivered again. "I mean who cares if she's *Hayley Mills*?"

Though bulging from the simple mock-habit sewn for the girl and torn (just like last time, by god . . .) from neck to belly button, were two of the most inviting prizes ever to quiver at the end of a bell-rope.

"But who cares if she's Jayne Mansfield or even June *Wilkinson*? C'mere you—" Again he had to carry the creature over one shoulder

as he descended the precarious ladder. And just as before her lewd bu-
zom was forced against his cheek or—when he tried to hold her away
from his sweat-soaked face—that tongueless mouth, and those large
eloquent eyes smiled at him so suggestively he was forced to confess
some grave doubts concerning the girl's reputed imbecility.

"But what I can't phathom," he panted, "is how you get up that
ladder and get *out* on that bell-rope that way."

A rung broke like a dry pistol crack; half-falling he grasped the
ladder pole with one hand and lurching snatched out to secure a bet-
ter purchase on his load with the other hand. Which fell full over one
of the full crimson nippled breasts. As soon as he regained a solid rung
once again he quickly resumed his former and more decorous hold
on his load.

He made no mention of the incident—it was an accident, a
slip!—to the Mother Superior nor to the anonymous ear that listened
to the mundane sins he droned into the confessional box. Nor even
thought of it again himself the rest of the day as he prepared his report
for the captain.

But in bed that evening, locked alone in his quarters, the discov-
ery finally burst loudly into his consciousness. "That—her—*it* felt
back!"

And barely slept at all that night for the listening out the window
across the bay.

Little love story just for variety.

I've still heard nothing from Estrella. Plan was he'd contact me
through alias at Telegrafo in Manzanillo. Don't know *what's* happen-
ing (fear Rohan didn't send cash. Lawyers someway always suspect
other lawyers being crooks. Wonder why.) But I like Estrella. He's
pompous and prideful and *just* right.

Did I ever thank you?

                                                                    Kesey

Lenny Bruce

*Comedian Lenny Bruce was the author of a down-to-earth chapter
called "Pills and Shit: The Drug Scene" in* The Essential Lenny
Bruce, *compiled and edited by John Cohen in 1967. As a drug
addict, Bruce was devoid of Leary's messianic zeal on the subject of
tripping. Instead, Bruce's painfully humorous nightclub monologues
gave the most honest account of the drug experience of any Sixties
writer. Using the example of his own life, he cautioned that taking
street drugs can get you arrested. They can also get you dead—in
1966 Bruce died at age forty of a morphine overdose.*

PILLS AND SHIT:
THE DRUG SCENE

OH! I GOT BUSTED since I've seen you. I'm going to lay that on you
first. I got two arrests. One: illegal use and possession of dangerous
drugs—which is a lie. They're *not,* they're *friendly.*

Lemme get serious with that for a moment. That's how weird I
am: I could never discuss or support anything I'm involved with.

I don't smoke pot at all. I don't dig the high. The reason I don't
smoke shit is that it's a hallucinatory high, and I've got enough shit
going around in my head; and second, it's a *schlafedicker* high, and I
like being *with* you all the time. So therefore I can talk about pot, and
champion it.

Marijuana is rejected all over the world. Damned. In England
heroin is all right for out-patients, but marijuana? They'll put your ass
in jail.

I wonder why that is? The only thing I can think of is De-
Quincy—the fact that opium is smoked and marijuana is smoked, and
there must be some correlation there. Because it's not a deterrent. In all
the codes you'll always see, "Blah-blah-blah with all the narcotics *except*
marijuana." So the legislature *doesn't* consider it a narcotic. Who does?

Well, first: I think that there's no *justification* for smoking shit. Al-
cohol? Alcohol has a medicinal justification. You can drink rock-and-

rye for a cold, pernod for getting it up when you can't get it up, blackberry brandy for cramps, and gin for coming around if she didn't come around.

But marijuana? The only reason could be: *To Serve The Devil— Pleasure!* Pleasure, which is a dirty word in a Christian culture. Pleasure is Satan's word.

> CONDEMNING VOICE: What are you doing! You're *enjoying* yourself? Sitting on the couch smoking shit and *enjoying* yourself? When your mother has *bursitis!* And all those people in China are suffering, too!
>
> GUILTY VOICE: I'm enjoying it a *little* bit, but it's bad shit, anyway. And I got a headache and I'm eating again from it.

If we were to give Man A three glasses of whiskey a day, and Man B were to smoke the necessary amount of marijuana to produce a euphoria like that the alcohol brings, and we do this now for ten years straight, stop them cold one day—Pow!

The guy who juiced will suffer some absence syndromes—he'll need a taste, physically need a taste. The guy that smoked the pot will suffer no discomfort. He is not addicted. Healthwise, the guy who juiced is a little screwed up; and the pot smoker may have a little bronchitis. Maybe.

Since marijuana is not a deterrent, no more than cigarettes, it seems inhumane that they *schlep* people and put them in jail with it.

> "Well, maybe marijuana's not *bad* for you, but it's a stepping stone. It leads to heavier drugs—heroin, etc."

Well, that syllogism has to work out this way, though. The heroin addict, the bust-out junkie that started out smoking pot, says to his cell-mate:

> "I'm a bust-out junkie. Started out smoking pot, look at me now. By the way, cell-mate, what happened to you? There's blood on your hands. How'd you get to murder those kids in that crap game? Where did it all start?"
>
> "Started with bingo in the Catholic Church."
>
> "I see."

Now lemme tell you something about pot. Pot will be legal in ten years. Why? Because in this audience probably every other one of you knows a law student who smokes pot, who will become a senator, who will legalize it to protect himself.

But then no one will smoke it any more. You'll see.

Do me a favor. I don't want to take a bust. The code reads that *I* talk, *you* smoke, *I* get busted. So don't smoke—drop a few pills, but don't smoke.

Did you see the *Post* reviews? It said that

"His regulars consist of mainlining musicians, call girls and their business managers."

Isn't that a little bit libelous?

I know that Californians are very concerned with the modern. Seven years ago there was a narcotics problem in New York, fifteen years ago in Los Angeles. Now in L.A. it's been like this:

They have a rehabilitation center, and they got this group to attack these narcotic drug addicts. Now, this group is attacking, and getting good at attacking. They mobilize. They get good at it, and better and better and better. First they learn the orthodox way to attack. Then, by hanging out with these deterrents, these felons, they learn *un*orthodox ways. They become bitchy-good attackers—unorthodox, orthodox—and they're wailing their ass off.

Suddenly:

CALIFORNIA LOSING ITS WAR
AGAINST DRUG ADDICTS

There are eighteen hundred empty beds at the rehabilitation center.

"*Schmuck,* you're winning!"
"No, we're *losing.* We gotta fill up the beds!"
"You didn't make one win? In fifteen years?"
"No. We're losing, we're losing!"

Well, I assume there's only one junkie left.

Narcotics? Now they've finished with heroin—I think in 1951 there were probably about fifty narcotic officers and seven thousand dope fiends in this state. Today, probably, there are about fifteen thousand narcotics officers and four dope fiends. Fifteen thousand Nalline testing stations, loop-o meters, and they got four dopey junkies left, old-time 1945 hippies.

O.K. One guy works for the county, undercover; the other guy works for the federal heat. O.K. So, finally, finally they went on strike:

JUNKIE: Look, we don*wanna* use dope any more. We're *tired!*
AGENT: Come on, now, we're just after the guys who sell it.
JUNKIE: *Schnook,* don'tya remembuh me? Ya arrested me last week. I'm the undercover guy for the federals.

It's like Sambo, running around the tree. *He* works for the federals, *he* works for the county.

AGENT: Look, we're after the guys who sold it to you. O.K.?
JUNKIE: But *nobody* sold it to me. I bought it from *him,* I told you that . . .
AGENT: Well, will ya just point out one of the guys?
JUNKIE: Don't you *know* him? There's four of us! I told ya that.
AGENT: Just tell us the names of the guys. Cooperate now. Tell us everybody.
JUNKIE [*gives up*]: O.K. He was a Puerto Rican. Drove a green Buick. Hangs out in Forster's.
AGENT: We'll wait for him.
JUNKIE: O.K.

Three days with the investigation:

AGENT: Is that him?
JUNKIE: No, I think it's, hm, ah, I think he was Hawaiian, anyway.
AGENT: O.K. Don't forget. If you hear from him—
JUNKIE: O.K. I'll call ya the first thing.
AGENT: O.K.

So now they've finished up that nonsense, and the guy says:

AGENT: You mean to tell me that you guys are gonna screw
up our rehabilitation program? If *you're* not using any
dope, you certainly *know* some people that need help.

JUNKIE: We don't know anybody. We don't know *anybody.*
Please. I can't use any more dope. I don't *like* it any more.

AGENT: Well, you really are selfish. You don't care about
anybody but yourself. Do you know we have a center
to rehabilitate people with fifteen hundred empty beds?

JUNKIE: I know, I'm shitty that way. I'll try.

I loved that when he got arrested. He was a dope fiend—Bela
Lugosi. It was the worst advertisement for rehabilitation: he was a
dope fiend for seven years; he cleaned up; and dropped dead.

There're no more narcotic drug addicts, so we're moving now to
dangerous drugs. Dangerous drugs—no opiates, nothing to send you
to that lethal mania, but the mood elevators, the amphetamines.

The big connections of the dangerous drugs are Squibb and
Park-Lilly, Olin Mathison and Merk and Wyeth. Do they know that?
Does the legislature know that? I wonder why they're not apprised of
that situation. Dangerous drugs—that's the legal phrase—relates to all
these medications that are mood elevators, not made for sores or boils.
They are made not in Guatemala, but in factories and for a purpose.

Then I said, "These senators, they come from the South. South-
erners don't take pills. Nor do Southern doctors prescribe pills." I'll
bet you that when all those people were dying of spinal meningitis at
Moffitt Field—and heretofore sulpha drugs had worked—you won-
dered what happened. Guys are dying there:

"They're spitting out the pills!"

"They're *what*? Whatsa matter with you guys? You're *dying*
and you're spitting out the sulpha drugs!"

"Look. I'm a Lockheed worker, and I read all about it in the
Herald Express, about those dangerous drugs. I'm not
filling my body fulla those poisons! I got spinal menin-
gitis, I'll get rid of it the natural way—take an enema,
I'll sweat and I'll run around. Not gonna take none of
that horseshit."

O.K. Now, dangerous drugs. Now, the insanity in that area is that
the reason that heroin is *verboten* is that it's no good for people. It de-

stroys the ego, and the only reason we get anything done in this country is that you want to be proud of it and build up to the neighbors. And if the opiate *schleps* all that away, then the guy goes up to the guy who builds a new building and he'll say,

DETACHED HIPPY VOICE: Hey, that's cool.

And that's it. So it's no good. And that's why it's out.

You know what I'd like to investigate? Zig-zag cigarette papers. Yeah. Bring the company up:

DEEP AGGRESSIVE VOICE: Now we have this report, Mr. Zig-zag . . . Certainly it must have seemed unusual to you, that Zig-zag papers have been in business for sixteen years, and Bugler tobacco has been out of business for five years! . . .

    This committee comes to the conclusion . . . that the people are using your Zig-zag cigarette papers, to . . . roll marijuana tobacco in it.

WITNESS: Oh, shit.

DEEP AGGRESSIVE VOICE: That's right. Lots of it—rolling it and smoking it.

Dig. The beautiful part about it is that so many neighborhood grocery stores have been kept in business for years—the *schmucks* don't know that, right?

YOUNG VOICE [*trying to sound nonchalant*]: O.K. I'll have Delsey toilet tissues, and, ah, another six cans of soup, and a broom, and, ah . . . some cigarette papers.

OLD JEWISH VOICE: I dunno, ve stay in business so long, it's terrific. All the markets—but ve screw em, we charge top prices, and the people come in here anyway. They *like* me.

O.K. where does this go on? At a place called Alfie's. Alfie's. Open 24 Hours. Cigarettes, cigars, old Jewish man behind the counter:

YOUNG WISE GUY: Pa?

OLD JEW: Yuh?

WISE GUY: Pa, do you sell many cigarette papers here?

OLD JEW: Uh.

WISE GUY: What do you assume that people are doing with the cigarette papers they're buying?

OLD JEW: De're rollink cigarettes.

WISE GUY: They're rolling cigarettes? In these flamboyant times you assume people are *rolling* cigarettes?

OLD JEW: Uhhh, so vut are you doink mit cigarette papuhs?

WISE GUY: You don't know?

OLD JEW: No.

WISE GUY: They're rolling *pot!*

OLD JEW: Vus?

WISE GUY: Pot.

OLD JEW: *Vus machts du* pop?

WISE GUY: Marijuana, *schmuck!*

OLD JEW: Marijuana? Hey! Uh, agh, *vus?* Hey—

Always talking to some *schmuck* in the back who's not there.

—you heard dot? Marijuana. All dese years I never knew dot. Marijuana. Sig-sag papuhs, marijuana, roll the marijuana, *meschugenah,* marijuana.

Next night an eighty-year-old pensioner walks to the stand:

OLD PENSIONER: Hullo? Hullo? Solly, in the bek? Hullo? Dingalingalingalinga?

OLD JEW: Hullo.

PENSIONER: Listen, gimme a peckege Bugler's and some Sig-sag papuhs.

OLD JEW: *Vus?* Sig-sag papuhs? Justa momunt . . . [*aside*] Hullo, policeman? Is gecamein a junkie!

All right. The kid, six years old, played by George Macready:

KID: Well, let's see now. I'm all alone in my room, and it's Saturday, and Mother's off in Sausalito freaking off with Juanita, so I'll make an airplane. Yes. What'll I do . . . I'll make, ah, an Me-110, that's a good structure. I'll get the balsa wood . . . cut it out there . . . there we go . . . rub it up . . . Now, I'll get a little airplane glue, rub it

on the rug, and, uh, uh, . . . hmmmmmm, I'm getting
loaded! . . . Is this possible? Loaded on airplane glue?
Maybe it's stuffy in here. I'll call my dog over.
Felika! Felika, come here, darling, and smell this rag. Smell
it! You freaky little doggy . . . smell the rag, Felika . . .
Felika! Felika! IT WORKED! I'M THE LOUIS PAS-
TEUR OF JUNKIEDOM! I'm out of my skull for a
dime!
 Well, there's much work to be done now . . . horse's
hooves to melt down, noses to get ready . . .

CUT TO, the toy store. The owner, Albert Wasserman. The kid
walks in:

> *tinglelingleling!*
> KID [*affected innocent voice*]: Hello, Mr. Shindler. It's a lovely
> store you've got here . . . Ah, why don't you let me
> have a nickel's worth of pencils, and a Big Boy tablet,
> hm! A Big-Little Book? Some nail polish remover, and,
> ah, [*voice changes to a driven madness*] *two thousand tubes of
> airplane glue!*
> OWNER [*old Jew*]: Dot's very unusual! Ve haff nefer sold so
> much airplane glue before. I'm an old man—don't
> bring no heat on the place! And save me a taste, you
> know? I vouldn't burn you for no bread, you know?

CUT TO Paul Cotes, Confidential File:

> COTES: This is Paul Cotes, Confidential File, and next to
> me, ladies and gentlemen of the viewing audience on
> television, is a young boy who's been sniffing airplane
> glue. Could be your kid, anybody's kid, whose life has
> been destroyed by the glue. I hope you can sleep
> tonight, Mr. LePage. Pretty rotten, a young kid like
> this. What's your name, sonny?
> KID: I'm Sharkey, from Palo Alto.
> COTES: Well, it's obvious that Sharkey feels a lot of hostility
> for the adult world. Sharkey, how did it all start, kid?
> How did you start on this road to ruin? With airplane
> glue.

KID: Well, I foist started chippying round wit small stuff—
like smellin' sneakuhs, doity lawndry, Mallomar
boxes. . .

COTES: A little Kraft-Ebbing in there . . . That's very inter-
esting, Sharkey. You've been sniffing it for six months?

KID: At'sright.

COTES: Are you hooked?

KID: No. I'm stuck.

This *schmuck* here was hooked on morphine suppositories. Like
that? Honest to God. If heroin is a monkey on the back, what's a
morphine suppository?

When I was in England all these faggots were strung out on
sleeping pill suppositories. *Emmis.* So I says to this cat, I says, "Do
they really make you sleep, man?"

He says, "Are you kidding? Before you get your *finger* outta your
athth you're *athleep,* Mary."

That's a beautiful ad:

> BEFORE YOU GET YOUR
> FINGER OUT OF
> YOUR ASS—
> YOU'RE ASLEEP!
> NEBYALTAL

"What is *that?* What did he need *that* for?"

"He's *weird,* that's all. He's on it, that's all. He's on it."

"How can you tell?"

"You can tell when they're on it. He's standing on it
right now. He *has* to have it. They gotta have it. They kill
their mothers for it in the mornings. They get the strength
of a madman."

How does he take it?

[*deep bass voice, with pride*] "I take it in the suppository
form."

Haha! I got high just before the show:

[*urgently*] "Get it up there, Phil!"
"O.K."
"Hurry up! Hurry up! Somebody's coming!"

Now the reason why I take it in the suppository form is that I have found that even with the most literate doctors, it's not the *substance,* it's the *method of administration,* because if this man would take a ton of opiates through a suppository, the imagery is: "If he takes rubicane in the arm, it's monstrous; but the guy takes it in the ass—what can it be? The *tuchus . . .*"

This is a Benzedrex inhaler. I know the inventor, who invented amphetamine sulphate, which was originally used for just shrinking the mucus membrane, you know, the air passage, but some fellows found out that you could crush these Benzedrine inhalers and— you've done it—and put them in coca-colas, and it would become a cerebral depressant. So, somehow they took out the Benzedrine and put in Benzedrex.

The old thing—one guy ruined it for the rest.

Now, if you notice, it has a date when it's exhausted. Your nose? No. The inhaler. Smith, Kline and French.

Now it's sort of weird, you know. I put this, and you know, sniff it up there. But it's about a year old, and it's probably exhausted; so I don't know if I just did that, or sticking things in my nose, you know? Or maybe I'm just hooked on smelling my pocket!

Actually, is it lewd? That goes back to taste. You know that it's just not good taste to blow your nose in public or put one of these in your nose in public. And I've never done it in front of anybody. But I just feel like I wanna do it tonight.

For the first time, being recorded on tape, a man sticking a Smith Kline French inhaler in his nose!

"Ladies and gentlemen, we're here at Fax No. Two. A hush is going over the crowd. He's reaching in his pocket. His neck is tightening. Some ladies sitting ringside, trau- matically, are sweating. He's taking it out, giggling ner- vously. Will he stick it up there? Nervous laughs emit from the crowd. He's a degenerate. Two D.A.R. women are throwing up. There go the people from the Mystery Bus Tour."

"We want our $5.75 back!"

"There he goes, folks, he's sniffing!"

"Hi, Howard, hi! Zowie! We're really high now, Howard. We certainly are. We've solved the world's problems."

And you're only twelve months old, you little bugger!

Exploitation Films present: I WAS A TEEN-AGE REEFER-SMOKING PREGNANT YORTSITE CANDLE. With Sal Mineo and Natalie Wood. See Sal Mineo as the trigger-happy Arty, the kid who knew but one thing—how to *love,* how to *kill!* And see Fatlay Good as Theresa, the girl who knew the other thing, tenderness, and love. And see Lyle Talbot as Gramps, who liked to watch. A picture with a message, and an original Hollywood theme—narcotics.

The film opens as we find Nunzio locked in the bathroom with the stuff, the *baccala,* the marijuana. Cut to the exterior—Youngstown kitchen, there's the wife, you know, the factory-worker wife, the whole bit. He comes home,

WIFE [*delighted*]: Put me down, you big nut! Oh, tee hee. . .

That scene, you know? Looking at her,

HUSBAND [*tenderly*]: Where's our son, where's Ralph?
WIFE [*concerned*]: He's in the bathroom again. And I dunno whatsamatter with him. He's nervous and listless, and he's not bothering with any of his friends, and he's falling off in his studies . . .
HUSBAND: In the bathroom again, eh? Tsk Tsk. Hmmm . . . [*knocks on the door*] Ralph? What are you doing in there?
RALPH [*sucking in a big drag, then trying to hold it in as he answers*]: Usta minud, I beyout in a minud.
WIFE: He's got asthma.
HUSBAND: Will you stop with that, you nitwit! He's on the stuff!

O.K. Suddenly we hear a knock at the door, a whistle; and he takes the marijuana, throws it in the toilet, rushes to the door—there's no one there! He's thrown it away! It's *gone,* it's *too late!* Beads of perspiration are breaking out on his forehead.

> RALPH: It's gone! There's only one thing left to do—*smoke the toilet!*

Jim Carroll

*By the end of the 1960s, as narcotics addiction spread in the inner-city ghettos, literature about the drug experience assumed a darker tone. Two writers who created memoirs describing their lives as teenage drug addicts are Jim Carroll and William S. Burroughs, Jr., the son of William S. Burroughs. Billy Burroughs was the author of two books—*Speed *(1970), an account of his physical and emotional deterioration as a methedrine "speed freak," and* Kentucky Ham *(1973), a description of his attempt to cure his habit at the Federal Narcotics Hospital in Lexington, Kentucky. In the concluding chapter of* Speed, *he described coming back to his grandmother's house in Palm Beach, Florida, in the fall of 1962, when he was fifteen, after hanging out in East Village crash pads for five months with his friends. A month earlier, unknown to Billy Burroughs, his father had become a literary celebrity at the Edinburgh Writers Conference, where* Naked Lunch *was championed by Mary Mc-Carthy and Norman Mailer (the novel was first published in Paris in 1959 by Olympia Press). In 1981 Billy died at the age of thirty-four from liver failure.*

In 1987, Jim Carroll published The Basketball Diaries, *a terse chronicle of his drug experiences from the fall of 1963 to the summer of 1966, when he was a rebellious New York City high school student. The book attracted a cult following among young readers and was made into a film in 1995 with an accompanying CD sound track featuring music by Jim Carroll with Pearl Jam, the Doors, and others.*

FROM *THE BASKETBALL DIARIES*

Summer 65

I'M GONNA BE FIFTEEN SOON and the summer's "Pepsi-Cola" heroin habit is tightening more and more around me. I'm getting that feeling for the first time since I lost my virgin veins at thirteen that I gotta start getting my ass together 'cause school's coming at me mighty quick and no way of doing that scene with a habit. A "Pepsi-Cola" is a small habit, a first habit that finally sneaks up on you while you're telling yourself, "Shit, I been fucking around with junk for three years and I know when to lay off and I ain't getting me no habit." But one morning you wake up, suddenly your nose is running and your eyes are tearing and the leg and back muscles start feeling tight and heavy. The laugh's on you finally, no matter how long you think you got it "under control." So now I look in the mirror and re-alize I better cut loose, no jiving myself any longer.

Shit it ain't easy. I've been on stuff almost everyday the last three months or so, and add that to the "off and on" tricks for these past three years. I got leg pains like I just played six ballgames on top of each other, eyes heavy and wet. But the worst part of all: that tiny voice reaching over your neck, feeding you all them anxieties, "First just one last one, you can start quitting tomorrow." Shit like that every second, you can't shake it loose. You see a spoon and all you think of is cooking up stuff on it, my arms and hands filled with tracks and I just gotta sit in chumpy Headquarters here, no one here for once in a blue moon, because one step outside and the pool-room's like a mag-net filled with dealers. And what about when Mancole or some other user gets back here and gets off in front of me? Can't even imagine what changes that's gonna hand me. I best get out to the country or shit, never gonna make it here . . . getting too nervous to even write about it. No use taking downers though, that just delays it, I got to do something to off that little voice, I can gladly take sore muscles but my mind can't handle the monkey back there. And I used to laugh at the corny monkey phrase too, I had it under "control" all the way to sitting and sneezing a lot on this fucking lice sofa wanting to scream my balls off.

Fall 65

Up in the country for the weekend and took some L.S.D. again with a friend at midnight. All night we walked on dirt roads and fields lit only by moon and star glow and I watched the trees to see which were friendly and which were evil. We could tell easily, and sat finally near a beautiful willow and watched its sad sway and its special glow hours until morning. At dawn light came in shafts and led me to some fields nearby to watch the tall reeds wave and then become fingers calling me over. I rolled in the dew drenched things as though they were lifting me across and through them with the fingers and my body did no work at all, in fact, I forgot all about any body I had and left it behind finally, thinking I was just a spirit flashing incredibly fast all through, wiping up the dew invisibly. I must have been there for hours and finally realized I had rolled far from the wild grass and was in the middle of a public golf course rolling for a good time while bunches of men were watching me like a moron. I saw them stare and just got up and smiled and walked off and found Willie again still near the tree, but he said the tree was very sad so we left and came back here to his little white room for music.

Summer 66

Was rapping with an old friend and dope hustling companion Franky Pinewater tonight up at Headquarters. He's got a beautiful head and we've spent a lot of nights together on acid on rooftops at night digging the star dome and rapping about the mystic. Thing is that Franky's about five years older than me so when we started using scag a few years back he didn't have school to hold him back from a heavy habit like me, so he did go all out from the beginning. Thus he's been very down and out for quite a while and I'm just feeling the pains of my first habit. I never thought he'd end up strung out, but like we were saying tonight: both peyote and opium grow from the earth, and though all the hip dudes are running around raving about all the knowledge of the cosmos peyote gives, who's to say the poppy has no secrets either . . . and though it was me that spouted that theory I don't think I really believe it.

Anyway Franky was telling me how his mother, a fanatical Irish Catholic like so many of the old ladies around here, was just so sick of all the cures he took that failed that she decided to drag him off to High Mass last Sunday and go through the whole bit. It seems Franky had been getting back into the Faith himself lately, reading a lot of Bible and all, and was all for a play at Mass again. What the hell, he tried every other cure in the book, he might as well take the religious route. Too bad, it all flopped. He said that as soon as he sat down (he hadn't had his morning fix yet so he was craving bad, if any miracle was gonna go down it was gonna have to be a biggie) there he was with a side altar to his right stacked with hundreds of those tiny thick candles in the red glass . . . just like the ones we clipped out of that same church to get a nice solid flame to cook up the dope on windy nights in the park (I got one right in the next room, in fact). So he's there staring at these candles imagining a little spoon or twist-off bottle cap over each with bubbling dope within. Then the altar boy walks toward the altar lugging a giant candle . . . and it's visions of glassine stamp holders the size of shopping bags and a ten foot long soup spoon over that candle cooking pounds of junk from powder to sweet juice. By this time his mother was looking at him funny, he's staring dead ahead in a trance like he's picking up a revelation from God, all this stuff floating around his head . . . DOPE. But the topper came when the priest started shaking the incense burner out to the people and Franky caught a good whiff. "It was the absolute, exact same smell as dope when it's cooking, no mistake about it," he rapped (and this is true, now that I think about it, dope cooking has that same heavy musty smell just like that thick church incense they use at funerals and stuff). "What happened then?" I asked him. "What the hell do you think happened, for Christ sake, I got up, left, and tore ass home to my bottom drawer and emptied my entire stock into the cooker and over the red candle . . . stoned."

Summer 66

In ten minutes it will make four days that I've been nodding on this ratty mattress up here in Headquarters. Haven't eaten except for three carrots and two Nestlé's fruit and nut bars and both my forearms sore as shit with all the little specks of caked blood covering them. My two sets of gimmicks right along side me in the slightly bloody water in the plastic cup on the crusty linoleum, probably used by every case of hepatitis in upper Manhattan by now. Totally zonked, and all the dope scraped or sniffed clean from the tiny cellophane bags. Four days of temporary death gone by, no more bread, with its hundreds of nods and casual theories, soaky nostalgia (I could have got that for free walking along Fifth Avenue at noon), at any rate, a thousand goofs, some still hazy in my noodle. In one nod I dreamt I was in a zoo, inside a fence where, down from a steep stone incline, was a green pond filled with alligators. It seemed at one point I was about to be attacked. About ten 'gators surfaced and headed slowly up the incline, staring directly at me. But just when I seemed pinned against the fence, instead of lunging at me, they just opened their huge jaws in slow motion and yelled, "Popcorn!" At this point a little zoo keeper shuffled out and tossed huge bags of popcorn onto the water. I ducked out through a hole that suddenly appeared in the fence.

Zonked, but I've been slugging away at orange juice all along, anyway, for vitamin C and dry mouth. I just crawl out of the bed at first; don't even attempt my human posture. Think about my conversation with Brian: "Ever notice how a junkie nodding begins to look like a foetus after a while?" "That's what it's all about, man, back to the womb." I get up and lean on a busted chair. Jimmy Dantone comes running in and grabs me, "Those guys that we sold the phony acid to the other day are after our asses if they don't get back the bread." "Go tell them I hate them," I tell him. He splits. A wasted peek into the mirror, I'm all thin as a wafer of concentrated rye. I wish I had some now with a little Cheez-Whiz on it. I can feel the window light hurting my eyes: it's like shooting pickle juice. What does that mean? Nice June day out today, lots of people probably graduating. I can see the Cloisters with its million in medieval art out the bedroom window. I got to go in and puke. I just want to be pure.

———

PART SIX

LIVING IN THE REVOLUTION: THE BEATS AND SOME OTHER LITERARY MOVEMENTS AT THE EDGE

What am I thinking about? I'm trying to figure out where I am between the established politicians and the radicals, between cops and hoods, tax collectors and vandals.

I'm not a Tax-Free, not a Hippie-Yippie—I must be a Bippie-in-the-Middle.

JACK KEROUAC, "AFTER ME, THE DELUGE" (1969)

BY THE END OF THE 1960S, as a staunch defender of America's involvement in Vietnam, Jack Kerouac had repudiated the counterculture movement his books had helped to inspire, but at the beginning of the 1960s, he was among the tens of thousands in the nation who welcomed cultural change as a breath of fresh air. One of the publishing events of the decade was *The New American Poetry,* an anthology edited by Donald M. Allen and issued in 1960 by Grove Press. Allen compiled a representative sampling of the work of forty-four poets, including Kerouac, all of whom had begun their careers after 1945 and none of whom were affiliated with academic institutions or mainstream publishing. The blurb on the back of the book linked this "new" American poetry as a cultural event to America's achievement in jazz and abstract expressionist painting.

Allen had long been associated as an editor with Grove Press and its magazine *Evergreen Review,* and he was familiar with the counterculture writers. In his introduction to the anthology, he stressed their connection with the experimental work of older generations of American poets: William Carlos Williams's *Paterson, The Desert Music and Other Poems,* and *Journey to Love;* Ezra Pound's *The Pisan Cantos, Section: Rock-Drill,* and *Thrones;* H.D.'s *Helen in Egypt;* and the recent books of e. e. cummings, Marianne Moore, and Wallace Stevens. As Allen explained, the younger poets he had chosen

> have written a large body of work, but most of what has been published so far has appeared only in a few little magazines, as broadsheets, pamphlets, and limited editions, or circulated in manuscript; a larger amount of it has reached its growing audience through poetry readings. As it has

emerged in Berkeley and San Francisco, Boston, Black Mountain, and New York City, it has shown one common characteristic: a total rejection of all those qualities typical of academic verse. Following the practice and precepts of Ezra Pound and William Carlos Williams, it has built on their achievements and gone on to evolve new conceptions of the poem. These poets have already created their own tradition, their own press, and their public. They are our avant-garde, the true continuers of the modern movement in American poetry.

Dividing the forty-four poets into five groups, Allen attempted to give a sense of their "primary alignment." First he listed the writers associated with the two literary magazines *Origin* and *Black Mountain Review*, including Charles Olson, Robert Duncan, Robert Creeley, and Denise Levertov. The second group comprised poets of the San Francisco Renaissance, including Lawrence Ferlinghetti and Lew Welch along with Robert Duncan, Brother Antoninus, Jack Spicer, and Philip Lamantia, among others. The Beat Generation writers were Allen's third group, which consisted of four poets: Jack Kerouac, Allen Ginsberg, Gregory Corso, and Peter Orlovsky, all from New York City but first attracting national attention in San Francisco, after Ginsberg read the first section of his poem-in-progress "Howl for Carl Solomon" on October 7, 1955, at the Six Gallery there. The New York poets, including John Ashbery, Kenneth Koch, and Frank O'Hara, were the fourth group. The fifth group lacked a geographical or aesthetic definition; Allen used it to include the poets whom he couldn't fit into his scheme of things in the four earlier groups.

Although Allen's five categories were provisional, they provided a useful frame of reference for new readers being introduced to the forty-four poets in his book. Allen's grouping also gave a sense of structure and solidity to this new wealth of experimental writing. Published during a time of cultural transition, *The New American Poetry* signaled what would become a sea change in our literature, anticipating the tumultuous social and political movements in the decade to come.

Charles Olson

The poet Charles Olson, previously rector of Black Mountain College, the distinguished but impoverished experimental school of the arts in North Carolina that had closed in 1957, was living in Gloucester, Massachusetts, in 1960. Allen placed examples of Olson's "open form" poetry first in The New American Poetry, which also included the poet's seminal essay "Projective Verse," written in 1950. There Olson defined what he called "COMPOSITION BY FIELD, as opposed to inherited line, stanza, overall form, what is the 'old' base of the non-projective. . . . From the moment [the poet] ventures into FIELD COMPOSITION— puts himself in the open—he can go by no track other than the one the poem under hand declares, for itself."

Although Olson was working on his epic Maximus poems, he found time to compose occasional verse, as in "The Hustings," written for the black poet LeRoi Jones (who later changed his name to Amiri Baraka), in November 1960, soon after the election of John Fitzgerald Kennedy to the presidency.

THE HUSTINGS

A poem written to LeRoi Jones
two days after the election
of John Fitzgerald Kennedy
to the Presidency of the
United States

the future sucks
all forward, the past
has been removed

by progress   Cuba
wishes to make its own
sugar   The Soviet Union

may have already
contaminated the Moon   China
wants to destroy

the United States   and LeRoi Jones
spits out the Nation
for its lies.

I do too
I stay at home   I don't go beyond
the West End

of main street I greet
the cop on the beat
in his topcoat   Ben Smith

the roommate
of the President   Joe at Tally's
makes fun of

my overshoes   The girl at the Waiting Station
says the colors
of my scarf and hat

clash I take em off
I say so she can
see me   I try to kiss my wife

as she boards
the bus and she says No
not on the street and I go off

feeling like the President
to receive the plaudits
of the populace on a day when LeRoi Jones

has asked me
it seems to me
to say why

one should continue
to live
in the United States

The new President
says long range
American views   Underneath the eyes

of the human race I see nothing
but the pasty-face of young girls and boys
and the cock lifts

in my pants
to me woman's
behind. The open-ended character of the future LeRoi
  Jones

says stay in the age
of your nation when all the new nations want
is what your own has

And with no abaissement
to the new child
of the President. France also

has been deprived
of itself   the youth of the world
wears wrist-watches. Do you believe

in the promises
of the use
of human beings? democracy

en masse on
transistors? It isn't the moon
which is in danger, it's the singleness

of the sun, which is neither soviet
nor capitalist, that it has been made into
a cheap one   LeRoi Jones

my name is Charles Olson
I live at 28 Fort Square
in Gloucester Massachusetts

in the world. I would like to die
with my eyes open as I imagine
God's eyes are, and that we don't have anything,

no matter what a future, except
that we musn't be blinded
by anything. If necessity exists—

and you and I are as much examples
as crowds demanding
youth taking

and the new inventing—

I don't think there is anywhere
where I am nearer, and I wire you

Please come immediately
There is no need to worry
We shall all eat   All is here

———————————

Lawrence Ferlinghetti

*By 1961 San Francisco poet, bookstore owner, and publisher
Lawrence Ferlinghetti had become solidly established through the
success of his own volumes of poetry published by New Directions in
New York City, his paperback bookshop City Lights in North*

Beach, and the flourishing sales of Ginsberg's Howl and Other Poems, *volume number 4 in the City Lights Pocket Poets series published by Ferlinghetti. Ginsberg's poem had been the subject of a sensational obscenity trial in San Francisco in 1956, when American Civil Liberties Union lawyers had helped Ferlinghetti convince the judge that the book had redeeming social importance. In 1961 and 1962, as publisher and friend, Ferlinghetti sent royalty checks and gave good advice in letters to Ginsberg, Gregory Corso, and Peter Orlovsky. While Ferlinghetti stayed at home to mind the store, the three City Lights poets were living abroad on their royalties and on Orlovsky's disabled Korean veteran's pension checks, planning to join Gary Snyder and his then-wife Joanne Kyger in India for further adventures together. In Ferlinghetti's letter of March 16, 1961, he addressed Ginsberg as "Alvah Irwin Garden Goldbooker," referring to names that Kerouac had called Ginsberg when Jack portrayed Allen as a character in various novels.*

LETTERS TO ALLEN GINSBERG, GREGORY CORSO, AND PETER ORLOVSKY

Dear Allen Alvah Irwin Garden Goldbooker. . . .   3/16/61
You crazy to give away original KADDISH ms. right now! Am sending it to you surface mail today, along with former mss. you sent me. This latter includes four or five of the principle poems in KADDISH as well as earlier version of KADDISH itself, and I beg you to lay this manuscreed on LIVING THEATRE and SAVE THE FINAL MS (which is in black folder) FOR YOURSELF. WHAT DO YOU FIGURE ANARCHISTS WILL HAVE TO EAT IN 1975? IF YOU WILL PLEASE SAVE THIS MANUSCRIPT UNTIL AT LEAST TEN YEARS FROM NOW YOU WILL EAT OFF OF IT FROM 1975 to 2000. EVEN RIGHT NOW YOU SHOULD (AND I COULD) GET AT LEAST MUCHOS $GRINGOS$ for it from a big library. PLEASE DO NOT THROW AWAY YOUR SHOES IN ORDER TO WALK BAREFOOT THRU INDIA, BECUZ WHEN YOU GIT BACK TO U.S. you will need dem shoes again. (By way, what did you do with original HOWL mss? I hope you still have IT?) . . . You crazy goofball. . . . Sending out re-

view copies to all new names you gave me/Books ready in gross here tomorrer! Trublu [Lawrence]

June 28 [19]61

Dear Gregory and Allen. . . . Enclosed resulted from editor meet in my attique and shows reaction to the things you & Gregory sent for JOURNAL (you kin tell purty easy who wrote which parts of enclosed) . . . Anyway, so do nut git mad if we feel you still ain't got the real idea of our magazoom. . . . Yr "PRESIDENT KENNEDY" would be great for the "old style" BigTableEvergruenRevewYugen-PoetryMagavantgarderscene—but we have this here new concept for JOURNAL, and we all feel that "Kennedy" poem and "History of Jewish Socialist Party in America" would not fit what we are trying to produce. We really want straightshot *essays* (like ones listed on top backside of enclosed). . . . (We also have, for instance, Camus' great speech THE ARTIST AS WITNESS OF FREEDOM.) . . . How about some LETTER FROM MOROCCO written by all three of youse, with actual observation of TANGIER streets, insides of houses, insides of lives behind hoods & veils; or Algeria seen from Tangier, or?

Paul Carroll writes that B[IG] T[ABLE] has folded and that, "anyway, the Revolution is over." So now it's our turn, and I tole him I thought "Revolution" was still in its early stages and was going to develop in direction we have in mind for JOURNAL. You Allen have already accomplished that "psychic breakthrough" (although halfass goonballreviewers, as in recent clip I sent you, aren't aware of it) so maybe now the thing is to bring that breakthrough back out of the ether and back down to people on earth (McClure's new "REVOLT" essay tends to do this). . . . You see as usual as publisher I am concerned with reaching that stupid crapper in his office routine, really getting across to the average stupid reader. . . .

Have written Gallimard Monique about Artaud, for JUDGEMENT and for possible book later . . . I wrote Gerodias for copy of your Spontaneous Declaration on Cuba but no answer and he has not sent it. I think we still might very well be able to use *it*.

I also wrote LeRoi [Jones] for corrected translation of Artaud JUDGEMENT, thanks. . . . I wrote Frechtman again about it and about doing Artaud book. . . . Will have royalty money for you and Gregory within a week—we have only $700 in bank, and I think maybe Allen's check will use of large part of it . . . but will scrape money together to pay all soon.

I can't do anything about those weirdies at Fantasy [Records]—
I've been over there several times and they say only that yes yes they
wrote people you set up for ads and that they haven't made you any
money report becus they don't owe you anything, due to last year's
advances and no sales, etc. etc. . . . .

Gregory, your own phrase is just what we want for JOURNAL:
"vast eyes on world *actual* scene". . . (but verse plays won't fit!)

Allen, I figure we shud maybe get going on yr next book in late
Fall—and get it out about January or Feb. OK? . . . KADDISH sale
has been a little disappointing—HOWL still outselling it—and it
looks like we won't be needing to reprint KADDISH for a few
months yet—which is too bad, what with typos to be corrected—but
we'll do it as soon as we possibly can—

OK. . . . all reet. . . . heaven sings [Lawrence]

Dear Allen & Peter . . . .   2 Feb 62

You'll get there yet—hope Gary is still there by then. (Your
meeting seems to be known all over the US, in the bookstore circuit,
that is. Everybody saying Allen got to India to meet Gary yet? Like
some kind of international sorcerer swamis' conjunction on Feb 4th
maybe? . . .) I sent you airmail letter to Ceylon address almost a
month ago—no money in it, but some enclosures of interest. So now
here's annual royalty report and checks: you sure sold a lot of copies.
Dig them totals. . . . Let me know if & when you get this check.

Yep, we have Bowles book almost to the printer, with title A
HUNDRED CAMELS IN THE COURTYARD, which is a quote
from proverb in story. Four stories altogether, one new. Thenku, he
wudnt have sent it if you hadnt writ him 3 letters. For this Spring I
also hope to have: Selected Poems (Mexican Cantinas etc) of Mal-
colm Lowry. (I am going to Vancouver BC by freighter tomorrow to
see ancient prof up there who has all Lowry mss. cornered; also to
give poetry reading at Univ of BC). . . . Also hope to have POEMS
OF THE THAW by Yevtushenko & Kirsanov (translated by Anselm
Hollo); also Robert Nicols, SLOW NEWSREEL OF MAN RID-
ING TRAIN (one long poem). Then your next book, which I am
just about to get ready for the printer. Don Allen has had your mss
and gone thru it for his new antho, but I don't know what he has
chosen from it. As far as you're concerned, are all these poems now
exactly as you want them, and can I go ahead and shoot them to Vil-
liers? [Ferlinghetti's printer.] Also tell me where you'll be about May
1st, so that I'll know where to send you proofs. . . . Am also working

toward that little Artaud volume but haven't had time to do any of the translation myself as yet. (I been writing plays) (More important to me) . . .

Well I guess that covers the world for the momento. See you in some temple.

Lawrence (over)

P.S. Since you might very well have a lot of trouble cashing even a Cashier's Check for this much ($509.64), I have gotten two cashier's checks

(1) One for	250.00
(2) The other for	<u>259.09</u>
Total	509.09

I will send *one* in this envelope & wait to see if you got it OK. Then let me know where & when to send other (which is already made out). OK?—L

Allen Ginsberg

In the 1960s, many books of Beat poetry as well as Beat poets were circulating throughout the world. During the cold war, they conveyed an irresistible dream of American spontaneity and personal freedom to readers in cities as diverse as Havana, Mexico City, Liverpool, Moscow, Benares, and Kyoto. Allen Ginsberg wrote his poem "Kral Majales" on May 7, 1965, describing his adventure as King of the May in Prague, before being expelled from Czechoslovakia by the Communist authorities. A few years later the small press Oyez in Berkeley printed this poem as a broadside, the text flanked by two matching black-and-white drawings of Ginsberg by the artist Robert La Vigne. The illustrations showed the poet standing in profile inside a very large cock, naked except for eye glasses and neatly laced tennis shoes, three hands improbably playing finger cymbals above his own rather small penis.

Such exuberant celebrations of Ginsberg's homosexuality and radical politics had helped to fuel conservative outrage against the so-called "beatnik" poets as a degenerative element in American society since the mid-1950s. As Eldridge Cleaver understood in Soul on Ice *(1968)*:

> . . . At about the same time that the blacks of Montgomery, Alabama, began their historic bus boycott (giving birth to the leadership of Martin Luther King, signifying to the nation that, with this initiative, this first affirmative step, somewhere in the universe a gear in the machinery had shifted), something, a target, came into focus. The tensions in the American psyche had torn a fissure in the racial Maginot Line and through this fissure, this tiny bridge between the Mind and Body, the black masses, who had been silent and somnolent since the '20s and '30s, were now making a break toward the dimly seen light that beckoned to them through the fissure. The fact that these blacks could now take such a step was perceived by the ostriches and owls as a sign of national decay, a sign that the System had caved in at that spot. And this gave birth to a fear, a fear that quickly became a focus for all the anxieties and exasperations in the Omnipotent Administrators' minds; and to embody this perceived decay and act as a lightning rod for the fear, the beatniks bloomed onto the American scene.

KRAL MAJALES

And the Communists have nothing to offer but fat cheeks
    and eyeglasses and lying policemen
and the Capitalists proffer Napalm and money in green
    suitcases to the Naked,
and the Communists create heavy industry but the heart is
    also heavy
and the beautiful engineers are all dead, the secret
    technicians conspire for their own glamour
in the Future, in the Future, but now drink vodka and
    lament the Security Forces,

and the Capitalists drink gin and whiskey on airplanes but
    let Indian brown millions starve
and when Communist and Capitalist assholes tangle the Just
    man is arrested or robbed or has his head cut off,
but not like Kabir, and the cigarette cough of the Just man
    above the clouds
in the bright sunshine is a salute to the health of the blue
    sky.
For I was arrested thrice in Prague, once for singing drunk
    on Narodni street,
once knocked down on the midnight pavement by a
    mustached agent who screamed out BOUZERANT,
once for losing my notebooks of unusual sex politics dream
    opinions,
and I was sent from Havana by plane by detectives in green
    uniform,
and I was sent from Prague by plane by detectives in
    Czechoslovakian business suits,
Cardplayers out of Cézanne, the two strange dolls that
    entered Joseph K's room at morn
also entered mine, and ate at my table, and examined my
    scribbles,
and followed me night and morn from the houses of lovers
    to the cafés of Centrum—
And I am the King of May, which is the power of sexual
    youth,
and I am the King of May, which is industry in eloquence
    and action in amour,
and I am the King of May, which is long hair of Adam and
    the Beard of my own body
and I am the King of May, which is Kral Majales in the
    Czechoslovakian tongue,
and I am the King of May, which is old Human poesy, and
    100,000 people chose my name,
and I am the King of May, and in a few minutes I will land
    at London Airport,
and I am the King of May, naturally, for I am of Slavic
    parentage and a Buddhist Jew
who worships the Sacred Heart of Christ the blue body of
    Krishna the straight back of Ram

the beads of Chango the Nigerian singing Shiva Shiva in a
   manner which I have invented,
and the King of May is a middleeuropean honor, mine in
   the XX century
despite space ships and the Time Machine, because I heard
   the voice of Blake in a vision,
and repeat that voice. And I am [the] King of May that
   sleeps with teenagers laughing.
And I am the King of May, that I may be expelled from my
   Kingdom with Honor, as of old,
To show the difference between Caesar's Kingdom and the
   Kingdom of the May of Man—
and I am the King of May, tho' paranoid, for the Kingdom
   of May is too beautiful to last for more than a month—
and I am the King of May because I touched my finger to
   my forehead saluting
a luminous heavy girl trembling hands who said "one
   moment Mr. Ginsberg"
before a fat young Plainclothesman stepped between our
   bodies—I was going to England—
and I am the King of May, returning to see Bunhill Fields
   and walk on Hampstead Heath,
and I am the King of May, in a giant jetplane touching
   Albion's airfield trembling in fear
as the plane roars to a landing on the gray concrete, shakes
   & expels air,
and rolls slowly to a stop under the clouds with part of blue
   heaven still visible.
And *tho'* I am the King of May, the Marxists have beat me
   upon the street, kept me up all night in Police Station,
   followed me thru Springtime Prague, detained me in
   secret and deported me from our kingdom by airplane.
Thus I have written this poem on a jet seat in mid Heaven.

May 7, 1965

Diane di Prima

A sense of the energy and uncertainty about the future in San Francisco and Berkeley during the Sixties demonstrations was captured in the poems of Diane di Prima. Di Prima dedicated her book Revolutionary Letters *to Bob Dylan. It was published in 1974 as number 27 in the City Lights Pocket Poets series.*

REVOLUTIONARY LETTER #1

I have just realized that the stakes are myself
I have no other
ransom money, nothing to break or barter but my life
my spirit measured out, in bits, spread over
the roulette table, I recoup what I can
nothing else to shove under the nose of the *maître de jeu*
nothing to thrust out the window, no white flag
this flesh all I have to offer, to make the play with
this immediate head, what it comes up with, my move
as we slither over this go board, stepping always
(we hope) between the lines

REVOLUTIONARY LETTER #3

store water; make a point of filling your bathtub
at the first news of trouble: they turned off the water
in the 4th ward for a whole day during the Newark riots;
or better yet make a habit
of keeping the tub clean and full when not in use
change this once a day, it should be good enough
for washing, flushing toilets when necessary
and cooking, in a pinch, but it's a good idea
to keep some bottled water handy too
get a couple of five gallon jugs and keep them full
for cooking

store food—dry stuff like rice and beans stores best
goes farthest. SALT VERY IMPORTANT: it's health and
energy
healing too, keep a couple pounds
sea salt around, and, because we're spoiled, some tins
tuna, etc. to keep up morale—keep up the sense
of 'balanced diet' 'protein intake' remember
the stores may be closed for quite some time, the trucks
may not enter your section of the city for weeks, you can
cool it indefinitely
with 20 lb brown rice
    20 lb whole wheat flour
    10 lb cornmeal
    10 lb good beans—kidney or soy
     5 lb sea salt
     2 qts good oil
dried fruit and nuts
add nutrients and a sense of luxury
to this diet, a squash or coconut
in a cool place in your pad will keep six months

remember we are all used to eating less
than the 'average American' and take it easy
before we
ever notice we're hungry the rest of the folk will be starving
used as they are to meat and fresh milk daily
and help will arrive, until the day no help arrives
and then you're on your own.

hoard matches, we aren't good
at rubbing sticks together any more
a tinder box is useful, if you can work it
don't count on gas stove, gas heater
electric light
keep hibachi and charcoal, CHARCOAL STARTER a
  help
kerosene lamp and candles, learn to keep warm
with breathing
remember the blessed American habit of bundling

REVOLUTIONARY LETTER #5

at some point
you may be called upon
to keep going for several days without sleep:
keep some ups around to be
clearheaded, avoid 'comedown' as much as possible,
take vitamin B along with amphetamines, try
powdered guarana root, available
at herb drugstores, it is an up
used by Peruvian mountainfolk, tastes
like mocha (bitter) can be put in tea
will clear your head, increase oxygen supply
keep you going past amphetamine wooziness

at some point
you may have to crash, under tension, keep some downs
on hand, you may have to cool out
sickness, or freak-out, or sorrow, keep some downs
on hand, I don't mean
tranquillizers, ye olde fashioned SLEEPING PILL
(sleep heals heads, heals souls) chloryll hydrate
(Mickey Finn) one of the best, but
nembutal, etc. OK in a pinch, remember
no liquor with barbiturates

at some point
you will need painkillers, darvon
is glorified shit, stash some codeine & remember
it's about five times more effective
if taken with aspirin

ups, downs & painkillers are
the essence: antibiotics
for extreme infections, any good
wide-spectrum one will do, avoid penicillin
too many allergies, speaking of which
cortisone is good for really bad attacks
(someone who freaks out asthma-style, or with hives)

USE ALL THESE AS LITTLE
as possible, side effects multifarious
and they cloud the brain
tend to weaken the body and obscure
judgment

ginseng tea, ginger compresses, sea salt,
prayer and love
are better healers, easier come by, save the others
for life and death trips, you will know
when you see one

REVOLUTIONARY LETTER #8

Everytime you pick the spot for a be-in
a demonstration, a march, a rally, you are choosing the
  ground
for a potential battle.
You are still calling these shots.
Pick your terrain with that in mind.
Remember the old gang rules:
stick to your neighborhood, don't let them lure you
to Central Park everytime, I would hate
to stumble bloody out of that park to find help:
Central Park West, or Fifth Avenue, which would you
choose?

go to love-ins
with incense, flowers, food, and a plastic bag
with a damp cloth in it, for tear gas, wear no jewelry
wear clothes you can move in easily, wear no glasses
contact lenses
earrings for pierced ears are especially hazardous

try to be clear
in front, what you will do if it comes
to trouble
if you're going to try to split stay out of the center
don't stampede or panic others
don't waver between active and passive resistance

know your limitations, bear contempt
neither for yourself, nor any of your brothers

NO ONE WAY WORKS, it will take all of us
shoving at the thing from all sides
to bring it down.

———————

Gary Snyder

*Gary Snyder included his poem "Poke Hole Fishing After the
March" in* Regarding Wave *(1970). The "March" he referred to
was the demonstration in Berkeley in May 1969, when activists
battled the police in an effort to save People's Park near the Univer-
sity of California campus. At the time, Snyder was also writing and
publishing sections of the long poem he regarded as his most impor-
tant work, the epic* Mountains and Rivers Without End, *begun
in 1956 as a response to East Asian landscape painting and com-
pleted forty years later. In the 1960s, Snyder published the sections
"Bubbs Creek Haircut" (1961), "Night Highway 99" (1962),
"The Market" (1964), "Journeys" (1965), "The Elwha River"
and* Six Sections from Mountains and Rivers Without End
*(1965), "Three Worlds, Three Realms, Six Roads" (1966),
"The Circumambulation of Mt. Tamalpais" (1966), and "The
Black-tailed Hare" and "The Blue Sky" (1968).*

POKE HOLE FISHING AFTER
THE MARCH

"Those pine shingles—gunpowder dry.
      if you want to save money on shingles
      go up to Petaluma

              a place called Wicks"
on anything; handling; pre-finished plywood;
"I got a house with those kind of walls."

Eel-fishing, poke-holing for blinnies
down cliffs through poison oak,
          a minus-two low tide.

          thirty thousand brothers and sisters
          bare-breasted girl on TV
          her braids whipping
          round about her head,

"A hawk with a fish or a bird, up in the air,
                 in his claws."

An older fatter short-haired man
Down fishing too—all catching nothing—
A roofing contractor.
Says "I'd like to stay down here all week."
11.30 AM now, tide's coming back in
                 rusty wrecked car on the rocks

After the People's Park march.
Monday, low tide.
          he sits with us down by the fire
          in the truck-high boulders, smoke
          stinging of salt
"Yeah I saw you guys on TV." Laugh, beer.

          as the sea moves in
          we all talk as friends;
          as if America wasn't in a war—

(Gone to the mountains
          gathering herbs
                 I do not know
                        when he will return—)

High tide.
Where the rocks were
Now there are fish.

N. of Slide Ranch

———————————————

Michael McClure

Jack Kerouac's discovery of what he called "spontaneous prose" and William Burroughs's "cut-up" method of writing prose were the two experimental techniques by Beat writers that received the most attention from readers and critics, but the poet Michael McClure also explored new ways of writing in the 1960s. McClure developed what he called "beast language," which he began to explore in broadsides, posters, and books such as Love Lion Lioness *(1964) and* Love Lion Book *(1966). McClure explained his approach in his essay "Poetry as a Muscular Principle," included as a preface to* Ghost Tantras, *a collection of his beast poems published in 1969 by Four Seasons Foundation in San Francisco. On the cover of the book was a photograph taken by artist Wallace Berman of McClure's face made up to resemble a lion's. McClure also recorded his voice reading the poems in* Ghost Tantras *after first rehearsing his performance before the lions at the San Francisco Zoo.*

FROM *GHOST TANTRAS*

Preface

POETRY IS A MUSCULAR PRINCIPLE and a revolution for the body-spirit and intellect and ear. Making images and pictures, even when speaking with melody, is not enough. There must be a poetry of pure beauty and energy that does not mimic but joins and exhorts reality and states the daily higher vision. To dim the senses and listen to inner energies a-roar is sometimes called the religious experience. It does not matter what it is called. Laughter as well as love is passion. The loveliness the nose snuffs in air may be translated to sound by interior perceptive organs. The touch of velvet on the fingertips may become a cry when time is stopped. Speed like calmness may become a pleasure or gentle muffled sound. A dahlia or fern might become pure speech in meditation. A woman's body might become the sound of worship. A goddess lies coiled at the base of man's body, and pure tantric sound might awaken her. There are no laws but living changing ones, and any system is a touch of death.

Read these poems as you would Lorca, or Mayakovsky, or Lawrence but READ ALOUD AND SING THEM.

These are spontaneous stanzas published in the order and with the natural sounds in which they were first written. If there is an "OOOOOOOOOOOOOOOH" simply say a long loud "oooh." If there is a "gahr" simply say gar and put an h in.

Look at stanza 51. It begins in English and turns into beast language—star becomes stahr. Body becomes boody. Nose becomes noze. Everybody knows how to pronounce NOH or VOOR-NAH or GAHROOOOO ME.

Pronounce sounds as they are spelled and don't worry about details—let individual pronunciations and vibrations occur and don't look for secret meanings. Read them aloud and there will be more pleasure.

I was born in the wheat and oil state of Kansas on October 20th, the same day as Rimbaud, in 1932. I grew up in Seattle on black beaches of the Pacific Ocean and returned to Wichita Kansas and blossomed in a Kansas college in an aura of jazz, William Blake, Swedenborg, and the Visionary Surrealists. I made trips to New York and spent a year in Arizona. I am an atheist who believes in Jesus and the Greek poet of joy, Anacreon. I am fascinated by Billy the Kid and Jean Harlow. In the nine years I've lived in San Francisco I've made a trip to the Orient (as merchant seaman), flights to New York, reading tours through the U.S., and two trips to Mexico (once to the mountains of Oaxaca to take films of the sacred mushroom). My poems and prose have appeared in *The Nation*, *Evergreen Review*, *Yugen*, *Poetry*, *Big Table*, *City Lights Journal* and *Kulchur*. I have an unpublished novel of a boy's 17th year titled THE MAD CUB.

My eyes are intense dark brown and sometimes insane. I believe in LIBERTY, BEAUTY, FREEDOM, AND THE CREATION OF MY SOUL AND HELPING OTHERS IN THE CREATION OF THEIRS through poetry.

Introduction

You've never heard anything like this before. These are my personal songs but anyone can sing them. Pronounce them as they are spelled and don't worry about details—use a natural voice and let the vibrations occur. They come from a swirling ball of silence that melds with outer sounds and thought. They were written in kitchens and bedrooms and frontrooms and airplanes and a couple in Mexico City. Their purpose is to bring beauty and change the shape of the universe.

I WAS HERE AND I LIKED IT!
It was all O.K.
I suffered.
There were scents, and flowers, and textures, beautiful women.
I was a handsome man. I invented love.
I radiated genius for those who saw me with loving eyes.
I was happy—I laughed and cried. Constantly new
sights and sounds. I trembled and sweated
at the sight of beauty. I laughed at strong
things because I loved them—wanting to kick them in
and make freedom. When I go I'M GONE.
Don't resurrect me
or the duplicates of my atoms.
It was perfect!
I am sheer spirit.

1
GOOOOOOR! GOOOOOOOOOO!
GOOOOOOOOOOR!
GRAHHH! GRAHH! GRAHH!
Grah gooooor! Ghahh! Graaarr! Greeeeer! Grayowhr!
Greeeeee
GRAHHRR! RAHHR! GRAGHHRR! RAHR!
RAHR! RAHHR! GRAHHHR! GAHHR! HRAHR!

BE NOT SUGAR BUT BE LOVE
looking for sugar!
GAHHHHHHHH!
ROWRR!
GROOOOOOOOOOH!

2

PLEASURE FEARS ME, FOOT ROSE, FOOT BREATH,
BY BLAHHR MOKGROOOOOOO TARRR
nowp tytath broooooooooooooooooooo

———

In the middle of the night I dreamed I was a creature
like the great Tibetan Yogi Milarepa.
I sang a song beginning:
"Home lies in front of you not in the past.
Follow your nose
to it."
It had great mystic import, both apparent and hidden.
I was pleased with it.
GOOOOOOOOOOR!
GROOOOOOOOOOOOOOOOOOOOH!
GOOOOOOOO.
ROOOOOOOOOOOH!
POWFF! RAHH! BLAHHR!

13

OH LOVELY LINE BETWEEN DAY AND DREAM.
We slip over and under thee
when we are pleased and richly placid.
REFUGE FOR ALL SENTIENT BEINGS!
WHO ART THOU, I, ME?
HOOOOOOO! HOOOOOO! GRAHH!
GROOOOOOOOOH! GROOOOOH! NAHHR
MHEE!
RRGAHH!
Grooor Kayve.
MWAHH!
Greeeeeeeeee-groooooo.
GARHRRROOOOOOOOOOOOOOH
WHOOG KLOWBB.

(What is not sentient? But I—more than all—
am a whole full universe.)
FULL. MAKE GROOOOR.

49

SILENCE THE EYES! BECALM THE SENSES!
Drive drooor from the fresh repugnance, thou whole,
thou feeling creature. Live not for others but affect thyself
from thy enhanced interior—believing what thou carry.
Thy trillionic multitude of grahh, vhooshes, and silences.
Oh you are heavier and dimmer than you knew
and more solid and full of pleasure.
Grahhr! Grahhhr! Ghrahhhrrr! Ghrahhr. Grahhrrr.
Grahhrr-grahhhhrr! Grahhr. Gahrahhrr Ghrahhhrrrr.
Ghrarrrr. Ghrahhr! Ghrarrrrr. Gharrrr. Ghrahhhrr.
Ghrahhrr. Ghrahr. Grahhr. Grahharrr. Grahhrr.
Grahhhhr. Grahhhr. Gahar. Ghrahhr. Grahhr. Grahhr.
Ghrahhr. Grahhhr. Grahhr. Gratharrr! Grahhr.
Ghrahrr. Ghraaaaaaahrr. Grhar. Ghhrarrr! Grahhrr.
Ghrahrr. Gharr! Ghrahhhhr. Grahhrr. Ghraherrr.

50

Gahr thy rooh gaharr eeem thah noolt eeeze
be me aiee grahorr im lowvell thee thy lips and hair
are stunning field byorr ayohh mah ahn teerz.
Ghroo ahn the green-blahk trees
are tall and brooding in the dark gray-pink
wet mist of night. All is flashes of silver
upon damp black by scroolt in theer.
THEE,
THEE,
THEE
mahk flooors pore reeer, thah noose eem rakd.
GAHARRRRR GAYRR RRAH MEEN LOOVEEE.
And all physicality is poesy
to demanding flesh.

Ring tailed cat.
Close Arcturus.
Heavenly visions of gentle rats with pink noses.

51

I LOVE TO THINK OF THE RED PURPLE ROSE
IN THE DARKNESS COOLED BY THE NIGHT.
We are served by machines making satins
of sounds.
Each blot of sound is a bud or a stahr.
Body eats bouquets of the ear's vista.
Gahhhrrr boody eers noze eyes deem thou.
NOH. NAH-OHH
hrooor. VOOOR-NAH! GAHROOOOO ME.
Nah droooooh seerch. NAH THEE!
The machines are too dull when we
are lion-poems that move & breathe.
WHAN WE GROOOOOOOOOOOOOOOR
hann dree myketoth sharoo sreee thah noh deeeeeemed ez.
Whan eeeethoooze hrohh.

67

((PALE PEARL PINK ON THE WALLS
AND OUR DAYDREAMS
projected outward in solid reality.
We hear, we touch, we breathe. Partitions rustle
and we do not care among the creakings and thumps
nah gayothorrs for we are incarnate joys.
ROGTRAYOMF! ROGTRAYOMF!
Each nostril is a booming perfection.
The blackened skulls and rusty bolts
are only a background
for
meat
warmth
that passes to something more.

———————————————————————

I like your eyes Liberty!

———————————————————————

Steam drips the windows in front of utter darkness
that's so deep it's cool and sweet. Forget it.
Take more wings love.))

Bob Kaufman

While The New American Poetry *introduced thousands of American readers to new names in contemporary poetry, Donald Allen was in some ways a conventional editor. Only four of his forty-four poets were women, and none represented the ethnic minorities who were beginning to find their voices as American poets. The African-American poet Bob Kaufman was not included in* The New American Poetry *(LeRoi Jones was the only black poet in the anthology). Kaufman was an active member of the group of Beat writers in San Francisco in the 1950s and 1960s. His poem "Grandfather Was Queer, Too" was included in his book* Solitudes Crowded with Loneliness, *published by New Directions in 1965.*

GRANDFATHER WAS QUEER, TOO

He was first seen in a Louisiana bayou,
Playing chess with an intellectual lobster.
They burned his linoleum house alive
And sent that intellectual off to jail.
He wrote home every day, to no avail.
Grandfather had cut out, he couldn't raise the bail.

Next seen, skiing on some dusty Texas road,
An intellectual's soul hung from his ears,
Discussing politics with an unemployed butterfly.
They hung that poor butterfly, poor butterfly.
Grandfather had cut out, he couldn't raise the bail.

Next seen on the Arizona desert, walking,
Applying soothing poultices to the teeth
Of an aching mountain.
Dentists all over the state brought gauze balls,
Bandaged the mountain, buried it at sea.
Grandfather had cut out, he couldn't raise the bail.

Next seen in California, the top part,
Arranging a marriage, mating trees,
Crossing a rich redwood and a black pine.
He was exposed by the Boy Scouts of America.
The trees were arrested on a vag charge.[1]
Grandfather cut out, he couldn't raise the bail.

Now I have seen him here. He is beat.
His girlfriend has green ears;
She is twenty-three months pregnant,
I kissed them both:
Live happily ever after.

———————

John Clellon Holmes

*Novelist and essayist John Clellon Holmes, who had become friends
with Jack Kerouac in New York in 1948 before either of them had
published his first novel, stayed close to Kerouac throughout his life.
Holmes kept a journal chronicling Kerouac's painful descent into his
alcoholic binges during his visits to Connecticut in the 1960s, a sad
contrast to his 1957 visit before the publication of* On the Road.
*"Visitor: Jack Kerouac in Old Saybrook" was published in 1981
as a chapbook by the unspeakable visions of the individual, a small
press in California, Pennsylvania.*

———————

1. Vagrancy charge.

VISITOR:
JACK KEROUAC IN OLD SAYBROOK

JACK HAD BEEN to Old Saybrook several times when Shirley[1] and I were weekending in my mother's capacious Victorian house on the Main Street. He had built chimney-roaring fires, we had downed bottles & talked incessantly, but, because I was still living in New York, I kept no journal entries of these visits, seeing him, as I did, almost every week.

This first entry describes, in brief terms, a long weekend that Jack & Allen Ginsberg & Peter Orlovsky spent with us in our still-being-self-renovated house in January of 1957. Jack arranged it, writing, "We must get together, drink, sing before glowing logs, play music, discuss, run yelling at the sea . . . So name the date old buddy boy." (December 13, 1956) That is what we did. The music was never off, the glasses were rarely empty, we played football in the snow, and Peter did perfect figure-eights on the ice-covered North Cove. One night we taped readings by the four of us: Allen did a part of *Howl*, Peter described his sexual initiation as a teen-ager, Jack read boozily from Shakespeare, and I read a section of Whitman's *Specimen Days* and a late, doomful poem of Robinson Jeffers. It was a fine time of friendship and fun, during which I snatched moments to read the first part of *Desolation Angels* and *Tristessa*, both still in manuscript. We all parted, quenched and affectionate.

> *January 22, 1957*
>   *There have been many things to do around here—wood, thawing cars, clearing driveways, etc.—and then we had Jack and Allen and Peter here this weekend. They didn't leave until yesterday. All seem in excellent shape, Jack particularly. There was a squib about them in this Sunday's Times, another piece will be in Mademoiselle soon. On the Road is coming out in the fall, under Viking imprint; another shorter novel will be published entire in a paperback anthology sometime in the spring. They seem set on going to Europe in a few weeks. Jack is, as I say, in a very calm, very objective mood, and, surprisingly (and thankfully!), this is not just*

---
1. Holmes's wife.

due to the breakthrough publishing-wise. He is a confirmed Buddhist of his own sort, has been for several years, and is remarkably well-read and thoughtful about it. Indeed, seems to know more than anyone I have ever met. He has learned to read (somewhat) Sanskrit, and has even made a new translation (into simpler English) of the Diamond Sutra ('The Diamondcutter of the Perfect Vow'), a sutra that I had never read before. He lives entirely like an itinerant poet, or even monk. With him, on the train, he brought everything he possesses: a few hardy, easily-kept clothes on his back; an army-knapsack with sleepingbag, cooking utensils, sewing kit, etc., and also a satchel of manuscripts which are still in progress. Last summer he spent all alone on the top of Desolation Mountain in the Great Cascades of Washington and Oregon, earning a little money as a government fire-watcher. He has written part of a book about his two and a half months of absolute solitude. He will go to Africa with Allen (and a few others), spend a few weeks there, and then go to Spain (somewhere in the South, a small village), get a rooftop (something he has been doing in Mexico), and think and work. We had fond, close hours over the weekend, and it was very good to see him again.

September 12, 1962

Jack here. The binge in its third day, 4th night. No certain end in sight. I am, already, beyond my limit. Yet care. Quarts of Courvoisier, no food, 2:00 in the afternoon. Poor Jack.

September 13, 1962

Good night's sleep. Jack up and drinking by 9:00. A day of feverish, good talk, as I cooled on the booze. He sleeps now—that incredible, lava-hot flow of memories, imaginations, perceptions, nonsense & humor temporarily stilled. We ranted & argued & laughed & got bitchy & good humored all day. Housewise (that is, his finding a house around here) the trip has been another huge, Kerouacian fiasco, a binge without end in sight. But we have talked, I've been close to that finally unapprochable core again, and I actually think that he's had a good time. He is probably the most prodigious, indefatigable drinker I've ever known. His genius is exhausting, unique, volcanic, and is fed somehow by booze. I've been spacing myself & feel goodish. But his strange amalgam of spurious ideas, verbal illumination, cornball politics, dead certain aesthetic feeling, huge relish for life, fatalistic physical strength—all that I

*knew so well once, has come back to me in a rush. The horrors lie
ahead for him tomorrow or Saturday, he knows it (having that queer
strain of self-knowledge that is part of all real talents in our time).
Our feelings towards one another remain ambiguous. We like one
another enormously, we are so utterly different & disagree with great
foaming screams. Anyway, I'm enjoying these wasteful, abusive
days of literally hours & hours of frantic, drunken talk—one flow-
ing into the other, all sequence & cohesion swept away sometime
days & days ago; I try to keep shaved & reasonably sweet-smelling.
Jack sits in torn blue pajama bottoms, a rank tee shirt, grimy socks
and Japanese slippers, unshaven in nearly a week, his hair never
combed till 5:00, growing headier & headier in the armpits, smok-
ing his little Camels, fixing his brandies & soda, padding around
with stiff, faltering old man's steps, talking in torrential gusts.*

*Around his chair (the big arm chair), reviews, letters, books,
old cigarette packets, ashes, matches and who knows what all else
accumulate. I sip scotch-and-milks & smoke cigarettes, and we
laugh and pop our eyes at one another & gabble. He drinks a fifth
of Courvoisier everyday, plus rations of scotch, beer & wine to fill it
out—all told considerably more than a quart of hard booze in every
24 hours. He sleeps 8 hours and drinks the other 16. He seems
very happy, and says this will probably go on for 10 days before he
has the horrors, the fears, the sweats, & has to take to his bed. I
don't think it will go on much more than a week, and he said today
we should go into NY on Monday or Tuesday. He has talked out
complete novels, with that utter recall, plus imaginative fire, that al-
ways astounds me. Too much to remember & set down now.*

September 16, 1962 (Sunday: 5:45)

*Jack left last night on one of those sudden whims, after having
had nothing but beer all day, & feeling better. Then he began on
brandy about 5:30, and suddenly wanted to go to Lowell, having
been phoning G. J. during the week, and it being Saturday night.
Before you knew it, he had gotten a cab (Shirley actually got it),
and was off on a mad $60 taxi ride 150 miles into the night, at
10:00, with a mason-jar of brandy & soda between his knees. We
had had a good day, but he was becoming bored, and, feeling a little
better, having shaved & cleaned himself up for the 1st time in a
week, and off he went, being unable to manage the train. He must
have spent close to $250 while here, most of it on brandy ($8.00 a
day), but a lot on food & drink for us. He phoned people in New*

York, or Lowell, at all hours of the night, and got fearfully, utterly drunk on Friday night. I went to bed, leaving Shirley, who lasted till 4:30 or so. I came down for milk at 6:00 & found him sitting up on the couch, sound asleep. Such boozing, a scary thing to behold.

We had our differences, but I screamed & ranted at him, and he grew passive & careful, and we parted close—as we really are despite the damage of the years. Sweet & tentative when sober, he becomes truculent, paranoiac, garrulous, stiff-jointed, wild-eyed, exhaustless, and amnesiac when drunk. Booze alone can seem to produce in him the "ecstasy" he needs to get thru time. You can see that coiled, complicated mind working behind the thickening good-looks, the dark brow, the calf-like tender eyes, the pouting mouth. His imagination is aflame, you'd think his very brains would cook & go up like tinder, one thing reminds him instantly of another, and when words will no longer come, gibberish (sheer sounds) do. He is a phenomenon, and those who knew him 10 years ago would be shocked & saddened now, to see him so recklessly burning himself up, vanishing in the swirl of his booze-heated mind, still a superb monologist, but almost incapable after 5:00 PM of "talk." I followed him fatalistically this week, but by Wednesday I had given up all hope of salvaging his house-buying reason for the trip, or much of anything else, and my only intention was to keep him out of trouble & reasonably alive. I let him go to Lowell because there was nothing further I could do for him, the driver was smart & hip, and I knew his buddies there would take care of him. I was going to take him into NY on Monday, if this hadn't happened, & deliver him to Lucien or someone who knows & loves him too, & wouldn't let him wander helplessly into further debacles. I broke my brains trying to conjure up what could be done, but came up with nothing, earned for my labors only an hour or two of surcease for him, saw nembutals fail to slow him down, tricked food into him, scolded & threatened, cajoled & ignored—all to no avail. He is mad, in that special, harmless, non-certifiable way of his, and he is an alcoholic—an unbeatable combination. Something of his genius has survived it all. He and Shirley got on very well, she was perfect—warm & understanding, and able to get thru to him her real affection for him. He and I are closer these last years, if possible, than before—perhaps because I am less of a mere shadow, and, in a ghoulish reversal, he has somewhat mellowed with all the money, all the drink.

Way deep down, I think, he wants to die, and no amount of self-abuse, disaster or sadness can expunge the feeling of loss & estrangement which has always scarred him, dogged him, driven him. He claimed, in his drink, that he was Christ, Satan, an Indian chieftain, various holy men of half a dozen cultures, the universal genius, and who knows who else, who can remember. The search for the role. The mile-deep puzzle of identity that goes on in someone who can imagine all alternatives, all roles. Sodden, a-stink, bent on oblivion, he still has more eccentric genius than anyone I've known. And yet he is impossible, or damn near impossible, to reach now. Poor Ti Jean. Off on one of those saddening Odysseys that must end in dreary, drunken tears at four in the morning. No real place for him. Such people leave a permanent mark on one's years.

Later, there was an abject letter, one of those letters that are only written by people who both waste themselves profligately and realize they are doing it, which said (in part): "No more cognac, for me. I find it depresses worse than anything except Irish Whiskey. O John, I'm so fucking sorry, there I was right in Saybrook and didn't do a damn thing. You know, living here, when I get to see the north and my friends again I go crazy. . . . No, no, no, I cant goof on like this—we've had our three day preliminary talk which went on for seven days . . . Because when you and I get together a kind of bell rings in my head that says GLUYR TIME FOR A DRINK . . . Same of course applies to when I see Lucien etc. etc. a thousand guys."

The following brief entry concerns Jack's last visit to Old Saybrook, a sudden whim on his part when two young, barroom friends in Florida offered to drive him up North. The backseat of their car was full of re-treaded tires. Jack was entering that final state where he needed to be cared-for. Something in his volcanic and creative spirit had been drowned. He had stopped striving. His vision was blurred and askew.

November 15, 1965

There was a scribble from Jack, or two friends of his, saying they would arrive "by Friday." They came at three-ish on Thursday: Jack tipsy & fatter & okay; and his two buddies, Cliff & Pat—Cliff good-looking & fast-talking, vain about his hair, but eager & likeable; Pat, big & plainer, affable, taking a back-seat.

They finally packed off for Lowell on Sunday afternoon, after a not-too-bad three days of more or less continual drink & talk,

most of it good, though I had a fairly bad hangover by Saturday, &
wasn't much good for the sort of frenetic, mind-storming attention
that Jack demands these days.

My feeling about him: he seems to be drinking less than he
was three years ago. He's off the brandy kick, and thus, although he
drinks more or less continually, he never gets into that wild, disasso-
ciated mental state that brandy creates. He drinks a lot of white
wine (10 or 15 bottles of it passed thru the house), and beer &
vodka. Physically, he is at last showing the signs of these years of
prodigious boozing: he looks (as Shirley said) rather like Balzac in
the body, his torso is enormous, a more or less unbroken belly &
huge chest & arms. I was reminded that his father was immensely
fat, & could see that Jack could become so too. His legs seemed
shorter, stumpier; he has a huge jowl now, a bad scar on the bridge
of his nose, & his features have blurred—just as Dylan Thomas's
did. But he was in good spirits, rarely morose, and only going into
furies over Jews, negroes, intellectuals, & most of the other racial &
class shibboleths which these years in the South, & off the road,
have made seem like menaces to him. At several points, he became
positively demented on the subject of the Jews—venomous, irra-
tional, sneering, parodying, ugly as a street corner tough. Then the
fury would go down (everyone disagreed with him vehemently), and
he would be warm, wacky & fun again. I saw fewer of those daz-
zling & scary mental flights of last time, fewer evidences of his old,
blazing creative flood, but still there were good enuf talks on this &
that. He was boyish (being with his boys), profane, goofy, confused
& changeable—as always. . . . A walk in hangover-withdrawal-
horror yesterday made me realize that a new life, on new basés, is
an essential for me. Some sane foundation for my ego & the next
years. I have striven so relentlessly, fighting out most of the inner-
battles alone (work-doubts, sanity-doubts, doubts about my ultimate
worth, plus the worth of existence) that I realize I need some basic
surcease now. . . . I fought the panics off with the clear, saving
thought (which came in the bath Sat. morning): "Nothing that you
think today will be true; no pre-vision of the-way-things-are will be
real," and kept going in the warm assurance of that thought. But
still, on my walk the next day, weary & trembling, sick with the
horrors of consciousness-without-rest, knowing that sleep might not
come even after the fourth mile, I looked ahead & could see nothing,
& had no strength to howl, & no belief in howling. Nothing but the
poison speaking in my inflamed consciousness, but out of such

trapped moments a "little death" always issues, & I can't afford
many of them. . . . Shirley says she now sees that Jack & I share
the same horror & hatred of "this world," and, of course, it's more
than a little true. Though I have no faith—silly or otherwise—to
sustain me. Will I only write well when I give it all up? Calm &
awareness & a slight bug at the fact that this week (of all weeks) the
car has finally given out & we'll probably have to get another.

We talked on the phone almost weekly thereafter; we corre-
sponded. I could feel some finality approaching. There was nothing I
could do. By then I was teaching to pay the bills, and besides Jack was
one of those people entrapped by the destiny of his special gifts, and
the conflicts of his nature. And then in 1969—

October 21, 1969 12:45 PM
    Jack is dead. I was reading about him in an old journal when
S. called out from downstairs, having heard it on the radio. There
were the bad, pointless moments waiting for a repeat of the news-
cast, there were the waves of awareness—coming up and then reced-
ing—death is only a word, it is an abrupt absence that has reality,
and you have to think a minute to realize that.
    The horror of his conscious life, with which I have lived for
years, came 1st. I realized how stubbornly, even bitterly, I had
wanted him to be happy, acknowledging nevertheless that there was
nothing you could do with such a brilliant, such a driven, man.
    Then, all of a sudden, I found myself weeping, because I have
always addressed my sentences to him, to his disapproving, canny
eye, and it would be different to write from now on. Allen G. called
(how thoughtful, knowing I would be heart-broken). By happen-
stance, he will be in New Haven tomorrow, & we will go down.
"He didn't live much beyond Neal," he said as a matter of interest.
"Only a year and a half." There was that attempt to be cheerful,
that warm, insinuative tone in the voice, that feeling of an old ca-
maraderie that should be acknowledged despite time & disputes. I
spoke to Gregory too—they were all at the Cherry Valley farm.
    I phoned Sterling,[2] who had been waked at 6:30. "He drank
himself to death," he said, & I felt that now (between Sterling & I)
it could be said, but neither of us had said it baldly out before, be-
cause of protectiveness for Jack, & both have known it (perhaps bet-

---

2. Sterling Lord, the literary agent for both Kerouac and Holmes.

ter than some of Jack's other friends) for years. We wired Memere &
Stella—hopeless, useless words.

If the funeral's in Lowell (as seems likely), I'll go, of course,
because—

Well, if love is total involvement, deep emotional clairvoyance
about the other's soul, fury & hunger all intermixed, he was the
only man I've ever loved. He changed my life irrevocably. Portents
of his death, somewhere, sometime, have plagued me for 8–10
years—as recently as last Thursday I thought of him dying in St.
Louis or Chicago, on some Kerouac-crazy trip.

I haven't dared think of his mind in its last hours. What can
one say? He's gone. It's over for him. I don't know what to do.

Words, words, words, words, words, words, words—

Richard Brautigan

*Richard Brautigan lived in the Bay Area and shared the West
Coast hippie ethos of the Beat writers, although in his fiction he re-
jected Kerouac's autobiographical approach to "true story novels"
and his spontaneous prose style. Instead Brautigan admired Hem-
ingway's literary style and wrote surreal fantasies, as in "The
Cleveland Wrecking Yard," a chapter in* Trout Fishing in Amer-
ica *(1967). He dedicated his book to the poets Jack Spicer and Ron
Loewinsohn. Brautigan's search for the ideal trout stream in this
book also suggests a satirical glance at the ultimate reaches of con-
sumer capitalism in the United States, as well as how much the
country had changed since Hemingway described fishing for trout in
"The Big Two-Hearted River" (1925).*

THE CLEVELAND WRECKING YARD

UNTIL RECENTLY my knowledge about the Cleveland Wrecking Yard had come from a couple of friends who'd bought things there. One of them bought a huge window: the frame, glass and everything for just a few dollars. It was a fine-looking window.

Then he chopped a hole in the side of his house up on Potrero Hill and put the window in. Now he has a panoramic view of the San Francisco County Hospital.

He can practically look right down into the wards and see old magazines eroded like the Grand Canyon from endless readings. He can practically hear the patients thinking about breakfast: *I hate milk,* and thinking about dinner: *I hate peas,* and then he can watch the hospital slowly drown at night, hopelessly entangled in huge bunches of brick seaweed.

He bought that window at the Cleveland Wrecking Yard.

My other friend bought an iron roof at the Cleveland Wrecking Yard and took the roof down to Big Sur in an old station wagon and then he carried the iron roof on his back up the side of a mountain. He carried up half the roof on his back. It was no picnic. Then he bought a mule, George, from Pleasanton. George carried up the other half of the roof.

The mule didn't like what was happening at all. He lost a lot of weight because of the ticks, and the smell of the wildcats up on the plateau made him too nervous to graze there. My friend said jokingly that George had lost around two hundred pounds. The good wine country around Pleasanton in the Livermore Valley probably had looked a lot better to George than the wild side of the Santa Lucia Mountains.

My friend's place was a shack right beside a huge fireplace where there had once been a great mansion during the 1920s, built by a famous movie actor. The mansion was built before there was even a road down at Big Sur. The mansion had been brought over the mountains on the backs of mules, strung out like ants, bringing visions of the good life to the poison oak, the ticks, and the salmon.

The mansion was on a promontory, high over the Pacific. Money could see farther in the 1920s, and one could look out and see whales and the Hawaiian Islands and the Kuomintang in China.

> The mansion burned down years ago.
> The actor died.
> His mules were made into soap.
> His mistresses became bird nests of wrinkles.

Now only the fireplace remains as a sort of Carthaginian homage to Hollywood.

I was down there a few weeks ago to see my friend's roof. I wouldn't have passed up the chance for a million dollars, as they say. The roof looked like a colander to me. If that roof and the rain were running against each other at Bay Meadows, I'd bet on the rain and plan to spend my winnings at the World's Fair in Seattle.

My own experience with the Cleveland Wrecking Yard began two days ago when I heard about a used trout stream they had on sale out at the Yard. So I caught the Number 15 bus on Columbus Avenue and went out there for the first time.

There were two Negro boys sitting behind me on the bus. They were talking about Chubby Checker and the Twist. They thought that Chubby Checker was only fifteen years old because he didn't have a mustache. Then they talked about some other guy who did the twist forty-four hours in a row until he saw George Washington crossing the Delaware.

"Man, that's what I call twisting," one of the kids said.

"I don't think I could twist no forty-four hours in a row," the other kid said. "That's a lot of twisting."

I got off the bus right next to an abandoned Time Gasoline filling station and an abandoned fifty-cent self-service car wash. There was a long field on one side of the filling station. The field had once been covered with a housing project during the war, put there for the shipyard workers.

On the other side of the Time filling station was the Cleveland Wrecking Yard. I walked down there to have a look at the used trout stream. The Cleveland Wrecking Yard has a very long front window filled with signs and merchandise.

There was a sign in the window advertising a laundry marking machine for $65.00. The original cost of the machine was $175.00. Quite a saving.

There was another sign advertising new and used two and three ton hoists. I wondered how many hoists it would take to move a trout stream.

There was another sign that said:

THE FAMILY GIFT CENTER,
GIFT SUGGESTIONS FOR THE ENTIRE FAMILY

The window was filled with hundreds of items for the entire family. *Daddy, do you know what I want for Christmas? What, son? A bathroom. Mommy, do you know what I want for Christmas? What, Patricia? Some roofing material.*

There were jungle hammocks in the window for distant relatives and dollar-ten-cent gallons of earth-brown enamel paint for other loved ones.

There was also a big sign that said:

USED TROUT STREAM FOR SALE.
MUST BE SEEN TO BE APPRECIATED.

I went inside and looked at some ship's lanterns that were for sale next to the door. Then a salesman came up to me and said in a pleasant voice, "Can I help you?"

"Yes," I said. "I'm curious about the trout stream you have for sale. Can you tell me something about it? How are you selling it?"

"We're selling it by the foot length. You can buy as little as you want or you can buy all we've got left. A man came in here this morning and bought 563 feet. He's going to give it to his niece for a birthday present," the salesman said.

"We're selling the waterfalls separately of course, and the trees and birds, flowers, grass and ferns we're also selling extra. The insects we're giving away free with a minimum purchase of ten feet of stream."

"How much are you selling the stream for?" I asked.

"Six dollars and fifty cents a foot," he said. "That's for the first hundred feet. After that it's five dollars a foot."

"How much are the birds?" I asked.

"Thirty-five cents apiece," he said. "But of course they're used. We can't guarantee anything."

"How wide is the stream?" I asked. "You said you were selling it by the length, didn't you?"

"Yes," he said. "We're selling it by the length. Its width runs between five and eleven feet. You don't have to pay anything extra for width. It's a big stream, but it's very pleasant."

"What kind of animals do you have?" I asked.

"We only have three deer left," he said.

"Oh . . . What about flowers?"

"By the dozen," he said.

"Is the stream clear?" I asked.

"Sir," the salesman said. "I wouldn't want you to think that we would ever sell a murky trout stream here. We always make sure they're running crystal clear before we even think about moving them."

"Where did the stream come from?" I asked.

"Colorado," he said. "We moved it with loving care. We've never damaged a trout stream yet. We treat them all as if they were china."

"You're probably asked this all the time, but how's fishing in the stream?" I asked.

"Very good," he said. "Mostly German browns, but there are a few rainbows."

"What do the trout cost?" I asked.

"They come with the stream," he said. "Of course it's all luck. You never know how many you're going to get or how big they are. But the fishing's very good, you might say it's excellent. Both bait and dry fly," he said smiling.

"Where's the stream at?" I asked. "I'd like to take a look at it."

"It's around in back," he said. "You go straight through that door and then turn right until you're outside. It's stacked in lengths. You can't miss it. The waterfalls are upstairs in the used plumbing department."

"What about the animals?"

"Well, what's left of the animals are straight back from the stream. You'll see a bunch of our trucks parked on a road by the railroad tracks. Turn right on the road and follow it down past the piles of lumber. The animal shed's right at the end of the lot."

"Thanks," I said. "I think I'll look at the waterfalls first. You don't have to come with me. Just tell me how to get there and I'll find my own way."

"All right," he said. "Go up those stairs. You'll see a bunch of doors and windows, turn left and you'll find the used plumbing department. Here's my card if you need any help."

"Okay," I said. "You've been a great help already. Thanks a lot. I'll take a look around."

"Good luck," he said.

I went upstairs and there were thousands of doors there. I'd never seen so many doors before in my life. You could have built an entire city out of those doors. Doorstown. And there were enough windows up there to build a little suburb entirely out of windows. Windowville.

I turned left and went back and saw the faint glow of pearl-colored light. The light got stronger and stronger as I went farther back, and then I was in the used plumbing department, surrounded by hundreds of toilets.

The toilets were stacked on shelves. They were stacked five toilets high. There was a skylight above the toilets that made them glow like the Great Taboo Pearl of the South Sea movies.

Stacked over against the wall were the waterfalls. There were about a dozen of them, ranging from a drop of a few feet to a drop of ten or fifteen feet.

There was one waterfall that was over sixty feet long. There were tags on the pieces of the big falls describing the correct order for putting the falls back together again.

The waterfalls all had price tags on them. They were more expensive than the stream. The waterfalls were selling for $19.00 a foot.

I went into another room where there were piles of sweet-smelling lumber, glowing a soft yellow from a different color skylight above the lumber. In the shadows at the edge of the room under the sloping roof of the building were many sinks and urinals covered with dust, and there was also another waterfall about seventeen feet long, lying there in two lengths and already beginning to gather dust.

I had seen all I wanted of the waterfalls, and now I was very curious about the trout stream, so I followed the salesman's directions and ended up outside the building.

O I had never in my life seen anything like that trout stream. It was stacked in piles of various lengths: ten, fifteen, twenty feet, etc. There was one pile of hundred-foot lengths. There was also a box of scraps. The scraps were in odd sizes ranging from six inches to a couple of feet.

There was a loudspeaker on the side of the building and soft music was coming out. It was a cloudy day and seagulls were circling high overhead.

Behind the stream were big bundles of trees and bushes. They were covered with sheets of patched canvas. You could see the tops and roots sticking out the ends of the bundles.

I went up close and looked at the lengths of stream. I could see some trout in them. I saw one good fish. I saw some crawdads crawling around the rocks at the bottom.

It looked like a fine stream. I put my hand in the water. It was cold and felt good.

I decided to go around to the side and look at the animals. I saw where the trucks were parked beside the railroad tracks. I followed the road down past the piles of lumber, back to the shed where the animals were.

The salesman had been right. They were practically out of animals. About the only thing they had left in any abundance were mice. There were hundreds of mice.

Beside the shed was a huge wire birdcage, maybe fifty feet high, filled with many kinds of birds. The top of the cage had a piece of canvas over it, so the birds wouldn't get wet when it rained. There were woodpeckers and wild canaries and sparrows.

On my way back to where the trout stream was piled, I found the insects. They were inside a prefabricated steel building that was selling for eighty-cents a square foot. There was a sign over the door. It said

INSECTS

Charles Bukowski

After Kerouac's death in 1969, Charles Bukowski became the counterculture's most prolific writer of autobiographical poetry and prose, perfecting a laconic style that was unmistakably his own. In 1960 he completed his first book, Flower, Fist, and Bestial Wail, *a twenty-eight-page chapbook of poems published by Hearse Press in an edition of two hundred copies. One of Bukowski's early publishers was R. R. Cuscaden, who said that he aimed "to find a legitimate response to the Corso/Ginsberg/Ferlinghetti syndrome (and imitators) on the one side and the tea-cozy* Poetry *magazine gang on the other side. Buk obviously was the answer."*

Later Bukowski's stream of poetry and fiction in books beauti-
fully designed and published by Black Sparrow Press sold widely
throughout the world, beginning in 1971 with his first novel, Post
Office. *In 1967 "the Buk" began writing a weekly column for the*
Los Angeles underground paper Open City *titled "Notes of a*
Dirty Old Man," collected in his early book Notes of a Dirty
Old Man *by City Lights Press in 1969. The excerpt in which he*
described how he pumped gas at an all-night gas station and be-
friended the local hookers was included in A Bukowski Sampler
(1969), edited by Douglas Blazek.

FROM *NOTES OF A DIRTY OLD MAN*

IT WAS A PLACE where the cabbies from this cab co. would come in
for gas. I would pump the gas, take the money and throw it into the
register. most of the night I sat in a chair. the job went all right the
first 2 or 3 nights. a little argument with the cabbies who wanted me
to change flats for them. some Italian boy got on the phone and raised
shit with the boss because I wouldn't do anything but I knew why I
was there—to protect the money, the old man had shown me where
the gun was, how to use it and be sure to make the cabbies pay for all
the gas and oil they used. but I had no desire to protect the $$$$$$ for
eighteen bucks a week and that was where Sunderson's thinking was
wrong. I would have taken the money myself, but the morals were all
fucked up: somebody had jobbed me with the crazy idea one time
that stealing was wrong, and I was having a hard time overcoming my
preconceptions. meanwhile I worked on them, against them, with
them, you know.

about the fourth night a little negress stood in the doorway. she
just stood there smiling at me. we must have been looking at each other
for about 3 minutes. "how you doing?" she asked. "my name's Elsie."

"I'm not doing very good. my name's Hank." she came in and
leaned against a little old desk in there. she seemed to have on a little
girl's dress. she had little girl movements and the fun in her eyes, but
she was a woman, throbbing and miraculous electric woman in a
brown and clean little girl's dress. "can I buy a soft drink?"

"sure."

she gave me the money and I watched her open the cover of the
soft drink box and, with much serious deliberation, she selected a
drink. then she sat on the little stool and I watched her drink it down.

the little bubbles of air floating through electric light, through the bottle. I looked at her body, I looked at her legs, I was filled with the warm brown kindness of her. it was lonely in that place just sitting in that chair night after night for eighteen bucks a week.

she handed me the empty bottle.

"thanks."

"yeh."

"mind if I bring some of my girl friends over tomorrow night?"

"if they're anything like you sweetie, bring them all."

the next night there were three or four of them, talking and laughing and buying and drinking soft drinks. jesus, I mean they were sweet, young, full of the thing, all young colored little girls, everything was funny and beautiful, and I mean it was, they make me feel that way. the next night there were eight or ten of them, the next night thirteen or fourteen. they began bringing in gin or whiskey and mixing it with the soft drinks. I brought my own. but Elsie, the first one was the finest of them all. she'd sit on my lap and then leap up and scream, "hey, Jesus Christ, you gonna shove my TESTINES out of the top of my head with that there FISHPOLE!" she'd act angry, real angry, and the other girls would laugh. and I'd just sit there confused, smiling, but in a sense I was happy. they had too much for me but it was a good show. I began to loosen up a bit myself. when a driver would honk, I'd stand up a bit leery, finish my drink, go find the gun, hand it to Elsie and say, "now look Elsie baby, you guard that god damned register for me, and if any of them girls makes a move toward it, you go on and shoot a hole in her pussy for me, eh?"

and I'd leave Elsie in there staring down at that big luger. it was a strange combo, the both of them, they could kill a man, or save him, depending upon which way it went. the history of man, woman and the world. and I'd walk out to pump the gas.

then the Italian cabbie, Pinelli, came in one night for a soft drink. I liked his name, but I didn't like him. he was the guy that bitched most about me not changing flats. I was not anti-Italian at all but it was strange that since I had landed in town that the Italian Faction was at the forefront of my misery. but I knew it was a mathematical, rather than a racial thing. in Frisco an old Italian woman had probably saved my life. but that was another story. Pinelli stalked in. and I mean STALKED. the girls were all around the place, talking and laughing. he walked over and lifted the lid of the soft drink container.

"GOD DAMN IT, ALL THE SOFT DRINKS ARE GONE

AND I'M THIRSTY! WHO DRANK ALL THE SOFT DRINKS?"

"I did," I told him.

it was very quiet. all the girls were watching. Elsie was standing right by me watching him. Pinelli was handsome if you didn't look too long or too deep. the hawk nose, the black hair, the Prussian officer swagger, the tight pants, the little boy fury.

"THESE GIRLS DRANK ALL THOSE SOFT DRINKS, AND THESE GIRLS AREN'T SUPPOSED TO BE IN HERE, THESE DRINKS ARE FOR TAXI DRIVERS ONLY!"

then he came close to me, stood there, spreading his legs like a chicken does, a bit, before it craps:

"YOU KNOW WHAT THESE GIRLS ARE WISE GUY?"

"sure, these girls are my friends."

"NO, THESE GIRLS ARE WHORES! THEY WORK IN THREE WHOREHOUSES ACROSS THE STREET! THAT'S WHAT THEY ARE—WHORES!"

nothing was said. we just all sat there looking at the Italian. it seemed like a long look. then he turned and walked out. the rest of the night was hardly the same, I was worried about Elsie. she had the gun. I walked over to her and took the gun.

"I almost gave that son of a bitch a new belly button," she said, "his mother was a whore!"

the next thing I knew the place was empty. I sat and had a long drink. then I got up and looked at the cash register. it was all there.

about 5 a.m. the old man came in.

"Bukowski."

"yes, Mr. Sunderson?"

"I gotta let you go." (familiar words)

"what's wrong?"

"the boys say you ain't been runnin' this place right, place full of whores and you here playin' around. them with their breasts out and snatches out and you suckin' and lickin' and tonguin'. is THAT what goes on around here early in the morning?"

"well, not exactly."

"well I'm gonna take your spot until I can find a more dependable man. got to find out what's going on around here."

"all right it's your circus, Sunderson."

I think it was two nights later that I was coming out of the bar and decided to walk past the old gas station. there were two or three police cars around.

I saw Marty, one of the cab drivers I got along with. I went up to him:

"what's up Marty?"

"they knifed Sunderson, and shot one of the cabbies with Sunderson's gun."

"jesus, just like a movie. the cabbie they shot, was it Pinelli?"

"yeah, how'd you know?"

"get it in the belly?"

"yeah, yeah, how'd you know?"

I was drunk. I walked away back towards my room. It was high New Orleans moon. I kept walking towards my room and soon the tears came, a great wash of tears in the moonlight. and then they stopped and I could feel the tear-water drying on my face, stretching the skin. when I got to my room I didn't bother with the light, got my shoes off, my socks off, and fell back on the bed without Elsie, my beautiful black whore, and then I slept, I slept through the sadness of everything and when I awakened I wondered what the next town would be, the next job. I got up, put on my shoes and socks, and went out for a bottle of wine. the streets didn't look very good, they seldom did. it was a structure planned by rats and men and you had to live within it. but like a friend of mine once said "nothing was ever promised you, you signed no contract." I walked into the store for my wine.

the son of a bitch leaned forward just a little, waiting for his dirty coins.

PART SEVEN

OUT OF THE FIRE:
THE BLACK ARTS MOVEMENT
AND THE RESHAPING OF
BLACK CONSCIOUSNESS

> *I can clear a beach or swimming pool without*
> *touching water.*
> *I can make a lunch counter become deserted*
> *in less than an hour.*
> *I can make property value drop by being seen*
> *in a realtor's tower. . . .*
> *I have Power,*
> *BLACK POWER.*

DON L. LEE, "STEREO" (1967)

IN MID-SEPTEMBER 1965, a month after the riots that had torched Watts and most of the black ghetto in southeast and central Los Angeles, the middle-aged screenwriter Budd Schulberg, then living in Beverly Hills, wanted to do what he could to help the situation. As a successful writer, he decided to start a creative writing workshop for high school dropouts in Watts. Making his way to the Westminster Neighborhood Association, a shabby two-story stucco social service building supported by the Presbyterian Church in a neighborhood where every other building had been burned to the ground, Schulberg put up a sign announcing his class in creative writing among the other notices offering instruction for unemployed teenagers and adults. Nobody came. Day after day, when he arrived at the community center in Watts, people glared at him in the hallways and muttered ugly things behind his back. "Dig the gray beast! What the fug you think he's up to?" Sometimes they taunted him directly with the words of Malcom X, "The white man's heaven is the black man's hell!"

Schulberg held his ground for a month, but still nobody ever showed up for his class. Then he got the idea of borrowing a sound projector and a 16-millimeter print of *On the Waterfront*, a film he had written about a longshoremen's strike, starring Marlon Brando. Schulberg figured that the kids would want to watch it, since there was no movie theater within twelve miles of Watts, and the teenagers who hung out at the Westminster Center seemed glued to the afternoon soap operas on their old television set. About thirty people showed up for his movie. They sat lethargically in the stuffy room, watching the flickering screen, when suddenly through the open windows came the sound of a commotion across the street at the local mortuary. Everyone in the audience stood up and headed outside, leaving Schulberg with his projector running in an empty room.

He followed them out of the building and was told that the funeral in progress was for a six-month-old infant who had died because an ambulance sent by the distant County General Hospital had arrived too late to save the baby. What Schulberg learned from the funeral that had interrupted what he called "the premiere" of his film in Watts continued to haunt him "as image and symbol of the true meaning of medical deprivation." He had finally experienced the reality of black life in America. Schulberg went back to his classroom, determined to teach the kids how to write about their lives. Over the next year he found his students, established the Watts Writers Workshop, and edited a collection of their poetry and fiction in *From the Ashes: Voices of Watts* for The New American Library in 1967.

The Watts Writers Workshop was something of an anomaly because it had been started by a white man. In the mid-1960s, most writing workshops in ghetto centers and community colleges were organized by militant black artists. As Maulana Karenga stated in 1968, "Black art, like everything else in the black community, must respond positively to the reality of the revolution." The struggle for black power had evolved into a separatist movement in which the "battle" was for the minds of black people. "It becomes very important then, that art plays the role it should play in Black survival and not bog itself down in the meaningless madness of the Western world wasted."

The new radical intellectual focus in the writing workshops derived from a program that originated during the spring of 1964 in Harlem, when a group of black East Coast artists led by writers LeRoi Jones, Charles Patterson, William Patterson, Clarence Reed, Johnny Moore, and others founded the Black Arts Repertory Theatre/School. They were inspired by the work of Franz Fanon, a Martinican psychiatrist who had written several important books about racism and colonialism, as well as by the writing of radical black American authors such as W. E. B. Du Bois, cofounder of the NAACP.

The Harlem group held poetry readings and concerts, but initially its most successful work was in the theater. Funded for three months by the Office of Economic Opportunity during President Lyndon Johnson's "Great Society" program of domestic subsidies, the

Black Arts Repertory Theatre/School brought its programs to the streets of New York City.

In the mid-1960s, the concept of Black Power also gave its impetus to the new Black Arts aesthetic. The meaning of the term "Black Power" was vague, but it originated during the 1966 March Against Fear in Greenwood, Mississippi, when Stokely Carmichael of SNCC gave a speech calling not for love or forbearance, but for "Black Power." The term caught on instantly, even if in the months to come, Carmichael continued to reach for new ways to explain it. However, the spirit behind his words was as clear, as historian Houston A. Baker, Jr., stated, "as the fingers of a clenched fist. Young black America was fed up with sitting in. The time had arrived for militant, outgoing, radical activism and revolt."

Despite their strident rhetoric, the writers associated with the Black Arts Movement did not speak for the entire black community. Poems that advocated violence, such as LeRoi Jones's "Black Art" and Nikki Giovanni's "The True Import of Present Dialogue: Black vs. Negro," were widely felt to be too extreme, even in the turbulent sixties. Giovanni herself did not reprint her poem in later collections of her work, referring to it in "My Poem" instead. Also troublesome for many readers was the anti-Semitism expressed by writers such as Larry Neal, LeRoi Jones, Haki R. Madhubuti, and Carolyn M. Rodgers. This has continued to be a problematic aspect of the Black Power agenda that has never been satisfactorily addressed.

While the Black Arts Movement gave a new sense of racial pride to a generation of young African-American dramatists, poets, and novelists, after the 1960s black writing blossomed in another direction in the United States. Books by Nobel Prize winner Toni Morrison, National Book Award winner Charles Johnson, and bestselling writers Terry McMillan and Walter Mosely, as well as many others, found an audience in the emergent black middle class and were also widely read by white Americans. The angry rhetoric of the Black Arts Movement continued to find its expression in the popular hip-hop and rap artists, whose recordings inevitably have their widest sales among white suburban adolescents.

Larry Neal

After the success of the Black Arts Repertory Theatre/School in the Harlem community, the writer Larry Neal wrote an essay describing the Black Arts Movement. It was published in the Summer 1968 issue of the Drama Review.

THE BLACK ARTS MOVEMENT

I

THE BLACK ARTS MOVEMENT is radically opposed to any concept of the artist that alienates him from his community. Black Art is the aesthetic and spiritual sister of the Black Power concept. As such, it envisions an art that speaks directly to the needs and aspirations of Black America. In order to perform this task, the Black Arts Movement proposes a radical reordering of the Western cultural aesthetic. It proposes a separate symbolism, mythology, critique, and iconology. The Black Arts and the Black Power concept both relate broadly to the Afro-American's desire for self-determination and nationhood. Both concepts are nationalistic. One is concerned with the relationship between art and politics; the other with the art of politics.

Recently, these two movements have begun to merge: the political values inherent in the Black Power concept are now finding concrete expression in the aesthetics of Afro-American dramatists, poets, choreographers, musicians, and novelists. A main tenet of Black Power is the necessity for Black people to define the world in their own terms. The Black artist has made the same point in the context of aesthetics. The two movements postulate that there are in fact and in spirit two Americas—one black, one white. The Black artist takes this to mean that his primary duty is to speak to the spiritual and cultural needs of Black people. Therefore, the main thrust of this new breed of contemporary writers is to confront the contradictions arising out of the Black man's experience in the racist West. Currently, these writers are re-evaluating Western aesthetics, the traditional role of the writer, and the social function of art. Implicit in this re-evaluation is the need to develop a "black aesthetic." It is the opinion of many Black writers, I among them, that the Western aesthetic has run its course: it is impossible to construct anything meaningful within its decaying structure. We advocate a cultural revolution in art and ideas. The cultural values inherent in Western history must either be radicalized or destroyed, and we will probably find that even radicalization is impossible. In fact, what is needed is a whole new system of ideas. Poet Don L. Lee expresses it:

> . . . We must destroy Faulkner, dick, jane, and other perpetuators of evil. It's time for DuBois, Nat Turner, and Kwame Nkrumah. As Frantz Fanon points out: destroy the culture and you destroy the people. This must not happen. Black artists are culture stabilizers; bringing back old values, and introducing new ones. Black Art will talk to the people and with the will of the people stop impending "protective custody."

The Black Arts Movement eschews "protest" literature. It speaks directly to Black people. Implicit in the concept of "protest" literature, as Brother [Etheridge] Knight has made clear, is an appeal to white morality:

> Now any Black man who masters the technique of his particular art form, who adheres to the white aesthetic, and who directs his work toward a white audience is, in one sense, protesting. And implicit in the act of protest is the belief that a change will be forthcoming once the masters are aware of the protestor's "grievance" (the very word connotes begging, supplications to the gods). Only when that belief has faded and protestings end, will Black art begin.

Brother Knight also has some interesting statements about the development of a "Black aesthetic":

> Unless the Black artist establishes a "Black aesthetic" he will have no future at all. To accept the white aesthetic is to accept and validate a society that will not allow him to live. The Black artist must create new forms and new values, sing new songs (or purify old ones); and along with other Black authorities, he must create a new history, new symbols,

myths and legends (and purify old ones by fire). And the Black artist, in creating his own aesthetic, must be accountable for it only to the Black people. Further, he must hasten his own dissolution as an individual (in the Western sense)— painful though the process may be, having been breast-fed the poison of "individual experience."

When we speak of a "Black aesthetic" several things are meant. First, we assume that there is already in existence the basis for such an aesthetic. Essentially, it consists of an African-American cultural tradition. But this aesthetic is finally, by implication, broader than that tradition. It encompasses most of the useable elements of Third World culture. The motive behind the Black aesthetic is the destruction of the white thing, the destruction of white ideas, and white ways of looking at the world. The new aesthetic is mostly predicated on an Ethics which asks the question: whose vision of the world is finally more meaningful, ours or the white oppressors'? What is truth? Or more precisely, whose truth shall we express, that of the oppressed or of the oppressors? These are basic questions. Black intellectuals of previous decades failed to ask them. Further, national and international affairs demand that we appraise the world in terms of our own interests. It is clear that the question of human survival is at the core of contemporary experience. The Black artist must address himself to this reality in the strongest terms possible. In a context of world upheaval, ethics and aesthetics must interact positively and be consistent with the demands for a more spiritual world. Consequently, the Black Arts Movement is an ethical movement. Ethical, that is, from the viewpoint of the oppressed. And much of the oppression confronting the Third World and Black America is directly traceable to the Euro-American cultural sensibility. This sensibility, anti-human in nature, has, until recently, dominated the psyches of most Black artists and intellectuals; it must be destroyed before the Black creative artist can have a meaningful role in the transformation of society.

It is this natural reaction to an alien sensibility that informs the cultural attitudes of the Black Arts and the Black Power movement. It is a profound ethical sense that makes a Black artist question a society in which art is one thing and the actions of men another. The Black Arts Movement believes that your ethics and your aesthetics are one. That the contradictions between ethics and aesthetics in western society is symptomatic of a dying culture.

The term "Black Arts" is of ancient origin, but it was first used in a positive sense by LeRoi Jones:

> We are unfair
> And unfair
> We are black magicians
> Black arts we make
> in black labs of the heart
>
> The fair are fair
> and deathly white
>
> The day will not save them
> And we own the night

There is also a section of the poem "Black Dada Nihilismus" that carries the same motif. But a fuller amplification of the nature of the new aesthetics appears in the poem "Black Art":

> Poems are bullshit unless they are
> teeth or trees or lemons piled
> on a step. Or black ladies dying
> of men leaving nickel hearts
> beating them down. Fuck poems
> and they are useful, would they shoot
> come at you, love what you are,
> breathe like wrestlers, or shudder
> strangely after peeing. We want live
> words of the hip world, live flesh &
> coursing blood. Hearts and Brains
> Souls splintering fire. We want poems
> like fists beating niggers out of Jocks
> or dagger poems in the slimy bellies
> of the owner-jews . . .

2

In the spring of 1964, LeRoi Jones, Charles Patterson, William Patterson, Clarence Reed, Johnny Moore, and a number of other Black artists opened the Black Arts Repertory Theatre /School. They produced a number of plays including Jones' *Experimental Death Unit # One*, *Black Mass*, *Jello*, and *Dutchman*. They also initiated a series of poetry readings and concerts. These activities represented the most advanced tendencies in the movement and were of excellent artistic quality. The Black Arts School came under immediate attack by the New York power structure. The Establishment, fearing Black creativity, did exactly what it was expected to do—it attacked the theatre and all of its values. In the meantime, the school was granted funds by OEO[1] though HARYOU-ACT. Lacking a cultural program itself, HARYOU turned to the only organization which addressed itself to the needs of the community. In keeping with its "revolutionary" cultural ideas, the Black Arts Theatre took its programs into the streets of Harlem. For three months, the threatre presented plays, concerts, and poetry readings to the people of the community. Plays that shattered the illusions of the American body politic, and awakened Black people to the meaning of their lives.

Then the hawks from the OEO moved in and chopped off the funds. Again, this should have been expected. The Black Arts Theatre stood in radical opposition to the feeble attitudes about culture of the "War On Poverty" bureaucrats. And later, because of internal problems, the theatre was forced to close. But the Black Arts group proved that the community could be served by a valid and dynamic art. It also proved that there was a definite need for a cultural revolution in the Black community.

With the closing of the Black Arts Theatre, the implications of what Brother Jones and his colleagues were trying to do took on even more significance. Black Art groups sprang up on the West Coast and the idea spread to Detroit, Philadelphia, Jersey City, New Orleans, and Washington, D.C. Black Arts movements began on the campuses of San Francisco State College, Fisk University, Lincoln University, Hunter College in the Bronx, Columbia University, and Oberlin College. In Watts, after the rebellion, Maulana Karenga welded the Black Arts Movement into a cohesive cultural ideology which owed much to the work of LeRoi Jones. Karenga sees culture as the most important element in the struggle for self-determination:

> Culture is the basis of all ideas, images and actions. To move
> is to move culturally, i.e. by a set of values given to you by

---

1. Office of Economic Opportunity.

your culture. Without a culture Negroes are only a set of re-
actions to white people. The seven criteria for culture are:

1. Mythology
2. History
3. Social Organization
4. Political Organization
5. Economic Organization
6. Creative Motif
7. Ethos

In drama, LeRoi Jones represents the most advanced aspects of
the movement. He is its prime mover and chief designer. In a poetic
essay entitled "The Revolutionary Theatre," he outlines the iconol-
ogy of the movement:

> The Revolutionary Theatre should force change: it should
> be change. (All their faces turned into the lights and you
> work on them black nigger magic, and cleanse them at hav-
> ing seen the ugliness. And if the beautiful see themselves,
> they will love themselves.) We are preaching virtue again,
> but by that to mean NOW, toward what seems the most
> constructive use of the word.

The theatre that Jones proposes is inextricably linked to the Afro-
American political dynamic. And such a link is perfectly consistent
with Black America's contemporary demands. For theatre is poten-
tially the most social of all of the arts. It is an integral part of the so-
cializing process. It exists in direct relationship to the audience it
claims to serve. The decadence and inanity of the contemporary
American theatre is an accurate reflection of the state of American so-
ciety. [Edward] Albee's *Who's Afraid of Virginia Woolf?* (1962) is very
American: sick white lives in a homosexual hell hole. The theatre of
white America is escapist, refusing to confront concrete reality. Into
this cultural emptiness come the musicals, an up-tempo version of the
same stale lives. And the use of Negroes in such plays as *Hello Dolly*
and *Hallelujah Baby* does not alert their nature; it compounds the
problem. These plays are simply hipper versions of the minstrel show.
They present Negroes acting out the hang-ups of middle-class white
America. Consequently, the American theatre is a palliative pre-
scribed to bourgeois patients who refuse to see the world as it is. Or,

more crucially, as the world sees them. It is no accident, therefore, that the most "important" plays come from Europe—Brecht, Weiss, and Ghelderode.[2] And even these have begun to run dry.

The Black Arts theatre, the theatre of LeRoi Jones, is a radical alternative to the sterility of the American theatre. It is primarily a theatre of the Spirit, confronting the Black man in his interaction with his brothers and with the white thing.

> Our theatre will show victims so that their brothers in the audience will be better able to understand that they are the brothers of victims, and that they themselves are blood brothers. And what we show must cause the blood to rush, so that prerevolutionary temperaments will be bathed in this blood, and it will cause their deepest souls to move, and they will find themselves tensed and clenched, even ready to die, at what the soul has been taught. We will scream and cry, murder, run through the streets in agony, if it means some soul will be moved, moved to actual life understanding of what the world is, and what it ought to be. We are preaching virtue and feeling, and a natural sense of the self in the world. All men live in the world, and the world ought to be a place for them to live.

The victims in the world of Jones' early plays are Clay, murdered by the white bitch-goddess [Lula] in *Dutchman*, and Walker Vessels, the revolutionary in *The Slave*. Both of these plays present Black men in transition. Clay, the middle-class Negro trying to get himself a little action from Lula, digs himself and his own truth only to get murdered after telling her like it really is:

> Just let me bleed you, you loud whore, and one poem vanished. A whole people neurotics, struggling to keep from being sane. And the only thing that would cure the neurosis would be your murder. Simple as that. I mean if I murdered you, then other white people would understand me. You understand? No. I guess not. If Bessie Smith[3] had killed

---

2. Michel de Ghelderode (1898–1962), Belgian playwright. Bertolt Brecht (1898–1956), German socialist playwright. Peter Weiss (b. 1916), German-Swiss playwright.
3. Blues singer (1894–1937).

some white people she wouldn't have needed that music. She could have talked very straight and plain about the world. Just straight two and two are four. Money. Power. Luxury. Like that. All of them. Crazy niggers turning their backs on sanity. When all it needs is that simple act. Just murder. Would make us all sane.

But Lula understands, and she kills Clay first. In a perverse way it is Clay's nascent knowledge of himself that threatens the existence of Lula's idea of the world. Symbolically, and in fact, the relationship between Clay (Black America) and Lula (white America) is rooted in the historical castration of Black manhood. And in the twisted psyche of white America, the Black man is both an object of love and hate. Analogous attitudes exist in most Black Americans, but for decidedly different reasons. Clay is doomed when he allows himself to participate in Lula's "fantasy" in the first place. It is the fantasy to which Frantz Fanon alludes in *The Wretched of the Earth* and *Black Skins, White Mask*: the native's belief that he can acquire the oppressor's power by acquiring his symbols, one of which is the white woman. When Clay finally digs himself it is too late. . . .

These plays are directed at problems within Black America. They begin with the premise that there is a well defined Afro-American audience. An audience that must see itself and the world in terms of its own interests. These plays, along with many others, constitute the basis for a viable movement in the theatre—a movement which takes as its task a profound reevaluation of the Black man's presence in America. The Black Arts Movement represents the flowering of a cultural nationalism that has been suppressed since the 1920's. I mean the "Harlem Renaissance"—which was essentially a failure. It did not address itself to the mythology and the life-styles of the Black community. It failed to take roots, to link itself concretely to the struggles of that community, to become its voice and spirit. Implicit in the Black Arts Movement is the idea that Black people, however dispersed, constitute a *nation* within the belly of white America. This is not a new idea. Garvey said it and the Honorable Elijah Muhammad[4] says it now. And it is on this idea that the concept of Black Power is predicated.

---

4. Leader of the Nation of Islam from the early 1930s until his death in 1975. Marcus Garvey (1887–1940), pioneer of black nationalism and founder of the Universal Negro Improvement Association, which advocated the return to Africa.

Afro-American life and history is full of creative possibilities, and the movement is just beginning to perceive them. Just beginning to understand that the most meaningful statements about the nature of Western society must come from the Third World of which Black America is a part. The thematic material is broad, ranging from folk heroes like Shine and Stagolee to historical figures like Marcus Garvey and Malcolm X. And then there is the struggle for Black survival, the coming confrontation between white America and Black America. If art is the harbinger of future possibilities, what does the future of Black America portend?

―――――――

Don L. Lee

Several so-called senior black authors joined the Black Arts Movement during the 1960s, such as Gwendolyn Brooks and Dudley Randall. In Randall's introduction to his anthology The Black Poets *(1971), he made clear the link of many of the contemporary Black Arts poets to their predecessors, writers like Langston Hughes and Robert Hayden. What distinguished the work of the younger poets was their nationalist impulse, their insistence on creating a myth of origins, a homeland, and an imagined common culture for Africans in America.*

Comparing the Black Arts Movement with the Harlem Renaissance of 1917–1930, Don L. Lee made the distinction that "the black arts movement in the twenties was of a minimal influence and virtually went unnoticed by the majority of black people in the country. More whites knew about what was happening than brothers and sisters." The major difference of the Black Arts Movement was "that among the black artists of today there is no such thing as being apolitical. To be apolitical, when our very lives are influenced and controlled by political power, is to be extremely fool-

ish. It is either not to care or to be in agreement with those who wish to systematically force us from this earth."

Although playwrights were the first successful artists of the Black Arts Movement, poets soon came to the forefront in the 1960s after the closing of the Black Arts Repertory Theatre/School in Harlem. They created a legacy of poetry that celebrated black spontaneous vernacular speech, expressing, as Lee wrote in his collection Think Black 1965–1967 (1967), what ordinary people "really meant to say."

FROM *THINK BLACK 1965–1967*

Introduction

I WAS BORN IN SLAVERY in Feb. of 1942. In the spring of that same year 110,000 persons of Japanese descent were placed in protective custody by the white people of the United States. Two out of every three of these were American citizens by birth; the other third were aliens forbidden by law to be citizens. No charges had been filed against these people nor had any hearing been held. The removal of these people was on racial or ancestral grounds only. World War II, the war against racism; yet no Germans or other enemy agents were placed in protective custody. There should have been Japanese writers directing their writings toward Japanese audiences.

Black. Poet. Black poet am I. This should leave little doubt in the minds of anyone as to which is first. Black art is created from black forces that live within the body. These forces can be lost at any time as in the case of Louis Lomax, Frank Yerby and Ralph Ellison. Direct and meaningful contact with black people will act as energizers for the black forces. Black art will elevate and enlighten our people and lead them toward an awareness of self, i.e., their blackness. It will show them mirrors. Beautiful symbols. And will aid in the destruction of anything nasty and detrimental to our advancement as a people. Black art is a reciprocal art. The black writer learns from his people and because of his insight and "know how" he is able to give back his knowledge to the people in a manner in which they can identify, learn and gain some type of mental satisfaction, e.g., rage or happiness. We must destroy Faulkner, dick, jane and other perpetuators of

evil. It's time for DuBois, Nat Turner and Kwame Nkruma. As Frantz
Fanon points out: destroy the culture and you destroy the people.
This must not happen. Black artists are culture stabilizers; bringing
back old values, and introducing new ones. Black art will talk to the
people and with the will of the people stop the impending "protec-
tive custody."

> America calling,
> negroes.
> can you dance?
> play foot/baseball?
> nanny?
> cook?
> needed now. negroes
> who can entertain
> ONLY.
> others not
> wanted.
> (& are considered extremely dangerous.)
>   d. l. l.

Haki R. Madhubuti

*Haki R. Madhubuti was the name taken by Don L. Lee as a
Black Arts writer, literary critic, publisher, and community activist.
In* Black Pride *(1968) and* Don't Cry, Scream *(1969), he
wrote in a direct language with considerable power. Madhubuti's
poem "Malcolm Spoke / who listened?" (1969) is an example of
his skill creating lines that seize the reader's attention.*

MALCOLM SPOKE/WHO LISTENED?

(this poem is for my consciousness too)

he didn't say
wear yr/blackness in
outer garments
& blk/slogans fr/the top 10.

he was fr a long
line of super-cools,
        doo-rag lovers &
        revolutionary pimps.
u are playing that
high-yellow game in blackface
minus the straighthair.
now
it's nappy-black
& air conditioned volkswagens
with undercover whi
te girls who studied faulkner at
smith
& are authorities on "militant"
knee / grows
selling u at jew town rates:[1]
        niggers with wornout tongues
        three for a quarter/or will consider a trade

the double-breasted hipster
has been replaced with a
dashiki wearing rip-off
who went to city college
majoring in physical education.

animals come in all colors.
dark meat will roast as fast as whi-te meat

---

1. A pejorative phrase directed at the Jewish economic establishments in African
   American communities.

especially in
the unitedstatesofamerica's
new
self-cleaning ovens.

if we don't listen.

———————

Etheridge Knight

*The poetry of Etheridge Knight embodied the ideals of the Black
Arts Movement and was an inspiration to many listeners who heard
him recite his work from memory. Born in Corinth, Mississippi, he
served in the U.S. Army from 1947 to 1951. Arrested for robbery
in 1960, Knight began to write poetry at the Indiana State Prison,
where he served eight years. Encouraged by Dudley Randall to pub-
lish his poetry, Knight debuted with* Poems from Prison, *pub-
lished by Randall's newly established Broadside Press in 1968.
"The Idea of Ancestry" is from that volume. For a time, Knight
was married to the Black Arts performer-poet Sonia Sanchez.
Knight also assembled the collection* Belly Song and Other Po-
ems *(1973), considered one of the most important books of the
Black Arts Movement.*

THE IDEA OF ANCESTRY

I

Taped to the wall of my cell are 47 pictures: 47 black
faces: my father, mother, grandmothers (1 dead), grand
fathers (both dead), brothers, sisters, uncles, aunts,
cousins (1st & 2nd), nieces, and nephews. They stare
across the space at me sprawling on my bunk. I know

their dark eyes, they know mine. I know their style,
they know mine. I am all of them, they are all of me;
they are farmers, I am a thief, I am me, they are thee.

I have at one time or another been in love with my mother,
1 grandmother, 2 sisters, 2 aunts (I went to the asylum),
and 5 cousins. I am now in love with a 7 yr old niece
(she sends me letters written in large block print, and
her picture is the only one that smiles at me).

I have the same name as 1 grandfather, 3 cousins, 3 nephews,
and 1 uncle. The uncle disappeared when he was 15, just
    took
off and caught a freight (they say). He's discussed each year
when the family has a reunion, he causes uneasiness in
the clan, he is an empty space. My father's mother, who
    is 93
and who keeps the Family Bible with everybody's birth
    dates
(and death dates) in it, always mentions him. There is no
place in her Bible for "whereabouts unknown."

II

Each Fall the graves of my grandfathers call me, the brown
hills and red gullies of mississippi send out their electric
messages, galvanizing my genes. Last yr / like a salmon
    quitting
the cold ocean—leaping and bucking up his birthstream / I
hitchhiked my way from L.A. with 16 caps[1] in my pocket
    and a
monkey on my back, and I almost kicked it with the
    kinfolks.
I walked barefooted in my grandmother's backyard / I
    smelled the old
land and the wood / I sipped cornwhiskey from fruit jars
    with the men /
I flirted with the women / I had a ball till the caps ran out
and my habit came down. That night I looked at my
    grandmother

---

1. A reference to units of heroin sold on the street to addicts.

and split / my guts were screaming for junk / but I was
  almost
contented / I had almost caught up with me.
The next day in Memphis I cracked a croaker's crib for a fix.

This yr there is a gray stone wall damming my stream, and
  when
the falling leaves stir my genes, I pace my cell or flop on my
  bunk
and stare at 47 black faces across the space. I am all of them,
they are all of me, I am me, they are thee, and I have no
  sons
to float in the space between.

Al Young

*Born in Ocean Springs, Mississippi, novelist and poet Al Young
was the son of a musician. He majored in Spanish at the University
of Michigan and debuted as an author in 1969 with his first
book of poetry,* Dancing, *which included "Conjugal Visits" and
"A Dance for Ma Rainey," a tribute to the black entertainer
(1886–1939) often called "the Mother of the Blues."*

CONJUGAL VISITS

By noon we'll be deep into it—
  up reading out loud in bed.
Or in between our making love
  I'll paint my toenails red.

Reece say he got to change his name
   from Maurice to Malik.
He thinks I need to change mine too.
   Conversion, so to speak.

"I ain't no Muslim yet," I say.
   "Besides, I like my name.
Kamisha still sounds good to me.
   I'll let you play that game."

"I'd rather play with you," he say,
   "than trip back to the Sixties."
"The Sixties, eh?" I'm on his case.
   "Then I won't do my striptease."

This brother look at me and laugh;
   he know I love him bad
and, worse, he know exactly how much
   loving I ain't had.

He grab me by my puffed up waist
   and pull me to him close.
He say, "I want you in my face.
   Or on my face, Miss Toes."

What can I say? I'd lie for Reece,
   but I'm not quitting school.
Four mouths to feed, not counting mine.
   Let Urban Studies rule!

I met him in the want ads,
   we fell in love by mail.
I say, when people bring this up,
   "Wasn't no one up for sale."

All these Black men crammed up in jail,
   all this I.Q. on ice,
while governments, bank presidents,
   the Mafia don't think twice.

They fly in dope and make real sure
    they hands stay nice and clean.
The chump-change Reece made on the street
    —what's that supposed to mean?

"For what it cost the State to keep
    you locked down, clothed and fed,
you could be learning Harvard stuff,
    and brilliant skills," I said.

Reece say, "Just kiss me one more time,
    then let's get down, make love.
Then let's devour that special meal
    I wish they'd serve more of."

They say the third time out's a charm;
    I kinda think they're right.
My first, he was the Ace of Swords,
    which didn't make him no knight.

He gave me Zeus and Brittany;
    my second left me twins.
This third one ain't about no luck;
    we're honeymooners. Friends.

I go see Maurice once a month
    while Moms looks after things.
We be so glad to touch again,
    I dance, he grins, he sings.

When I get back home to my kids,
    schoolwork, The Copy Shop,
ain't no way Reece can mess with me.
    They got his ass locked up.

A DANCE FOR MA RAINEY

I'm going to be just like you, Ma
Rainey this monday morning
clouds puffing up out of my head

like those balloons
that float above the faces of white people
in the funnypapers

I'm going to hover in the corners
of the world, Ma
& sing from the bottom of hell
up to the tops of high heaven
& send out scratchless waves of yellow
& brown & that basic black honey
misery

I'm going to cry so sweet
& so low
& so dangerous,
Ma,
that the message is going to reach you
back in 1922
where you shimmer
snaggle-toothed
perfumed &
powdered
in your bauble beads
hair pressed & tied back
throbbing with that sick pain
I know
& hide so well
that pain that blues
jives the world with
aching to be heard
that downness
that bottomlessness
first felt by some stolen delta nigger
swamped under with redblooded american agony;
reduced to the sheer shit
of existence
that bred
& battered us all,
Ma,
the beautiful people
our beautiful brave black people

who no longer need to jazz
or sing to themselves in murderous vibrations
or play the veins of their strong tender arms
with needles
to prove that we're still here

———————

Nikki Giovanni

*Very different in style is the poetry of black activist Nikki Gio-
vanni, who asked in her 1968 lyric "The True Import of Present
Dialogue: Black vs. Negro,"*

> *Can you poison*
> *Can you stab-a-jew*
> *Can you kill huh?*

Giovanni urged her readers,

> *Learn to kill niggers*
> *Learn to be Black men*

*As the critic Houston Baker recognized, Giovanni's "un-
abashed advocacy of murderous militancy as a proper black response
to white oppression brought her instant fame." She published three
books of poetry that sold widely among black audiences:* Black
Feeling *(1967);* Black Judgment *(1968), which included "My
Poem"; and* Re:Creation *(1970).*

MY POEM

i am 25 years old
black female poet
wrote a poem asking

nigger can you kill
if they kill me
it won't stop
the revolution

i have been robbed
it looked like they knew
that i was to be hit
they took my tv
my two rings
my piece of african print
and my two guns
if they take my life
it won't stop
the revolution

my phone is tapped
my mail is opened
they've caused me to turn
on all my old friends
and all my new lovers
if i hate all black
people
and all negroes
it won't stop
the revolution

i'm afraid to tell
my roommate where i'm going
and scared to tell
people if i'm coming
if i sit here
for the rest
of my life
it won't stop
the revolution

if i never write
another poem
or short story
if i flunk out

of grad school
if my car is reclaimed
and my record player
won't play
and if i never see
a peaceful day
or do a meaningful
black thing
it won't stop
the revolution
the revolution
is in the streets
and if i stay on
the 5th floor

it will go on
if i never do
anything
it will go on

————————

Carolyn M. Rodgers

*Women were among the most talented writers in the Black Arts
Movement, despite the sexism endemic at the time that often lim-
ited their opportunities for recognition. Sonia Sanchez was a gradu-
ate of Hunter College in New York City and working for the
Congress of Racial Equality when she heard a speech by Malcolm
X and decided to become a poet. Early in her career, in the 1960s,
Toni Morrison began to develop the theme of racial self-loathing in
a story that turned into the novel* The Bluest Eye. *Her novel was
published in 1970, and later Morrison credited what she called
"the reclamation of racial beauty in the Sixties" as the source of her*

idea for the book, which "tried to hit the raw nerve of racial self-contempt, expose it, then soothe it not with narcotics but with language. . . . The struggle was for writing that was indisputably black."

Carolyn M. Rodgers was one of the founders of Third World Press, one of the many successful publishing companies of the Black Arts Movement, along with Drum and Spear Press and Dudley Randall's Broadside Press. Rodgers has said that "I've been compared to Phillis Wheatley. But I like to think of myself as a female Langston Hughes and a quasi Zora N. Hurston. I'm probably not as good as either, but I have my aspirations." Educated at Roosevelt University and at creative writing workshops at Chicago's Organization of Black American Culture, Rodgers was also inspired by the writing of the poet Gwendolyn Brooks, one of her instructors. Third World Press published both of her earliest books of poetry, Paper Soul (1968) and Songs of a Black Bird (1969). "It Is Deep," written in 1969, was included in How I Got Ovah, published by Doubleday in 1975.

IT IS DEEP

(don't never forget the bridge that you crossed over on)

Having tried to use the
witch cord
that erases the stretch of
thirty-three blocks
and tuning in the voice which
   woodenly stated that the
   talk box was "disconnected"

My mother, religiously girdled in
her god, slipped on some love, and
laid on my bell like a truck,
blew through my door warm wind from the south
concern making her gruff and tight-lipped
        and scared
that her "baby" was starving
she, having learned, that disconnection results from
                non-payment of bill(s).

She did not
recognize the poster of the
grand le-roi[1] (al) cat on the wall
had never even seen the book of
Black poems that I have written
thinks that I am under the influence of
             communists
when I talk about Black as anything
other than something ugly to kill it befo it grows
      in any impression she would not be
considered "relevant" or "Black"
                        but
there she was, standing in my room
not loudly condemning that day and
not remembering that I grew hearing her
curse the factory where she "cut uh slave"
and the cheap j-boss[2] wouldn't allow a union,
not remembering that I heard the tears when
they told her a high school diploma was not enough,
and here now, not able to understand, what she had
been forced to deny, still—

she pushed into my kitchen so
she could open my refrigerator to see
what I had to eat, and pressed fifty
bills in my hand saying "pay the talk bill and buy
some food; you got folks who care about you . . ."

My mother, religious-negro, proud of
having waded through a storm, is very obviously,
a sturdy Black bridge that I
crossed over, on.

1. LeRoi Jones.
2. Cheap Jew-boss.

Amiri Baraka

In "It Is Deep," Rodgers mentions a poster of LeRoi Jones on the wall of her room. LeRoi Jones, who changed his name to Amiri Baraka, was what historians refer to as "a principal architect" of the Black Arts Movement. His activist role began when he involved himself in his Black Arts theater group, after he left his children and his white wife, Hettie Jones, and moved uptown to Harlem.

The turning point for Jones was his earlier visit to Cuba sponsored by the New York chapter of the Fair Play for Cuba Committee in 1960, after he had published his poem January 1 1959: Fidel Castro. *In Cuba he met third-world intellectuals who forced him to question his allegiance to America; they called him a "cowardly bourgeoisie individualist" for wanting to write poems about his soul. The Mexican poet Jaime Shelly told him, "You want to cultivate your soul? In that ugliness you live in, you want to cultivate your soul? Well, we've got millions of starving people to feed, and that moves me enough to make poems out of."*

Back in the United States, Jones published two volumes of poetry, Preface to a Twenty Volume Suicide Note *(1961) and* The Dead Lecturer *(1965), as well as a book on the blues,* Blues People *(1963), and several plays. In 1964 he vented his anger at white society in his play* Dutchman. *It dramatized the conflict over race and gender between a predatory white woman and a middle-class black man in a New York City subway car, and won an Obie Award for best Off-Broadway production. The following year, after Malcolm X's assassination, he relocated himself in Harlem with the Black Arts Repertory Theatre/School. In 1966 he moved to Newark and established the community center "Spirit House," and he continued to publish throughout the Sixties. "Numbers, Letters" is from* Black Magic: Poetry 1961–1967 *(1969). After Jones changed his name to Baraka, he coedited* Black Fire: An Anthology of Afro-American Writing *(1968) with Larry Neal.*

NUMBERS, LETTERS

If you're not home, where
are you? Where'd you go? What
were you doing when gone? When
you come back, better make it good.
What was you doing down there, freakin' off
with white women, hangin' out
with Queens, say it straight to be
understood straight, put it flat and real
in the street where the sun comes and the
moon comes and the cold wind in winter
waters your eyes. Say what you mean, dig
it out put it down, and be strong
about it.

I can't say who I am
unless you agree I'm real

I can't be anything I'm not
Except these words pretend
to life not yet explained,
so here's some feeling for you
see how you like it, what it
reveals, and that's Me.

Unless you agree I'm real
that I can feel
whatever beats hardest
at our black souls

I am real, and I can't say who
I am. Ask me if I know, I'll say
yes, I might say no. Still, ask.
I'm Everett LeRoi Jones, 30 yrs old.

A black nigger in the universe. A long breath singer,
wouldbe dancer, strong from years of fantasy
and study. All this time then, for what's happening

now. All that spilling of white ether, clocks in ghostheads
lips drying and rewet, eyes opening and shut, mouths
   churning.

I am a meditative man. And when I say something it's all
   of me
saying, and all the things that make me, have formed me,
   colored me
this brilliant reddish night. I will say nothing that I feel is
lie, or unproven by the same ghostclocks, by the same riders
always move so fast with the word slung over their backs or
in saddlebags, charging down Chinese roads. I carry some
   wors,
some feeling, some life in me. My heart is large as my mind
this is a messenger calling, over here, over here, open your
   eyes
and your ears and your souls; today is the history we must
   learn
to desire. There is no guilt in love.

———————————

Ishmael Reed

Ishmael Reed began his career as a journalist in 1960 after drop-
ping out of the State University of New York at Buffalo in his ju-
nior year. As a reporter for Buffalo's Empire Star Weekly, *Reed*
wrote about Civil Rights issues and interviewed Malcolm X. Mov-
ing to New York City in the early 1960s, Reed helped to start the
underground newspaper East Village Other *while writing his first*
novel, The Free-Lance Pallbearers *(1967). By the end of the*
Sixties, he had settled in Los Angeles, where he published his sec-
ond novel, Yellow Back Radio Broke-Down *(1969), a spoof*
on the American Western that had a religious African-American
cowboy, Loop Garoo, as hero.

*Reed's individual style flowered in many books during the fol-
lowing decades, culminating in the selections chosen for* The Reed
Reader *(2000), which includes his tribute to black activist El-
dridge Cleaver.*

ELDRIDGE CLEAVER—WRITER

THOUGH THE YOUNG African American hip-hop intellectuals pic-
ture Malcolm X as an apostle of armed resistance—their favorite
poster is that of a rifle-bearing Malcolm, peering out from behind
curtains, preparing to do battle with his enemies—the revolutions
that both Malcolm X and Martin Luther King, Jr., precipitated were
textbook Sun Tzu. They produced change, King in the law, Malcolm
in consciousness—without throwing a punch (at whites), or firing a
shot. And though they are regarded as opposites, it was Malcolm's
threats that were partially responsible for the establishment's agreeing
to some of King's demands.

Malcolm made wolfing and jive into an art form, and though his
battles were fought on television (Marshall McLuhan referred to him
as "the electronic man") and his weapons were words, he was a sym-
bol of black manhood; "our shining prince" was the way Ossie Davis
put it, in a eulogy delivered at Malcolm's funeral. Black men were in
need of such a prince, manhood being very much on the minds of
black men during the sixties. Their frustration was heightened when
some black children were blown to bits during church services in
Birmingham, Alabama; King Jr.'s macho critics thought that he had
"punked out" when he used children in one of his nonviolent
demonstrations.

Black nationalist poet Askia Muhammed Toure wondered aloud,
"But who will protect the women's quarters?" the desperate cry of
men whose women were being poked with cattle prods and beaten to
the ground by white thugs in uniform. I wrote a long noisy rambunc-
tious poem entitled "Fanfare for an Avenging Angel," dedicated to
Malcolm, and, after reading it, Malcolm told me, charitably, that it re-
minded him of works by "Virgil and Dante."

That's how we saw Malcolm X. He would make them pay. Pay
for the humiliations we suffered in a racist country. Young black intel-
lectuals were out for revenge. They were in a Kikukyu warrior mode.
On the west coast, a young black prisoner was using the Spanish
dungeon of the sort that used to hold slaves as his personal library.

Eldridge Cleaver was also impressed with Malcolm X and took Malcolm X's position over that of Elijah Muhammad, whose generation called whites devils, because they had come out of the southern racist hell where the whites had shown themselves to be capable of the most fiendish acts.

As in the case of his hero, Malcolm X, Eldridge Cleaver went to school in jail, reading, writing, meditating, and practicing his intellectual style on mentors, who were obviously no match for his probing, hungry intellect. In his book *Soul on Ice*, he confessed to a former career as a rapist and admitted to relationships with white women (still the cardinal taboo in the eyes of white and black nationalists).

He assured his readers, especially the eastern Left, which had the power to make celebrities of those who supported its issues, that he was a recovering racist, a former black Muslim, who read and admired Norman Mailer's *The White Negro* (the usual bit of Noble Savage gibberish), but the recurrent theme in the book is that of an eternal struggle between the black supermasculine menial and the white omnipotent administrator—a struggle that continues in various forms, to this day. While white males were on the receiving end of criticism by black writers during the sixties and early seventies, some white male writers and media commentators have since gotten even by bonding with the black feminist movement and criticizing the treatment of black women by black men.

In this war, women are regarded as bargaining chips and loot for both sides, the black ones, Amazons, the white ones, gullible Barbie dolls. A white guard objected to Cleaver having pictures of a white woman on his cell wall. This guard, like many white men, regarded all white women as their property, while black men feel that black women belong to them. Both groups were upset when the women declared that they owned their own bodies, their souls, and their minds. In *Soul on Ice* the women are either Madonnas or whores. In some gushy, heart-wringing letters, Cleaver professed his love for his lawyer, Beverly Axelrod, and her responses, printed in the book, were equally cloying.

Cleaver was first pushed as a celebrity by the New York Old Left and its branches in Northern California and Los Angeles. They had given up on the worker (at the time depicted by Robert Crumb and other underground cartoonists as a bigoted, flagwaving, Budweiser-guzzling hard hat and incipient Reagan Democrat) and in his place substituted the black prisoner as proxy in their fight against capitalism. In the *New York Times Magazine*, in an article that was preceded by a quote of mine that if Thomas Jefferson were around he'd be reading Eldridge Cleaver, Old Lefter Harvey Swados referred to Cleaver as the quintessential American. And he is, in the sense that Tom Sawyer, Huckleberry Finn, Ellison's Rinehart, Gerald Vizenor's Bearheart, and the creatures in those African–Native American animal tales who use guile, wit, and flattery to accomplish their ends are quintessential Americans. (In a classic tale a snake says to a benefactor, who expresses dismay after being bitten by the creature it has rescued, "You knew I was a snake.")

I was in Leonard Bernstein's apartment the week before he gave a party for the Black Panthers (a party made notorious by Thomas Wolfe, in whose latest book, *The Bonfire of the Vanities*, blacks are likened to rats) and Bernstein, pointing to Cleaver's book on the coffee table, asked me had I read him. I hadn't read him at the time, but figured that the New York Left was going to make use of Cleaver and the Panthers, for whom he became Minister of Information. I said so publicly. I was hip to the eastern intelligentsia which was dabbling in Marxism at the time and knew of the intelligentsia's "contradictions." Leonard Bernstein, who was sympathetic to the Panthers' cause, was having trouble with black musicians like Arthur Davis, who accused the conductor of discriminating against black musicians.

After the collapse of the Black Panther party, Cleaver, like Doug Street in Wendell Harris's extraordinary film *Chameleon Street*, went through different changes. In *Soul on Ice* he refers to himself as though he were different people: "I was very familiar with the Eldridge who came to prison, but that Eldridge no longer exists. And the one I am now is a stranger to me." He went into exile and lived in Cuba, Algeria, and France (where it was rumored that he shared a mistress with a prime minister), returned to become a fundamentalist minister, campaigned for the Republican senatorial nomination, designed clothes that highlighted the penis, and began a church devoted to the male reproductive organs and the preservation of sperm. Recently, he was criticized for poaching curbside recyclables, on behalf of his "Church of the Great Taker," that were intended for the nonprofit Berkeley Ecology Center. Once in a while he appears in the local newspapers, in trouble with the law over some petty charge, or for assisting an elderly white woman from being evicted from her house. Sometimes the local media uses him for comic relief.

He wrote a second book, *Soul on Fire*, which in many ways was as absorbing as *Soul on Ice*. But, like Till Eulenspiegel, he had worked his tricks too many times; the book was ignored and his description of his conversion to Christianity, mocked (he said that he joined the fundamentalists because they had brought him from exile, and if the Panthers had brought him home he would have sided with them).

Each group of Cleaver's supporters claimed that it had been taken by the head of the Church of the Great Taker, but it could be argued that they did quite a bit of betraying themselves. Besides, if they had read *Soul on Ice* instead of marveling at the fact that a black prisoner could hold such a gifted mind they would have learned that Cleaver's most persistent intellectual quality is doubt. And doubters aren't followers and are distrustful of structures, which is what perhaps inspired Amiri Baraka to describe Eldridge Cleaver as a "bohemian anarchist," a highfalutin name for the trickster.

His supporters used him, but he used them too. And who could blame a black man for using his wits to get out of one of these Nazi-like pits, often guarded by depraved sadists, where this society had cast him to rot and die at the age of twenty-two? Today, thousands of young black men like Cleaver languish in the country's prisons while the inside traders receive light sentences for nearly wrecking the economic system, while the Justice Department spends millions of dollars to trap a black mayor on a misdemeanor charge, while the BCCI money-laundering enterprise, perhaps the biggest drug scandal in history, is ignored, and in a society where most of the S&Lers won't even come to trial.

Had Cleaver remained in prison without the publicity that ultimately led to his release, he'd probably be dead.

By the end of the sixties the Left and the Right, like lovers, began to trot toward each other so that at the beginning of the eighties they were in bed together. Cleaver hurt James Baldwin (so did I) who was deemed politically incorrect by the young lions who were so paranoid about their manhood. Baldwin was also considered a sellout, and "radical chic" was the expression introduced by the late Seymour Krim to chastise Baldwin for permitting *The Fire Next Time* to be published in the *New Yorker*, the epitome of uptown pretensions and snobbery. Baldwin pretended that he didn't care. Baldwin used to tell me that he didn't mind my criticisms of him because, "Ishmael, you're a writer, but that Cleaver. . . ." Cleaver and Baldwin underestimated each other. Far from being a clown, Cleaver is a writer, too, and though Baldwin comes in for some vicious criticism from Cleaver, it is obvious that *Soul on Ice* is influenced by Baldwin's flamboyantly eloquent taxidermist's style, just as Baldwin's *If Beale Street Could Talk* reminds one of Eldridge Cleaver.

But Baldwin proved to be more reliable than Norman Mailer, who is championed in this book. Baldwin went to his grave protesting the injustices committed against the underdogs of the world by forces and institutions more powerful than they, while, by the end of the sixties, Norman Mailer was saying that he was "tired of Negroes and their rights," and there is only a thin intellectual partition between his recent comments blaming blacks for the drug trade and those of the new policy elite at the *New Republic* (whose neoconservative about-face can be gauged by the fact that an endorsement from the pre–Right wing *New Republic* appears on the paperback edition of *Soul on Ice*. The publisher, Martin Peretz, who seems to spend all of his waking hours making up fibs about the "underclass," formerly had ties with SDS, wouldn't you know). Cleaver supporter, the *New York Review of Books*, which, during the sixties, carried instructions on how to make a Molotov cocktail, now prints long, unreadable pieces by Andrew Hacker denouncing affirmative action and seeking to divide Asian Americans from black Americans with ignorant comments about the model minority.

The New Left, which sought to use the Black Panthers to foment a violent revolution, by the late seventies had joined the Reagan consensus, or had begun to wallow in a selfish consumerism. Others became Second Thoughters, denouncing the Panthers before neoconservative banquets of the sort that get carried on C-Span. Sylvia Ann Hewlett describes the spirit of postrevolutionary America as that of "a therapeutic mentality . . . which focuses on the self rather than a set of external obligations."

Cleaver believed that the younger generation of whites would be wooed away from their omnipotent administrator fathers by African American dance and music. Whites began to dance better, but that didn't make them more humanistic. Rock and roll made billions for white artists and became the entertainment at white-power rallies and accompanied the black-hating lyrics of Axl Rose. Even the creator of the Willie Horton campaign, Lee Atwater, received a better review in the *New York Times* for his rock and roll music than Miles Davis. *Rolling Stone*, which was the voice of the counterculture during the sixties, went Republican and upscale, and Malcolm X, the symbol of black sixties manhood, has been "outed" in a new book by Bruce Perry.

The groups that are the subjects of so much abuse in *Soul on Ice*, women and gays (the Cleaver of *Soul on Ice* considers homosexuality to be a disease), have placed their oppression front and center and

have even made villains of the former black male machos who fanta-
sized a revolution (while borrowing their strategies). These groups
could even be accused of trivializing the oppression of the white and
black underclass because once you propose that all women, including
Queen Elizabeth, or all gays, including Malcolm Forbes, are op-
pressed, then everybody is oppressed, even the omnipotent administ-
trator—white males with Ph.D.s, the new oppressed, whom the
media would have us believe are being set upon by a politically cor-
rect multiculturalism.

And now Hollywood, which poured money into Black Panther
coffers, will get its money back with interest, with a slew of films now
in the works about the Black Panthers demonstrating that Cleaver's
scientific socialism was no match for the witchcraft of capitalism.
(One of these films is being scripted by Anna Hamilton Phelan, the
writer for *Gorillas in the Mist*, the favorite film of the gestapo wing of
the LAPD.) Capitalism could even transform a group that once advo-
cated its overthrow into box office receipts and T-shirt revenue.

I always wondered what would have happened if Cleaver and
Huey Newton and the Panthers hadn't been used as pawns in a strug-
gle between the white Right, who destroyed them, and the white
Left, who piled an agenda on them that went way beyond their origi-
nal community concerns, and who viewed them as cannon fodder.
(They wanted "a nigger to pull the trigger" as one Panther put it.)
Thanks to the Panthers, the downtown Oakland political establish-
ment is black but that doesn't seem to prohibit the police from con-
tinuing to beat the shit out of black people in Oakland (and as
elsewhere in the case of these black ceremonial governments, the cash
is controlled by whites). They also elected a Congressman.

Huey Newton was shot dead in the gutter and was bitterly
denounced, before his body was even cold, by a post–New Left
Berkeley "alternative" newspaper whose editorial line mirrors the
confusion of the Left—one week printing a long piece sympathetic to
still-imprisoned Panther Geronimo Pratt, another week printing an
article favorable to University of California anthropologist Vincent
Sarvich, a member of the new oppressed, who maintains that women
and blacks are intellectually deficient because of their small brain size
(the same argument that Hitler's "scientists" used to advance against
the professor's ancestors).

In this political and cultural environment Cleaver seems a has-
been and the villains in his book, Lyndon Johnson (promoter of the
Great Society) and Barry Goldwater (who challenged the CIA's min-

ing of the Nicaraguan harbor)—in comparison to the sinister crowd in power now—seem like populists from the quaint old days of the American Weimar.

But I suspect that history is not finished with Eldridge Cleaver. If he never does another thing in his life, he wrote this book. It's not just a book about the sixties like those books and films written by his former white allies that prove that the authors were white nationalists all along because they omit, or give scant attention to, the role of blacks, who created the political and cultural matrix for that decade. The conclusion of one recent film, Mark Kitchell's *Berkeley in the Sixties*, most of whose narrators are white women, seems to be that the significance of the political and cultural upheaval of the sixties was that it led to the formation of the middle class feminist movement.

The reissue of Eldridge Cleaver's *Soul on Ice* will challenge the current bleaching out of the black influence on the cultural and political climate of the sixties. This book is a classic because it is not merely a book about that decade, regarded as demonic by some and by others as the most thrilling and humanistic of this century. *Soul on Ice* is the sixties. The smell of protest, anger, tear gas, and the sound of skull-cracking billy clubs, helicopters, and revolution are present in its pages.

The old cover's image of the lilies juxtaposed with the young prisoner's rugged face and unkempt hair is apt.

Out of the manure that American society can often be for black men, the growth and beauty of their genius cannot be repressed. Cannot be denied.

———

Eldridge Cleaver

As Minister of Information for the radical Black Panther Party, Eldridge Cleaver was the author of the bestselling memoir Soul on Ice *(1968). Having served twelve years in California state prisons, he left the United States in 1968 rather than face a return to prison because of his involvement in a Black Panther gun battle with the Oakland police. Critical of the work of authors like Baraka and Reed, Cleaver did not consider himself a member of the Black Arts Movement. This excerpt from* Soul on Ice *is from the chapter "The White Race and Its Heroes."*

FROM *SOUL ON ICE*

THIS MOST ALIENATED VIEW of America was preached by the Abolitionists, and by Harriet Beecher Stowe in her *Uncle Tom's Cabin*. But such a view of America was too distasteful to receive wide attention, and serious debate about America's image and her reality was engaged in only on the fringes of society. Even when confronted with overwhelming evidence to the contrary, most white Americans have found it possible, after steadying their rattled nerves, to settle comfortably back into their vaunted belief that America is dedicated to the proposition that all men are created equal and endowed by their Creator with certain inalienable rights—life, liberty and the pursuit of happiness. With the Constitution for a rudder and the Declaration of Independence as its guiding star, the ship of state is sailing always toward a brighter vision of freedom and justice for all.

Because there is no common ground between these two contradictory images of America, they had to be kept apart. But the moment the blacks were let into the white world—let out of the voiceless and faceless cages of their ghettos, singing, walking, talking, dancing, writing, and orating *their* image of America and Americans—the white world was suddenly challenged to match its practice to its preachments. And this is why those whites who abandon the *white* image of America and adopt the *black* are greeted with such unmitigated hostility by their elders.

For all these years whites have been taught to believe in the myth they preached, while Negroes have had to face the bitter reality of what America practiced. But without the lies and distortions, white Americans would not have been able to do the things they have done. When whites are forced to look honestly upon the objective proof of their deeds, the cement of mendacity holding white society together swiftly disintegrates. On the other hand, the core of the black world's vision remains intact, and in fact begins to expand and spread into the psychological territory vacated by the non-viable white lies, i.e., into the minds of young whites. It is remarkable how the system worked for so many years, how the majority of whites remained effectively unaware of any contradiction between their view of the world and that world itself. The mechanism by which this was rendered possible requires examination at this point.

Let us recall that the white man, in order to justify slavery and, later on, to justify segregation, elaborated a complex, all-pervasive myth which at one time classified the black man as a subhuman beast of burden. The myth was progressively modified, gradually elevating the blacks on the scale of evolution, following their slowly changing status, until the plateau of separate-but-equal was reached at the close of the nineteenth century. During slavery, the black was seen as a mindless Supermasculine Menial. Forced to do the backbreaking work, he was conceived in terms of his ability to do such work—"field niggers," etc. The white man administered the plantation, doing all the thinking, exercising omnipotent power over the slaves. He had little difficulty dissociating himself from the black slaves, and he could not conceive of their positions being reversed or even reversible.

Blacks and whites being conceived as mutually exclusive types, those attributes imputed to the blacks could not also be imputed to the whites—at least not in equal degree—without blurring the line separating the races. These images were based upon the social function of the two races, the work they performed. The ideal white man was one who knew how to use his head, who knew how to manage and control things and get things done. Those whites who were not in a position to perform these functions nevertheless aspired to them. The ideal black man was one who did exactly as he was told, and did it efficiently and cheerfully. "Slaves," said Frederick Douglass, "are generally expected to sing as well as to work." As the black man's position and function became more varied, the images of white and black, having become stereotypes, lagged behind.

The separate-but-equal doctrine was promulgated by the Supreme Court in 1896. It had the same purpose domestically as the Open Door Policy toward China in the international arena: to stabilize a situation and subordinate a non-white population so that racist exploiters could manipulate those people according to their own selfish interests. These doctrines were foisted off as *the epitome of enlightened justice, the highest expression of morality*. Sanctified by religion, justified by philosophy and legalized by the Supreme Court, separate-but-equal was enforced by day by agencies of the law, and by the

KKK & Co. under cover of night. Booker T. Washington, the Martin Luther King of his day, accepted separate-but-equal in the name of all Negroes. W. E. B. DuBois denounced it.

Separate-but-equal marked the last stage of the white man's flight into cultural neurosis, and the beginning of the black man's frantic striving to assert his humanity and equalize his position with the white. Blacks ventured into all fields of endeavor to which they could gain entrance. Their goal was to present in all fields a performance that would equal or surpass that of the whites. It was long axiomatic among blacks that a black had to be twice as competent as a white in any field in order to win grudging recognition from the whites. This produced a pathological motivation in the blacks to equal or surpass the whites, and a pathological motivation in the whites to maintain a distance from the blacks. This is the rack on which black and white Americans receive their delicious torture! At first there was the color bar, flatly denying the blacks entrance to certain spheres of activity. When this no longer worked, and blacks invaded sector after sector of American life and economy, the whites evolved other methods of keeping their distance. The illusion of the Negro's inferior nature had to be maintained.

One device evolved by the whites was to tab whatever the blacks did with the prefix "Negro." We had *Negro* literature, *Negro* athletes, *Negro* music, *Negro* doctors, *Negro* politicians, *Negro* workers. The malignant ingeniousness of this device is that although it accurately describes an objective biological fact—or, at least, a sociological fact in America—it concealed the paramount psychological fact: that to the white mind, prefixing anything with "Negro" automatically consigned it to an inferior category. A well-known example of the white necessity to deny due credit to blacks is in the realm of music. White musicians were famous for going to Harlem and other Negro cultural centers literally to steal the black man's music, carrying it back across the color line into the Great White World and passing off the watered-down loot as their own original creations. Blacks, meanwhile, were ridiculed as *Negro* musicians playing inferior coon music.

The Negro revolution at home and national liberation movements abroad have unceremoniously shattered the world of fantasy in which the whites have been living. It is painful that many do not yet see that their fantasy world has been rendered uninhabitable in the last half of the twentieth century. But it is away from this world that the white youth of today are turning. The "paper tiger" hero, James Bond, offering the whites a triumphant image of themselves, is saying what many whites want desperately to hear reaffirmed: *I am still the White Man, lord of the land, licensed to kill, and the world is still an empire at my feet.* James Bond feeds on that secret little anxiety, the psychological white backlash, felt in some degree by most whites alive. It is exasperating to see little brown men and little yellow men from the mysterious Orient, and the opaque black men of Africa (to say nothing of these impudent American Negroes!) who come to the UN and talk smart to us, who are scurrying all over *our* globe in their strange modes of dress—much as if they were new, unpleasant arrivals from another planet. Many whites believe in their ulcers that it is only a matter of time before the Marines get the signal to round up these truants and put them back securely in their cages. But it is away from this fantasy world that the white youth of today are turning.

In the world revolution now under way, the initiative rests with people of color. That growing numbers of white youth are repudiating their heritage of blood and taking people of color as their heroes and models is a tribute not only to their insight but to the resilience of the human spirit. For today the heroes of the initiative are people not usually thought of as white: Fidel Castro, Che Guevara, Kwame Nkrumah, Mao Tse-tung, Gamal Abdel Nasser, Robert F. Williams, Malcolm X, Ben Bella, John Lewis, Martin Luther King, Jr., Robert Parris Moses, Ho Chi Minh, Stokely Carmichael, W. E. B. DuBois, James Forman, Chou En-lai.

The white youth of today have begun to react to the fact that the "American Way of Life" is a fossil of history. What do they care if their old baldheaded and crew-cut elders don't dig their caveman mops? They couldn't care less about the old, stiffassed honkies who don't like their new dances: Frug, Monkey, Jerk, Swim, Watusi. All they know is that it feels good to swing to way-out body-rhythms instead of dragassing across the dance floor like zombies to the dead beat of mind-smothered Mickey Mouse music. Is it any wonder that the youth have lost all respect for their elders, for law and order, when for as long as they can remember all they've witnessed is a monumental bickering over the Negro's place in American society and the right of people around the world to be left alone by outside powers? They have witnessed the law, both domestic and international, being spat upon by those who do not like its terms. Is it any wonder, then, that they feel justified, by sitting-in and freedom riding, in breaking laws made by lawless men? Old funny-styled, zipper-mouthed political night riders know nothing but to haul out an investigating committee *to look into the disturbance* to find the cause of the unrest among the youth. Look into a mirror! The cause is you, Mr. and Mrs. Yesterday, you with your forked tongues.

A young white today cannot help but recoil from the base deeds of his people. On every side, on every continent, he sees racial arrogance, savage brutality toward the conquered and subjugated people, genocide; he sees the human cargo of the slave trade; he sees the systematic extermination of American Indians; he sees the civilized nations of Europe fighting in imperial depravity over the lands of other people—and over possession of the very people themselves. There seems to be no end to the ghastly deeds of which his people are guilty. *GUILTY.* The slaughter of the Jews by the Germans, the dropping of atomic bombs on the Japanese people—these deeds weigh heavily upon the prostrate souls and tumultuous consciences of the white youth. The white heroes, their hands dripping with blood, are dead.

The young whites know that the colored people of the world, Afro-Americans included, do not seek revenge for their suffering. They seek the same things the white rebel wants: an end to war and exploitation. Black and white, the young rebels are free people, free in a way that Americans have never been before in the history of their country. And they are outraged.

There is in America today a generation of white youth that is truly worthy of a black man's respect, and this is a rare event in the foul annals of American history. From the beginning of the contact between blacks and whites, there has been very little reason for a black man to respect a white, with such exceptions as John Brown and others lesser known. But respect commands itself and it can neither be given nor withheld when it is due. If a man like Malcolm X could change and repudiate racism, if I myself and other former Muslims can change, if young whites can change, then there is hope for America. It was certainly strange to find myself, while steeped in the doctrine that all whites were devils by nature, commanded by the heart to applaud and acknowledge respect for these young whites—despite the fact that they are descendants of the masters and I the descendant of slaves. The sins of the fathers are visited upon the heads of the children—but only if the children continue in the evil deeds of the fathers.

Allen Polite

*What happened in the early 1960s, before the Black Arts Move-
ment, when an African-American poet decided that he would no
longer tolerate the racial prejudice he encountered in the United
States? Like W. E. B. Du Bois, Richard Wright, and James Bald-
win before him, the writer and artist Allen Polite left the country in
1964 to settle in Europe. Born in 1932 in Newark, New Jersey,
Polite served in Japan during the Korean War. A boyhood friend of
LeRoi Jones, Polite settled in Greenwich Village after his discharge
and began studying aesthetics and Asian philosophy at Columbia
University on the GI Bill. He also worked for the United Nations
as a code scrambler, where he was given a special line to the UN
secretary-general in case of emergency.*

In The Autobiography of LeRoi Jones, *Amiri Baraka de-
scribed visiting Polite and his wife, Charlene, at their apartment on
Bedford Street in the late 1950s. "When Charlene, Allen's wife at
the time, served cheese omelet and black bread along with ale, it was
a work of art, it was the sheerest revelation. The conversations one
heard in this home, which, both in their form and content, were in-
triguing and positive, were something to be found out and emu-
lated." In Baraka's 1969 poem "Numbers, Letters," he could have
been thinking of Allen Polite living in Scandinavia five years after
he had left New York City.*

*Jotting down poems on notepads, receipts, and envelopes, Po-
lite reworked them over and over again on flimsy typewriting paper
with multiple corrections. Jones took a few of them for the magazine*
Yugen, *which he published with his wife, Hettie. Other poems by
Polite were included in Paul Bremon's anthology* Sixes and Sevens
(1962) and Langston Hughes's New Negro Poets *(1964). That
year Polite organized and sponsored the exhibition "10 American
Negro Artists Living and Working in Europe" at Den Frie, the
largest gallery in Copenhagen. In Polite's introduction to the cata-
log, he wrote that*

> *Europe is realizing here through this exhibition an
> unprecedented phenomenon in art experiences. Ten*

Americans, not just any ten, but ten Black Americans,
that is ten social curios with their "circus animals all on
show," are gathered under one tent, which tent is pitched
rather far from their shores. There is something in that, I
am certain, but what?

Supporting himself as a theatrical set designer and painter, Po-
lite settled in Stockholm, Sweden. After his death from pancreatic
cancer in 1993, his widow, Helene Polite, edited two collections of
Allen Polite's poetry—Poems *(1996) and* Looka Here, Now!
(1997). The selections here are from these volumes.

SONG

When I sing this song without accompaniment
      I can hear the silence the emptiness
When I sing this song in which the only instrument
      is my voice

                my voice which comes over the lips
      as a man comes out of a desert
            just near death then near life

      I know why man sang before he talked
        Why he sings before he walks
        Why he hates to be a slave
        Why he is singing in the grave

I know what it is to long for
      that which we have never known

      I know why man sang before he talked
        Why he sings before he walks
        Why he hates to be a slave
        Why he is singing in the grave

When your voice joins mine, as something coming
      to meet the dead
See we then the genius of man? See him strike the first
instrument?
See him paint paradise as bird song?
See him paint wings on loaves of bread?

I know why man sang before he talked
    Why he sings before he walks
    Why he hates to be a slave
    Why he is singing in the grave

And when we sing together without effort
    the stops in the greatest organ are like child's play
When we are singing into each others mouths and
hearing
      songs
Unison is night changing to day—

I know why man sang before he talked
    Why he sings before he walks
    Why he hates to be a slave
    Why he is singing in the grave

WHY THEY ARE IN EUROPE?

In the artist's unwritten tradition
he very often wonders as he goes abroad
from where he is
and thereby embellishes, through his images
of the eccentricities of cultures, his art.
His search is for meaning, for truth,
for beauty, for god.
Each is an artist first and has no
flags in his pocket

[WE KNEW OUR LONELINESS
AND TOLD IT]

We knew our loneliness and told it.
Always man, we talked of things
That we had known in the other lands,
And missed.

Men speak of cars and shoes,
Of houses and joints, of jobs and

Professions, of the Arts,
Of women.
We speak of everything man!

Always
We talked and played
And bitched and laughed
And sweat and hurt,
And cried, and always,
Man, we laughed!

That's how we sprang to
That new life, and will
Spring to others; like
Young lions; strong and
Tumbled down, and
Loud and boastful.

———————————————

PART EIGHT

WITH OUR ARMS UPRAISED: THE WOMEN'S MOVEMENT AND THE SEXUAL REVOLUTION

*In America, recent events have forced us to acknowledge at last that
the relationship between the sexes is indeed a political one. . . .
What goes largely unexamined, often unacknowledged (yet is insti-
tutionalized nonetheless) in our social order, is the birthright prior-
ity whereby males rule females. . . . However muted its present
appearance may be, sexual dominion obtains nevertheless as per-
haps the most pervasive ideology of our culture and provides its
most fundamental concept of power.*

KATE MILLETT, SEXUAL POLITICS (1969)

THE EMINENT WOMEN'S RIGHTS ADVOCATE Pauli Murray believed
that "the catalytic event which signaled the rebirth of feminism in the
United States" was a meeting between former First Lady Eleanor
Roosevelt and President John F. Kennedy early in 1961. As historian
Lynne Olson described the event in *Freedom's Daughters* (2001):

> Roosevelt, who had supported women's rights as fervently
> as she had endorsed the black civil rights struggle, was an-
> gered by what she considered Kennedy's abysmal record on
> appointing women to positions in his administration. He
> was the first President since Herbert Hoover not to select a
> woman for his cabinet and had named only ten women to
> policy-making jobs, none of them especially high-ranking
> or visible. That was unacceptable, Roosevelt told the young
> President, and presented him with a three-page list of the
> names of women who she said should be considered for ex-
> ecutive appointments. Kennedy countered her proposal with
> one of his own: He was about to announce the formation of
> a presidential commission on the status of women. Would
> Mrs. Roosevelt be its chair?
>
> The seventy-six-year-old Roosevelt was seriously ill,
> but she agreed to Kennedy's request. He may have thought
> he was getting rid of two troublesome birds with one stone:
> silencing the outspoken former First Lady by bringing her
> into the administration tent and ridding himself of the

"woman question" by creating a commission that would meet for years and accomplish nothing. What happened instead was an unprecedented national focus on the role of women in America, and the creation of a nationwide women's network, under Eleanor Roosevelt's aegis, to seek changes in the way women were treated.

In 1963, the President's Commission on the Status of Women issued a report that made recommendations for constructive action on employment, insurance, tax laws, and legal treatment, stating unequivocally that women were discriminated against in almost every area of American life. The report sold more than sixty-four thousand copies and hastened the drafting of new legislation and the formation of a new Women's Rights Movement. That same year, another book about the status of women sold even more copies and reached even more people.

Betty Friedan

In 1963 Betty Friedan published The Feminine Mystique, *an eloquent plea for all Americans to reconsider the myth that women were fulfilled in their role as housewives. Friedan's book, as the critic Alan Wolfe remarked, "remains one of the most powerful works of popular nonfiction written in America. Not only did the book sell in the millions but it has long been credited with launching the contemporary feminist movement."*

In Friedan's preface, she described her confusion as a college-educated mother of three small children, discovering that she felt guilty spending time away from home. She had embarked upon a research project, interviewing her classmates fifteen years after their graduation from Smith College, in an effort to find out if they were satisfied with their lives. Friedan had come to feel that "there was a strange discrepancy between the reality of our lives as women and the image to which we were trying to conform, the image that I came to call the feminine mystique. I wondered if other women faced this schizophrenic split, and what it meant."

Drawing upon the work of distinguished European women intellectuals, especially the French writer Simone de Beauvoir, whose book The Second Sex *(1949) had argued that women's roles are imposed upon them by society, not determined by biology, Friedan translated her research about the nature-versus-nurture controversy into language understood by a popular audience.*

The critic Daniel Horowitz has argued that just as the radical politics of the 1940s and 1950s shaped the Civil Rights Movement, they also influenced the emergence of feminism in Friedan's writing of The Feminine Mystique. *During the 1940s, Friedan worked as a labor journalist and author of pamphlets, attending meetings of the United Electrical, Radio and Machine Workers of America, known as UE, one of the most radical American unions in the postwar era. In 1952, she wrote the pamphlet* UE Fights for Women Workers, *a brilliant manual for fighting wage discrimination, in which she argued that the women in the union shouldn't be treated as an inferior species. Friedan has denied that her feminism arose from her earlier advocacy of left-wing ideology, maintaining that the men involved in union politics "were every bit as male chauvinist as the rest of the world." As Horowitz understands, most readers of Friedan's book prefer to view her as a "self-actualizing individual shaped primarily by personal experiences as a suburban housewife and mother. They like Friedan's own version of her life because they advocate a feminism grounded in middle-class experience, humanist psychology, and a celebration of the ability of the heroic and isolated self to discover truth that is more personal than political or at least not political in terms set by socialist feminists."*

In an article titled "It Changed My Life" (1976), Friedan offered her view of how she got the inspiration for The Feminine Mystique: *"In a certain sense it was almost accidental—coincidental—that I wrote* The Feminine Mystique, *and in another sense my whole life had prepared me to write that book; all the pieces of my own life came together for the first time in the writing of it."*
"The Problem That Has No Name" is the opening chapter of her book.

FROM *THE FEMININE MYSTIQUE*

The Problem That Has No Name

THE PROBLEM LAY BURIED, UNSPOKEN, FOR MANY years in the minds of American women. It was a strange stirring, a sense of dissatisfaction, a yearning that women suffered in the middle of the twentieth century in the United States. Each suburban wife struggled with it alone. As she made the beds, shopped for groceries, matched slipcover material, ate peanut butter sandwiches with her children, chauffeured Cub Scouts and Brownies, lay beside her husband at night—she was afraid to ask even of herself the silent question—"Is this all?"

For over fifteen years there was no word of this yearning in the millions of words written about women, for women, in all the columns, books and articles by experts telling women their role was to seek fulfillment as wives and mothers. Over and over women heard in voices of tradition and of Freudian sophistication that they could desire no greater destiny than to glory in their own femininity. Experts told them how to catch a man and keep him, how to breastfeed children and handle their toilet training, how to cope with sibling rivalry and adolescent rebellion; how to buy a dishwasher, bake bread, cook gourmet snails, and build a swimming pool with their own hands; how to dress, look, and act more feminine and make marriage more exciting; how to keep their husbands from dying young and their sons from growing into delinquents. They were taught to pity the neurotic, unfeminine, unhappy women who wanted to be poets or physicists or presidents. They learned that truly feminine women do not want careers, higher education, political rights—the independence and the opportunities that the old-fashioned feminists fought for. Some women, in their forties and fifties, still remembered painfully giving up those dreams, but most of the younger women no longer even thought about them. A thousand expert voices applauded their femininity, their adjustment, their new maturity. All they had to do was devote their lives from earliest girlhood to finding a husband and bearing children.

By the end of the nineteen-fifties, the average marriage age of women in America dropped to 20, and was still dropping, into the teens. Fourteen million girls were engaged by 17. The proportion of women attending college in comparison with men dropping from 47 per cent in 1920 to 35 per cent in 1958. A century earlier, women had fought for higher education; now girls went to college to get a husband. By the mid-fifties, 60 per cent dropped out of college to marry, or because they were afraid too much education would be a marriage bar. Colleges built dormitories for "married students," but the students were almost always the husbands. A new degree was instituted for the wives—"Ph.T." (Putting Husband Through).

Then American girls began getting married in high school. And the women's magazines, deploring the unhappy statistics about these young marriages, urged that courses on marriage, and marriage counselors, be installed in the high schools. Girls started going steady at twelve and thirteen, in junior high. Manufacturers put out brassieres with false bosoms of foam rubber for little girls of ten. And an advertisement for a child's dress, sizes 3–6x, in the *New York Times* in the fall of 1960, said: "She Too Can Join the Man-Trap Set."

By the end of the fifties, the United States birthrate was overtaking India's. The birth-control movement, renamed Planned Parenthood, was asked to find a method whereby women who had been advised that a third or fourth baby would be born dead or defective might have it anyhow. Statisticians were especially astounded at the fantastic increase in the number of babies among college women. Where once they had two children, now they had four, five, six. Women who had once wanted careers were now making careers out of having babies. So rejoiced *Life* magazine in a 1956 paean to the movement of American women back to the home.

In a New York hospital, a woman had a nervous breakdown when she found she could not breastfeed her baby. In other hospitals, women dying of cancer refused a drug which research had proved might save their lives: its side effects were said to be unfeminine. "If I have only one life, let me live it as a blonde," a larger-than-life-sized picture of a pretty, vacuous woman proclaimed from newspaper, magazine, and drugstore ads. And across America, three out of every ten women dyed their hair blonde. They ate a chalk called Metrecal, instead of food, to shrink to the size of the thin young models. Department-store buyers reported that American women, since 1939, had become three and four sizes smaller. "Women are out to fit the clothes, instead of vice-versa," one buyer said.

Interior decorators were designing kitchens with mosaic murals and original paintings, for kitchens were once again the center of women's lives. Home sewing became a million-dollar industry. Many women no longer left their homes, except to shop, chauffeur their children, or attend a social engagement with their husbands. Girls were growing up in America without ever having jobs outside the home. In the late fifties, a sociological phenomenon was suddenly remarked: a third of American women now worked, but most were no longer young and very few were pursuing careers. They were married women who held part-time jobs, selling or secretarial, to put their husbands through school, their sons through college, or to help pay the mortgage. Or they were widows supporting families. Fewer and fewer women were entering professional work. The shortages in the nursing, social work, and teaching professions caused crises in almost every American city. Concerned over the Soviet Union's lead in the space race, scientists noted that America's greatest source of unused brain-power was women. But girls would not study physics: it was "unfeminine." A girl refused a science fellowship at Johns Hopkins to take a job in a real-estate office. All she wanted, she said, was what every other American girl wanted—to get married, have four children and live in a nice house in a nice suburb.

The suburban housewife—she was the dream image of the young American women and the envy, it was said, of women all over the world. The American housewife—freed by science and labor-saving appliances from the drudgery, the dangers of childbirth and the illnesses of her grandmother. She was healthy, beautiful, educated, concerned only about her husband, her children, her home. She had found true feminine fulfillment. As a housewife and mother, she was respected as a full and equal partner to man in his world. She was free to choose automobiles, clothes, appliances, supermarkets; she had everything that women ever dreamed of.

In the fifteen years after World War II, this mystique of feminine fulfillment became the cherished and self-perpetuating core of contemporary American culture. Millions of women lived their lives in the image of those pretty pictures of the American suburban housewife, kissing their husbands goodbye in front of the picture window, depositing their stationwagonsful of children at school, and smiling as they ran the new electric waxer over the spotless kitchen floor. They baked their own bread, sewed their own and their children's clothes, kept their new washing machines and dryers running all day. They changed the sheets on the beds twice a week instead of once, took the rug-hooking class in adult education, and pitied their poor frustrated mothers, who had dreamed of having a career. Their only dream was to be perfect wives and mothers; their highest ambition to have five children and a beautiful house, their only fight to get and keep their husbands. They had no thought for the unfeminine problems of the world outside the home; they wanted the men to make the major decisions. They gloried in their role as women, and wrote proudly on the census blank: "Occupation: housewife."

For over fifteen years, the words written for women, and the words women used when they talked to each other, while their husbands sat on the other side of the room and talked shop or politics or septic tanks, were about problems with their children, or how to keep their husbands happy, or improve their children's school, or cook chicken or make slipcovers. Nobody argued whether women were inferior or superior to men; they were simply different. Words like "emancipation" and "career" sounded strange and embarrassing; no one had used them for years. When a Frenchwoman named Simone de Beauvoir wrote a book called *The Second Sex*, an American critic commented that she obviously "didn't know what life was all about," and besides, she was talking about French women. The "woman problem" in America no longer existed.

If a woman had a problem in the 1950's and 1960's, she knew that something must be wrong with her marriage, or with herself. Other women were satisfied with their lives, she thought. What kind of a woman was she if she did not feel this mysterious fulfillment waxing the kitchen floor? She was so ashamed to admit her dissatisfaction that she never knew how many other women shared it. If she tried to tell her husband, he didn't understand what she was talking about. She did not really understand it herself. For over fifteen years women in America found it harder to talk about this problem than about sex. Even the psychoanalysts had no name for it. When a woman went to a psychiatrist for help, as many women did, she would say, "I'm so ashamed," or "I must be hopelessly neurotic." "I don't know what's wrong with women today," a suburban psychiatrist said uneasily. "I only know something is wrong because most of my patients happen to be women. And their problem isn't sexual." Most women with this problem did not go to see a psychoanalyst, however. "There's nothing wrong really," they kept telling themselves. "There isn't any problem."

But on an April morning in 1959, I heard a mother of four, having coffee with four other mothers in a suburban development fifteen miles from New York, say in a tone of quiet desperation, "the problem." And the others knew, without words, that she was not talking about a problem with her husband, or her children, or her home. Suddenly they realized they all shared the same problem, the problem that has no name. They began, hesitantly, to talk about it. Later, after they had picked up their children at nursery school and taken them home to nap, two of the women cried, in sheer relief, just to know they were not alone.

Gradually I came to realize that the problem that has no name was shared by countless women in America. As a magazine writer I often interviewed women about problems with their children, or their marriages, or their houses, or their communities. But after a while I began to recognize the telltale signs of this other problem. I saw the same signs in suburban ranch houses and split-levels on Long Island and in New Jersey and Westchester County; in colonial houses in a small Massachusetts town; on patios in Memphis; in suburban and city apartments; in living rooms in the Midwest. Sometimes I sensed the problem, not as a reporter, but as a suburban housewife, for during this time I was also bringing up my own three children in Rockland County, New York. I heard echoes of the problem in college dormitories and semi-private maternity wards, at PTA meetings and luncheons of the League of Women Voters, at suburban cocktail parties, in station wagons waiting for trains, and in snatches of conversation overheard at Schrafft's. The groping words I heard from other women, on quiet afternoons when children were at school or on quiet evenings when husbands worked late, I think I understood first as a woman long before I understood their larger social and psychological implications. . . .

It is no longer possible to ignore that voice, to dismiss the desperation of so many American women. This is not what being a woman means, no matter what the experts say. For human suffering there is a reason; perhaps the reason has not been found because the right questions have not been asked, or pressed far enough. I do not accept the answer that there is no problem because American women have luxuries that women in other times and lands never dreamed of; part of the strange newness of the problem is that it cannot be understood in terms of the age-old material problems of man: poverty, sickness, hunger, cold. The women who suffer this problem have a hunger that food cannot fill. It persists in women whose husbands are struggling internes and law clerks, or prosperous doctors and lawyers; in wives of workers and executives who make $5,000 a year or $50,000. It is not caused by lack of material advantages; it may not even be felt by women preoccupied with desperate problems of hunger, poverty or illness. And women who think it will be solved by more money, a bigger house, a second car, moving to a better suburb, often discover it gets worse.

It is no longer possible today to blame the problem on loss of femininity: to say that education and independence and equality with men have made American women unfeminine. I have heard so many women try to deny this dissatisfied voice within themselves because it does not fit the pretty picture of femininity the experts have given them. I think, in fact, that this is the first clue to the mystery: the problem cannot be understood in the generally accepted terms by which scientists have studied women, doctors have treated them, counselors have advised them, and writers have written about them. Women who suffer this problem, in whom this voice is stirring, have lived their whole lives in the pursuit of feminine fulfillment. They are not career women (although career women may have other problems); they are women whose greatest ambition has been marriage and children. For the oldest of these women, these daughters of the American middle class, no other dream was possible. The ones in their forties and fifties who once had other dreams gave them up and threw themselves joyously into life as housewives. For the youngest, the new wives and mothers, this was the only dream. They are the ones who quit high school and college to marry, or marked time in some job in which they had no real interest until they married. These women are very "feminine" in the usual sense, and yet they still suffer the problem. . . .

The fact is that no one today is muttering angrily about "women's rights," even though more and more women have gone to college. In a recent study of all the classes that have graduated from Barnard College, a significant minority of earlier graduates blamed their education for making them want "rights," later classes blamed their education for giving them career dreams, but recent graduates blamed the college for making them feel it was not enough simply to be a housewife and mother; they did not want to feel guilty if they did not read books or take part in community activities. But if education is not the cause of the problem, the fact that education somehow festers in these women may be a clue.

If the secret of feminine fulfillment is having children, never have so many women, with the freedom to choose, had so many children, in so few years, so willingly. If the answer is love, never have women searched for love with such determination. And yet there is a growing suspicion that the problem may not be sexual, though it must somehow be related to sex. I have heard from many doctors evidence of new sexual problems between man and wife—sexual hunger in wives so great their husbands cannot satisfy it. "We have made women a sex creature," said a psychiatrist at the Margaret Sanger marriage counseling clinic. "She has no identity except as a wife and mother. She does not know who she is herself. She waits all day for her husband to come home at night to make her feel alive. And now it is the husband who is not interested. It is terrible for the women, to lie there, night after night, waiting for her husband to make her feel alive." Why is there such a market for books and articles offering sexual advice? The kind of sexual orgasm which Kinsey found in statistical plenitude in the recent generations of American women does not seem to make this problem go away.

On the contrary, new neuroses are being seen among women—and problems as yet unnamed as neuroses—which Freud and his followers did not predict, with physical symptoms, anxieties, and defense mechanisms equal to those caused by sexual repression. And strange new problems are being reported in the growing generations of children whose mothers were always there, driving them around, helping them with their homework—an inability to endure pain or discipline or pursue any self-sustained goal of any sort, a devastating boredom with life. Educators are increasingly uneasy about the dependence, the lack of self-reliance, of the boys and girls who are entering college today. "We fight a continual battle to make our students assume manhood," said a Columbia dean.

A White House conference was held on the physical and muscular deterioration of American children: were they being over-nurtured? Sociologists noted the astounding organization of suburban children's lives: the lessons, parties, entertainments, play and study groups organized for them. A suburban housewife in Portland, Oregon, wondered why the children "need" Brownies and Boy Scouts out here. "This is not the slums. The kids out here have the great outdoors. I think people are so bored, they organize the children, and then try to hook everyone else on it. And the poor kids have no time left just to lie on their beds and daydream."

Can the problem that has no name be somehow related to the domestic routine of the housewife? When a woman tries to put the problem into words, she often merely describes the daily life she leads. What is there in this recital of comfortable domestic detail that could possibly cause such a feeling of desperation? Is she trapped simply by the enormous demands of her role as modern housewife: wife, mistress, mother, nurse, consumer, cook, chauffeur; expert on interior decoration, child care, appliance repair, furniture refinishing, nutrition, and education? Her day is fragmented as she rushes from dishwasher to washing machine to telephone to dryer to station wagon to supermarket, and delivers Johnny to the Little League field, takes Janey to dancing class, gets the lawnmower fixed and meets the 6:45. She can never spend more than 15 minutes on any one thing; she has no time to read books, only magazines; even if she had time, she has lost the power to concentrate. At the end of the day, she is so terribly tired that sometimes her husband has to take over and put the children to bed.

This terrible tiredness took so many women to doctors in the 1950's that one decided to investigate it. He found, surprisingly, that his patients suffering from "housewife's fatigue" slept more than an adult needed to sleep—as much as ten hours a day—and that the actual energy they expended on housework did not tax their capacity. The real problem must be something else, he decided—perhaps boredom. Some doctors told their women patients they must get out of the house for a day, treat themselves to a movie in town. Others prescribed tranquilizers. Many suburban housewives were taking tranquilizers like cough drops. "You wake up in the morning, and you feel as if there's no point in going on another day like this. So you take a tranquilizer because it makes you not care so much that it's pointless."

It is easy to see the concrete details that trap the suburban house-wife, the continual demands on her time. But the chains that bind her in her trap are chains in her own mind and spirit. They are chains made up of mistaken ideas and misinterpreted facts, of incomplete truths and unreal choices. They are not easily seen and not easily shaken off.

How can any woman see the whole truth within the bounds of her own life? How can she believe that voice inside herself, when it denies the conventional, accepted truths by which she has been living? And yet the women I have talked to, who are finally listening to that inner voice, seem in some incredible way to be groping through to a truth that has defied the experts.

I think the experts in a great many fields have been holding pieces of that truth under their microscopes for a long time without realizing it. I found pieces of it in certain new research and theoretical developments in psychological, social and biological science whose implications for women seem never to have been examined. I found many clues by talking to suburban doctors, gynecologists, obstetricians, child-guidance clinicians, pediatricians, high-school guidance counselors, college professors, marriage counselors, psychiatrists and ministers—questioning them not on their theories, but on their actual experience in treating American women. I became aware of a growing body of evidence, much of which has not been reported publicly because it does not fit current modes of thought about women—evidence which throws into question the standards of feminine normality, feminine adjustment, feminine fulfillment, and feminine maturity by which most women are still trying to live.

I began to see in a strange new light the American return to early marriage and the large families that are causing the population explosion; the recent movement to natural childbirth and breastfeeding; suburban conformity, and the new neuroses, character pathologies and sexual problems being reported by the doctors. I began to see new dimensions to old problems that have long been taken for granted among women: menstrual difficulties, sexual frigidity, promiscuity, pregnancy fears, childbirth depression, the high incidence of emotional breakdown and suicide among women in their twenties and thirties, the menopause crises, the so-called passivity and immaturity of American men, the discrepancy between women's tested intellectual abilities in childhood and their adult achievement, the changing incidence of adult sexual orgasm in American women, and persistent problems in psychotherapy and in women's education.

If I am right, the problem that has no name stirring in the minds of so many American women today is not a matter of loss of femininity or too much education, or the demands of domesticity. It is far more important than anyone recognizes. It is the key to these other new and old problems which have been torturing women and their husbands and children, and puzzling their doctors and educators for years. It may well be the key to our future as a nation and a culture. We can no longer ignore that voice within women that says: "I want something more than my husband and my children and my home."

PUBLICATION OF *The Feminine Mystique* helped to spur the recognition that women played a secondary role in American society. In 1964 Title VII of the Civil Rights Act, attempting to implement the recommendations in the report of the President's Commission on the Status of Women, barred employment discrimination by private employers, employment agencies, and unions on the basis of race, color, religion, sex, and national origin. Its enforcement was not an easy task, as the Equal Employment Opportunity Commission (EEOC) formed to deal with complaints and penalties soon learned. Two years later, after tens of thousands of complaints about gender had been received, the EEOC's inaction led to the founding of the National Organization for Women (NOW), with Betty Friedan elected president through the remainder of the 1960s.

New organizations proliferated in the early years of the Women's Movement. In 1967, the Chicago Convention of the New Left's National Conference for a New Politics resulted in the formation of two new women's liberation groups: the Westside Group in Chicago and the New York Radical Women (NYRW). In 1968 NYRW organized meetings of women who gathered to share their life stories, a process that was called "consciousness raising." These CR groups quickly spread throughout the United States and led to the formation of other radical feminist encounter groups.

By 1970 mass-market paperbacks like the New American Library's anthology *Voices from Women's Liberation,* edited by Leslie B. Tanner, included pages of "Feminist Organizations, Journals, and Newspapers" in the back of the book, including (among others) Tooth & Nail in Berkeley; Redstockings, The Group, N.Y. Radical

Feminists, Up From Under, and Rat in New York City; Southern Female Rights Union in New Orleans; Lilith in Seattle; Sojourner Truth's Disciples in Philadelphia; Ain't I A Woman? in Iowa City; and No More Fun and Games in Somerville, Massachusetts.

Kate Millett

As a Columbia University graduate student, Kate Millett was active in a number of women's liberation groups in New York City. Her book Sexual Politics, *published in 1969, was written originally as a doctoral dissertation. Millett's thesis was that "sex has a frequently neglected political aspect." Doubleday's cover for the book was a severe white, black, and red design with bold typography used for the title and author's name. In much smaller letters, almost giving the appearance of the charts used by optometrists, was the statement in capital letters:*

A
SURPRISING
EXAMINATION
OF
SOCIETY'S
MOST
ARBITRARY
FOLLY

In Sexual Politics, *Millett took on the writings of Sigmund Freud, D. H. Lawrence, Henry Miller, Norman Mailer, and Jean Genet in order to expose these authors' insidious patriarchal biases. Her intense scrutiny of their texts suggested dissection rather than analysis. Millett's book aroused a storm of controversy that intensified the debate started by other outspoken authors such as Betty Friedan and the Australian radical feminist Germaine Greer, whose* The Female Eunuch *was also a bestseller in 1969.*

FROM *SEXUAL POLITICS*

FREUD ASSUMED that the female's discovery of her sex is, in and of itself, a catastrophe of such vast proportions that it haunts a woman all through life and accounts for most aspects of her temperament. His entire psychology of women, from which all modern psychology and psychoanalysis derives heavily, is built upon an original tragic experience—born female. Purportedly, Freud is here only relaying the information supplied by women themselves, the patients who furnished his clinical data, the basis of his later generalities about all women. It was in this way, Freud believed, he had been permitted to see how women accepted the idea that to be born female is to be born "castrated":

> As we learn from psycho-analytic work, women regard themselves as wronged from infancy, as undeservedly cut short and set back; and the embitterment of so many daughters against their mothers derives, in the last analysis, from the reproach against her of having brought them into the world as women instead of as men.[1]

Assuming that this were true, the crucial question, manifestly, is to ask why this might be so. Either maleness is indeed an *inherently* superior phenomenon, and in which case its "betterness" could be empirically proved and demonstrated, or the female misapprehends and reasons erroneously that she is inferior. And again, one must ask why. What forces in her experience, her society and socialization have led her to see herself as an inferior being? The answer would seem to lie in the conditions of patriarchal society and the inferior position of women within this society. But Freud did not choose to pursue such a line of reasoning, preferring instead an etiology of childhood experience based upon the biological fact of anatomical differences.

My critique of Freud's notions of women is indebted to an unpublished summary by Frances Kamm.

1. Freud, "Some Character Types Met With in Psycho-Analysis Work" (1915) *Collected Papers of Sigmund Freud*, edited by Joan Riviere (New York: Basic Books, 1959), Vol. IV, p. 323.

While it is supremely unfortunate that Freud should prefer to bypass the more likely social hypothesis to concentrate upon the distortions of infantile subjectivity, his analysis might yet have made considerable sense were he sufficiently objective to acknowledge that woman is born female in a masculine-dominated culture which is bent upon extending its values even to anatomy and is therefore capable of investing biological phenomena with symbolic force. In much the same manner we perceive that the traumatizing circumstance of being born black in a white racist society invests skin color with symbolic value while telling us nothing about racial traits as such.

In dismissing the wider cultural context of feminine dissatisfaction and isolating it in early childhood experience, Freud again ignored the social context of childhood by locating a literal feminine "castration" complex in the child's discovery of the anatomical differentiation between the sexes. Freud believed he had found the key to feminine experience—in that moment when girls discover they are "castrated"—a "momentous discovery which little girls are destined to make":

> They notice the penis of a brother or playmate, strikingly visible and of large proportions, at once recognize it as the superior counterpart of their own small and inconspicuous organ, and from that time forward fall a victim to envy for the penis.[2]

There are several unexplained assumptions here: why is the girl instantly struck by the proposition that bigger is better? Might she just as easily, reasoning from the naïveté of childish narcissism, imagine the penis is an excrescence and take her own body as norm? Boys clearly do, as Freud makes clear, and in doing so respond to sexual enlightenment not with the reflection that their own bodies are peculiar, but, far otherwise, with a "horror of the mutilated creature or triumphant contempt for her."[3] Secondly, the superiority of this "superior counterpart," which the girl is said to "recognize at once" in the penis, is assumed to relate to the autoerotic satisfactions of childhood; but here again the child's experience provides no support for such an assumption.

---

2. Freud, "Some Psychological Consequences of the Anatomical Distinction Between the Sexes" (1925), *Collected Papers*, Vol. V, p. 190.

3. *Ibid.*, p. 191.

Much of Freudian theory rests upon this moment of discovery and one is struck how, in the case of the female, to recapitulate the peculiar drama of penis envy is to rehearse again the fable of the Fall, a Fall that is Eve's alone.[4] As children, male and female first inhabit a paradisiacal playground where roles are interchangeable, active and passive, masculine and feminine. Until the awesome lapsarian moment when the female discovers her inferiority, her castration, we are asked to believe that she had assumed her clitoris a penis. One wonders why. Freud believes it is because she masturbated with it, and he assumes that she will conclude that what is best for such purposes must be a penis.[5] Freud insists upon calling the period of clitoral autoeroticism "phallic" in girls.

Moreover, the revelation which Freud imagined would poison female life is probably, in most cases, a glimpse of a male playmate urinating or having a bath. It is never explained how the girl child makes the logical jump from the sight of bathing or urination to knowledge that the boy masturbates with this novel article. Even should her first sight of the penis occur in masturbatory games, Freud's supposition that she could judge this foreign item to be more conducive to autoerotic pleasure than her own clitoris (she having no possible experience of penile autoeroticism as males have none of clitoral) is groundless. Yet Freud believed that female autoeroticism declines as a result of enlightenment, finding in this "yet another surprising effect of penis-envy, or of the discovery of the inferiority of the clitoris."[6] Here, as is so often the case, one cannot separate Freud's account of how a child reasons from how Freud himself reasons, and his own

---

4. Not only has Adam grace within his loins to assure him he belongs to a superior species, but even his later fears of castration which come to him after a glimpse of the "mutilated creature" cause him to repress his Oedipal desires (out of fear of a castrating father's revenge) and in the process develop the strong super-ego which Freud believes accounts for what he took to be the male's inevitable and transcendent moral and cultural superiority.

5. Because she feels free, equal, and active then, Freud says "the little girl is a little man." "Femininity," p. 118. So strong is Freud's masculine bias here that it has obliterated linguistic integrity: the autoerotic state might as well, in both cases, be called "clitoral" for all the light shed by these terms. Freud's usage is predicated on the belief that masturbation is the active pursuit of pleasure, and activity masculine *per se*. "We are entitled to keep to our view that in the phallic phase of girls the clitoris is the leading erotogenic zone." *Ibid*.

6. "Some Psychological Consequences of the Anatomical Distinction Between the Sexes," p. 193.

language, invariably pejorative, tends to confuse the issue irremediably. Indeed, since he has no objective proof of any consequence to offer in support of his notion of penis envy or of a female castration complex,[7] one is struck by how thoroughly the subjectivity in which all these events are cast tends to be Freud's own, or that of a strong masculine bias, even of a rather gross male-supremacist bias.[8]

This habitual masculine bias of Freud's own terms and diction, and the attitude it implies, is increased and further emphasized by his followers: Deutsch refers to the clitoris as an "inadequate substitute" for the penis; Karl Abraham refers to a "poverty in external genitals" in the female, and all conclude that even bearing children can be but a poor substitute for a constitutional inadequacy.[9] As Klein observes in her critique of Freud, it is a curious hypothesis that "one half of humanity should have biological reasons to feel at a disadvantage for not having what the other half possess (but not vice versa)."[10] It is especially curious to imagine that half the race should attribute their clear and obvious social-status inferiority to the crudest biological reasons when so many more promising social factors are involved.

It would seem that Freud has managed by this highly unlikely hypothesis to assume that young females negate the validity, and even, to some extent, the existence, of female sexual characteristics altogether. Surely the first thing all children must notice is that mother

---

7. The entirety of Freud's clinical data always consists of his analysis of patients and his own self-analysis. In the case of penis envy he has remarkably little evidence from patients, and his description of masculine contempt and feminine grief upon the discovery of sexual differences is extraordinarily autobiographical. Little Hans (Freud's own grandson), a five-year-old boy with an obsessive concern for his "widdler," furnishes the rest of the masculine data. Though an admirable topic of precise clinical research, it was and is remarkably difficult for Freud, or anyone else, to make generalizations about how children first come to sexual knowledge, family and cultural patterns being so diverse, further complicated by the host of variable factors within individual experience, such as the number, age, and sex of siblings, the strength and consistency of the nakedness taboo, etc.

8. Ernest Jones aptly described Freud's attitude here as "phallocentric." There is something behind Freud's assumptions reminiscent of the ancient misogynist postulate that females are but incomplete or imperfect males—e.g., deformed humans, the male being accepted as the norm—a view shared by Augustine, Aquinas, etc.

9. Karl Abraham, "Manifestations of the Female Castration Complex," *International Journal of Psychoanalysis*, Vol. 3, March 1922.

10. Klein, *op. cit.*, pp. 83–84.

has breasts, while father has none. What is possibly the rather impressive effect of childbirth on young minds is here overlooked, together with the girl's knowledge not only of her clitoris, but her vagina as well.

In formulating the theory of penis envy, Freud not only neglected the possibility of a social explanation for feminine dissatisfaction but precluded it by postulating a literal jealousy of the organ whereby the male is distinguished. As it would appear absurd to charge adult women with these values, the child, and a drastic experience situated far back in childhood, are invoked. Nearly the entirety of feminine development, adjusted or maladjusted, is now to be seen in terms of the cataclysmic moment of discovered castration.

So far, Freud has merely pursued a line of reasoning he attributes, rightly or wrongly, to the subjectivity of female youth. Right or wrong, his account purports to be little more than description of what girls erroneously believe. But there is prescription as well in the Freudian account. For while the discovery of her castration is purported to be a universal experience in the female, her response to this fate is the criterion by which her health, her maturity and her future are determined through a rather elaborate series of stages: "After a woman has become aware of the wound to her narcissism, she develops, like a scar, a sense of inferiority. When she has passed beyond her first attempt at explaining her lack of a penis as being a punishment personal to herself and has realized that that sexual character is a universal one, she begins to share the contempt felt by men for a sex which is the lesser in so important a respect."[11] The female first blames her mother, "who sent her into the world so insufficiently equipped" and who is "almost always held responsible for her lack of a penis."[12] Again, Freud's own language makes no distinction here between fact and feminine fantasy. It is not enough the girl reject her own sex however; if she is to mature, she must redirect her self positively toward a masculine object. This is designated as the beginning of the Oedipal stage in the female. We are told that the girl now gives up the hope of impregnating her mother, an ambition Freud attributes to her. (One wonders how youth has discovered conception, an elaborate and subtle process which children do not discover by them-

---

11. "Some Psychological Consequences of the Anatomical Distinction Between the Sexes," p. 192.
12. *Ibid.*, p. 193.

selves, and not all primitive adults can fathom.) The girl is said to assume her female parent has mutilated her as a judgment on her general unworthiness, or possibly for the crime of masturbation, and now turns her anxious attention to her father.[13]

At this stage of her childhood the little girl at first expects her father to prove magnanimous and award her a penis. Later, disappointed in this hope, she learns to content herself with the aspiration of bearing his baby. The baby is given out as a curious item; it is actually a penis, not a baby at all: "the girl's libido slips into position by means—there is really no other way to put it—of the equation 'penis-child.' "[14] Although she will never relinquish some hope of acquiring a penis ("we ought to recognize this wish for a penis as being *par excellence* a feminine one")[15] a baby is as close to a penis as the girl shall get. The new penis wish is metamorphosed into a baby, a quaint feminine-coated penis, which has the added merit of being a respectable ambition. (It is interesting that Freud should imagine the young female's fears center about castration rather than rape—a phenomenon which girls are in fact, and with reason, in dread of, since it happens to them and castration does not.) Girls, he informs us, now relinquish some of their anxiety over their castration, but never cease to envy and resent penises[16] and so while "impotent" they remain in the world a constant hazard to the well-provided male. There are overtones here of a faintly capitalist antagonism between the haves and the have nots. This seems to account for the considerable fear of women inherent in Freudian ideology and the force of an accusation of penis envy when leveled at mature women.

The Freudian "family romance," domestic psychodrama more horrific than a soap opera, continues. The archetypal girl is now flung into the Oedipal stage of desire for her father, having been persuaded of the total inadequacy of her clitoris, and therefore of her sex and her self. The boy, meanwhile, is so aghast by the implications of sexual enlightenment that he at first represses the information. Later, he can absorb it only by accompanying the discovery of sexual differenti-

---

13. The description of female psychological development is from Freud's *Three Contributions to the Theory of Sex*, "Femininity," "Some Psychological Consequences of the Anatomical Distinction Between the Sexes," and "Female Sexuality."

14. "Some Psychological Consequences of the Anatomical Distinction Between the Sexes," p. 195.

15. "Femininity," p. 128.

16. See "Female Sexuality" (1931), *Collected Works*, Vol. V, pp. 252–72.

ation with an overpowering contempt for the female. It is difficult to understand how, setting aside the social context, as Freud's theory does so firmly, a boy could ever become this convinced of the superiority of the penis. Yet Freud assures us that "as a result of the discovery of women's lack of a penis they [females] are debased in value for girls just as they are for boys and later perhaps for men."[17]

Conflict with the father warns the boy that the castration catastrophe might occur to him as well. He grows wary for his own emblem and surrenders his sexual desires for his mother out of fear.[18] Freud's exegesis of the neurotic excitements of nuclear family life might constitute, in itself, considerable evidence of the damaging effects of this institution, since through the parents, it presents to the very young a set of primary sexual objects who are a pair of adults, with whom intercourse would be incestuous were it even physically possible.

While Freud strongly prescribes that all lingering hopes of acquiring a penis be abandoned and sublimated in maternity, what he recommends is merely a displacement, since even maternal desires rest upon the last vestige of penile aspiration. For, as she continues to mature, we are told, the female never gives up the hope of a penis, now always properly equated with a baby. Thus men grow to love women, or better yet, their idea of women, whereas women grow to love babies.[19] It is said that the female doggedly continues her sad phallic quest in childbirth, never outgrowing her Oedipal circumstance of wanting a penis by having a baby. "Her happiness is great if later on this wish for a baby finds fulfilment in reality, and quite especially so if the baby is a little boy who brings the longed-for penis with him."[20] Freudian logic has succeeded in converting childbirth, an impressive female accomplishment, and the only function its rationale permits her, into nothing more than a hunt for a male organ. It somehow becomes the male prerogative even to give birth, as babies are but surrogate penises. The female is bested at the only function Freudian theory recommends for her, reproduction. Furthermore, her libido is actually said to be too small to qualify her as a constructive agent here, since Freud repeatedly states she has less sexual drive than the male.

---

17. "Femininity," p. 127.
18. "Some Psychological Consequences of the Anatomical Distinction Between the Sexes" and elsewhere in connection with the Oedipus complex in males.
19. "Femininity," p. 134.
20. *Ibid.*, p. 128.

Woman is thus granted very little validity even within her limited existence and second-rate biological equipment: were she to deliver an entire orphanage of progeny, they would only be so many dildoes.

Muriel Rukeyser

In the early years of the Women's Movement in the United States, poetry rather than fiction was the genre preferred by writers. Best-selling American feminist novels such as Sue Kaufman's Diary of a Mad Housewife *(1967) were the exception in the 1960s. To the next decade belongs the outpouring of fiction and nonfiction books exploring the radicalization of women's consciousness and the evolution of new gender roles that has continued to our own day, beginning not only with mainstream novels as popular as Erica Jong's bestseller* Fear of Flying *(1973), but also "casebooks" as obscure as M. F. Beal's small-press study of Patricia Hearst in* Safe House: A Casebook Study of Revolutionary Feminism in the 1970's *(1976).*

In the Sixties, women writers from an earlier generation, such as the English novelist Doris Lessing in The Golden Notebook *(1962) and the American poet Muriel Rukeyser in "Poem," voiced their reaction to the twentieth century's unprecedented violence and destruction, expressing their need to describe the social realities of the immediate present along with their desire to forge relationships on a new basis. In Rukeyser's preface to her* Collected Poems *(1976), she reflected on the social changes from when she first began to read collections of poetry as a young girl: "I loved the collected poems I found—they invited me through the poems of all the years of a loved poet. There were two differences then from today's books: the poets were all dead, and all were men."*

POEM

I lived in the first century of world wars.
Most mornings I would be more or less insane,
The newspapers would arrive with their careless stories,
The news would pour out of various devices
Interrupted by attempts to sell products to the unseen.
I would call my friends on other devices;
They would be more or less mad for similar reasons.
Slowly I would get to pen and paper,
Make my poems for others unseen and unborn.
In the day I would be reminded of those men and women
Brave, setting up signals across vast distances,
Considering a nameless way of living, of almost unimagined
    values.
As the lights darkened, as the lights of night brightened,
We would try to imagine them, try to find each other.
To construct peace, to make love, to reconcile
Waking with sleeping, ourselves with each other,
Ourselves with ourselves. We would try by any means
To reach the limits of ourselves, to reach beyond ourselves,
To let go the means, to wake.

I lived in the first century of these wars.

Sylvia Plath

*The two American women poets whose work in the 1960s perhaps
most dramatically suggested the radical disjunctions of women's lives
in the postwar era before the emergence of the Women's Movement*

are Anne Sexton and Sylvia Plath. In 1970 Sexton told the story of their friendship in a candid essay, "The Barfly Ought to Sing." Both grew up in Wellesley, a suburb of Boston, but they met for the first time and became friends after they had graduated from college, when they both audited Robert Lowell's late-afternoon creative writing class at Boston University in the winter-spring of 1959. Another young poet, George Starbuck, was with them. As Sexton remembered,

> *. . . we orbited around the class silently. Silence was wiser, when we could command it. We tried, each one in his own manner; sometimes letting our poems come up, as for a butcher, as for a lover. Both went on. We kept as quiet as possible in view of the father.*
>
> *Then, after the class, we would pile in the front seat of my old Ford and I would drive quickly through the traffic to, or near, The Ritz. I would always park illegally in a LOADING ONLY ZONE, telling them gaily, "It's okay, because we are only going to get loaded!" Off we'd go, each on George's arm, into The Ritz to drink three or four or two martinis. George even has a line about this in his first book of poems,* Bone Thoughts. *He wrote,* I weave with two sweet ladies out of The Ritz. *Sylvia and I, such sleep mongers, were those two sweet ladies.*

Hoping that the white-coated waiters who seated them on "red leather chairs around polite little tables" would think them celebrities, the three poets piled their books and manuscripts on the thick carpet at their feet and made themselves comfortable before they ordered their first round of martinis. Hungry and wired after their class with Lowell, they sipped their drinks while they ferociously sampled the free potato chips in the silver bowl at the center of their table. Sometimes they devoured five bowls of chips before they left the Ritz to walk to a cheap restaurant nearby in downtown Boston, where they pooled their remaining money to order the seventy-cent dinner special.

Over their martinis at the Ritz, Sexton recalled, she and Sylvia often "would talk at length about our first suicides; at length, in detail and in depth between the free potato chips . . . It is a wonder that we didn't depress George with our egocentricity. Instead, I think, we three were stimulated by it, even George, as if

*death made each of us a little more real at the moment." In her es-
say, Sexton tried to explain their mutual fascination with suicide by
inserting a poem she had written for Sylvia, "Wanting to Die,"
which included the lines*

> *But suicides have a special language.*
> *Like carpenters they want to know* which tools.
> *They never ask* why build.

*Sexton understood how hard Plath worked on her poetry, be-
cause along with their obsessive interest in suicide, both women
shared the desire to become great writers. In the class with Lowell,
Plath wasn't impressed with her instructor. Near the end of the se-
mester, in May 1959, she wrote in her journal, "How few of my
superiors do I respect the opinions of anyhow? Lowell a case in
point. How few, if any, will see what I am working at, overcoming?
How ironic, that all my work to overcome my easy poeticisms merely
convinces them that I am rough, anti-poetic, unpoetic. My God."*

*Lowell never thought of Plath as his student, but she made a
vivid impression on him. Six years later, when he wrote the fore-
word to Plath's posthumously published last collection,* Ariel
*(1966), he remembered that "she was willowy, long-waisted,
sharp-elbowed, nervous, giggly, gracious—a brilliant tense presence
embarrassed by restraint. . . . I sensed her abashment and distinc-
tion, and never guessed her later appalling and triumphant fulfill-
ment." He thought that Plath's prodigious gifts as a poet and
fascination with suicide made her "one of those super-real, hypnotic,
great classical heroines." Plath's poem "Lady Lazarus," written in
1962, was included in* Ariel.

LADY LAZARUS

I have done it again.
One year in every ten
I manage it—

A sort of walking miracle, my skin
Bright as a Nazi lampshade,
My right foot

A paperweight,
My face a featureless, fine
Jew linen.

Peel off the napkin
O my enemy.
Do I terrify?—

The nose, the eye pits, the full set of teeth?
The sour breath
Will vanish in a day.

Soon, soon the flesh
The grave cave ate will be
At home on me

And I a smiling woman.
I am only thirty.
And like the cat I have nine times to die.

This is Number Three.
What a trash
To annihilate each decade.

What a million filaments.
The peanut-crunching crowd
Shoves in to see

Them unwrap me hand and foot—
The big strip tease.
Gentlemen, ladies

These are my hands
My knees.
I may be skin and bone,

Nevertheless, I am the same, identical woman.
The first time it happened I was ten.
It was an accident.

The second time I meant
To last it out and not come back at all.
I rocked shut

As a seashell.
They had to call and call
And pick the worms off me like sticky pearls.

Dying
Is an art, like everything else.
I do it exceptionally well.

I do it so it feels like hell.
I do it so it feels real.
I guess you could say I've a call.

It's easy enough to do it in a cell.
It's easy enough to do it and stay put.
It's the theatrical

Comeback in broad day
To the same place, the same face, the same brute
Amused shout:

"A miracle!"
That knocks me out.
There is a charge

For the eyeing of my scars, there is a charge
For the hearing of my heart—
It really goes.

And there is a charge, a very large charge
For a word or a touch
Or a bit of blood

Or a piece of my hair or my clothes.
So, so, Herr Doktor.
So, Herr Enemy.

I am your opus,
I am your valuable,
The pure gold baby

That melts to a shriek.
I turn and burn.
Do not think I underestimate your great concern.

Ash, ash—
You poke and stir.
Flesh, bone, there is nothing there——

A cake of soap,
A wedding ring,
A gold filling.

Herr God, Herr Lucifer
Beware
Beware.

Out of the ash
I rise with my red hair
And I eat men like air.

23–29 October 1962

———

Anne Sexton

Four years older than Plath, and quicker to find her voice as a poet, Anne Sexton was also a pioneer Sixties "suicide heroine." Both she and Plath were vivid illustrations of Betty Friedan's thesis, that intelligent, educated, and married middle-class women could disas-

trously fail to find fulfillment in the roles that society expected of them in the 1960s. Even more outspoken than Plath, Sexton wrote about a wide range of women's experiences not often discussed openly in her time. "The Abortion" is from Sexton's early book All My Pretty Ones *(1962); "The Addict" is from* Live or Die *(1966); and "The Ballad of the Lonely Masturbator" is from* Love Poems *(1969).*

THE ABORTION

Somebody who should have been born
is gone.

Just as the earth puckered its mouth,
each bud puffing out from its knot,
I changed my shoes, and then drove south.

Up past the Blue Mountains, where
Pennsylvania humps on endlessly,
wearing, like a crayoned cat, its green hair,

its roads sunken in like a gray washboard;
where, in truth, the ground cracks evilly,
a dark socket from which the coal has poured,

Somebody who should have been born
is gone.

the grass as bristly and stout as chives,
and me wondering when the ground would break,
and me wondering how anything fragile survives;

up in Pennsylvania, I met a little man,
not Rumpelstiltskin, at all, at all . . .
he took the fullness that love began.
Returning north, even the sky grew thin
like a high window looking nowhere.
The road was as flat as a sheet of tin.

Somebody who should have been born
is gone.

Yes, woman, such logic will lead
to loss without death. Or say what you meant,
you coward . . . this baby that I bleed.

THE ADDICT

Sleepmonger,
deathmonger,
with capsules in my palms each night,
eight at a time from sweet pharmaceutical bottles
I make arrangements for a pint-sized journey.
I'm the queen of this condition.
I'm an expert on making the trip
and now they say I'm an addict.
Now they ask why.
Why!

Don't they know
that I promised to die!
I'm keeping in practice.
I'm merely staying in shape.
The pills are a mother, but better,
every color and as good as sour balls.
I'm on a diet from death.

Yes, I admit
it has gotten to be a bit of a habit—
blows eight at a time, socked in the eye,
hauled away by the pink, the orange,
the green and the white goodnights.
I'm becoming something of a chemical
mixture.
That's it!

My supply
of tablets
has got to last for years and years.
I like them more than I like me.
Stubborn as hell, they won't let go.
It's a kind of marriage.
It's a kind of war
where I plant bombs inside
of myself.

Yes
I try
to kill myself in small amounts,
an innocuous occupation.
Actually I'm hung up on it.
But remember I don't make too much noise.
And frankly no one has to lug me out
and I don't stand there in my winding sheet.
I'm a little buttercup in my yellow nightie
eating my eight loaves in a row
and in a certain order as in
the laying on of hands
or the black sacrament.

It's a ceremony
but like any other sport
it's full of rules.
It's like a musical tennis match where
my mouth keeps catching the ball.
Then I lie on my altar
elevated by the eight chemical kisses.

What a lay me down this is
with two pink, two orange,
two green, two white goodnights.
Fee-fi-fo-fum—
Now I'm borrowed.
Now I'm numb.

THE BALLAD OF THE LONELY
MASTURBATOR

The end of the affair is always death.
She's my workshop. Slippery eye,
out of the tribe of myself my breath
finds you gone. I horrify
those who stand by. I am fed.
At night, alone, I marry the bed.

Finger to finger, now she's mine.
She's not too far. She's my encounter.
I beat her like a bell. I recline
in the bower where you used to mount her.
You borrowed me on the flowered spread.
At night, alone, I marry the bed.

Take for instance this night, my love,
that every single couple puts together
with a joint overturning, beneath, above,
the abundant two on sponge and feather,
kneeling and pushing, head to head.
At night, alone, I marry the bed.

I break out of my body this way,
an annoying miracle. Could I
put the dream market on display?
I am spread out. I crucify.
My little plum is what you said.
At night, alone, I marry the bed.

Then my black-eyed rival came.
The lady of water, rising on the beach,
a piano at her fingertips, shame
on her lips and a flute's speech.
And I was the knock-kneed broom instead.
At night, alone, I marry the bed.

She took you the way a woman takes
a bargain dress off the rack
and I broke the way a stone breaks.
I give back your books and fishing tack.
Today's paper says that you are wed.
At night, alone, I marry the bed.

The boys and girls are one tonight.
They unbutton blouses. They unzip flies.
They take off shoes. They turn off the light.
The glimmering creatures are full of lies.
They are eating each other. They are overfed.
At night, alone, I marry the bed.

Denise Levertov

While Denise Levertov never considered herself a feminist, her poetry in the 1960s manifested her belief that politics had a central place in her poetry. In poems like "About Marriage," from her collection O Taste and See *(1964), she insisted on her personal space within the confines of domesticity. She wanted to remain solitary and free not only to experience the mystery of a close encounter with nature in a city park, but also to interpret it in a poem for others, including her husband. In "The Mutes," from* The Sorrow Dance *(1966), Levertov ruminated on women's sensitivity to men's responses to them on the street, as she seamlessly integrated the language of everyday speech with imaginative poetic metaphors.*

ABOUT MARRIAGE

Don't lock me in wedlock, I want
marriage, an
encounter—

I told you about the
green light of
May

       (a veil of quiet befallen
       the downtown park,
       late

       Saturday after
       noon, long
       shadows and cool

       air, scent of
       new grass,
       fresh leaves,

       blossom on the threshold of
       abundance—

       and the birds I met there,
       birds of passage breaking their journey,
       three birds each of a different species:

       the azalea-breasted with round poll, dark,
       the brindled, merry, mousegliding one,
       and the smallest, golden as gorse and wearing
       a black Venetian mask

       and with them the three douce hen-birds
       feathered in tender, lively brown—

I stood
a half-hour under the enchantment,
no-one passed near,
the birds saw me and

let me be
near them.)

It's not
irrelevant:
I would be
met

and meet you
so,
in a green

airy space, not
locked in.

THE MUTES

Those groans men use
passing a woman on the street
or on the steps of the subway

to tell her she is a female
and their flesh knows it,

are they a sort of tune,
an ugly enough song, sung
by a bird with a slit tongue

but meant for music?

Or are they the muffled roaring
of deafmutes trapped in a building that is
slowly filling with smoke?

Perhaps both.

Such men most often
look as if groan were all they could do,
yet a woman, in spite of herself,

knows it's a tribute:
if she were lacking all grace
they'd pass her in silence:

so it's not only to say she's
a warm hole. It's a word

in grief-language, nothing to do with
primitive, not an ur-language;
language stricken, sickened, cast down

in decrepitude. She wants to
throw the tribute away, dis-
gusted, and can't,

it goes on buzzing in her ear,
it changes the pace of her walk,
the torn posters in echoing corridors

spell it out, it
quakes and gnashes as the train comes in.
Her pulse sullenly

had picked up speed,
but the cars slow down and
jar to a stop while her understanding

keeps on translating:
"Life after life after life goes by

without poetry,
without seemliness,
without love."

Diane Wakoski

Born in California, Diane Wakoski came to New York City in 1960 after earning her B.A. degree at the University of California at Berkeley. She supported herself as a junior high school teacher while she wrote poetry accepted by magazines as diverse as Po-etry, The New Yorker, Coyote's Journal, *and* Fuck You: A Magazine of the Arts. *In 1962 Wakoski published* Coins and Coffins, *the first of her nearly twenty collections of poetry. "Belly Dancer" was included in* Discrepancies and Apparitions *(1966). "Ringless" appeared in* Inside the Blood Factory *(1968). Its references to George Washington suggest Wakoski's mythological dramatizations in her poetry of her imaginative en-counters with historical figures who embody patriarchal power.*

BELLY DANCER

Can these movements which move themselves
be the substance of my attraction?
Where does this thin green silk come from that covers my
   body?
Surely any woman wearing such fabrics
would move her body just to feel them touching every part
   of her.

Yet most of the women frown, or look away, or laugh stiffly.
They are afraid of these materials and these movements
in some way.
The psychologists would say they are afraid of themselves,
   somehow.
Perhaps awakening too much desire—
that their men could never satisfy?
So they keep themselves laced and buttoned and made up
in hopes that the framework will keep them stiff enough
   not to feel

the whole register.
In hopes that they will not have to experience that
   unquenchable
desire for rhythm and contact.

If a snake glided across this floor
most of them would faint or shrink away.
Yet that movement could be their own.
That smooth movement frightens them—
awakening ancestors and relatives to the tips of the arms and
   toes.

So my bare feet
and my thin green silks
my bells and finger cymbals
offend them—frighten their old-young bodies.
While the men simper and leer—
glad for the vicarious experience and exercise.
They do not realize how I scorn them;
or how I dance for their frightened,
unawakened, sweet
women.

RINGLESS

I cannot stand the man who wears
a ring
on his little finger/ a white peacock walking on the moon
and splinters of silver dust his body;
but the great man, George, cracked in half in my living
   room
one day and I saw he was made of marble
with black veins. It does not justify the ring to say
someone gave it to you and the little finger is the only one
it will fit;
it does not justify to say Cocteau wore one
and still made the man burst silently through the mirror—
many beautiful
poems have been made with rings worn on the little finger.
That
isn't the point.

Flaubert had jasper; Lorca had jade; Dante had
amber; and Browning had carnelian;
George Washington had solid gold—even Kelly once wore
    a scarab there;
but I am telling you I cannot stand the man
who wears a ring
on his little finger. He may indeed
run the world;
that does not make him any better in
my needlepoint eyes.
Why
is a story.

> There were heaps of fish lying, shimmering in the
>   sun
> with red gashes still heaving
> and the mouths of medieval lovers.
> There were gold and green glass balls bobbing in
>   their
> nets on the waves.
> There were black-eyed men with hair all over their
>   bodies
> There were black-skirted ladies baking bread
> and there were gallons and gallons of red wine.
> A girl spilled one drop of hot wax on her lover's neck
> as she glanced at his white teeth and thick arms.
> There were red and silver snakes coiling around
>   the legs
> of the dancers.
> There was hot sun and there was no talk.
> How do I reconcile these images with our cool
>   president,
> George Washington, walking the streets? Every
>   bone
> in my body is ivory and has the word "America"
> carved on it, but
> my head takes me away from furniture and pewter
> to the sun tugging at my nipples and trying to
>   squeeze
> under my toes.
> The sun appeared in the shape of a man and he
>   had

a ring made of sun around his little finger.
"It will burn up your hand," I said.
But he made motions in the air and passed by.
The moon appeared in the shape of a young negro
    boy,
and he had a ring made of dew around his little
    finger.
"You'll lose it," I said,
but he touched my face,
not losing a drop and passed away. Then I saw
Alexander Hamilton, whom I loved,
and he had a ring on his little finger,
but he wouldn't touch me.
And Lorca had rings around both little fingers,
and suddenly everyone I knew appeared,
and they all had rings on their little fingers,
and I was the only one in the world left without
    any
rings
on any
of my fingers whatsoever.
And worst of all,
there was George Washington
walking down the Senate aisles
with a ring on his little finger—managing
the world,
managing *my* world.
This is what I mean—you wear a ring on your
        little finger
        and you manage the world,
        and I am ringless
        ringless . . .
I cannot stand the man who wears
a ring
on his little finger;

not even if it is you.

Hettie Jones

*In the Sixties, radical women who challenged their conventional
roles as wives and mothers in American society came from many dif-
ferent walks of life. In the memoir* How I Became Hettie Jones
*(1990), Hettie Jones described herself on a typical day in the fall of
1961 when she was the young white wife of the black writer LeRoi
Jones. At the time, Hettie had just ended her full-time job as edito-
rial assistant at* Partisan Review *in order to stay at home and care
for their two small daughters, Lisa and Kellie, when she figured out
that she would have more money every week from her unemploy-
ment checks than she would have from her* Partisan Review *salary
after paying the babysitter. Sitting in a park in lower Manhattan
while her children played nearby, she dreamed of someday having
the time for herself to develop her talent as a writer.*

*The decade of the Sixties would be long past before Hettie
Jones had the time to write her memoir, but another Jewish writer,
Tillie Olsen, living in California, understood her predicament. In
October 1965, Olsen published an article titled "Silences: When
Writers Don't Write" in* Harper's *magazine. In 1961 Olsen had
gained recognition with four stories collected in* Tell Me a Riddle,
*but she became identified as a champion of the reemerging feminist
movement with "Silences." In the article, she described how the ne-
cessity to raise and support her four children cut short her promising
career as a novelist before her marriage. Olsen was a Utopian social-
ist, and as the daughter of political refugees from czarist Russia, she
was bitterly disappointed with what she considered to be the limita-
tions of American society, not least for its failure to provide child care
for working mothers. In "Silences," she wrote:*

> More than in any human relationship, overwhelmingly
> more, motherhood means being instantly interruptible,
> responsive, responsible. Children need one now (and
> remember, in our society, the family must often be the
> center for love and health the outside world is not). The
> very fact that these are needs of love, not duty, that one
> feels them as one's self; that there is no one else to be

> *responsible for these needs, gives them primacy. It is*
> *distraction, not meditation, that becomes habitual;*
> *interruption, not continuity; spasmodic, not constant*
> *toil. The rest has been said here. Work interrupted,*
> *deferred, postponed, makes blockage—at best, lesser*
> *accomplishment. Unused capacities atrophy, cease to be.*

Tillie Olsen took more than fifteen years to complete Silences
(1978), her book of essays exploring the different circumstances that
obstruct or silence literary creation. Hettie Jones's musings in the
East River Park in 1961 about her sense of her thwarted creativity
as a mother who wanted time to be a writer could have come out of
Olsen's pages.

FROM *HOW I BECAME HETTIE JONES*

AT THE CURB on a corner of Fourteenth and First, late one fall after-
noon. It's beginning to rain. Hurrying people eddy around me, I'm a
convoy in a traffic dilemma: I've got a baby carriage on the sidewalk,
a shopping cart piled with clean laundry in the street, and a fallen
sheet getting mucky in the gutter. I hate to let go of the carriage be-
cause it's collapsible and tends to fulfill this function, making it some-
thing to operate more than just steer, and thus requiring sensitivity,
careful attention, and quick, firm decision—from me, like everything
else in my life. Lisa, for one: she was propped on a pillow under the
hood, but slid down on the trip up the curb. Now I hear her insistent
wah wah, which I know won't stop of itself, since she's the kind who
must *see*—everything, at all times. Often, to make dinner, in these
days before infant seats, I tie her onto me with pieces of fabric. It's
easier. But is it? Experience distances, leads you to the clean, dry air
of generalization. I'd be the first to say (when not stuck in the rain)
that such a will as Lisa's is nothing to thwart, that I'd encourage it in
anyone, and obviously did in Kellie, who, in a seat clamped across the
top of the carriage, has twisted around to offer advice, further tipping
our tenuous balance and also—incidentally?—her hard shoes are an
inch from her sister's head.

I'm not a convoy, I'm a thrumming blinking bleating switch-
board.

Given my attachment to the living cargo, these adorable small ganglia of human complication, even though one is yelling at me, and I'm about to yell at the other, I let go not of them but of the shopping cart. By now the sheet is nothing I can put on my bed tonight. The wasted effort, the extra quarter to dry it pass my mind in a wave of disgust, I hate *applying* myself to it again. Nevertheless, clutching the carriage handle like an unstable ballet barre I plié toward it, when suddenly—

Just under my outstretched arm, the veined, spotted hands of an elderly woman appear. Snatching the sheet she flips it onto the stack of damp clothes, brushes it off, and then with surprising strength jams the stack into the cart and hauls the whole thing onto the sidewalk. She's wearing an old blue coat with military buttons, and above her beautiful Irish face her white hair is a thick ropy pile. She's dismissing my thanks, too, because there's something bitter on her mind. "The men, they don't know about this," she says. "They don't know and they don't care to know, them with their lives, their damned *lives.*" And then she's gone.

At the northern tip of East River Park there's an overgrown quarter acre with some benches facing the water and a neglected, sinking monument to the dead of World War II. In 1961, when Stuyvesant Towners never ventured south, and people from the Jacob Riis housing project seldom went north, the solitude was impressive.

I was there one day, sitting apart from the children in order to pay attention to myself, impossible in their immediate presence: if they demanded they also seduced, like the TV that captures because it's on. We'd left Roi at home, typing in his windowless box of a room. When I'd looked in to say good-bye he was grinning. Through Joyce [Johnson], who was now working at the publisher William Morrow, he'd just met an editor with whom he'd discussed a book about the blues, a critical study of the music, its antecedents, contexts, the lives of the people who made it. The editor thought the project exciting and novel, not least because it would be the first full-length work on the subject by a *Negro*. Negroes were now newsworthy. A trend had been spotted. Book sales could be predicted. Joyce was sure Roi's proposal would go through, that it was just a matter of his writing it. All week he'd been bouncing his chair and stamping his feet and yelling "Yeah! Yeah!"—the way he'd always applaud a good solo (you can hear him on some of the Monk records made at the Five Spot). Like the kids he was a bundle of jumpy good humor, demanding instant gratification. Yesterday evening, while I was bathing Kellie, he'd come dashing into the bathroom with a poem. "Look at this! Read this!" he cried. I dried my hands and grabbed it—why not?

Today, everything in the landscape seemed in an act of relation, reflected in and reflecting. Shadows of trees dappled the water; the river, refracting sun, played on the tree trunks. The children were part of the pattern too, their eyes were on each other. And what, then, of me? Would there ever be a way to balance Roi?

I began to try to sort myself out. I'd graduated *Partisan*. I'd finished bearing children. I was growing out my hair, and my head had outgrown what my hand could sew. Life as wife and mother was fine because of other pleasures—the unemployment insurance in my pocket, the promise, from friends in publishing, of free-lance editorial work. *Yugen* 7 was out, a sixty-six-page issue; Totem Press had eleven titles. These were now printed with money advanced by Corinth, but we—mostly me—still ran our business (when Ted Wilentz had first offered to back us, he'd joked to Roi that he was giving him money only because he trusted his wife).

Still I knew what was missing, and what that white-haired woman on the corner had meant. All told, I was an energetic young person of twenty-seven, serving others.

The monument to the dead of World War II brought to mind my first love, my second-youngest uncle, fixer of my father's comb-case machine. Though he'd married and moved to the Bronx, the telegram announcing his death in the war came to Laurelton; arriving home from Newark one night we found it under the door: *We regret to inform you* . . . I was ten when he died, but dead he refused to die, and in my mind descended again and again the stairway where I'd seen him last. At seventeen, desperate to set him to rest, I wrote him a poem. It worked.

Since then only the future had ever obsessed me, as if art were not work but a simple act of faith, and only by *seeing* myself at it would I ever make it happen. Though I admired poets like Denise Levertov and Barbara Guest, I felt I could never write like they did, with astonishing, sophisticated metaphor, and anyway I only wanted to write like William Carlos Williams, with tones and repetitions, a kind of melody line, the language equivalent to Miles's pretty, ambivalent notes. Like Creeley's:

> *Let me be my own fool*
> *of my own making, the sum of it*
> *is equivocal.*

Kellie was calling. "Mommy!"

I went to look. Lisa was moving every muscle, as if jumping or running, and her mouth was working too, like "Wow! Wow! Wow!"—and all because of the same reflections I'd noticed, the riverlight on the trees. Kellie, perceiving this response as opinion, and thus some progress in consciousness, exclaimed, proudly, "They look *good* to her!"

Only the verb in this sentence differs from a line in a poem by Williams. That night—reconvinced—I started a book for children. I figured I'd just go back to where I left off, before the kids, Totem, *Yugen,* Roi. . . . I thought it would be good training, and felt stubborn about the method, even if writers were supposed to have more on their minds, and even if Gregory Corso, continuing a current argument in *Yugen* 7, had suggested that the idea of writing nursery rhymes would produce a "stark" poetry.

Inevitably we all write for our children or end up talking to ourselves, but the book I began remained unfinished; ten years would pass before my first published children's book; and in thinking that I'd commenced with myself, I was—extremely as usual—mistaken. I even lost the manuscript, probably in the pile on my desk, most of which weren't mine during this time. Publishers paid me to read Beckett, Burroughs, Marguerite Duras, Fanon, Genet, and many more. I thought about all of it. But my feelings—with never anything literary to them and all I ever wanted to write about—were left tangled for lack of time, like the long hair I grew but then twisted up carelessly. There are different reasons for silences, but the Russian poet Marina Tsvetayeva, describing her own, came closest to mine: "It's precisely for feeling that one needs time, and not for thought." Anyway, now I think I'm lucky to have, from Fourteenth Street, the one poem that mattered, which offered at last what the gypsies could never have seen—a future I'd invented and therefore couldn't disappoint—the rest of my life from prophetic twenty-seven:

> *I've been alive since thirty-four*
> *and I've sung every song*
> *since before the War*

> *Will the press of this music*
> *warp my soul*
> *till I'm wrinkled and gnarled*
> *and old and small—*

A crone in the marshes
singing and singing

A crone in the marshes singing
and singing

and singing
and singing
and singing
and singing
and singing

———————————

Valerie Solanas

In "What's Happening in America (1966)," Susan Sontag ended her article by praising the radicalism of young people involved in the sexual revolution. "To sympathize, of course, you have to be convinced that things in America really are as desperately bad as I have indicated. This is hard to see; the desperateness of things is obscured by the comforts and liberties that America does offer." Three years later, Sontag's remarks seemed right on target after members of the organization Students for a Democratic Society (SDS) formed the Weather Underground to espouse terrorism and violent revolution. Also in 1969, in Greenwich Village, gays protested a raid by the police vice squad at the Stonewall Inn on Sheridan Square, causing a riot that led to the formation of the Gay Liberation Movement.

Perhaps the most radical document by a woman at the time was created by Valerie Solanas in her SCUM Manifesto, which she wrote and self-published in New York City in 1967. As a radical lesbian, Solanas invented a hypothetical organization she called the Society for Cutting Up Men (SCUM), which she insisted was "a state of mind. In other words, women who think a certain way

are in SCUM. Men who think a certain way are in the men's aux-
iliary of SCUM." Although her extremism was rejected by most
feminists, in 1968 Solanas became famous after shooting Andy
Warhol. She served a short prison sentence and spent years in and
out of mental institutions before dying of pneumonia in a San Fran-
cisco welfare hotel in 1989. I Shot Andy Warhol, a film drama-
tizing her life, was produced by American Playhouse in 1995.

FROM *SCUM MANIFESTO*

LIFE IN THIS SOCIETY BEING, at best, an utter bore and no aspect of
society being at all relevant to women, there remains to civic-minded,
responsible, thrill-seeking females only to overthrow the government,
eliminate the money system, institute complete automation, and de-
stroy the male sex.

It is now technically possible to reproduce without the aid of
males (or, for that matter, females) and to produce only females. We
must begin immediately to do so. Retaining the male has not even
the dubious purpose of reproduction. The male is a biological acci-
dent: the Y (male) gene is an incomplete X (female) gene, that is, has
an incomplete set of chromosomes. In other words, the male is an in-
complete female, a walking abortion, aborted at the gene stage. To be
male is to be deficient, emotionally limited; maleness is a deficiency
disease and males are emotional cripples.

The male is completely egocentric, trapped inside himself, inca-
pable of empathizing or identifying with others, of love, friendship,
affection, or tenderness. He is a completely isolated unit, incapable of
rapport with anyone. His responses are entirely visceral, not cerebral;
his intelligence is a mere tool in the service of his drives and needs; he
is incapable of mental passion, mental interaction; he can't relate to
anything other than his own physical sensations. He is a half-dead,
unresponsive lump, incapable of giving or receiving pleasure or happi-
ness; consequently, he is at best an utter bore, an inoffensive blob,
since only those capable of absorption in others can be charming. He
is trapped in a twilight zone halfway between humans and apes, and is
far worse off than the apes because, unlike the apes, he is capable of a
large array of negative feelings—hate, jealousy, contempt, disgust,
guilt, shame, doubt—and moreover he *is aware* of what he is and isn't.

Although completely physical, the male is unfit even for stud
service. Even assuming mechanical proficiency, which few men have,

he is, first of all, incapable of zestfully, lustfully, tearing off a piece, but is instead eaten up with guilt, shame, fear, and insecurity, feelings rooted in male nature, which the most enlightened training can only minimize; second, the physical feeling he attains is next to nothing; and, third, he is not empathizing with his partner, but is obsessed with how he's doing, turning in an A performance, doing a good plumbing job. To call a man an animal is to flatter him; he's a machine, a walking dildo. It's often said that men use women. Use them for what? Surely not pleasure.

Eaten up with guilt, shame, fears, and insecurities and obtaining, if he's lucky, a barely perceptible physical feeling, the male is, nonetheless, obsessed with screwing; he'll swim a river of snot, wade nostril-deep through a mile of vomit, if he thinks there'll be a friendly pussy awaiting him. He'll screw a woman he despises, any snaggle-toothed hag, and, furthermore, pay for the opportunity. Why? Relieving physical tension isn't the answer, as masturbation suffices for that. It's not ego satisfaction; that doesn't explain screwing corpses and babies.

Completely egocentric, unable to relate, empathize, or identify, and filled with a vast, pervasive, diffuse sexuality, the male is psychically passive. He hates his passivity, so he projects it onto women, defines the male as active, then sets out to prove that he is ("prove he's a Man"). His main means of attempting to prove it is screwing (Big Man with a Big Dick tearing off a Big Piece). Since he's attempting to prove an error, he must "prove" it again and again. Screwing, then, is a desperate, compulsive attempt to prove he's not passive, not a woman; but he is passive and does want to be a woman.

Being an incomplete female, the male spends his life attempting to complete himself, to become female. He attempts to do this by constantly seeking out, fraternizing with, and trying to live through and fuse with the female, and by claiming as his own all female characteristics—emotional strength and independence, forcefulness, dynamism, decisiveness, coolness, objectivity, assertiveness, courage, integrity, vitality, intensity, depth of character, grooviness, etc.—and projecting onto women all male traits—vanity, frivolity, triviality, weakness, etc. It should be said, though, that the male has one glaring area of superiority over the female—public relations. (He has done a brilliant job of convincing millions of women that men are women and women are men.) The male claim that females find fulfillment through motherhood and sexuality reflects what males think they'd find fulfilling if they were female.

Women, in other words, don't have penis envy; men have pussy envy. When the male accepts his passivity, defines himself as a woman (males as well as females think men are women and women are men), and becomes a transvestite he loses his desire to screw (or to do anything else, for that matter; he fulfills himself as a drag queen) and gets his cock chopped off. He then achieves a continuous diffuse sexual feeling from "being a woman." Screwing is, for a man, a defense against his desire to be female. Sex is itself a sublimation.

The male, because of his obsession to compensate for not being female combined with his inability to relate and to feel compassion, has made of the world a shitpile. He is responsible for:

WAR . . .

<hr>

Gloria Steinem

In the December 2, 2001, issue of the New York Times Maga- *zine, the novelist Jane Smiley reflected on the "Women's Crusade" as presented by Laura Bush after the first lady had made a public statement that the United States deserved credit for liberating women in Afghanistan during our country's war against terrorism there in the months after September 11. Smiley observed that "she can ally herself with women for whom any sort of life other than imprisonment is a liberation but protect herself from feminists . . . because her position doesn't require any theory or analysis that might reflect on the corporate or multinational goals of G.O.P. sponsors or the failures of American foreign policy over the years." Reflecting back on thirty years of the Women's Movement, Smiley acknowledged the naïveté of the early feminists and what she called the "dangerous business" of women's liberation:*

> *When we were sitting around in consciousness-raising groups and talking about jobs and boyfriends and sister-*

hood, we were new to the moral complexities and poten-
tial risks of liberating women. For one thing, we didn't
know that our drive to define the meaning of our own
lives would call out a conservative backlash, that we
would be accused of destroying the family and tearing up
the fabric of American life by the very party now trum-
peting its determination to have Afghan women at the
negotiating table where the future Afghan government is
decided. We didn't know how much some men would
resent sharing power and how stubborn their resentment
would be. We didn't know that our ideas weren't univer-
sally good and that women in other parts of the world
would have different needs and use different methods to
liberate themselves.

In 1971, the year before she founded Ms. magazine, feminist
leader Gloria Steinem gave a talk at Harvard University that was
one of the most balanced and insightful accounts of the goals of the
Women's Movement in the United States at the time. "A New
Egalitarian Life Style" was published in the Op-Ed section of the
New York Times on August 26, 1971. It was included in
About Women (1973), a paperback anthology edited by S. Berg
and S. J. Marks.

A NEW EGALITARIAN LIFE STYLE

THE FIRST PROBLEM for all of us, men and women, is not to learn,
but to unlearn. We are filled with the popular wisdom of several cen-
turies just past, and we are terrified to give it up. Patriotism means
obedience, age means wisdom, woman means submission, black
means inferior: these are preconceptions imbedded so deeply in our
thinking that we honestly may not know that they are there.

Whether it's woman's secondary role in society or the paternalis-
tic role of the United States in the world, the old assumptions just
don't work any more.

Part of living this revolution is having the scales fall from our
eyes. Every day, we see small obvious truths that we had missed be-
fore. Our histories, for instance, have generally been written for and
about white men. Inhabited countries were "discovered" when the
first white male set foot there, and most of us learned more about any

one European country than we did about Africa and Asia combined.

We need Women's Studies courses just as much as we need Black Studies. We need courses on sexism and American law just as much as we need them on racism. The number of laws that discriminate against women is staggering. At least to women.

"Anonymous," as Virginia Woolf once said bitterly, "was a woman."

If we weren't studying white paternalistic documents, after all, we might start long before Charlemagne in history, or Blackstone in law. More than 5,000 years before, in fact, when women were treated as equals or superiors. When women were the gods, and worshipped *because* they had the children. Men didn't consider child-bearing a drawback, and in fact imitated that envied act in their ceremonies. It was thought that women bore fruit when they were ripe, like trees.

When paternity was discovered—a day I like to imagine as a gigantic light bulb over someone's head, as he says, "Oh, *that's* why"—the idea of ownership of children began. And the possibility of passing authority and goods down to them. And the origin of marriage—which was locking women up long enough to make sure who the father was. Women were subjugated, the original political subjugation and the pattern which others were to follow, as the means of production. They were given whatever tasks the men considered odious, and they became "feminine," a cultural habit which has continued till today.

When other tribes or groups were captured, they were given the least desirable role: that of women. When black people were brought to these shores as slaves, for instance, they were given the legal status of wives; that is, chattel. Since then, our revolutions have followed, each on the heels of the other.

I don't mean to equate women's problems with the sufferings of slavery. Women lose their identities: black men lose their lives. But, as Gunnar Myrdal pointed out more than thirty years ago, the parallel between women and blacks—the two largest second-class groups—is the deepest truth of American life.

We suffer from the same myths—childlike natures, smaller brains, naturally passive, lack of objectivity (Harvard Law School professors are still peddling that), inability to govern ourselves, identity as sex objects, supernatural powers—usually evil, and special job skills. We're great at detail work for instance, as long as it's poorly paid, but brain surgery is something else.

When we make a generalization about women, it helps if we

substitute black, or Chicano or Puerto Rican. Then we see what we are saying.

The truth is that women are so much more durable than men at every stage of life, so much less subject to diseases of stress, for instance. Child-bearing shouldn't mean child-rearing. Motherhood is not all-consuming, nor is fatherhood a sometime thing. In fact, there are tribes in which the fathers rear the children, and the famous mother instinct turns out to be largely cultural.

The problem is achieving a compassionate balance, something this society has not done. It's clear that most American children suffer from too much mother and too little father.

Women employees in general lose no more time from work than men do, even including childbirth. They change jobs less, since they have less chance of trading upward, and tend to leave only after long periods of no promotion; thus benefiting male employes by financing their retirement plans.

Women don't want to imitate the male pattern of obsessive work ending up with a heart attack and an engraved wrist watch. We want to humanize the work pattern, to make new, egalitarian life styles.

We are not more moral, we are only less corrupted by power. But we haven't been culturally trained to feel our identity depends on money, manipulative power, or a gun.

From now on, no man can call himself liberal, or radical, or even a conservative advocate of fair play, if his work depends in any way on the unpaid or underpaid labor of women at home, or in the office. Politics doesn't begin in Washington. Politics begins with those who are oppressed right here.

And maybe, if we live this revolution every day, we will put a suitable end to this second 5,000-year period: that of patriarchy and racism. Perhaps we have a chance for a third and new period—one of humanism.

PART NINE

IN DEFENSE OF THE EARTH: THE ENVIRONMENTAL MOVEMENT

There are no fish in the water.
There are few deer or bear in the woods.
Only the bright blue damsel flies
On the reeds in the daytime. . . .

KENNETH REXROTH, FROM "TIME IS THE
MERCY OF ETERNITY" (1956)

IN 1962 A BOOK BY A WOMAN started the Environmental Movement in the United States, just as a book by another woman was to restart the Women's Movement soon afterward. Trained as a marine biologist, **Rachel Carson** had worked for fourteen years as a writer of pamphlets and radio scripts for the U.S. Fish and Wildlife Service, eventually becoming editor in chief of the service's publication program before she wrote the bestsellers *The Sea Around Us* (1951) and *The Edge of the Sea* (1955).

In 1958 Carson received a letter from Olga Owens Huckins, in Duxbury, Massachusetts. A journalist for the *Boston Post*, Huckins said she had noticed that the state's widespread aerial pesticide spraying of DDT to eliminate mosquitoes was also killing birds—or, as Carson eloquently described the letter—Huckins "told me of her own bitter experience of a small world made lifeless, and so brought my attention sharply back to a problem with which I had long been concerned. I then realized I must write this book." The result was *Silent Spring*, excerpted in *The New Yorker* before it was published as a book.

Carson's work aroused a storm of controversy. Major chemical companies tried to suppress it, attacking its author as being hysterical and extremist for speaking out, as Carson stated in her introduction, "against the reckless and irresponsible poisoning of the world that man shares with all other creatures." The attack on Carson reminded many of her readers of the assault on Charles Darwin for publishing *The Origin of Species* in 1855 and the vilification campaign against Harriet Beecher Stowe for her novel *Uncle Tom's Cabin* in 1852. When Carson came to Washington, D.C., in 1963 to testify on the dangers of pesticides, Senator Abraham Ribicoff introduced her to Congress as "the lady who started all this," echoing President Abraham Lincoln's welcome to Stowe when she visited him in the White House during the Civil War.

Before the publication of *Silent Spring*, the Environmental Movement did not have a national spokesperson who could engage the attention of a national audience. After 1962, as critic Tom Bissell observed, American culture was enriched by "a tradition of reflection upon nature and a stubborn activism upon its behalf that extended from Henry David Thoreau to John Muir to Rachel Carson." The opening section of *Silent Spring* was a dramatic introduction to Carson's subject. She titled it "A Fable for Tomorrow."

Rachel Carson

FROM *SILENT SPRING*

A Fable for Tomorrow

THERE WAS ONCE A TOWN in the heart of America where all life seemed to live in harmony with its surroundings. The town lay in the midst of a checkerboard of prosperous farms, with fields of grain and hillsides of orchards where, in spring, white clouds of bloom drifted above the green fields. In autumn, oak and maple and birch set up a blaze of color that flamed and flickered across a backdrop of pines. Then foxes barked in the hills and deer silently crossed the fields, half hidden in the mists of the fall mornings.

Along the roads, laurel, viburnum and alder, great ferns and wildflowers delighted the traveler's eye through much of the year. Even in winter the roadsides were places of beauty, where countless birds came to feed on the berries and on the seed heads of the dried weeds rising above the snow. The countryside was, in fact, famous for the abundance and variety of its bird life, and when the flood of mi-grants was pouring through in spring and fall people traveled from great distances to observe them. Others came to fish the streams, which flowed clear and cold out of the hills and contained shady pools where trout lay. So it had been from the days many years ago when the first settlers raised their houses, sank their wells, and built their barns.

Then a strange blight crept over the area and everything began to change. Some evil spell had settled on the community: mysterious maladies swept the flocks of chickens; the cattle and sheep sickened and died. Everywhere was a shadow of death. The farmers spoke of much illness among their families. In the town the doctors had be-come more and more puzzled by new kinds of sickness appearing among their patients. There had been several sudden and unexplained deaths, not only among adults but even among children, who would be stricken suddenly while at play and die within a few hours.

There was a strange stillness. The birds, for example—where had they gone? Many people spoke of them, puzzled and disturbed. The feeding stations in the backyards were deserted. The few birds seen anywhere were moribund; they trembled violently and could not fly. It was a spring without voices. On the mornings that had once throbbed with the dawn chorus of robins, catbirds, doves, jays, wrens, and scores of other bird voices there was now no sound; only silence lay over the fields and woods and marsh.

On the farms the hens brooded, but no chicks hatched. The farmers complained that they were unable to raise any pigs—the litters were small and the young survived only a few days. The apple trees were coming into bloom but no bees droned among the blossoms, so there was no pollination and there would be no fruit.

The roadsides, once so attractive, were now lined with browned and withered vegetation as though swept by fire. These, too, were silent, deserted by all living things. Even the streams were now lifeless. Anglers no longer visited them, for all the fish had died.

In the gutters under the eaves and between the shingles of the roofs, a white granular powder still showed a few patches; some weeks before it had fallen like snow upon the roofs and the lawns, the fields and streams.

No witchcraft, no enemy action had silenced the rebirth of new life in this stricken world. The people had done it themselves.

This town does not actually exist, but it might easily have a thousand counterparts in America or elsewhere in the world. I know of no community that has experienced all the misfortunes I describe. Yet every one of these disasters has actually happened somewhere, and many real communities have already suffered a substantial number of them. A grim specter has crept upon us almost unnoticed, and this imagined tragedy may easily become a stark reality we all shall know.

What has already silenced the voices of spring in countless towns in America? This book is an attempt to explain.

———

Peter Matthiessen

Shortly before the publication of Rachel Carson's Silent Spring, *another book was published that helped to give impetus to the Environmental Movement in the United States.* Wildlife in America *(1959) was the first book by Peter Matthiessen, who had set out on his own in a Ford convertible after his graduation from Yale University to explore America's wildlife refuges and to write about the state of its natural environment, believing that "the concept of conservation is a far truer sign of civilization than that spoliation of a continent which we once confused with progress."*

Wildlife in America began with the chapter "The Outlying Rocks." There Matthiessen imagined in impressive, chilling detail how hunters killed the last great auks in 1844, the first birds native to North America to have been extinguished by human beings.

FROM *WILDLIFE IN AMERICA*

The Outlying Rocks

IN EARLY JUNE OF 1844, a longboat crewed by fourteen men hove to off the skerry called Eldey, a stark, volcanic mass rising out of the gray wastes of the North Atlantic some ten miles west of Cape Reykjanes, Iceland. On the islets of these uneasy seas, the forebears of the boatmen had always hunted the swarming seabirds as a food, but on this day they were seeking, for collectors, the eggs and skins of the garefowl or great auk, a penguinlike flightless bird once common on the ocean rocks of northern Europe, Iceland, Greenland, and the Maritime Provinces of Canada. The great auk, slaughtered indiscriminately across the centuries for its flesh, feathers, and oil, was vanishing, and the last birds, appearing now and then on lonely shores, were granted no protection. On the contrary, they were pursued more intensively than ever for their value as scientific specimens.

At the north end of Eldey, a wide ledge descends to the water, and, though a sea was running, the boat managed to land three men, Jon Brandsson, Sigourour Isleffson, and Ketil Ketilsson. Two auks, blinking, waddled foolishly across the ledge. Isleffson and Brandsson each killed a bird, and Ketilsson, discovering a solitary egg, found a crack in it and smashed it. Later, one Christian Hansen paid nine pounds for the skins, and sold them in turn to a Reykjavik taxidermist named Möller. It is not known what became of them thereafter, a fact all the more saddening when one considers that, on all the long coasts of the northern ocean, no auk was ever seen alive again.

The great auk is one of the few creatures whose final hours can be documented with such certainty. Ordinarily, the last members of a species die in solitude, the time and place of their passage from earth unknown. One year they are present, striving instinctively to maintain an existence many thousands of years old. The next year they are gone. Perhaps stray auks persisted a few years longer, to die at last through accident or age, but we must assume that the ultimate pair fell victim to this heedless act of man.

One imagines with misgiving the last scene on desolate Eldey. Offshore, the longboat wallows in a surge of seas, then slides forward in the lull, its stern grinding hard on the rock ledge. The hunters hurl the two dead birds aboard and, cursing, tumble after, as the boat falls away into the wash. Gaining the open water, it moves off to the eastward, the rough voices and the hollow thump of oars against wood tholepins unreal in the prevailing fogs of June. The dank mist, rank with marine smells, cloaks the dark mass, white-topped with guano, and the fierce-eyed gannets, which had not left the crest, settle once more on their crude nests, hissing peevishly and jabbing sharp blue bills at their near neighbors. The few gulls, mewing aimlessly, circle in, alighting. One banks, checks its flight, bends swiftly down upon the ledge, where the last, pathetic generation of great auks gleams raw and unborn on the rock. A second follows and, squalling, they yank at the loose embryo, scattering the black, brown, and green shell segments. After a time they return to the crest, and the ledge is still. The shell remnants lie at the edge of tideline, and the last sea of the flood, perhaps, or a rain days later, washes the last piece into the water. Slowly it drifts down across the sea-curled weeds, the anchored life of the marine world. A rock minnow, drawn to the strange scent, snaps at a minute shred of auk albumen; the shell fragment spins upward, descends once more. Farther down, it settles briefly near a *littorina,* and surrounding mollusks stir dully toward the stimulus. The periwinkle scours it, spits the calcified bits away. The current takes the particles, so small as to be all but invisible, and they are borne outward, drifting down at last to the deeps of the sea out of which, across slow eons of the Cenozoic era, the species first evolved.

For most of us, its passing is unimportant. The auk, from a practical point of view, was doubtless a dim-witted inhabitant of Godforsaken places, a primitive and freakish thing, ill-favored and ungainly. From a second and a more enlightened viewpoint, the great auk was the mightiest of its family, a highly evolved fisherman and swimmer, an ornament to the monotony of northern seas, and for centuries a crucial food source for the natives of the Atlantic coasts. More important, it was a living creature which died needlessly, the first species native to North America to become extinct by the hand of man. It was to be followed into oblivion by other creatures, many of them of an aesthetic and economic significance apparent to us all. Even today, despite protection, the scattered individuals of species too long persecuted are hovering at the abyss of extinction, and will vanish in our lifetimes.

The slaughter, for want of fodder, has subsided in this century, but the fishes, amphibians, reptiles, birds, and mammals—the vertebrate animals as a group—are obscured by man's dark shadow. Such protection as is extended them too rarely includes the natural habitats they require, and their remnants skulk in a lean and shrinking wilderness. The true wilderness—the great woods and clear rivers, the wild swamps and grassy plains which once were the wonder of the world—has been largely despoiled, and today's voyager, approaching our shores through the oiled waters of the coast, is greeted by smoke and the glint of industry on our fouled seaboard, and an inland prospect of second growth, scarred landscapes, and sterile, often stinking, rivers of pollution and raw mud, the whole bedecked with billboards, neon lights, and other decorative evidence of mankind's triumph over chaos. In many regions the greenwood not converted to black stumps no longer breathes with sound and movement, but is become a cathedral of still trees; the plains are plowed under and the prairies ravaged by overgrazing and the winds of drought. Where great, wild creatures ranged, the vermin prosper.

The concept of conservation is a far truer sign of civilization than that spoliation of a continent which we once confused with progress. Today, very late, we are coming to accept the fact that the harvest of renewable resources must be controlled. Forests, soil, water, and wildlife are mutually interdependent, and the ruin of one element will mean, in the end, the ruin of them all. Not surprisingly, land management which benefits mankind will benefit the lesser beasts as well. Creatures like quail and the white-tailed deer, adjusting to man, have already shown recovery. For others, like the black-footed ferret and the California condor, it is probably much too late, and the grizzly bear dies slowly with the wilderness.

This book is a history of North American wildlife, of the great auk and other creatures present and missing, of how they vanished, where, and why; and of what is presently being done that North America may not become a wasteland of man's creation, in which no wild thing can live.

"Everybody knows," one naturalist [Aldo Leopold] has written, "that the autumn landscape in the north woods is the land, plus a red maple, plus a ruffed grouse. In terms of conventional physics, the grouse represents only a millionth of either the mass or the energy of an acre. Yet substract the grouse and the whole thing is dead."

The finality of extinction is awesome, and not unrelated to the finality of eternity. Man, striving to imagine what might lie beyond the long light years of stars, beyond the universe, beyond the void, feels lost in space; confronted with the death of species, enacted on earth so many times before he came, and certain to continue when his own breed is gone, he is forced to face another void, and feels alone in time. Species appear and, left behind by a changing earth, they disappear forever, and there is a certain solace in the inexorable. But until man, the highest predator, evolved, the process of extinction was a slow one. No species but man, so far as is known, unaided by circumstance or climatic change, has ever extinguished another, and certainly no species has ever devoured itself, an accomplishment of which man appears quite capable. There is some comfort in the notion that, however *Homo sapiens* contrives his own destruction, a few creatures will survive in that ultimate wilderness he will leave behind, going on about their ancient business in the mindless confidence that their own much older and more tolerant species will prevail.

The *Terra Incognita*, as cartographers of the Renaissance referred to North America, had been known to less educated Eurasians for more than ten thousand years. Charred animal bones found here and there in the West, and submitted to the radiocarbon test, have been ascribed to human campfires laid at least twenty-five thousand years ago. Thus one might say that the effect of man on the fauna of North America commenced with the waning of the glaciers, when bands of wild Mongoloid peoples migrated eastward across a land bridge now submerged by the shoal seas of the Bering Strait. In this period—the time of transition between the Pleistocene and Recent epochs—the mastodons, mammoths, saber-toothed tigers, dire wolves, and other huge beasts which had flourished in the Ice Age disappeared forever from the face of the earth, and the genera which compose our modern wildlife gained ascendancy.

Man was perhaps the last of the large mammals to find the way from Asia to North America. In any case, many species had preceded him. The members of the deer family—the deer, elk, moose, and caribou—had made the journey long before, as had the bison, or buffalo, and the mountain sheep. Among all modern North American hoofed mammals, in fact, only the pronghorn antelope emerged originally on this continent. The gray wolf, lynx, beaver, and many other animals also have close relations in the Old World, so close that even today a number of them—the wolverine and the Eurasian glutton, for example, and the grizzly and Siberian brown bear—are widely considered to be identical species. Similarly, many bird species are common to both continents, including the herring gull, golden plover, mallard, and peregrine falcon. The larger groupings—the genera and families which contain those species and many others—are widespread throughout the Northern Hemisphere. Even among the songbirds, which are quite dissimilar on the two continents in terms of individual species, the only large American family which has no counterpart in Eurasia is that of the colorful wood warblers, *Parulidae*.

Since the American continents are connected overland, it seems rather strange that the faunas of North America and Eurasia are more closely allied than the faunas of North and South America. One must remember, however, that the Americas were separated for fifty million years or more in the course of the present geologic era, and during this time their creatures had evolved quite differently. It is only in recent times, in geological terms—two million years ago, perhaps—that the formation of the huge icecaps, lowering the oceans of the world, permitted the reappearance of the Panama bridge between Americas.

The animals moved north and south across this land bridge, just as they had moved east and west across the dry strait in the Arctic. But the South American forms, become senile and overspecialized in their long period of isolation, were unable to compete with the younger species which were flourishing throughout the Northern Hemisphere. Many archaic monkeys, marsupials, and other forms were rapidly exterminated by the invaders. Though a certain interchange took place across the land bridge, the northern mammalian genera came to dominate both continents, and their descendants comprise virtually all the large South American animals of today, including the cougar, jaguar, deer, peccaries, and guanacos.

The armadillo, opossum, and porcupine, on the other hand, are among the primitive creatures which arrived safely from the opposite direction and are still extending their range. A large relation of the armadillo, *Boreostracon,* and a mighty ground sloth, *Megatherium,* also made their way to North America. These slow-witted beasts penetrated the continent as far as Pennsylvania, only to succumb to the changes in climate which accompanied the passing of the Ice Age.

The mass extermination of great mammals at this time occurred everywhere except in Africa and southern Asia. Alteration of environment brought about by climatic change is usually held accountable, but the precise reasons are as mysterious as those offered for the mass extinction of the dinosaurs some seventy million years before. Even among large animals the extinctions were by no means uniform: in North America the moose and bison were able to make the necessary adaptations, while the camel and horse were not. The camel family survived in South America in the wild guanaco and vicuña, but the horse was absent from the Western Hemisphere until recent centuries, when it returned with the Spaniards as a domestic animal.

Large creatures of the other classes were apparently less affected than the mammals. Great Pleistocene birds such as the whooping crane and the California condor prevail in remnant populations to this day, and many more primitive vertebrates, of which the sharks, sturgeons, sea turtles, and crocodilians are only the most spectacular examples, have persisted in their present form over many millions of years. For these, the slow wax and wane of the glacial epoch, which witnessed the emergence of mankind, was no more than a short season in the long history of their existence on the earth.

The last mastodons and mammoths were presumably hunted by man, who may have been hunted in his turn by *Smilodon,* the unsmiling saber-toothed tiger. Possibly the demise of these creatures at the dawn of the Recent epoch was significantly hastened by nomadic hunters whose numerous tribes were wandering east and south across the continent. The red men were always few in number and, the Pueblo peoples of the Southwest excepted, left little sign of their existence. They moved softly through the wilderness like woodland birds, rarely remaining long enough in one locality to mar it.

The visits by Vikings, few records of which have come down from the Dark Ages, were transient also, and the forest green soon covered their crude settlements, leaving only a few much-disputed traces. These fierce warriors, whose sea-dragon galleys were the most exotic craft ever to pierce the North Atlantic fogs, had colonized Greenland by the tenth century and were thus the earliest white discoverers of the Western Hemisphere. That they also discovered North America by the year 1000 seems hardly to be doubted, and the Norse colonists of an ill-defined stretch of northeast coast were the first to record the resources of the new continent. In addition to the wild grapes for which the country was called Vinland, "there was no lack of salmon there either in the river or in the lake, and larger salmon than they had ever seen before," according to the chronicle of Eric the Red. But they concerned themselves chiefly with the export of timber and fur, and in their murderous dealings with the Skrellings, as they called the red men, established a precedent firmly adhered to in later centuries by more pious invaders from France, England, Spain, and Holland. The last Vinland colony, in 1011, was beset less by Skrellings than by civil strife; in the following spring, the survivors sailed away to Greenland, and the history of Vinland, brief and bloody, came to an end.

The modern exploitation of North American wildlife, then, commenced with Breton fishermen who, piloting shallops smaller still than the very small *Santa María,* were probably appearing annually on the Grand Banks off Newfoundland before the voyage of Columbus, and certainly no later than 1497, the year that Americus Vespucius and the Cabots explored Vinland's dark, quiet coasts. "The soil is barren in some places," Sebastian Cabot wrote of Labrador or Newfoundland, "and yields little fruit, but it is full of white bears, and stags far greater than ours. It yields plenty of fish, and those very great, as seals, and those which commonly we call salmons: there are soles also above a yard in length: but especially there is great abundance of that kind of fish which the savages call baccalaos." The baccalao, or cod, abounding in the cold offshore waters of the continental shelf, formed the first major commerce of what Vespucius, in a letter to Lorenzo de' Medici, would term the New World; in its incidental persecution of seabirds, this primitive fishery was to initiate the long decline of North American fauna.

Though the Breton fishermen left no records, it must be assumed that they located almost immediately the great bird colonies in the Magdalen Islands and at Funk Island, a flat rock islet thirty-odd miles off Newfoundland. Since many seabirds, and especially those of the alcid family—the auks, puffins, guillemots, and murres—are of general distribution on both sides of the North Atlantic and nest on the rock islands of Brittany even today, these sailors were quick to recognize their countrymen. A concept of the plenty they came upon may still be had at Bonaventure Island, off the Gaspé Peninsula of Quebec, where the four-hundred-foot cliffs off the seaward face form one vast hive of alcids. The birds swarm ceaselessly in spring and summer, drifting in from the ocean in flocks like long wisps of smoke and whirring upward from the water to careen clumsily along the ledges. Above, on the crest, the magnificent white gannets nest, and the kittiwakes and larger gulls patrol the face, their sad cries added to a chittering and shrieking which pierce the booming of the surf in the black sea caves below. At the base of the cliff the visitor, small in a primeval emptiness of ocean, rock, and sky, feels simultaneously exalted and diminished; the bleak bird rocks of the northern oceans will perhaps be the final outposts of the natural profusion known to early voyagers, and we moderns, used to remnant populations of creatures taught to know their place, find this wild din, this wilderness of life, bewildering.

The largest alcid, and the one easiest to kill, was the great auk. Flightless, it was forced to nest on low, accessible ledges, and with the white man's coming its colonies were soon exterminated except on remote rocks far out at sea. The size of a goose, it furnished not only edible eggs but meat, down and feathers, oil, and even codfish bait, and the Micmac Indians were said to have valued its gullet as a quiver for their arrows. The greatest colony of garefowl was probably at Funk Island, where Jacques Cartier, as early as 1534, salted down five or six barrels of these hapless birds for each ship in his expedition. In 1536 an Englishman named Robert Hore improved upon old-fashioned ways by spreading a sail bridge from ship to shore and marching a complement of auks into his hold. Later voyagers, sailing in increasing numbers to the new continent, learned quickly to augment their wretched stores in similar fashion, not only at Funk Island but at Bird Rocks in the Magdalens and elsewhere. The great auk is thought to have nested as far south as the coast of Maine, with a wintering population in Massachusetts Bay, but the southern colonies were probably destroyed quite early.

As a group, the alcids have always been extraordinarily plentiful—the Brünnich's murre and the dovekie, which may be the most numerous of northern seabirds, each boast colonies in Greenland of two million individuals or more—and the great auk was no exception. The relative inaccessibility of its North Atlantic rookeries deferred its extinction for three centuries, but by 1785, when the frenzy of colonization had subsided, George Cartwright of Labrador, describing the Funks, was obliged to take note of the bird's decline: "it has been customary of late years, for several crews of men to live all summer on that island, for the sole purpose of killing birds for the sake of their feathers; the destruction which they have made is incredible. If a stop is not soon put to that practice, the whole breed will be diminished to almost nothing, particularly the penguins: for this is now the only island they have left to breed upon." Cartwright does not mention the complementary industry of boiling the birds in huge try-pots for their oil, an enterprise made feasible on the treeless Funks by the use of still more auks as fuel.

The naturalists of the period, unhappily, did not share Cartwright's alarm. Thomas Pennant, writing in the previous year, makes no mention of auk scarcity, and Thomas Nuttall, as late as 1834, is more concerned with the bird's demeanor than with its destruction. "Deprived of the use of wings," he mourns, "degraded as it were from the feathered ranks, and almost numbered with the amphibious monsters of the deep, the Auk seems condemned to dwell alone in those desolate and forsaken regions of the earth. . . . In the Ferröe isles, Iceland, Greenland and Newfoundland, they dwell and breed in great numbers." Though Nuttall pointed out, somewhat paradoxically, that recent navigators had failed to observe them, his contemporary, Mr. Audubon, was persuaded of their abundance off Newfoundland and of their continued use as a source of fish bait. In 1840, the year after Audubon's account, the auk is thought to have become extinct off Newfoundland, and two decades later Dr. Spencer F. Baird was of the opinion that, as a species, the bird was rather rare. His remark may well have been the first of a long series of troubled observations by American naturalists in regard to the scarcity of a creature which was, in fact, already extinct.

"All night," wrote Columbus, in his journal for October 9, 1492, "they heard birds passing." He was already wandering the eastern reaches of the Caribbean, seeking in every sign of life a harbinger of land. The night flyers mentioned were probably hosts of migratory birds, traversing the Caribbean from North to South America, rather than native species of the Greater Antilles or Hispaniola. Columbus could not have known this, of course, nor did he suspect that the birds seen by day which raised false hopes throughout the crossing were not even coastal species, but shearwaters and petrels, which visit land but once a year to breed.

Certain shearwaters, storm petrels, and alcids are still very common in season off the Atlantic coasts, but it is no coincidence that the great auk and two species of petrel were the first North American creatures to suffer a drastic decline. The Atlantic islands, rising out of the endless fetch of the wide, westward horizon, were much frequented by ships, and often provided new ship's stores for the last leg of the voyage. Fresh meat was usually supplied by seabirds, incredibly plentiful on their crowded island nesting grounds; in temperate seas, the shearwaters and petrels, like the great auks farther north, were conscripted commonly as a supplementary diet.

In spite of local plenty, the bird communities of islands around the world are often early victims of extermination. The breeding range of island species is small and therefore vulnerable, and the species themselves may be quite primitive. Some are relict populations of forms which, on the mainland, have long since succumbed in the struggle for survival. Other species, freed from competition and mammalian predation, grow overspecialized, diminished in vitality, and thus are ill equipped to deal with new factors in their environment.

In the 1960s, poetry by Beat writers such as Diane di Prima, Gary Snyder, and Lew Welch contributed to the raising of their readers' consciousness about the inextricable connection of all natural systems in the universe. Jack Kerouac first dramatized the hippie creed of simplifying life by going "back to the land" in *The Dharma Bums* (1958), a novel that has inspired generations of "rucksack revolutionaries." In *Desolation Angels* (1965), Kerouac described his summer job in 1956 as a fire spotter in the mountains of Washington State, where he spent seventy days attempting to free his mind, meditating and writing spontaneously in a journal in an effort to achieve what he considered a direct perception of nature, "pointing out things directly, purely, concretely, no abstractions or explanations." Many readers considered section 12 of the part of the book that Kerouac called "Desolation in Solitude" as their introduction to the Environmental Movement.

In a few paragraphs, Kerouac described a mystical moment when he believed that he saw nature in its pure state, existing outside of time and space, after he unexpectedly had a vision of the Chinese poet Hanshan, whose writing Snyder had translated and shown him in Berkeley. Active in the seventh or eighth century A.D., Hanshan was characterized by Snyder as "a mountain madman in an old Chinese line of ragged hermits." Hanshan became an Immortal through his poetry and his presence in later Zen paintings, always pictured with "the scroll, the broom, the wild hair and laughter." Stories about him related that Hanshan lived alone in a place called Cold Mountain, and that he often went down to a nearby temple, where his friend Shihte saved him scraps of food. In *Desolation Angels,* Kerouac described his sudden vision of Hanshan and Shihte in his "little peaked wood outhouse on Starvation Ridge in the High Cascades."

Diane di Prima

Diane di Prima described her fears of widespread ecological destruction in "Revolutionary Letter #16," written in the late 1960s and included in her series of Revolutionary Letters *published by City Lights in 1974.*

REVOLUTIONARY LETTER #16

we are eating up the planet, the New York Times
takes a forest, every Sunday, Los Angeles
draws its water from the Sacramento Valley
the rivers of British Columbia are ours
on lease for 99 years

every large factory is an infringement
of our god-given right to light and air
to clean and flowing rivers stocked with fish
to the very possibility of life

for our children's children, we will have to
look carefully, i.e., do we really want/
need
electricity and at what cost in natural resource
human resource
do we need cars, when petroleum
pumped from the earth poisons the land around
for 100 years, pumped from the car
poisons the hard-pressed cities, or try this
statistic, the USA
has 5% of the world's people uses over
50% of the world's goods, our garbage
holds matter for survival for uncounted
"underdeveloped" nations

———————

Gary Snyder

*Gary Snyder included "What You Should Know to Be a Poet"
and "Revolution in the Revolution in the Revolution" in* Regarding Wave *(1970). Snyder distributed his poem "Smokey the Bear
Sutra" in San Francisco at the Sierra Club Wilderness Conference
in 1969 as a free broadside to raise environmental consciousness.*

WHAT YOU SHOULD KNOW TO BE A POET

all you can about animals as persons.
the names of trees and flowers and weeds.
names of stars, and the movements of the planets
                and the moon.

your own six senses, with a watchful and elegant mind.

at least one kind of traditional magic:
divination, astrology, the *book of changes,* the tarot;

dreams.
the illusory demons and illusory shining gods;

kiss the ass of the devil and eat shit;
fuck his horny barbed cock,
fuck the hag,
and all the celestial angels
                    and maidens perfum'd and golden—

& then love the human; wives   husbands   and friends.

children's games, comic books, bubble-gum,
the weirdness of television and advertising.

work, long dry hours of dull work swallowed and accepted
and livd with and finally lovd.   exhaustion,
                  hunger, rest.

the wild freedom of the dance, *extasy*
silent solitary illumination, *enstasy*

real danger.   gambles.   and the edge of death.

REVOLUTION IN THE REVOLUTION IN THE REVOLUTION

The country surrounds the city
The back country surrounds the country

"From the masses to the masses" the most
Revolutionary consciousness is to be found
Among the most ruthlessly exploited classes:
Animals, trees, water, air, grasses

We must pass through the stage of the
"Dictatorship of the Unconscious" before we can
Hope for the withering-away of the states

And finally arrive at true Communionism.

If the capitalists and imperialists
    are the exploiters, the masses are the workers.
        and the party
        is the communist.

If civilization
    is the exploiter, the masses is nature.
        and the party
        is the poets.

If the abstract rational intellect
    is the exploiter, the masses is the unconscious.
        and the party
        is the yogins.

& POWER
comes out of the seed-syllables of mantras.

SMOKEY THE BEAR SUTRA

Once in the Jurassic about 150 million years ago,
the Great Sun Buddha in this corner of the Infinite
Void gave a Discourse to all the assembled elements
and energies: to the standing beings, the walking beings,
the flying beings, and the sitting beings—even grasses,
to the number of thirteen billion, each one born from a
seed, assembled there: a Discourse concerning
Enlightenment on the planet Earth.

"In some future time, there will be a continent called
America. It will have great centers of power called
such as Pyramid Lake, Walden Pond, Mt. Rainier, Big Sur,
Everglades, and so forth; and powerful nerves and channels
such as Columbia River, Mississippi River, and Grand
  Canyon.

The human race in that era will get into troubles all over
its head, and practically wreck everything in spite of
its own strong intelligent Buddha-nature.

"The twisting strata of the great mountains and the pulsings
of volcanoes are my love burning deep in the earth.
My obstinate compassion is schist and basalt and
granite, to be mountains, to bring down the rain. In that
future American Era I shall enter a new form; to cure
the world of loveless knowledge that seeks with blind
  hunger:
and mindless rage eating food that will not fill it."

And he showed himself in his true form of

SMOKEY THE BEAR.

A handsome smokey-colored brown bear standing
on his hind legs, showing that he is aroused and watchful.

Bearing in his right paw the Shovel that digs to the
truth beneath appearances; cuts the roots of useless attach-
ments, and flings damp sand on the fires of greed and war;

His left paw in the Mudra of Comradely Display—
indicating that all creatures have the full right to live to their
limits and that deer, rabbits, chipmunks, snakes, dandelions,
and lizards all grow in the realm of the Dharma;

Wearing the blue work overalls symbolic of slaves
and laborers, the countless men oppressed by a civilization
that claims to save but often destroys;

Wearing the broad-brimmed hat of the West,
symbolic of the forces that guard the Wilderness, which is
the Natural State of the Dharma and the True Path of man
on earth: all true paths lead through mountains—

With a halo of smoke and flame behind, the forest
fires of the kali-yuga, fires caused by the stupidity of those

who think things can be gained and lost whereas in truth all
is contained vast and free in the Blue Sky and Green Earth
of One Mind;

Round-bellied to show his kind nature and that the
great earth has food enough for everyone who loves her
and trusts her;

Trampling underfoot wasteful freeways and needless
suburbs; smashing the worms of capitalism and
totalitarianism;

Indicating the Task: his followers, becoming free of
cars, houses, canned foods, universities, and shoes, master
the Three Mysteries of their own Body, Speech, and Mind;
and fearlessly chop down the rotten trees and prune out the
sick limbs of this country America and then burn the
leftover trash.

Wrathful but Calm. Austere but Comic. Smokey the Bear
  will
Illuminate those who would help him; but for those who
  would
hinder or slander him,

HE WILL PUT THEM OUT.

Thus his great Mantra:

Namah samanta vajranam chanda maharoshana
            Sphataya hum traks ham mam

"I DEDICATE MYSELF TO THE UNIVERSAL DIAMOND
BE THIS RAGING FURY DESTROYED"

And he will protect those who love woods and rivers,
Gods and animals, hobos and madmen, prisoners and sick
people, musicians, playful women, and hopeful children:

And if anyone is threatened by advertising, air pollution,
  television,

or the police, they should chant SMOKEY THE BEAR'S
WAR SPELL:

DROWN THEIR BUTTS
CRUSH THEIR BUTTS
DROWN THEIR BUTTS
CRUSH THEIR BUTTS

And SMOKEY THE BEAR will surely appear to put the
    enemy out
with his vajra-shovel.

Now those who recite this Sutra and then try to put it in
            practice will accumulate merit as countless as the
            sands of Arizona and Nevada.
Will help save the planet Earth from total oil slick.
Will enter the age of harmony of man and nature.
Will win the tender love and caresses of men, women, and
            beasts.
Will always have ripe blackberries to eat and a sunny spot
            under a pine tree to sit at.
AND IN THE END WILL WIN HIGHEST PERFECT
ENLIGHTENMENT.

            thus have we heard.

                                (*may be reproduced free forever*)

— — —

Lew Welch

In Lew Welch's posthumously published Selected Poems *(1976),
Gary Snyder wrote a preface in which he connected his friend's writ-
ing to the emerging Environmental Movement in the 1960s. Sny-
der also underscored the dark quality in the bare-bones appeal of
Welch's open-form poetry:*

Ultimately Lew's poems are devotional songs to the Goddess Gaia: Planet Earth Biosphere: and he is truly one of the few who have Gone Beyond, in grasping the beauty of that ecstatic Mutual Offering called the Food Chain.

Lew and I were brothers and fellow-workers from early. Poets are the sons of witches; understanding the tradition of Muses is contingent on that. Living with the image of the Teeth Mother was the darker side of Lew's songs. He drank far too much, had a way with guns, and took one with him into the woods, never to be seen again, in May of 1971.

This selection from Welch's Hermit Poems *was included in* Selected Poems. *The entire set was originally published in 1965 by Four Seasons Foundation in San Francisco as* Hermit Poems. *"The Song Mt. Tamalpais Sings" was published as a broadside in 1969.*

HERMIT POEMS

(For Lloyd Reynolds)

Preface To *Hermit Poems*, The Bath

At last it is raining, the first sign of spring.
The Blue Jay gets all wet.

Frost-flowers, tiny bright and dry like
inch high crystal trees or sparkling silver mold,
acres of them, on heaps of placer boulders all around me,
are finally washing away. They were beautiful.
And the big trees rising, dark, behind them.

This canyon is so steep we didn't get sun since late
   November,
my "CC" shack and I. Obsolete. The two of us.
He for his de-funct agency.
I for this useless Art?

> *"Oughtta come by more often, Lewie,*
> *you get shack simple."*

big winter boom of the river
crunch of boots on the icy trail to it

kerosene lantern even in the daytime   golden light

inside

I think I'll bathe in
Spring-rain tin-roof clatter of it
all begins to melt away.
The bath a ritual here, the way it used to be.

> *Vat & Cauldron*
> *Kettle Pot & Tub*
> *Stoke the Stove till Cherry*

Naked, he clambers over boulders to his spring.
He dips two buckets full and scampers back.
Filling the many vessels on his stove, he starts
to rave.

> I hear Incantations!
> I hear voices of the Wise Old Men and
> songs of the Addled Girls!

> Moss! Astonishing green!
> All that time the rocks were, even.

> Hopping on it, wet, that Crested Blue!

Robin bedraggled.   Warm rain finally.   Spring.

[I Know a Man's Supposed to Have His Hair Cut Short]

I know a man's supposed to have his hair cut short,
but I have beautiful hair.
I like to let it grow into a long bronze mane.

In my boots. In my blue wool shirt.
With my rifle slung over my shoulder
among huge boulders in the dark ravine,

I'm the ghost roan stallion.
Leif Ericson.
The beautiful Golden Girl!

In summer I usually cut it all off.
I do it myself, with scissors and a
little Jim Beam.

How disappointed everybody is.

Months and months go by before they can
worry about my hairdo

and the breeze
is so cool

[Apparently Wasps]

Apparently wasps
work all their only summer at the nest,
so that new wasps work
all their only summer at the nest,
et cetera.

All my lizards lost their tails, mating.
Six green snakes ate all my frogs.
Butterflies do very odd things with their tongues.

There seems to be no escaping it.
I planted nine tomato plants and water them.
I replaced my rotten stoop with a
clean Fir block.

Twelve new poems in less than a week!

[I Burn Up the Deer in My Body]

I burn up the deer in my body.
I burn up the tree in my stove.

I seldom let a carrot go to seed, and I
grind up every kind of grain.

How can I be and never be an
inconvenience to others, here,

where only the Vulture is absolutely pure

and in the Chicago River
are carp?

[Whenever I Make a New Poem]

Whenever I make a new poem,
the old ones sound like gibberish.
How can they ever make sense in a book?

Let them say:
"He seems to have lived in the mountains.
He traveled now and then.
When he appeared in cities,
he was almost always drunk.

"Most of his poems are lost.
Many of those we have were found in
letters to his friends.

"He had a very large number of friends."

Step out onto the Planet.
Draw a circle a hundred feet round.

Inside the circle are
300 things nobody understands, and, maybe
nobody's ever really seen.

How many can you find?

THE SONG MT. TAMALPAIS SINGS

This is the last place. There is nowhere else to go.

> Human movements,
> > but for a few,
> are Westerly.
> Man follows the Sun.

This is the last place. There is nowhere else to go.

> Or follows what he thinks to be the
> movement of the Sun.
> It is hard to feel it, as a rider,
> on a spinning ball.

This is the last place. There is nowhere else to go.

> Centuries and hordes of us,
> from every quarter of the earth,
> now piling up,
> and each wave going back
> to get some more.

This is the last place. There is nowhere else to go.

> "My face is the map of the Steppes,"
> she said, on this mountain, looking West.

> My blood set singing by it,
> to the old tunes,
> Irish,
> among these Oaks.

This is the last place. There is nowhere else to go.

> Once again we celebrate the great Spring Tides.
> Beaches are strewn again with Jasper,

Agate, and Jade.
The Mussel–rocks stand clear.

This is the last place. There is nowhere else to go.

Once again we celebrate the
Headland's huge, cairn–studded, fall
into the Sea.

This is the last place. There is nowhere else to go.

For we have walked the jeweled beaches
at the feet of the final cliffs
of all Man's wanderings.

This is the last place

There is nowhere else we need to go.

Wendell Berry

Through his many books of poetry and essays, Wendell Berry, who taught at the University of Kentucky while he reclaimed a worn-out hill farm in his native Kentucky, has become one of the most prominent ecological spokesmen in the United States. Berry has said that he finds his discipline in poetry, farming, and family. "To the Unseeable Animal," a poem inspired by a conversation with his young daughter, was included in Farming: A Hand Book *(1970).*

TO THE UNSEEABLE ANIMAL

My daughter: "I hope there's an animal
somewhere that nobody has ever seen.
And I hope nobody ever sees it."

Being, whose flesh dissolves
at our glance, knower
of the secret sums and measures,
you are always here,
dwelling in the oldest sycamores,
visiting the faithful springs
when they are dark and the foxes
have crept to their edges.
I have come upon pools
in streams, places overgrown
with the woods' shadow,
where I knew you had rested,
watching the little fish
hang still in the flow;
as I approached they seemed
particles of your clear mind
disappearing among the rocks.
I have waked deep in the woods
in the early morning, sure
that while I slept
your gaze passed over me.
That we do not know you
is your perfection
and our hope. The darkness
keeps us near you.

Edward Abbey

Like the iconoclasts Gary Snyder and Jack Kerouac before him, Edward Abbey also learned much as a writer from his seasonal job in a nature preserve in the western part of the United States. At the end of the 1950s, Abbey worked for three springs and summers (April through September) as a park ranger in Arches National Monument in southeast Utah. Ten years later, in his introduction to Desert Solitaire: A Season in the Wilderness *(1968), Abbey said, "I would have returned . . . each year thereafter but unfortunately for me the Arches, a primitive place when I first went there, was developed and improved so well that I had to leave."*

While keeping a journal of his experiences in Utah, Abbey tried to be as accurate as possible in recording his impressions of nature, "since I believe that there is a kind of poetry, even a kind of truth, in simple fact." Aware that he was often dealing with the surface of things, he confessed that surfaces pleased him:

> *In fact they alone seem to me to be of much importance. Such things for example as the grasp of a child's hand in your own, the flavor of an apple, the embrace of friend or lover, the silk of a girl's thigh, the sunlight on rocks and leaves, the feel of music, the bark of a tree, the abrasion of granite and sand, the plunge of clear water into a pool, the face of the wind—what else is there? What else do we need?*

Near the end of Desert Solitaire, *in a chapter entitled "Polemic: Industrial Tourism and the National Parks," Abbey vented his anger at the way that the National Park Service and the Department of the Interior "developed" the natural landscape into national parks. Abbey cautioned his readers that most of what he wrote about Arches National Monument "is already gone or going under fast. This is not a travel guide but an elegy. A memorial. You're holding a tombstone in your hands. A bloody rock. Don't drop it on your foot—throw it at something big and glassy. What do you have to lose?" "The Serpents of Paradise" is an early chap-*

*ter describing how Abbey settled into his house trailer at the begin-
ning of his stay at the Arches.*

THE SERPENTS OF PARADISE

THE APRIL MORNINGS ARE BRIGHT, clear and calm. Not until the afternoon does the wind begin to blow, raising dust and sand in funnel-shaped twisters that spin across the desert briefly, like dancers, and then collapse—whirlwinds from which issue no voice or word except the forlorn moan of the elements under stress. After the reconnoitering dust-devils comes the real, the serious wind, the voice of the desert rising to a demented howl and blotting out sky and sun behind yellow clouds of dust, sand, confusion, embattled birds, last year's scrub-oak leaves, pollen, the husks of locusts, bark of juniper. . . .

Time of the red eye, the sore and bloody nostril, the sand-pitted windshield, if one is foolish enough to drive his car into such a storm. Time to sit indoors and continue that letter which is never finished— while the fine dust forms neat little windrows under the edge of the door and on the windowsills. Yet the springtime winds are as much a part of the canyon country as the silence and the glamorous distances; you learn, after a number of years, to love them also.

The mornings therefore, as I started to say and meant to say, are all the sweeter in the knowledge of what the afternoon is likely to bring. Before beginning the morning chores I like to sit on the sill of my doorway, bare feet planted on the bare ground and a mug of hot coffee in hand, facing the sunrise. The air is gelid, not far above freezing, but the butane heater inside the trailer keeps my back warm, the rising sun warms the front, and the coffee warms the interior.

Perhaps this is the loveliest hour of the day, though it's hard to choose. Much depends on the season. In midsummer the sweetest hour begins at sundown, after the awful heat of the afternoon. But now, in April, we'll take the opposite, that hour beginning with the sunrise. The birds, returning from wherever they go in winter, seem inclined to agree. The pinyon jays are whirling in garrulous, gregarious flocks from one stunted tree to the next and back again, erratic exuberant games without any apparent practical function. A few big ravens hang around and croak harsh clanking statements of smug satisfaction from the rimrock, lifting their greasy wings now and then to probe for lice. I can hear but seldom see the canyon wrens singing their distinctive song from somewhere up on the cliffs: a flutelike de-

scent—never ascent—of the whole-tone scale. Staking out new nest-
ing claims, I understand. Also invisible but invariably present at some
indefinable distance are the mourning doves whose plaintive call sug-
gests irresistibly a kind of seeking-out, the attempt by separated souls
to restore a lost communion:

Hello . . . they seem to cry, *who . . . are . . . you?*

And the reply from a different quarter. *Hello* . . . (pause) *where . . .
are . . . you?*

No doubt this line of analogy must be rejected. It's foolish and
unfair to impute to the doves, with serious concerns of their own, an
interest in questions more appropriate to their human kin. Yet their
song, if not a mating call or a warning, must be what it sounds like, a
brooding meditation on space, on solitude. The game.

Other birds, silent, which I have not yet learned to identify, are
also lurking in the vicinity, watching me. What the ornithologist
terms l.g.b.'s—little gray birds—they flit about from point to point on
noiseless wings, their origins obscure.

As mentioned before, I share the housetrailer with a number of
mice. I don't know how many but apparently only a few, perhaps a sin-
gle family. They don't disturb me and are welcome to my crumbs and
leavings. Where they came from, how they got into the trailer, how they
survived before my arrival (for the trailer had been locked up for six
months), these are puzzling matters I am not prepared to resolve. My
only reservation concerning the mice is that they do attract rattlesnakes.

I'm sitting on my doorstep early one morning, facing the sun as
usual, drinking coffee, when I happen to look down and see almost
between my bare feet, only a couple of inches to the rear of my heels,
the very thing I had in mind. No mistaking that wedgelike head, that
tip of horny segmented tail peeping out of the coils. He's under the
doorstep and in the shade where the ground and air remain very cold.
In his sluggish condition he's not likely to strike unless I rouse him by
some careless move of my own.

There's a revolver inside the trailer, a huge British Webley .45,
loaded, but it's out of reach. Even if I had it in my hands I'd hesitate to
blast a fellow creature at such close range, shooting between my own
legs at a living target flat on solid rock thirty inches away. It would be
like murder; and where would I set my coffee? My cherrywood walk-
ing stick leans against the trailerhouse wall only a few feet away but
I'm afraid that in leaning over for it I might stir up the rattler or spill
some hot coffee on his scales.

Other considerations come to mind. Arches National Monument is meant to be among other things a sanctuary for wildlife—for all forms of wildlife. It is my duty as a park ranger to protect, preserve and defend all living things within the park boundaries, making no exceptions. Even if this were not the case I have personal convictions to uphold. Ideals, you might say. I prefer not to kill animals. I'm a humanist; I'd rather kill a *man* than a snake.

What to do. I drink some more coffee and study the dormant reptile at my heels. It is not after all the mighty diamondback, *Crotalus atrox*, I'm confronted with but a smaller species known locally as the horny rattler or more precisely as the Faded Midget. An insulting name for a rattlesnake, which may explain the Faded Midget's alleged bad temper. But the name is apt: he is small and dusty-looking, with a little knob above each eye—the horns. His bite though temporarily disabling would not likely kill a full-grown man in normal health. Even so I don't really want him around. Am I to be compelled to put on boots or shoes every time I wish to step outside? The scorpions, tarantulas, centipedes, and black widows are nuisance enough.

I finish my coffee, lean back and swing my feet up and inside the doorway of the trailer. At once there is a buzzing sound from below and the rattler lifts his head from his coils, eyes brightening, and extends his narrow black tongue to test the air.

After thawing out my boots over the gas flame I pull them on and come back to the doorway. My visitor is still waiting beneath the doorstep, basking in the sun, fully alert. The trailerhouse has two doors. I leave by the other and get a long-handled spade out of the bed of the government pickup. With this tool I scoop the snake into the open. He strikes; I can hear the click of the fangs against steel, see the stain of venom. He wants to stand and fight, but I am patient; I insist on herding him well away from the trailer. On guard, head aloft—that evil slit-eyed weaving head shaped like the ace of spades— tail whirring, the rattler slithers sideways, retreating slowly before me until he reaches the shelter of a sandstone slab. He backs under it.

You better stay there, cousin, I warn him; if I catch you around the trailer again I'll chop your head off.

A week later he comes back. If not him, his twin brother. I spot him one morning under the trailer near the kitchen drain, waiting for a mouse. I have to keep my promise.

This won't do. If there are midget rattlers in the area there may be diamondbacks too—five, six or seven feet long, thick as a man's wrist, dangerous. I don't want *them* camping under my home. It looks as though I'll have to trap the mice.

However, before being forced to take that step I am lucky enough to capture a gopher snake. Burning garbage one morning at the park dump, I see a long slender yellow-brown snake emerge from a mound of old tin cans and plastic picnic plates and take off down the sandy bed of a gulch. There is a burlap sack in the cab of the truck which I carry when plucking Kleenex flowers from the brush and cactus along the road; I grab that and my stick, run after the snake and corner it beneath the exposed roots of a bush. Making sure it's a gopher snake and not something less useful, I open the neck of the sack and with a great deal of coaxing and prodding get the snake into it. The gopher snake, *Drymarchon corais couperi,* or bull snake, has a reputation as the enemy of rattlesnakes, destroying or driving them away whenever encountered.

Hoping to domesticate this sleek, handsome and docile reptile, I release him inside the trailerhouse and keep him there for several days. Should I attempt to feed him? I decide against it—let him eat mice. What little water he may need can also be extracted from the flesh of his prey.

The gopher snake and I get along nicely. During the day he curls up like a cat in the warm corner behind the heater and at night he goes about his business. The mice, singularly quiet for a change, make themselves scarce. The snake is passive, apparently contented, and makes no resistance when I pick him up with my hands and drape him over an arm or around my neck. When I take him outside into the wind and sunshine his favorite place seems to be inside my shirt, where he wraps himself around my waist and rests on my belt. In this position he sometimes sticks his head out between shirt buttons for a survey of the weather, astonishing and delighting any tourists who may happen to be with me at the time. The scales of a snake are dry and smooth, quite pleasant to the touch. Being a cold-blooded creature, of course, he takes his temperature from that of the immediate environment—in this case my body.

We are compatible. From my point of view, friends. After a week of close association I turn him loose on the warm sandstone at my doorstep and leave for a patrol of the park. At noon when I return he is gone. I search everywhere beneath, nearby and inside the trailerhouse, but my companion has disappeared. Has he left the area entirely or is he hiding somewhere close by? At any rate I am troubled no more by rattlesnakes under the door.

The snake story is not yet ended.

In the middle of May, about a month after the gopher snake's disappearance, in the evening of a very hot day, with all the rosy desert cooling like a griddle with the fire turned off, he reappears. This time with a mate.

I'm in the stifling heat of the trailer opening a can of beer, bare-footed, about to go outside and relax after a hard day watching cloud formations. I happen to glance out the little window near the refrigerator and see two gopher snakes on my verandah engaged in what seems to be a kind of ritual dance. Like a living caduceus they wind and unwind about each other in undulant, graceful, perpetual motion, moving slowly across a dome of sandstone. Invisible but tangible as music is the passion which joins them—sexual? combative? both? A shameless *voyeur*, I stare at the lovers, and then to get a closer view run outside and around the trailer to the back. There I get down on hands and knees and creep toward the dancing snakes, not wanting to frighten or disturb them. I crawl to within six feet of them and stop, flat on my belly, watching from the snake's-eye level. Obsessed with their ballet, the serpents seem unaware of my presence.

The two gopher snakes are nearly identical in length and coloring; I cannot be certain that either is actually my former household pet. I cannot even be sure that they are male and female, though their performance resembles so strongly a *pas de deux* by formal lovers. They intertwine and separate, glide side by side in perfect congruence, turn like mirror images of each other and glide back again, wind and unwind again. This is the basic pattern but there is a variation: at regular intervals the snakes elevate their heads, facing one another, as high as they can go, as if each is trying to outreach or overawe the other. Their heads and bodies rise, higher and higher, then topple together and the rite goes on.

I crawl after them, determined to see the whole thing. Suddenly and simultaneously they discover me, prone on my belly a few feet away. The dance stops. After a moment's pause the two snakes come straight toward me, still in flawless unison, straight toward my face, the forked tongues flickering, their intense wild yellow eyes staring directly into my eyes. For an instant I am paralyzed by wonder; then, stung by a fear too ancient and powerful to overcome I scramble back, rising to my knees. The snakes veer and turn and race away from me in parallel motion, their lean elegant bodies making a soft hissing noise as they slide over the sand and stone. I follow them for a short distance, still plagued by curiosity, before remembering my place and the requirements of common courtesy. For godsake let them go in peace, I tell myself. Wish them luck and (if lovers) innumerable offspring, a life of happily ever after. Not for their sake alone but for your own.

In the long hot days and cool evenings to come I will not see the gopher snakes again. Nevertheless I will feel their presence watching over me like totemic deities, keeping the rattlesnakes far back in the brush where I like them best, cropping off the surplus mouse population, maintaining useful connections with the primeval. Sympathy, mutual aid, symbiosis, continuity.

How can I descend to such anthropomorphism? Easily—but is it, in this case, entirely false? Perhaps not. I am not attributing human motives to my snake and bird acquaintances. I recognize that when and where they serve purposes of mine they do so for beautifully selfish reasons of their own. Which is exactly the way it should be. I suggest, however, that it's a foolish, simple-minded rationalism which denies any form of emotion to all animals but man and his dog. This is no more justified than the Moslems are in denying souls to women. It seems to me possible, even probable, that many of the nonhuman undomesticated animals experience emotions unknown to us. What do the coyotes mean when they yodel at the moon? What are the dolphins trying so patiently to tell us? Precisely what did those two enraptured gopher snakes have in mind when they came gliding toward my eyes over the naked sandstone? If I had been as capable of trust as I am susceptible to fear I might have learned something new or some truth so very old we have all forgotten it.

They do not sweat and whine about their condition,
They do not lie awake in the dark and weep for their sins. . . .

All men are brothers, we like to say, half-wishing sometimes in secret it were not true. But perhaps it is true. And is the evolutionary line from protozoan to Spinoza any less certain? That also may be true. We are obliged, therefore, to spread the news, painful and bitter though it may be for some to hear, that all living things on earth are kindred.

N. Scott Momaday

N. Scott Momaday first published "The Way to Rainy Mountain"
as an essay in the Reporter *in 1967. Two years later it was*
reprinted as the introduction to his book The Way to Rainy
Mountain, *where he described his return as a member of the*
Kiowa Native American tribe to his homeland.

FROM *THE WAY TO RAINY MOUNTAIN*

A SINGLE KNOLL rises out of the plain in Oklahoma, north and west
of the Wichita Range. For my people, the Kiowas, it is an old land-
mark, and they gave it the name Rainy Mountain. The hardest
weather in the world is there. Winter brings blizzards, hot tornadic
winds arise in the spring, and in summer the prairie is an anvil's edge.
The grass turns brittle and brown, and it cracks beneath your feet.
There are green belts along the rivers and creeks, linear groves of
hickory and pecan, willow and witch hazel. At a distance in July or
August the steaming foliage seems almost to writhe in fire. Great
green and yellow grasshoppers are everywhere in the tall grass, pop-
ping up like corn to sting the flesh, and tortoises crawl about on the
red earth, going nowhere in the plenty of time. Loneliness is an aspect
of the land. All things in the plain are isolate; there is no confusion of
objects in the eye, but *one* hill or *one* tree or *one* man. To look upon
that landscape in the early morning, with the sun at your back, is to
lose the sense of proportion. Your imagination comes to life, and this,
you think, is where Creation was begun.

I returned to Rainy Mountain in July. My grandmother had died
in the spring, and I wanted to be at her grave. She had lived to be
very old and at last infirm. Her only living daughter was with her
when she died, and I was told that in death her face was that of a
child.

I like to think of her as a child. When she was born, the Kiowas
were living the last great moment of their history. For more than a
hundred years they had controlled the open range from the Smoky

Hill River to the Red, from the headwaters of the Canadian to the fork of the Arkansas and Cimarron. In alliance with the Comanches, they had ruled the whole of the southern Plains. War was their sacred business, and they were among the finest horsemen the world has ever known. But warfare for the Kiowas was preeminently a matter of disposition rather than of survival, and they never understood the grim, unrelenting advance of the U.S. Cavalry. When at last, divided and ill-provisioned, they were driven onto the Staked Plains in the cold rains of autumn, they fell into panic. In Palo Duro Canyon they abandoned their crucial stores to pillage and had nothing then but their lives. In order to save themselves, they surrendered to the soldiers at Fort Sill and were imprisoned in the old stone corral that now stands as a military museum. My grandmother was spared the humiliation of those high gray walls by eight or ten years, but she must have known from birth the affliction of defeat, the dark brooding of old warriors.

Her name was Aho, and she belonged to the last culture to evolve in North America. Her forebears came down from the high country in western Montana nearly three centuries ago. They were a mountain people, a mysterious tribe of hunters whose language has never been positively classified in any major group. In the late seventeenth century they began a long migration to the south and east. It was a journey toward the dawn, and it led to a golden age. Along the way the Kiowas were befriended by the Crows, who gave them the culture and religion of the Plains. They acquired horses, and their ancient nomadic spirit was suddenly free of the ground. They acquired Tai-me, the sacred Sun Dance doll, from that moment the object and symbol of their worship, and so shared in the divinity of the sun. Not least, they acquired the sense of destiny, therefore courage and pride. When they entered upon the southern Plains they had been transformed. No longer were they slaves to the simple necessity of survival; they were a lordly and dangerous society of fighters and thieves, hunters and priests of the sun. According to their origin myth, they entered the world through a hollow log. From one point of view, their migration was the fruit of an old prophecy, for indeed they emerged from a sunless world.

Although my grandmother lived out her long life in the shadow of Rainy Mountain, the immense landscape of the continental interior lay like memory in her blood. She could tell of the Crows, whom she had never seen, and of the Black Hills, where she had never been. I wanted to see in reality what she had seen more perfectly in the mind's eye, and traveled fifteen hundred miles to begin my pilgrimage.

Yellowstone, it seemed to me, was the top of the world, a region of deep lakes and dark timber, canyons and waterfalls. But, beautiful as it is, one might have the sense of confinement there. The skyline in all directions is close at hand, the high wall of the woods and deep cleavages of shade. There is a perfect freedom in the mountains, but it belongs to the eagle and the elk, the badger and the bear. The Kiowas reckoned their stature by the distance they could see, and they were bent and blind in the wilderness.

Descending eastward, the highland meadows are a stairway to the plain. In July the inland slope of the Rockies is luxuriant with flax and buckwheat, stonecrop and larkspur. The earth unfolds and the limit of the land recedes. Clusters of trees, and animals grazing far in the distance, cause the vision to reach away and wonder to build upon the mind. The sun follows a longer course in the day, and the sky is immense beyond all comparison. The great billowing clouds that sail upon it are shadows that move upon the grain like water, dividing light. Farther down, in the land of the Crows and Blackfeet, the plain is yellow. Sweet clover takes hold of the hills and bends upon itself to cover and seal the soil. There the Kiowas paused on their way; they had come to the place where they must change their lives. The sun is at home on the plains. Precisely there does it have the certain character of a god. When the Kiowas came to the land of the Crows, they could see the dark lees of the hills at dawn across the Bighorn River, the profusion of light on the grain shelves, the oldest deity ranging after the solstices. Not yet would they veer southward to the caldron of the land that lay below; they must wean their blood from the northern winter and hold the mountains a while longer in their view. They bore Tai-me in procession to the east.

A dark mist lay over the Black Hills, and the land was like iron. At the top of a ridge I caught sight of Devil's Tower upthrust against the gray sky as if in the birth of time the core of the earth had broken through its crust and the motion of the world was begun. There are things in nature that engender an awful quiet in the heart of man; Devil's Tower is one of them. Two centuries ago, because they could not do otherwise, the Kiowas made a legend at the base of the rock. My grandmother said:

> *Eight children were there at play, seven sisters and their brother. Suddenly the boy was struck dumb; he trembled and began to run upon his hands and feet. His fingers became claws, and his body was covered with fur. Directly there was a bear where the boy had*

been. The sisters were terrified; they ran, and the bear after them.
They came to the stump of a great tree, and the tree spoke to them.
It bade them climb upon it, and as they did so it began to rise into
the air. The bear came to kill them, but they were just beyond its
reach. It reared against the tree and scored the bark all around with
its claws. The seven sisters were borne into the sky, and they became
the stars of the Big Dipper.

From that moment, and so long as the legend lives, the Kiowas have kinsmen in the night sky. Whatever they were in the mountains, they could be no more. However tenuous their well-being, however much they had suffered and would suffer again, they had found a way out of the wilderness.

My grandmother had a reverence for the sun, a holy regard that now is all but gone out of mankind. There was a wariness in her, and an ancient awe. She was a Christian in her later years, but she had come a long way about, and she never forgot her birthright. As a child she had been to the Sun Dances; she had taken part in those annual rites, and by them she had learned the restoration of her people in the presence of Tai-me. She was about seven when the last Kiowa Sun Dance was held in 1887 on the Washita River above Rainy Mountain Creek. The buffalo were gone. In order to consummate the ancient sacrifice—to impale the head of a buffalo bull upon the medicine tree—a delegation of old men journeyed into Texas, there to beg and barter for an animal from the Goodnight herd. She was ten when the Kiowas came together for the last time as a living Sun Dance culture. They could find no buffalo; they had to hang an old hide from the sacred tree. Before the dance could begin, a company of soldiers rode out from Fort Sill under orders to disperse the tribe. Forbidden without cause the essential act of their faith, having seen the wild herds slaughtered and left to rot upon the ground, the Kiowas backed away forever from the medicine tree. That was July 20, 1890, at the great bend of the Washita. My grandmother was there. Without bitterness, and for as long as she lived, she bore a vision of deicide.

Now that I can have her only in memory, I see my grandmother in the several postures that were peculiar to her: standing at the wood stove on a winter morning and turning meat in a great iron skillet; sitting at the south window, bent above her beadwork, and afterwards, when her vision failed, looking down for a long time into the fold of her hands; going out upon a cane, very slowly as she did when the weight of age came upon her; praying. I remember her most often at prayer. She made long, rambling prayers out of suffering and hope, having seen many things. I was never sure that I had the right to hear, so exclusive were they of all mere custom and company. The last time I saw her she prayed standing by the side of her bed at night, naked to the waist, the light of a kerosene lamp moving upon her dark skin. Her long, black hair, always drawn and braided in the day, lay upon her shoulders and against her breasts like a shawl. I do not speak Kiowa, and I never understood her prayers, but there was something inherently sad in the sound, some merest hesitation upon the syllables of sorrow. She began in a high and descending pitch, exhausting her breath to silence; then again and again—and always the same intensity of effort, of something that is, and is not, like urgency in the human voice. Transported so in the dancing light among the shadows of her room, she seemed beyond the reach of time. But that was illusion; I think I knew then that I should not see her again.

Houses are like sentinels in the plain, old keepers of the weather watch. There, in a very little while, wood takes on the appearance of great age. All colors wear soon away in the wind and rain, and then the wood is burned gray and the grain appears and the nails turn red with rust. The windowpanes are black and opaque; you imagine there is nothing within, and indeed there are many ghosts, bones given up to the land. They stand here and there against the sky, and you approach them for a longer time than you expect. They belong in the distance; it is their domain.

Once there was a lot of sound in my grandmother's house, a lot of coming and going, feasting and talk. The summers there were full of excitement and reunion. The Kiowas are a summer people; they abide the cold and keep to themselves, but when the season turns and the land becomes warm and vital they cannot hold still; an old love of going returns upon them. The aged visitors who came to my grandmother's house when I was a child were made of lean and leather, and they bore themselves upright. They wore great black hats and bright ample shirts that shook in the wind. They rubbed fat upon their hair and wound their braids with strips of colored cloth. Some of them painted their faces and carried the scars of old and cherished enmities. They were an old council of warlords, come to remind and be reminded of who they were. Their wives and daughters served them well. The women might indulge themselves; gossip was at once the mark and compensation of their servitude. They made loud and elaborate talk among themselves, full of jest and gesture, fright and false alarm. They went abroad in fringed and flowered shawls, bright beadwork and German silver. They were at home in the kitchen, and they prepared meals that were banquets.

There were frequent prayer meetings, and great nocturnal feasts. When I was a child I played with my cousins outside, where the lamplight fell upon the ground and the singing of the old people rose up around us and carried away into the darkness. There were a lot of good things to eat, a lot of laughter and surprise. And afterwards, when the quiet returned, I lay down with my grandmother and could hear the frogs away by the river and feel the motion of the air.

Now there is a funeral silence in the rooms, the endless wake of some final word. The walls have closed in upon my grandmother's house. When I returned to it in mourning, I saw for the first time in my life how small it was. It was late at night, and there was a white moon, nearly full. I sat for a long time on the stone steps by the kitchen door. From there I could see out across the land; I could see the long row of trees by the creek, the low light upon the rolling plains, and the stars of the Big Dipper. Once I looked at the moon and caught sight of a strange thing. A cricket had perched upon the handrail, only a few inches away from me. My line of vision was such that the creature filled the moon like a fossil. It had gone there, I thought, to live and die, for there, of all places, was its small definition made whole and eternal. A warm wind rose up and purled like the longing within me.

The next morning I awoke at dawn and went out on the dirt road to Rainy Mountain. It was already hot, and the grasshoppers began to fill the air. Still, it was early in the morning, and the birds sang out of the shadows. The long yellow grass on the mountain shone in the bright light, and a scissortail hied above the land. There, where it ought to be, at the end of a long and legendary way, was my grandmother's grave. Here and there on the dark stones were ancestral names. Looking back once, I saw the mountain and came away.

———————

TEN ELEGIES
FOR THE SIXTIES

for

ERNEST HEMINGWAY
(1899–1961)

Archibald MacLeish

HEMINGWAY

"In some inexplicable way an accident."

Mary Hemingway

Oh, not inexplicable. Death explains,
that kind of death: rewinds remembrance
backward like a film track till the laughing man
among the lilacs, peeling the green stem,
waits for the gunshot where the play began;

rewinds those Africas and Idahos and Spains
to find the table at the Closerie des Lilas,
sticky with syrup, where the flash of joy
flamed into blackness like that flash of steel.

The gun between the teeth explains.
The shattered mouth foretells the singing boy.

for

MARILYN MONROE
(1926–1962)

Michael McClure

FROM *GHOST TANTRAS*

39
MARILYN MONROE, TODAY THOU HAST PASSED
THE DARK BARRIER
—diving in a swirl of golden hair.
I hope you have entered a sacred paradise for full
warm bodies, full lips, full hips, and laughing eyes!
AHH GHROOOR. ROOOHR. NOH THAT OHH!
OOOH . . .
Farewell perfect mammal.
Fare thee well from thy silken couch and dark day!
AHH GRHHROOOR! AHH ROOOOH. GARR
nah ooth eeze farewell. Moor droon fahra rahoor
rahoor, rahoor. Thee ahh-oh oh thahrr
noh grooh rahhr.

(August 6, 1962)

f o r

JOHN F. KENNEDY
(1917–1963)

Eric Von Schmidt

KENNEDY BLUES

Lay down, lay down, lay down about midday.
I lay down, lay down, lay down about midday.
When I woke up they'd stole a man away.

Could not believe, believe what my friend said.
Could not believe, believe what my friend said.
He said, "The President's been shot," said "The President's
dead."

Then George turned to me, tears all in his eyes,
Well, George turned to me, tears all in his eyes,
Sayin', "I ain't puttin' you on man, the President's dyin'."

"The President's dyin'."

Mountain run to the river, river run to the, run to the,
run to the sea.
Mountain run to the river, river runnin' to the sea.
When I heard the news I said I'd lost a part of me.

Well, I'd heard about Dallas, about how it was so great.
I'd heard about Dallas, about how it was so great.
Now I know about your Dallas, your city full of hate.

Had your opera down in Dallas when the President was
                                          dead and cold,
Had your opera down in Dallas when the President was
                                          dead and cold.
I could not hear the music, the blues was cryin' in my soul.
I lay down, I lay down, lay down about midday.
I lay down, lay down, lay down about midday.
When I woke up they'd stole a man away.

for

SYLVIA PLATH
(1932–1963)

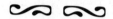

John Berryman

FROM *THE DREAM SONGS*

172

Your face broods from my table, Suicide.
Your force came on like a torrent toward the end
of agony and wrath.
You were christened in the beginning Sylvia Plath
and changed that name for Mrs Hughes and bred
and went on round the bend

till the oven seemed the proper place for you.
I brood upon your face, the geography of grief,
hooded, till I allow
again your resignation from us now
though the screams of orphaned children fix me anew.
Your torment here was brief,

long falls your exit all repeatingly,
a poor exemplum, one more suicide
to stack upon the others
till stricken Henry with his sisters & brothers
suddenly gone pauses to wonder why he
alone breasts the wronging tide.

for

MALCOLM X
(1925–1965)

❧ ❧

Etheridge Knight

THE SUN CAME

And if sun comes
How shall we greet him?

—GWEN BROOKS

The sun came, Miss Brooks,—
After all the night years.
He came spitting fire from his lips.
And we flipped—We goofed the whole thing.
It looks like our ears were not equipped
For the fierce hammering.

And now the Sun has gone, has bled red,
Weeping behind the hills.
Again the night shadows form.
But beneath the placid face a storm rages.
The rays of Red have pierced the deep, have struck
The core. We cannot sleep.
The shadows sing: Malcolm, Malcolm, Malcolm.
The darkness ain't like before.

The Sun came, Miss Brooks.
And we goofed the whole thing.
I think.
(Though ain't no vision visited my cell.)

for

MARTIN LUTHER KING, JR.
(1929–1968)

∽ ∽

Don L. Lee

ASSASSINATION

it was wild.
the
bullet hit high
      (the throat-neck)

& from everywhere:
     the motel, from under bushes and cars,
     from around corners and across streets,
     out of the garbage cans and from rat holes
     in the earth
they came running.
with
guns
drawn
they came running
toward the King—
        all of them
        fast and sure—
as if
the King
was going to fire back.
they came running,
fast and sure,
in the
wrong
direction.

for

ROBERT F. KENNEDY
(1925–1968)

Lawrence Ferlinghetti

ASSASSINATION RAGA

Tune in to a raga
on the stereo
and turn on Death TV
without its sound
Outside the plums are growing in a tree
"The force that through the green fuse
drives the flower"
drives Death TV
"A grief ago"
They lower the body soundlessly
into a huge plane in Dallas
into a huge plane in Los Angeles
marked "United States of America"
and soundlessly
the "United States of America"
takes off
& wings away with that Body
Tune out the TV sound
& listen soundlessly
to the blind mouths of its motors
& a sitar speaking on the stereo
a raga in a rage
at all that black death
and all that bad karma

La illaha el lill Allah
There is no god but God
The force that through the red fuze
drives the bullet
drives the needle in its dharma groove
and man the needle
drives that plane
of the "United States of America"
through its sky full of shit & death
and the sky never ends
as it wings soundlessly
from those fucked-up cities
whose names we'd rather not remember
Inside the plane
inside the plane a wife
lies soundlessly
against the coffin
Engine whines as sitar sings outrageously
La illaha el lill Allah
There is no god but God?
There is no god but Death
The plums are falling through the tree
The force that drives the bullet
through the gun
drives everyone
as the "United States of America"
flies on sightlessly
through the swift fierce years
with the dead weight of its Body
which they keep flying from Dallas
which they keep flying from Los Angeles
And the plane lands
without folding its wings
its shadow in mourning for itself
withdraws into itself
in death's draggy dominion
La illaha el lill Allah
There is no god but Death
The force that through the green fuze
drove his life
drives everyone

And they are driving the Body
they are driving the Body
up Fifth Avenue
past a million people in line
"We are going to be here a long time"
says Death TV's spielman
The cortège passes soundlessly
"Goodbye! Goodbye!" some people cry
The traffic flows around & on
The force that drives the cars
combusts our karma
La illaha el lill Allah
There is no god but Death
The force that drives our life to death
drives sitar too
so soundlessly
And they lift the Body
They lift the Body
of the United States of America
and carry it into a cathedral
singing Hallelujah He Shall Live
For ever & ever
And then the Body moves again
down Fifth Avenue
Fifty-seven black sedans after it
There are people with roses
behind the barricades
in bargain-basement dresses
And sitar sings & sings nonviolence
sitar sounds in us its images of ecstasy
its depth of ecstasy
against old dung & death
The force that strikes its strings
strikes us
And the funeral train
the silver train
starts up soundlessly
at a dead speed
over the hot land
an armed helicopter over it
They are clearing the tracks ahead of assassins

The tracks are lined with bare faces
A highschool band in New Brunswick plays
The Battle Hymn of the Republic
They have shot it down again
They have shot him down again
& will shoot him down again
& take him on a train
& lower him again
into a grave in Washington
Day & night journeys the coffin
through the dark land
too dark now to see the dark faces
Plums & planes are falling through the air
as sitar sings the only answer
sitar sings its only answer
sitar sounds the only sound
that still can still all violence
There is no god but Life
Sitar says it Sitar sounds it
Sitar sounds on us to love love & hate hate
Sitar breathes its Atman breath in us
sounds & sounds in us its lovely *om om*
At every step the pure wind rises
People with roses
behind the barricades!

*First read, to an evening raga, at "The Incredible Poetry Reading,"
Nourse Auditorium, San Francisco, June 8, 1968, the day Robert
Kennedy was buried.*

*"The force that through the green fuse drives the flower" & "A grief
ago": from Dylan Thomas. "La illaha el lill Allah": variation of a
Sufi ecstatic chant.*

for

NEAL CASSADY
(1926–1968)

Allen Ginsberg

ON NEAL'S ASHES

Delicate eyes that blinked blue Rockies all ash
nipples, Ribs I touched w/ my thumb are ash
mouth my tongue touched once or twice all ash
bony cheeks soft on my belly are cinder, ash
earlobes & eyelids, youthful cock tip, curly pubis
breast warmth, man palm, high school thigh,
baseball bicept arm, asshole anneal'd to silken skin
all ashes, all ashes again.

August 1968

f o r

JANIS JOPLIN
(1943–1970)

∽ ∾

Marilyn Hacker

ELEGY

for Janis Joplin

Crying from exile, I
mourn you, dead singer, crooning and palming
your cold cheeks, calling you: You.
A man told me you died; he was
foreign, I felt for the first time, drunk, in his car, my
throat choked: You won't sing for me
now. Later I laughed in the hair between
his shoulder blades, well enough
loved in a narrow
bed; it was
your Southern Comfort
grin stretching my
mouth. You were in me
all night,

shouting our pain, sucking off
the mike, telling a strong-headed
woman's daily beads to dumb kids
creaming on your high
notes. Some morning at wolf hour
they'll know.
Stay in my
gut, woman lover I never

touched, tongued, or sang to; stay
in back of my
throat, sandpaper
velvet, Janis, you
overpaid your
dues, damn it, why are you dead?

Cough up your whiskey gut
demon, send him home howling
to Texas, to every
fat bristle-chinned
white motel keeper on
Route 66, every half-
Seminole waitress with a
crane's neck, lantern-jawed
truck driver missing a
finger joint, dirt farmer's
blond boy with asthma and sea dreams,
twenty-one-year-old
mother of three who got far
as Albuquerque once.

Your veins were
highways from
Coca-Cola flatland,
dust and dead
flies crusting the
car window till it rained.
Drive! anywhere
out of here, the
ratty upholstery smelling
of dog piss and cunt,
bald tires swiveled and
lurched on slicked macadam
skidding the funk in your mouth
to a Black woman's tongue.

Faggots and groupies and
meth heads loved you, you
loved bodies and booze
and hard work, and more

than that, fame. On your
left tit was a tattooed
valentine, around your
wrist a tattooed filigree; around
your honeycomb brain webbed
klieg lights and amp circuits screamed
Love Love and the booze-
scag-and-cocaine baby twisted your
box, kicked your
throat and the songs came.

I wanted to write your
blues, Janis, and put my
tongue in your mouth that way.
Lazy and grasping and
treacherous, beautiful
insomniac freaking the ceiling,
the cold smog went slowly blue, the cars
caught up with your heartbeat, maybe you were not
alone, but the ceiling told you
otherwise, and scag said:
You are more famous than anyone
out of East Texas, your hair is a
monument, your voice preserved
in honey, I love you, lie down.

I am in London and
you, more meat than Hollywood
swallowed, in Hollywood, more
meat. You got me through
long nights with your coal-scuttle
panic, don't be scared
to scream when it hurts
and oh mother it hurts, tonight
we are twenty-seven, we are
alone, you are dead.

for

JACK KEROUAC
(1922–1969)

The Harvard Crimson
October 23, 1969

KEROUAC, 1922–1969

WOULDN'T YOU KNOW IT? Kerouac is dead. Neal Cassady is dead, and now Kerouac, of a "massive hemorrhage." He drank too much. He couldn't seem to make the transition to the flower-power scene. He was too much the dirty bum, the dope fiend, the sinner redeemed through his sin, innocent the whole way, embarrassingly sincere, impatient, hostile, one of the most generous souls of his time, a creator of the American underground, avatar of the ones who could not fight the Nova Police because there were too few of them, and they would have been crushed: William Burroughs, Gregory Corso, Neal Cassady, Allen Ginsberg, Kerouac. So they ran.

It seems that these days, after the myth of the possibility of a congenial and happy world has been ripped from our grasp by the maudlin and ranting politicos, that maybe the spirit of the Beats is the only viable one for those of us who are tired of waiting around for a fight we don't want, who agree with Kerouac that stupidity is prolific, who are just not naive enough any longer to be hip, who just want to *live,* and stop playing magician with the realities of our lives, pulling revolutions out of thin air, pulling our personalities from the pages of underground newspapers and half-baked talk, turning nonsense into our daily bread, like some mad troupe of sorcerer's apprentices-Cum-epileptic Luther.

According to his friends, Kerouac was almost never tired and always hopeful. No one went to visit him in his time; we were embarrassed by our writing teachers who told us that Kerouac's prose was bad. It isn't. Now he's dead; but he was a good man, and the ideas for which he was mocked, that "bad prose" which liberated so many, are still good. We should say a prayer for him: God give us strength to be as alive as Kerouac was. Send us more to help burn away the bullshit.

SELECTED BIBLIOGRAPHY

Armstrong, Gregory, ed. *Protest: Man Against Society*. New York: Bantam Books, 1969.

Baker, Houston A., Jr. "The Black Arts Movement: 1960–1970." In *The Norton Anthology of African American Literature*, ed. Henry Louis Gates, Jr., and Nellie Y. McKay. New York: Norton, 1997.

Baldwin, James. *The Fire Next Time*. New York: Dial, 1963.

Bambara, Toni Cade. *The Black Woman: An Anthology*. New York: New American Library, 1970.

Banes, Sally. *Greenwich Village 1963: Avant-Garde Performance and the Effervescent Body*. Durham, N.C.: Duke University Press, 1993.

Beauvoir, Simone de. *The Second Sex*. Ed. and trans. H. M. Parshley. New York: The Modern Library, 1968.

Belfrage, Sally. *Freedom Summer*. New York: Viking, 1965.

Berkeley, Kathleen C. *The Women's Liberation Movement in America*. Westport, Conn.: Greenwood Press, 1999.

Berman, Paul. *A Tale of Two Utopias*. New York: Norton, 1996.

Blackman, Allan. *Face to Face with Your Draft Board*. Berkeley, Calif.: World Without War Council, 1969.

Bloom, Alexander, and Wini Breines, eds. *"Takin' It to the Streets."* New York: Oxford University Press, 1995.

Boston Women's Health Book Collective. *Our Bodies, Ourselves*. New York: Simon and Schuster, 1969.

Boyle, Kay. *The Long Walk at San Francisco State*. New York: Grove Evergreen, 1970.

Branch, Taylor. *Parting the Waters: America in the King Years, 1954–1963*. New York: Simon and Schuster, 1988.

Brody, Leslie. *Red Star Sister: Between Madness and Utopia.* Saint Paul, Minn.: Hungry Mind Press, 1998.

Bromell, Nick. *Tomorrow Never Knows: Rock and Psychedelics in the 1960s.* Chicago: University of Chicago Press, 2000.

Brown, Claude. *Manchild in the Promised Land.* New York: Macmillan, 1965.

Burroughs, William S. *The Adding Machine: Collected Essays.* London: John Calder, 1985.

Burroughs, William S., Jr. *Speed/Kentucky Ham.* New York: Overlook Press, 1993.

Candida Smith, Richard. *Utopia and Dissent: Art, Poetry and Politics in California.* Berkeley: University of California Press, 1995.

Carmichael, Stokely, and Charles Hamilton. *Black Power: The Politics of Liberation.* New York: Random House, 1967.

Carson, Clayborne, et al. *The Eyes on the Prize: Civil Rights Reader.* New York: Penguin Books, 1997.

Chapman, Abraham, ed. *Black Voices.* New York: New American Library, 1968.

Clay, Steven, and Rodney Phillips. *A Secret Location on the Lower East Side: Adventures in Writing, 1960–1980.* New York: New York Public Library/ Granary Books, 1998.

Cohen, Allen, ed. *The* San Francisco Oracle: *The Psychedelic Newspaper of the Haight-Ashbury, 1966–1968.* Berkeley, Calif.: Regent Press, 1991.

Cook, Mercer, and Stephen E. Henderson. *The Militant Black Writer.* Madison: University of Wisconsin Press, 1969.

Davidson, Sara. *Loose Change: Three Women of the Sixties.* New York: Doubleday, 1977.

Dickstein, Morris. *Gates of Eden: American Culture in the Sixties.* Cambridge, Mass.: Harvard University Press, 1997.

Didion, Joan. *The White Album.* New York: Simon and Schuster, 1979.

Doctorow, E. L. *The Book of Daniel.* New York: Plume, 1971.

DuPlessis, Rachel Blau, and Ann Snitow, eds. *The Feminist Memoir Project: Voices from Women's Liberation.* New York: Three Rivers Press, 1998.

Echols, Alice. *Daring to Be Bad: Radical Feminism in America, 1967–1975.* Minneapolis: University of Minnesota Press, 1989.

———. *Shaky Ground: The Sixties and Its Aftershocks.* New York: Columbia University Press, 2002.

Ehrenreich, Barbara, and John Ehrenreich. *Long March, Short Spring: The Student Uprising*. New York: Monthly Review Press, 1969.

Eisen, Jonathan. *Altamont*. New York: Avon, 1970.

Ellis, Julie. *Revolt of the Second Sex*. New York: Lancer Books, 1970.

Farber, Jerry. *The Student as Nigger*. New York: Pocket Books, 1970.

Ferlinghetti, Lawrence. *Where Is Vietnam?* San Francisco: City Lights, 1965.

Foley, Jack. *O Powerful Western Star: Poetry and Art in California*. Oakland, Calif.: Pantograph Press, 2000.

Franklin, H. Bruce, ed. *The Vietnam War*. Boston: Bedford Books, 1996.

Friedman, Leon, ed. *The Civil Rights Reader: Basic Documents of the Civil Rights Movement*. New York: Walker and Co., 1967.

Ginsberg, Allen. *Deliberate Prose*. Edited by Bill Morgan. New York: HarperCollins, 2000.

Gitlin, Todd. *The Sixties: Years of Hope, Days of Rage*. New York: Bantam, 1987.

Goines, David Lance. *The Free Speech Movement: Coming of Age in the 1960s*. Berkeley, Calif.: Ten Speed Press, 1993.

Goodman, Mitchell. *The Movement Toward a New America*. New York: Knopf, 1970.

Goodman, Paul. *Growing Up Absurd: Problems of Youth in the Organized Society*. New York: Random House, 1960.

Greer, Germaine. *The Female Eunuch*. London: MacGibbon and Kee, 1970.

———. *The Madwoman's Underclothes: Essays and Occasional Writings*. New York: The Atlantic Monthly Press, 1986.

Grier, William H.; and Price M. Cobbs. *Black Rage*. New York: Basic Books, 1968.

Griffin, John Howard. *Black Like Me*. Boston: Houghton Mifflin, 1961.

Grinspoon, Lester, and James B. Balakar. *Psychedelic Drugs Reconsidered*. New York: Basic Books, 1979.

Gruen, John. *The New Bohemia*. New York: Shorecrest, 1966.

Hardwick, Elizabeth. *Bartleby in Manhattan & Other Essays*. New York: Random House, 1983.

Hay, John. *In Defense of Nature*. Boston: Little, Brown, 1969.

Himes, Chester. *Pinktoes*. Paris: Olympia Press, 1961.

Hoffman, Abbie. *Revolution for the Hell of It*. New York: Dial, 1968.

Holmes, John Clellon. *Nothing More to Declare*. New York: Dutton, 1967.

Horowitz, Daniel. *Betty Friedan and the Making of* The Feminine Mystique: *The American Left, the Cold War, and Modern Feminism*. Amherst: University of Massachusetts Press, 1998.

Hughes, Langston. *Fight for Freedom: The Story of the NAACP*. New York: Norton, 1962.

———. *Good Morning Revolution: Uncollected Social Protest Writings*. Edited by Faith Berry. New York: Lawrence Hill & Co., 1973.

———. *The Panther & the Lash: Poems of Our Times*. New York: Knopf, 1967.

Huxley, Aldous. *The Doors of Perception* and *Heaven and Hell*. London: Penguin, 1961.

Jamison, Andrew, and Ron Eyerman. *Seeds of the Sixties*. Berkeley: University of California Press, 1994.

Jones, LeRoi. *Home: Social Essays*. New York: Morrow, 1966.

Joplin, Laura. *Love, Janis*. New York: Villard Books, 1992.

Kandel, Lenore. *The Love Book*. San Francisco: Stolen Paper Review Editions, 1966.

Kasher, Steven. *The Civil Rights Movement: A Photographic History, 1954–68*. New York: Abbeville, 1996.

Kaufman, Sue. *Diary of a Mad Housewife*. New York: Random House, 1967.

Kerouac, Jack. *Big Sur*. New York: Farrar, Straus and Giroux, 1962.

———. *Desolation Angels*. New York: Coward McCann, 1965.

———. *Satori in Paris*. New York: Grove Press, 1966.

Kesey, Ken. *One Flew Over the Cuckoo's Nest*. New York: Viking, 1962.

Kornbluth, Jesse, ed. *Notes from the New Underground: An Anthology*. New York: Viking, 1968.

Kupferberg, Tuli. *1001 Ways to Live Without Working*. New York: Grove Press, 1967.

Laing, R. D. *The Politics of Experience*. New York: Pantheon Books, 1967.

Leamer, Laurence. *The Paper Revolutionaries: The Rise of the Underground Press*. New York: Simon and Schuster, 1972.

Leary, Timothy, G. M. Weil, and Ralph Metzner. *The Psychedelic Reader*. New Hyde Park, N.Y.: University Books, 1965.

Lee, Martin A., and Bruce Shlain. *Acid Dreams: The Complete Social History of LSD, the CIA, and Beyond*. New York: Grove Press, 1986.

Levertov, Denise. *The Poet in the World*. New York: New Directions, 1973.

Levy, Peter B., ed. *America in the Sixties—Right, Left, and Center*. Westport, Conn.: Praeger, 1998.

Lewis, Anthony, and the *New York Times*. *Portrait of a Decade: The Second American Revolution*. New York: Random House, 1964.

Lewis, Roger. *Outlaws of America: The Underground Press and Its Context*. New York: Penguin, 1972.

Lowenfels, Walter, ed. *Where Is Vietnam? American Poets Respond*. New York: Anchor Books, 1967.

McClure, Michael. *The Beard*. Berkeley, Calif.: Oyez, 1965.

———. *Freewheelin' Frank, Secretary of the Angels* (with Frank Reynolds). New York: Grove Press, 1967.

———. *Scratching the Beat Surface*. San Francisco: North Point, 1982.

Macedo, Stephen, ed. *Reassessing the Sixties*. New York: Norton, 1997.

McNeill, Don. *Moving Through Here*. New York: Knopf, 1970.

McPhee, John. *The Pine Barrens*. New York: Farrar, Straus and Giroux, 1967.

Margolis, Jon. *The Last Innocent Year: America in 1964*. New York: Morrow, 1999.

Marwick, Arthur. *The Sixties*. London: Oxford University Press, 1998.

Matthiessen, Peter. *The Peter Matthiessen Reader*. New York: Random House, 1999.

Mead, Margaret, and Frances Balgley Kaplan, eds. *American Women: The Report of the President's Commission on the Status of Women and Other Publications of the Commission*. New York: Charles Scribner's Sons, 1965.

Metzner, Ralph, ed. *The Ecstatic Adventure*. Foreword by Alan Watts. New York: Macmillan, 1968.

Miller, Arthur. "Miracles." In *Echoes Down the Corridor: Collected Essays, 1944–2000*. New York: Viking, 2000.

Miller, James. *"Democracy Is in the Streets": From Port Huron to the Siege of Chicago*. New York: Simon and Schuster, 1987.

Mitchell, Angelyn. *Within the Circle*. Durham, N.C.: Duke University Press, 1994.

Morgan, Robin. *Going Too Far: The Personal Chronicle of a Feminist*. New York: Random House, 1970.

———, ed. *Sisterhood Is Powerful: An Anthology of Writings from the Women's Movement*. New York: Random House, 1970.

Morrison, Toni. Afterword (1993) to *The Bluest Eye* (1970). New York: Knopf, 1993.

Mottram, Eric. *William Burroughs: The Algebra of Need.* London: Marion Boyars, 1977.

Obst, Lynda R. *The Sixties.* New York: Random House/Rolling Stone Press, 1977.

Ogden, Samuel R., ed. *America the Vanishing: Rural Life and the Price of Progress.* Brattleboro, Vt.: The Stephen Greene Press, 1969.

Olson, Lynne. *Freedom's Daughters: The Unsung Heroines of the Civil Rights Movement, from 1830 to 1970.* New York: Scribner, 2001.

O'Nan, Stewart, ed. *The Vietnam Reader.* New York: Doubleday, 1998.

Palmer, Cynthia, and Michael Horowitz, eds. *Sisters of the Extreme: Women Writing on the Drug Experience.* Rochester, Vt.: Park Street Press, 2000.

Peck, Abe. *Uncovering the Sixties: The Life and Times of the Underground Press.* New York: Citadel Press, 1991.

Piercy, Marge. *Braided Lives.* New York: Simon and Schuster, 1982.

———. *Living in the Open.* New York: Knopf, 1969.

Polsgrove, Carol. *Divided Minds: Intellectuals and the Civil Rights Movement.* New York: Norton, 2001.

Pynchon, Thomas. *Slow Learner.* Boston: Little, Brown, 1984.

———. *Vineland.* Boston: Little, Brown, 1990.

Quetchenbach, Bernard W. *Back from the Far Field: American Nature Poetry in the Late Twentieth Century.* Charlottesville: University Press of Virginia, 2000.

Redstockings. *Notes from the First Year.* New York: Redstockings, 1968.

———. *Notes from the Second Year.* New York: Redstockings, 1970.

Reed, Ishmael. *The Last Days of Louisiana Red.* New York: Random House, 1974.

Rexroth, Kenneth. *The Heart's Garden/The Garden's Heart.* Cambridge, Mass.: Pym-Randall Press, 1967.

Rips, Geoffrey. *Unamerican Activities: The Campaign Against the Underground Press.* San Francisco: City Lights, 1981.

Romm, Ethel G. *The Open Conspiracy.* New York: Avon Books, 1970.

Rorabaugh, W. J. *Berkeley at War: The Sixties.* New York: Oxford University Press, 1989.

Roszak, Theodore. *The Making of a Counter Culture*. New York: Doubleday, 1969.

Roth, Philip. "Writing American Fiction." In *Reading Myself and Others*. New York: Farrar, Straus and Giroux, 1975.

Sann, Paul. *The Angry Decade: The Sixties*. New York: Crown, 1979.

Saroyan, Aram. *Genesis Angels: The Saga of Lew Welch and the Beat Generation*. New York: Morrow, 1979.

Scigaj, Leonard. *Sustainable Poetry: Four American Ecopoets*. Lexington: The University Press of Kentucky, 1999.

Selby, Hubert, Jr. *Last Exit to Brooklyn*. New York: Grove Press, 1964.

Showalter, Elaine, ed. *Women's Liberation and Literature*. New York: Harcourt Brace Jovanovich, 1971.

Shulman, Alix Kates. *Memoirs of an Ex–Prom Queen*. New York: Knopf, 1969.

Sklar, Morty, and Jim Mulac. *Editor's Choice: Literature & Graphics from the U.S. Small Press, 1965–1977*. Iowa City: Spirit That Moves Us Press, 1980.

Snyder, Gary. *Riprap & Cold Mountain Poems*. San Francisco: Four Seasons Foundation, 1965.

Solotaroff, Theodore. *The Red Hot Vacuum and Other Pieces on the Writing of the Sixties*. New York: Atheneum, 1970.

Spitz, Robert. *Barefoot in Babylon: The Creation of the Woodstock Festival*. New York: Viking, 1979.

Stambler, Sookie. *Women's Liberation: Blueprint for the Future*. New York: Ace Books, 1970.

Stein, Arnold, ed. *Theodore Roethke: Essays on the Poetry*. Seattle: University of Washington Press, 1965.

Stone, Robert. *A Hall of Mirrors*. Boston: Houghton Mifflin, 1966.

Streitmatter, Roger. *Unspeakable: The Rise of the Gay and Lesbian Press in America*. Boston: Faber and Faber, 1995.

———. *Voices of the Revolution: The Dissident Press in America*. New York: Columbia University Press, 2001.

Sullivan, James D. *On the Walls and in the Streets: American Poetry Broadsides from the 1960s*. Urbana: University of Illinois Press, 1997.

Tanner, Leslie B., ed. *Voices from Women's Liberation*. New York: Signet, 1971.

Teale, Edwin Way. *Wandering Through Winter*. New York: Dodd, Mead, 1965.

Thompson, Mary Lou. *Voices of the New Feminism*. Boston: Beacon Press, 1970.

Van Devanter, Lynda. *Home Before Morning: The Story of an Army Nurse in Vietnam*. New York: Beaufort Books, 1983.

Vendler, Helen. *Poems Poets Poetry*. Boston: Bedford Books, 2002.

Vollers, Maryanne. *Ghosts of Mississippi: The Murder of Medgar Evers, the Trials of Byron de la Beckwith, and the Haunting of the New South*. Boston: Little, Brown, 1993.

Vonnegut, Mark. *The Eden Express*. New York: Praeger, 1975.

Walker, Alice. *Meridian*. New York: Harcourt Brace Jovanovich, 1976.

Whitfield, Stephen J. *A Death in the Delta: The Story of Emmett Till*. New York: Macmillan, 1988.

Williams, Juan. *Eyes on the Prize: America's Civil Rights Years, 1954–1965*. New York: Viking, 1987.

Wolfe, Burton. *The Hippies*. New York: Signet Books, 1968.

Wolfe, Tom. *The Electric Kool-Aid Acid Test*. New York: Farrar, Straus and Giroux, 1968.

———. *In Our Time*. London: Pan Books, 1980.

Woodcock, George. *Thomas Merton, Monk and Poet*. New York: Farrar, Straus and Giroux, 1978.

ACKNOWLEDGMENTS

R. G. Davis: "The Minstrel Show" from *The San Francisco Mime Troupe: The First Ten Years* by R. G. Davis (Ramparts Press). Copyright © R. G. Davis. Reprinted by permission of R. G. Davis.

Diane di Prima: Revolutionary Letters #1, #3, #5, #8, and #16 from *Revolutionary Letters* by Diane di Prima (City Lights Books, 1971) and "The Holidays at Millbrook—1966." Reprinted by permission of the author.

Bob Dylan: "The Lonesome Death of Hattie Carroll." Copyright © 1964 by Warner Bros., Inc. Copyright renewed 1992 by Special Rider Music. All rights reserved. International copyright secured. Reprinted by permission of Special Rider Music.

Lee Felsenstein: "Put My Name Down." Copyright © 1964 by Lee Felsenstein. Used by permission of Fantasy Records.

Lawrence Ferlinghetti: "Assassination Raga" from *These Are My Rivers* by Lawrence Ferlinghetti. Copyright © 1969 by Lawrence Ferlinghetti. Reprinted by permission of New Directions Publishing Corp. Letters to Gregory Corso, Allen Ginsberg, and Peter Orlovsky. Excerpt from "One Thousand Fearful Words for Fidel Castro." Published as a broadside by City Lights Books, 1961. Reprinted by permission of Lawrence Ferlinghetti.

Betty Friedan: Excerpt from *The Feminine Mystique* by Betty Friedan. Copyright © 1983, 1974, 1973, 1963 by Betty Friedan. Used by permission of W. W. Norton & Company, Inc.

Dave Genesen: Excerpt from "Free Speech Demonstration Talking Blues" by Dave Genesen. Used by permission of Fantasy Records.

Allen Ginsberg: "Demonstration or Spectacle As Example . . ." from *Deliberate Prose: Selected Essays 1952–1995* by Allen Ginsberg. Copyright © 1999 by Allen Ginsberg Trust. "Kral Majales" copyright © 1965 by Allen Ginsberg. Copyright renewed 1993 by Allen Ginsberg. "On Neal's Ashes" copyright © 1973 by Allen Ginsberg. Both from *Collected Poems 1947–1980* by Allen Ginsberg. Reprinted by permission of HarperCollins Publishers Inc.

Nikki Giovanni: "My Poem" from *Black Feeling, Black Talk, Black Judgment* by Nikki Giovanni. Copyright © 1968, 1970 by Nikki Giovanni. Reprinted by permission of HarperCollins Publishers Inc.

David Lance Goines: "Here they come! Get ready" and "Let Sleeping Dogs Lie" from *The Free Speech Movement: Coming of Age in the 1960s* by David Lance Goines. Copyright © 1993 by David Lance Goines. Reprinted by permission of Ten Speed Press, Berkeley, California.

Andrew Gordon: "Smoking Dope with Thomas Pynchon" from *The Vineland Papers: Critical Takes on Pynchon's Novels*, edited by Geoffrey Green, Donald J. Greiner, and Larry McCaffery. Copyright © 1994 by Dalkey Archive Press. Reprinted by permission of Dalkey Archive Press.

Emmett Grogan: Excerpt from *Ringolevio* by Emmett Grogan. Copyright © 1972 by Eugene Leo Michael Emmett Grogan. Used by permission of Little, Brown and Company (Inc.).

Marilyn Hacker: "Elegy" from *Presentation Piece* by Marilyn Hacker (Viking Press). Copyright © 1974 by Marilyn Hacker. Used by permission of the author.

The Harvard Crimson: "Kerouac, 1922-1969" appeared in *The Harvard Crimson,* October 23, 1969. Used by permission of *The Harvard Crimson.*

Michael Herr: Excerpt from *Dispatches* by Michael Herr. Copyright © 1977 by Michael Herr. Used by permission of Alfred A. Knopf, a division of Random House, Inc.

Abbie Hoffman: "Che's Last Letter" reprinted by permission of Four Walls Eight Windows, New York, publisher of *The Best of Abbie Hoffman* (1989), edited by Dan Simon.

John Clellon Holmes: "Visitor: Jack Kerouac in Old Saybrook" originally published in *the unspeakable visions of the individual,* vol. 11. Copyright © 1980 by John Clellon Holmes. Reprinted by permission of Liz Von Vogt.

Robert Hunter: "New Speedway Boogie." Copyright © 1969 by Ice Nine Publishing Company, Inc. Reprinted by permission of Ice Nine Publishing Co., Inc.

Charles Johnson: Excerpt from *Dreamer* by Charles Johnson, reprinted with the permission of Scribner, a division of Simon & Schuster, Inc. Copyright © 1998 by Charles Johnson.

Hettie Jones: Excerpt from *How I Became Hettie Jones* by Hettie Jones. Copyright © 1990 by Hettie Jones. Used by permission of Grove/Atlantic, Inc.

Richard Kampf: "Hey Mr. Newsman." Copyright © 1964 by Fantasy/Galaxy Records. Used by permission of Fantasy Records.

Bob Kaufman: "Grandfather Was Queer, Too" from *Solitudes Crowded with Loneliness* by Bob Kaufman. Copyright © 1965 by Bob Kaufman. Reprinted by permission of New Directions Publishing Corp.

Ken Kesey: "Letters from Mexico." Published in *Ararat,* Autumn 1968. Reprinted by permission of the author.

Martin Luther King, Jr.: "Letter from a Birmingham Jail." Copyright © Martin Luther King 1963, copyright renewed 1991 Coretta Scott King. Reprinted by arrangement with the Estate of Martin Luther King, Jr., c/o Writers House as agent for the proprietor.

Etheridge Knight: "The Idea of Ancestry" and "The Sun Came" from *The Essential Etheridge Knight* by Etheridge Knight. Copyright © 1986 by Etheridge Knight. Reprinted by permission of the University of Pittsburgh Press.

Yusef Komunyakaa: "2527th Birthday of the Buddha," "Facing It," "Hanoi Hannah," "Nude Interrogation," "Prisoners," "Tunnels," and " 'You and I Are Disappearing' " from *Pleasure Dome: New and Collected Poems* by Yusef Komunyakaa. Copyright © 2001 by Yusef Komunyakaa. Reprinted by permission of Wesleyan University Press.

Ron Kovic: Excerpt from *Born on the Fourth of July* by Ron Kovic. Copyright © 1976 by Ron Kovic. Reprinted by permission of The McGraw-Hill Companies.

Timothy Leary: "Turning On the World." First published in *Esquire* magazine, 1968. Reprinted courtesy of *Esquire* and the Hearst Corporation.

Don L. Lee: "Assassination" and excerpt from introduction to *Think Black 1965–1967*, both from *Directionscore* by Don L. Lee (Broadside Press). Copyright © 1968 by Don L. Lee. Reprinted by permission of Haki R. Madhubuti, Chicago, Illinois.

Denise Levertov: "About Marriage," "Life at War," and "The Mutes" from *Poems 1960–1967* by Denise Levertov. Copyright © 1966 by Denise Levertov. "Overheard over S.E. Asia" from *Poems 1968–1972* by Denise Levertov. Copyright © 1972 by Denise Levertov. Reprinted by permission of New Directions Publishing Corp.

Robert Lowell: "For the Union Dead" from *For the Union Dead* by Robert Lowell. Copyright © 1959 by Robert Lowell. Copyright renewed © 1987 by Harriet Lowell, Caroline Lowell, and Sheridan Lowell. Reprinted by permission of Farrar, Straus and Giroux, LLC.

Michael Lydon: "The Rolling Stones—At Play in the Apocalypse." Reprinted by permission of the author.

Archibald MacLeish: "Hemingway" from *Collected Poems 1917–1982* by Archibald MacLeish (Houghton Mifflin). Copyright © 1985 by the Estate of Archibald MacLeish. Reprinted by permission of William H. MacLeish.

Haki R. Madhubuti: "Malcolm Spoke / who listened?" from *Don't Cry, Scream* by Haki R. Madhubuti. Copyright © 1969 by Haki R. Madhubuti. Reprinted by permission of Third World Press, Inc., Chicago, Illinois.

Norman Mailer: Excerpt from *The Armies of the Night* by Norman Mailer. Copyright © Norman Mailer, 1968. Used by permission of Dutton, a member of Penguin Putnam Inc.

Malcolm X: "The Ballot or the Bullet" from *Malcolm X Speaks* by Malcolm X (Pathfinder Press). Copyright © 1989 by Betty Shabazz. Reprinted by permission of John Hawkins & Associates, Inc.

Dave Mandel: "Battle of Berkeley Talking Blues." Copyright © 1964 by Fantasy/Galaxy Records. Reprinted by permission of Fantasy Records.

Peter Matthiessen: "The Outlying Rocks" from *Wildlife in America* by Peter Matthiessen. Copyright © Peter Matthiessen, 1959. Copyright renewed Peter Matthiessen, 1987. Used by permission of Viking Penguin, a division of Penguin Putnam Inc.

Michael McClure: Selections from *Ghost Tantras* by Michael McClure (City Lights Books, 1964). Reprinted by permission of the author.

Country Joe McDonald: "I Feel Like I'm Fixin'-to-Die Rag" and "Superbird." Copyright © 1965, renewed 1993 by Alkatraz Corner Music (BMI). "Janis." Copyright © 1967, renewed 1995 by Joyful Wisdom Music (BMI). "Talking Non-Violence." Copyright © 1964, renewed 1992 by Alkatraz Corner Music (BMI). Reprinted by permission of Country Joe McDonald.

Thomas Merton: "Original Child Bomb" from *The Collected Poems of Thomas Merton*. Copyright © 1962 by The Abbey of Gethsemani. Reprinted by permission of New Directions Publishing Corp.

Kate Millett: Excerpt from *Sexual Politics* by Kate Millett (Doubleday). Copyright © 1969, 1970, 1990, 2000 by Kate Millett. Reprinted by permission of Georges Borchardt, Inc., for the author.

Janice Mirikitani: "Attack the Water." Reprinted by permission of the author.

N. Scott Momaday: Excerpt from *House Made of Dawn* by N. Scott Momaday. Copyright © 1966, 1967, 1968 by N. Scott Momaday. Reprinted by permission of HarperCollins Publishers Inc. Excerpt from *The Way to Rainy Mountain* by N. Scott Momaday. Reprinted by permission of University of New Mexico Press.

Anne Moody: Excerpt from *Coming of Age in Mississippi* by Anne Moody. Copyright © 1968 by Anne Moody. Used by permission of Doubleday, a division of Random House, Inc.

Larry Neal: "The Black Arts Movement" from *Visions of a Liberated Future* by Larry Neal. Copyright © 1989 by Larry Neal. Reprinted by permission of the publisher, Thunder's Mouth Press.

Tim O'Brien: "The Man I Killed" from *The Things They Carried* by Tim O'Brien. Copyright © 1990 by Tim O'Brien. Reprinted by permission of Houghton Mifflin Company. All rights reserved.

Charles Olson: "The Hustings" from *The Collected Poems of Charles Olson*, edited by George F. Butterick. Copyright © 1987 University of Connecticut. Used with permission.

Dan Paik: "There's a Man Taking Names." Copyright © 1964 by Fantasy/Galaxy Records. Reprinted with permission of Fantasy Records.

Rosa Parks: Excerpt from *Rosa Parks: My Story* by Rosa Parks with Jim Haskins. Copyright © 1992 by Rosa Parks. Used by permission of Dial Books for Young Readers, an imprint of Penguin Putnam Books for Young Readers, a division of Penguin Putnam Inc.

Sylvia Plath: "Lady Lazarus" from *Ariel* by Sylvia Plath. Copyright © 1963 by Ted Hughes. Reprinted by permission of HarperCollins Publishers Inc.

Allen Polite: "Song," ["We Knew Our Loneliness and Told It"], and "Why They Are in Europe?" Reprinted by permission of Helen Polite.

Dudley Randall: "Ballad of Birmingham" from *Cities Burning*, edited by Doughtry Long (Broadside Press, 1968). Reprinted by permission of Vivian B. Randall.

Ishmael Reed: "Eldridge Cleaver—Writer" from *The Reed Reader* (Basic Books, 2000). Reprinted by permission of the author.

Carolyn M. Rodgers: "It Is Deep" from *How I Got Ovah* by Carolyn M. Rodgers. Copyright © 1968, 1969, 1970, 1971, 1972, 1973, 1975 by Carolyn M. Rodgers. Used by permission of Doubleday, a division of Random House, Inc.

Muriel Rukeyser: "Poem" from *The Collected Poems of Muriel Rukeyser* (McGraw-Hill). Copyright © 1978 by Muriel Rukeyser. Reprinted by permission of International Creative Management, Inc.

Edward Sanders: "Yeats in the Gas" from *1968: A History in Verse* by Edward Sanders. Copyright © 1997 by Edward Sanders. Reprinted with permission of Black Sparrow Press.

Richard Schmorleitz and Dan Paik: "I Walked Out in Berkeley." Copyright © 1964 by Fantasy/Galaxy Records. Used by permission of Fantasy Records.

Anne Sexton: "The Abortion" from *All My Pretty Ones* by Anne Sexton. Copyright © 1961, 1962 by Anne Sexton. "The Addict" from *Live or Die* by Anne Sexton. Copyright © 1966 by Anne Sexton. "The Ballad of the Lonely Masturbator" from *Love Poems* by Anne Sexton. Copyright © 1967, 1968, 1969 by Anne Sexton. Reprinted by permission of Houghton Mifflin Co. All rights reserved.

Gary Snyder: "Poke Hole Fishing After the March," "Revolution in the Revolution in the Revolution," and "What You Should Know to Be a Poet" from *Regarding Wave* by Gary Snyder. Copyright © 1970 by Gary Snyder. Reprinted by permission of New Directions Publishing Corp.

Valerie Solanas: Excerpt from *SCUM Manifesto* by Valerie Solanas. Copyright © AK Press. By permission of AK Press, 674-A 23rd Street, Oakland, California 94612.

Susan Sontag: "What's Happening in America (1966)" from *Styles of Radical Will* by Susan Sontag. Copyright © 1967, 1969 by Susan Sontag. Reprinted by permission of Farrar, Straus and Giroux, LLC.

Gloria Steinem: "A New Egalitarian Life Style" published in *The New York Times*, August 26, 1971. Copyright © 1971 by Gloria Steinem. Reprinted by permission of the author.

Hunter Thompson: Excerpt from *Hell's Angels* by Hunter S. Thompson. Copyright © 1966, 1967 by Hunter S. Thompson. Used by permission of Random House, Inc.

Sally Tomlinson: "Psychedelic Rock Posters: History, Ideas, and Art" published in *High Societies: Psychedelic Rock Posters of Haight-Ashbury* (San Diego Museum of Art). Reprinted by permission of the author.

Calvin Trillin: "The March" published in *The New Yorker*, September 7, 1963. Copyright © 1963 by The New Yorker Magazine, Inc. Reprinted by permission of the publisher.

Eric Von Schmidt: "Kennedy Blues." Used by permission of Eric Von Schmidt/Minglewood.

Diane Wakoski: "Belly Dancer" and "Ringless" from *Emerald Ice: Selected Poems, 1962–1987* by Diane Wakoski. Copyright © 1988 by Diane Wakoski. Reprinted with permission of Black Sparrow Press.

Alice Walker: "The Civil Rights Movement: What Good Was It?" from *In Search of Our Mothers' Gardens: Womanist Prose* by Alice Walker. Copyright © 1967 by Alice Walker. Reprinted by permission of Harcourt, Inc.

Lew Welch: ["Apparently Wasps"], ["I Burn Up the Deer in My Body"], ["I Know a Man's Supposed to Have His Hair Cut Short"], "Preface To *Hermit Poems*, The Bath," "The Song Mt. Tamalpais Sings," ["Step Out onto the Planet"], and ["Whenever I Make a New Poem"] from *Ring of Bone* by Lew Welch. By permission of Grey Fox Press.

Eudora Welty: "Where Is the Voice Coming From?" First appeared in *The New Yorker*, June 11, 1963. Copyright © 1963 by Eudora Welty, renewed 1991 by Eudora Welty. Reprinted by permission of Russell & Volkening as agents for the author.

Al Young: "Conjugal Visits." Copyright © 1996, 2001 by Al Young. "A Dance for Ma Rainey." Copyright © 1969, 1992 by Al Young. Reprinted with permission of the author.

ILLUSTRATION CREDITS

Page 207: "Wanted: Hip Cops." Berkeley, California, street handout (circa 1966).

Page 279: "A Minstrel Show." R. G. Davis, *The San Francisco Mime Troupe: The First Ten Years* (1975).

Page 439: Drawing by Charles Bukowski. From Charles Bukowski, *A Bukowski Sampler* (1969).

Page 570: Handwritten poem by Lew Welch. From Lew Welch, *Hermit Poems* (1965).

ALPHABETICAL LIST OF
AUTHORS AND TITLES